PENGUIN BOOKS
THE BANKIMCHANDRA OMNIBUS
VOLUME 1

Radha Chakravarty is a Reader in English at Gargi College, University of Delhi. Her doctoral thesis is a cross-cultural study of contemporary women writers. Her translations include *Crossings: Stories from Bangladesh and India*, Rabindranath Tagore's *Chokher Bali* and *Shesher Kabita: Farewell Song*, and Mahasweta Devi's *In the Name of the Mother*.

*

Marian Maddern has lectured in Literature in the Faculty of Education at the University of Melbourne and has translated variously from Bengali prose and poetry.

*

Soumyendra Nath Mukherjee has taught History at Oxford, Cambridge and Sydney. Author of several books on India, S.N. Mukherjee has also edited a number of translations from Bengali.

*

Sreejata Guha has an MA in Comparative Literature from State University of New York at Stony Brook. She has translated Saradindu Bandyopadhyay's *Picture Imperfect* and *Band of Soldiers*, Taslima Nasrin's *French Lover*, Rabindranath Tagore's *Chokher Bali: A Grain of Sand* and *Home and the World*, and Saratchandra Chattopadhyay's *Devdas* for Penguin.

PENGUIN BOOKS

THE BANKIMCHANDRA OMNIBUS

VOLUME

BANKIMCHANDRA CHATTOPADHYAY

The Bankimchandra Omnibus

Volume 1

KAPALKUNDALA

Translated by Radha Chakravarty

BISHABRIKSHA (THE POISON TREE)

Translated by Marian Maddern

INDIRA

Translated by Marian Maddern

KRISHNAKANTA'S WILL

Translated by S.N. Mukherjee

RAJANI

Translated by Sreejata Guha

PENGUIN BOOKS

PENGUIN BOOKS
Published by the Penguin Group
Penguin Books India Pvt Ltd, 11 Community Centre, Panchsheel Park, New Delhi 110 017, India
Penguin Group (USA) Inc., 375 Hudson Street, New York, New York 10014, USA
Penguin Group (Canada), 90 Eglinton Avenue East, Suite 700, Toronto, Ontario, M4P 2Y3, Canada (a division of Pearson Penguin Canada Inc.)
Penguin Books Ltd, 80 Strand, London WC2R 0RL, England
Penguin Ireland, 25 St Stephen's Green, Dublin 2, Ireland (a division of Penguin Books Ltd)
Penguin Group (Australia), 250 Camberwell Road, Camberwell, Victoria 3124, Australia (a division of Pearson Australia Group Pty Ltd)
Penguin Group (NZ), cnr Airborne and Rosedale Roads, Albany, Auckland 1310, New Zealand (a division of Pearson New Zealand Ltd)
Penguin Group (South Africa) (Pty) Ltd, 24 Sturdee Avenue, Rosebank, Johannesburg 2196, South Africa

Penguin Books Ltd, Registered Offices: 80 Strand, London WC2R 0RL, England

First published by Penguin Books India 2005

10 9 8 7 6 5 4 3 2 1

ISBN: 0144 000555 ISBN: 9780144000555

Typeset in *Perpetua* by Mantra Virtual Services, New Delhi
Printed at Baba Barkhanath Printers, New Delhi

CONTENTS

Kapalkundala

PART 1

1

At the Estuary

Floating straight obedient to the stream.

—*The Comedy of Errors*

EARLY IN THE SEVENTEENTH CENTURY, LATE ONE NIGHT IN THE MONTH OF Magh, a passenger boat was on its way back from Gangasagar. It was customary those days for passenger boats to travel together in groups, to protect themselves from the Portuguese and other pirates. But this boat was unaccompanied, because in the dense fog that had enveloped the horizon in the wee hours, the sailors, losing their orientation, had steered the vessel away from the rest of the fleet. Now they had no idea where they were headed, or in which direction. Many of the passengers were asleep. Only two men remained awake: one was old, the other young. They were engaged in conversation.

'How far can we travel tonight?' the old man broke off, to inquire of the sailors.

'I couldn't say,' replied the oarsman, after some hesitation.

Enraged, the old man began to rant at the oarsman.

'Sir, when matters are in God's hands, even learned men cannot predict what might transpire,' the young man intervened. 'How can this illiterate man say anything for certain? Please don't agitate yourself.'

'Not be agitated?' exclaimed the old man sharply. 'How is that possible, when rascally robbers have snatched away the paddy from twenty to twenty-five acres of my land? What will my children survive on, all year?'

He had received these tidings after he was already at the estuary, from travellers who arrived there subsequently.

'I did point out earlier that it was not a good idea for Sir to have come on this pilgrimage, because his household has no other guardian,' the young man reminded him.

'Not come on this pilgrimage?' exclaimed the old man as sharply as before. 'With three-quarters of my lifespan over already? When should I build my store of virtue for the life to come, if not at this stage?'

'If I understand the scriptures correctly,' observed the young man, 'it's possible to prepare for the afterlife in one's own home, just as well as on a pilgrimage.'

'Then why did you undertake this journey?' the old man demanded.

'As I've said before, I had a great desire to see the ocean,' replied the young man. 'That is why I came here.'

'Ah! What a vision!' he mused, in a softer voice. 'Never to be forgotten in all eternity!' In Sanskrit, he quoted:

Behold the remote blue shore, densely encircled by tal and tamal!
And there, like a long, dark stain, stretch the salt waters of the deep.

The old man paid no attention to the poetry. He was listening with rapt attention to the conversation of the sailors.

'O bhai, my brother! What a terrible thing we've done!' one sailor was saying to another. 'Are we now in the open seas? Or are we approaching some unknown land? I couldn't say!'

The speaker sounded very frightened. The old man realized that there was cause for anxiety.

'What's the matter?' he asked the oarsman, fearfully.

The oarsman made no reply. But the young man stepped out on deck without waiting for an answer. He found that it was almost dawn. The world, all around, was enveloped in dense fog; sky, stars, moon, shore, nothing could be seen. He realized that the sailors had lost their way. Unable to ascertain the direction in which they were going, they were terrified of drowning in the open seas.

The passengers within the boat had remained unaware of all this, because of a screen draped over the front of the cabin, to protect them from the cold. But the young traveller understood their predicament, and explained it to the old man. This caused a huge commotion on board. Some of the female passengers, aroused from slumber by the sound of voices, began to scream as soon as they heard the news.

'To the shore! To the shore! To the shore!' cried the old man.

'If we knew where the shore was, would we be in such grave danger?' asked the young man, with a faint smile.

At this, the passengers began to scream even more loudly. The young traveller somehow managed to calm them down.

'There's no cause for anxiety,' he assured the sailors. 'Day has broken. In a few hours, the sun will be up. The boat will certainly not be destroyed in two or three hours. Stop rowing now, and let the boat drift with the current. Later, once the sun comes up, we can discuss what is to be done.'

The sailors accepted his advice and proceeded accordingly.

For a long time, the sailors sat idle. The passengers were half-dead with fright. There was not much of a breeze, so they could not really sense the undulation of the waves. All the same, everyone assumed that death was close at hand. The men began to silently chant Goddess Durga's name, the women wailed in many voices. Only one woman did not weep: she had sacrificed her child to the waters of the Gangasagar estuary, having failed to lift him out of the water after the holy dip.

They waited until morning seemed close at hand. Suddenly, the sailors created a great uproar, calling upon the five pirs of the ocean.

'What is it? What is it? Tell us, oarsman, what has happened?' cried the passengers.

'The sun is up! The sun is up! Land ahoy!' cried the oarsmen, in a babble of voices.

All the passengers came out on deck, curious to see where they had arrived, and to ascertain the truth about their predicament. They found that the sun was up. The air was now completely clear of the fog's shadow. The day was well advanced. The boat had not drifted out into the open seas, but had merely reached the river's mouth. At this point, though, the river was at its widest. On one side, the shore was very close to the boat, indeed—in fact, within about thirty feet of it; but the opposite shore could not be seen at all. In every direction, wherever one looked, stretched a vast expanse of water, sparkling in the playful sunshine, extending to the horizon, where it merged with the sky. The water, seen at close range, had a river's usual muddy hue, but acquired a bluish gleam where it stretched into the distance. The passengers concluded with certainty that they had reached the high seas; but they counted themselves fortunate that, due to the proximity of the beach, they had no cause for anxiety. They determined their orientation from the position of the sun. The stretch of land facing them was readily identified as the western shore of the sea. Along the beach, not far from the boat, was the mouth of a river, flowing gently into the sea like a stream of gold. To the right of the estuary, countless birds of all varieties could be seen, frolicking on the wide stretch of sand. This river is today known as the Rasulpur.

2
On the Beach

Ingratitude! Thou marble-hearted friend!

—*King Lear*

WHEN THE PASSENGERS' EXCITED BABBLE HAD SUBSIDED, THE SAILORS proposed that while high tide was still far away, they could cook their meal on the beach facing them. Afterwards, as soon as the tide came in, they could proceed on their homeward journey. The passengers accepted this suggestion. Once the sailors had brought the boat to the shore, the travellers alighted, and busied themselves with their daily ablutions.

Ablutions completed, when they began preparations for cooking, another difficulty presented itself: there was no firewood on board. For fear of tigers, nobody was willing to fetch firewood from the embankment above. Finally, the old man, realizing they would all starve, addressed the young man we have spoken of earlier:

'Nabakumar, my son! If you don't tackle the situation, all of us will die.'

'Very well, I shall go,' decided Nabakumar, after a brief hesitation. 'I need an axe, and someone to accompany me with a da—a chopping blade.'

Nobody was willing to accompany Nabakumar.

'When it's time to eat, we'll see who joins me,' remarked Nabakumar. Girding his waist, he picked up the axe and set off alone in search of firewood.

Clambering up the embankment, Nabakumar found no trace of human habitation, anywhere within sight. Only forests were to be seen, not graced with rows of giant trees, nor densely wooded, but consisting instead of clusters of small shrubs, covering the land in patches. Unable to spot any firewood worth collecting, Nabakumar had to walk far inland, away from the riverbank, in search of suitable trees. Finally, having located a tree that would suit his purpose, he gathered all the wood he required. He found the load very difficult to carry. As he was not a poor man's son, Nabakumar was unaccustomed to such chores; having gone in search of firewood without considering the consequences, he now found his load very burdensome. All the same, having once taken on a task, it was not in Nabakumar's nature to give up easily; so he began to somehow stagger back with his burden of firewood. He would go a little way, then sit and rest awhile, before moving on again, making his way back in this fashion.

Nabakumar's return was thus delayed. Meanwhile, his companions grew anxious, fearing that Nabakumar had been killed by a tiger. After a reasonable time had elapsed, they were convinced in their hearts that this was indeed what had happened. Yet, no one had the courage to climb the embankment and advance inland in search of him.

While the travellers speculated thus, a tumult broke out in the waters. The sailors realized that the tide had turned. They were well aware that in such places, the waves at high tide buffet the shore so violently, that any boat or other river-craft that happen to be within range are smashed to bits. So, they rapidly untied the boat and began to row away towards the middle of the river. No sooner had the boat moved away, than the stretch of sand before them was inundated with water. The terrified travellers had barely managed to scramble on board; the rice, with all other items placed on the beach, was swept away in the tide. Unfortunately, the sailors, lacking expertise, could not control the boat, which was carried by the torrent, out into the middle of the Rasulpur river.

'But we've left Nabakumar behind!' cried one of the passengers.

'Oh, as if your Nabakumar is still alive!' scoffed a sailor. 'He has been devoured by jackals.'

The force of the tide was carrying the boat midstream, far out into Rasulpur river. It would be difficult to steer it back. The sailors struggled with all their might to pull out of the current. Even in the cold month of Magh, sweat began to pour down their foreheads. With incredible effort, they managed to pull out of Rasulpur river, but as soon as the boat emerged into the open waters, it encountered even stronger currents which spun the vessel around, propelling it northwards with the speed of an arrow. The sailors could not control its movements at all. The boat did not return.

When the tide subsided sufficiently for the vessel's speed to be brought under control, they had travelled far beyond the mouth of the Rasulpur. They now had to decide whether or not it would be possible to return in search of Nabakumar. It must be mentioned at this juncture that Nabakumar's fellow-travellers were merely his neighbours, not his close friends. After considering the situation, they concluded that to turn back from their present position meant waiting for the tide to ebb again. Night would descend after that, making navigation impossible; they would have to await the next day's high tide. Until then, all of them would starve. Two days without food would bring them close to death. Besides, the sailors were unwilling to turn back; they were not under the passengers' command. The sailors insisted that Nabakumar had been killed by tigers. That was the likeliest possibility. So, why inflict such suffering on themselves?

Considering all this, the travellers thought it wise to proceed on their homeward journey without Nabakumar, who was left to survive somehow on that dreadful seashore.

If someone, hearing this account, should vow never to fetch firewood for others who are starving, such a person deserves to be ridiculed. Those naturally predisposed to banish their benefactor to the forest, will always do so. But one naturally predisposed to fetch firewood for others, will continue to do so, even if repeatedly banished to the forest. Why should someone else's ignoble nature deter one from aspiring to nobility?

3
In the Wilderness

Life's a veil
Which if withdrawn, would but disclose the frown
Of one who hates us, so the night was shown
And grimly darkled o'er their faces pale
And hopeless eyes.

—*Don Juan*

NOT FAR FROM THE SPOT WHERE THE TRAVELLERS HAD ABANDONED Nabakumar, two tiny villages, named Daulatpur and Dariapur, have now appeared. But during the period in question, there was no trace of human habitation in that area, which was a complete wilderness. But unlike other parts of Bengal, the land in this region was not flat and free of undulations. For several miles, from the mouth of the Rasulpur to the Subarnarekha, stretches an unbroken chain of sandhills. If they were slightly higher, these hillocks could have been described as a low, sandy mountain range. Today, people call them sand dunes. Viewed from afar, the white crests of these dunes shine gloriously in the afternoon sunlight. No tall trees grow there. The sand dunes are scantily wooded at the base, but their middle and upper portions shine with a stark, white beauty, free of any shade. The vegetation covering the base of the sand dunes consists mainly of scrub, wild tamarisk and wildflowers.

In this cheerless place, Nabakumar had been abandoned by his companions. Returning to the riverbank with his load of firewood, he could not see the boat. He felt a sudden, wild surge of terror, but did not imagine that his fellow-travellers had permanently deserted him. Convinced that they had moved the boat to some nearby protected spot when the beach was flooded at high tide, he was sure they would soon seek him out. In this expectation, he lingered for a while on the sandy shore, waiting for the boat, but it did not return. Nor did any of the passengers reappear. Nabakumar was famished. Unable to wait any longer, he scoured the shores of the river for the boat. Finding no trace of it anywhere, he returned to the original spot. The boat still nowhere in sight; he concluded that it must have been carried away at high tide, and that his fellow-travellers, on their way back to fetch him, were taking a long time to row against the current. But even the tide receded. Now he was convinced the boat, unable to turn back against the force of the tide, was surely coming back for him now, at ebb tide. But the tide continued to ebb, the day wore on, and eventually, it was sunset. If the boat was to return, it should have done so by now.

Then it dawned on Nabakumar that either the rough waves at high tide had caused the boat to sink, or else his companions had abandoned him in this desolate place.

There was no village in sight, no refuge, no signs of human life, nor any food or drink; the river water was unbearably salty, but he was wracked by hunger and thirst. There was no place to seek shelter from the cold, not even a warm wrap to shield his body. Sans refuge, sans any protective clothing, he would have to sleep under the open sky, exposed to the dampness of the falling dew, on this ice-cold, windswept riverbank. At night, he was likely to chance upon a beast of prey. Death seemed inevitable.

Nabakumar was too agitated to remain in one place for long. Abandoning the shore, he clambered up the embankment and began to roam about aimlessly. Night descended. In the dew-laden sky, silent stars appeared, exactly as in Nabakumar's own home-country. Darkness enveloped this desolate place. Earth, sky and sea were utterly silent: only the roar of the ocean could be heard, and occasionally, the call of some wild beast. Still, Nabakumar wandered among the sand dunes, under that dark, chilly sky. He meandered in the valleys and plateaux, at the foot of the sandhills and across their crests. At every step, he could have been attacked by some beast of prey. But to remain in one fixed spot would expose him to the same danger.

As he wandered about, Nabakumar began to feel exhausted, the more so for having gone without food all day. He rested against a sand dune. His warm, cosy bed at home came to mind. In a state of physical and mental exhaustion, one's thoughts are sometimes overcome by drowsiness. Lost in thought, Nabakumar drifted off to sleep. But for this law of human nature, the unchecked flood of our worldly troubles would often seem too much for us to tolerate.

4

On the Crest of the Sand-dune

He beheld in surprise, not far away, a vision that filled him with dread.

—Meghnadbadh

THE NIGHT WAS FAR ADVANCED WHEN NABAKUMAR AWAKENED FROM HIS slumber. He was amazed to find himself still alive, not yet devoured by tigers. He looked around for approaching tigers. Far ahead, in the distance, he suddenly spotted a light. To make sure his eyes were not deluding him, he gazed at the light with full concentration. Gradually, the light seemed to grow larger and brighter; he was convinced it was the glow of a fire. The realization instantly revived Nabakumar's hopes of survival. The glow could only signal the presence of some human habitation, for this was not the season for forest-fires. Rising to his feet, Nabakumar raced towards the light.

'Is this a ghostly light?' he wondered, for a moment. 'It might be. But if daunted by fear, how can we protect our lives?'

Having arrived at this conclusion, he advanced fearlessly towards the light, obstructed at every step by trees, creepers and mounds of sand. Trampling upon the undergrowth, stepping over sand-heaps, Nabakumar forged ahead. Nearing the light's source, he saw a fire burning on the crest of a sand dune, and revealed by its glow, silhouetted against the sky, a seated human form. Determined to approach this man on the sand dune's crest, Nabakumar proceeded without slowing his pace. He began to ascend the slope. He felt some pangs of anxiety now, but continued his ascent with unfaltering firmness of tread. What he saw when he came face-to-face with the man on the crest of the mound, made his hair stand on end. He could not decide whether to stay, or to retreat.

Eyes closed, the man seemed lost in meditation. At first, he did not see Nabakumar. Inspecting his appearance, Nabakumar surmised that he must be about fifty years old. He could see no clothing on the man's body, which was wrapped in a leopard-skin from waist to knee. On his neck, the man wore a string of rudraksha beads, and his broad countenance was framed by dense, tangled locks of hair. Before him was a heap of burning logs, whose glow had guided Nabakumar to that spot. A terrible stench assailed Nabakumar's nostrils, and glancing at the place occupied by the stranger, he could sense its source. The man with the coiling locks was seated on a rotting, headless corpse. Nabakumar was even more terrified when he saw, placed before the meditating figure, a human skull containing a crimson fluid. Scattered all around were human bones; in fact, even the beads of the rudraksha necklace were interspersed with tiny bits of bone. Nabakumkar stared at the scene, transfixed. He was in two minds whether to advance or to abandon the spot. He had heard of kapaliks, followers of the ascetic cult of Goddess Kali. This man, he realized, was a member of that dreaded sect.

When Nabakumar arrived at the spot, the kapalik, immersed in holy ritual, prayer or meditation, took no notice of the young man.

'Who are you?' he asked in Sanskrit, after a long time.

'A Brahmin,' replied Nabakumar.

'Wait,' instructed the kapalik, and busied himself with the same rituals as before. Nabakumar remained standing.

An hour and a half went by. Then, rising to his feet, the kapalik addressed Nabakumar in Sanskrit, as before. 'Follow me,' he ordered.

At any other time, Nabakumar would certainly not have accompanied him. But now he complied, because hunger and thirst had made him desperate.

'As you say, sir,' he answered. 'But I am starving. Where could I find some food, by your leave?'

'The goddess has sent you to me,' answered the kapalik, in Sanskrit. 'Follow me; you will be satisfied.'

Nabakumar followed the kapalik. They trudged a long distance, the two of them, without speaking a word to each other. At last, they reached a thatched hut. Entering first, the kapalik allowed Nabakumar in, and by some mysterious means incomprehensible to the young man, ignited a piece of firewood. By the light of that flame, Nabakumar saw that the entire hut was built of keya leaves. Within the hut were some tiger-skins, a pitcher of water and some fruit.

Having lit a fire, the kapalik said, 'You may have all the fruit, and use a cupped leaf to drink from the pitcher. Recline on the tiger-skins if you so desire. You may rest in peace, for there is no fear of tigers here. You will see me again after a while; until then, don't leave this hut.'

With these words, the kapalik departed. Nabakumar ate the fruits and drank the slightly brackish water, with immense satisfaction. Stretching out on a tiger-skin, exhausted after the events of the day, he soon fell into a deep slumber.

5

On the Seashore

In you, no sign of spiritual influence can be seen;
Your aspect is sad, like Mrinalini, suffering from the cold.

—*Raghuvamsha*

WHEN HE AWAKENED AT DAWN, NABAKUMAR INSTINCTIVELY STRUGGLED TO find a means of returning home. He thought it especially unwise to remain in the proximity of this kapalik. But how, at this juncture, was he to escape from this pathless forest? And how would he find his way back home? The kapalik surely knew the way: would he not offer directions, if requested? Since the kapalik, so far, had not displayed any threatening tendencies towards him, why should Nabakumar be afraid? On the other hand, the kapalik had forbidden him to leave the hut until they met again, and was likely to be angered if his injunctions were disobeyed. Having heard that kapaliks possessed the magic powers to accomplish the impossible, Nabakumar deemed it unwise to disobey this man. All things considered, he decided to remain in the hut for the time being.

But the day wore on, and the kapalik did not return. After a whole day of fasting, the lack of food this morning made Nabakumar acutely hungry. The previous night, he had already devoured all the fruit that he had found in the hut. Now, if he did not venture forth in search of fruits and vegetables, he would surely die of starvation. With just a few hours of daylight remaining, Nabakumar set out to gather some fruit.

He scoured the sandhills for fruit. Sampling the fruits on the few trees that grew in that sandy soil, he quelled his hunger-pangs with a particular fruit that had the delicious flavour of almonds.

As the stretch of sand dunes was rather narrow, Nabakumar crossed the dunes in a very short time. He now found himself in a dense forest, devoid of sand. Anyone who has spent a short time roaming in an unfamiliar forest would know how easy it is to lose one's way in a pathless jungle. So it was with Nabakumar. Having walked a short distance, he could not remember the way back to the ashram. Hearing the deep sound of turbulent waters, he recognized it as the roar of the ocean. Soon after, he suddenly found himself out of the forest, facing the sea. His heart leapt with joy at the sight of this vast, blue expanse of water. He reclined on the sandy shore. Before him stretched the ocean, foaming, blue, limitless. On both sides, as far as the eye could see, was a line of froth, flung onshore by the breaking waves, like a garland of bunched white blossoms deposited on the golden sand, a hair-ornament to adorn the earth's green tresses. Foaming waves broke the blue surface of the water in a thousand places. Only a storm violent enough to displace thousands of stars, swirling them against the azure backdrop of the sky, could match the sight of the waves churning in the ocean. At this moment, one segment of the blue water shone like molten gold in the gentle rays of the setting sun. Faraway, a European merchant vessel breasted the waves, white sails outspread, winging its way like some gigantic bird.

Nabakumar had no idea how long he remained on the seashore, gazing at the beauty of the ocean. Then, the darkness of dusk descended upon the black waters. It now struck Nabakumar that he must locate the hut. He rose to his feet with a sigh. Why he sighed, I cannot say, for there is no telling what happy memories awakened in his heart at that moment. Rising to his feet, he turned away from the sea. At once, he beheld an extraordinary apparition. At the edge of the wave-resonant ocean, on the sandy shore, in the blurred glow of twilight, stood an exquisite female figure! Outlined against her heavy tresses—her thick, unbraided locks, coiled like snakes, cascading down to her ankles—her body glowed like a jewel, a picture framed by its backdrop. Though partially concealed by the profusion of her hair, her countenance glowed like moonlight glimpsed through a gap in the clouds. Her large eyes were calm, tender and intense, yet bright as the gentle moonbeams that played upon the ocean's breast. Her shoulders were completely obscured from view by her cascading hair, but the unblemished beauty of her arms was partially visible. Her body was free of ornament. The magic of her beauty was indescribable. The enchanting effect of her complexion, resembling the gleam of the crescent moon, offset by the tangled webs of her dark hair, had to be viewed against the backdrop of that wave-resonant seashore, in the twilight glow, for its true impact to be felt.

Suddenly encountering this divine figure in the midst of such a wilderness, Nabakumar stood transfixed. Robbed of speech, he gazed at her in silence. She, too, fixed the unwavering, unblinking gaze of her enormous eyes on Nabakumar's face. But Nabakumar's eyes bore a startled expression, while the young woman showed no signs of surprise; instead, her gaze expressed acute anxiety.

There the two of them remained, on the vast ocean's desolate shore, gazing at each other in this way, for a very long time. After a prolonged silence, the young woman's voice was heard.

'Traveller, have you lost your way?' she asked, very softly.

Her voice struck the chords in Nabakumar's heart. The strings of our heart's extraordinary instrument sometimes grow too slack to be tuned to harmony, try as one might. But at a single sound, at the musical note in a woman's voice, the dissonance is instantly rectified. All the strings fall into tune. At such a moment, the journey of life seems to resemble a blissful stream of music. The sound of her voice fell upon Nabakumar's ears with just such an effect.

'Traveller, have you lost your way?' The sound of the words entered his ears. What they meant, what reply he should offer, he did not know. The sound seemed to spread everywhere, bringing a shiver of joy; it seemed to fill the breeze and murmur through the leaves on the trees, fading away to blend with the ocean's booming sound. The earth, girdled with the sea, was beautiful; beautiful, too, was the woman, and also the sound of her voice. The heart's instrument began to resonate with the rhythms of harmony.

'Come with me,' invited the maiden, when she received no reply to her question. With these words, she walked away, leaving no footprints. With invisible footsteps she moved, like a white cloud wafted on the slow spring breeze; like a clockwork toy, Nabakumar followed. At a certain place, where they had to skirt a small wood, the beautiful maiden disappeared behind a clump of trees. Having trudged around the forested area, Nabakumar found himself standing before a hut.

6
With the Kapalik

Alas, why are you in chains? I shall take you hence, forthwith!

—*Ratnabali*

ENTERING THE HUT, NABAKUMAR CLOSED THE DOOR AND SANK TO THE floor, clasping his head in his hands. He did not raise his head for a long time.

'Is she a goddess, a human being, or merely an illusion conjured up by the kapalik?' Frozen, immobile, he turned this question over and over in his mind, uncomprehending.

Preoccupied as he was, Nabakumar failed to notice something else. Inside the hut, even before his arrival, there was already a burning torch. The improbability of it struck him only afterwards, late at night, when he remembered that his evening ablutions had not been performed, his reverie disrupted by the task of fetching water. In the hut, he found not only a lighted torch, but also some rice and other provisions. He was not surprised, taking it for another sign of the kapalik's diligence. In this place, nothing seemed surprising anymore. Having completed his evening chores, Nabakumar dined on rice, cooked in an earthen vessel that he found in the hut.

The next morning, as soon as he left his bed, made of animal skin, he headed for the seashore. Thanks to the previous day's explorations, he did not have much trouble finding his way. Once there, morning ablutions over, he waited. Who was he waiting for? How intensely Nabakumar longed for last evening's enchantress to reappear at this spot, I cannot say for certain; but he was unable to leave the place. The day advanced, but no one appeared. Nabakumar began to roam about restlessly. He searched in vain, unable to detect the faintest trace of human habitation. He came back to the same spot as before. The sun set and it grew dark. Despondently, Nabakumar retraced his steps to the hut. Returning from the seashore at dusk, he found the kapalik seated silently on the floor of the hut. The kapalik did not return Nabakumar's greetings.

'Why was I denied access to the master until now?' asked Nabakumar.

'I was occupied with my own religious rituals.'

Nabakumar then expressed his desire to return to his homeland. 'I don't know the way,' he explained. 'Nor have I any provisions for the journey. I have been surviving on the hope that a meeting with the master will indicate my next course of action.'

'Come with me,' was all the kapalik said. He rose to his feet with an indifferent air. Nabakumar followed him, hoping to find some proper means of making his way back home.

The glow of twilight had not yet faded. The kapalik strode on ahead, with Nabakumar following behind. Suddenly, Nabakumar felt a tender touch on his back. Turning, he froze at the sight that met his eyes. It was the same goddess of the wilderness, she of the dense, ankle-length tresses! As before, she was silent and utterly still. From where had this vision suddenly appeared? The maiden had placed a finger on her lips; Nabakumar realized she was warning him against blurting out anything. Not that any warning was required. What could Nabakumar have said? Wonderstruck, he remained rooted to the spot. The kapalik walked on ahead, unaware. Once he was out of earshot, the maiden spoke, in a low, gentle voice.

'Where are you going?' Nabakumar heard her murmur. 'Stop! Turn back! Run away!'

The words were barely out of her mouth before she moved away, without waiting for a reply. For a while, Nabakumar remained rooted to the spot, stupefied. He was anxious to turn back, but could not determine the direction in which the maiden had vanished.

'Who has cast this magic spell?' he began to wonder. 'Or have I become disoriented? The words I heard are frightening, indeed, but what is the cause for fear? Tantrics are capable of anything. Should I run away, then? But why should I escape? If I could survive yesterday's events, I shall survive today, as well. The kapalik is a man, and so am I.'

As he pondered these things, Nabakumar saw the kapalik returning in search of him.

'Why do you tarry?' demanded the kapalik.

At this second call, Nabakumar followed the kapalik without a word.

Having trudged a short distance, they came upon a mud-walled hut. It could even be called a small house, but that does not concern us. Immediately behind was the sandy shore of the sea. Skirting the house, the kapalik led Nabakumar towards that shore. Suddenly, with the speed of an arrow, the maiden darted past the young man.

'Escape, even now!' she whispered into his ear in passing. 'Don't you know a tantric's prayers are never complete without an offering of human flesh?'

Nabakumar's forehead broke out in sweat. Unfortunately, the maiden's words had reached the ears of the kapalik.

'Kapalkundala!' he roared.

His voice fell upon Nabakumar's ears like the rumble of thunder in the clouds. But Kapalkundala offered no reply.

The kapalik began to drag Nabakumar by the hand. At his deadly touch, the blood began to pound in Nabakumar's veins, and he recovered the courage he had lost.

'Release my hand,' he demanded. The kapalik made no reply.

'Where are you taking me?' Nabakumar persisted.

'To the place for prayer,' answered the kapalik.

'Why?'

'To sacrifice you.'

Swiftly, Nabakumar tried to wrench his hand away from his grasp. The force of his action should not only have freed his hand, but also flung an ordinary mortal to the ground. But the kapalik did not budge an inch;

Nabakumar's wrist remained fast within his grip. The young man's bones and tendons seemed to crumble under the pressure. Nabakumar realized that force would not save him. Subterfuge was the need of the hour.

'Very well, we'll see what happens,' he decided, allowing the kapalik to drag him along.

Once they reached the appointed spot in the middle of the sandy stretch, Nabakumar saw a huge log fire burning there, as before. Arranged around the fire were the trappings of a tantric ritual, including liquor-filled human skulls, but no corpse. He gathered that he was meant to serve as the corpse.

Some dry, sinewy vines had already been placed there. The kapalik proceeded to bind Nabakumar's limbs tightly with them. Nabakumar tried to resist with all his might, but to no effect. Even at this advanced age, the kapalik had the strength of a mad elephant, he realized.

'You fool!' exclaimed the kapalik, observing Nabakumar's attempts to assert his strength. 'Why do you try to show your might? Today, your life has become worthwhile. To surrender your flesh to the worship of the goddess—what better fortune could a man like you desire?'

Having bound Nabakumar securely, the kapalik flung him down on the sand. He then busied himself with prayers and rituals, in preparation for the human sacrifice. Meanwhile, Nabakumar struggled to free himself; but the dry vines were too tough for him, the bonds too strong. Death was near at hand! Nabakumar now turned his mind to prayer. He remembered, in a flash, his birthplace, his comfortable home, his long-departed parents. He shed a few teardrops, instantly absorbed by the sand. Preliminary rituals over, the kapalik rose to his feet, looking for the scimitar with which the sacrifice was to be performed. But the scimitar was not where he had placed it. How extraordinary! The kapalik was rather surprised. He distinctly remembered having put the scimitar in its proper place that afternoon, and he had not removed it since. Where could it have gone? The kapalik searched here and there, but the scimitar was nowhere to be found. Then, turning towards the aforementioned cottage, he shouted for Kapalkundala, but his repeated calls went unanswered. The kapalik's eyes grew fiery red, his eyebrows twisted in a frown. He strode off in the direction of his own abode. Nabakumar took this opportunity to try once more to break free of the wild vines that bound him; but even these attempts were futile. Then he heard gentle footsteps on the sand. This was not the kapalik's tread. Turning around, Nabakumar beheld the same enchantress as before—Kapalkundala! In her hand, swaying to and fro, was the scimitar.

'Shh! Don't say a word!' she cautioned him. 'I have the scimitar—I stole it!'

With these words, wielding the scimitar, she began to quickly sever the bonds that tied Nabakumar. In an instant, he was free.

'Run away!' she urged. 'Follow me, I'll show you the way.'

Swift as an arrow, she sped on ahead, leading the way. Nabakumar raced after her.

7
The Hunt

And the great Lord of Luna
Fell at that deadly stroke;
As falls on mount Alvemus
A thunder-smitten oak.

—*Lays of Ancient Rome*

MEANWHILE, THE KAPALIK, HAVING SCOURED THE INTERIOR OF HIS HUT without finding either the scimitar or Kapalkundala, returned to the sand dunes in a suspicious frame of mind. He was astounded to discover that Nabakumar had vanished. Soon, he noticed the severed fragments of the vines that had bound the young man. As realization dawned on him, the kapalik rushed away in search of Nabakumar. But in the desolate wilderness, it was hard to determine which way the fugitives may have gone. Unable to see anyone in the dark, he wandered here and there for a while, listening for voices. But he could hear no voices, either. To scrutinize his surroundings, he now climbed to the top of a high sand dune. He ascended the slope on one side, unaware that the flow of water had eroded the base of the sand dune on the opposite side. As soon as he reached the top, the kapalik's body-weight caused the dune's crest to collapse with a resounding crash. Like a bull dislodged from a mountain-peak, the kapalik, too, fell with the descending mass of sand.

8
Refuge

And that very night—
Shall Romeo bear thee to Mantua.

—*Romeo and Juliet*

BREATHLESSLY THEY RACED INTO THE FOREST, THE TWO OF THEM, IN THE darkness of that moonless night. Unfamiliar with the forest tracks, Nabakumar had no choice but to follow the path taken by his young female companion, keeping her in sight. 'Fate had this too, in store for me!' he thought to himself. Nabakumar did not know that Bengalis are slaves of circumstance, not masters of their situation. Else, he would not have felt so aggrieved.

Gradually, they slackened their pace. In the darkness, nothing could be seen, but for the white crest of an occasional sand dune, outlined indistinctly in the starlight, or the shape of a tree trunk, adorned with its garland of foliage.

Kapalkundala led her fellow-traveller into a desolate garden. The night was far advanced. Before them, in the darkness, a tall temple-dome loomed above the trees of the forest. Near it, they could also see a house made of brick, encircled by a wall. Approaching the wall, Kapalkundala knocked on the gate.

'Who is that?' called a male voice from within, after repeated knocking. 'Is it Kapalkundala?'

'Open the door!' cried Kapalkundala.

The door was opened by the man who had answered from within. About fifty years of age, he was the officiating priest who attended upon the deity of the temple. Drawing down his hairless head, Kapalkundala brought her lips close to his ear and briefly explained her companion's predicament. For a long while, the priest pondered, resting his head in his hands.

'This is a terrible affair,' he presently declared. 'Once he makes up his mind, the kapalik is capable of anything. Anyway, by the grace of Ma, our presiding deity, no harm will come to you. Where is the person in question?'

Kapalkundala called out to Nabakumar, who had remained out of sight. Upon her invitation, he entered the house.

'Hide here today,' advised the priest. 'Tomorrow at dawn, I shall take you to the road that leads to Medinipur.'

In the course of conversation, it dawned on the priest that Nabakumar was starving. He busied himself preparing a meal for the young man, but Nabakumar had no appetite, and begged only for a place to rest. The priest arranged a bed for him in his own kitchen. When Nabakumar had retired for the night, Kapalkundala prepared to return to the seashore.

'Please don't leave!' begged the priest, looking at her with affection. 'Wait a little. I have a humble request.'

'What is it?'

'Ever since I set my eyes on you, I have addressed you as "Ma",' pleaded the priest. 'I touch the deity's feet and swear that I adore you as my mother, and more. You will not spurn my request, will you?'

'I will not.'

'I beseech you not to return to that place.'

'Why not?'

'You cannot save yourself if you do.'

'Indeed, I know that's true.'

'Then why ask for reasons?'

'Where else can I go?'

'Go with this traveller to another part of the country.'

Kapalkundala remained silent.

'What are you thinking, Ma?' asked the priest.

'When your disciple had come here earlier, you had said that it was inappropriate for a young woman to accompany a young man. Now, why do you ask me to do the same thing?'

'I had not feared for your life at that time. What's more important, there was no proper solution available at that time, but such a solution may be possible now. Come, let's seek the deity's consent.'

Lamp in hand, the priest went to the door of the temple and unlocked it. Kapalkundala joined him. Inside the temple was the awesome image of Goddess Kali in human form. They offered their devotion, the two of them, at the deity's feet. The priest performed some preliminary rituals before chanting a prayer over an intact triad of belpata, wood-apple leaves, which he placed at the idol's feet. He gazed at the leaves for a while.

'Look, Ma, the devi has accepted our offering,' he pointed out to Kapalkundala. 'The leaves didn't fall off, which means the wish I made while making the offering is bound to come true. You may proceed with this traveller with no misgivings. But I know the ways of worldly men. If you accompany him as an appendage, he will find the company of an unknown young woman a social embarrassment. People will also treat you with contempt. You tell me this man is a Brahmin; I see he wears a sacred thread. It would be best for everyone concerned if he were to marry you. Otherwise, even I cannot bring myself to say that you should accompany him.'

'M-a-r-r-y!' Kapalkundala pronounced the word very slowly. 'I hear all of you speak of marriage, but I don't know exactly what it means. What does marriage require of me?'

'Marriage is a woman's only stepping-stone to dharma, the observance of her sacred duty,' explained the priest, with a faint smile. 'That is why a wife is called a sahadharmini, a man's partner in his pursuit of dharma. Even Jaganmata, divine mother of the world, is married to Shiva.'

The priest thought he had explained everything. Kapalkundala thought she had understood everything.

'So let it be,' she assented. 'But I don't feel like abandoning my foster-father. After all, he has taken care of me, all this time.'

'Don't you know why he has taken such care of you?'

The priest tried to explain to Kapalkundala, in a roundabout way, the role of a woman in tantric prayer rituals. Kapalkundala did not understand anything of this, but she felt very frightened.

'Very well, let the marriage take place, then,' she faltered.

They emerged from the temple. Leaving Kapalkundala in one of the rooms, the priest approached the sleeping Nabakumar.

'Are you asleep, sir?' he inquired.

'No, sir,' answered Nabakumar. Unable to sleep, he was worrying about his own predicament.

'Sir, I have come to request an introduction,' the priest explained. 'Are you a Brahmin?'

'Yes, sir.'

'Of what category?'

'Radhi.'

'We, too, are Radhi Brahmins. Don't take us for Utkal Brahmins. By birth, I am head-priest of my clan, but at this moment, I have taken refuge at the deity's feet. What is sir's name?'

'Nabakumar Sharma.'

'Place of residence?'

'Saptagram.'

'Which village do you come from?'

'Bandyaghoti.'

'How many families do you have?'

'Just one.' Nabakumar did not disclose the entire truth. Actually, he did not have even one family. He had married Padmavati, daughter of Ramgobinda Ghoshal. After the wedding, Padmavati had remained in her paternal home for some time, visiting her in-laws occasionally. When she was thirteen, her father had taken his family on a pilgrimage to the shrine of Purushottam. At this time, the Pathans, expelled from Bengal by Emperor Akbar, had collectively settled in Orissa. Emperor Akbar was now systematically engaged in the task of curbing them. When Ramgobinda Ghoshal set out on his journey back from Orissa, fighting had broken out between the Mughals and the Pathans. On the way, he fell into the hands of the Pathan army. The Pathans, at that time, did not discriminate between the respectable and the disreputable; they tried to threaten the innocent traveller, in the hope of extorting money. Somewhat aggressive by nature, Ramgobinda began to shower abuses upon them. As a result, he and his family were taken captive. Ultimately, they saved themselves by converting to Islam, surrendering their faith.

Ramgobinda Ghoshal returned alive, along with his family; but as a Muslim, he was now ostracized by his own community. Under these circumstances, Nabakumar's father, who was alive at the time, had no choice but to disown his daughter-in-law and also her father, for having lost their caste purity. Nabakumar did not see his wife again.

Cast out by his family and his community, Ramgobinda Ghoshal could not remain in his hometown for long. For this reason, and also from an ambitious desire to attain a high position in the royal household, he moved with his family to the capital city, and settled in the royal palace there. Having converted to Islam, he and his family had adopted Muslim names. Once they had moved into the royal palace, Nabakumar had no way of finding out what became of the father and his daughter; and indeed, up to this time, he had no information about them. He was too detached to marry again. That is why I say, Nabakumar had no family at all.

The temple attendant was unaware of these facts. 'Why should a kulin Brahmin object to having two families?' he thought.

Outwardly, he said: 'I had come to make a request. This young woman who saved your life has wasted her life in the service of another. The holy man who has given her refuge is a person to be dreaded. If she returns to him, she will meet the same fate that was designed for you. Can't you think of a way out for her?'

Nabakumar sat up. 'That's what I had feared,' he confessed. 'You know the whole story: please suggest a solution. I am willing to lay down my life if required, by way of reciprocating her goodwill. I am thinking of going back to that murderer, to surrender myself to him. That should save her life.'

'You are insane!' laughed the official. 'What good would that do? You would lose your life, but that would not reduce the holy man's ire against this girl. There is only one solution to the problem.'

'What is it?'

'She must run away with you. But that is very difficult to accomplish. If she remains here with me, she will be captured within a couple of days. The holy man visits this temple regularly. It seems apparent to me that fate doesn't augur well for Kapalkundala.'

'Why would it be so difficult for her to escape with me?' demanded Nabakumar, eagerly.

'You know nothing about her—her parentage, her caste. Would you accept her as your companion? Even if you did, would you offer her a place in your home? And if you don't let her stay with you, where will this orphan go?'

'There's nothing I cannot do for the person who saved my life,' answered Nabakumar, after pausing briefly to consider. 'She will live with me as a member of my family.'

'Very well. But when your relatives want to know whose wife she is, what answer will you offer?

Nabakumar paused again to consider. 'Please explain her parentage to me,' he requested. 'That is how I shall introduce her to everyone.'

'Fine ' replied the priest. 'But how will a young man and a young woman travel unchaperoned across the border from one region to another? What will people say? How will you explain this to your relatives? And having adopted this girl as my Ma, how can I send her off to some faraway place in the company of an unknown young man?'

The matchmaker was quite skilled at his job!

'You could accompany us,' Nabakumar suggested.

'Accompany you? Who would offer daily prayers to Goddess Bhavani then?'

'Can you think of no solution, then?' demanded Nabakumar, aggrieved.

'There can be only one solution. It depends on your magnanimity.'

'What is it? Is there anything I would refuse? Please tell me what the solution might be!'

'Then listen. She is the daughter of a Brahmin. I know the entire story of her life. In her childhood, she was abducted by a band of dreaded Christian brigands, who abandoned her on this seashore after their carriage broke down. Later, you can ask her for a detailed account of this story. The kapalik found her, and brought her up with the intention of using her to fulfil the requirements of his religious practice. In the near future, he would have satisfied his own needs. She is still chaste, pure of nature. Marry her and take her home with you. Nobody can raise any objections then. I shall conduct the wedding rites according to the scriptures.'

Nabakumar rose to his feet and began to pace swiftly up and down. He offered no reply.

'Please go back to sleep,' advised the temple attendant after a while. 'I shall wake you at dawn. You may travel alone if you wish. I shall show you the road to Medinipur.'

With these words, he took his leave. 'Have I forgotten the art of matchmaking which I learnt in the land of Radh?' he wondered to himself, as he departed.

9

In the Temple

Kanwa: Weep no more. Be calm. Walk this way, watching your step.

—*Shakuntala*

AT DAWN, THE PRIEST APPROACHED NABAKUMAR, TO FIND THAT THE YOUNG man had not slept at all.

'What is to be our course of action?' the priest inquired.

'From today, Kapalkundala shall be my wife,' declared Nabakumar. 'For her sake, I could even renounce the world. Who will give away the bride?'

The expert matchmaker's countenance glowed with joy. 'At last, by the grace of Goddess Jagadamba, my little Kapalini seems to have found a way out of her predicament!' he thought to himself. Outwardly, he said:

'I shall give away the bride.'

The priest returned to his bedroom, where a few worn and faded palm-leaf parchments had been stored inside a khungi, a small cane casket. Inscribed on the palm-leaves was the almanac, which charted auspicious days, astronomical calculations, etc. Having closely scrutinized the almanac, he emerged from his room and announced:

'Today is not a date earmarked for weddings, but there are no obstacles indicated for a marriage ceremony on this day. At dusk, I shall perform the kanyadaan ritual to give away the bride. A daylong fast is all you need observe. Ensure that all other family rituals are performed after you return to your own home. There is a place where I can conceal the two of you for a day. If the kapalik comes here today, he will not find you. Once married, you can leave for home at daybreak tomorrow, accompanied by your wife.'

Nabakumar agreed to this proposal. The ceremony was performed, following the prescribed rules as closely as the present circumstances permitted. At dusk, Nabakumar was married to the hermit-woman, the kapalik's foster-daughter.

There was no sign of the kapalik. Early next morning, the three of them prepared to set out on their journey. The priest would accompany them up to the road to Medinipur.

When it was time to leave, Kapalkundala went to pay her last respects to the image of Kali. In deep devotion, she bowed in obeisance; then, taking an intact belpata triad from the flower-basket, she placed it at the deity's feet, and fixed her gaze upon it. The belpata fell off.

Kapalkundala was deeply religious. She was terrified to see the triple leaf fall away from the feet of the idol. She informed the priest, who was also perturbed.

'There is nothing to be done, now,' he told her. 'Your husband is now your sole object of devotion. If he heads for the cremation ground, even there you must follow him. So, you must now proceed quietly on your journey.'

The three of them trudged on in silence. The day was far advanced when they arrived at the road to Medinipur. The priest took his leave of them. Kapalkundala burst into tears. She was parting with the person dearest to her in the whole world.

The priest also began to weep. Then, wiping away his tears, he whispered to Kapalkundala: 'Ma! You know that, by the grace of the goddess, I do not lack for means. The goddess receives prayer-offerings from everyone in Hijli, old or young. Use what I have knotted into the end of your sari—give it to your husband, and ask him to hire a palanquin for you. Think of me as your son!'

Weeping, he departed. Also in tears, Kapalkundala proceeded on her journey.

Part 2

1
On the Highway

There—now lean on me:
lace your foot here—

—*Manfred*

WHEN THEY ARRIVED AT MEDINIPUR, NABAKUMAR ARRANGED A PALANQUIN for Kapalkundala, using the money donated by the priest to hire a maid, a bodyguard and palanquin-bearers. Due to a paucity of funds, he himself proceeded on foot. Nabakumar was exhausted after the strain of the previous day. After their noontime meal, the palanquin bearers outstripped him, leaving him far behind. As evening approached, daylight waned. The sky was overcast with light winter clouds. Then, twilight faded, too, and darkness enveloped the earth. It began to drizzle. Nabakumar now grew anxious to catch up with Kapalkundala. He was certain that he would find her at the first serai or wayside inn, but there was no serai in sight at present. The hour was late. Nabakumar strode on swiftly. Suddenly, he trod on something hard; it broke under his weight with a loud, cracking sound. Nabakumar paused, then walked on. The same thing happened again. He bent to pick up the object he had stepped on. It looked like a broken plank of wood.

Even on a cloudy night, it is not usually dark enough out in the open for a solid shape to remain entirely invisible. Before him lay a giant object, which Nabakumar realized was a broken palanquin. At once, he was filled with apprehensions of some danger having befallen Kapalkundala. As he advanced towards the palanquin, his foot again touched something. This time, the substance felt different, like the touch of tender human flesh. Kneeling to stroke the form that lay on the ground, he found that it was indeed a human body. It was extremely cold to the touch; his fingers felt something wet. He could not find the pulse: was the person dead? But when he listened carefully, the sound of breathing could be heard. If breath remained, why was there no pulse? Was this person ill? Placing his hand close to the nostrils, he could feel no breath. Then why that sound? Perhaps there was also a living person present on the scene.

'Is there a living person here?' he asked.

'There is,' came the reply, in a low voice.

'Who are you?'

'Who are *you*?' demanded the voice, in return.

The voice sounded like a woman's.

'Kapalkundala, is that you?' asked Nabakumar, in great agitation.

'Who Kapalkundala is, I don't know,' replied the woman. 'I am a traveller, with no kundals or earrings to my name at present, thanks to the bandits who have robbed me.'

Her wit lightened Nabakumar's mood somewhat. 'What's the matter?' he asked.

'The bandits have smashed my palanquin,' replied the woman. 'They have killed one of the bearers, and the others have run away. Having robbed me of all the jewels I was wearing, the bandits have tied me up and left me here inside the palanquin.'

Groping in the dark, Nabakumar found that there was indeed a woman lying inside the palanquin, trussed up by some garments. Swiftly, he untied her bonds.

'Can you get up?' he asked.

'They struck me with a stick,' the woman replied. 'My leg hurts. But with a bit of help, I think I can stand up.'

Nabakumar extended his hand, and with his support, the woman rose to her feet.

'Can you walk?' asked Nabakumar.

'Did you see any other traveller following you?' the woman inquired, without answering his question.

'No.'

'How far is it to the chati, the wayside resting place?' she wanted to know.

'I couldn't say exactly, but I suppose it's not far away.'

'It's no use sitting alone here, out in the open,' decided the woman. 'I should go with you up to the chati. I can probably hobble along with some support.'

'It's foolish to harbour scruples in times of crisis,' declared Nabakumar. 'You can lean on my shoulder.'

The woman was not foolish enough to hesitate; she began to walk, leaning on his shoulder for support.

The chati was indeed not far away. Those days, bandits were not afraid to commit robberies even near a chati. Within a short time, Nabakumar arrived at the resting place, along with his companion.

There, he found Kapalkundala. Her attendants had hired a room for her. Nabakumar hired an adjoining room for his fellow-traveller, and ensconced her there. At his request, the landlady's daughter brought in a lighted oil lamp. Bathed in the stream of lamplight, his companion's form struck Nabakumar as extraordinarily beautiful. Her voluptuous beauty resembled the surging waves of a river in the monsoon flood.

2
The Wayside Inn

Who is this woman, so restless by nature?

—*Uddhavduta*

IF THIS WOMAN'S BEAUTY HAD BEEN FLAWLESS, I WOULD HAVE SAID: 'OH male reader! She is as beautiful as your own wife. And oh my beautiful female reader! She is as lovely as your own image in the mirror.' Her appearance would need no further description. Unfortunately, she was not beautiful in every respect; hence I cannot adopt that course.

She was not a flawless beauty: firstly, she was slightly above medium height; secondly, her lips were rather thin; and thirdly, she was not really fair of complexion.

She was rather tall, indeed, but her limbs and bosom were full and well rounded. Like trees and vines in the rainy season, her body rippled with its own voluptuousness, the fullness lending grace even to her tall figure. A truly fair complexion resembles either the light of the full moon, or the rosy light of dawn. I do not describe this woman as truly fair because her complexion resembled neither; but her colouring was no less attractive. She was dusky, but hers was not the dark complexion evoked by the names of 'Shyama Ma,' the Goddess Kali, or 'Shyam Sundar,' the Lord Krishna. Her skin had the deep hue of molten gold. If the light of the full moon or the rays of the golden sun are similes for the fair-complexioned, then the glory of vernal foliage may be an apt analogy for the complexion of this dusky woman. Many of my esteemed readers may celebrate the complexion of fair-skinned women, but if anyone comes under the spell of such a dark-complexioned woman, I would not call him colour-blind. If anyone should quarrel with this view, let him imagine this woman, her locks clustered about her dark, glowing forehead like bees hovering about the petals of a newly-blossomed flower; her eyebrows, arching up to her hairline beneath her crescent-shaped brow; her cheeks, bright as flowers in full bloom, and her small, rosy mouth. Visualizing her thus, he is bound to find this unknown woman beautiful, on the whole. Her eyes were not large, but they were extremely bright, and framed by lovely, curling lashes. Their gaze was calm, yet penetrating. Her glance would instantly make you feel that she had the power to look into the interior of your heart. The expression of those penetrating eyes would change from moment to moment, now melting with tender affection, now full of sweet languor, as if the god of Love himself lay dreaming there. At times, her eyes would be dilated with desire, intoxicated with romance; and at other times, a heartless sidelong glance would dart from the corners of her eyes, like a flash of lightning in the clouds. Two ineffable elements irradiated her countenance: the stamp of intelligence, and her self-esteem. From her posture, the arch of her swan-neck, it was clear that she was a queen among women.

This beautiful woman was twenty-seven years old, in the full flush of youth, like a river in flood during the month of Bhadra. Her sensuous beauty brimmed over, like a river surging against its banks in the rains. Even more than her complexion, her eyes, and all her individual features, this flood tide of voluptuousness rendered her enchanting. Youthful vitality made her body restless, as a river in autumn ripples even without a breeze; from moment to moment, this restless energy revealed some new facet of her loveliness. Nabakumar gazed, transfixed, at this ever-changing display of charm.

'What are you staring at? My beauty?' inquired the beautiful woman, observing his unblinking stare.

Nabakumar was a bhadralok, a gentleman; embarrassed, he lowered his gaze.

Seeing that he was speechless, the unknown woman smiled. 'Have you never seen a woman before?' she persisted, 'or do you find me so very beautiful?'

Because she smiled, what would normally have seemed a reprimand sounded merely like a sarcastic remark. Nabakumar realized that she was extremely articulate. Why should he not engage in repartee with such a loquacious woman?

'I have indeed seen other women,' he replied. 'But I have not seen anyone so lovely.'

'Not even one?' she inquired, with pride.

In his mind's eye, Nabakumar saw a vision of Kapalkundala. 'I wouldn't quite say that,' he answered, with equal arrogance.

'That's not so bad, then. Is she your wife, the other one?'

'Why? Why should you imagine her to be my wife?'

'Bengalis find their own wives most beautiful.'

'I am a Bengali. You sound like a Bengali, too. Where are you from?'

'Yours truly is not fortunate enough to be a Bengali,' replied the young woman, glancing at her own attire. 'I am a Muslim from the western region.'

Inspecting her appearance, Nabakumar realized that her garb was indeed that of a Muslim woman from the west. But she spoke Bengali exactly as if it were her mother tongue.

'Sir, you have taken my measure in repartee,' she continued, after a pause. 'Now please gratify me by disclosing your identity. Where is the home of which that woman of unparalleled beauty is the mistress?'

'I live in Saptagram,' answered Nabakumar.

The woman—this stranger from elsewhere—did not reply. Suddenly, she bent over the lamp and busied herself trying to turn up its flame.

'My name is Moti,' she informed him after a while, without raising her head. 'May I not know yours?'

'Nabakumar Sharma.'

The lamp went out.

3

A View of Female Beauty

. . . O goddess, as divine enchantress let yourself appear!
By your leave, with ornaments diverse,
Your beauteous form I shall adorn!

—*Meghnadbadh*

NABAKUMAR ORDERED THE LANDLORD TO FETCH ANOTHER LAMP. BEFORE the lamp arrived, he heard a sigh. Soon after, a Muslim in attendant's livery entered the room.

'What's this!' exclaimed the female stranger. 'Why did you take so long, all of you? Where are the others?'

'The bearers were drunk!' replied the attendant. 'While we struggled to herd them together, your palanquin left us far behind. Afterwards, discovering the smashed palanquin, and no sign of you anywhere, we almost fainted with shock. Some of them are still at that spot; others have scattered here and there in search of you. I came here looking for you.'

'Get them to this place!' ordered Moti.

Saluting her, the attendant departed. The woman from elsewhere remained lost in thought for a while, resting her cheek on her hand.

Nabakumar prepared to leave. Like a sleepwalker, Moti rose to her feet.

'Where will you stay?' she asked, resuming her earlier tone.

'In the very next room.'

'I saw a palanquin near that room. Do you have a companion?'

'My wife accompanies me.'

'Is she the one, the woman of unparalleled beauty?' asked Moti, finding another opportunity for banter.

'If you see her, you will know.'

'Would it be possible to see her?'

'What's the harm?' replied Nabakumar, after some thought.

'Do me a favour, then. I am very curious to see this woman, this matchless beauty. I want to speak of her when I get to Agra. But not now. Please leave me now. I shall send word to you after some time.'

Nabakumar left. Soon after, a large contingent arrived there, including attendants, maidservants, and bearers carrying chests and other items of luggage. With them came a palanquin, bearing a maidservant. Then Nabakumar received a message: 'Bibi, her ladyship, is thinking of you.'

Nabakumar returned to Motibibi. Once again, he found her transformed. She had shed her earlier garb, and was now attired in embroidered garments, embellished with gold and pearls; her person, previously bare of ornament, was now bedecked with jewellery. Gold, diamonds and precious stones flashed from every part of her body, from her tresses and braided hair-knot to her forehead, temples, ears, throat, bosom, and both her arms. Nabakumar's eyes were dazzled. Like a garland of stars adorning the sky, the profusion of jewellery seemed appropriate for her voluptuous body, enhancing her charm.

'Come, sir, let's get acquainted with your wife,' she invited Nabakumar.

'There was no need for you to adorn yourself with jewels for that purpose,' Nabakumar informed her. 'My wife has no ornaments at all.'

'Perhaps I have worn my jewellery to show it off. If a woman possesses ornaments, she can't resist displaying them. Let's go.'

Nabakumar escorted Motibibi from the room. Accompanying them was Peshaman, the maidservant who had arrived in the palanquin.

They found Kapalkundala alone, on the damp, earthen floor of the room that served as the shop. The room was faintly lit by a single lamp. Her form was framed by the dark backdrop of her heavy, unbound tresses. Glancing at her for the first time, Motibibi showed faint signs of amusement, a slight smile playing at the corners of her mouth and the edges of her eyes. She raised the lamp to take a closer look at Kapalkundala. All her amusement evaporated, and her expression grew grave. She gazed, unblinking. Both were silent—Moti spellbound, Kapalkundala slightly surprised.

After a while, Moti began to take off her jewellery. One by one, she removed her ornaments, and adorned Kapalkundala with them. Kapalkundala said nothing.

'What are you doing?' Nabakumar expostulated.

Moti offered no reply.

'You were indeed right,' she remarked to Nabakumar, when she had parted with all her ornaments. 'Such a flower does not blossom even in the garden of a king. It is my regret that I could not display this profusion of beauty at the capital city. These ornaments are befitting only for her figure—that's why I have bedecked her with them. I hope that you, too, will sometimes adorn her with these jewels, and remember me—this woman from an alien land, so skilled at repartee.'

'Impossible!' cried Nabakumar, thunderstruck. 'These jewels are priceless! Why should I accept them?'

'By the grace of God, I have more. I shall not be bereft of ornaments. If it gives me happiness to adorn her with these jewels, why should you object?'

With these words, Motibibi departed, along with her maid.

'Bibijaan! Who is this man?' demanded Peshaman as soon as they were alone.

'Mera shauhar,' replied the young Muslim lady. 'He is my husband!'

4

The Palanquin Ride

. . . Swiftly, I discard
My bangles, necklace, hair-ornament, choker
Earrings, anklets, girdle.

—*Meghnadbadh*

LET ME TELL YOU THE FATE OF THOSE ORNAMENTS. MOTIBIBI SENT A SILVER-enamelled ivory casket for storing the jewellery. The robbers had taken only a few of her ornaments, unable to grab anything beyond what they found close at hand.

Leaving a few of the ornaments on Kapalkundala's person, Nabakumar transferred the rest to the casket. The next morning, Motibibi left for Bardhaman, and Nabakumar for Saptagram, accompanied by his wife. Nabakumar helped Kapalkundala into the palanquin, and handed her the casket of jewels. The bearers soon outstripped Nabakumar and proceeded on their way. Kapalkundala opened the palanquin door to observe the scene around her. Seeing her, a beggar began to walk alongside the palanquin, asking for alms.

'But I have nothing,' Kapalkundala protested. 'What can I offer you?'

'How can you say that, Ma!' cried the beggar, pointing at the few ornaments she wore. 'Bedecked with diamonds and pearls, you say you have nothing to give!'

'If I gave you these ornaments, would you be satisfied?' asked Kapalkundala.

The beggar was surprised. His greed knew no bounds. 'I would be satisfied, indeed!' he instantly replied.

Artlessly, Kapalkundala handed him the jewellery, casket and all. She even gave away the ornaments on her person.

For a moment, the beggar was overwhelmed. The attendants remained unaware of what had taken place. The beggar's hesitation lasted but an instant. Then, glancing quickly all about him, he made off with the jewellery at top speed.

'Why did the beggar run away?' wondered Kapalkundala to herself.

5

Back Home

These words, though sayable before her female companions,
I'd whisper only in her ear, just for the pleasure of her touch.

—Meghdoot

ACCOMPANIED BY KAPALKUNDALA, NABAKUMAR RETURNED TO HIS OWN place of domicile. Fatherless, he lived with his widowed mother and his two sisters. The elder of the two was a widow; the reader will not have the opportunity of making her acquaintance. Though married, the second sister, Shyamasundari, was no better off than a widow, because her husband was a kulin Brahmin. She will make a few brief appearances in the story.

When Nabakumar returned home under altered circumstances, married to a hermit-woman of unknown extraction, there is no saying whether his relatives would have approved. But as it turned out, he did not have to suffer much on this account. Everyone had given up hope of his ever coming back, for upon their return, Nabakumar's fellow-travellers had spread rumours about his having been killed by a tiger. The esteemed reader may think that these truth-sayers had reported what they believed to be a fact; but this would be an underestimation of their imaginative powers. Many of the travellers who had returned, swore that they had actually seen Nabakumar fall into the tiger's clutches. They argued about the dimensions of the tiger, some estimating its length at about twelve feet, while others insisted that it was almost twenty-one feet long.

'Anyway, I had a narrow escape!' declared the old traveller we have encountered earlier. 'The tiger chased me first, but I eluded him. Nabakumar was not as brave: he didn't manage to get away.'

When these rumours reached the ears of Nabakumar's mother and sisters, the sound of wailing that arose within the house did not subside for several days. The news of her only son's demise brought his mother to the brink of death. In this situation, when Nabakumar returned home accompanied by a wife, no one thought to inquire about his spouse's caste or parentage. They were blind with joy, all of them. Nabakumar's mother cordially performed the boron ritual to welcome the bride into the house.

Nabakumar was overjoyed to find Kapalkundala so warmly accepted as a member of the household. Fearing that she might be rejected by his family, he had expressed neither tenderness nor desire towards Kapalkundala even after she became his wife. Yet, it was her image that filled his heart. It was this worry that had held him back from instantly agreeing to the proposed marriage with Kapalkundala. Indeed, it was this apprehension that had deterred him from expressing his love for her even once, from the time they were married, until they reached his home. He had not allowed the slightest wave to rock the ocean of his love, though it was full to flooding. But now, his anxieties were dispelled. Like the wild torrent that gushes forth when a rock obstructing the water's flow is shattered, the sea of love in Nabakumar's heart surged and spilled over.

This love did not always express itself in words. It revealed itself in the expression in Nabakumar's eyes whenever he looked at Kapalkundala, for he would gaze at her transfixed, his eyes brimming with tears; in the way he sought her out on some imaginary pretext, even when there was no need; in his attempts to bring Kapalkundala's name into the conversation, even when it was out of context; in his striving, day and night, to ensure

Kapalkundala's happiness and comfort; in the way he ceaselessly paced up and down, lost in thought. Even his personality began to change. In place of restlessness, a new gravity was born; in place of gloom, cheerfulness appeared; Nabakumar's countenance was now ever-happy. Now that his heart was filled with love, he felt more affection for others; he grew less hostile towards those who tested his patience; he now loved every human being; it seemed to him that the world had been created only for good deeds; the whole world seemed to him a beautiful place. Such is love! Love transforms the harsh into the tender, evil into good, vice into virtue, darkness into light!

And Kapalkundala, what of her? What was her state of mind? Come, reader, let us take a look.

6
In Seclusion

Why, in your youth, shed all finery to wrap yourself in tree-bark?
Say, at dusk, can the starry, moonlit night seek out the sun?

—*Kumarasambhava*

IN OLDEN DAYS, AS WE KNOW, SAPTAGRAM WAS A VERY PROSPEROUS TOWN. It was once a trade centre for merchants from every country, from Java to Rome. But in the tenth or eleventh century of the Bengali calendar, the ancient glory of Saptagram began to decline, mainly because the river that skirted the edge of the town had become too narrow for large vessels to navigate. As ships could no longer access the town, its flourishing business began to disappear. If a trade centre loses its business, it loses everything. Saptagram lost everything. In the eleventh century of the Bengali calendar, Hooghly, in its growing splendour, became its rival. Having begun trading in Hooghly, the Portuguese drained the economy of Saptagram, luring away Dhanalakshmi, the town's presiding goddess of wealth. But even then, Saptagram had not entirely lost its charm. Important administrators, including military officials, still resided there; but already, many parts of the town, now ugly and abandoned, had begun to acquire a provincial air.

Nabakumar lived in an isolated suburb of the town. With Saptagram in ruins, this place now was rarely frequented by people. The main street was overrun with weeds and creepers. Just behind Nabakumar's house was a dense, extensive forest. In front of the house, almost a mile away, flowed a narrow canal, skirting a tiny field to enter the forest at the rear. The house, made of brick, was no mean structure, considering the time and place of its construction. Though double-storeyed, it was not unduly high: nowadays, single-storeyed houses are often of the same height.

On the terrace of this house stood two young women, gazing at the view. Dusk had descended. The scene that presented itself all around them was indeed a feast for the eyes. Close at hand, on one side, was a dense forest, resonant with the chirping of countless birds. Opposite the forest was the canal, narrow as a silver thread. Far away, in the distance, one could see the beautiful silhouettes of innumerable mansions, full of townspeople yearning for a touch of the fresh spring breeze. On the other side, far, far away, the darkness deepened on the immense trees that lined the shores of the river Bhagirathi, its surface adorned with boats.

Of the two young women on the terrace, one had a complexion like the glimmer of moonlight; she was half-concealed by her mass of unbound tresses. The other woman, dark-skinned, was a beautiful sixteen, with slender frame and tiny face, the upper portion of her countenance framed by wisps of curly hair like the petal-encircled heart of a blue lotus. Her wide eyes were pale and tender like a small saphari fish; her delicate fingers caressed her companion's wavy hair. The esteemed reader would have guessed that she of the moonlight glow was Kapalkundala. Let me add that the dark-skinned one was her nanad, her sister-in-law Shyamasundari.

Shyamasundari addressed her sister-in-law sometimes as 'Bou' or bride, sometimes affectionately as 'Bon' or sister, and sometimes as 'Mrino'. Kapalkundala being such a formidable name, the family had renamed her

Mrinmayi, Mrino for short. We, too, shall sometimes refer to her as Mrinmayi.

Shyamasundari was reciting a verse learnt in childhood:

The lotus-flower, she hides her face in sand,
But seeing her loved one, she blooms to attract the bee.
And the wild vine spreads her leaves to reach out to the tree;
And at flood-tide, the river-waters descend to the sea.
In moonlight blooms the flower, without being coy;
The bride sheds all restraint upon entering the nuptial bed.
What's this? A quirk of fate, for sure! How bittersweet is love!
Modesty forgotten, we blossom at another's touch!

'Would you remain a loner, then, in your holy pursuit of abstinence?'

'Why, what holy pursuit am I engaged in?' demanded Mrinmayi.

'Won't you braid this mass of hair?' asked Shyamasundari, lifting up Mrinmayi's wavy tresses with both hands.

With a faint smile, Mrinmayi merely pulled away the locks of hair from Shyamasundari's grasp.

'Please keep my wish,' Shyamasundari persisted. 'Dress like a housewife, just for once. How long will you remain a female ascetic—a yogini?'

'Before I met this man, descendant of Brahmins, I was indeed a yogini,' replied Kapalkundala.

'Not any more.'

'Why not?'

'Why not? Do you really want to know? I shall disrupt your holy pursuit. Do you know what a touchstone is?'

'No,' confessed Mrinmayi.

'Its touch can convert even tin to gold.'

'So what?'

'Women possess a touchstone, too.'

'What's that?'

'A man. The company of a man can turn even a yogini into a housewife.

You have touched that stone. Wait and see:

I'll make you braid your hair, dress you in finery,
Place a swaying flower-garland in your hair,
An ornament in your parting, a girdle round your waist,
And earrings on your ears.
With kumkum, sandalwood, scent and paan-supari
I'll tint your rosy countenance.
In your lap I'll cast a golden doll, a son,
And we'll see if you like it or not!

'I understand perfectly,' responded Mrinmayi. 'Let us suppose that the touchstone turns me to gold. Suppose I braid my hair, deck myself out in finery, wear flowers in my hair, a girdle around my waist, and ornaments in my ears; let us go as far as the sandalwood, kumkum, scent, paan, and even the golden doll of a son. Let us imagine it all. But even then, how will it make me happy?'

'Tell me, what about the happiness of a flower that bursts into bloom?'

'That would make people happy, but what would the flower gain from blooming?'

Shyamasundari's countenance grew grave; like blue lotuses stirred by the early morning breeze, her wide-eyed gaze wavered.

'What about the flower?' she wondered. 'I couldn't say! I have never bloomed like a flower, but had I been a bud like you, I would have blossomed with joy.'

'Very well, if this does not appeal to you,' persisted Shyamasundari, when Mrinmayi remained silent, 'then tell me what makes you happy?'

'I can't say,' replied Mrinmayi, after considering for a while. 'Perhaps it would make me happy to wander in those forests by the seashore.'

Shyamasundari was surprised. She felt rather offended, even angry, at Mrinmayi's lack of gratitude towards those who had looked after her.

'How would you return there, now?' she asked.

'There can be no return.'

'Then what will you do?'

'"As I am bidden, so shall I act," the priest at the temple used to say.'

Shyamasundari covered her face with the end of her sari, stifling a smile. 'As you say, Mr Bhattacharya, sir!' she mimicked. 'So, what next?'

'Fate will determine my actions,' sighed Mrinmayi. 'Whatever destiny has in store for me, will happen.'

'Why, what could fate have in store for you? Happiness is your destiny. Why do you sigh, then?'

'Listen,' explained Mrinmayi. 'The day I set out on my journey with my husband, I offered a triple belpata at the Goddess Bhavani's feet. I would never undertake any task without offering a triple leaf at Ma's lotus-like feet. If destiny decreed a positive outcome for my endeavour, Ma would accept the offering; if an inauspicious outcome was likely, the belpata would fall off her pedestal. I was apprehensive about travelling to unknown lands, accompanied by a stranger. I went to Ma for an indication of the future, to find out whether it boded ill or well for me. Ma did not accept my triple leaf offering, so I'm not sure what the future holds in store for me.'

Mrinmayi fell silent. Shyamasundari shivered.

PART 3

1
In the Past

The role of a servant is very painful.

—*Ratnabali*

AFTER NABAKUMAR LEFT THE CHATI WITH KAPALKUNDALA, MOTIBIBI changed her route and headed for Bardhaman. While she is on her way, let us recount the story of her past. Moti's character was tainted with deep sin, but also graced by great virtues. A detailed account of such a person's character will not displease the esteemed reader.

When her father converted to Islam, her Hindu name was changed to Lutfunnissa. She was not called Motibibi at all, but sometimes, she adopted that name while travelling in disguise from place to place. When he reached Dhaka, her father entered royal service. But the place was frequented by many people from his own region. After having lost their social position, not everyone would like to continue in their original place of domicile. Hence, having gradually gained the favour of the subedar, he obtained letters of reference from numerous rich umraos and moved to Agra with his family. No person of talent could fail to attract Emperor Akbar's attention. He soon took note of this gentleman's expertise. In a short time, Lutfunnissa's father rose in the ranks to become one of the chief umraos of Agra.

Meanwhile, Lutfunnissa was growing up. In Agra, she became well-versed in Persian, Sanskrit, dance, music and the arts. She was ranked foremost among the innumerable beautiful and talented women of Agra. Unfortunately, her training in religious matters did not match her expertise in learned subjects. As she grew up, she began to display a wild, uncontrollable temperament. She had neither the ability, nor the inclination, to curb her sensuous appetites. When it came to questions of morality, it was exactly the same. She did exactly as she pleased, without first considering the rightness or wrongness of an action. She performed good deeds and evil deeds as it pleased her heart. Her nature developed the flaws that appear when youthful instincts run wild, without control. As her former husband was alive, none of the umraos, royal courtiers, were willing to marry her. She, too, showed no particular desire for marriage. 'Why clip the wings of the bee that flits from flower to flower?' she thought, in her heart of hearts. At first there were rumours, then, ultimately, scandal. Her father threw her out of the house in disgust.

Crown Prince Salim was one of the secret recipients of Lutfunnissa's favours. Salim, until now, had not made Lutfunnissa part of his harem, for fear of incurring the wrath of his impartial father if this unchaste woman brought family dishonour upon one of the umraos. Now, he found his opportunity. The sister of the Rajput king Raja Mansingh was the Crown Prince's chief consort. The Crown Prince appointed Lutfunnissa her chief companion. Officially, Lutfunnissa was the begum's companion, but in private, she became a beneficiary of the Crown Prince's largesse.

As we can easily imagine, a clever woman like Lutfunnissa quickly won the prince's heart. So completely did she dominate his affections, eliminating all competition, that she developed a firm resolve to become his reigning queen at the appropriate time. This was not only Lutfunnissa's own resolve; everyone in the royal palace also perceived this as a likely possibility. Lutfunnissa passed her days, rapt in these rosy dreams, when all of a sudden, she was rudely awakened. Mehrunnissa, daughter of Khaja Ayesh, treasurer to Emperor Akbar, was the reigning beauty of the Muslim community. One day, the treasurer invited Prince Salim to his home, along with other eminent personages. That day, Salim met Mehrunnissa, and gave her his heart. What happened thereafter is well known to readers of history. The treasurer's daughter was already betrothed to a very powerful umrao named Sher Afghan. Blinded by love, Salim beseeched his father to break that engagement, but all he received was a scolding from his fair-minded parent. For the time being, Salim had to desist, but he did not give up hope. Sher Afghan married Mehrunnissa. But Lutfunnissa understood all the nuances of Salim's psychology. She knew for sure that there would be no escape for Sher Afghan, even if he was blessed with a thousand lives. As soon as Emperor Akbar passed away, Sher Afghan would die, and Mehrunnissa would become Salim's queen. Lutfunnissa gave up her designs on the throne.

Akbar, the pride of the reigning Muslim dynasty, reached the end of his lifespan. The sun that had irradiated the entire region from Turkey to the Brahmaputra, was now about to set. At this time, to preserve her position of eminence, Lutfunnissa made a daring resolve.

The Rajput ruler Raja Mansingh's sister was Salim's chief consort. Khusrau was her son. One day, in the course of a discussion with her about Emperor Akbar's illness, Lutfunnissa congratulated her on the prospect of a Rajput's daughter becoming the reigning queen.

'A woman may indeed consider her life worthwhile if she becomes the Emperor's wife, but the Emperor's mother is senior to all,' retorted Khusrau's mother.

A novel strategy immediately suggested itself to Lutfunnissa's mind.

'Why not?' she responded. 'That, too, is within your control.'

'How is that?' wondered the begum.

'Give the throne to Khusrau, the Crown Prince's son!' proposed the clever woman.

The begum did not reply. The matter was not mentioned again that day, but neither of them forgot it. The begum was not averse to the idea that her son, rather than her husband, should ascend the throne; Salim's infatuation with Mehrunnissa was as much a thorn in the flesh for her, as it was for Lutfunnissa. Why should Mansingh's sister take kindly to the idea of being ordered about by an upstart daughter of a Turk? Lutfunnissa also had her own secret reasons for aiding and abetting this plan. The matter was raised again, another day. The two of them came to an agreement.

It did not seem impossible to dismiss Salim, in order to establish Khusrau on Akbar's throne. Lutfunnissa took great pains to convince the begum of this.

'The Mughal empire is sustained by the might of the Rajputs,' she argued. 'Raja Mansingh, the leading light of the Rajput clan, is Khusrau's mama, his maternal uncle; and Khan Azim, leader of the Muslims and chief minister to the emperor, is Khusrau's father-in-law; if these two men are ready to accept the arrangement, who would not follow them? And with whose support would the Crown Prince ascend the throne? It is your responsibility to commit Raja Mansingh to this undertaking. It is mine, to enlist the support of Khan Azim and the other Muslim umraos. With your blessings, I shall succeed, but I fear that Khusrau, having ascended the throne, might expel this errant woman from the fort.'

The begum understood her companion's intentions.

'You will be accepted by any umrao in Agra whose wife you wish to become,' she smiled. 'Your husband will become a royal official on a salary of five thousand.'

Lutfunnissa was satisfied. This, indeed, had been her motive. What joy in clipping the wings of the bee that flitted from flower to flower, to live in the royal palace as a humble housewife? If freedom must be surrendered, what pleasure would she derive from being slave to Mehrunnissa, her childhood playmate? More glorious by far, to marry some important royal functionary, to become the centre of his existence.

It was not merely this temptation that spurred Lutfunnissa to adopt such a course of action. She also wanted to avenge herself because Salim had ignored her and showered all his attention on Mehrunnissa.

Khan Azim and the other umraos of Agra and Delhi were very much under Lutfunnissa's thumb. It was hardly surprising that Khan Azim should promote the interests of his son-in-law. He and the other umraos agreed to the plan.

'Suppose things go wrong and our plot does not succeed?' Khan Azim urged Lutfunnissa. 'There will be no saving us then. So, it's best to devise some means of saving our lives.'

'What would you advise?'

'There is no refuge but Orissa,' Khan Azim declared. 'That is the only place where the hold of the Mughal administration is weak. It is necessary to have the Orissa army within our control. Your brother is an official in

Orissa; tomorrow, I shall spread word that he has been injured in battle. On the pretext of going to see him, you must leave for Orissa tomorrow itself. Come back as soon as your mission there is accomplished.'

Lutfunnissa consented to this proposal. The esteemed reader has encountered her on her journey back from Orissa.

2
Change of Route

We fall to the ground but rise again, with the earth's support;
Whoever dies of despair at a single blow of misfortune?
The storm has brought me low but I shall not give up hope;
Though thwarted today, my efforts may bear fruit tomorrow.

—*Nabin Tapaswini*

HAVING TAKEN LEAVE OF NABAKUMAR, MOTIBIBI ALIAS LUTFUNNISSA SET OUT for Bardhaman, but she could not reach her destination on the same day. She spent the night at a different chati. That evening, she chatted with Peshaman.

'Peshaman! What did you think of my husband?' Motibibi suddenly wanted to know.

'Why, what should I think of him?' asked Peshaman, rather surprised.

'Isn't he handsome?'

Peshaman had developed a special aversion to Nabakumar. She had once coveted the ornaments that Motibibi had given Kapalkundala, hoping that one day, the jewels would be hers for the asking. But now that this hope had been shattered, Peshaman felt a tremendous hostility towards Kapalkundala and her husband.

Hence, she replied: 'How can one think of an impoverished Brahmin as either handsome or ugly?'

'If the impoverished Brahmin becomes an umrao, would he not appear handsome?' laughed Moti, sensing her companion's mood.

'What's that supposed to mean?'

'Why, don't you know the begum has agreed to appoint my husband as an umrao if Khusrau becomes emperor?'

'I know that, indeed. But why should your former husband become an umrao?'

'What other husband do I have?'

'Your husband-to-be.'

'Two husbands for a chaste woman like me? What an impertinent thought!' protested Moti with a faint smile. 'Who goes there?' she called out suddenly.

Peshaman recognized the person in question as a resident of Agra, a trusted member of Khan Azim's entourage. The two women grew agitated. Peshaman called out to the man. Approaching them, he greeted Lutfunnissa and handed her a letter.

'I was carrying this letter to Orissa,' he told her. 'It's very urgent.'

Motibibi's hopes evaporated as she read the letter. This was what it said:

> Our efforts have been fruitless. Even at the time of his death, Akbar Shah has defeated us with his intelligence. He has now left us for his heavenly abode. By his orders, Prince Salim has become Jehangir Shah, the emperor. Please do not worry about Khusrau. To ensure that no one acts against you in this matter, please return to Agra as fast as possible.

How Akbar Shah handled this conspiracy, history books have recounted; there is no need to go into those details here.

Having dismissed the messenger with a tip, Moti read the letter aloud to Peshaman.

'What should we do now?' wondered Peshaman.

'There's nothing we can do now,' replied Moti.

'Well, what harm in that?' pronounced Peshaman, after some thought. 'You may as well continue as before, for any woman who belongs to the royal establishment enjoys more importance than even the reigning queen of some other state.'

'That's not possible anymore,' Moti explained, with a faint smile. 'I can no longer remain in that palace. Jehangir will waste no time in marrying Mehrunnissa. I have known Mehrunnissa since adolescence. Once she enters the palace, she will become the emperor, and Jehangir will remain Badshah only in name. She will discover that I had tried to obstruct her path to the throne. What will be my fate, then?'

'What will happen, now?' Peshaman was almost in tears.

'There is only one hope. What are Mehrunnissa's feelings for Jehangir? Such is her firmness of character, that if she cares more for her husband than for Jehangir, then she will not surrender her heart to Jehangir even if he were to murder a hundred Sher Afghans. But if Mehrunnissa is genuinely in love with Jehangir, then there is no hope for us.'

'How will you discover the secrets of Mehrunnissa's heart?'

'What can Lutfunnissa not accomplish?' smiled Moti. 'Mehrunnissa is my childhood companion. Tomorrow, I shall set out for Bardhaman, to spend a couple of days with her.'

'If Mehrunnissa is in love with the Badshah, what will you do?'

'My father used to say: "The situation will determine our course of action".'

For a while, they were silent. A faint smile began to play upon Moti's lips.

'Why do you smile?' asked Peshaman.

'A new idea has occurred to me.'

'What is it?'

Moti did not tell Peshaman what it was. We, too, shall withhold it from the reader. Eventually, the truth will reveal itself.

3
In the Rival's Home

Shyam alone, and none but he, rules over my heart.

—*Uddhavduta*

AT THIS TIME, SHER AFGHAN WAS THE OFFICIAL IN CHARGE OF THE BARDHAMAN administration, under the authority of the subedar of Bengal. Having arrived at Bardhaman, Motibibi presented herself at his house. Sher Afghan, along with his family, welcomed her warmly as a household guest. When Sher Afghan and his wife Mehrunnissa were residents of Agra, Moti had been one of their close acquaintances, particularly intimate with Mehrunnissa. Afterwards, the two of them had become rivals in their designs upon the throne of Delhi.

'Which of us is destined to rule India?' Mehrunnissa wondered, now that they were reunited. 'Only Fate knows the answer, and Salim; and if anyone else is in the know, it would be Lutfunnissa. Let's see if Lutfunnissa has anything to reveal!' Motibibi, too, was trying to decipher Mehrunnissa's frame of mind.

At that time, Mehrunnissa was renowned as the most beautiful and talented woman in India. Indeed, very few women like her have been born into this world. Every historian has acknowledged her prominent place amongst the legendary beauties of this world. Among the men of her time, few could match her at any skill. Her talent for music and dance was unparalleled; in poetry and the visual arts as well, she could hold her audience enthralled. Her gift for conversation was even more captivating than her physical beauty. In all these aspects, Moti, too, was in no way less talented. These two enchantresses were now keen to understand each other's minds.

Mehrunnissa was in the special parlour, painting a picute. Peering over her shoulder was Lutfunnissa, chewing paan, betel leaf, as she watched her paint.

'What do you think of my painting?' asked Mehrunnissa.

'It is typical of your artistry. It's a pity nobody else can boast of your artistic skills.'

'If that is indeed true, then why is it a pity?'

'If others had your artistic talent, they could paint your image as a keepsake.'

'In my grave, my image will be entombed.'

Mehrunnissa pronounced these words with gravity.

'My sister!' cried Moti. 'Why are you in such low spirits today?'

'Low spirits? Of course not! But how can I forget that you leave at dawn tomorrow? Why should you not gratify me by staying a couple of days longer?'

'Who doesn't fancy a life of pleasure? Would I leave, if I had my way? But I must act as others decree: how can I linger here?'

'You don't love me anymore, else you would have extended your stay. If you could travel to this place, why can't you stay on?'

'I have told you everything. My brother, a mansabdar in the Mughal army, was grievously injured in a skirmish with the Pathans of Orissa. When I received tidings of his condition, I travelled to this region to visit him, with the begum's permission. I have spent too much time in Orissa, but now I should delay no more. I spent these two days with you because we had not met for a very long time.'

'By which date have you promised the begum that you will return?'

Moti realized that Mehrunnissa was being sarcastic. She could not match Mehrunnissa in the art of polished, yet piercing irony. But she, too, was never at a loss for words.

'Is it possible to fix a date when embarking on a three-month-long journey? But I have delayed too long; any further delay might incur displeasure.'

'Whose displeasure do you fear?' inquired Mehrunnissa with her captivating smile. 'The Crown Prince's, or his consort's?'

'Would you embarrass me, shameless person that I am?' responded Moti, slightly discomfited. 'Both could be displeased.'

'But why not assume the title of begum yourself, may I ask? I hear that Prince Salim is to marry you, as his special consort. How far have those plans advanced?'

'I am easily subjugated. Why should I surrender the little freedom I have? As the begum's companion, I could easily travel to Orissa; but as Salim's begum, could I have done the same?'

'For one who will be the reigning queen of Delhi, what need to travel to Orissa?'

'I would never dare aspire to become Salim's reigning queen. In Hindustan, only Mehrunnissa is fit to reign supreme over the heart of Delhi's ruler.'

Mehrunnissa lowered her head. 'My sister!' she pleaded, after a short silence, 'I shall not try to ascertain whether you uttered these words to hurt my feelings, or to know my mind. But when you speak to me, I beg you not to forget that I am Sher Afghan's wife, his devoted slave in body, mind and soul.'

Far from being put out by this admonition, the brazen Moti took this opportunity to advance her argument.

'That you are a devoted wife, I know only too well,' she persisted. 'That is why I have dared to raise this subject indirectly. My aim is to make you aware that Salim has been unable to forget the magic of your beauty. Please remain careful.'

'Now I understand. But what have I to fear?'

'Widowhood,' declared Moti, after some hesitation.

As she spoke, Moti fixed her gaze upon Mehrunnissa's countenance, but could detect no trace of fear or joy.

'Fear of widowhood!' cried Mehrunnissa proudly. 'Sher Afghan is not incapable of protecting himself! Under the rule of Akbar Shah, even the emperor's own son would not be spared if he destroyed an innocent life.'

'True, indeed. But according to the latest news from Agra, Akbar Shah is no more. Salim has ascended the throne. Who can stop the monarch of Delhi?'

Mehrunnissa said no more. Tremors shook her entire body. Once more she lowered her head; tears flowed from her eyes.

'Why do you weep?' asked Moti.

'Salim enthroned as the emperor of India, and what about me?' sighed Mehrunnissa.

Moti's purpose was fulfilled.

'Have you not been able to forget the Crown Prince completely, even now?' she inquired.

'Forget? Who am I supposed to forget?' cried Mehrunnissa, in a choking voice. 'I may forget my own life, but I can never forget the Crown Prince. But listen, my sister! I have suddenly opened the doors of my heart to you. You have heard what I just said, but by my word, let this matter not reach the ears of any other person.'

'Very well, so it shall be,' promised Moti. 'But when Salim hears of my visit to Bardhaman, he will certainly want to know what Mehrunnissa had to say about him. How shall I answer him, then?'

'Tell him that Mehrunnissa will dwell upon his image, which she cherishes in her heart,' instructed Mehrunnissa, after some thought. 'She will give up her life for him, if necessary. But she will never sacrifice her family honour. As long as her husband, her Lord and master, remains alive, this humble slave will never show her face to the emperor of Delhi. And if her husband's death is engineered by the monarch of Delhi, then she will never give herself to her husband's murderer, not as long as she lives.'

With these words, Mehrunnissa left the room. Motibibi gazed after her in wonder. But the victory was Motibibi's. She had fathomed the state of Mehrunnissa's heart, but Mehrunnissa had not understood Motibibi's hopes and plans at all. Even she—the woman who, by dint of her own intelligence, would rule the heart of Delhi's ruler—was outwitted by Motibibi. This was because Mehrunnissa was a woman in love, while Motibibi, in this instance, was guided solely by self-interest.

Motibibi was familiar with the vagaries of the human heart. The conclusions she drew after considering Mehrunnissa's words, proved in time to be entirely accurate. She realized that Mehrunnissa was genuinely in love with Jehangir; whatever she may say now in a spirit of womanly pride, she would not be able to restrain her wayward heart once the path was clear. She would surely submit to the emperor's desires.

Having reached this conclusion, Moti's hopes and dreams evaporated. But did this cast her into a state of extreme grief? Not at all! In fact, she felt rather happy. At first, Moti could not understand why this impossible joy should arise in her heart. She headed for Agra. The journey took a few days. During that time, she became acquainted with her own state of mind.

4

At the Royal Palace

Think not of me as your wife, henceforth.

—*Birangana Kavya*

MOTI ARRIVED IN AGRA. THERE IS NO NEED TO REFER TO HER AS MOTI anymore, for in a few days, her attitudes and inclinations had been utterly transformed.

She met Jehangir. He welcomed her with warmth, as before, asking after her brother's health and hoping she had had a good journey. What Lutfunnissa had predicted to Mehrunnissa proved true. After some desultory conversation, the subject of Bardhaman came up.

'You say you spent a couple of days with Mehrunnissa; what did she say about me?' inquired Jehangir.

Artlessly, Lutfunnissa told him about Mehrunnissa's love for him. The emperor listened in silence; a few tears fell from his wide-open eyes.

'My Lord!' beseeched Lutfunnissa, 'Your humble slave has brought you good tidings. But you have not yet announced a reward for her.'

'Bibi! Your desires are limitless!' laughed the emperor.

'My Lord! How is your humble slave to blame?'

'I have made the Badshah of Delhi your vassal, and you still want more rewards?'

'Women have many desires,' laughed Lutfunnissa.

'What is your latest desire?'

'Let Your Highness declare, first, that this humble slave's plea will be granted.'

'Yes, if it does not hamper the process of governance.'

'A single person cannot hamper the official work of the emperor of Delhi,' smiled Lutfunnissa.

'In that case, I consent. Tell us what it is you desire.'

'I fancy getting married.'

'A novel desire, indeed!' guffawed Jehangir. 'Has a match been fixed?'

'Indeed it has. We only await your royal consent. Without the emperor's consent, no match can be finalized.'

'What is the need of my consent? Who is this man you intend to sweep away on this tide of joy?'

'Your humble slave may have served the emperor of Delhi, but that doesn't make her an unfaithful woman. Your slave wants permission to marry her own husband.'

'Is that so, indeed! And what will be the fate of yours truly, your old retainer?'

'As a parting gift, I shall present to you Mehrunnissa, Empress of Delhi.'

'Who is Mehrunnissa, Empress of Delhi?'

'She is the empress-to-be.'

Privately, Jehangir took this to mean that Lutfunnissa considered it inevitable that Mehrunnissa would become Empress of Delhi. Her heart's desire thwarted, she seemed to be seeking release from her confinement in the royal establishment, because it no longer held any charm for her. Hurt at what he inferred to be her mindset, Jehangir remained silent.

'Does Your Highness object to this proposal?' urged Lutfunnissa.

'I have no objection. But why must you remarry your husband?'

'The first time we were married, my husband did not accept me as his wife—such was my misfortune. This time, he cannot reject Your Highness's humble slave.'

The Badshah laughed merrily, then grew grave.

'My love!' he said, 'There is nothing I would not grant you. If you are so inclined, please act accordingly. But why must you leave me? Don't the sun and moon inhabit the same sky? Can't two flowers bloom on the same stalk?'

'That may be true of tiny flowers, but one stem cannot support two lotuses,' answered Lutfunnissa, fixing her wide gaze upon the Badshah. 'Why should I remain a thorn beneath your bejewelled throne?'

Lutfunnissa returned to her own quarters. She had not revealed to Jehangir the reasons underlying her heart's desire. Jehangir was satisfied with what he could sense about her feelings from her behaviour. He understood nothing of the deep, concealed facts of the matter. Lutfunnissa's heart was made of stone. Even Salim's royal bearing, which won the hearts of women, had failed to captivate her. But now, a worm had found its way into the stone.

5

In the Temple of the Self

A lifetime of gazing at his beauty, and my eyes haven't had their fill;
Hearing his sweet words, my ears still crave the sound of his voice.
So many tender nights together, but my heart desires him still;
For a thousand centuries I held him in my heart, yet I have no peace.
Vidyapati says, of all the interesting men in this world,
Not one in a million is as enchanting as he.

—*Vidyapati*

BACK HOME, LUTFUNNISSA CHEERFULLY SENT FOR PESHAMAN AND discarded her finery.

'You may have this costume,' she told Peshaman, removing her gold-and-pearl-encrusted attire.

Peshaman was rather surprised. The outfit had been stitched very recently, at great expense.

'Why are you giving me this dress?' she asked. 'What's the news?'

'Good news, indeed,' replied Lutfunnissa.

'That is obvious. Have you overcome your apprehensions regarding Mehrunnissa?'

'I have. We have no cause for worry on that account.'

'So that makes me the begum's handmaiden!' exclaimed Peshaman, overjoyed.

'If you wish to be the begum's handmaiden, I shall refer you to Mehrunnissa.'

'What's this you say? But you tell me there is no likelihood of Mehrunnissa becoming the Badshah's begum.'

'I told you nothing of the sort. I said I was not worried on that account.'

'Isn't there cause for worry? If you don't become sole Empress of Agra, all is lost.'

'I shall sever all links with Agra.'

'What's that supposed to mean? I can't make head or tail of all this. Please explain today's glad tidings to me.'

'The glad news is that I am leaving Agra for good.'

'Where will you go?'

'I shall move to Bengal. If possible, I shall marry a gentleman, a bhadralok.'

'Such sarcasm is novel, indeed, but it sets my heart atremble.'

'I'm not joking. I am really leaving Agra for good. I have taken leave of the emperor.'

'What made you think of such a terrible idea?'

'It is not a bad idea. I had such a long sojourn in Agra, but to what avail? Ever since I was a child, I had an intense thirst for happiness. To quench that thirst, I travelled here, all the way from Bengal. To obtain that precious jewel, was there any fortune I would not squander, any sin I would not commit? And as for my aims in going to such lengths, was there any purpose that I failed to accomplish? Wealth, property, riches, glory, prestige—I have enjoyed all these in abundance, after all. But ultimately, what did I gain for all my efforts? As I sit here, recapitulating all those days, I can declare that I never enjoyed any happiness, not for a single day, not even for a single moment. I never felt fulfilled; my craving only continued to grow. I can attain even greater wealth and property if I make the effort, but to what end? If these things were a source of happiness, then in all these days, I would have found happiness at least once, just for a single day. This desire for happiness is like a mountain waterfall; it emerges at first from a desolate place, as a pure, narrow stream, concealed in its own womb, unbeknownst to all, babbling to itself, unheard by anyone. The further it flows, the wider and murkier it becomes. Sometimes, the wind blows, too, generating waves; crocodiles and turtles come to inhabit the waters. The stream expands, grows even more muddy and salty; countless sandbanks and deserts appear upon the river's bosom; its pace slackens. Where this murky river-body will find a place to hide in the endless ocean now, who can tell?'

'I haven't understood any of this. Why do you not find happiness in such things?'

'I have at last realized why these things don't make me happy. In a single night, on my way back from Orissa, I experienced the happiness I could not find in the three years that I have spent in the shadow of this royal palace. This has made me realize the truth.'

'What have you realized?'

'All this while, I was like a Hindu idol, outwardly embellished with gold and jewels, but inwardly, made of stone. I have braved the fires of worldly life, seeking the pleasures of the senses, but the flames have never touched me. Now let me see if I can search within the stone to find a heart made of flesh and blood.'

'I don't understand any of this, either.'

'Have I ever loved anyone here, in Agra?'

'No one at all!' whispered Peshaman.

'Am I not a woman with a heart of stone, then?'

'Well, why don't you fall in love now, if you so desire?'

'That is indeed my desire. That's why I am leaving Agra.'

'What need of that? Is there a dearth of people in Agra that you should turn to a region full of scoundrels? Why not love the Badshah himself, now, if he loves you? When it comes to appearance, wealth, splendour, or what you will, is there anyone in the world who can surpass the Badshah of Delhi?'

'Why does water flow downwards when the moon and stars are in the sky above?'

'Why?'

'It's destiny.'

Lutfunnissa did not disclose the entire truth. The fire had made its way into the stone, which was dissolving in the heat.

6
Obeisance

Body, mind and heart, to you I surrender;
Enjoy a royal feast at your female slave's abode.

—*Birangana Kavya*

WHEN SEEDS ARE SOWN IN THE FIELD, THEY SPROUT OF THEIR OWN ACCORD. Nobody can sense, or witness, their sprouting. Once the seed is sown, wherever its planter might be, it gradually grows from a seedling into a tree. Today, the plant might be tiny, finger-sized, escaping the beholder's eye. Then, little by little, it grows, until it is a foot-and-a-half, then a yard in height. Even then, if it does not seem useful to anyone's selfish needs, overlooked even when it is within sight. Days pass, then months and years; gradually, it begins to catch the eye. There is no ignoring it now: slowly, the tree grows taller, its shadow destroying other trees, until no other vegetation can survive in that field.

Lutfunnissa's love had expanded in the same way. First, there was the sudden encounter with her beloved. At that moment, the seed of love was sown, though she was not particularly aware of it. Afterwards, she did not meet him again. But, in his absence, she repeatedly recalled his face, taking pleasure in conjuring up his image in her memory. The seedling sprouted. She began to love that image. It is a law of human nature that, the oftener we perform a mental task, the more we relish it; eventually, such activity acquires the semblance of a natural, inborn trait. Day and night, Lutfunnissa began to nurture that image in her heart. She felt a desperate urge to see him; it now became hard to control her natural desires. Even the temptation of capturing the throne of Delhi seemed less important in comparison. The throne seemed to her to be encircled with flames produced by the arrows of Manmatha, god of Love. Throwing kingdom, capital and royal throne to the winds, she rushed to meet her beloved. The man she loved was Nabakumar.

This was why even the disclosures of Mehrunnissa, which sounded the death-knell to her own aspirations, had not disheartened Lutfunnissa; this was why, upon her return to Agra, she made no effort to safeguard what was hers; why she took leave of the Badshah forever.

Lutfunnissa arrived in Saptagram. She took up residence in a mansion within the city, not far from the royal highway. Travellers on the road noticed that the mansion was suddenly full of servants in gold-trimmed livery. The decor in every room was exquisite. Fragrant substances, sprayed perfume and flower petals were scattered everywhere with gay abandon. Gold and silver decorations, inlaid with ivory, brightened every corner of the mansion. In one such ornate chamber sat Lutfunnissa, with lowered countenance; opposite her, on a separate mat, was Nabakumar. Lutfunnissa had met Nabakumar in Saptagram a couple of times before this; their conversation on this present occasion will reveal the extent to which those earlier meetings had helped Lutfunnissa attain her ends.

'I shall take your leave, then,' said Nabakumar after a short silence. 'Please don't send for me again.'

'Please don't go!' pleaded Lutfunnissa. 'Stay a little longer. I haven't finished what I had to say.'

Nabakumar waited, but Lutfunnissa did not continue.

'What else do you have to say?' asked Nabakumar after a while.

Lutfunnissa did not reply. Observing that she was weeping silently, Nabakumar rose to his feet. Lutfunnissa clutched at the end of his garment.

'Tell me, what is the matter?' demanded Nabakumar, rather irritated.

'What do you want?' asked Lutfunnissa. 'Is there nothing in the world that you desire? Wealth, property, prestige, love, amusement, mystery—I offer you all the things that are associated with happiness in this life, expecting nothing in return. I only want to be your slave. I don't ask for the privilege of becoming your wife, I only want to be your slave!'

'I am a poor Brahmin,' replied Nabakumar. 'And in this life, a poor Brahmin I shall remain. I cannot accept your gifts of wealth and property, to become the paramour of a Yavanakanya, daughter of a different faith.'

Paramour of a Yavanakanya! Nabakumar was not aware, even now, that this woman was his own wife. Lutfunnissa hung her head. Nabakumar extricated the end of his garment from her grasp.

'Very well, then, let it be!' cried Lutfunnissa, clutching at the corner of his dhoti once more. 'If the Lord so desires, let me drown all my longings and inclinations in the bottomless deep. I ask nothing more of you, but that sometimes, you will pass this way. Think me your slave and appear to me now and then, so I can merely feast my eyes upon you!'

'You are a Yavani, a woman of a different faith, and wife of another man. Even this mode of interaction with you would be sinful. We shall never meet again.'

There was a short silence. A storm raged in Lutfunnissa's heart. Like an image carved in stone, she remained immobile. Then she released the corner of Nabakumar's dhoti.

'Go!' she said.

Nabakumar turned to leave. He had barely walked a few paces, when, like a storm-uprooted plant, Lutfunnissa cast herself at his feet.

'Oh heartless one!' she cried, twining her arms, vine-like, around his ankles. 'For your sake, I gave up the throne of Agra to come here. Please don't abandon me!'

'Please go back to Agra,' Nabakumar insisted. 'As for me, you may as well give up hope.'

'Not as long as I live!' declared Lutfunnissa proudly, springing to her feet, swift as an arrow. 'As long as I live, I shall not give up hope of receiving your love.'

Head held high, neck slightly arched, with her unflinching gaze fixed on Nabakumar's countenance, stood the woman who had stolen the heart of the king of kings. The inflexible pride that had melted in the flames of passion, again shone forth; the invincible strength of mind that had remained undaunted at the prospect of governing the Indian empire, was again restored to her person, which love had earlier made weak. The veins in her forehead swelled, in an exquisite tracery of lines; her bright eyes glittered like the ocean's surface in sunlight; her nostrils quivered. As a swan frolicking in the river current arches her neck to confront the one who obstructs her play, as a snake raises her hood to strike the one who has trodden upon her head, so stood this wild, enraged Yavani, poised, with her head held high.

'Not as long as I live!' she declared. 'You shall be mine alone.'

The vision of this woman, so like a ferocious serpent, frightened Nabakumar. Lutfunnissa's indescribable voluptuousness struck him as never before. But the magic of that beauty was like a flash of lightning, predicting thunder; it was a sight to terrify the soul. About to leave, Nabakumar suddenly recalled the image of a fiery-spirited woman. One day, annoyed with his first wife Padmavati, he had threatened to expel her from the bedroom. The twelve-year-old girl had then turned upon him, her posture exuding fierce pride; just so, her eyes had flashed fire; just so, the veins in her forehead had swelled; just so had her nostrils quivered; just so had she tilted her head. It was ages since he had recalled this image; but now it came to mind. The resemblance seemed exact.

'Who are you?' asked Nabakumar slowly, in a halting voice, his heart assailed with doubt.

The pupils in the Yavani's eyes grew even more dilated.

'I am Padmavati!'

Without waiting for a reply, Lutfunnissa swept out of the room. Troubled and preoccupied, Nabakumar made his way home.

7
On the Outskirts of the City

. . . I am settled, and bend up,
Each corporal agent to this terrible feat.

—*Macbeth*

RUSHING INTO ANOTHER CHAMBER, LUTFUNNISSA BOLTED THE DOOR. FOR two days, she did not emerge. In these two days, she determined what she should do, and what she must avoid. Having decided upon her course of action, she was firm in her resolve. The sun was declining as Lutfunnissa, aided by Peshaman, began to dress. What an extraordinary costume! There was no trace of the feminine in her attire.

'Tell me, Peshaman, am I recognizable?' she asked, inspecting her clothes in the mirror.

'Who would recognize you now?'

'I'll be on my way, then. Let no attendants accompany me.'

'Please forgive your humble slave's impertinence, but may I ask a question?' asked Peshaman, rather hesitantly.

'What is it?'

'What purpose do you have in mind?'

'Kapalkundala's permanent separation from her husband, to begin with. Afterwards, he shall be mine.'

'Bibi! Please think carefully. The woods are dense, it's almost dark, and you will be all alone.'

Without offering any reply, Lutfunnissa left the house. She headed for the desolate, forested outskirts of Saptagram, where Nabakumar lived. It grew dark by the time she got there. The esteemed reader may recall the deep forest not far from Nabakumar's home. Having reached the edge of that forest, she rested beneath a tree. For a while, she thought about the daring plan she had set out to execute. As it happened, help arrived in an unprecedented form.

From her resting place, Lutfunnissa could hear a continuous, monotonous sound emitted by a human voice. Rising to her feet and looking all about her, she saw a light within the forest. Lutfunnissa was braver than a man; she advanced towards the light. First, she observed the scene from behind a tree, to ascertain the situation. The light, she realized, came from the flames of a sacrificial fire; the sound she had heard was the chanting of a prayer. Listening to the words of the prayer, she recognized one word for a name. As soon as she heard that name, Lutfunnissa went up to the person performing the ritual, and took her place beside him.

There let her remain, for the present. It has been a long time since the esteemed reader received news of Kapalkundala; we must now offer him some information about her.

Part 4

1

Inside the Bedchamber

Break, I beseech you, the shackles that bind Radhika!

—*Brajangana Kavya*

IT HAD TAKEN LUTFUNNISSA ALMOST A YEAR TO TRAVEL TO AGRA, AND THENCE to Saptagram. For over a year, Kapalkundala had been Nabakumar's wife. That evening, while Lutfunnissa wandered in the forest, Kapalkundala rested in her bedroom, in rather an absent frame of mind. This was not the same Kapalkundala—unadorned, with flowing, unbound tresses—whom the esteemed reader had encountered on the seashore. Shyamasundari's prediction had come true; the magic of the touchstone had transformed the female ascetic into a housewife. Those heavy locks, cascading to her ankles in intricate coils like countless gleaming black serpents, were now confined in a heavy braid down her back. Even the braid was artfully contrived; her fine, ornamental hairstyle revealing Shyamasundari's expert touch. Nor had flower-garlands been forgotten, for they were twined about her hair, encircling the braid like a crown. The locks of hair that escaped the braid did not lie smoothly; in clusters of curls, they graced her head in fine, black, wavy lines. Her countenance, no longer half-concealed by heavy tresses, was now visible in all its glowing beauty, touched only in places by tiny tendrils of hair with beads of moisture on them. Her complexion still resembled the glimmer of moonbeams on a half-moon night. Gold earrings dangled at her earlobes now, a diamond necklace graced her neck. Her ornaments did not appear faded against the brightness of her complexion; they were like the nocturnal blossoms that grace the moonlight-enshrouded lap of the earth on a half-moon night. She was attired in white, the pale fabric resembling the flimsy white clouds that adorn the sky in the light of the crescent moon. Her complexion still glowed like the crescent moon, but appeared somewhat dimmer than before, as if dark clouds had appeared somewhere on the horizon.

Kapalkundala was not alone. She was engaged in conversation with her companion Shyamasundari. The esteemed reader must overhear part of their exchange.

'How long will our Thakurjamai, your husband, remain here?' Kapalkundala wanted to know.

'He leaves tomorrow,' Shyamasundari replied. 'Ah! If only I had plucked the medicinal herb tonight, I could still have cast my spell upon him and fulfilled all my life's desires. But after being chastised for venturing out of doors last night, how can I step out again tonight?'

'Can't you pluck it in the daytime?'

'How would it work if plucked in the daytime? One must pluck it exactly at midnight, with one's hair unbound. Well, my friend, my innermost desire must remain buried in my heart.'

'But this morning I identified the herb, and also the place where it grows in the forest. There is no need for you to venture out tonight; I shall go and fetch the herb alone.'

'Once is enough. There's no need for you to go out again at night.'

'Why worry on that account? Haven't you heard that nocturnal wandering is my childhood habit? Just think, but for that habit of mine, you and I would never have set our eyes upon each other.'

'I am afraid to speak of that. But is it a good idea for the wives and daughters of gentlefolk to wander alone in the woods at night? Considering the chastisement I had to suffer even when the two of us went out together, would there be any saving you if you went out alone?'

'What's the harm? Do you, too, believe that the simple act of going out at night will make a loose woman of me?'

'I don't believe that. But wicked people will say wicked things.'

'Let them say what they will. That won't make me a wicked person.'

'Indeed it won't. But if people speak ill of you, it will hurt our feelings deeply.'

'Don't let such unjust aspersions hurt your feelings.'

'That, too, I can handle. But why make Dada, my elder brother, unhappy?'

Kapalkundala glanced obliquely at Shyamasundari with her bright, tender eyes. 'If it makes him unhappy, how can I help it?' she said. 'Had I known that marriage, for a woman, means slavery, I would never have married at all.'

Shyamasundari thought it best to say no more. She went away to resume her household duties.

Kapalkundala busied herself with essential domestic chores. The housework done, she went out in search of the medicinal herb. The hour was late. It was a moonlit night. From his window in the outer chamber, Nabakumar saw Kapalkundala leave the house. Stepping outside, he caught her by the arm.

'What is the matter?' asked Kapalkundala.

'Where are you going?' There was no trace of admonition in his voice.

'Shyamasundari wants to seduce her husband with the help of a medicinal herb. I am going in search of the herb.'

'Fine, but you had gone out last night, too, hadn't you?' asked Nabakumar, his tone as gentle as before. 'Why again, tonight?'

'Last night, I couldn't find the herb. I shall search again tonight.'

'Very well, but couldn't you search in the daytime?' suggested Nabakumar, very softly, his voice full of tenderness.

'The medicine doesn't work in the daytime.'

'Why must you hunt for the medicine? Tell me the name of the herb. I shall fetch it for you.'

'I recognize the plant, but I don't know its name. And it won't work if you pluck it. A woman must pluck it, with her hair undone. Please don't hinder me when I try to help another.'

Kapalkundala sounded offended. Nabakumar raised no more objections.

'Let's go,' he said. 'I shall accompany you.'

'Come, see for yourself whether I am unfaithful or not!' retorted Kapalkundala proudly.

Nabakumar was silenced. With a sigh, he relinquished Kapalkundala's arm and went back into the house. Kapalkundala entered the forest alone.

2
In the Woods

Tender is the night
And haply the Queen moon is on her throne,
Clustered around by all her starry fays;
But here there is no Light.

—*Keats*

AS WE HAVE MENTIONED EARLIER, THIS PART OF SAPTAGRAM WAS HEAVILY forested. At a short distance from the village was a dense jungle. All by herself, Kapalkundala went there in search of the medicinal herb, following a narrow forest track. The night was exquisitely beautiful, utterly silent, devoid of the slightest sound. In the honey-sweet night-sky, the moon rose silently above the scattered white clouds, spreading its tender glow; on earth, silently, the trees and vines of the forest rested in the cold moonlight; and in silence, the leaves on the trees reflected that moonlit glow. Amidst the vines and creepers, white flowers blossomed in silence. The birds and beasts were silent. Occasionally, one could hear the wing-flaps of a bird disturbed in slumber; once in a while, the sound of a dry leaf falling, somewhere; at rare intervals, the slithering sound of a reptile's movement; and every now and then, the distant barking of dogs. Not that the air was still: the languorous spring breeze played upon the body. It was the faintest hint of a breeze, secret and silent, stirring only the outermost leaves on the trees; only the dark vine drooping to the earth was swayed by it; only the tiny fragments of cloud in the blue sky floated slowly in that breeze. Stirred by the same breeze, indistinct memories of former bliss awakened faintly in the heart.

Such memories were awakening in Kapalkundala's heart, as well; she remembered the moisture-laden vernal sea breeze, playing upon her long tresses as she stood on the sand dune's crest; gazing at the pure, limitless blue sky, she recalled the ocean, which mirrored that pure, endless blue. Lost in memories of the past, Kapalkundala proceeded on her way.

She walked on absent-mindedly, unmindful of where she was going and why. The path she had taken became gradually inaccessible; the forest thickened; the tangle of branches overhead blocked out the moonlight almost totally; the forest track was obscured from view. Unable to see the way, Kapalkundala came out of her reverie. Looking all around, she saw a light in the midst of this dense forest. Lutfunnissa, too, had seen the same light earlier. At such moments, Kapalkundala, by force of habit, was fearless, but curious. Advancing slowly towards the light, she found nobody at the spot where the fire was burning. But not far away was a broken building, invisible from a distance because the forest was so dense. The house, though brick-built, was a very small and humble abode, consisting of just one room. Human voices could be heard from within. With silent tread, Kapalkundala approached the house. As soon as she came near, she sensed that two persons were engaged in a cautious dialogue. At first, she understood nothing of what they said. Then, as her hearing grew sharper with concentrated effort, she overheard the following:

'To kill is my aim,' declared one. 'If you do not concur, I shall not help you. You, too, need not help me.'

'I am not a well-wisher, either,' replied the other. 'But lifelong exile for her is all I would agree to. I shall have no hand in a murder; rather, I would act to prevent it.'

'You are ignorant, and extremely foolish!' cried the first speaker. 'Let me apprise you of some facts. Listen to me carefully: I am about to narrate a deep secret. Go and check our surroundings first: I seem to hear the sound of human breathing.'

Kapalkundala had indeed positioned herself very close to the walls of the house, the better to hear their conversation. From acute anticipation combined with fear, her breath fell thick and fast.

At his companion's request, one of the men within the house stepped out, and immediately spotted Kapalkundala. In the bright moonlight, Kapalkundala also had a clear view of the man's approaching figure. She could not decide whether to be frightened, or overjoyed, at what she saw. She saw that he was dressed like a Brahmin in a simple dhoti, a shawl gracefully draped around his body. The Brahmin youth was of a very tender age, his countenance unlined. His face was exquisitely beautiful, as lovely as a woman's, but distinguished by a fiery arrogance not usually found in women. His hair was not trimmed by the barber's shearing-blade as was customary for men; like a woman's tresses, his uncut hair cascaded over his shawl, flowing in serpent-like coils down his back, shoulders, arms and chest. His forehead was broad, slightly distended, graced by a single visible vein at its centre. His eyes flashed like lightning. In his hand was a long, unsheathed sword. But his handsome image exuded a terrible aspect, as if some destructive desire had cast its shadow upon his golden complexion. His piercing glance, which seemed to probe the depths of her innermost being, struck terror into Kapalkundala's heart.

For a while, the two of them gazed at each other. Kapalkundala was the first to lower her eyes.

'Who are you?' asked the young man who had appeared on the scene.

If this question had been put to Kapalkundala a year earlier, amidst the keya forests of Hijli, she would have answered immediately, with composure. But now, having acquired some of the attitudes of a housewife, Kapalkundala could not reply at once. When she failed to respond, the stranger in Brahmin's attire addressed her severely.

'Kapalkundala!' he said. 'Why have you entered this dense forest at night?'

Hearing her name on the lips of a stranger in the night, Kapalkundala was startled, but also afraid. She could not reply immediately.

'Did you overhear our conversation?' demanded the stranger in Brahmin's attire, once again.

Suddenly, Kapalkundala found her tongue.

'I have the same query!' she declared, without answering his question.

'In this dense forest, so late at night, what conspiracy were the two of you hatching?'

For a while, the person in Brahmin's attire remained lost in thought, without offering any reply. A new means of attaining his ends seemed to have occurred to him. Grasping Kapalkundala's hand, he began to drag her away from the ruined building. Angrily, Kapalkundala snatched her hand away.

'What are you worried about?' whispered the one dressed as a Brahmin, in a very low voice, close to Kapalkundala's ear. 'I am not a man.'

Kapalkundala was even more amazed. These words restored some of her faith, but she was not completely convinced. She went along with the woman disguised as a Brahmin.

When they were out of sight of the ruined house, the Brahmin-impersonator whispered to Kapalkundala: 'Would you like to hear about our conspiracy? It was about you.'

'Yes I would!' cried Kapalkundala, her eagerness greatly heightened.

'Wait here, then, until I return.'

With these words, the woman in disguise returned to the ruined house. Kapalkundala waited at the same place for a while. But she was rather frightened at what she had seen and heard. Now, as she waited alone in the dark forest, her anxiety began to grow. Why had this person in disguise left her there to wait—who could tell? Perhaps she only wished to fulfil her evil intentions, now that an opportunity had presented itself. The Brahmin-impersonator was taking a very long time to return. Unable to wait any longer, Kapalkundala rose to her feet and started walking swiftly homewards.

The sky grew cloudy, dark as ink; even the faint light in the forest began to fade. Kapalkundala could delay no more. She began to run, emerging from the depths of the forest. As she ran, she seemed to hear footsteps behind her. But when she turned back to look, she could see nothing in the darkness. The Brahmin-impersonator was pursuing her, Kapalkundala told herself. Leaving the woods, she came out onto the narrow forest track described earlier. It was not so dark there; one could detect a human being within one's range of vision. But no one could be seen. She ran on. But again, very distinctly, she heard the sound of footsteps. The sky, full of inky clouds, grew even more threatening. Kapalkundala ran faster. Home was not far away, but she was barely within close range of it when a tremendous thunderstorm rent the skies with a fearsome sound. Kapalkundala raced ahead. The person behind her was running hard, too, by the sound of it. Before the house came into view, the terrible storm broke over Kapalkundala's head. The clouds rumbled, accompanied by frequent bolts of thunder. Lightning flashed, again and again. Rain came down in torrents. Somehow managing to shield herself, Kapalkundala reached home. Crossing the courtyard, she entered her room. The door had been left open for her. She turned, facing the courtyard, to shut the door. She felt she saw a tall male figure standing in the courtyard. There was a flash of lightning. In that single flash, she recognized the man: he was the kapalik who lived on the shores of the sea.

3
In the World of Dreams

I had a dream, which was not all a dream.

—Byron

SLOWLY, KAPALKUNDALA CLOSED THE DOOR. SLOWLY, SHE ENTERED THE bedchamber, and slowly lay down on the bed. The human heart is a boundless ocean; when the wild winds rage, who can count the chain of waves they produce? Who could count the waves that surged in the ocean of Kapalkundala's heart?

That night, Nabakumar was too distressed to visit the antarpur, the inner chambers of his house. Kapalkundala went to bed alone, but she could not sleep. All around her, even in the dark, she saw that countenance, framed in coils of windswept, rain-drenched hair. Kapalkundala began to relive the events of the past. She was reminded of her behaviour towards the kapalik at the time when she had deserted him; the monstrous deeds committed by the kapalik in the depths of the forest: his worship of Goddess Bhairavi, the way he had taken Nabakumar captive, she remembered all those things. Kapalkundala shuddered. She also recalled the events of the present night: Shyama's desire for the medicinal herb, Nabakumar's admonition, Kapalkundala's own heated rejoinder, and afterwards, the moonlit beauty of the forest, the darkness of the woods, the fellow-wanderer she had encountered in the forest, and the terrifying beauty of the stranger's appearance.

As dawn broke in all its glory, Kapalkundala dozed off. In that light slumber, she began to dream. She seemed to be adrift on a boat in the ocean's bosom, the same ocean she had seen before. The boat was beautifully decorated with bright yellow pennants; the oarsmen, bedecked with garlands, sang erotic songs about Radha and Shyam. From the western sky, the sun rained down a shower of gold. The ocean rejoiced in its glow; in the skies, the frolicking clouds bathed in it. Suddenly, it grew dark; the sun was nowhere to be seen. All the golden clouds had vanished. Heavy, inky clouds covered the entire sky. It was no longer possible to figure out directions at sea. The sailors turned the boat back, but could not decide which way to go. They ceased their music, and tore the garlands off their necks. The bright yellow pennants slipped down and fell into the ocean of their own accord. The wind rose; waves, high as trees, reared their heads; arising from the waves, the giant figure of a man with coiling locks lifted Kapalkundala's boat in his left hand, and made as if to cast it into the sea. At this juncture, the awe-inspiring Brahmin-impersonator appeared, and took hold of the boat.

'Should I save you, or drown you?' he asked.

'Drown me!' said Kapalkundala suddenly.

The Brahmin-impersonator relinquished the boat. Now, the boat, too, acquired a voice.

'I can bear this burden no longer!' it declared. 'Let me enter the netherworld.'

With these words, the boat cast her into the waters and descended into the netherworld.

Bathed in sweat, Kapalkundala awakened from her dream and opened her eyes. She saw that it was dawn. Through the open window, the spring breeze wafted in; birds were singing in the gently swaying boughs of trees. Over the window hung some beautiful wild vines, laden with fragrant flowers. In her womanly way, Kapalkundala began to arrange the vines tidily. As she bound them together, she found a letter amidst the vines. Kapalkundala had been trained by the temple priest; she knew how to read. She read the following:

> Tonight, after sundown, you must meet the Brahmin youth. You will learn of urgent matters concerning yourself, which you wanted to know. I am the one disguised as a Brahmin.

4
Hints and Signals

I will have grounds
More relative than this.

—*Hamlet*

ALL DAY, UNTIL SUNSET, KAPALKUNDALA TRIED SINGLE-MINDEDLY TO determine whether or not it was advisable for her to meet the Brahmin-impersonator. Her hesitation did not arise from the belief that it was improper for a devoted young wife to meet a strange man alone, at night. She was sure that such a meeting was harmless, unless intended for a wrongful purpose. Just as persons of the same sex had the right to meet each other, so also, she felt, should persons of the opposite sexes enjoy the mutual right to intermingle. As it was also doubtful whether the Brahmin-impersonator was a man, such inhibitions were redundant. All the same, Kapalkundala hesitated for a long time, uncertain whether the outcome of such a meeting would be good or evil. First, the words uttered by the Brahmin-impersonator, then her vision of the kapalik, and afterwards, her dream: all these factors had aroused in her heart a strong apprehension that some evil fate awaited her in the near future. It did not seem far-fetched, moreover, to suspect that this impending doom was linked to the kapalik's arrival. Since this Brahmin-impersonator seemed to be the kapalik's accomplice, Kapalkundala's rendezvous with him could help that evil destiny to materialize, bringing about her downfall. After all, the Brahmin-impersonator had made it perfectly clear that Kapalkundala herself had been the subject of their conspiracy. But it was also possible that, at their meeting, he might announce his repudiation of that plot. The young Brahmin had been secretly conferring with another person, probably the kapalik. Their conversation had indicated the decision to do away with someone, or to banish someone to permanent exile, at the very least. Whose fate had they been discussing? The Brahmin-impersonator had clearly stated, after all, that Kapalkundala herself was the target of their evil conspiracy. So, it was her death or eternal banishment that they were plotting. What of that? And then there was the dream—what did it signify? In her dream, the Brahmin-impersonator had come to her aid at a time of great trouble; the same seemed to be proving true in practice. The Brahmin-impersonator wanted to reveal the entire truth to her. 'Drown her!' he had said, in the dream. Would he say the same in reality, as well? No, no—the Goddess Bhavani, so benevolent to her devotees, had tried to protect Kapalkundala by offering her guidance in the form of a dream, implying that the Brahmin-impersonator wanted to come to her rescue: if Kapalkundala rejected his help, she would drown. Kapalkundala, therefore, decided to meet him, after all. It is doubtful if a wise person would have arrived at such a decision; but the decisions of wise men are not our concern. Not being particularly wise, Kapalkundala did not arrive at a wise decision. Hers was the decision of a woman overwhelmed by curiosity, a young woman craving for sight of an awesomely attractive man, a woman who enjoyed nocturnal wanderings because she had been reared by a hermit, a woman held captive by her devotion to the Goddess Bhavani. It was the decision of an insect about to plunge into the flames of a burning fire.

When it was dark, Kapalkundala, having completed some domestic chores, headed for the forest, as before. Before setting out, she turned up the flame of the lamp in her bedroom. As soon as she left the room, the light went out.

On her way, Kapalkundala realized she had forgotten something. Where had the Brahmin-impersonator asked her to meet him? She must re-read his letter. Returning to the house, she searched for the letter, but it was not where she had left it. She recalled having placed the letter in her hair-knot while braiding her hair, in order to carry it with her. She probed within her hair-knot, searching for the letter. When her fingers did not feel the letter, she loosened her hair-knot, but still, the letter was not to be found. Then she looked for it elsewhere in the house. Unable to find it anywhere, she finally decided that their rendezvous would probably be at their former meeting-place. Once more, she set forth. Due to lack of time, she had not been able to re-braid those voluminous tresses. So, tonight, Kapalkundala proceeded on her way, framed by the mass of her unbound hair, as in the days of her adolescence.

5
On the Threshold

Stand you a while apart,
Confine yourself but in a patient list.

—Othello

JUST BEFORE DUSK, WHILE KAPALKUNDALA WAS BUSY WITH HER DOMESTIC chores, the letter had slipped out of her hair-knot and fallen to the ground, without her knowledge. It had caught Nabakumar's eye. He was surprised to see a letter fall out of her hair-knot. When Kapalkundala moved away to attend to another task, he picked up the letter, carried it outdoors, and read it. The contents of the letter could only lead to one conclusion. '*You will learn of the urgent matters concerning yourself, which you wanted to know.*' What were the urgent matters she wanted to know about? Matters of the heart? Was the person in Brahmin's attire Mrinmayi's paramour? To someone who did not know what had transpired the previous night, no other conclusion could suggest itself.

When a devoted wife wishing to join her husband in death—or any other living person, impelled by some other motive—ascends the funeral pyre and sets it alight, he or she is at first encircled by a thick cloud of smoke. The smoke obscures one's vision; the world grows dark. Later, as the logs begin to burn, a few flames reach upwards, like serpent-tongues, to lick the body here and there. Then, roaring flames envelop the entire body. Ultimately, with an explosive noise, the fire lights up the sky, soaring above one's head and reducing the body to a heap of ashes.

Such was Nabakumar's mental state upon reading the letter. At first, he was mystified; then he was assailed by doubt, followed by certainty, and ultimately, heartburn. The human heart cannot cope immediately with an excess of pain or joy; it can only accept such emotions gradually. Nabakumar was first encircled by a cloud of smoke; then, flames began to scorch his heart, and finally, the fire began to consume his heart, burning it to ashes. Prior to this, Nabakumar had already noticed that Kapalkundala disobeyed him in some matters. He had noted, in particular, that she would go alone, whenever and wherever she wished, even when he forbade her. She mingled freely with all and sundry, and would roam alone in the woods at night, ignoring his injunctions. This would have made another person suspicious; but, knowing that to entertain doubts about Kapalkundala would be like the scorpion's fatal bite, Nabakumar had never harboured any suspicions for a single day. Today, too, he would not have allowed doubt to prevail, but this time he was confronted, not with suspicion, but with concrete fact.

When the first surge of agony had subsided, Nabakumar wept in silence for a long while, finding some consolation in his tears. Then, he resolutely decided upon his course of action. Tonight, he would say nothing to Kapalkundala, but when she made for the woods at dusk, he would follow her secretly. Having witnessed her utterly sinful behaviour, he would end his life. Rather than admonish Kapalkundala, he would take his own life instead. What else could he do? He would not have the strength to bear the burden of such a life.

Having come to this decision, he fixed his gaze upon the rear exit of the house, awaiting Kapalkundala's departure. After she had emerged, and walked some distance, Nabakumar also prepared to step out. But seeing her return for the letter, he moved out of sight. Once Kapalkundala had re-emerged and travelled a short distance, Nabakumar was again about to follow her, when he saw tall male figure blocking the doorway. Who the person was, why he was standing there, Nabakumar had not the slightest wish to know. Even when he saw the man, he failed to notice his face, anxious only to keep Kapalkundala in view. He placed his hand on the stranger's chest, to push him aside; but he could not make the man budge.

'Who are you?' demanded Nabakumar. 'Move aside—let me go!'

'Don't you know who I am?' The stranger's voice assailed the ears like the roar of the ocean. Nabakumar looked at him, and recognized the same kapalik he had encountered before, the ascetic with his tangled coils of hair.

Nabakumar started, but was not afraid. Suddenly, his face brightened. 'Is it you Kapalkundala is going to meet?' he wanted to know.

'No,' replied the kapalik.

The lamp of hope extinguished as soon as it had been ignited, Nabakumar's countenance clouded over, as before.

'Let me go, then!' he demanded.

'I'll let you go,' the kapalik answered, 'but there is something I must tell you. Hear me first.'

'What could you have to say to me?' Nabakumar protested. 'Have you come here to destroy my life, again? You may take my life; this time, I shall offer no resistance. Wait here; I shall be back soon. Why did I not sacrifice myself to please the gods? Now I have paid the price, ruined by the very person who had rescued me. Kapalik! Don't mistrust me this time. I shall return forthwith to surrender my life to you.'

'I have not come with the intention of killing you,' the kapalik informed him. 'That is not the wish of Goddess Bhavani. The task I have come here to accomplish will meet with your approval. Come inside, and listen to what I have to say.'

'Not now!' declared Nabakumar. 'I shall listen to you after some time; for the moment, you must wait. I have an urgent task to perform; as soon as it is accomplished, I shall return.'

'My son, I know everything!' exclaimed the kapalik. 'You will follow the sinful woman. I know where she will go: I shall take you there, and show you what you want to see. Now, listen to me. Have no fear.'

'I have nothing to fear from you now,' Nabakumar told him. 'Come with me.'

With these words, Nabakumar escorted the kapalik into the house, offered him a floor-mat, and took his place beside him.

'Tell me what you have to say,' he demanded.

6
Re-encounter

Proceed there, and your divine task accomplish.

—*Kumarasambhava*

HAVING TAKEN HIS PLACE ON THE FLOOR-MAT, THE KAPALIK HELD OUT HIS arms for Nabakumar to view. Nabakumar saw that both his arms were broken.

The esteemed reader may recall that, on the night when Kapalkundala and Nabakumar had escaped from the seashore, the kapalik, while hunting for them, had fallen off the crest of a sand dune. Falling, he had tried to land on his arms in order to protect his body from injury; this saved his body, indeed, but he fractured both his arms. Narrating the entire episode to Nabakumar, the kapalik told him:

'I don't have much difficulty in performing my daily tasks. But there's no strength left in these arms of mine. In fact, it is difficult even to collect firewood.

'Not that I realized instantly that my fall had broken my arms, leaving the rest of my body intact,' he continued. 'As soon as I fell, I fainted. At first, I remained unconscious for a stretch of time. Then, I drifted in and out of consciousness. How long I continued in this state, I cannot say. For two nights and a day, perhaps. Dawn was breaking when I completely regained consciousness. Just before that, I had been dreaming. As if the Goddess Bhavani . . .' As he spoke, the kapalik's hair stood on end. 'As if the Goddess Bhavani had appeared before my eyes. Frowning in anger, she admonished me: "Oh evil one, it is your impurity of mind that has disrupted your worship of me in this manner. Having fallen prey to your sensual desires, you have not yet offered up this maiden's blood to me. Because of this maiden, all the fruits of your previous spiritual labour have been destroyed. I shall never again accept your prayers!" When I fell weeping at her feet upon hearing her words, she was pleased. "My good man! I shall decree the only possible penance for this sin. You must sacrifice the very same Kapalkundala to me. Until you accomplish this task, don't offer me any prayers."

'How long I took to recover, and by what means, I need not recount here. Eventually, having regained my health, I began my efforts to obey the goddess's decree. I found that my arms lacked even the strength of an infant. Without the physical power of my arms, my efforts would be futile. An accomplice was therefore necessary. But in matters of religion, human beings are narrow-minded. In this depraved age called Kaliyuga, this sinful era of Yavana rule, nobody is willing to act as an accomplice in such an undertaking. After much searching, I managed to locate the sinful woman's abode. But lacking strength in my arms, I have not been able to carry out Bhavani's decree. I can only continue my tantric prayer rituals, to accomplish my purpose. Last night, I was performing the fire ritual in the forest nearby, when with my own eyes I witnessed Kapalkundala's tryst with a Brahmin youth. Tonight, as well, she is on her way to meet him. If you wish to observe the scene, come with me, and I will show you.

'My son! Kapalkundala deserves to be sacrificed; I shall destroy her, as Bhavani has decreed. Kapalkundala has betrayed you, too; she deserves death at your hands, as well. So, give me the help I need. Capture this unfaithful woman; let us take her to the place of sacrifice. There, destroy her with your own hands. This will earn me forgiveness for my offence against the deity; your holy deed will earn you immortal virtue for your afterlife; the treacherous woman will be punished; it will be the ultimate revenge.'

The kapalik ended his speech. Nabakumar did not reply.

'My son!' urged the kapalik, seeing that he was silent. 'Now come and witness the scene I had promised to show you.'

Bathed in sweat, Nabakumar accompanied the kapalik.

7

In Conversation with the Co-wife

Be at peace; it is your sister that addresses you. Requite Lucretia's love.

—Lucretia

EMERGING FROM HER HOUSE, KAPALKUNDALA ENTERED THE FOREST. SHE went first to the ruined hut, where she met the Brahmin. Had it been daylight, she would have noticed that his countenance had lost much of its brightness.

'It is not advisable to say anything here, for the kapalik might arrive,' the Brahmin-impersonator told Kapalkundala. 'Let's go somewhere else.'

In the midst of the forest was a small clearing, with a path leading away from it. There the Brahmin-impersonator led Kapalkundala.

'Let me introduce myself first,' The Brahmin-impersonator said, once both of them were seated. 'You can judge for yourself how far to trust my words. En route from Hijli, travelling with your husband, you had encountered a Muslim woman one night. Do you recall the incident?'

'Was she the one who gave me her jewellery?'

'I am that Muslim woman!' declared the Brahmin-impersonator.

Kapalkundala was stunned.

'I have something even more amazing to reveal,' Lutfunnissa informed her. 'I am your co-wife!'

'Really!' cried Kapalkundala, astounded.

Lutfunnissa began to recount the story of her past. She spoke of her marriage, conversion, how she was rejected by her husband, of Dhaka, Agra, Jehangir, Mehrunnissa, her departure from Agra and residence in Saptagram, her encounter with Nabakumar, his behaviour towards her, her arrival in the woods in disguise the previous day, her meeting with the performer of the fire-ritual—she narrated everything.

'Why did you wish to visit our house in disguise?' asked Kapalkundala at this point.

'To bring about your eternal separation from your husband,' replied Lutfunnissa.

Kapalkundala pondered over this. 'How would you have accomplished that?' she wanted to know.

'To begin with, I would have made your husband doubt your chastity. But what is the use of saying of such things now? I have abandoned that plan. Now, if you do as I say, I can fulfil my aim through you; and yet, it will be for your own benefit.'

'Whose name did you hear from the person who was performing the fire-ritual?'

'Your own name. To gauge whether he was praying for your harm or benefit, I touched his feet in obeisance, and waited by his side. There I remained, until his ritual was complete. Then, I asked him why he was offering prayers in your name. After speaking to him for a while, I realized that he had performed the ritual with malignant intent towards you. My needs were the same. When I confided this to him, we immediately decided to assist each other. He took me into the ruined house for a special consultation. There, he revealed his plan to me. It was your death he desired, but I had no such aim in mind. I have led a sinful life, but in taking the path of moral degradation, I have not fallen so low as to will the death of an innocent young girl. I refused to consent to his plan. At this juncture, you appeared on the scene. I think you may have overheard something.'

'Indeed, I overheard an argument of the kind you have described.'

'Taking me for an ignorant fool, that man wanted to offer me some advice. I left you concealed in the woods to go and listen to his intended plan, so as to brief you accordingly.'

'Then why didn't you come back?'

'He spoke at length; it took a long time to hear his extended narrative. You know that man particularly well. Can you guess who he is?'

'The kapalik, my former foster-parent!'

'Indeed, it is he. First, the kapalik acquainted me with the facts: how you were found on the seashore, how he brought you up in that place, the arrival of Nabakumar, your escape with him. He also described all that had happened after your departure. You don't know about all those developments. I shall give you a detailed account, so that you know what transpired.'

Lutfunnissa proceeded to tell her about the kapalik's fall from the sand dune crest, the injury to his arms, and his dream. Hearing about the dream, Kapalkundala started, and trembled, agitated as if lightning had struck her heart.

'The kapalik has firmly resolved to follow the dictum of Bhavani,' continued Lutfunnissa. 'Because his arms have lost their strength, he desperately needs someone to help him. Taking me for the son of a Brahmin, he told me the entire story in the hope of making me his accomplice. Until now, I have not agreed to join him in this evil enterprise. I cannot vouch for my fickle heart, but I hope that I shall never consent to his plan. Rather, it is my intention to resist his resolve; that is why I have arranged this rendezvous with you. But I have not taken this step for purely unselfish motives. I am offering to save your life, but you must do something for me in return.'

'What can I do for you?' Kapalkundala wondered.

'Save my life, as well. Leave your husband.'

For a long time, Kapalkundala said nothing.

'Where should I go, once I have left my husband?'

'To other lands, far away. I shall give you a mansion to live in, wealth, an army of servants; you shall live like a queen.'

Once again, Kapalkundala fell into contemplation. In her mind's eye she scanned the whole world, but could see nobody who mattered. She looked within her own heart, but there, too, she found nobody, not even Nabakumar. Then why should she block the path to Lutfunnissa's happiness?

'Whether you have done me any good, I still cannot determine,' she told Lutfunnissa. 'I do not need a mansion, or wealth, or an army of servants. Why should I obstruct the path to your happiness? May your desire be fulfilled! From tomorrow, you will hear no tidings of the woman who stood in your way. I was once a wanderer in the wilds. To the wilds, as a wanderer, I shall return again.'

Lutfunnissa was wonderstruck; she had not hoped for such swift compliance.

'My sister!' she cried. 'May you live forever, for you have just granted me the boon of life! But only on one condition shall I let you go: tomorrow, at dawn, I'll send you a trusted, intelligent maidservant. Go with her. There is a woman of eminence in Bardhaman, a close friend of mine. She will look after all your needs.'

So intent were Lutfunnissa and Kapalkundala in their conversation, that they remained oblivious to immediate dangers. They failed to detect the hostile gaze of the kapalik and Nabakumar, who stood at the end of the forest path leading away from the clearing in which the two women had taken refuge.

Nabakumar and the kapalik were watching them, but unfortunately, from such a distance, they could hear nothing of their conversation. Had the range of human hearing matched the scope of human sight, who can tell whether the tide of human sorrow would have risen or declined? Creation is so exquisitely complicated! Nabakumar observed that Kapalkundala's hair was unbound, flowing free. In the days before she became his, she used to leave her hair unbraided. Again, he noticed that her heavy tresses had cascaded down to the young Brahmin's back, to mingle with his shoulder-length locks. So massive was the weight of Kapalkundala's hair, and so closely did they lean towards each other as they conducted their whispered conversation, that Kapalkundala's locks had fallen across Lutfunnissa's back. The two women had not noticed it. But the sight caused Nabakumar to slowly sink to the ground.

Seeing this, the kapalik produced a coconut shell from his waistband. 'My son!' he urged. 'You are losing your valour. Drink this sacred potion, blessed by Bhavani. It will revive you.'

The kapalik held the container to Nabakumar's lips. Absent-mindedly, he drank from it to quench his acute thirst. Nabakumar was not aware that this delicious fluid was an extraordinarily potent liquor, brewed by the kapalik himself. Drinking it, he at once felt stronger.

Meanwhile, Lutfunnissa continued to address Kapalkundala in a low voice, as before: 'My sister! It is beyond my power to repay you for what you have done. Still, if you remember me always, even that would make me happy. The jewellery I gave, you have donated in charity, I'm told. I have nothing on me at this moment. To take care of other needs that might arise tomorrow, I had carried a ring concealed in my hair, but by the Lord's grace, I need no longer pursue that evil plan. Keep this ring. Wear it, and when you look at the ring, think of your sister, the Yavani. Tonight, if your husband wants to know where you got this ring, tell him that Lutfunnissa gave it to you.'

With these words, Lutfunnissa removed a jewel-encrusted ring from her finger, and handed it to Kapalkundala. This, too, was witnessed by Nabakumar. The kapalik, who had been supporting him, felt his body tremble again, and once more offered him the liquor to drink. The spirit went to Nabakumar's head, and began to play havoc with his nature, uprooting even the tender seedling of affection.

Taking her leave of Lutfunnissa, Kapalkundala headed back for her own home. By the secret path that Lutfunnissa had taken, Nabakumar and the kapalik began to trail Kapalkundala.

8
On the Way Home

No spectre greets me—no vain shadow this.

—Wordsworth

SLOWLY, KAPALKUNDALA WALKED HOMEWARDS. VERY SLOWLY SHE WALKED, with a gentle tread, for she was lost in deep thought. Lutfunnissa's words had utterly transformed Kapalkundala's frame of mind. She was ready to sacrifice her life. Sacrifice her life, for whom? For Lutfunnissa? It was not so.

In matters of the heart, Kapalkundala was the child of a tantric. Just as a tantric does not hesitate to kill others in the hope of earning Goddess Kali's blessings, so was Kapalkundala ready to sacrifice her own life to fulfil the same desire. Not that Kapalkundala had shared the kapalik's single-minded pursuit of shakti, the divine gift of spiritual power. All the same, exposed day and night to the sight, sound and practice of shakti-worship, she had developed in her heart a special devotion to Kali. She was strongly convinced that Bhairavi was the ruler of the created world, as well as its liberator. Her compassionate heart could not bear to see the place for Kali-worship flooded with human blood, but in all other respects, she spared no effort to express her devotion. Now, the same Bhairavi, ruler of the universe, arbiter of human joys and sorrows, liberator of the soul, had appeared in a dream to decree that Kapalkundala should surrender her life. Why should Kapalkundala not obey that decree?

You and I don't wish to die. Whatever we may say in moments of anger, this world is full of happiness. It is the hope of finding happiness, and not in search of sorrow, that we spin around the world like a ball on a playground. If ever, as a consequence of our own misdeeds, that hope is frustrated, we at once break into loud protests about our sorrows. Sorrow is, therefore, not a law of life, but a deviation from the normal and customary. For you and me, there is happiness everywhere. For the sake of happiness, we remain rooted in this world, not wishing to relinquish it. But love is the primary strand in the ties that bind us to life. Kapalkundala did not have such ties—she had no ties at all. So, there was no holding her back.

A person without any ties proceeds with unchecked speed. When the waterfall descends from the mountain-crest, who can restrain its flow? If Kapalkundala's heart grew restless, who could restore her tranquillity? When a young elephant is in heat, who can calm it down?

'Why should I not surrender this body at the Goddess Jagadiswari's feet?' Kapalkundala asked herself. 'Of what use are the five senses to me?'

She asked herself these questions, but was unable to arrive at any definite answers. Even in the absence of all other worldly ties, the senses bind one to life.

Kapalkundala walked on with lowered head. When the heart is overcome with some monstrous emotion, this single obsession makes one oblivious to external surroundings. In this state, even insubstantial things seem to take on a material shape. Such was Kapalkundala's condition at this time.

'My child!' she seemed to hear a voice call out, from above. 'I shall show you the way.'

Startled, Kapalkundala looked up. Etched in the clouds that had just formed in the sky, she saw what looked like the outline of a figure. A stream of blood flowed from the garland of human skulls around the neck of this apparition; encircling her waist was a girdle of human arms; in her left hand was a human skull; rivulets of blood streamed down her body; and adorning her forehead, at the outer edge of her extraordinarily bright, fiery eye, hung the crescent moon! Right arm upraised, Bhairavi seemed to beckon to Kapalkundala.

Gazing skywards, Kapalkundala went on her way. Before her, leading the way, that figure, resembling a new-formed mass of clouds, moved across the pathways of the sky. Sometimes the shape of the apparition, with her garland of skulls, was hidden by clouds; sometimes, it was clearly visible to the eye. Gazing at her, Kapalkundala walked on.

Nabakumar and the kapalik had not seen the apparition. Fuelled by alcohol, Nabakumar's heart was on fire.

'Kapalik!' he exclaimed to his companion, losing patience at the slowness of Kapalkundala's tread.

'What is it?'

'Give me something to drink!' he demanded.

Once again, the kapalik offered him liquor.

'Why wait any longer?' asked Nabakumar.

'Why wait?' the kapalik repeated.

'Kapalkundala!' roared Nabakumar, in a booming voice.

The sound of his voice startled Kapakundala. Of late, nobody had addressed her by that name. She turned around. Nabakumar and the kapalik came up, to stand face-to-face with her. At first, Kapalkundala could not recognize them.

'Who are you?' she asked. 'Are you messengers from hell?'

The next instant, she recognized them. 'No, no, you are my father!' she exclaimed. 'Have you come to offer me up in sacrifice?'

Nabakumar took hold of her arm, with a grip of iron.

'Come with us, my child!' invited the kapalik, in tender, honeyed tones.

With these words, he headed for the cremation grounds, leading the way.

Kapalkundala glanced up, in the direction where she had seen the terrible figure of the goddess who ranged the sky. She saw the goddess burst into peals of laughter, pointing with a long trident at the path taken by the kapalik. Wordlessly, like one blind to her fate, Kapalkundala followed the kapalik. Gripping her arm tightly as before, Nabakumar walked on.

9
In the Land of Spirits

In her collapse, she brought her husband down, as well,
As the oil, when it drips from the lamp, brings the flame down, too.

—*Raghuvamsha*

THE MOON SANK BENEATH THE HORIZON. THE UNIVERSE WAS PLUNGED IN darkness. The kapalik led Kapalkundala to his place of worship. It was a wide stretch of sand on the shores of the Ganga. Facing it was an even larger stretch of sand, the cremation ground. At high tide, an expanse of shallow water separated the two sandy tracts; at low tide, the wet area disappeared. At this time, the space was free of water. The part of the cremation ground facing the Ganga was far above the river. To enter the river at that point would mean plunging from a height, straight into deep waters. The sandy shore, moreover, had been eroded by the continuous assault of waves cast ashore by the relentless breeze. From time to time, a chunk of earth would break off, crashing down into the bottomless waters.

There was no lamp at the place of worship, only a flaming torch. By its light, the cremation ground, indistinctly seen, appeared even more monstrous. Arrangements had been made for prayers, the havan or fire ceremony and the ritual human sacrifice. The heart of the immense river stretched out in the dark. The Chaitra wind blew with unchecked force across the Ganga's breast; the sky resounded with the noise of crashing waves, whipped to turbulence by the wind. Every now and then, from the cremation ground, the hoarse call of scavenging beasts could be heard.

Having positioned Nabakumar and Kapalkundala on suitably-arranged reed-mats, the kapalik began his devotional rites as prescribed by tantric law. At the appropriate time, he instructed Nabakumar to take Kapalkundala for a ritual bath. Taking her by the hand, Nabakumar led Kapalkundala across the cremation ground. Bones pierced the soles of their feet. A water-filled funeral pitcher cracked under Nabakumar's foot when he trod on it. Close to it lay the corpse of an unfortunate wretch for whom nobody had performed the last rites. Their feet touched the corpse. Kapalkundala walked around it, while Nabakumar stepped on it as he proceeded on his way. Circling the area, the scavenging animals called out loudly at the approach of the two humans; some advanced to attack them, others retreated with a noisy tread. Nabakumar's hand was trembling, Kapalkundala discovered; but she herself was fearless and steady.

'Are you afraid?' she asked him.

Nabakumar's intoxication was waning.

'Afraid, Mrinmayi?' he replied, very gravely. 'No, that is not the reason.'

'Then why do you tremble?'

Only a woman's voice can capture the tone in which she asked this question. Only a woman who melts in compassion can speak in such a tone. Who would have expected such a tone of voice from Kapalkundala here, at the cremation ground, when her own death was imminent?

'It is not fear,' asserted Nabakumar. 'I tremble in rage because I am unable to weep.'

'Why should you weep?'

Once more, the same tone of voice.

'Why should I weep? What would you know, Mrinmayi! After all, the sight of beauty has never driven you mad . . .' As he spoke, Nabakumar's voice choked with agony. 'You have never come to the cremation ground to tear out your own heart and throw it away.'

Suddenly, Nabakumar burst into a loud wail, and flung himself at Kapalkundala's feet.

'Mrinmayi! Oh Kapalkundala! Save me! I fall at your feet. Tell me, just once, that you are not unfaithful! Say it just once, and I shall clasp you to my heart and carry you home.'

Kapalkundala took Nabakumar by the hand and helped him to his feet.

'You never asked me about it,' she reminded him gently.

As they spoke, the two of them had reached the water's edge. Kapalkundala was ahead, standing with her back to the river, just a step away from the water. The tide was rising; Kapalkundala was standing on the brink, at the edge of the river's vertical bank.

'You never asked me,' she said.

'I have lost my senses—what am I to ask you?' cried Nabakumar, like one driven insane. 'Tell me, Mrinmayi, tell me, tell me, tell me! Accept me. Come home with me!'

'I shall answer your question. The person you saw tonight is Padmavati. I have not been unfaithful. I tell you this by way of information. But I shall not return home again. I have come here to surrender this body at Goddess Bhavani's feet; I shall fulfill my resolve. You must go home. I go to my death. Don't even grieve for me.'

'No, Mrinmayi! No!' With a loud cry, Nabakumar stretched out his arms to clasp Kapalkundala to his breast. But his arms never reached her. Spurred by the Chaitra wind, an enormous wave crashed upon the shore, where Kapalkundala had been standing. Instantly, with a deafening crash, the chunk of earth fell into the river current, carrying Kapalkundala with it. Nabakumar heard the sound of the collapsing landmass, and saw Kapalkundala vanish. At once, he plunged into the water. He was not a bad swimmer. For a while, he swam about, searching for Kapalkundala. He did not find her, nor did he emerge from the water.

In the river's endless flow, tossed about by the waves surging in the stormy winds of spring, where did Kapalkundala and Nabakumar disappear?

BISHABRIKSHA

1
Nagendra's Boat-journey

NAGENDRA DATTA WAS TRAVELLING BY BOAT. IT WAS THE MONTH OF JYAISHTHA, the time of typhoons—his wife Suryamukhi had adjured him most earnestly: 'See that you take care on the boat, and if you see a typhoon, stop. Never stay on the boat during a storm.' Nagendra promised this before embarking, otherwise Suryamukhi would not have let him go. And it was impossible for him not to go to Kolkata: there was much to be done there.

Nagendranath was a very wealthy man: a zamindar. He lived in Govindapur. I shall not reveal the name of the district in which this village was situated, but shall refer to it as Haripur. Nagendra Babu[1] was a mature man, just thirty years of age. He was travelling on his own barge. The first few days passed smoothly; Nagendra watched as he went: the river water flowed past in continual motion; it ran fast, it danced in the breeze, it laughed in the sunlight, its eddies gurgled. The water was timeless, endless, full of sport. Beside the river, on the banks and in the fields, herdsmen were tending cattle, or sitting under trees singing, or smoking, or scuffling among themselves; others were eating bhuja. Peasants were ploughing, flogging their oxen with rods: most human abuse is directed at oxen, though peasants receive a share as well. On the landings, the peasants' womenfolk too were to be seen, with pitchers, torn kanthas, rotten mats, silver amulets, nose-pins, brass bangles, clothes dirty from two months of wearing, complexions blacker than soot, and harsh, dry hair. Among them a beauty would be scouring her head with mud. Some were thrashing boys, some were arguing about the whereabouts of some missing unnamed neighbour, some were beating clothes on wood.

On the ghats of the occasional higher-class villages, women of good families brightened the shore. Older women chatted; middle-aged women were worshipping Shiva; young women, veiled, were bathing; and boys and girls were shouting, spreading mud, collecting flowers for their puja, swimming, splashing everyone with water, and sometimes running off with the clay Shiva that stood in front of some housewife sitting with eyes closed, absorbed in meditation. Brahmins, like harmless good men, were chanting hymns to the Ganga in their minds, offering puja, sometimes gazing stealthily at some young woman submerged up to her neck. In the sky, white clouds flew past, heated by the sun; under them, black dots of birds were flying; a kite sat in a coconut tree looking around in all directions like a king's chief minister to see on whom, and how, he could swoop to kill. The cranes were the small people, wandering about, stirring up mud. Waterfowl were the jokers, diving and plunging. Other birds were light-weight people, merely flying about. Market boats were chugging along—they needed to. Ferry boats moved majestically—for others' needs. Goods boats were not moving at all—they depended on their owners' whims.

For the first four days, Nagendra watched as he went. On the fifth day, clouds covered the sky, the river's water turned black, the tops of the trees looked brownish, cranes flew in the lap of the clouds, and the river became stuporous. Nagendra ordered the boatmen: 'Moor the boat to the bank.' Helmsman Rahamat Molla was at his prayers and did not answer. Rahamat had not always followed the profession of a boatman—his maternal grandfather's cousin had been the daughter of a boatman and taken in by that he had chosen the profession of a boatman, finding, fortunately, that it fulfilled all his desires. Rahamat had a ready tongue—once his prayers were finished he turned towards the Babu and said, 'No need to worry, sir, stay calm.' The reason for such courage on the part of Rahamat Molla was this, that the bank was very close and the boat reached it almost immediately. Then the boatmen disembarked and made fast the hawsers.

Perhaps there was some dispute between the Almighty and Rahamat Molla—the storm arrived with considerable speed. First the wind arrived. After it had wrestled for a while with the foliage of the trees, it called to its brother, the rain. The two brothers started a drunken revelry. Brother rain flew about riding on brother wind's shoulders. The two brothers seized and bent the heads of the trees, broke branches, tore creepers, destroyed flowers, sent the river water flying, and made all kinds of mischief. One brother went flying off with Rahamat Molla's topi, the other brother turned his beard into a fountain. The oarsmen sat wrapped in the sails. The Babu closed all the shutters. The servants set themselves to save the boat's equipment.

Nagendra found himself in a knotty problem. If he disembarked from the boat, the boatmen would think him a coward—if he did not disembark, he would be forsworn to Suryamukhi. Some will ask, 'What is wrong with that?' I do not know, but Nagendra considered it wrong. At this point, Rahamat Molla himself said: 'Sir, the hawsers are old, I do not know what might happen, the storm has got much worse, you had better get off the boat.' So Nagendra disembarked.

Without shelter one could not stand upright easily on the river bank in the wind and rain. A kind of twilight had fallen and the storm had not abated; so, judging that it was necessary to go in search of shelter, Nagendra set off in the direction of the village. The village was some distance away from the river bank; Nagendra went on foot along a muddy path. The rain stopped; the wind, too, abated somewhat, but the sky was full of clouds; so it was probable that there would be further wind and rain during the night. Nagendra went on: he did not turn back.

Because of the heavy clouds, darkness was extreme as soon as night fell. Village, house, path, river—nothing could be seen. Only the tree branches, adorned with thousands of fireflies, shone like artificial trees inlaid with diamonds. From time to time, pale lightning flashed among the white and black clouds whose roaring had diminished—women's anger does not subside all at once. Only the frogs were making merry, rejoicing in the freshly gathered water. Crickets could be heard, if one listened for them, like Ravana's funeral pyre, endlessly sounding, but if one did not pay attention to them they were unnoticeable. There was also the sound of drops of water falling from the treetops; the sound of droplets of water dislodged from leaves falling on to the rainwater standing under the trees; the sound of jackals' feet moving through the standing pools of water on the paths; occasionally, the sound of birds perched in the trees shaking their wings to dislodge the water from them. From time to time, there was a howl from the nearly-subsided wind, together with the sound of the falling of multiple droplets of water dislodged from the leaves of the trees. In due course, Nagendra saw a light in the distance. Moving over the water-drenched earth, soaked by the water falling from the trees, controlling his fear of the jackals under the trees, Nagendra toiled on towards the light. Slowly, he drew near. He saw that the light issued from an old brick dwelling. The door was not bolted. Leaving his servant outside, Nagendra entered the house. He saw that it was in a terrible condition.

2
The Lamp Goes Out

THE HOUSE WAS NOT AT ALL A COMMON ONE. BUT NOW THERE WAS NO SIGN in it of wealth. The rooms were all dilapidated, dirty, and devoid of any signs of human habitation. It was inhabited by ants, mice and various kinds of insects and worms. Light burned only in one small room. Nagendra entered that room. He saw that there were in the room only a few articles fit for human use, and even these suggested poverty. One or two pots—a broken stove—several metal utensils—that was all. The walls were discoloured, there were sooty cobwebs in the corners; and everywhere cockroaches, spiders, lizards and rats wandered about. An old man was lying on torn bedding. He seemed to be at death's door. His eyes were dim, his breath sharp, his lips trembled. By the bedside, on a brick fallen from the house, stood an earthenware lamp, in need of oil; so too was the lamp of life supine on the bed. Beside the bed was yet another lamp—a beautiful, fair and graceful girl, as if full of tender light.

Whether because of the dullness of the lamp's light or because the two people were deeply engrossed in their situation, neither saw Nagendra when he came in. Nagendra, standing at the door, listened to all the words that came from the old man in the sorrow of his dying moments. These two people, young and old, were without help in this populous world. Once they had had riches, kinspeople, manservants and maidservants, resources, and all the luxuries of life—everything. But together with the favours of fickle Lakshmi, everything had gradually been lost. Under the oppression of this newly-arrived poverty, the children's faces grew paler day by day like lotuses parched with cold; the mother was the first to go to her pyre by the river. All the other stars went out together with that moon. The scion of the house, the jewel of his mother's eye, the hope of his father's declining years, he too lay on his pyre before his father's eyes. No one was left, save the old man and one beautiful daughter, who came to live in this lonely, dilapidated house surrounded by the forest. They were each other's sole support. Kundanandini passed the age to be married but her father suffered from the blindness of his sixty years; there was now only one knot remaining of the bonds of his family; while the old man lived he could not give her up to another. 'Let a little more time pass—if I give Kunda away where shall I live? How shall I live?' Thus the old man used to think if the subject of her marriage came to his mind. It did not occur to him to ask where Kunda would be left when the call came for him. And now, all at once, Death's messenger had come and was standing by his bedside. He was going. Where would Kundanandini stand tomorrow?

The deep, inexorable suffering of the dying man was manifest in his words. Tears fell ceaselessly from eyes soon to be closed. And by his head, like a stone image, the thirteen-year-old girl watched with fixed gaze the death-shadowed face of her father. Oblivious of herself, oblivious of where she would go tomorrow, she looked only at the face of him who was about to depart. Gradually, the old man's speech became less clear. The breath caught in his throat, his eyes dimmed; the suffering spirit obtained release from suffering. In that private room, by the dim lamp, Kundanandini remained sitting alone, holding her father's dead body in her arms. The night was veiled in thick darkness; outside, drops of rain were still falling, one could hear their sound on the tree leaves; from time to time, the wind howled—all these sounds came through the door of the dilapidated house. Within the house was the lamp's unsteady, thin, nearly extinguished light, which alternately flickered on the corpse's face or left it in darkness. There were not many minutes worth of oil left in the lamp. And then, with one last flare of brightness, the lamp went out.

Then Nagendra, with soundless steps, withdrew from the house.

3
Coming Events Cast Their Shadow Before

IT WAS MIDNIGHT. INSIDE THE DILAPIDATED HOUSE WERE KUNDANANDINI and the body of her father. Kunda called, 'Father!' No one answered. Once she thought, 'Father is sleeping', then again she thought, 'He must be dead'—but Kunda could not bring herself to say this word. At last, Kunda could neither call nor think any more. In the darkness, fan in hand, she began to stir the air where her living father had been lying, where now his dead body lay. She finally decided that he was asleep; for, if he had died, what would her situation be? Drowsiness, from her daily vigil and present trouble, came upon the girl. Kunda had stayed awake day and night to tend her father. Sleep overcoming her, Kundanandini, fan in hand, resting her head on an arm more delicate and beautiful than a lotus stalk, went to sleep on the cold, hard floor of the room.

Then Kundanandini had a dream. She saw the night become full of radiant moonlight. The sky was bright blue, and it seemed as if that glowing blue sphere of the sky was the manifestation of a great moon-halo. Its radiance, too, was very bright, yet soothing to the eyes. But within this beautiful great lunar aureole there was no moon; instead, Kunda saw within it a strange, light-filled, heavenly form. Then the moon-halo, with its bright form, seemed to leave the sky and slowly, gradually descend. Eventually the halo, glowing with a thousand cool rays, was above Kundanandini's head. Kunda saw that the beautiful light-filled form within the aureole, with diadem, bracelets and ornaments, had the form of a woman. Her lovely face was filled with compassion; a tender smile trembled on her lips. Kunda, with fear and joy, saw that this compassionate one bore the form of her long-dead mother. The bright figure, with tender face, lifted Kunda from the earth and took her on her lap. And motherless Kunda, with the word 'Mother' on her lips after so long a time, felt as if all her dreams were fulfilled. Then the figure in the moon-halo kissed Kunda and said, 'Child! You have had much sorrow. Leave the world and come with me.' To this Kunda replied, 'Where should I go?' Kunda's mother, pointing to the radiant, bright firmament, said, 'To that realm.' Kunda, looking at the unknown realm of stars as if from beyond fair, timeless, endless seas, said, 'I cannot go so far; I have no strength.' At these words, a slight frown of displeasure appeared on her mother's compassion-bright yet serious face, and in a soft, deep voice she said, 'Child, do what you will. But it would be better to come with me. In time to come, gazing towards the sky, you will long to go there. I will show myself to you once more. When, stricken to the ground in mental agony, you think of me and weep to come to me, then I will appear to you again, and then: come with me. Now, look at the sky's edge where my finger points. I will show you the figures of two people. These two people will be the causes of your weal and woe in this world. If you can, when you see them, reject them like poisonous snakes. Whatever paths they take, you must not take those paths.'

Then the radiant one pointed with her finger towards the horizon. Kunda, following, saw, drawn on the background of the sky, the figure of a god-like man. He had a fine, noble, tranquil brow; a candid, compassionate look; his swan-like long neck was slightly curved; and, seeing in him all the indications of a great man, nobody would believe that he could be a source of misgiving. Then that image gradually faded like a bubble from the background of the sky. Kunda's mother said to her, 'Do not be charmed by the sight of that divinely beautiful form. Even though he is noble-minded, he is the cause of your misfortune. Therefore, renounce him as a poisonous snake.' Then the radiant one, saying again, 'Look at this,' pointed to the horizon; and Kunda saw a second figure delineated on the blue background of the sky. But this time it was not the figure of a man. Kunda saw there a bright, dark-complexioned young girl, with eyes like lotus-petals. Kunda felt no fear at the sight of her, either. Her mother said, 'This is a demon in the form of a dark-skinned woman. If you see her, flee.'

As she said this, the sky suddenly became dark, the great moon-halo vanished from the sky, and, with it, disappearing within it, the burning figure vanished, too. Kunda woke up.

4

'That is the One'

NAGENDRA WENT INTO THE VILLAGE. HE LEARNED THAT THE VILLAGE'S NAME was Jhumjhumpur. At his request and with his help, some of the villagers came and started to prepare for the cremation of the dead. A neighbouring woman stayed with Kundanandini. When Kunda saw her father being taken away to be cremated, she believed at last that he was dead, and began to weep ceaselessly.

In the morning, the neighbour returned to her own housework. She sent her daughter, Champa, to comfort Kundanandini. Champa was about Kunda's age, and a friend. When she arrived, she set herself to comfort Kunda by talking to her of various things. But she saw that Kunda was not listening to anything she said; she was weeping and from time to time looking longingly towards the sky. Champa asked curiously, 'What do you see, gazing a hundred times at the sky?'

Then Kunda said, 'Yesterday, my mother came from the sky. She called me, saying, "Come with me". I was so foolish, I was afraid, and I didn't go with my mother. Now I am wondering why I didn't go. If she comes back again now I will go with her. That is why I keep looking towards the sky.'

Champa said, 'Oh! Do dead people come back?' Then Kunda told her all about her dream. Champa, listening, was astonished and said, 'Did you recognize the man and the woman whose forms you saw in the sky?'

Kunda said, 'No, I have never seen them before. Surely there can't be a man as beautiful as that anywhere. I have never seen such beauty.'

Meanwhile, Nagendra rose from his bed in the morning, and calling all the people of the village together, asked them, 'What will become of the daughter of the dead man? Where will she live? What family does she have?' To this everyone answered, 'She has no place to stay; she has no one.' Nagendra said, 'Then let some from among you adopt her. Arrange a marriage for her, and I will pay the expense. And as long as she lives with you, I will give you some money each month to pay for her food and clothing.'

If Nagendra had produced some money in cash, many would have agreed to his proposal. Then, once Nagendra had gone away, they would have sent Kunda away or made her a servant. But Nagendra was not so naive. Consequently, seeing no cash, no one came forward.

Then, seeing Nagendra at a loss, someone said, 'An aunt of hers has a house in Shyambazar. Binod Ghosh is her uncle-in-law. You are going to Kolkata: if you take her with you, you can leave her there; then this Kayastha girl will be looked after, and you will have done your duty.'

Having no alternative, Nagendra accepted this idea. And he sent for Kunda in order to tell her of it. Champa set out, bringing Kunda with her.

As they came, Kunda, seeing Nagendra from a distance, came suddenly to a standstill, and took not another step. With astonished eyes, as if mesmerized, she stood gazing at Nagendra.

Champa said, 'What is it? Why have you stopped?'

Kunda pointed and said, 'That is the one.'

Champa said, 'Who?'

Kunda said, 'The one my mother showed me in the night, in the sky.'

Then Champa, too, stood there astonished and alarmed. Seeing the girls hesitating to move forward, Nagendra came to them and explained everything to Kunda. Kunda could give no answer; she just kept gazing at Nagendra, her eyes wide with amazement.

5
Of Different Matters

HAVING NO ALTERNATIVE, NAGENDRA TOOK KUNDA WITH HIM TO KOLKATA. The first thing he did was to search for her uncle-in-law, Binod Ghosh. He could find no one by the name of Binod Ghosh in Shyambazar. He found a Binod Das—but he denied any relationship. So Kunda remained as a burden on Nagendra's shoulders.

Nagendra had a sister. She was younger than him. Her name was Kamalamani. Her father-in-law's house was in Kolkata. Her husband's name was Shrishchandra Mitra. Shrish Babu was a commercial agent in the firm of Plander Faerlie. This was an important firm—Shrishchandra was very wealthy. He and Nagendra were on good terms. Nagendra took Kundanandini there. Calling Kamala, he told her all about Kunda.

Kamala was eighteen years old. She resembled Nagendra in appearance. Brother and sister were both very good-looking. But Kamala was renowned for her learning as well as for her great beauty. Nagendra's father had taken pains to educate Kamalamani and Suryamukhi, and had employed a governess by the name of Miss Temple for them. Kamala's mother-in-law was still alive. But she was living in Shrishchandra's ancestral home. It was Kamala who was the mistress of the house at Kolkata.

Having introduced Kunda, Nagendra said, 'If you do not keep her, there is nowhere for her to stay. Later, when I go home, I will take her with me to Govindapur.'

Kamala was very mischievous. As soon as Nagendra, having said this, turned away, Kamala lifted Kunda in her arms and ran off. There was a tub with some warm water in it, and into this, without warning, she dropped Kunda. Kunda was very frightened. Laughing, Kamala took up some sweet-smelling soap and started to wash Kunda's body. A servant-girl, seeing Kamala herself engaged in such a task, came quickly running up, saying, 'I will do it, I will do it'—Kamala sprayed the servant with warm water, and she fled.

Kamala scrubbed and bathed Kunda with her own hands—Kunda emerged as beautiful as a lotus bathed in dew. Then Kamala dressed her in beautiful white clothes; smoothed her hair with fragrant oil; and, having given her several ornaments to wear, said, 'Now, come and pay your respects to my brother. And mind, don't pay your respects to the master of the house. If he sees you, he will want to marry you!'

Nagendranath wrote all about Kunda to Suryamukhi. He had a close friend called Haradev Ghoshal who lived in a distant province—Nagendra, writing to him also, spoke of Kundanandini thus:

> Tell me, then, at what age is a woman beautiful? You will say, after forty, since your Brahmini is a year or so older than that. The girl called Kunda of whom I have told you—she is thirteen. Seeing her, I think that this is the time of beauty. The sweetness and simplicity which precedes the first transition to adolescence diminishes afterwards. Kunda's simplicity is wonderful; she understands nothing. Even now, she runs out to play with the girls of the street; if she is forbidden, she is frightened, and refrains. Kamala is teaching her to read and write. Kamala says she shows great intelligence at it. But she understands nothing else. If I say: how big and blue your eyes are—your two eyes are like autumn lotuses floating in eternally clear water—those two eyes remain gazing at my face—she says nothing—looking at those eyes, I lose my train of thought and can no longer explain anything. You will smile at this revelation of what my mental strength amounts to; you, especially, tearing your hair, have issued writs for the mockery of infatuations; but if I could make you stand in front of those two eyes, you would learn what

your own mental strength is. I have not yet been able to decide what kind of eyes they are. I have not seen them look the same twice; it seems to me that they are not of this world, they do not seem to see the things of this world well; they seem to be engaged in looking at what can be seen in the heavens. It is not that Kunda is beautiful without flaw. In comparison with others, her appearance would probably not be praised; yet it seems to me that I have never seen anyone so beautiful. It seems to me that there is in Kundanandini something beyond this earth, as if she is not made of flesh and blood; as if moonlight fashioned her by embodying the beauty of the flowers. Comparisons do not readily come to mind. She is incomparable, a manifestation of mental peace—if you imagine the rays of an autumn moon falling on a clear lake, you will have some idea of what she is like. I cannot think of anything else to compare her with.

Several days after Nagendra had written to Suryamukhi, he received an answer. The answer was thus:

I do not know what fault your servant has committed. If you are to stay for so long in Kolkata, why can I not come to you and serve you? This is my humble prayer; if you send word, I will come immediately.

Have you forgotten me, having acquired a young girl? Many things are favoured when they are immature. It is the green coconut that is refreshing. Perhaps we lowly women, too, are only sweet when young? Otherwise, why would you forget me on acquiring this young girl?

Enough of such jesting. Have you entirely given away any claim to the girl? If not, I would beg her from you. I have some say in what is to be done with her. It is proper for me to have some authority over anything you might acquire, but I see that these days it is your sister who has it all.

What will I do with the girl? I will give her in marriage to Taracharan. If Providence has brought you a good girl, then do not disappoint me. If Kamala lets her go, bring Kundanandini with you when you return. I have written to Kamala, too, with this request. I have been engaged in having ornaments made, and other preparations for a wedding. Do not delay in Kolkata: a man who stays six months in Kolkata is a fool, is he not? And if you still want to marry Kunda yourself, I will set about preparing a welcome!

I will reveal Taracharan's identity later. But whoever he was, both Nagendra and Kamala agreed to Suryamukhi's proposal. Therefore, it was decided that Nagendra would take Kunda with him when he returned home. Everyone being happily agreed, Kamala, too, had some ornaments made for Kunda. Yet mankind is ever blind! A day would come when Kamalamani and Nagendra, stricken to the dust and beating their brows, would think: What an evil hour it was in which we acquired Kundanandini! What an evil hour it was in which we agreed to Suryamukhi's letter.

So Kamalamani, Suryamukhi and Nagendra, all three together, planted the poison-seed. All three would, in time to come, lament.

Then Nagendra had the boat prepared, and, taking Kunda with him, set out for Govindapur.

Kunda nearly forgot her dream. Once, on the journey with Nagendra, she thought of it. But considering Nagendra's kindly, charming countenance and his affectionate character, Kunda could not believe for a minute that any harm would come to her from him. Some people have the self-destroying impulse of moths, which seeing a blazing fire, rush headlong into it.

6
Taracharan

THE POET KALIDASA KNEW A GARDENER WOMAN, WHO USED TO SUPPLY HIM with flowers. Kalidasa was a poor Brahmin, and could not pay the price of the flowers—in exchange, he used to recite to the gardener poems composed by himself. One day, a wonderful lotus opened in the gardener's pool; she brought it and presented it to Kalidasa. As a reward, the poet began to recite the *Meghaduta*. The *Meghaduta* is an ocean of delights, but everyone knows that its opening verses are somewhat dry. The gardener did not like them—she grew angry and got up to go. The poet asked, 'Friend gardener! Are you going away?'

The gardener said, 'Where is the savour in your poetry?'

The poet said, 'Gardener! You will never reach heaven.'

The gardener said, 'Why?'

The poet said, 'There are stairs to heaven. One reaches heaven after traversing a hundred thousand stairs. There are also stairs to this *Meghaduta* of mine—these savourless verses are those stairs. You could not traverse these humble stairs—so how will you be able to traverse a hundred thousand stairs?'

Then the gardener, in fear of losing heaven through a Brahmin's curse, listened to the *Meghaduta* from beginning to end. Delighted at hearing it, the following day she fashioned the many-coloured garland called madanmohini, brought it to the poet and placed it on his head.

This humble work of mine is no heaven—neither has it a hundred thousand stairs. Its savours are few, and its stairway small. This dry chapter is some of that stairway. If among my readers there are some of the gardener's disposition, I warn them that without traversing this stairway they will not reach the savour.

Suryamukhi's father's home was in Konnagar. Her father was an upper-class Kayastha; he was a treasurer in some firm in Kolkata. Suryamukhi was his only child. During her childhood, a widow called Shrimati lived in the house as servant to the Kayastha girl, and looked after her. Shrimati had a child whose name was Taracharan. He was the same age as Suryamukhi. Suryamukhi used to play with him during their childhood, and because of their childhood companionship, she grew as fond of him as of a brother.

Shrimati was extremely beautiful, and consequently she soon fell into danger. Coming under the eyes of a rich man of bad character in the village, she left Suryamukhi's father's house. No one could discover exactly where she went. But Shrimati never returned.

Shrimati left Taracharan behind. Taracharan remained in Suryamukhi's father's house. Suryamukhi's father was of a very compassionate disposition. He raised the orphaned boy as his own child, and far from employing him in any such lowly occupation as that of a servant, taught him to read and write. Taracharan studied at a free missionary school.

Later, Suryamukhi was married. Several years after that, her father died. By then, Taracharan had learned English after a fashion, but had been unable to obtain any position. Having nowhere to live after the death of Suryamukhi's father, he went to live with Suryamukhi. Suryamukhi had induced Nagendra to establish a school in the village. Taracharan was employed there as a master. These days, by the power of grants-in-aid,[2] there are meek, love-song singing schoolmasters with parted hair in every village; but at that time 'Master Babus' were not commonly seen. Consequently, Taracharan became one of the village deities. He read the *Citizen of the World* and the *Spectator*; and word was widely circulated in the market that he had read three books of geometry. By virtue of all this, he became a member of the Brahmo Samaj[3] of the zamindar of Devipur, Devendra, and was accepted into the society of Babus. Taracharan wrote many essays on widow remarriage, the education of women, and the evils of idolatry, read them every week to the Samaj, and made many long speeches beginning with 'O most gracious Lord of all!' Some he copied from the *Tattvabodhini*, some he took from the writings of other pundits. He was always saying, 'Discard your worship of bricks and stones; arrange marriages for your uncles' widows; teach your daughters to read and write—why do you keep them in cages? Let your daughters out.' The particular reason for his liberality towards women was the fact that there was no woman in his own house. He was still unmarried; Suryamukhi had made many efforts to get him married, but because the story of his mother's leaving her home was known in Govindapur, no upper-class Kayastha had agreed to give him his daughter. Many dark-skinned, ugly daughters of low-class Kayasthas were available. But Suryamukhi thought of Taracharan as a brother; how could she call the daughter of some low-class person sister-in-law? With this in her mind, she had not accepted them. She was searching for the beautiful daughter of some upper-class Kayastha; and at this point, learning from Nagendra's letter of the beauty and virtues of Kundanandini, she determined to arrange a marriage between her and Taracharan.

7

You, With Eyes Like Lotus Petals! Who Are You?

KUNDA, WITH NAGENDRA DATTA, CAME TO GOVINDAPUR. AT THE SIGHT OF Nagendra's residence, Kunda was speechless. She had never seen such a large establishment. It had three outer buildings and three inner ones. Each building was like a palace. Through an iron gateway, one entered the principal outer building, which was surrounded by high, painted iron railings. Having entered, one passed along a fine, grass-free, well-made red path. On each side of the path, was a plot of earth filled with soft, new grass, a paradise for cows. In these were circular beds, made beautiful by blossoming trees with flowers and leaves of all hues. Ahead was the very tall, one-and-a-half-storeyed reception hall. It was reached by a very fine flight of steps. Along its veranda, were great fluted columns; its floor was of marble. Above the cornice, in the centre, was a huge terracotta lion with flowing mane and tongue lolling out. This was Nagendra's reception hall. On either side of the plots of earth with their grass and flowers, that is, one to the left and one to the right, were two rows of single-storeyed buildings. In one row were the records room and the office. In the other were the storage room and the servants' quarters. On each side of the gate was a gatekeeper's room. This first outer building was called the 'kachari building'. Beside it was the 'puja building'. In the puja building was a hall for big festivals, as prescribed; and on three sides were two-storeyed buildings around a big courtyard, according to custom. No one lived in this building. At the time of Durga puja, it was filled with ceremonious activities, but now grass was growing through the tiles in the courtyard, the hall and the covered ways were filled with pigeons, the compartments were stacked with all the furniture, and the doors were locked. Beside this was the thakur bari. Housed therein was a painted shrine, a beautiful stone hall for devotional dancing; and on three sides were rooms, one each for cooking food for the deities, for the priests, and for guests. There was no lack of people in this building. There were groups of priests with garlands around their necks and tilaks of sandal-paste, and groups of cooks; people were bringing trays of flowers, bathing the images of the gods, ringing bells, arguing, preparing sandal-paste, and cooking. Servants were bringing water on carrying poles, cleaning the rooms, bringing washed rice, and quarrelling with the Brahmins. Somewhere in the guest-rooms, an ash-smeared sannyasi, having untied his matted hair, was lying on his back. An ascetic with one arm raised was dispensing medicine in the maidservants' building of the Datta establishment. A white-bearded brahmachari, wearing a red-ochred loincloth and swinging a rosary, was reading the Bhagavad Gita written by hand in the Devanagari script. Some greedy sadhu was causing a disturbance by helping himself to measures of ghee and flour. A group of bairagis, wearing garlands of tulsi around their withered necks and tilaks on their foreheads, were playing drums, the tufts of long hair on the crowns of their shaven heads swaying; and with noses moving from side to side were singing kirtans: 'I did not get to speak—elder brother Balai was with me . . .' Vaishnavis, wearing the Vaishnavi streak of mud on the bridges of their noses, were singing to the rhythm of tambourines songs such as 'Of sweet ears' or 'Yatra-leader Govinda'. Young, modern Vaishnavi girls sang with the old-fashioned ones, middle-aged women joined their voices with the elderly. In the middle of the dancing hall, the neighbourhood's idle boys were wrestling, quarrelling and hitting each other, and directing various kinds of refined abuse at each other's parents.

These were the three outer buildings. Behind these three buildings were the three inner buildings. The building behind the office building was the building used by Nagendra himself. Only he and his wife lived in it, with the maidservants who attended on them. And their personal things were kept there. This building was new, built by Nagendra himself, and its construction was very well-ordered. Beside it, behind the puja building, stood the original building. It was old, and poorly-constructed; the rooms were low, small, and dirty. This old house was filled day and night with the continuous loud talking of countless daughters of kinsmen, maternal aunts and their cousins, paternal aunts and their cousins, widowed maternal aunts, married nieces, wives of paternal aunts' brothers, daughters of maternal aunts' brothers, and other such female relations, like a banyan tree full of crows. And it was constantly filled with various kinds of outcry, laughing, joking, quarrelling, arguments, stories, gossip, the fighting of boys and the weeping of girls, calls of 'Bring me water', 'Pass the clothes', 'You haven't washed the rice', 'The boy hasn't eaten', 'Milk and curds', and other such sounds, like a troubled sea. Beside this, and behind the building for worship, was the kitchen. There was even more of a to-do over there. A cook, wearing metal ornaments on her ankles and heating a bowl of rice, was giving an account to her neighbour of the pomp at her son's wedding. Another, with eyes streaming with tears from smoke as she blew on green wood, was slandering the establishment's steward, and advancing various kinds of evidence for his intention of stealing money by providing sappy wood. A young beauty, putting fish in hot oil, was grimacing horribly with eyes closed, showing rows of teeth, because the heated oil had spattered onto her body; someone else, with oil-smeared, unruly locks from bathing bound on the top of her hair-parting, was stirring dal with a stick—like a cowherd prodding cows with a club. With big blades fixed in pieces of wood set out front of them, Bami, Kshemi, Gopal's mother, Nepal's mother, Lau, Kumra, Bartaku and Patala were cutting up vegetables; from this came sounds of swishing and crunching, and from their mouths gossip of the neighbourhood and about the master, and abuse of each other. And there was discussion of various matters such as that Golapi had become widowed very young, Chandi's husband was a great drunkard, Kailasi's son-in-law had got an excellent job—he was a police clerk—there were no plays in the world like those of Gopal Ure, there was not another boy as naughty as Parvati's son in all Bengal, were not the English a race of demons, how Bhagirath had brought the Ganga, and whether the Bhattacharyas' daughter's lover was Shyam Bishwas. A dark-skinned, fat woman was killing fish at a stroke with a knife-and-board set up on an ash-heap in the courtyard; the kites, seeing the pride of her huge-limbed body and the dexterity of her hands, did not, in fear, come close, but neither did they forbear to swoop down once or twice. A grey-haired woman was fetching water; an ugly woman was pounding spices. Somewhere in the storehouse, a maidservant, a cook and the storehouse-keeper were engaged in a terrible brawl. The storehouse-keeper was arguing that the ghee she had given out was the right amount—the cook was arguing that it was insufficent. The maidservant was arguing that if the storehouse was left unlocked then they could give out enough. Many boys, girls, beggars and dogs were sitting around, hoping for some rice. The cats did not hope—whenever opportunity presented itself, they would 'sinfully enter another's house'[4] and take food without permission. And a cow which had entered without sanction, was chewing calabashes, eggplant and cucumber stalks, and banana leaves, with eyes closed, savouring the nectar of the gods.

Beyond these three inner buildings, was a flower-garden. Beyond the flower-garden was a fine lake, like a piece of blue cloud. The lake was surrounded by a wall. Between the three inner buildings and the flower-garden was a path to the postern gate. It was by this path that one entered the three inner buildings.

Outside the establishment were the stables, the elephant stalls, the kennels, the cowsheds, the aviary, and so on.

Kundanandini, looking with amazed eyes upon Nagendra's immense wealth, entered the inner buildings in a palanquin. She was brought to Suryamukhi, and touched her feet. Suryamukhi blessed her.

Perceiving Nagendra's similarity to the image of the man she had seen in her dream, Kundanandini had started to feel sure that his wife would have the appearance of the image of the woman she had seen after that; but the sight of Suryamukhi put that suspicion to flight. Kunda saw that Suryamukhi was not dark-skinned like the woman she had seen against the sky. Suryamukhi's complexion was that of liquid gold, like the full moon. Her eyes were beautiful, indeed, but not the kind of eyes that Kunda had seen in her dream. Suryamukhi's eyes were long, sheltered by brows almost meeting her hair, between gracefully-curved lashes, with wide, dark pupils, circular and a little expanded, bright but slow moving. The eyes of the dark-skinned woman in the dream did not have such heavenly charm. Neither was Suryamukhi's figure like hers. The woman in the dream was short; Suryamukhi was rather tall, and swayed with the beauty of a creeper moved by the breeze. The woman in the dream was beautiful, but Suryamukhi was a hundred times more beautiful. And the woman in the dream was probably not more than twenty—Suryamukhi was nearly twenty-six. Seeing no similarity between Suryamukhi and the image of that woman, Kunda became easy in her mind.

Having greeted Kunda cordially, Suryamukhi called her servants and gave them orders. And to the foremost among them she said, 'I am going to arrange a marriage between this Kunda and Taracharan. So you will treat her as my brother's wife.'

The maidservant acquiesced. She took Kunda with her to another room. All this time, Kunda had been gazing at her. As she looked, her flesh prickled, and she became bathed in perspiration. The form of the woman which, in her dream, following her mother's pointing finger, she had seen against the sky, was that of this lotus-petal-eyed, dark-skinned maidservant!

Kunda, beside herself with fear, in a faint, uneven voice asked, 'Who are you?'

The maidservant said, 'My name is Hira.'

8
A Reason for Great Anger on the Part of the Gentle Reader

HERE THE GENTLE READER WILL BE VERY DISPLEASED. IT IS THE CUSTOM IN romances for the wedding to come at the end; I have put Kundanandini's wedding at the beginning. Another time-honoured custom is that the man whom the heroine marries should be extremely handsome, adorned with all the virtues, and a great hero; and should be head-over-heels in love with the heroine. Poor Taracharan was none of these things—as far as beauty goes, he was copper-coloured and snub-nosed; his heroism was displayed only in the boys' room of the schoolhouse—and I cannot say how far from being in love with Kundanandini he was, only that she was to him something like a tame monkey.

However that may be, after Kundanandini was taken to Nagendra's home, she was married to Taracharan. Taracharan took his beautiful wife home. But in doing so he fell into difficulties. The gentle reader will remember that essays by Taracharan on the education of women and the breaking of the seclusion of women would often be read in the salon of Devendra Babu himself. Taracharan always used to say boastfully during discussions, 'If my time ever comes I will offer the first example of these reforms. If I marry, I will present my wife to everyone.' Now he was married—the fame of Kundanandini's beauty had spread to the men's quarters. Everyone, referring to his favourite theme, said, 'Where is your promise?' Devendra said, 'What is this, then, are you, too, of the old fold? Why do you not let us talk with your wife?' Taracharan was very ashamed. He could not escape the torment of Devendra's requests and comments. He consented to arrange a meeting between Devendra and Kundanandini. But he was terrified that Suryamukhi would hear of it and be angry. In such crises, the year's end came and went. After that, in order to avoid more crises, he sent Kunda to Nagendra's house, on the pretext of having repairs made to his own house. The house was repaired. Kunda returned. Then one day, Devendra himself arrived very quietly at Taracharan's place. And he started to mock Taracharan for his boastful lies. Then, having no option, Taracharan had Kundanandini dressed up and brought out to converse with Devendra. What did Kundanandini say to Devendra? After standing there veiled for some moments, she fled weeping. But Devendra, seeing the great beauty of her newly-adolescent movements, was enchanted. He never forgot this beauty.

A few days after this, there was a ceremony at Devendra's house. A girl came from his house with an invitation for Kunda. But Suryamukhi came to hear of this and forbade her to go. So she did not go.

After this, Devendra came once again to Taracharan's house to speak again with Kunda. Suryamukhi heard people talking of this, too. She rebuked Taracharan so severely that from then on communications between Devendra and Kundanandini were closed.

In this way, three years passed after the marriage. Then Kundanandini became a widow. Taracharan died of typhoid. Suryamukhi took Kunda to live with her. She sold the house which she had given to Taracharan, and gave the money to Kunda.

The gentle reader will indeed have been very displeased, but now the tale has commenced. Now the seed of the poison tree has been planted.

9
Haridasi the Vaishnavi

SOME TIME PASSED WITH THE WIDOWED KUNDANANDINI LIVING IN Nagendra's home. One day, after midday, all the women of the household were sitting in the old inner building. By the mercy of God, there were many of them, and there was easily obtainable village women's work to suit the preference of each of them, in which they were engaged. There was everyone from young girls not yet out of childhood to grey-haired old women. Some were dressing their hair, some were dressing others' hair; some were having their heads looked at, some were looking at others' heads, and with little cries were killing lice; some were having white hairs culled, some with rice stalks in hand were culling them. A young beauty was making a coloured patchwork bedcover for her son; someone else was suckling her son. Another beauty was plaiting her hair into a braid; someone else was thrashing her son who, with mouth wide open, was drowning three villages with the noise of his wailing that ranged over the seven notes of the scale. A lovely woman was weaving a carpet; others were examining the spread-out palms of their hands. An expert painter, preparing for someone's wedding, was covering a low wooden seat with designs in rice-pigment; a scholarly appreciator of good books was reading Dasharath's *Panchalis*.[5] An old woman was gratifying her listeners by upbraiding her son; a young humorist was describing to her intimates, in a low voice, the amorous frolics of her husband, and expressing her pain at his absence. Some were gossiping about the mistress of the house, some about the agent, some about their neighbours; very many were praising themselves. Someone who had been gently reprimanded that morning for her foolishness by Suryamukhi was advancing many examples of her cleverness; someone in whose cooking the amount of salt was hardly ever correct was giving a long speech about her culinary skills. A woman whose husband was the most utterly stupid of all in the village was astonishing her companions with songs of praise of his wonderful scholarship. A woman whose children were dark-skinned and lumpish was bragging about their excellence. Suryamukhi was not present at this gathering. She was a little proud, and usually did not sit with these groups; moreover, her presence would have hindered the enjoyment of all the others. Everyone feared her; in her presence no one could speak freely. But Kundanandini used to be there; and she was present on this occasion. At his mother's request, she was teaching a boy the letters of the Bengali alphabet. Kunda had told her student to look at the sweetmeat held in the hand of another boy;

consequently, he was making a particular effort to learn.

At this point, a Vaishnavi entered the circle of that gathering of women and, with the words 'Victory to Radha',[6] stood there.

Every day, guests were served in Nagendra's thakur bari, and rice was distributed every Sunday; but apart from that, no Vaishnavi beggar was allowed into the inner apartments. So, hearing 'Victory to Radha' within the inner apartments, a woman of the house said, 'What are you doing inside, woman? Go to the worship building.' But as she spoke, she turned her head and saw the Vaishnavi, and did not finish her speech. Instead she said, 'O mother! What sort of Vaishnavi is this!'

Everyone was astonished to see that the Vaishnavi was a young woman, and looked it. Even in that circle of many beautiful women, no one except Kundanandini was more beautiful than she. Her glowing lips, as beautiful as bimba fruit, her well-formed nose, her wide, lotus-like eyes, her eyebrows like drawn lines, her smooth forehead, her arms like lotus-stalks and her complexion like a garland of champak flowers—all these were rare beauties in women. Yet if there had been some judge of beauty present, they would have said that there was a fault in the Vaishnavi's beauty. Her movements, her gait and deportment were all masculine.

There was the Vaishnava streak of mud on the Vaishnavi's nose, her hair was parted on her head, she wore a Simla dhoti and held a tambourine in her hand. There were brass bangles on her arms, and above these, thin bangles with wavy designs.

An elder among the women said, 'Well, then, who are you?'

The Vaishnavi said, 'My name is Haridasi Vaishnavi. Would the ladies like to hear a song?'

From all around, from young and old, came the sound of, 'We would like to, yes, we would like to.' With tambourine in hand, the Vaishnavi came and sat near the women. The spot where she sat was where Kunda had been teaching the boy. Kunda was extremely fond of singing, and hearing that the Vaishnavi was going to sing, she came a little closer to her. Her student, seizing the opportunity, got up, and, snatching the sweetmeat from the hand of the boy who was eating it, ate it himself.

The Vaishnavi asked, 'What shall I sing?' Her audience began to make various requests; some wanted 'Govinda the Prince'—some 'One of Gopal Ure's songs'.[7] The one who had been reading Dasharath's *Panchalis* wanted something from that. One or two older ones ordered something about Krishna. In response to that, those of middle-age expressed their different opinions, saying, 'The confidante's story' and 'Estrangement'. Someone said, 'The grazing ground'—a shameless young woman said, 'Sing some amorous songs—if you don't, I won't listen.' An inarticulate little girl, with the intention of instructing the Vaishnavi, sang, 'Methingers, do dot, do dot, do dot go.'

Having heard all the requests, the Vaishnavi shot a glance like a flash of lightning towards Kunda and said, 'Well, then—you made no request.' Kunda smiled a little, her face bashfully downcast, and made no reply. But then she whispered to one of her friends, 'Why don't you ask for a kirtan?'

Then her friend said, 'Kunda says to ask for a kirtan.' Hearing this, the Vaishnavi started a kirtan. Kunda was very embarrassed at the Vaishnavi's passing over the requests of all the others in favour of hers.

First, Haridasi Vaishnavi stroked the tambourine once or twice gently with her fingers, as if in play. Then she started the tune with a humming deep in her throat like the humming of bees newly come in spring—as if a bashful girl was opening her mouth to express her first words of love to her husband. Then, suddenly, from that humble tambourine came forth a sound as deep as clouds rumbling, like the sound from the fingers of an instrumental virtuoso, and to that accompaniment, thrilling the flesh of the listeners, came the sound of a singing voice more beautiful than that of an apsara. The women listened with amazement and enchantment as the Vaishnavi's incomparable voice rose towards the sky, building up a palace of sound. What would the ignorant women of the household understand of the structure of that song? If they had had the power, they would have understood that this was a song of a meticulously refined fusion of all the elements of rhythm and melody, not just a matter of a beautiful voice. Whoever the Vaishnavi might be, she was extraordinarily well-taught in musical theory and, at a young age, an expert.

The Vaishnavi finished her song; her listeners asked her to sing again. Then Haridasi, looking with thirsty, wistful eyes towards Kundanandini's face, started to sing another kirtan:

Auspicious lotus-faced one—I want to see you,
So I have come to this pasture.
Give me a place, Radha, at your feet.
You are honoured with a wealth of honour,
So I have disguised myself as a stranger,
Now speak, Radha, and let me live,
Touching your feet I come home.
I want to fill my eyes with the sight of you,
So I play my flute from house to house.
When Radha says: the flute plays,
Then I am flooded with tears.
If you do not want to come back,
Then I will go to the Yamuna's bank,
I will break my flute and abandon my life;
Now let your honour be broken.
Radha has given Braja's joy to the water,
I gave myself to your feet,
Now I bind your anklets round my neck,
And enter the water of the Yamuna.

When the song was finished, the Vaishnavi looked towards Kundanandini and said, 'My mouth has become dry from singing. Give me a little water.'

Kunda brought water in a pot. The Vaishnavi said, 'I shall not touch your pot. Come and pour water into my hands. I am not a Vaishnavi by birth.'

By this she made it understood that she had formerly been of some unclean caste and had now become a Vaishnavi. Hearing these words, Kunda went after her to the place where water was drawn. This was at such a distance from the other women that softly-spoken words could not be overheard. Kunda poured water into the Vaishnavi's hands and the Vaishnavi washed her hands and face.

As she did so, she spoke, her voice unheard by anyone else, 'You are Kunda, are you not?'

Kunda, astonished, asked, 'Why?'

The Vaishnavi said, 'Have you ever seen your mother-in-law?'

Kunda said, 'No.'

Kunda had heard that her mother-in-law, after her disgrace, had left the region.

The Vaishnavi said, 'Your mother-in-law has come here. She is at my house, she weeps to see you just once—Oh! No matter what she is, she is your mother-in-law. Having returned here she cannot show her dishonoured face to the mistress of your household—so why not come with me just once and let her see you?'

Although Kunda was simple, she understood that to agree to meet her mother-in-law was improper. So she only shook her head in refusal at the Vaishnavi's words.

But the Vaishnavi did not give up—again and again she repeated her urgings. Then Kunda said, 'I cannot go without the mistress's permission.'

Haridasi forbade this. She said, 'Do not speak to the mistress. She would not let you go. Perhaps she would send for your mother-in-law. Then your mother-in-law would flee the region.'

However much the Vaishnavi persisted, Kunda would not consent at all to going without Suryamukhi's permission. Then, having no alternative, Haridasi said, 'Very well, but mind you speak well to the mistress. I will come another day to fetch you, but see that you speak well; and weep a little, otherwise nothing will come of it.'

Kunda did not agree with this, but she said neither yes nor no to the Vaishnavi. Then Haridasi, having finished washing her hands and face, went back to the others and asked for her payment. At this point, Suryamukhi arrived. The idle chatter stopped completely, and everyone, old and young, took up their work.

Suryamukhi looked Haridasi over from head to foot and said, 'Who are you, then?' A maternal aunt of Nagendra's said, 'She is a Vaishnavi, she came to sing. She sings beautifully. I have never heard such beautiful songs, Mother. Do you want to hear one? Sing, then, sing, Haridasi! Sing a song of the goddess.'

Suryamukhi was enchanted and delighted at the wonderful Sakta lyric Haridasi sang, and paid her before dismissing her.

The Vaishnavi touched her feet, glanced once again at Kunda, and went away. Once Suryamukhi was screened from her eyes, she played a khemta dance softly on her tambourine and went away singing in a soft voice:

Come, O piece of the moon.
I will give you flower-nectar to drink and gold to wear.
I will give you a flask of attar
I will give you a spray of rose-water
And filling the box for you myself
I will give you rolls of betel-leaf.[8]

For a long time after the Vaishnavi had gone, the women talked of nothing else but her. At first, they began to praise her highly. Then, gradually, a few defects emerged. Viraj said, 'That may be, but her nose was a bit flat.' Then Bama said, 'Her complexion was very pallid.' Chandramukhi said, 'Her hair was like ropes of jute.' Champa said, 'Her forehead was a bit high.' Pramada said, 'The woman's chest was like those of the confidantes in a play; despicable to see.' In this manner, the beautiful Vaishnavi was quickly found to be second to none in ugliness. Then Lalita said, 'However she looked, the woman sang well.' But there was no deliverance there. Chandramukhi said, 'Perhaps, but the woman's voice was rough.' Muktakeshi said, 'You are right—the woman roared like a bull.' Ananga said, 'The woman didn't know her songs, she couldn't sing one of Dasharath's songs.' Kanak said, 'The woman had no sense of rhythm.' In due course it was found that Haridasi Vaishnavi was not only second to none in ugliness—she was worse than anyone else at singing, too.

10
Babu

LEAVING THE DATTA ESTABLISHMENT, HARIDASI VAISHNAVI WENT IN THE direction of the village of Devipur. In Devipur stood a flower-garden, surrounded by iron-railings. Here there were many kinds of flowering trees, and, in the middle, a lake beside which stood a house. Haridasi entered the garden. And, going into the house, she went to a private room and took off her clothes. Suddenly, that braided hair with its thick tresses fell from her head—it was only a wig. The two breasts dropped from her torso—they were made of cloth. The Vaishnavi took off and threw down the brass bangles and the thin ones with their wavy design, and washed off the tilak. Then, in appropriate clothing, the Vaishnavi's female guise having disappeared, there stood an unusually beautiful young man. He was twenty-five years old, but as chance would have it there was no sign of hair on his face. His face and figure were those of a boy. His beauty was very great. This young man was Devendra Babu. He has already been briefly introduced.

Devendra and Nagendra were both of the same family; but over the generations, the family had divided into two branches, to the extent that there was no converse between the Babus of Devipur and the Babus of Govindapur. There had been litigation between the two branches for generations. Nagendra's grandfather had defeated Devendra's grandfather in a big court case, and the Devipur Babus had become powerless. They lost everything through the execution of a decree—the Govindapur Babus bought up all their property. Since then, Devipur had become of little account, and Govindapur had prospered. There was no reconciliation between the two families; Devendra's father sought a means to rebuild something of their wealth and pride. Another zamindar, called Ganesh Babu, lived in the Haripur district. His only child was Haimavati. He gave Haimavati to Devendra in marriage. Haimavati had many qualities—she was ugly, garrulous, disagreeably-spoken and selfish. Up to the time of

Devendra's marriage to her, his character had been spotless. He put particular effort into his studies, and his nature was gentle and truthful. But this marriage was his ruin! When he reached adulthood, he saw that because of his wife's qualities there was no hope of happiness for him at home.

By the tendencies natural to his age, a thirst for beauty awoke in him, but this was not allayed in his own home. By the tendencies natural to his age, the desire for conjugal love awoke in him—but this desire fled at the very sight of the disagreeably-spoken Haimavati. Devendra saw that it was hard for him to even live at home, let alone be happy, because of the pain caused by Haimavati's poisonous words. One day, Haimavati said a filthy word to Devendra; Devendra had borne much—he bore no more. He seized Haimavati by the hair and kicked her. And from that day on, he forsook the house, and, giving orders for a building fit for him to live in to be built in the flower-garden, he went to Kolkata. Devendra's father had already died. So Devendra was now independent. In Kolkata he became engaged in slaking his unappeased thirst for dalliance. A certain personal dissatisfaction arose from this, which he repeatedly tried to wash away with wine. Finally, there was no longer any need for this—he began to develop a taste for sin itself. After some time, having become very well educated in the ways of Babus, Devendra returned to the country and, taking up residence in the garden-house, devoted himself to such pursuits.

Devendra came back from Kolkata having acquired many affectations. On returning to Devipur, he announced himself to be a reformer. First, he established a Brahmo Samaj. Many Brahmos, including Taracharan, gathered; there was no end to their eloquence. From time to time there was a lot of noise about starting a school for girls, but not much was done about it. There was great enthusiasm for widow remarriage. So much so that marriages were arranged for several lower-class widows; but the bridegrooms were of the same quality as the brides. Devendra agreed with Taracharan on the subject of breaking the chains of the prison of the zenana—both used to say: 'Bring out your daughters.' In this matter, Devendra Babu became particularly active—but his 'bringing out' was in a special sense.

After returning from Govindapur, divesting himself of his Vaishnavi clothes, and resuming his own form, Devendra went and sat down in the adjoining room. A servant, Shramhari, prepared tobacco and gave him a pipe; Devendra spent some time serving the Tobacco Goddess, destroyer of all fatigue. He who has not enjoyed the happiness of the favour of this great goddess is not a human being. O pleaser of the minds of all people, fascinator of the world! May our worship of you be constant. May your vehicles, the hubble-bubble, the hookah, the water-pipe and your other heavenly attendants be always before our eyes: the very sight of them is salvation to us. O hookah! O hubble-bubble! O emitters of coiling smoke! O serpent of a tube, surpassing snakes! O beautiful one, crowned with silver! How the fringe slipping from your diadem sparkles! How beautiful is the curved end of your mouthpiece, ornamented with chain-like rings! How deep is the sound of the cool waters in your inner parts! O satisfier of the universe! You take away the fatigue of all men, care for the idle, destroy the mental disturbance of those scolded by their wives, give courage to those in fear of their masters! What do fools know of your greatness? You give consolation to those who mourn, hope to the fearful, understanding to the foolish, peace to the enraged. O giver of favours! O giver of all happiness! May you be unfailingly present in my house. May your fragrance increase from day to day! May the sound of the tumult of your inner waters, like the roaring of clouds, be always there! May your mouthpiece be never separated for an instant from my lips.

Devendra, addicted to pleasure, abundantly enjoyed the favour of this great goddess—but he was not satisfied by that. He prepared to worship another great power. A servant appeared, carrying a straw-covered bottle in his hands. Then, on a soft, spread-out white bed, on a silver-plated seat, with a colour like that of ruddy clouds in an evening sky, in a demonish vessel called a decanter, the great Liquor Goddess appeared. A cut-glass worship vessel was put down, and a plated jug became the ceremonial copper pot; and from the kitchen a black-bearded priest brought a fragrant heap of flowers, called 'roast mutton', on a ritual flower container called a 'hot-water plate'. Then Devendra Datta, devoutly, according to the scriptures, sat down to worship the goddess.

Afterwards, a group of singers and musicians, with tabla, sitar and other instruments, came in. They performed the music necessary for worship.

Finally, a pleasant, graceful young man of Devendra's own age came in and sat down. This was Surendra, the son of Devendra's maternal uncle; he was, in his qualities, the opposite of Devendra in all respects. Even Devendra loved him for his natural qualities. Devendra heeded no one in his family except for him. Surendra came once every evening to hear Devendra's news. But he did not stay long, because of the alcohol. When everyone else had gone, Surendra asked Devendra, 'How is your health?'

Devendra said, 'The body is the temple of disease.'

Surendra said, 'Especially yours. Did you take your temperature today?'

Devendra said, 'No.'

Surendra asked, 'And that pain in your liver?'

Devendra said, 'The same as before.'

Surendra persisted, 'Then wouldn't it be better to stop all this, now?'

Devendra said, 'What—drinking wine? How long will you keep saying this? Wine is my most faithful companion.'

Surendra asked, 'How so? It did not come with you—nor will it go with you. Many give it up—why don't you give it up too?'

Devendra retorted, 'What would I gain by giving it up? Those who give it up have other happinesses—they give it up in the hope of gaining them. I have no other happiness.'

Surendra persisted, 'Then give it up in the hope of living, in the desire for life.'

Devendra said, 'Let those who enjoy living give up wine in the hope of life. What benefit to me is there in living?'

Surendra's eyes overflowed with tears. Then, filled with a friend's affection, he said, 'Then give it up because I ask you to.'

Tears came to Devendra's eyes too. He said, 'There is no longer anyone except you who asks me to walk the right path. If I ever do give up wine it will be because you ask me to. And—'

'And what?'

Devendra said, 'And if you ever bring me the news of my wife's death—then I will give up wine. Otherwise, it's the same to me whether I live or die.'

Surendra, with tears in his eyes, cursing Haimavati a hundred times in his heart, left the house.

11
Suryamukhi's Letter

DEAREST KAMALAMANI, MAY YOU LIVE FOR EVER—

I am ashamed to write this blessing to you again. Now you, too, are someone—the mistress of a house. However that may be, I cannot think of anything to talk to you about except my young sister. I brought you up. I taught you to write your first 'A, B, C', but seeing your handwriting I am ashamed to send you these scribblings of mine. What is the point of feeling this shame? Those days are gone. If they had not, why would I be in this state?

Which state? This is not to be told to anyone—it both saddens me and shames me to tell it. But unless I tell someone, I cannot bear the pain which is in my heart. And whom can I tell? You are the sister of my soul—no one loves me as you do. And I cannot speak of your brother to anyone except you.

I myself have prepared my own funeral pyre. If Kundanandini had died of starvation, how would that have harmed me? God helps so many people, would he not have arranged for her relief? Why did I bring her home and feed her myself?

When you saw that unfortunate, she was a girl. Now she is seventeen or eighteen years old. That she is beautiful, I acknowledge. That beauty has become my ruin.

If there is any happiness for me in this world, it is my husband; if

I am aware of anything in this world, it is my husband; if I have any wealth in this world it is my husband: Kundanandini is snatching my husband away from my heart. If I have any desire in this world, it is for my husband's affection. Kundanandini is cheating me of that affection.

Do not think ill of your brother. I am not blaming him. He is virtuous, and even an enemy could not malign him. Every day I can see how he exerts every ounce of strength to control his mind. As far as he can, he never casts his eyes in Kundanandini's direction. Except when it is absolutely necessary, he does not utter her name. He even treats her harshly. I have even heard him rebuke her for no fault.

But why do I bother you with all these details? It would be very hard to explain this matter to a man, if he asked; but you are a woman, you will have understood already. If Kundanandini was as other women in his eyes, why would he be so eager not to look at her? Why would he be so careful not to say her name? Because of Kundanandini he feels himself to be guilty. That is why he sometimes rebukes her without reason. His anger is not at her but at himself. He rebukes himself, not her. I understand this. I have been devoted to him for so long, I have watched only him—I can tell the words of his heart from seeing his shadow—what could he hide from me? Sometimes, absent-mindedly, his eyes seek here and there—do I not understand that? Seeing, he becomes confused again and turns his eyes away; do I not understand? At mealtimes, with food in his hand, he turns his head to hear the sound of her voice; do I not understand? The rice in his hand stays in his hand, he cannot get it to his mouth, but he turns his head to listen—why? Then as soon as he hears Kunda's voice, he starts to cram food into his mouth: do I not understand? My beloved always looked bright—why is he now so absent-minded? If I speak to him, the words do not reach him and he answers, absent-mindedly, 'Hm.' If I say, angrily, 'I am dying,' he answers without listening, 'Hm.' Why such absentmindedness? If I ask him, he says, 'I am preoccupied with a legal case.' I know that legal cases have no place in his mind. When he speaks of legal cases, he speaks laughingly. Another thing—one day a group of old women from the neighbourhood were speaking of Kunda, and pitying her for being a young widow and an orphan. Your brother was there. Screened from view, I saw that his eyes filled with tears—suddenly he went away quickly.

We have now a new maidservant. Her name is Kumud. My husband calls her, by her name. Sometimes instead of 'Kumud' he says 'Kunda.' And he becomes so embarrassed! Why embarrassed?

I cannot say that he is careless or lacking in affection towards me. Rather he shows me more care and affection than before. I understand the reason for this. He feels himself guilty towards me. Care is one thing, love is another—we women readily understand the difference between them.

Another ironic thing—there is this great pandit in Kolkata called Ishwar Vidyasagar,[9] who has brought out another book on widow remarriage. If he who advocates widow remarriage is a pandit, who is a fool? Now when Bhattacharya Brahmins[10] come to the reception hall, they have heated arguments about this book. On one such day, a logic-chopping Brahmin, like Saraswati's favourite, argued the case for widow remarriage and went away with ten rupees from my husband for the repair of the school. The day after this, the Brahmin Sarvabhaum objected to widow remarriage. I had nine hundred grains of gold made into bangles for his daughter's wedding. No one else was much in favour of widow remarriage.

I have inflicted this long story of my misery on you. I do not know how much angry you will be. But what can I do, sister—if I do not tell you, whom can I tell? My story is still not finished—but out of consideration for you I have stopped. Do not tell anyone about all this. Do not, I adjure you, show this letter to my brother-in-law, either.

Will you come to see us? Do come—your presence would be

a great comfort in my distress.

Write with news of your son, and of your husband, soon.

Yours
Suryamukhi

P.S. Another thing. If the offender could be sent away, I could live. Where could I send her? Could you take her? Or would you be afraid?

In reply, Kamala wrote:

You are mad. Otherwise, why would you doubt your husband's heart? Do not lose faith in your husband. And if indeed you cannot retain your faith—then go and drown yourself in the lake. I, Kamalamani, offer a logical prescription: tie a pitcher to yourself to help you drown. She who cannot retain faith in her husband—it is better for her to die.

12
The Seed Sprouts

WITHIN A FEW DAYS, NAGENDRA'S WHOLE CHARACTER CHANGED. CLOUDS appear in a clear sky—like a summer sky at evening, his character became overcast. Seeing this, Suryamukhi wiped her eyes with the end of her sari.

Suryamukhi thought, 'I will follow Kamala's advice. Why should I doubt my husband's heart? His mind is as steady as a mountain—it is I who am mistaken. He must have some disease.' Suryamukhi was building a dyke of sand.

There was a doctor of sorts in the house. Suryamukhi was the mistress of the house. She spoke to everyone from behind a screen, which hung beside the veranda; Suryamukhi would stand behind that screen. The individuals she spoke to stayed on the veranda; between them a maidservant was stationed; Suryamukhi spoke through her. In this way, Suryamukhi spoke to the doctor. Having called him, Suryamukhi asked, 'The master is ill, why do you not give him some medicine?'

The doctor said, 'What illness, I know nothing of it. I have heard nothing about any illness.'

Suryamukhi said, 'The master has said nothing?'

The doctor said, 'No—what illness?'

Suryamukhi said, 'You are the doctor, if you do not know, how should I know?'

The doctor was embarrassed at this. 'I will go and ask,' he said, and prepared to depart; but Suryamukhi called him back and said, 'Do not ask the master anything—give me some medicine.'

The doctor thought that that was not a bad way of proceeding. 'Certainly, madam, there's no problem about medicine,' he said, and fled. Then he went to his dispensary and mixed together a little soda, a little port wine, a little syrup of iron salts and a little of this and that, filled a bottle with it, stuck on a label and wrote this prescription on it: Take twice a day. Suryamukhi gave the medicine to Nagendra; Nagendra looked at the bottle in his hand and threw it at a cat—the cat fled—its tail sent the medicine flying.

Suryamukhi said, 'You will not take the medicine—tell me, what illness do you have?'

Nagendra asked angrily, 'What illness?'

Suryamukhi said, 'Look at what has happened to your body,' and held a mirror in front of him. Nagendra took the mirror from her hand and threw it away. The mirror broke into many pieces.

Tears fell from Suryamukhi's eyes. Seeing this, Nagendra's eyes turned red with anger, and he got up and went away. Going to the parlour, he beat a servant for no fault. That beating fell on Suryamukhi's limbs.

Previously, Nagendra had been exceedingly mild-tempered. Now every word enraged him.

Not only rage. One day, the time for the evening meal had passed but Nagendra had not come to the inner building. Suryamukhi sat waiting for him. It became very late. By the time Nagendra returned it was quite late; Suryamukhi was astonished at the very sight of Nagendra. His face was flushed, his eyes bloodshot—he had been drinking. Nagendra never touched wine. Suryamukhi was astounded.

From then on, it was the same every day. One day, Suryamukhi clasped Nagendra's feet, and, somehow repressing her tears, pleaded with him; she said, 'If only for me, give it up.' Nagendra asked, 'What's the harm in it?'

The manner of his question forbade any answer. Yet Suryamukhi answered, 'I do not know what harm. What you do not know, I do not know either. I know only my plea.'

Nagendra answered again, 'Suryamukhi, I am a drunkard; drunkards are respected, respect me. Otherwise let it go.'

Suryamukhi left the room. Ever since the servant had been beaten, she had sworn not to weep in front of Nagendra.

The steward sent word: 'Speak to the mistress—the property is melting away, there will be nothing left.'

'Why?'

'The master sees to nothing. In the city and the country, the clerks do as they like. In the absence of interest on the master's part, they pay no attention to me.'

Suryamukhi said, 'If he whose property it is maintains it, it will remain. If not, let it go.'

Previously Nagendra had supervised everything himself.

One day, three or four thousand tenants came to Nagendra's office building and stood there with hands joined in respect. 'Save us, Lord—we cannot survive under the rent-collectors' oppression. They have robbed us of everything we have. Who will save us if you do not?'

Nagendra ordered, 'Drive them all away.'

Earlier, one of his rent-collectors had beaten one of his tenants and taken one rupee from him. Nagendra had deducted ten rupees from the rent-collector's salary and given it to the tenant.

Haradev Ghoshal wrote to Nagendra, 'What has happened to you? What are you doing? I do not know what to think. I receive no letters from you. If I do receive one, it is only two lines, with nothing in them. There is no news. Are you angry with me? Why do you not say so? Have you lost a lawsuit? Why do you not tell me? Whatever else you do or don't tell me, tell me whether you are well or not.'

Nagendra wrote back, 'I am not angry with you—I am driven to destruction.'

Haradev was very experienced. Having read the letter, he thought, 'What is this? Money problems? Estrangement from friends? Devendra Datta? Or, is this love?'

Kamalamani received another letter from Suryamukhi. At the end was this: 'Please come! Kamalamani! Sister! I have no other friend than you. Please come.'

13
A Great Battle

KAMALAMANI'S ATTITUDE CHANGED. SHE COULD STAY AWAY NO LONGER. Kamalamani was a jewel of a woman. So she went to her husband.

Shrishchandra was in the inner building, going through the office accounts book. Beside him, sitting on a mattress, their one-year-old son Satishchandra had taken possession of an English newspaper. First, Satishchandra had tried to see if he could eat the newspaper, but not being able to accomplish that, he had spread it out and was now sitting on it.

Kamalamani went up to her husband, put her arms around his neck and then prostrated herself at his feet. Joining her hands together she said, 'Salaam to the Great King!'

(Recently the play 'Govinda the Prince'[11] had been performed at the house.)

Shrishchandra laughed and said, 'Has another cucumber been stolen?'

Kamala said, 'Neither cucumber nor pumpkin. This time a very important thing has been stolen.'

Shrishchandra asked, 'What has been stolen, and where?'

Kamala said, 'The theft has occurred at Govindapur. There was one farthing in my brother's golden box, and someone has taken it.'

Shrishchandra, puzzled, said, 'Your brother's golden box is Suryamukhi—but what is the farthing?'

Kamalamani said, 'Suryamukhi's intelligence.'

Shrishchandra said, 'Well, people say that if you gamble, you can gamble with a farthing. Suryamukhi bought your brother with that same farthing—and if you have as much intelligence—' Kamalamani pinched Shrishchandra's mouth shut. Freeing himself, Shrishchandra said, 'Who has stolen that farthing?'

Kamala said, 'I don't know—but reading her letter, I can see that that farthing has been stolen—otherwise why would the woman write such a letter?'

Shrishchandra said, 'Can I see the letter?'

Kamalamani put Suryamukhi's letter into Shrishchandra's hand and said, 'Read it. Suryamukhi forbade me to tell you about all this—but I can't breathe properly when I haven't told you everything. I couldn't sleep unless I showed you the letter—or I would fall ill.'

Shrishchandra took the letter, thought, and said, 'Since you were forbidden, I won't look at the letter. I won't ask you to tell me the contents, either. Just tell me what is to be done.'

Kamalamani said, 'This is what is to be done—Suryamukhi's little bit of intelligence is gone—she is in need of some. Who else is there who can give her some intelligence—Satish Babu has it all. So his aunt has written to ask him to go to Govindapur.'

During all this, Satish Babu had upset a vase of flowers and was looking at the inkpot. Seeing this, Shrishchandra said, 'He is a worthy bestower of intelligence, indeed! However that may be, I gather he has been invited to your mother-in-law's house. If Satish must go, then Kamalamani will go too. If Suryamukhi's farthing were not lost, why would she write any such thing?'

Kamalamani said, 'Is that all? Satish is invited, I am invited and you are invited.'

Shrishchandra asked, 'Why am I invited?'

Kamala said, 'Should I go alone? Who will carry our baggage?'

Shrishchandra said, 'This is very unjust of Suryamukhi. If she only needs a brother-in-law to carry pots and towels, then I can show her a two-day brother-in-law.'

Kamalamani became very angry. She frowned, made a face at Shrish, tore up the piece of paper Shrishchandra was writing on and threw it away. Shrish laughed and said, 'Why did you go and do that?'

Then Kamalamani angrily shook her fist at Shrishchandra. Biting her lower lip with teeth as white as lotus petals, she clenched her small hand into a small fist and shook it at him.

Seeing her fist, Shrishchandra undid Kamalamani's hair. Then Kamalamani, with increased anger, tipped the ink from Shrishchandra's inkwell into the spittoon.

In a fit of passion, Shrishchandra, moving quickly, kissed Kamalamani. Impassionately also, impatiently, Kamalamani kissed Shrishchandra. Seeing this, Satishchandra was much amused. He knew that the leasehold on kissing was his. So seeing this profusion of it, he clutched his mother's knee and stood up, with the intention of collecting the king's share; and looking towards the faces of both he gave rise to a wave of laughter. How sweet that laughter sounded in Kamalamani's ears! Kamalamani lifted Satish onto her lap and kissed him again and again. Then Shrishchandra took him from Kamala's lap and kissed him again and again. In due course, Satish Babu, having thus collected the king's share, got off; and catching sight of his father's gold pencil he ran to carry it off. Then, holding it in his hands and thinking it would be a tasty snack, put it to his mouth and started licking it.

During the war of the Kurus, Bhagadatta and Arjuna fought a grand battle. Bhagadatta threw a weapon which would not miss its target, Arjuna;

knowing that Arjuna was powerless to ward it off, Krishna presented his own breast, received the weapon and subdued it. Similarly, in this great battle between Kamalamani and Shrishchandra, Satishchandra, by taking all their mighty weapons on his own face, stopped the fight. But this war and peace of theirs was like the rains of a rainy day—coming and passing repeatedly.

Then Shrishchandra said, 'Must you indeed go to Govindapur? How will I manage being alone?'

Kamalamani said, 'As I manage being alone. Let us both go. Go and finish all your office work, and if you take too long, Satish and I will sit on each side of you and weep.'

Shrishchandra protested, 'How can I go? It is the time for us to buy linseed. You go alone.'

Kamalamani said, 'Come, Satish! Come, we will sit on either side of him and weep.'

Satish heard his mother's call; giving up his pencil-sucking he gave rise to waves of joyous laughter, and consequently Kamala did not weep this time. Instead, she kissed Satish—and following her example, Shrishchandra kissed him also. Satish, demonstrating his skill, sent up another wave of laughter. When all these important matters had been concluded, Kamala said again, 'Now what are your orders?'

Shrishchandra said, 'You go. I don't forbid it, but how can I go during the linseed season?

At this, Kamalamani turned her head away in pique. She said no more.

There was a little ink in Shrishchandra's pen. Shrishchandra took the pen and coming from behind her put a mark on Kamala's forehead.

Then Kamala laughed and said, 'Dearest one, how I love you.' She put her arms round his neck and kissed him, so that the ink mark was transferred to Shrishchandra's cheek.

After the latest battle had been won in this way, Kamala said, 'If you really can't go, then make arrangements for me to go.'

Shrishchandra asked, 'When will you return?'

Kamalamani said, 'Why do you ask? If you don't go, will I be able to stay long?'

Shrishchandra arranged Kamalamani's journey to Govindapur. But I have reliable information that Shrishchandra's employers did not make much profit from their trade in linseed that season. The firm's officials told me in confidence that this was Shrish Babu's fault. He did not put his mind to his work much on this occasion. He just sat in his room staring at the rafters. Shrishchandra, hearing this story one day, said, 'Exactly! I was abandoned by Lakshmi then.' His listeners turned away saying, 'Fie! How uxorious!' Shrish heard this. He happily called the servants and said, 'Prepare the meal well. These gentlemen will be eating here today.'

14
Found Out

IN GOVINDAPUR, IN THE DATTA HOUSEHOLD, IT WAS AS IF A FLOWER HAD bloomed in the darkness. At the sight of Kamalamani's smiling face, even Suryamukhi's tears dried up. Kamalamani had barely set foot in the house when she sat down to do something about Suryamukhi's hair. Suryamukhi had not dressed her hair for many days. Kamalamani said, 'Shall I twine in a couple of flowers?' Suryamukhi pinched her cheek. Kamalamani said, 'No! No!' and secretly put in two flowers. When people came she said, 'Look, the woman is wearing flowers in her hair at her age!'

Neither was the light-bringer's light overshadowed by the clouds of Nagendra's countenance. As soon as she saw Nagendra, Kamalamani touched, and pinched, his feet. Nagendra said, 'Where have you come from?' Kamala bowed her head and said, like an inoffensive, good-hearted person, 'May it please you, Khoka brought me.' Nagendra said, 'Indeed! Beat the rascal!' With these words he took Khoka on his lap and kissed him by way of punishment. Khoka reciprocated by dribbling on him and pulling his moustache.

Kamalamani's conversation with Kundanandini went thus: 'Aha, Kundi—Kundi Mudi Dundi—are you well, then, Kundi?'

Kundi did not speak. After thinking for a while, she said, 'Yes.'

'"Yes, Didi"—you should call me Didi—if you don't, I'll set fire to your hair while you're asleep. Or else I'll throw cockroaches all over you.'

Kunda now began calling her 'Didi'. When Kunda had stayed with Kamala in Kolkata, she did not address Kamala by any terms. Nor did she say much at all. But it was from that time that she had started to love Kamala for her constantly loving nature. She had forgotten her somewhat in the intervening years, not having seeing her. But now, because of Kamala's nature, and Kunda's also, that love sprang up afresh.

Her affection intensified. Meanwhile, Kamalamani prepared to return to her husband's house. Suryamukhi said, 'No, dear! Stay another couple of days! If you leave, I can't go on. Talking with you gives me peace.' Kamala said, 'I won't go without settling your business.' Suryamukhi said, 'What business will you settle?' Kamala said aloud, 'Your funeral'; to herself she said, 'Your deliverance from difficulty.'

When Kundanandini heard that Kamala was going, she hid herself in her room and wept; Kamalamani followed secretly behind her; while Kundanandini wept, her head on the pillow, Kamalamani bound up her hair. Hair-dressing was an addiction with Kamala.

Having finished styling Kunda's hair, Kamala lifted Kunda's head and took it on her lap. With the end of her sari, she wiped Kunda's eyes. After all this, she finally asked, 'Kundi, why were you weeping?'

Kunda said, 'Why are you leaving?'

Kamalamani smiled a little. But that smile did not prevent two teardrops from forming. Silently, they ran down Kamalamani's cheeks, falling over her smile. Rain fell over the sunshine.

Kamalamani said, 'Why do you weep for that?'

Kunda said, 'You at least love me.'

Kamala asked, 'Why—doesn't anyone else love you?'

Kunda remained silent.

Kamala said, 'Who doesn't love you? The mistress doesn't love you—yes? Don't hide from me.'

Kunda was silent.

Kamala said, 'My brother doesn't love you?'

Kunda was silent.

Kamala said, 'If I love you—and you love me, then why not come with me?'

Still Kunda said nothing. Kamala said, 'Will you come?' Kunda shook her head. 'No.'

Kamala's cheerful face became serious.

Then Kamalamani affectionately lifted and held Kundanandini's head to her breast, and affectionately stroking her cheek said, 'Kunda, will you tell me truthfully?'

Kunda said, 'What?'

Kamala said, 'What I ask you? I am your elder sister—don't hide from me—I will not tell anyone else.' To herself Kamala said, 'If I tell anyone, it will be the king's minister, Shrish Babu. And Khoka.'

Kunda said, 'What are you saying?'

Kamala said, 'You love my brother very much—yes?'

Kunda did not answer. Hiding her face in Kamalamani's breast, she started to weep.

Kamala said, 'I understand—you have suffered. There is no harm in your suffering—but what if other people suffer with you?'

Kundanandini lifted her head and gazed fixedly at Kamala's face. Kamalamani understood her question. She said, 'Unlucky girl, have you not seen? Can you not see that—' The words remained unspoken—Kunda's raised head turned again to Kamalamani's breast. Kundanandini's tears flooded over Kamalamani's heart. Kundanandini wept silently for a long time—she wept inconsolably, like a child. She wept, and her companion's tears soaked her hair.

Kamala knew what love was. In her heart of hearts she grieved for Kundanandini's sorrow, and was happy in her happiness. Wiping Kundanandini's eyes she said, 'Kunda!'

Kunda lifted her head again and looked at her.

Kamala said, 'Come with me.'

Tears started to fall again from Kunda's eyes. Kamala said, 'Will you come? Think—'a paradise for cows,

After a long time, Kunda wiped her eyes, sat up and said, 'I will come.'

Why after a long time? Kamala understood. She understood that Kundanandini was sacrificing her own heart's desire in the temple of the good of others. For Nagendra's good, for Suryamukhi's good, she was agreeing to forget Nagendra. That was why it had taken so long. And her own good? Kamala understood that Kundanandini could not understand what was for her own good.

15
Hira

AT ABOUT THIS TIME, HARIDASI VAISHNAVI CAME AND SANG:

I went to pick the flower of disgrace in the thorn thicket,
My companion was the black flower of disgrace.
I wore a garland on my head, earrings in my ears.
My companion was the flower of disgrace.

On this occasion, Suryamukhi was present. She sent someone to call Kamala to hear the singing. Kamala came to listen, bringing Kunda with her. The Vaishnavi began to sing:

Come what may, the thorns blossom,
I will steal and eat the flower's nectar,
I wander, seeking for where blossom
New buds.

Kamalamani frowned and said, 'Sister Vaishnavi—let rubbish infect your mouth—and you will die. Don't you know any other songs?'

Haridasi Vaishnavi said, 'Why?' Kamala became even angrier; she said, 'Why? Bring a thorny acacia branch here, then—I will show you how much pleasure thorns are, woman!'

Suryamukhi said gently to Haridasi, 'We do not like those songs—sing respectable songs in a family house.'

Haridasi said, 'Very well.' She started to sing:

I will read the smriti shastras, begging
them from the Bhattacharyas.
I will learn piety and impiety, no young woman will reproach me.

Kamala frowned and said, 'Mistress of the house—listen to your Vaishnavi's songs yourself if you want to; I am leaving.' With these words, Kamala went away—Suryamukhi too, with a displeased expression, got up and went away. The other women, following their own inclinations, either went away or stayed; Kundanandini stayed. The reason for this was that Kundandini had understood nothing of the substance of the songs—she had not even listened much—she was abstracted and merely stayed where she was. Haridasi sang no more songs. Idle chatter arose here and there. Seeing that there was no further singing, everyone got up and went away. Only Kundanandini did not get up—it was doubtful whether she had any strength left in her legs. Then, having Kunda to herself, Haridasi talked to her a great deal. Kunda listened only to some of it.

Suryamukhi was watching all this from a distance. When she saw that the two of them seemed to be talking with rapt attention, she called Kamala to see them. Kamala said, 'What is this, then? Let them talk. They are only women.'

Suryamukhi said, 'Isn't that woman a man?'

Kamala was astonished and said, 'What?'

Suryamukhi said, 'I think that is some man in disguise. I will find out straight-away—but how sinful Kunda is.'

'Wait. I will fetch an acacia branch. I will show the chap the pleasure of thorns.' With these words, Kamala went in search of an acacia branch. On the way she met Satish—Satish had taken possession of his aunt's box of vermilion and was lavishly painting his own cheeks, nose, chin and belly—seeing him, Kamala forgot all about the Vaishnavi, the acacia branch, Kundanandini and the rest.

Then Suryamukhi sent for Hira.

Hira's name has been mentioned already. Now some information about her is necessary.

Nagendra and his father were particularly keen in employing maidservants of very good character in the house. With this intention, both agreed to pay good wages, and tried to employ women from fairly upper-class homes. In their house, maidservants lived happily and with honour, and consequently the daughters of many poor gentlefolk accepted service with them. Among those of this sort, Hira was the foremost. Many of the maidservants were Kayasthas—Hira, too, was a Kayastha—Nagendra's father had brought her grandmother from her village. Initially, it was her grandmother who was employed—Hira was then a child who came with her. Later, when Hira was old enough, the grandmother gave up her job and with the money she had saved, built a small house to live in in Govindapur—Hira took employment in the Datta household.

Hira was now twenty years old. She was younger than most of the other maidservants. Because of her intelligence and character, she was now considered the best of the maidservants.

Hira was known as a child widow in Govindapur. No one had ever heard any reference to her husband. But no one had heard of any stain on Hira's character either. Yet Hira was very talkative, dressed her hair like a married woman's, and was very fond of nice clothes.

Hira was beautiful, as well—with glistening dark limbs, and eyes like lotus petals. She was short in stature; her face was like a cloud-covered moon; her tresses swung like a cobra's hood. Hira sang songs behind a screen; she started quarrels among the servants in order to watch the show; she frightened the cooks in the dark; she incited the boys to ask for marriages; if she saw someone taking a nap she would paint them like clowns with lime and ink.

But Hira had many more faults. These will be revealed as the story progresses. For the time being, I will content myself by saying that Hira would no sooner see some attar of roses than she would steal it.

Suryamukhi sent for Hira and said, 'Do you know this Vaishnavi?'

Hira said, 'No. I never go beyond this neighbourhood—how would I know a Vaishnavi beggar? Ask the women of the thakur bari. Karuna or Shitala may have brought her.'

Suryamukhi said, 'She is not a Vaishnavi of the thakur bari. I want you to find out who this Vaishnavi is. Who she is, and where she lives. And why there is such a friendship between her and Kunda. If you can find out all this and tell me, I will give you a new Benarasi sari and let you go and see the processions.'

At the mention of a Benarasi sari, Hira drew a deep breath, and asked, 'When am I to go and find out?'

Suryamukhi said, 'When you please. But if you don't follow her now, you won't discover her address.'

Hira answered, 'Very well.'

Suryamukhi warned her, 'But see that the Vaishnavi doesn't suspect anything. And that no one else does either.'

At this point, Kamala returned. Suryamukhi told her all about her plan. Kamala was happy to hear it. She said to Hira, 'And if you can, give the woman a couple of blows with acacia thorns.'

Hira said, 'I can do all this, but I want more than just a Benarasi sari.'

Suryamukhi asked, 'What do you want?'

Kamala said, 'She wants a husband. Arrange a marriage for her.'

Suryamukhi said, 'Very well, that can be arranged—do you fancy my brother-in-law? If so, Kamala will negotiate for you!'

Hira said, 'I will see. But there is a husband to my liking at home.'

Suryamukhi asked, 'Who, then?'

Hira said, 'Death.'

16
'No'

THAT EVENING, KUNDANANDINI SAT BESIDE THE LAKE IN THE GARDEN. THE lake was very wide; its water was very clear, and always shining blue. The reader may remember that behind this lake was a flower-garden. Within the flower-garden was a marble pergola. In front of the pergola was a flight of steps descending to the lake. These steps were made of stone-like bricks, very well made and smooth, and on either side, were two huge, old bakul trees. Under these trees, on the steps, alone in the twilight, sat Kundanandini, watching the reflection of the sky with all its stars in the heart of the lake. Here and there crimson flowers could be seen indistinctly in the darkness. On the other three sides of the lake, amra, kantal, rose-apple, citrus, lychee, coconut, kul, bel and other flowering trees, merging in dense rows, looked like an uneven-topped wall in the darkness. Occasionally, a machar bird in the branches gave a great cry which resounded over the still lake. A cool breeze across the lake set the lotus buds faintly trembling, quivered the image of the sky, murmured in the leaves of the bakul trees over Kundanandini's head and spread the fragrance of the bakul flowers, opened by the heat, all around. Bakul flowers dropped silently on Kundanandini's limbs and all around her. From behind came the fragrance of innumerable mallika, yuthika and kamini flowers. All around in the darkness, fireflies rose, fell, lifted, dropped over the clear water. One or two bats called—one or two jackals barked a warning—one or two clouds were wandering in the sky, having lost their way—one or two stars fell sorrowfully. Sorrowfully, Kundanandini was thinking. What thoughts she was thinking! Thus—'Well, then, everyone has died already—my mother died, my brother died, my father died—why did I not die? Since I didn't die, why did I come here? Well, then, do people become stars when they die?' Kunda no longer thought at all of the dream she had seen on the night of her father's death; it was never in her mind, and was not now. Only a hint of it came to her. Only this was in her mind, that she had once seen her mother in a dream and that her mother had seemed to speak to her from the stars. Kunda thought, 'Well, then, do people become stars when they die? Then have Father, Mother and everyone become stars? But which stars are they? That one? Or that one? Who is which? How shall I know? Can I see which is which? I weep so much—let that go, let me not think of it any more—I should weep again. What good is weeping? Weeping is my fate—if not, Mother—that word again! Let it go—well, then—how about dying? How? By drowning? Fine! If I die, I shall become a star—then what will happen? I shall see—day after day I shall see—whom? Can I not say whom? Why can I not say his name, then? There is no one here—no one will hear. Shall I say his name once? There is no one here—I name my heart's longing. Na—Nag—Nagendra! Nagendra, Nagendra, Nagendra. Nagendra, Nagendra, Nagendra! Nagendra, my Nagendra! Oh! My Nagendra? Who am I? Suryamukhi's Nagendra! What difference does it make however many times I say it? Well—if he hadn't married Suryamukhi, if he'd married me—let it go—let me drown myself. Well, if I drown myself now—tomorrow I'll float to the surface—then everyone will hear of it—Nagendra will hear—Nagendra!—Nagendra!—Nagendra! I will say it again—Nagendra, Nagendra, Nagendra—what will Nagendra think when he hears? I won't drown myself—I should become all swollen—I should look like a demon. If he saw me? Can I die by poison? What poison shall I take? Where would I get it—who would get it for me? If they did—would I be able to die? I can—but not just yet—let me for once think of satisfying my longing—he loves me. What was Kamala about to say? It was that. Well, then, is it true? But how would Kamala know? I could not disgrace myself by asking. Does he love me? How could he love me? What does he love about me, my appearance or my qualities? Appearance? Let me see.' (With these words, she looked to see her own image in the dark, clear face of the lake, but she could see nothing, and resumed her former position.) 'Let it go, why do I think of what is not so? Suryamukhi is more beautiful than I; Haramani is more beautiful than I; Vishu, Chandra, Prasanna, Bama, and Pramada are more beautiful; even

Hira the maidservant is more beautiful. Even Hira is more beautiful? Yes; what if her complexion is dark—her face is more beautiful than mine. So my appearance is of no account—what about qualities? Well, let me think—I can think of nothing. Who knows! But I will not die, I've decided that. It is a useless idea! I think it is a useless idea. I shall think of a better idea. But to go to Kolkata—I cannot go: I won't be able to see him. I cannot go—I cannot go—I cannot go. But if I don't go, what shall I do? If what Kamala said is true, then I am bringing ruin on those who have done so much for me. I can understand something of what is in Suryamukhi's mind. Whether it is true or false, I must therefore go to Kolkata. I cannot do it. So let me drown myself. I must die. O Father! Did you leave me so that I might drown myself—'

Then Kunda put her hands over her eyes and wept. Suddenly, like a light in a dark house, the details of that dream of hers came into her mind. Kunda stood up as if touched by lightning. 'I forgot everything—why did I forget? My mother showed me—knowing my destiny, my mother told me to go to that world of stars—why did I not listen to her—why did I not go! Why am I still not dying? I will die now.' With this thought, Kunda slowly started to descend the steps. Kunda was very weak—very timid-natured—at every step she was afraid—at every step her limbs trembled. But determinedly, with the purpose of obeying her mother's command, slowly she went. And then someone behind her very slowly touched her back. 'Kunda!' Kunda saw—in the darkness she instantly recognized—Nagendra. Kunda did not die that day.

And Nagendra! Is this your long-standing good character? Is this your long-standing learning? Is this your return for Suryamukhi's self-denying love! Fie! Fie! Look, you are a thief! Even worse than a thief. What would a thief have done to Suryamukhi? He would have stolen her ornaments and gone off with her money, but you have stolen her life. A thief, to whom Suryamukhi has given nothing, simply steals. Suryamukhi has given you everything—and you have stolen more than a thief would. Nagendra, it would be better if you were dead. If you have the courage, then go and drown yourself.

And fie! Fie, Kundanandini! Why did you tremble at the touch of a thief? Fie! Fie, Kundanandini!—why did a thief's words make your body shiver? Kundanandini!—Look, the water of the lake is clear, cool, and fragrant—within it, the stars tremble in the wind's waves. Will you sink into it? Will you not drown yourself? Kundanandini does not want to die.

The thief said, 'Kunda! Are you going to Kolkata?'

Kunda said nothing—she wiped her eyes—she said nothing.

The thief said, 'Kunda! Are you going of your own will?'

Of her own will? Oh God! Kunda wiped her eyes again—she said nothing.

'Kunda—why are you weeping?' At this, Kunda burst into tears. Then Nagendra said, 'Listen, Kunda! I have borne much suffering for so long, but I can bear it no longer. I cannot say through what suffering I have gone. Fighting with myself I have been wounded. I have sunk low, I drink wine. I cannot go on. I cannot give you up. Listen, Kunda! Widow remarriage is taking place these days—I will marry you. I will marry you at a word from you!'

Now Kunda spoke. She said, 'No.'

Again Nagendra spoke. 'Why, Kunda? Is widow remarriage against the shastras?' Kunda said again, 'No.'

Nagendra said, 'Then why not? Speak, speak—speak—will you become mistress of my house or not? Do you love me or not?'

Kunda said, 'No.'

Then, as if with a thousand mouths, how many unchecked, heart-piercing, love-filled words did Nagendra utter! Kunda said, 'No.'

Then Nagendra looked and saw that the lake was clear and cool—scented with flowers—with stars trembling within it in the undulating breeze—and he thought, 'How would it be to lie there?'

It was as if Kunda said from the sky, 'No.' Widow remarriage is in the shastras. It was not that. But why did Kunda not drown herself? Clear water—cool water—stars dancing below—why did Kunda not drown herself?

17
Birds of a Feather

HARIDASI VAISHNAVI CAME TO THE GARDEN-HOUSE, WAS TRANSFORMED INTO Devendra Babu, and sat down. Beside him on one side was a hubble-bubble. This hubble-bubble, bound with garlands of decorated silver chains, offering the delight of sweet warbling music, stretched out its beautiful long lips for a kiss—on top of its head the fire of affection burned. On the other side, in a crystal container, a golden-complexioned daughter of confusion shone clearly. Before him, seated near the dishes of food like a tame tomcat, was a sycophant, his nostrils distended with his desire for favour. The hookah said, 'Look! Look! I am offering my mouth!' The maiden said, 'Caress me first! See how fair I am! Come, come! Take me first!' The nose of the one desiring favour said, 'Give something to the one I belong to.'

Devendra complied with all the requests. He kissed the hubble-bubble—its love rose in smoke. He took the daughter of confusion into his belly, and she rose slowly to his head. He satisfied Master Tomcat's nose—which, after several glasses, began to rumble. The servants, addressing him as, 'Teacher, teacher,' removed him to another room.

Then Surendra came and sat by Devendra, and after asking about his health and so on, said, 'Where did you go again today?'

Devendra said, 'Has even this come to your ears?'

Surendra said, 'You are making yet another mistake. You think that you hide everything—that no one can find you out; but the drum sounds from quarter to quarter.'

Devendra said, 'By God! I don't want to deceive anyone at all—which bugger should I deceive?'

Surendra answered, 'Do not consider that is to your credit, either. If you had some shame, then we would have some hope for you. If you had some shame, would you any more go from village to village in a Vaishnavi's garb, behaving scandalously?'

Devendra laughed, 'But such an interesting Vaishnavi, brother? Seeing the Vaishnavi mark, weren't you interested?'

Surendra said, 'I have not seen that disgraceful face; if I had seen it, I would have destroyed the Vaishnavi's Vaishnava play with two whips.'

Then, snatching away the wine-container from Devendra's hand, Surendra said, 'Now stop for a bit, and while you still have your senses, listen to one or two things. After that, drink.'

Devendra said, 'Speak on, brother! It seems I see great rancour now—has Haimavati's wind touched your body, or what?'

Surendra, not listening to the foul-mouth's words, said, 'Whom do you wish to destroy, that you disguised yourself as a Vaishnavi?'

Devendra said, 'Do you not know that? Don't you remember that Taracharan married a divine girl? That girl is now a widow, and is shut up in the Datta establishment. So I went to see her.'

Surendra said, 'Why, are you not sated with so much wrongdoing that you must work the downfall of that protectorless girl? See here, Devendra, you are so very sinful, so cruel, so outrageous that I believe I can no longer live with you.'

Surendra spoke these words with such firmness that Devendra was struck silent. Then Devendra said, seriously, 'Do not be angry with me. I can't control my mind. I can give up everything, but I cannot give up hoping for this woman. From the day I first saw her in Taracharan's house, I have been stricken by her beauty. In my eyes, there is no such beauty elsewhere. The kind of thirst a sick person suffers in fever—since then, that is the kind of thirst I suffer in longing for her. Since then, I have employed so many strategems in order to see her, but have not been able to. Until now, I have not been able to—finally, I have used this Vaishnavi garb. You need have no misgivings—the woman is very virtuous.'

Surendra asked, 'Then why do you go?'

Devendra said, 'Only to see her. I cannot tell you what satisfaction there is for me in seeing her, speaking with her, singing songs for her.'

Surendra said, 'I tell you truly—I am not jesting. If you will not give up this wicked behaviour—if you go along this path again—then your converse with me is finished from now on. I, too, become your enemy.'

Devendra said, 'You are my only friend. I can do without half my things, but not without you. But if I must do without you, I must: I cannot give up seeing Kundanandini.'

Surendra said, 'So be it. This is my last meeting with you.'

With these words Surendra, with a sorrowful heart, went away. Devendra, greatly saddened by the loss of his only friend, sat there morosely for some time. Finally, after careful thought, he said, 'Let it go! Who has what in this world! I have myself!' With this, he filled his glass and drank some brandy. Under its influence, he soon became cheerful. Then Devendra, lying back and closing his eyes, began to sing:

My name is Hira Gardener
I live in Radha's bower, my sister-in-law is humpbacked.
Ravana says—Chandrabali,
you are my lotus bud,
hearing this Krishna strikes down the bamboo
and rescues Draupadi!

Then, all his companions having gone, Devendra, like a raft on the bosom of a river without boats, sat alone and rose and sank in the waves of pleasure. Whales and monsters, in the form of diseases, hid in such waters—there was only evil water and evil moonlight!

At this point, there came a kind of rustling sound from the direction of the window—as if someone had lifted the Venetian blind to look in, and had suddenly let it go. Perhaps Devendra was hoping for someone—he said, 'Who is shaking the blind?' Receiving no answer, he looked towards the window, and saw a woman running away. Seeing the woman fleeing, Devendra opened the window, jumped out, and ran staggering after her.

The woman could easily have escaped, but whether it was that she did not want to escape or whether she lost her way in the garden in the darkness, it is impossible to say. Devendra seized her and looked into her face, but was unable to recognize her in the darkness. In a slurred voice, besotted with wine, he said, 'Help! From what tree have you come?' Then he dragged her into the house, and, holding a light, looked at her from one side and then the other, and said in the same way, 'Whose spirit are you, then?' Finally, not being able to decide on anything, he said, 'I couldn't! Go away now, at new moon I'll offer bread and a goat and give a puja—now, just drink a little brandy and go.' With this, the drunkard sat the woman down in the sitting room and put a glass in her hand.

Not accepting it, the woman put it down.

Then the drunkard brought the light close to the woman's face. Moving the light, he solemnly examined her from this direction, that direction, and all around; and finally, suddenly throwing the light down, he began to sing,—'O who are you, I know you—I have seen you somewhere.'

Then the woman, thinking that she had been found out, said, 'I am Hira.'

Saying 'Hurrah! Three cheers for Hira!' the drunkard jumped up. Then, lying on the floor again, he touched Hira's feet and, with glass in hand, started to sing a hymn of praise:

Obeisance obeisance obeisance
To the goddess in the form of shadow
under the banyan tree.
Obeisance obeisance obeisance
To the goddess in the form of Hira
in the Datta's house.
Obeisance obeisance obeisance
To the goddess with basket in hand
on the bank of the pool.
Obeisance obeisance obeisance
To the goddess with crown in hand
at the door of the house.
Obeisance obeisance obeisance
To the goddess in the form of a hag
in my house
Obeisance obeisance obeisance.[12]

'So—Aunt Gardener! what do you think?'

Before this, Hira, following the Vaishnavi in daylight, had discovered that Haridasi Vaishnavi and Devendra Babu were the same person. But why was Devendra coming and going to and from the Datta household disguised as a Vaishnavi? It was not easy to discover this. After some thought, Hira had boldly resolved to come to Devendra's house at this time. She had secretly entered the garden, stood at the window, and listened to Devendra's talk. Having heard from concealment Devendra's conversation with Surendra, Hira had been going away, her question answered, when she had carelessly let fall the Venetian blind—and thus made her mistake.

Now Hira was impatient to escape. Devendra again put a glass of wine in her hand. Hira said, 'Drink it yourself.' Devendra swallowed it immediately. That glass filled Devendra to capacity—he swayed once or twice—then fell to the floor. Then Hira got up and fled. And Devendra sang drowsily:

Her age is sixteen
She is dark to look at and hear,
Next mouth she will die
And I'll burn at home.

That night Hira did not return to the Datta house, but went to her own house and slept there. At dawn on the following day, she went to Suryamukhi and told her about Devendra. Devendra went to and fro in Vaishnavi garb on account of Kunda. That Kunda was innocent Hira did not say, nor did Suryamukhi understand this. Why Hira hid this point—the reader will in due course come to know. Suryamukhi had seen Kunda talking secretively with the Vaishnavi—consequently, Suryamukhi believed her to be guilty. Hearing Hira's story, Suryamukhi's lotus-petal-like eyes became red with anger. The veins in her forehead swelled and stood out. Kamala also heard everything. Suryamukhi sent for Kunda. When she came, Suryamukhi said, 'Kunda! We have learned who Haridasi Vaishnavi is. We know who she is to you. You knew who she was! We do not give room in our house to women like you. Go from this house immediately. Or Hira will drive you away with a broom.'

Kunda's body trembled. Kamala saw that she was about to fall. Kamala took her to her bedroom. There she comforted her affectionately, and said, 'Let that woman say what she likes; I do not believe a single word she says.'

18
Protectorless

IN THE DEAD OF NIGHT, WHEN EVERYONE IN THE HOUSE WAS ASLEEP, Kundanandini opened the door of her bedroom and came out. With only the clothes she stood up in, she left the house. In that deep night, in her simple clothes, the seventeen-year-old, protectorless girl plunged alone into the ocean of the world.

The night was very dark. Little by little clouds gathered; where was the path?

Who would tell her where the path was? Kundanandini had never been outside the Datta establishment. She knew not which path led where. And where indeed should she go?

The great dark body of the buildings loomed against the sky's body—Kundanandini began to circle that darkness. It was in her mind that she would be able to see the light from Nagendra's bedroom windows. She would console her eyes with one look at that light before she went away.

She knew his bedroom—as she went on she could see it—light was coming from its windows. The shutters were open—the sashes were closed—the three windows shone in the darkness. Against them flying insects fell. Seeing the light, they flew towards it, but unable to enter—the path being closed—they dashed themselves against the glass.

Kundanandini's heart suffered for those tiny insects.

Kundanandini stared with fascinated eyes at the light from the windows—she was unable to leave that light. There were several tamarisk trees in front of the bedroom—Kundanandini sat down under them, facing the windows. The night was dark, all around was darkness, in the trees the glitter of fireflies, in thousands, blossomed, went out; went out, blossomed. In the sky, black clouds chased black clouds—after them even blacker clouds chased—and after them, even blacker ones still. There were only one or two stars in the sky, sometimes diving into the clouds, sometimes floating. All around the house were rows of tamarisk trees which stood like nocturnal ghouls lifting their heads into that cloud-filled sky. In the lap of night, these terrible beings spoke, at the wind's touch, in their own ghoulish language, above Kundanandini's head. Even the owls, in fear of the terrible night, seldom spoke. As the wind blew, the open shutters of the windows would rap once against the wall. A screech owl, perched on top of the building, called. Occasionally a dog, seeing some other animal, ran quickly forward. Now and then, tamarisk leaves or flowers fell. In the distance, the dark tops of the coconut palms slowly tilted: from the distance, the rustle of the leaves of the tal trees came to her ears; above all, the light of that row of windows shone—and the insects came again and again towards it. Kundanandini kept gazing towards it.

Slowly, a window-sash was opened. The shape of a man became outlined against the light. Hari! Hari! It was Nagendra's shape. Nagendra—Nagendra! If you could see the small Kunda-blossom in the darkness at the foot of that tamarisk tree! If you could hear the sound of her heartbeats—thud! thud!—as she gazes at you through the window! If you could know how her happiness at seeing you is spoiled by the fear that you will move away again now and become invisible! Nagendra! You are standing in front of the lamp—stand, just once, with the lamp in front of you! Stand there—do not move—Kunda is very miserable. Stand there—then she will no longer think of the clear, cool water of the lake, and the reflections of the stars in its depths.

Listen to that! The screech owl calls! If you move away, you will frighten

Kundanandini! It is lightning you see! Do not move away—you will frighten Kundanandini! Look at the battle between the black clouds pressed by the wind. There will be much rain. Who will offer shelter to Kunda?

Look—you have opened the window and clusters of insects have come and entered your bedroom. Kunda wonders what, in this world, is needed to be born as an insect. Kunda! The insects are burned and die! Kunda desires that. She thinks, 'Why did I not burn and die?'

Nagendra closed the sash and moved away. Pitiless one! What a wound that inflicts! No, you have no business to be awake in the night—go to sleep—or you will become unwell. If Kundanandini dies, let her die. Kundanandini desires that you should not fall ill.

Now it was as if the light-filled window became dark. Gazing, gazing, gazing, wiping tears from her eyes, Kundanandini got up. She moved slowly along the path she found in front of her. Where was she going? The nocturnal ghouls asked in the murmuring of the tamarisk trees, 'Where are you going?' The tal trees, rustling, asked: 'Where are you going?' The owl's deep voice said, 'Where are you going?' The bright row of windows said, 'You may as well go—we will not show you Nagendra again.' Yet Kundanandini, foolish Kundanandini, kept turning back to look at them.

Kunda went on, went on—only went on. Even more clouds raced into the sky—the clouds all gathered into one and made darkness in the sky, too—lightning laughed—and laughed again—and again! The wind roared, the clouds roared—the wind and the clouds, merged into one, roared. The sky and the night, merged into one, roared. Kunda! Where will you go?

The storm grew. First, sound, then the dust rose, then the wind itself came, tearing away the leaves of the trees! Finally, pitter-pat, plop, plop, whoosh! The rain came! Kunda! Where will you go?

By the flash of the lightning, Kunda saw beside the path a small house. The four walls of the house were of clay; above them was a small thatched roof. Kundanandini, coming to its shelter, sat beside the door. At the touch of her back, the door made a sound. The occupant of the house was awake, and heard the sound of the door. She thought, 'It is the storm'; but a dog was lying beside the door—it rose and started to bark. Then the occupant of the house was afraid. Fearfully, she opened the door to look. She saw it was only a shelterless woman. She asked, 'Who are you, then?'

Kunda said nothing.

'Who are you, woman?'

Kunda said, 'I stopped because of the rain.'

The occupant of the house said, anxiously, 'What? What? What? Say that again?'

Kunda said, 'I stopped because of the rain.'

The occupant of the house said, 'I know that voice. Don't I? Come into the house, then.'

The occupant of the house took Kunda inside. She kindled a light. Then Kunda saw—Hira.

Hira said, 'I understand that you have fled from recriminations. Don't be afraid. I shall tell no one. Stay in this place of mine for a couple of days.'

19
Hira's Anger

HIRA'S HOUSE WAS ENCLOSED WITH A WALL. THERE WERE TWO NEAT, EARTHEN rooms. On them were designs painted in rice flour—lotuses—birds—gods. The courtyard was swabbed with a solution of cow-dung—on one side were red vegetables, near them were dopati and mallika flowers, and roses. The gardener at the Babu's house had himself brought and planted seedlings of flowering plants—if she had wanted it, he would probably have moved the garden itself to her house. Amongst the gardener's gains was this, that Hira prepared tobacco for him with her own hands. The gardener went home at night thinking of Hira, wearing thin black bangles, holding in her hands the hookah and offering it to him.

Hira lived with her grandmother; the grandmother slept in one room, and Hira in the other. Hira made a bed for Kunda with her for the night. Kunda lay down—she did not sleep. The next day, Hira kept her there. She said, 'Stay here now for a couple of days; see whether they are still angry, then go wherever you like.' Kunda stayed. Following Kunda's wishes, Hira kept her concealed. She gave Kunda the key, without her grandmother seeing her. Then she went to work at the Babu's house. When the grandmother went to bathe, at the second prahar, Hira came and bathed Kunda and gave her food. Then, giving her the key again, she went away. In the evening she returned and, when Kunda unlocked the door, the two of them made up their beds.

Chink—chink—chink—jingle—clang! The outer door's chains cautiously stirred. Hira was surprised. Only one person sometimes stirred the chains. That was the gatekeeper at the Babu's house, who came in the dead of night calling and shaking the chains. But in his hands the chains shook and said, 'Clang, clang, jangle! Bolt and socket and shank stay firm!' This was not what the chains were saying. They were saying, 'Clink, clink, jingle! Let me see how my Hira is! Chink, chang, chonk. My Hira rise up! Tink, tink, tinky, tingle—Come, my jewel of a Hira.' Hira got up and went to see; opening the outside door, she saw a woman. At first she did not recognize her, and then she did—'What fortune is this! Is it you, Ganga Water!'[13] Hira's Ganga Water was Malati Goyalini. Malati Goyalini's home was Devipur—near Devendra's house—and she had a very fine sense of humour. She was thirty years old, wore a sari, had bangles on her arms, and a paan-stained mouth. Malati Goyalini was nearly fair-complexioned—a little ruddy—with reddish spots on her face and a snub nose—and a tattoo on her forehead. There were tobacco stains at the corners of her mouth. Malati Goyalini was not a servant of Devendra's—she was one of his dependants—but she was very devoted to him and to his many orders—what others could not do, Malati would accomplish. Seeing Malati, crafty Hira said, 'Dear Ganga Water! May I see you in my last moments! But why now?'

Ganga Water whispered, 'Devendra summons you.'

Hira, slinging mud, said smilingly, 'Will you not get something for this?'

Malati poked Hira with two fingers and said, 'Oh hell! Think what you like! Now come!'

Hira wanted to. She said to Kunda, 'I must go to my father's house—he has sent for me; who knows why?' She put out the lamp, skilfully dressed herself in the dark and went with Malati. In the darkness, the two of them joined their voices:

I strive to get a jewel to my liking
Churning the sea, I will raise up a lover
and my body will fall.

They went along singing this song.

Hira went alone to Devendra's sitting room. Devendra was worshipping the goddess, but this time with more restraint. His mind was alert. He conversed with Hira in a different manner. He sang no hymn of praise. He said, 'Hira, that evening I had drunk a lot of wine and could not understand anything of the significance of what you said. Why had you come? I sent for you in order to ask you this.'

Hira said, 'I came only to see you.'

Devendra smiled. He said, 'You are very intelligent. Nagendra Babu was fortunate to get a maidservant like you. I know that you had come in search of Haridasi Vaishnavi. You came to find out what was in my mind. You came to find out why I dress as a Vaishnavi, why I go to the Datta house. And you went away having found this out, in a fashion. Nor will I hide these things from you. No doubt you received a reward from your master for doing this. Now do something for me: I, too, will reward you.'

It is very painful to write down clearly all the words uttered by those whose characters are steeped in mortal sin. Devendra, observing that Hira had a great desire for much wealth, spoke of her selling Kunda to him. Hearing this, Hira's eyes became red and her ears turned hot with anger. She got up and said, 'Sir! You have spoken to me as to a servant. I cannot give you an answer. I will tell my master. He will give you a fitting answer.'

With these words, Hira swiftly went away. For some moments, Devendra, embarrassed and discouraged, was silent. Then his spirits lifted and he drank two glasses of brandy. After that, restored to his normal self, he sang softly:

> A young heifer came to eat oil-cake
> in a strange cowshed—

20
Hira's Malice

AT DAWN, HIRA GOT UP AND WENT TO WORK. FOR THE PAST TWO DAYS there had been disturbance in the Datta household—Kunda could not be found. Everyone in the household knew that she had gone away in anger; of the people in the neighbourhood, some knew and some did not. Nagendra heard that Kunda had left the house and gone away—why she had gone away, no one told him. Nagendra thought, 'After what I said to her, Kunda went away because she thought it improper to stay any longer in my house. If that was so, why did she not go with Kamala?' Nagendra's face was sombre. No one had the courage to go near him! No one knew what Suryamukhi had done wrong, but there was no communication between him and Suryamukhi. He sent out women messengers secretly in search of Kundanandini, from village to village and neighbourhood to neighbourhood.

Although Suryamukhi was overwhelmed with anger and jealousy, she was greatly distressed when she learned of Kunda's flight. Particularly when Kamalamani explained that nothing that Devendra said was ever trustworthy. For if Kunda had secretly had an affection for Devendra, it would never have remained undisclosed. Kunda's nature was such that this was most unlikely. Devendra was a drunkard, and, under the influence of wine, uttered boastful lies. Suryamukhi understood all this, and her remorse became stronger. Because of this, she suffered even more inner pain at her husband's continuing displeasure. A hundred times she reproached Kunda; a thousand times she reproached herself. She, too, sent people out to search for Kunda.

Kamala postponed her return to Kolkata. She reproached no one—even to Suryamukhi she uttered not the slightest reproof. She took off her necklace and said to everyone in the household, 'I will give this necklace to the person who brings Kunda back.'

Sinful Hira saw and heard all this, but said nothing. At the sight of Kamala's necklace she felt a few pangs of desire—but she restrained these. For the second day, after work, at the second prahar, after her grandmother's bath-time, she fed Kunda. Then, when night came, the two of them made up their beds and lay down. Neither Kunda nor Hira slept—Kunda lay awake because of the sorrow in her heart. Hira lay awake because of the happiness and sorrow in her own heart. She, too, like Kunda, lay in bed thinking. What she was thinking could not be expressed in words—it was a deep secret.

O Hira! Fie! Fie! Hira! Her face was not ill to look at—she was so young, so why was there so much cruel deceit in her heart? Why? Why had God cheated her? God had cheated her and she in turn wanted to cheat everyone else. If she had been put in Suryamukhi's place, would Hira have been cruelly deceitful? Hira says 'No.' It was because Hira was put in Hira's place that she was Hira. People say, 'Everything is the fault of the wicked.' The wicked say, 'I would have been a good person—but I became wicked through the fault of others.' People say, 'Why was five not seven?' Five says, 'I would have been seven—but seven is five plus two—if God, or people created by God, had given me another two, then I would have been seven.' So Hira was thinking.

Hira thought—'Now what will I do? If God had given me the chance, then everything would not be spoilt as it is, through His own fault.

Meanwhile, if I take Kunda back to the Datta house, then Kamala will give me her necklace, and the mistress will also give me something—and will I exempt the master himself? And if I give Kunda into Devendra's hands, then I will receive a lot of money. But I could not bear that. Well, then, does Kunda seem so beautiful to Devendra? We eat only by working hard; if we ate well, dressed well and lived in separate rooms like the ease-loving women in paintings, then we too could look like that. And could such a weak-hearted, whining, whimpering one understand Devendra Babu's heart? The lotus does not flower without mud; and if Kunda were not there, Devendra Babu would not be attracted to her! Why am I angry at what is somebody's fate? Why am I angry? Ha! Fate! What is the use any more of hiding my feelings from myself? I used to laugh at the talk of love. I used to say, "All that is only words, only people's set phrases." Now I no longer laugh. I used to think, "Let those who love, call it love, I will never love any one." God said, "Stay, I show you pleasure." In the end, I bathed in the water of the Ganga under duress. Catching another's thief, my own life has been stolen. What a face! What a figure! What a voice! Has anyone else such attributes? And the fellow says to me, "Bring Kunda and give her to me!" As if he doesn't have to say more! I will punch his nose. Aha, it would be a pleasure to punch his nose. Let it go, let all this go. On that path, too, are the thorns of religion. For a long time, I have attributed to God the happiness and suffering of this life. Because of that, I cannot give Kunda into Devendra's hands. The very thought of it sets my body aflame; rather, I will do whatever may prevent Kunda from falling into his hands. What will achieve that? If Kunda stayed where she was, she would be out of his hands. Let him dress as a Vaishnavi, let him dress up as Vasudeva himself, he could not seize her in his teeth in that house. So that means returning Kunda there. But Kunda will not go—she will not consider turning towards that house again. But if everyone together called her "dear child" and took her back, then she could go. And there's another idea in my mind; will God do it! Will Suryamukhi's pride be humbled? If God acts, even that may happen. Well, why am I so angry with Suryamukhi? She has never done me any harm; rather, she has favoured me and treated me well. So why am I angry? Does Hira not know that? Does Hira not know? Will I say why? Suryamukhi is happy and I am miserable; this is why I am angry. She is important; I am insignificant. She is the employer, I am the servant. Therefore, I am very angry with her. If you say, God made her important, what fault is it of hers? Why do I harm her?—To that I say, God has harmed me, for what fault of mine? Even so, I do not actually want to harm her; yet if I harm her I shall profit, so why not? Who does not seek their own good? So, let me work it out; how can it be done? Now, I need some money, and I can't be a servant anymore. Where will the money come from? Apart from the Datta household, where is there money? So here is a way of taking money from the Dattas—everyone knows that Nagendra's eye has fallen on Kunda—the Babu worships Kunda now. He is an important man, he can do whatever he wants. It is only because of Suryamukhi that he cannot. If there were to be a quarrel between the two of them, then he would no longer take much notice of Suryamukhi. Now I must do something which will result in their quarrelling.

'If that happens, the Babu will literally worship Kunda. Now, Kunda is a silly woman; I am a clever one; I shall soon be able to manage Kunda. A lot of preparation has been made already. If I put my mind to it, I shall be able to make her do whatever I want. And if the Babu starts to worship Kunda, then he will become obedient to her. I will make Kunda obedient to me. So I, too, shall get the fruits of worship. If I am no longer a servant, and this is what happens, then I shall be all right. Let us see what Goddess Durga has in mind. I will give Kundanandini to Nagendra. But not straightaway. I will hide her for a few days first, and see. Love ripens through estrangement. Through estrangement the Babu's love will ripen. Then I will bring Kunda out and present her. If Suryamukhi's luck does not break then, she has very strong luck! During that time, I will sit and practise making Kunda "Sit" and "Get up". Before that I will send my grandmother to Kamarghat; otherwise I shall not be able to keep Kunda hidden.'

Sinful Hira put into practice what she had planned. She sent her grandmother to kinsfolk in Kamarghat village, on a pretext; and kept Kunda well-hidden in her own house. Kunda, seeing her care and friendliness, began to think, 'There is no one like Hira. Even Kamala does not love me so much.'

21
Hira's Quarrel—the Poison Tree Buds

SO IT HAPPENED. KUNDA WAS BROUGHT UNDER HIRA'S THUMB. BUT UNLESS Suryamukhi became as poison in Nagendra's eyes, nothing would come of that. That was the basic work. Hira was now engaged in an attempt to separate their two hearts.

One day, after dawn, sinful Hira went to her employer's house and started her housework. Another maidservant by the name of Kaushalya worked at the Datta household, and envied Hira because of her position, and the favour and rewards that she received from the master and mistress. Hira said to her, 'Kushi, sister! I am not very well today, you do my work—' Kaushalya was afraid of Hira and, unable to object, said, 'Of course I will. Everyone's health has its ups and downs—we are servants of the same master—of course I will do it.' Hira's intention was that, no matter what answer Kaushalya gave, she would use it as the pretext for a quarrel. Hence, she leaned over her and said, scoldingly, 'What's this, Kushi—what's this impudence I hear? You insult me!' Kaushalya, astonished, said, 'Oh help! When did I insult you?'

Hira said, 'Oh pest! Do you ask, when did you insult me? Why did you speak of bad health? Am I at death's door? I suppose you think that when I am dying people will say that's a blessing! May *your* health fail.'

Kaushalya retorted, 'Well, let it. Why should that make you angry? We have to die one day—Death won't forget either you or me.'

Hira said, 'Let him never forget you in the day's first words! You'll die of envying me! Die quickly, die, die, and go to destruction! May you see nothing!'

Kaushalya could bear no more. She too raised her voice, 'May you see nothing! You die! Let Death not forget you! Unfortunate one! Ill-fated one! A hundred times miserable!' Kaushalya was more skilful in quarrelling than Hira. So Hira received these brickbats.

Then Hira went to the mistress to make a complaint. If anyone had observed Hira as she went, they would have seen that she showed no sign of anger; rather, there was a little smile at the corners of her lips. When she reached Suryamukhi, she showed many signs of anger—and let fly, first, woman's God-given weapon; that is, she wept floods of tears.

Suryamukhi responded to her request to hear her complaint, and made a proper judgement. She perceived that the fault was Hira's. Yet, at Hira's request, she allotted a little blame to Kaushalya. Hira, not satisfied with this, said, 'Dismiss that woman, otherwise I will not stay.'

Then Suryamukhi became angry with Hira. She said, 'Hira, you have been shown great favour! You started the abuse—the fault is all yours—shall I dismiss her because you say so? I cannot perpetrate such injustice—if you want to go, go; I will not tell you to stay.'

This was what Hira wanted. She said, 'All right, I will go,' and with tears pouring down her face she went to the Babu, to the reception hall—he now lived there, alone. Seeing Hira weeping, Nagendra said, 'Hira, why are you weeping?'

Hira sobbed, 'Tell them to calculate what I am owed for the month.'

Nagendra, astonished, said, 'What is this? What has happened?'

Hira said, 'I have been dismissed. The mistress dismissed me.'

Nagendra asked, 'What did you do?'

Hira replied, 'Kushi insulted me—I made a complaint. The mistress believed her, and dismissed me.'

Nagendra laughed, and shook his head, and said, 'That's not what it's about, Hira; tell me what the real issue is.'

Then Hira said, candidly, 'The real issue is that I will not stay here.'

Nagendra asked, 'Why?'

Hira said, 'The mistress has become unreliable in what she says—what she says to people is sometimes not right.'

Nagendra frowned, and said, sharply, 'What is this?'

Now Hira said what she had come to say: 'The way she spoke to mistress Kunda that day. It was after that that mistress Kunda left the place. We are afraid that some day she will speak like that to us—we could not bear that. So I am going first.'

Nagendra asked, 'What did she say?'

Hira said, 'I am ashamed to say it to your face.'

Hearing this, Nagendra's brow darkened. He said to Hira, 'Go home now. I will send for you tomorrow.'

Hira's desire was accomplished. It was for this that she had engineered the quarrel with Kaushalya.

Nagendra got up and went to Suryamukhi. Hira tiptoed behind him.

Having taken Suryamukhi somewhere secluded, Nagendra asked her, 'Did you dismiss Hira?' Suryamukhi said, 'I did.' Then she gave a detailed account of Hira's and Kaushalya's stories. Nagendra said, 'Plague take it! What did you say to Kundanandini?'

Nagendra saw that Suryamukhi's face paled! In a stifled voice, Suryamukhi said, 'What did I say?'

Nagendra demanded, 'What evil words?'

Suryamukhi was silent for a while. Then she said what was right; she said, 'You are my everything. You are my life now, and my life hereafter. Why should I hide anything from you? I have never hidden anything from you; why should I now hide something about someone else from you? I spoke harshly to Kunda. Lest you should be angry with me, I did not confide in you. Forgive my fault. I will tell you everything.'

Suryamukhi frankly narrated everything, from the discovery of Haridasi Vaishnavi to the rebuking of Kundanandini. At the end, she said, 'By driving Kundanandini away I have wounded you to the heart. I have sent people in search of her from province to province. If I find her, I will bring her back. Do not hold my fault against me.'

Then Nagendra said, 'There is no particular fault in you; which gentlewoman, hearing the kind of scandal against Kunda that you did, would have said nothing to her, or allowed her a place in the house? But it would have been better if you had asked yourself whether it was true or not.'

Suryamukhi said, 'I did not think of that at the time. I do now.'

Nagendra asked, 'Why did you not think of it?'

Suryamukhi said, 'I was under an illusion.'

As she spoke, Suryamukhi—devoted to her husband—a faithful wife—fell to the ground at Nagendra's feet, and holding his feet in her hands moistened them with her tears. Then, lifting her head, she said, 'You are dearer to me than life. I will not hide anything in this sinful mind from you. Will you still not hold my fault against me?'

Nagendra said, 'You need not say it. I know that you have suspected that I am attracted to Kundanandini.'

Suryamukhi hid her face against Nagendra's feet and wept. Then she raised her sorrow-stricken face, like a lotus wet with dew, and, gazing at her all-sorrow-relieving husband's face, she said, 'What can I say to you? Can I tell you the sorrow I have felt? The only reason I have not died is that it might increase your pain. Otherwise, when I learned that another shared your heart—I wanted to die. Not just in words—not as everyone says they want to die; I really, in my heart, sincerely wanted to die. Do not hold my fault against me.'

For a long while Nagendra remained still; finally, he let out a deep sigh and said, 'Suryamukhi! The fault is all mine. You have no fault at all. I am in truth a traitor to you. In truth, I forgot you, and in Kundanandini—what shall I say? The pain I have suffered, the pain I am suffering—how can I tell you? You thought that I made no effort to control my mind; do not think that. You can never reproach me as much as I have reproached myself. I am a sinful soul—I could not control my mind.'

Suryamukhi could bear no more; joining her hands together, she said in a pained voice, 'Let what is in your mind stay there—do not tell me any more. Every word you say pierces my breast—whatever happened has happened—I do not want to hear any more. I should not hear all this.'

'No. That is not so, Suryamukhi! You must hear more. If I can find the words, let me speak my mind—for I have been trying for a long time. I am going to leave this life. Not die—but I will go to another province. There is no longer any happiness for me here, at home. There is no longer any happiness for me in you. I am not a worthy husband for you. If I stay, I shall only give you more pain. I will go from province to province in search of Kundanandini. You remain here, as mistress of this house. Think of yourself as a widow—is not she whose husband is so vile as good as a widow? But whether I am vile or whatever I am, I will not deceive you. My heart has become another's—I say this to you clearly, before I leave. If I can forget Kundanandini, I will come back! Otherwise I shall never see you again!'

What could Suryamukhi say to these piercing words? For some moments she stayed staring at the ground like a stone image. Then she fell face down on the ground. Hiding her face in the earth—did she weep? Like the killer tiger watching the pain of the dying animal, Nagendra, standing motionless, watched. He thought, 'She will die—what is there for her now? It is the will of God—what can I do? Can I think of any redress to offer her? I could die, but would that help her to live?'

No, Nagendra! Your death would not help Suryamukhi to live, yet it would be good for you to die.

After half an hour, Suryamukhi rose. Again touching her husband's feet, she said, 'One request.'

Nagendra said, 'What?'

Suryamukhi said, 'Stay here for just one month more. If by then Kundanandini is not found, then go. I will not forbid it.'

Nagendra silently went away. In his mind he consented to stay another month. Suryamukhi understood this. She gazed after Nagendra's departing figure. In her mind she was thinking, 'My whole wealth! I can give my life for removing the thorn from your foot. Will you leave home for the sake of sinful Suryamukhi? Which is the nobler act?'

22

Highway Robbery on Top of Theft

HIRA THE MAIDSERVANT HAD LOST HER JOB, BUT SHE HAD NOT LOST HER connection with the Datta household. Hira was continually eager for the household's news. She would get hold of people from the house, sit them down, and engage them in gossip. Through her trickery with words she came to know of Nagendra's attitude towards Suryamukhi. On days when she met no one, she would go to the house itself on some pretext. She would achieve her aim by listening to the varied talk in the servants' quarters, and go away again.

In this way, several days passed. But one day the possibility of a disturbance arose.

Since Hira's acquaintance with Devendra, Malati Goyalini had started coming somewhat more often to Hira's house. Malati saw that Hira was not very happy about this. She saw, moreover, that one of the rooms was nearly always shut. This room, due to Hira's sagacity, was always fastened from outside with chains, which were held by a padlock; but one day, Malati came and saw to her surprise that the padlock was open. At once Malati took off the chains and pushed at the door. She found that the door was locked from the inside. Then she knew that there was a person inside.

Malati said nothing to Hira, but she started to wonder—who was that person? At first she thought it must be a man. But who could it be: Malati knew everyone—she did not give that idea much room. Finally, a suspicion came into her mind—that it was Kunda who was there. Malati had heard all about Kunda's disappearance. Now, she quickly found a way to test her suspicion. Hira had brought a fawn from the Babu's house. Because it was very restless, it was kept tied up. One day, Malati was feeding it. While she was feeding it, she untied its tether, hiding this from Hira's sight. As soon as the fawn was free, it quickly ran away. Seeing this, Hira ran after it to catch it.

As soon as Hira ran off, Malati called in an eager voice, 'Hira! O Hira! O Ganga Water!' Once Hira had disappeared into the distance, Malati fell to the ground and wept, 'O Mother! Why has my Ganga Water gone like this?' Saying this and weeping, she beat on Kunda's door and said in a distressed voice, 'Mistress Kunda! Kunda! Come out quickly! Ganga Water is ill!' So Kunda opened the door. Malati looked at her and ran away giggling.

Kunda closed the door. She said nothing to Hira, lest Hira should reproach her.

Malati went to Devendra and told him of her discovery. Devendra decided to go to Hira's house himself to find out what was going on, for good or ill. But there was a 'party' that day—so he could not go just then. He would go the following day.

23
The Caged Bird

KUNDA WAS NOW A CAGED BIRD—'INCESSANTLY RESTLESS'. TWO OPPOSING currents, constantly checking each other, increase the force of their flow. It was so in Kunda's heart too. In one direction was great shame—disgrace—reproof—no way of showing her face—Suryamukhi had sent her away from the house. But against this current of shame rose a current of love. Beating against each other, it was the stream of love which became the greater. Small rivers are overwhelmed by great ones. The disgrace caused by Suryamukhi was gradually submerged. Suryamukhi no longer held a place in her mind—Nagendra was everywhere. Gradually, Kunda started to think, 'Why did I come away from that house? What harm could a few words do me? I used to see Nagendra. Now I do not see him even once. Will I go back to that house? If no one chases me away, then I will. But what if they do chase me away?' Kundanandini thought of this day and night. She no longer thought much about whether it was proper to return to the Datta household—she decided within a couple of days that it was—otherwise she would die. But whether, if she went back, Suryamukhi would send her away again; this had to be considered. Finally, Kunda reached such a miserable state that she decided she would go regardless of whether Suryamukhi sent her away, or of anything else.

But how could Kunda go and stand again in that courtyard? She was ashamed to go alone—she could go if she took Hira with her. But she was ashamed to speak to Hira about it. She could not speak of it.

And her heart could no longer bear not seeing him who was dearer than life. One day, about an hour before dawn, Kunda left her bed and got up. Silently, she opened the door and went out. The last sliver of the waning moon was floating at the edge of the sky like a beautiful young girl thrown into the ocean. Mounds of darkness hid within the shelter of the trees. The gentle breeze did not stir into waves the lotus-leaf and algae-covered water of the lake beside the path. The deep, blue sky was beautiful above the dimly visible treetops. Dogs were asleep beside the path. The earth was beautiful in its cool solemnity. With doubtful, slow steps, feeling her way, Kunda went towards the Datta house. She no longer had any other purpose in going—if only by some chance she could once see Nagendra. It was not possible to return to the Datta house—when it became possible, it would happen—in the meantime, where was the harm in coming for once and hiding and watching? But where would she see him? How? After some thought, Kunda decided that she would go all around the Dattas' house while it was still night—by some chance she would see Nagendra, at a window or in the building, or in the courtyard, or on a path. Nagendra used to get up at dawn; Kunda should be able to see him. As soon as she had seen him she would go back.

Thinking these thoughts, Kunda went towards Nagendra's house, at the end of the night. Nearing the buildings, she saw that dawn was a little way off. Kunda looked along the path and saw that Nagendra was not there—she looked towards the rooftop—Nagendra was not there either—nor was he at the window. Kunda thought, 'He has probably not yet got up—it is not yet time to get up. I will sit under the tamarisk trees until dawn.' Kunda sat down under the tamarisk trees. Under the tamarisk trees it was very dark. Several tamarisk flowers and leaves fell gently into the water. The birds in the trees overhead shuffled their wings. Occasionally, the sounds of the gatekeepers of the house unlocking and banging the gates could be heard. The cool wind presaging the arrival of dawn blew.

Then the hawk-cuckoo called, setting the sky ringing overhead. A little after, the kokil in the tamarisk tree called. Finally, all the birds joined together in a tumult. Then Kunda's hope faded—she could no longer stay sitting under the tamarisk trees; dawn had come—someone would see her. Kunda got up to go back. One hope grew strong in her mind. Sometimes Nagendra would get up at dawn and go to take the air in the flower-garden adjoining the inner buildings. Perhaps Nagendra had all this time been walking there. Kunda could not go back without once looking there. But that garden was enclosed with a wall. Unless the garden gate was open, there was no way of entering it. Nor was it possible to see it from outside. Kunda went to see whether the gate was open or closed.

She saw that the gate was open. Drawing forth courage, Kunda went in. And slowly coming to the end of the garden, she stood in the shelter of a bakul tree.

The garden was thickly surrounded with many trees, creepers and shrubs. Amongst the rows of trees were beautifully made paths; in different places, trees and other plants were embellished with many flowers—white, red, blue, yellow—and on these, groups of bees, enticed by the dawn nectar, were circling, settling, rising and humming. And, in imitation of human nature, they were descending in flocks on certain flowers particularly rich in nectar. Tiny coloured birds riding like fruit on clusters of fully-opened flowers were drinking their nectar; from the throats of some issued mingled notes of the musical scale. Slender branches weighed down with blossoms, swayed in the gentle current of the dawn wind—the flowerless branches did not sway, for they did not bend. Master Kokil, hiding his black complexion in the bakul tree, enchanted everyone with the music from his throat.

In the middle of the garden was a marble pavilion for creepers to climb on. On its support, many kinds of creepers held up their flowers, and beside it, in borders of earth, were planted rows of flowering shrubs.

Standing in the shelter of the bakul tree, Kundanandini looked about at the garden but could not see the tall, god-like figure of Nagendra. Casting a glance within the pavilion, she saw that someone was lying on its cool stone; Kundanandini supposed it to be Nagendra. In order to see better, she went forward slowly from the shelter of one tree to another. Unfortunately, at that moment, the person within the pavilion got up and came out. Unlucky Kunda saw that it was not Nagendra but Suryamukhi.

Kunda, terrified, stood in the shelter of a flowering kamini tree. In her fear, she could not move forward—nor could she retreat. She saw that Suryamukhi was moving around the garden picking flowers. Suryamukhi was gradually approaching the place where Kunda was hidden. Kunda realized that she would be discovered. At last Suryamukhi saw Kunda. From a distance she did not recognize her, and asked, 'Who is that?'

Kunda remained silent in fear—and did not move a step. Then Suryamukhi came near—saw—recognized Kunda. In amazement she said, 'Why, is this not Kunda?'

Still Kunda could not answer. Suryamukhi took Kunda's hand. She said, 'Kunda! Come—come, sister. And I will not reproach you.'

With these words, Suryamukhi led Kunda into the inner building.

24
Descent

THAT EVENING, DEVENDRA DATTA, IN DISGUISE, HIS EYES REDDENED FROM drinking, appeared at Hira's house in search of Kundanandini. Looking into this room and that, he saw that Kunda was not there. Hira covered her mouth and laughed. Devendra, enraged, asked, 'Why do you laugh?'

Hira said, 'Seeing your sorrow. The caged bird has escaped—even a police search of my house would not produce her.'

Then, at Devendra's questions, Hira related what she knew, from beginning to end. Finally she said, 'At dawn, when I saw she was not here, I looked everywhere, and, searching, I saw her at the Babu's house—this time she was warmly welcomed.'

Devendra was turning away, crestfallen, but his suspicions were not dispelled. He wanted to stay a little longer and learn more. There was a gathering of clouds in the sky; seeing this, he said, 'There seems to be rain coming.' He stammered a little. Hira wanted Devendra to stay for a while—but she was a woman—she was there alone—it was night—she could not ask him to stay. If she did, she would be taking another step downwards; that, too, was in her destiny. Devendra said, 'Is there an umbrella in your house?'

There was no umbrella in Hira's house. Devendra said, 'Will anyone think anything of it if I sit here for a while with you because of the rain?'

Hira said, 'Why would they not? But the offence of your coming to my house at night has already been committed.'

Devendra said, 'Then I can sit down.'

Hira did not answer. Devendra sat down.

Then Hira made up a very neat bed on a plain cot, for Devendra to sit on. And she took from a chest a small silver-bound hookah. With her own hands, she filled it with cold water, prepared tobacco for it, fixed on the lid and the pipe, and gave it to him.

Devendra took from his pocket a flask of brandy, drank from it, and, kindled by it, saw that Hira's eyes were very beautiful. Indeed, her eyes were beautiful. Her eyes were wide, deep black, shining, and quick-moving.

Devendra said to Hira, 'You have the eyes of a goddess!' Hira laughed softly. Devendra noticed that a damaged violin was lying in a corner. Devendra, humming a song, took up the violin and set the bow to it. The violin was out of tune. Devendra asked, 'Where did you get this violin?'

Hira said, 'I bought it from a beggar.' Devendra took the violin, tuned it so that it was roughly tolerable, and, mingling his voice with it, sang sweet songs of sweet sentiments. Hira's eyes grew even brighter. For a few moments Hira completely forgot herself. She forgot that she was Hira, that he was Devendra. She thought, 'He is my husband—I am his wife.' It seemed to her that God had created them for each other, that they had been joined long since, that they had been happy for ages in each other's love. Overwhelmed by this illusion, Hira spoke aloud the words in her mind. Devendra heard in Hira's half-articulate speech that in her mind Hira was offering herself to him.

After she had spoken, Hira came to herself, her head spinning. Then, like a madwoman, in distress, she said to Devendra, 'Go away from my house at once!'

Devendra, astonished, said, 'What is this, Hira?'

Hira said, 'Go away at once—or I will go.'

Devendra said, 'What is this, why are you driving me away?'

Hira repeated, 'Go away—or I will call someone—why did you come here to ruin me?'

Hira was out of control, like a woman gone mad.

Devendra said, 'This is woman's nature!'

Hira was enraged—she said, 'Woman's nature? Woman's nature is not bad. It is the nature of men like you that is so evil. You have no knowledge of virtue—you do not care about the good or ill of others—you seek only your own pleasure—you only go about trying to find out how to ruin some woman. Otherwise, why did you sit down in my house? Did you not intend to ruin me? You considered me a prostitute, otherwise how would you dare to sit here? But I am not a prostitute. We miserable people, we earn our food by physical labour—we do not have the leisure to become prostitutes—whether we would if we were the wives of important men I cannot say.' Devendra frowned. Hira was glad to see it. Then, raising her face towards Devendra and looking at him unwaveringly, she said, 'Lord, I became maddened by the sight of your beauty. But do not judge me to be a prostitute. I am happy only to look at you. It was for this that I could not forbid you when you asked to sit down in my house—but women are weak—was it proper for you to sit down just because I could not forbid you? You are a great sinner; you tried to ruin me by entering my house by means of this strategem. Now go away at once!'

Devendra drank another mouthful of brandy, and said, 'Very good, very good. Hira, you have made a good speech. Will you give a speech one day at our Brahmo Samaj?'

Hira was mortified at this taunt, and said in a voice distressed by anger, 'I do not deserve your taunts—if even a very lowly person loves you, it is not good to make a joke of their love. I am not religious, I do not understand religion—I do not think about religion. But I am proud that I am not a prostitute, because I have promised myself that I will not court disgrace in the desire for your love. If you had loved me even a little, I would not have made that promise—I count shame as a straw in comparison to your love. But you do not love me—for what happiness, then, would I court disgrace? For what gain would I discard my pride? You never reject a young woman who is available, so you would accept me too, but tomorrow you would forget me, or, if you did remember me, you would joke about me to your friends—so why should I become your slave-girl? But if you ever come to love me, on that day I will become your servant and worship at your feet.'

Devendra listened to these words of Hira's. He understood her state of mind. He thought to himself, 'I know you; I can make you dance to my tune. When I choose to, I will finish my work with you.' With these thoughts, he went away.

Devendra had not fully come to know Hira.

25
Good News

IT WAS THE SECOND PRAHAR. SHRISH BABU WAS AWAY AT HIS OFFICE. EVERYONE in the house was sleeping after the meal. The reception room was closed.

A cross-bred kind of terrier was sleeping outside the reception room, on the doormat, with her head between her paws. Seizing the opportunity, a lovesick maidservant, sitting beside a lively manservant, was smoking tobacco, and chattering away in a whisper. Kamalamani was sitting relaxed in the bedroom with needle in hand, embroidering a carpet—her hair was a little dishevelled—there was no one about, only Satish Babu sat there uttering various kinds of sounds and dribbling onto his chest. Satish Babu had at first approached his mother and tried to make off with the wool, but seeing that the guard was very strict, he had become engaged in licking the head of an earthenware tiger. At a distance, lying with paws spread out, a cat was observing them both. Her thoughts were very deep; on her face were the signs of great learning; and her thoughts were as unperturbed as a yogin's. Probably the cat was thinking, 'The state of mankind is really terrible; their minds are always engaged in such trivial pursuits as embroidering carpets and playing with dolls; they have no propensity for good deeds; their minds are not on the business of procuring food for cats; so what will become of them in the afterlife?'

Elsewhere, a lizard was hanging on the wall, gazing at an insect in front of it. No doubt, it too was thinking to itself how bad the character of insects was. A butterfly was flying about; the place where Satish Babu had sat eating a sandesh was seething with insects—ants, as well, had started to form a queue.

After a while, the lizard, unable to seize the insect, moved away in another direction. The cat, too, seeing no signs of human character changing for the present, yawned and went away slowly. The butterfly flew outside. Kamalamani, dissatisfied, put the carpet aside and started a conversation with Satish Babu.

Kamalamani said, 'O Satu Babu, can you tell me why people go to the office?'

Satu Babu said, 'Illy-ly-ly.'

Kamalamani said, 'Satu Babu, don't ever go to office.'

Satu said, 'Kiss!'

Kamalamani said, 'What's this idea of yours of kissing? You won't have to go to the office to kiss. Don't go to office—if you do, your wife will sit down at noon and weep.'

Satu Babu understood the word 'wife', for Kamalamani used to frighten him by saying that when his wife came, she would beat him. Satu Babu now answered, 'Wife—beat.'

Kamala said, 'Remember that. If you go to office, your wife will beat you.'

For how long the conversation might have gone on in this way, it is impossible to say, for at this point a maidservant, rubbing the sleep from her eyes, came and handed a letter to Kamala. Kamala saw that the letter was from Suryamukhi. She opened it. She read it, and read it again. Having read it again, she sat sorrowfully silent. The letter went thus:

> Dearest! Since you returned to Kolkata you have forgotten us—otherwise why have you written only one letter? Don't you know that I am always eager for your news?
>
> You asked about Kundanandini. She has been found—you will be happy to hear this—give thanks to the goddess Sashthi. Apart from that, there is another piece of good news—my husband is going to marry Kunda. I am arranging this marriage myself. Widow remarriage is in the shastras—so what fault is there in this? The wedding will be in a couple of days. You will not be able to come to it—otherwise I would have invited you. If you can, then come for the flower-bed ceremony. For I have a great desire to see you.

Kamalamani could make nothing of this letter. Thinking it over, she asked Satish Babu for advice. Satish had been chewing the corner of a Bengali book in front of her; Kamalamani read the letter out to him—she asked, 'What is the meaning of this, tell me, Satu Babu?' Satu Babu understood banter; he stood up, with the support of his mother's hand, and started to eat Kamalamani's nose. So Kamalamani forgot Suryamukhi. Once Satu Babu had finished his nose-eating, Kamalamani read Suryamukhi's letter again. She said to herself, 'This is not a matter for Satu

Babu, this needs that counsellor of mine. Haven't the counsellor's office hours finished? Come now, Satu Babu, let us be angry.'

In due course, Counsellor Shrishchandra returned from the office and took off his office clothes. Kamalamani gave him some water, and finally, taking Satish, she angrily went and lay down on a cot. Shrishchandra, seeing her anger, laughed, took a hookah, and went to sit on a couch at a distance. Addressing the hookah as a witness, he said, 'O hookah! You hold Ganga water in your body and fire in your head! Witness this: those who are angry with me shall speak to me—shall speak, shall speak! Or else I will put fire on your head and sit here and smoke ten pipe-bowls full of tobacco!'

Hearing this, Kamalamani sat up, and, turning her eyes in mock anger, said, 'And ten bowls of tobacco will not obey you! I do not get to speak a word through the flames of one bowlful—am I then to be even more overwhelmed by ten bowlfuls!' With these words she got up from the bed, took the hookah-bowl and sacrificed it in the sacred fire to the Tobacco God.

Once Kamalamani's great pique had been thus assuaged, she made known the cause of it by offering him Suryamukhi's letter to read, and said, 'Interpret this, otherwise I will cancel your monthly counsellor's salary.'

Shrish said, 'Rather, give me an advance. I will make sense of it.'

Kamalamani brought her face close to Shrishchandra's, and Shrishchandra collected his salary. Then he read the letter and said, 'This is a joke.'

Kamala said, 'What is the joke? Your words, or the letter?'

Shrish said, 'The letter.'

Kamala said, 'I will now dismiss my counsellor. Haven't you any sense? Could a woman utter that kind of a joke?'

Shrish said, 'Then can what is not a joke be really true?'

Kamala said, 'In life's troubles, it can. I believe it is true.'

Shrish exclaimed, 'What! True?'

Kamala said, 'If not, I'll eat my head.'

Shrishchandra pinched Kamala's cheek. Kamala said, 'All right, if not, I'll eat my co-wife's head.'

Shrish said, 'Then you'll just have to starve.'

Kamala said, 'All right, I've eaten no one's head—now it seems God is eating Suryamukhi's head. Do you think my brother is being forced to marry?'

Shrishchandra became preoccupied. He said, 'I cannot understand it at all. Shall I write to Nagendra? What do you say?'

Kamalamani agreed to this. Shrishchandra wrote a joking letter. What Nagendra wrote in reply was this:

> Brother! Do not despise me—but what is the use of begging this? You will certainly despise the despicable. I am going through with this marriage. If everyone in the world casts me off, I will still make it happen. Otherwise I should go mad—that is all.
>
> Having said this, there is probably no need to say anything further. You, too, probably will, after this, say nothing, and cut me off completely. If you do speak, then I, too, am ready to debate.
>
> If anyone says that widow remarriage is contrary to the Hindu religion, I offer him Vidyasagar's essay to read. When such a great scholar, learned in the shastras, says that widow remarriage is in accordance with the shastras, then who can say that it is un-shastric? And if you say, even if it is in accordance with the shastras, it is not in accordance with society, that I shall, if I make this marriage, be dismissed from society, the answer to that is, who in this village of Govindapur is capable of dismissing me from society: where it is I who am society, what dismissal from society is possible? Yet in order to comply with your wishes I will marry privately—for the present, no one knows of it.
>
> You will not make all these objections. You will say that to marry twice is contrary to justice. Brother, how do you know that this is contrary to justice? You have learned this from the English; this is not an Indian idea. But are the English infallible? The English have this notion because it is a Jewish law—but you and I do not accept Jewish law as the word of God. Then why should I say for this reason that for a man to marry twice is against justice?

You will say that if a man may have two wives, then should not a woman have two husbands? The answer is, that if a woman had two husbands there would be the likelihood of much harm occurring; there is not that likelihood in the case of a man marrying twice. If a woman had two husbands, then it would not be certain who the father of her child was—it is the father who is the child's supporter—from that uncertainty, social anarchy might arise. But in the case of a man with two wives, there is no uncertainty about who is the mother. As well as this, many more things could be said.

It is that which is harmful to the majority of the people which is contrary to justice. If you consider that a man's marriage is contrary to justice, then you must demonstrate that it is harmful to the majority of the people.

You will give me the argument of disputes in the home. I will put forward one argument. I am childless. If I were to die, the name of my father's line would be lost. If I make this marriage, there is the possibility of a child—is this not an argument?

A final objection—Suryamukhi. Why do I give a loving wife the thorn of a co-wife? The answer is that Suryamukhi is not saddened by this marriage. It is she who has proposed the marriage—she who has induced me to make it—she who is arranging it. Then who else has any objection?

Then for what reason is this marriage of mine censurable?

26
Who Has Any Objection?

KAMALAMANI READ THE LETTER AND SAID, 'FOR WHAT REASON CENSURABLE? God knows. But what a mistake! It seems men understand nothing.

However that may be, let my counsellor dress himself. We must go to Govindapur.'

Shrish said, 'Will you be able to prevent the marriage?'

Kamala said, 'If I can't, I'll die in front of my brother.'

Shrish laughed, 'You can't do that. But we shall be able to cut off your brother's new wife's nose. Come, let's go with that purpose.'

Then they both prepared to set out for Govindapur. The next day, in the morning, they boarded a boat. In due course, they arrived in Govindapur.

Even before they entered the house, they met maidservants and village womenfolk; many of them, indeed, came to fetch Kamalamani from the boat. Both she and her husband were extremely anxious to know whether the marriage had taken place or not, but neither of the two asked anyone this—how could they open their mouths to ask other people such a shameful thing?

Extremely anxious, Kamalamani entered the inner building; she forgot that now Satish was left behind. Having entered the house, she asked the maidservants, in a clear voice, bereft of courage, 'Where is Suryamukhi?' She was afraid lest someone should say that the marriage had taken place—lest someone should say that Suryamukhi was dead.

The maidservants told her that Suryamukhi was in her bedroom. Kamalamani ran to the bedroom.

She went in, and at first could see no one. For a moment she looked from one side to the other. Finally, she saw that in a corner of the room near a window, a woman was sitting with her head down. Kamalamani could not see her face; but she knew that it was Suryamukhi. Then Suryamukhi, hearing her step, got up and came over to her. Seeing Suryamukhi, Kamalamani could not ask whether the marriage had taken place or not—Suryamukhi's shoulder-blades stood out—Suryamukhi's young-deodar-like body was like a broken bow; Suryamukhi's shining, lotus-petal eyes were sunken—Suryamukhi's lotus-face had lengthened. Kamalamani understood that the marriage had taken place. She asked, 'When did it happen?' Suryamukhi said in the same gentle voice, 'Yesterday.'

Then the two women sat there silently and wept—neither saying anything. Suryamukhi hid her face in Kamala's lap and wept—Kamalamani's tears fell on her breast and on her hair.

Meanwhile, Nagendra was sitting in his reception hall thinking, 'Kundanandini! Kunda is mine! Kunda is my wife! Kunda! Kunda! Kunda! She is mine!' Shrishchandra was sitting nearby—Nagendra could not speak to him properly. From time to time, he thought, 'Suryamukhi has arranged the marriage—so who else has any objection to this happiness of mine!'

27
Suryamukhi and Kamalamani

WHEN, IN THE TWILIGHT, BOTH CALMED DOWN AND WERE ABLE TO SPEAK clearly to each other, Suryamukhi told Kamalamani the whole story of Nagendra's marriage. Kamalamani was astonished at it and said, 'It was by your efforts that this marriage took place—why did you yourself make arrangements for your own death?'

Suryamukhi smiled and said, 'Who am I?'—she gave this answer with a soft, thin smile—as lightning shows through torn clouds at the edge of the sky after rain, smiling a smile like that—she answered, 'Who am I? Come and look at your brother just once—come and see the joy which fills his face—then you will know how happy he is. If I see him so happy, is not my life successful? In the hope of what happiness could I keep happiness away from him? I saw day and night the unhappiness in him, the sight of whose unhappiness for an hour makes me want to die—he was preparing to leave home, renouncing all happiness—but would any happiness for me have remained? I said, "Lord! It is your happiness which is my happiness—marry Kunda—I shall be happy"—so he married her.'

Kamala said, 'And are you happy?'

Suryamukhi said, 'Why do you question my words again; who am I? If

I ever saw a pebble under my husband's foot, I would think, "Why didn't I lay my breast there, so that my husband could rest his foot on my breast."'

Saying this, Suryamukhi remained silent for a while—her clothes were soaked with her tears—then suddenly she lifted her head and asked, 'Kamala, in which country do they kill girls?'

Kamala understood what was on her mind and said, 'What if we are girls—that which is in our destiny will happen!'

Suryamukhi said, 'Whose destiny is better than mine? Who is so fortunate? Who has such a husband? Beauty, wealth, property—and all those are trifles—whose husband has such qualities? My destiny is a fortunate one—yet why has it turned out like this?'

Kamala replied, 'This, too, is destiny.'

Suryamukhi said, 'Yet why is my mind in this torment?'

Kamala said, 'You are happy to see your husband's now joy-filled face—yet you say, why is your mind in such torment? Are both things true?'

Suryamukhi answered, 'Both are true. I am happy in his happiness—but that he should kick me aside, that he should have such joy in kicking me aside!—'

Suryamukhi could say no more, her voice choked—her eyes overflowed; but Kamalamani understood her unfinished words. She said, 'Your heart's pain is because he has kicked you aside. So why do you say, "Who am I?" Your mind is still half-full of yourself; otherwise why, even after renouncing yourself, would you speak thus?'

Suryamukhi said, 'I do not repent. I have no doubt that I have done well. But it is still painful to die. Reckoning my death good, I have died by my own hand. But even so, shall I not weep at the time of my death?'

Suryamukhi wept. Kamala held her head to her own heart. Not everything was said in words—but heart spoke to heart. Heart to heart, Kamalamani understood how miserable Suryamukhi was. Heart to heart, Suryamukhi understood that Kamalamani understood her misery.

Both checked their weeping and wiped their eyes. Then Suryamukhi stopped speaking of herself and spoke of others. She had Satishchandra fetched, and cuddled him, and had a conversation with him. She spoke long with Kamala of Satish and Shrishchandra. There was much happy discussion of Satishchandra's education, marriage and so on. Thus they both talked until late into the night; then Suryamukhi warmly embraced Kamala, and took Satishchandra on her lap and kissed him. As she said goodnight to both of them, Suryamukhi's tears again became unrestrainable. Weeping, she blessed Satish, saying, 'Child! I wish for you the imperishable qualities of your uncle. I know no greater blessing.'

Suryamukhi spoke in her natural gentle voice, but Kamalamani was startled at her tone. She said, 'Sister! What is in your mind—what? Tell me?'

Suryamukhi said, 'Nothing.'

Kamalamani said, 'Do not hide from me.'

Suryamukhi answered, 'I have hidden nothing from you.'

Then Kamala went to her bed with an easy mind. But Suryamukhi had hidden one thing. Kamala found that out in the morning. In the morning, she went to Suryamukhi's bedroom in search of her, and saw that Suryamukhi was not there, but there was a letter on her unslept bed. When she saw the letter, Kamalamani's head spun—she did not need the letter—she understood without reading it. She understood that Suryamukhi had fled. She had no desire to open the letter and read it—she crushed it in her hand. Hitting her head with her hand, she sat down on the bed. She said, 'I am mad. Otherwise, why did I not understand yesterday when I was leaving her?' Satish was standing near her; seeing his mother strike her forehead and weep, he too began to wail.

28
Letter of Blessing

ONCE THE FIRST SPATE OF GRIEF HAD BEEN CHECKED, KAMALAMANI OPENED the letter and read it. It was addressed to her. The letter went thus:

On the very day that I heard from my husband's lips that he had no more pleasure in me, that he would go mad, or die, on account of Kundanandini, I resolved that if I ever found Kundanandini I would give her hand to my husband to make him happy. Having given my husband to Kundanandini, I would myself leave the house; for I should not be able to look at my husband who had become Kundanandini's. Now I have found Kundanandini and given her to my husband. And I have left the house.

I would have left the house the night before last, after the wedding. But I wanted to see with my own eyes the happiness of my husband, for which I have sacrificed my life. And I wanted to see you once more before I went. I wrote to you to come—I knew that you would be sure to come. Now these two desires have been fulfilled. I have seen that he who is dearer than life to me is happy. I have said farewell to you. Now I have gone.

By the time you read this letter I shall be far away. The reason I did not tell you that I was going was that if I had, you would not have let me go. Now I beg this of you all, that you do not search for me.

There is no hope that I shall ever see you again. I will not come back to this place while Kundanandini is alive—it is no use searching for me. I have now become a beggar on the roads—I shall wander from place to place in the guise of a beggar-woman—I shall live by begging—who will recognize me? I could have taken money with me, but I have not. I have gone away, giving up my husband—should I take gold and silver with me?

Do one thing for me. Convey to my husband my thousand, thousand obeisances at his feet. I tried many times to write to him of my going, but I could not. I could not see the letter for tears—the paper became soaked and spoilt. I tore up the paper and threw it away, and wrote again—again tore it up—and again—but the words to say what I had to say could not be written in any letter. Give him this news of me in whatever way seems best to you.

Explain to him that I have not gone away in anger at him. I am not angry at him, I never shall be. How can there be anger at him whom it is a joy to think of ? The unchanging devotion that I have towards him remains, and will remain for as long as this clay is not mingled with the earth. For I can never forget his thousand virtues. No one else has so many virtues. It is because no one else has such virtues that I am his servant. If I could forget his thousand virtues because of one fault I should not be worthy of being his servant. I have said farewell to him for the rest of this life. You will be able to understand with what sorrow I have left everything, having said farewell to my husband for the rest of this life.

I have said farewell to you for the rest of this life too; I pray that your husband and son will live long and that you will be always happy. And I pray that you will die before you lose your husband's love. No one prayed that prayer for me.

29
What Is the Poison Tree?

THE POISON TREE FROM THE SOWING OF WHOSE SEED TO THE BEARING OF whose fruit and its consumption I have been expounding, grows in everyone's courtyard. Its seed is the power of the six deadly vices. Circumstances ensure that it is scattered in every field. There is no person whose mind is untouched by passion, envy, lust, anger and the rest. Even wise people, according to circumstances, are troubled by all these vices. But the difference between one person and another is this, that some can control their inflamed faculties and keep steady: such an individual is a great soul; others do not control their own minds; it is for these that the seed of the poison tree is sown. Inability to control the mind is its shoot, and from that the poison tree grows. This tree is very strong; once it is nourished, it cannot be destroyed. And its beauty is greatly pleasing to the eye; from a distance its multicoloured leaves and opening buds are very pleasant to see. But its fruit is poisonous; those who eat it, die.

In different fields there are varied fruits on the poison tree. In different people they produce different effects—disease, grief, and so on. In the matter of controlling the mind, first the desire to control the mind, and second the power to control the mind is necessary. Of these, power is born of practice; and desire is born of education. Habit, too, depends on education. Consequently, it is education which is the foundation of controlling the mind. But I am not speaking only of education by the teachings of a guru; it is the heart's suffering which is the best education.

Nagendra had never had this education. God had put him on this earth in possession of all happiness. Graceful form; untold wealth; healthy body; wide-ranging intelligence; amiable character; faithful, affectionate wife: all these rarely fall to the lot of one person. They had fallen to Nagendra. Most importantly, Nagendra had always been happy in the virtues of his own character: he was truthful yet fair-spoken; philanthropic yet just; generous yet thrifty; affectionate yet resolute in doing his duty. While his father and mother were still alive he was extremely devoted and loving towards them; he was extremely devoted to his wife; he was a benefactor to his friends; compassionate towards his servants; a protector of those who served him, and free of enmity towards his enemies. He was wise in his advice; straightforward in his deeds; polite in conversation; eloquent in repartee. The reward of such a character is untroubled happiness—since his infancy this had been so for Nagendra. He had honour at home; fame abroad; obedient servants; devotion from his tenants; and from Suryamukhi unwavering, unstinted affection. If it had not been his fate to have been so happy, he would never have become so miserable.

If he had not become miserable, he would not have fallen into temptation. Temptation lies in that wherein there is a lack. Before looking at Kundanandini with covetous eyes, Nagendra had never fallen into temptation, for he had never known the lack of anything. Consequently, he had not had the mental practice or the education necessary for controlling temptation. Because of this, he was incapable of controlling his mind either. Untroubled happiness is the foundation of misery; without previous unhappiness, stable happiness does not develop.

I do not say that Nagendra was without fault. His fault was heavy; his also-heavy penance was beginning.

30
The Search

IT IS SUPERFLUOUS TO SAY THAT WHEN THE NEWS OF SURYAMUKHI'S FLIGHT spread through the house, people were speedily sent out to search for her. Nagendra sent people out in all directions, Shrishchandra sent people out, Kamalamani sent people out in all directions. The senior maidservants threw down their water-pitchers and ran; the Hindustani doorkeepers went with clubs in their hands, waistcoats of French chintz stuffed with cotton on their bodies, and their slippers making scuffling sounds—the table-servants, with napkins on their shoulders and ornamental girdles round their waists, went out to bring back the mistress. Many of her own people took carriages and went out on the main roads. The village people searched the fields and the landings; or formed committees under trees and smoked tobacco. The gentlefolk, too, sat in conference in such places as the festival place, the temple of Shiva's terrace, and the school of the logic-chopping Brahmins. The lower-class women turned the bathing ghat into a court of petty sessions. There was a solemn festival in the boys' building; many boys started to hope that there would be a vacation from school.

At first, Shrishchandra offered hope to Nagendra and Kamala, saying, 'She has never travelled on foot—how far could she go? She will be sitting down somewhere, having gone about a mile and a half; this present search will find her.' But when two or three hours had elapsed, and still there was no news of Suryamukhi, Nagendra himself went out in search of her. After searching for a while in the sun, he thought, 'I am out here searching, but perhaps all this time Suryamukhi has been brought home.' So he went back. Returning home, he saw that there was no news of Suryamukhi. He went out again. Again he returned. So the whole day passed.

In fact, what Shrishchandra had said was true. Suryamukhi had never gone outside the house on foot. How far could she go? She had lain down in a mango grove beside a pool a mile away from the house. A steward, who used to go to and from the inner buildings, came there during the search and saw her. He recognized her and said, 'Mistress, come!'

Suryamukhi gave no answer. He said again, 'Mistress, come! Everyone at the house is very anxious.' Then Suryamukhi said angrily, 'Who are you to make me go back?' The steward became nervous. Yet he stayed standing there. Suryamukhi said, 'If you keep standing there, I will drown myself in the pool.'

Unable to do anything, the steward went quickly and told Nagendra. Nagendra took a palanquin there. But by then Suryamukhi was no longer there. He searched nearby, but in vain.

Suryamukhi had got up and gone from there, and sat down in a forest. There she met an old woman. The old woman had come to collect wood—but because there might be a reward if she could find Suryamukhi, she too was searching. When she saw Suryamukhi, she said, 'Hello, aren't you our mistress?'

Suryamukhi said, 'No!'

The old woman said, 'Yes, you are our mistress.'

Suryamukhi said, 'Who is your mistress, then?'

The old woman said, 'The wife in the Babu's house.'

Suryamukhi said, 'Is there a golden necklace around my neck that I should be the wife in the Babu's house?'

The old woman thought, 'That's true, isn't it?'

She went off, to gather wood in another forest.

Thus the whole day passed fruitlessly. Neither did the night produce any result. Nothing was accomplished the next day, or the day after, either—yet there was no slackening in the search. Most of the people searching did not know Suryamukhi—they brought many beggars and poor people before Nagendra. Finally, it became dangerous for the daughters of the gentlefolk to go along the path to the landing, to bathe. Seeing them alone, Nagendra's faithful Hindustanis would chase them, calling, 'Mistress' and preventing them from bathing, would bundle them into a palanquin and take them to Nagendra. Many had never ridden in a palanquin, and took the opportunity of a free ride.

Shrishchandra could no longer stay. He returned to Kolkata and started a search from there. Kamalamani stayed back, searching in Govindapur.

31

All Happiness Has Bounds

THE HAPPINESS WHICH KUNDANANDINI HAD NEVER HOPED FOR HAD become hers. She had become Nagendra's wife. On the day of the marriage, Kundanandini thought, 'This happiness has no bounds, no measure.' After that, Suryamukhi left. Then she felt remorse—she thought, 'Suryamukhi looked after me in my hard times—if she had not, where would I have gone—but now she has left home on my account. It would have been better if I had died instead of becoming happy.' She saw that there are bounds to happiness.

In the evening, Nagendra came and lay down on the bed—Kundanandini sat at his head and fanned him. Both were silent; this was not a good sign; there was no one else there—yet the two of them were silent—if their happiness had been complete, this would not have been so.

But since Suryamukhi's flight, where was this complete happiness?

Kundanandini was ceaselessly thinking, 'How can things be made as they were again?' Now, today, Kundanandini asked this aloud, 'How can things be made to be as they were, once again?'

Nagendra said angrily, 'As they were? Do you regret that I married you?'

Kundanandini was hurt. She said, 'Did I ever hope for the happiness you gave me by marrying me? I am not saying that—I am saying, how can Suryamukhi be brought back?'

Nagendra said, 'Do not say that again. It torments me to hear Suryamukhi's name on your lips—it was because of you that Suryamukhi left me.'

Kundanandini had known this—but she was hurt by Nagendra's words. She thought, 'What is this rebuke? I have an evil fate—but I have done nothing wrong. It was Suryamukhi herself who arranged this marriage.' Kunda said nothing more, but went on fanning. Seeing Kundanandini silent for so long, Nagendra said, 'Why aren't you saying anything? Are you angry?' Kunda said, 'No.'

Nagendra persisted, 'You say only one little "No" and then you are silent again. Don't you love me anymore?'

Kunda said, 'I love you lots and lots.'

Nagendra mimicked, '"I love you lots and lots"! That's childish cajolery. Kunda, I believe you never did love me.'

Kunda said, 'I have loved you always.'

Nagendra did not understand that this was not Suryamukhi. It was not that Kundanandini did not love as Suryamukhi did—but Kunda did not know the words for it. She was a child, timid-natured; she did not know the words: what else should she say? But Nagendra did not understand this, and he said, 'Suryamukhi loved me always. Why put a pearl necklace round a monkey's neck?—An iron chain would be better.'

Now Kundanandini could not restrain her tears. Slowly she got up and went out. There was no one to weep with her. Since Kamalamani's arrival, Kunda had not gone near her. Thinking herself guilty of this marriage, Kundanandini had not been able, for shame, to show her face. But in her present pain she wished to talk to the compassionate, affectionate Kamalamani. On the day when she had despaired of love, Kamalamani had been sorrowful at her sorrow, had taken her on her lap and wiped away her tears—remembering that day, she went to weep with her. Kamalamani was displeased to see Kundanandini—seeing Kunda approach she was surprised and said nothing. Kunda sat down near her and started to weep. Kamalamani said nothing; nor did she ask what had happened. So Kundanandini herself was silent. Then Kamala said, 'I have work to do.' And she got up and went away.

Kundanandini saw that indeed all happiness has bounds.

32

The Fruit of the Poison Tree

(NAGENDRA DATTA'S LETTER TO HARADEV GHOSHAL)

> You wrote that of all the things I have done on this earth, marrying Kundanandini is the greatest mistake. I acknowledge this. By doing this, I lost Suryamukhi. To have Suryamukhi as a wife was the greatest good fortune. Everyone digs in the earth, but only one is fated to find the Kohinoor diamond. Suryamukhi is that Kohinoor. How could Kundanandini fill her place?
>
> Then why did I install Kundanandini in her place? Mistake, mistake! Now I am aware of it. Kumbhakarna woke up to die. I, too, have woken from this sleep of illusion to die. Where shall I ever find Suryamukhi?
>
> Why did I marry Kundanandini? Did I love her? I did love her, of course—I was going mad because of her—was losing my life. But I understand now that it was only a superficial love. Otherwise

why would I say, just fifteen days after marrying her, 'I did love her'? Why did I love her? I still love her—but where has Suryamukhi gone? I had intended to write to you on many things, but I cannot. I am in great distress.

Haradev Ghoshal's reply:

I understand your heart. It is not that you did not love Kundanandini—you still love her; but you said rightly that this was only a superficial love. Your deepest affection is towards Suryamukhi—it was overlaid only for two days by Kundanandini's shadow. Now, having lost Suryamukhi, you understand that. While the sun is uncovered, we are scorched by its rays, and welcome the clouds. But once the sun has set, we understand that it is the sun which is the eye of the world. Without the sun, the world is dark.

Not understanding your heart, you committed this big mistake—I will not reproach you any more for this—for the error you fell into is one which is very difficult to dispel. There are many sensations in the mind which people call love. But it is the state of mind in which we are ready of our own accord to sacrifice our own happiness for the happiness of another is correctly called love. 'Ready of our own accord', that is, not because of knowing our duty or in the desire for virtue. Consequently, the desire to enjoy the beauty of a beautiful woman is not love. As you cannot call the hunger of a hunger-stricken man for food, love, so you cannot call the mental agitation of a man stricken with lust for a beautiful woman, love. The great poets described this mental agony as being caused by the arrows of Madan. The propensity whose fancied incarnation is Madan, who broke the meditation of Shiva, by whose favour, in the poets' descriptions, the bucks rub their bodies on the does, and the male elephants break lotus stalks and give them to the she-elephants, that is this illusion born just of beauty. This propensity, too, is sent by God; it is by means of it, too, that the world's desires are realized, and it fascinates all creatures. Kalidasa, Byron, and Jayadeva are its poets; *Vidyasundara*[14] distorts it. But it is not love. Love is based on the faculties of the mind. When the qualities of one who is an object of love are apprehended by the faculties of the mind, and the heart, becoming enchanted by these qualities, is drawn towards that person and is moved, then the desire for union with the person who holds these qualities is born, and devotion towards that person grows. The result is sympathy, and in the end, self-forgetfulness, and self-renunciation. This is truly love. Shakespeare, Valmiki, and the author of the *Bhagavata Purana* are its poets. It is not born of beauty. First comes the apprehending of the qualities of the mind, and after that, the desire for union; once union is realized, there is companionship, and as a result of this, love, and from love, self-renunciation. It is this that I call love. At least, this is my judgement concerning the love of men and women. I believe that the root of other loves, too, is there. Yet, affection is not present as a cause. But all causes are in the faculties of the mind. At least, without the affection that arises from the faculties of the mind it will not be permanent. Fascination born of beauty is not so. The intensity of all the upheaval of the mind which arises from the sight of beauty becomes less with recurrence. That is, it is allayed by repetition. This is not so with what arises from qualities. For beauty is a single thing—every day, it is manifested in the same way; qualities manifest themselves newly day by day in new actions. Love arises both from beauty and qualities—for from both arises the desire for union. If both are united then love arises quickly; but once love and companionship are deep-rooted, it is the same whether beauty remains or not. Affections towards the beautiful and the ugly are constant sources of illustrations of this.

Love which arises from qualities is indeed everlasting—but it takes time to recognize qualities. For this reason, this love does not acquire strength all at once—it grows gradually. But the fascination born of beauty will achieve its full strength all at once. Its strength is such that it is difficult to subdue: all the other faculties are crushed by it. Is this fascination—is this lasting love, or not—the power of discerning this is lost. It is judged to be everlasting love. You judged it to be that—in the first strength of this fascination, your lasting love towards Suryamukhi became invisible to your eyes. This was your mistake. Human nature is very proficient at making this mistake. So I will not reproach you. Rather, I offer you advice: try to be happy in it.

You need not despair. Suryamukhi will certainly return—how long can she go without seeing you? While she does not return, be affectionate to Kundanandini. As far as I can understand from your letters, and so on, it seems that she, too, is not lacking in qualities. Never mind about the fascination arising from beauty; in time, lasting love will develop. That being so, you will be able to be happy with her, and if you never see your first wife again, then you will even be able to forget her. Moreover, your second wife loves you. Never neglect love, for mankind's only pure and imperishable happiness is in love. It is love which is the ultimate means of humanity's progress—if only people would love one another, there would be no more damage done by humanity on earth.

Nagendranath's rejoinder:

I have received your letter, and as to the cause of my mental suffering, I have nothing to add. I have understood all that you have written; and that your advice is true advice, that also I know. But I cannot remain mentally calm at home. A month ago my Suryamukhi left me and went away; I have resolved that I too, will take that path. I, too will leave home. I will wander from place to place in search of her. If I find her, I will bring her back; otherwise I will not return. I cannot stay at home with Kundanandini. She has become a torment to my eyes. It is not her fault—the fault is mine—but I can no longer bear to see her face. Before, I said nothing—now, I constantly reproach her—she weeps—what should I do? I have set out, and shall soon be with you. After seeing you, I will go elsewhere.

Nagendra did as he had written. Entrusting the management of his affairs to the steward, he left home and set out on his travels without delay. Kamalamani had already returned to Kolkata. So of all the characters described in this story, Kundanandini alone remained in the inner building of the Datta establishment, with Hira the maidservant to look after her.

That well-appointed building of the Dattas' became dark. As a theatre, bright with many lamps, filled with people, and pervaded with the sound of music, becomes empty and silent when the play is finished, so that great building, abandoned by Suryamukhi and Nagendra, became dark. As a child, playing one day with a painted doll, throws the doll away when it breaks, and the doll lies where it fell on the earth, and earth falls on it, and grass and plants grow over it, so Kundanandini, abandoned like a broken doll by Nagendra, remained alone and uncared for in that great building. As in a forest fire, a nest and its young being burnt, the mother bird, returning with food, sees that there is no tree left, no nest, no young; and then, uttering high calls of distress, flies circling over the burnt forest in search of her nest, so Nagendra went wandering from place to place in search of Suryamukhi. As a pearl once fallen into the depthless waters of the endless ocean is seen no more, so difficult to find had Suryamukhi become.

33
As a Sign of Love

LIKE A BURNING COAL IN COTTON CLOTH, DEVENDRA'S MATCHLESS FORM burnt through layer on layer in Hira's heart. Many times, Hira's fear of religion and public disgrace were on the point of floating away on the tide of love; but Devendra's affectionless and sensual character would come into her mind and check her. Hira was able to control her mind very well, and because of this she had easily been able to preserve her chastity, even though she was not particularly religious. By that power, knowing her strong attraction towards Devendra to be unworthy, she was easily able to keep it under control. Rather, Hira decided, as a means of controlling her mind, to resort to becoming a maidservant again. If she was engaged daily in the chores of someone else's house, then, preoccupied with other thoughts, she would be able to obliterate the pain, like a scorpion's sting, of this fruitless attraction. When Nagendra set out on his travels, Hira begged for a position, on the strength of her former allegiance. Knowing Kunda's preference, Nagendra appointed Hira to look after her.

There was another reason for Hira's acceptance of the position of maidservant again. Believing that Kunda had become Nagendra's best-beloved, Hira had previously, in her desire for wealth and so on, taken care to bring her under her own control. She thought that Nagendra's wealth would come into Kunda's hands, and that the wealth that came into Kunda's hands would become Hira's. Now Kunda had become the mistress of Nagendra's house. Kunda had not acquired any particular control of any wealth, but this fact did not now occupy a place in Hira's mind, either. Hira no longer thought of money, and if she had, she would have considered money obtained from Kunda as poison.

Hira could bear the pain of her own fruitless love, but she could not bear Devendra's desire for Kundanandini. When she heard that Nagendra was going to wander in other parts, and that Kundanandini would be the mistress of the house, she remembered Haridasi Vaishnavi and became pervaded with fear. Hira came to guard against Haridasi Vaishnavi's comings and goings, and to create obstacles in her path.

Hira was not motivated by a desire for Kundanandini's welfare. Overcome by envy, Hira was so enraged with Kunda that, far from being concerned with her welfare, she would have been delighted to witness her ruin. Hira guarded Nagendra's wife out of a fear born of envy lest there should be a meeting between Kunda and Devendra.

Hira became one more cause of Kunda's suffering. Kunda saw that Hira was not so caring, so affectionate or so fair-spoken. She saw that, having become her maidservant, Hira was always showing disrespect towards her, and reproving and insulting her. Kunda was very gentle-natured; even though she suffered much from Hira's rough behaviour, she did not ever say anything to her. Kunda's nature was peaceful, Hira's was violent. For this reason, even though Kunda was the master's wife, she was like a servant to her servant, and even though Hira was the maidservant, she became the master of the master's wife. Seeing Kunda's suffering, the other women in the house would sometimes reproach Hira, but no rhythm could establish itself against Hira's thunder. The steward, hearing all this, said to Hira, 'Take yourself off. I dismiss you.' At this, Hira, with rage-expanded eyes, said to the steward, 'Who are you to dismiss me? The master appointed me. I will not go unless the master tells me to. I have the same power to dismiss you as you have to dismiss me.' The steward did not speak again for fear of insults. Without Suryamukhi, no one could manage Hira.

One day, after Nagendra had left, Hira was lying alone in a pavilion of creepers in the flower-garden next to the inner buildings. Since Nagendra and Suryamukhi had left, all these pavilions of creepers had fallen into Hira's possession. Twilight had passed. A nearly-full moon shone in the sky. Its beams were reflected in the bright leaves of the garden's trees. The moon beams penetrated the gaps in the creepers' leaves and fell on the floor of the white marble building, and danced on the clear water of the nearby lake, whipped by the evening wind. The fragrance of the garden flowers intoxicated the sky. Suddenly Hira saw, among the creeper pavilions, the figure of a man. Gazing at it, she saw that it was Devendra. Today, Devendra was not in disguise; he had come in his own garb.

Hira, astonished, said, 'You are very daring. If anyone sees you, you will be beaten.'

Devendra said, 'What fear have I where Hira is?' Saying this, Devendra sat down beside Hira. Hira was pleased. After a while, she said, 'Why have you come here? You will not see the one you came hoping to see.'

'But I have. I came hoping to see you.'

Hira was not deceived by the hypocritical words of the greedy flatterer. She laughed and said, 'I did not know such pleasure was in my fate. However that may be, if my fortune has turned, let us go and sit somewhere safe where I can satisfy my mind by looking at you. There are many dangers here.'

Devendra said, 'Where shall we go?'

Hira said, 'Where there is nothing to fear. Let us go to that arbour of yours.'

Devendra said, 'You need not fear for me.'

Hira said, 'If I don't fear for you, I fear for myself. If someone sees me with you, what will my situation be?'

Devendra said diffidently, 'Then go. Is there a possibility of conversing once with your new mistress?'

In the dim light, Devendra did not see clearly the malicious glance which Hira cast at him when she heard this. Hira said, 'How can you meet her?'

Devendra said modestly, 'By your favour, all is possible.'

Hira said, 'Then wait here and be careful; I will go and call her.'

With those words, Hira went out of the pavilion. Having gone some distance, she sat down in beneath a tree, and her pent-up tears began to flow. Then she got up and went into the house, but she did not go to Kundanandini. She went out and said to the gatekeepers, 'Come quickly, there's a thief in the flower-garden.'

Then all the gatekeepers, with thick bamboo clubs in their hands, ran through the inner building towards the flower-garden. Devendra heard the sound of their shoes and slippers from a distance, and from a distance saw their great black beards; and leaping from the pavilion, he quickly fled. The tribe of gatekeepers followed a little behind. They did not quite catch Devendra. But Devendra did not get away without some reward. I cannot say for certain whether or not he received a taste of the bamboo clubs, but I have heard that he was referred to by the gatekeepers as 'Bastard', 'Bugger' and other such sweet terms of endearment. And one day, having drunk a ration of leftover brandy, his servant told his concubine that the following day 'while I was massaging the Babu, I saw that there was a bruise on his back'.

Having reached home, Devendra resolved two things. First, that he would not go to the Dattas' house while Hira remained there. Second, that he would be revenged on Hira. In the end, he did wreak great retribution on Hira. Hira's great sin was severely punished. Hira's punishment was so severe that, seeing it, finally, even Devendra's stony heart was pierced. This is not to be described in detail; I will briefly narrate those events later.

34

By the Roadside

IT WAS THE RAINY SEASON. THE WEATHER WAS FOUL. IT HAD BEEN RAINING all day. The sun had not come out even once. The sky was covered with clouds. The surface of lime on the main road to Kashi had become rather slippery. There was hardly anyone on the road—who travels when it is soaking wet? Only one traveller was moving along the road. The traveller's garb was that of a brahmachari. He wore ochre-coloured clothes—there was a rosary around his neck—a streak of sandal-paste on his brow—no great display of matted hair, only small, somewhat whitened locks of hair. In one hand he held a palm-leaf umbrella, and in the other, a metal vessel—rain-soaked, the brahmachari travelled on. The very day had been dark, and now night had fallen, so that the earth was black—the traveller could scarcely make out which was road and which was not. Yet the traveller moved on, unravelling the road—for he had renounced the world, he was a brahmachari. For him who has renounced the world, darkness, light, a bad road, a good road: all are equal.

It was late at night. The earth was dark—there was a dark covering over the sky's face. The treetops could be made out only as domes of denser darkness. It was only by the gaps in the treetops that the line of the path could be perceived. Drops of rain were falling. Now and again lightning flashed—darkness was better than that light. The world did not look so terrible in the darkness as it did in the lightning flashing briefly in the darkness.

'Oh, Mother!'

As he was proceeding in the darkness, the brahmachari suddenly heard in the middle of the road this faint, drawn-out, sighing call. The call was unearthly—nevertheless, one could tell that it came from a human throat. The call was very soft, yet one could tell that it expressed great pain. The traveller stood still on the road. He stood waiting for the next flash of lightning. Streaks of lightning were coming in quick succession. By the next flash, the traveller saw that something had fallen by the roadside. Was it a person? The traveller thought so. But he waited for another flash of lightning. By its light, he decided that it was indeed a person. Then the traveller called out, 'Who are you, fallen on the road?'

No one answered. Again he asked—this time an inarticulate distressed utterance briefly reached his ears. Then the brahmachari put down his umbrella and rosary on the ground, noted the place, and began to reach out from side to side. Soon his hands touched the soft body of a person. 'Who are you?' His hands touched the head, and found a sheaf of long hair. 'Durga! It is a woman!'

Then the brahmachari, not waiting for an answer, lifted the dying or unconscious woman in his arms. His umbrella and rosary remained where they were on the road. The brahmachari left the road and went across the dark fields in the direction of a village. The brahmachari knew the roads, landings, and villages of this region extremely well. He was not strong, but he moved over that difficult-to-traverse path carrying the dying woman like a child in his arms. Those who help others, whose love for others is strong, never feel the want of physical strength!

The brahmachari reached a thatched hut on the outskirts of the village.

He went to the door of that hut, with the solitary woman in his arms. He called, 'Hara, child, are you at home?' A woman called from within the hut, 'That's the guru's voice I hear. When did you arrive?'

The brahmachari said, 'Just now. Open the door quickly—I am in great difficulty.'

Haramani opened the door of the hut. Then the brahmachari told her to light a lamp, and gently he laid the woman on the floor within the hut. Hara lit a lamp and brought it close to the face of the dying woman; and, looking at her closely, they both saw that she was not old. But her physical state was such that they could not estimate her age. Her body was extremely emaciated—and showed signs of terrible suffering. She might once have been beautiful, but now there was no trace of beauty. Her wet clothes were very dirty—and torn in a hundred places. Her dishevelled hair was rough. Her eyes were sunken. Now those eyes were closed. She was breathing—but unconscious. She seemed near death.

Haramani asked, 'Where did you find her?'

The brahmachari told her everything, and said, 'She looks to be near death. But perhaps with warmth and fomentations she may live. Do as I say.'

Then Haramani, following the brahmachari's directions, skilfully changed the wet clothes for dry ones of her own. She dried the water from the limbs and hair with a dry cloth. Then, preparing a fire, she applied heat. The brahmachari said, 'She probably has not eaten for a long time. If there is milk in the house, try and see if you can feed her milk, a little at a time.'

Haramani had a cow—there was milk in the house. She warmed some milk and gave it to the woman sip by sip. The woman drank it. As the warmth penetrated her body, her eyes opened. Seeing this, Haramani said, 'Mother, where have you come from?'

The now-conscious woman said, 'Where am I?'

The brahmachari said, 'I found you in a state of near-death on the road, and brought you here. Where are you going?'

The woman said, 'A long way.'

Haramani said, 'There is a conch-shell bracelet on your arm. Have you a husband?'

The woman frowned. Haramani was abashed.

The brahmachari said, 'Child, what shall I call you? What is your name?'

The helpless woman hesitated a little and said, 'My name is Suryamukhi.'

35

In Hope

THERE WAS NO HOPE OF SURYAMUKHI'S RECOVERY. THE BRAHMACHARI, NOT being able to interpret the signs of her illness, sent for the village physician the next morning.

Ramakrishna Ray was very learned. He was a great scholar of Ayurveda. He was famous in the village for his remedies. He noted the symptoms and said, 'She has tuberculosis. She is feverish. The illness is deadly, it is true. But it is possible that she may survive.'

All this was said out of Suryamukhi's hearing. The physician prepared some medicine—seeing the helpless woman, Ramakrishna Ray said nothing about fees. Ramakrishna Ray was not a money-grubber. When the physician had taken his leave, the brahmachari sent Haramani away to another job, and sat down by Suryamukhi in order to speak uninterruptedly with her. Suryamukhi said, 'Sir! Why are you taking so much trouble for me? There is no need to worry about me.'

The brahmachari said, 'What trouble am I taking? It is my work. I have no one. I am a brahmachari. My obligation is to care for others. If I were not engaged in doing things for you, I would be doing things for someone else like you.'

Suryamukhi said, 'Then leave me, and go and help someone else. You may be able to help someone else—you cannot help me.'

The brahmachari asked, 'Why?'

Suryamukhi said, 'It will not benefit me if I survive. It is dying which will do me good. When I fell on the road last night—I hoped very much that I would die. Why did you save me?'

The brahmachari said, 'I do not know how great your sorrow is—but however great your sorrow, it is a great sin to kill yourself. Never think of killing yourself. Killing yourself is as sinful as killing another.'

Suryamukhi said, 'I did not try to kill myself. Death had itself come to me—that was what I hoped for. But my happiness is not in death.'

'Happiness is not in death'—at those words Suryamukhi's voice choked. Tears fell from her eyes.

The brahmachari said, 'I have seen that whenever there is talk of death, tears fall from your eyes. Yet you want to die. Ma, I am like your child. Think of me as a son, and tell me the desires of your heart. If there is a way to dispel your sorrow, I will do so. It was to say this to you that I sent Haramani away and came and sat with you alone. From your speech, I know that you must be the daughter of gentlefolk. I know, too, that you are suffering from terrible mental agony. Why not tell me what it is? Think of me as your child, and tell me.'

With tears in her eyes, Suryamukhi said, 'I am waiting to die. Why should I be bashful now? And my sorrow is nothing—only the sorrow of not seeing my husband's face as I die. My happiness is in dying—but if I die without seeing his face, then there will be misery in dying, too. If I could see his face once more, then I would be happy to die.'

The brahmachari wiped his eyes. He said, 'Where is your husband? There is no way now of taking you to him. But if, receiving word, he can come here, I will write to him.'

There was a flash of joy in Suryamukhi's illness-ravaged face. Then, despondent again, she said, 'He might come, but I do not know whether he would or not. I have offended him greatly—yet he is compassionate towards me—he might forgive me. But he is very far away—will I survive so long?'

The brahmachari asked, 'How far away is he?'

Suryamukhi said, 'The district of Haripur.'

The brahmachari said, 'You will.'

Saying this, the brahmachari fetched a paper and pen, and, with Suryamukhi's help, wrote a letter:

> I am unknown to you. I am a Brahmin—a brahmachari. Neither do I know who you are. I know only this, that Shrimati Suryamukhi is your wife. She is here in this village of Madhupur, critically ill, in Haramani Vaishnavi's house. She has been given treatment—but there is no sign of her recovering. I write this letter to inform you of this. Her wish is to see you once before she dies. If you can forgive her offence, then please come to this place. I address her as 'Mother'. I write this letter, as a son, with her permission. She has not the strength to write herself.
>
> If you consent to come, then take the road to Raniganj. Ask at Raniganj for Shriman Madhavachandra Goswami. If you mention my name, he will send someone to accompany you. Then you need not wander around searching for Madhupur.
>
> If you come, come quickly; if you delay, your purpose will not be achieved.
>
> Shri Shivaprasad Sharma.

Having written the letter, the brahmachari asked, 'To whom shall I address it?'

Suryamukhi said, 'I will tell Haramani.'

After Haramani had come back, the brahmachari addressed the letter to Nagendranath Datta, and took it with him to post.

When the brahmachari had gone away with the letter to post it, Suryamukhi, with tears in her eyes, folded hands, and uplifted face, begged God with body and mind, 'O great Lord! If you are true, if I am devoted to my husband, may this letter bear fruit. I know nothing but to serve my husband always—if there is virtue in that, then I do not ask for heaven as a reward. I ask only this, that I may see my husband's face before I die.'

But the letter did not reach Nagendra. When it reached Govindapur, Nagendra had long since set out on his travels. The postman took it to the steward.

Nagendra's instructions to the steward were: 'When I get to where I am going, I will write to you from there. When you receive my orders, send letters addressed to me there.' Nagendra had, a while before, written a letter from Patna, saying, 'I am going to Kashi by boat. I will write from Kashi. When you get that letter, send my letters and so on there.' Awaiting that news, the steward kept the brahmachari's letter locked in a box.

In due course, Nagendra reached his residence in Kashi. Having arrived, he sent word to the steward. Then the steward sent off Brahmachari Shivaprasad's letter, together with other letters. Having received the letter and grasped its contents, Nagendra clutched his brow and said, stricken, 'God! Keep me conscious for a moment longer.' These words reached God's ears; for a moment Nagendra remained conscious; calling the overseer, he ordered, 'I must go to Raniganj this very night—spend whatever you have to, but arrange it.'

The overseer went away to make the arrangements. Then Nagendra fell to the ground and lay unconscious in the dust.

That night, Nagendra left Kashi behind. Varanasi, beauty of the universe, what happy man could leave you behind with satisfied eyes on such an autumn night? The night was moonless. Thousands of stars burned in the sky—standing above the waves on the heart of the Ganga, in whatever direction one looked, there were stars in the sky!—with ceaseless fire, from eternity they shone—endlessly they shone, without rest. On the earth was a second sky!—the steady blue heart of the waves was like a blue cloth; on the banks, on the flights of steps and in the buildings like endless rows of hills, a thousand lights burned. Houses after houses, and after them more houses, endless lines of houses were thus adorned with rows of lights. And all these were reflected in the clear river. Nagendra wiped his eyes. He could not now bear earth's beauty. Nagendra knew that Suryamukhi's letter had been a long time in reaching him—where was Suryamukhi now?

36

Hira's Poison Tree Flowers

ON THE DAY THE GATEKEEPERS, WITH THICK BAMBOO CLUBS IN THEIR HANDS, chased Devendra away, Hira laughed uproariously to herself. But after that, she repented deeply. Hira thought to herself, 'I did not do well to cause him that indignity. I do not know how angry he is with me. I had not achieved a place in his heart; now all my hopes are gone.'

Devendra, too, was engaged in fulfilling the hope of achieving his heart's desire, born of malice, to punish Hira. He sent for Hira, through Malati. Hira hesitated for a couple of days, and finally went. Devendra showed no anger at all—he made no reference to the recent occurrence. As a spider weaves a net for a fly, Devendra started to spread out a net for Hira. The greedy-hearted Hira-fly easily fell into the trap. She was captivated by Devendra's sweet talk, and deceived by his flattery. She thought that this was love; that Devendra loved her. Hira was clever, but here her intelligence was dim. Under the influence of that power which the ancient poets hymned, describing it as being able to break the meditation of those who have subdued their passions and conquered death, Hira's intelligence disappeared.

Abandoning words, Devendra took up a tanpura and, stimulated by wine, began to sing. Then Devendra, with his skill and his heavenly voice, created such nectar-filled waves of music that Hira, overwhelmed by the sound, was totally enchanted. Her heart trembled; and her mind melted with love for Devendra. In her eyes, Devendra seemed then the most beautiful thing in the world, more precious than anything, most worthy of being appreciated by beautiful women. Tears of love streamed from Hira's eyes.

Devendra set down the tanpura, and with the hem of his own garment tenderly wiped Hira's eyes. Hira's body trembled with pleasure. Then Devendra, kindled by wine, started to utter such sweet words, mixed with wit and humour, and again spoke in such love-drenched, poetically-allusive phrases that foolish, rustic Hira thought, 'This is the happiness of heaven.' If Hira's mind had been clear, and her intelligence refined through good company, she would have thought, 'This is hell.' As for words of love—Devendra had never felt anything of what people call love—Hira knew more of it—but Devendra was an expert in the clichés of the ancient poets. Hearing the praises of love's ineffable glory from Devendra's lips, Hira thought him superhumanly accomplished—and her whole body was suffused with love. Then Devendra again prepared to sing, humming like the first solitary bee in spring. Hira, overpowered by love, joined with it the sound of her own sweet, womanly voice. Devendra asked Hira to sing. Then Hira, with love-softened mind, widening her wine-flushed lotus-eyes, making play with her finely-drawn brows, her face blooming, started to sing full-throatedly. Because of the exuberance of her state of mind, her voice rose high and strong. What Hira sang spoke of love—it was full of pleading for love.

Then, in that sinful house, the two sinful hearts, overwhelmed by sinful desire, pledged eternal love, in the form of eternal sin, to each other. Hira knew how to control her mind, but because she did not do so, she easily went, insect-like, into the flames. Knowing Devendra not to be in love with her she had controlled her mind, though only to a small extent; but she had acted in accordance with her own desires. When she had had Devendra under her control, she had, even though laughingly admitting her love to him, warded him off from dalliance. Again, she had only quelled that love, which ate into her heart like a worm in a flower, by engaging herself in work in another's house. But when she believed that Devendra loved her, she no longer restrained her mind. By this lack of restraint, the fruit for her eating ripened on the poison tree.

People say that punishment for sin is not evident in this life. Whether this is true or not, you will see that people who do not control their minds do not, in this world, eat the fruit of the poison tree.

37

News of Suryamukhi

THE RAINS PASSED. AUTUMN CAME. NOW AUTUMN, TOO, WAS PASSING. THE water in the fields dried up. The rice was ripening. Lotuses bloomed in the ponds. In the mornings, dew dropped from the leaves of the trees. In the evenings, there was mist over the fields. At such a time, in the month of Kartik, there came one morning on the Madhupur road a palanquin. Seeing a palanquin in the village, the local boys dropped their games and stood in a large crowd beside it. The maidservants, young wives, and women of the village, with water pitchers on their hips, stood at a little distance—and stared speechlessly at the palanquin. The young wives lowered their veils from their eyes and looked—the other womenfolk stared openly. The peasants were harvesting the rice—letting the rice fall, with sickles in their hands and turbans on their heads, they gazed gaping at the palanquin. The headmen of the village community sat together in committee. A booted foot emerged from within the palanquin. Everyone concluded that a sahib had come—the boys were certain that his wife had come too.

Nagendra emerged from the palanquin. Half-a-dozen people salaamed him—for he wore trousers, and there was a hat on his head! Some thought he must be a police inspector; some thought a naval captain had come.

Addressing an old man amongst the onlookers, Nagendra asked for news of Shivaprasad Brahmachari. The individual addressed was certain that there must be some deposition in a murder case involved here—so it would not be a good idea to give a truthful answer. He said, 'Sir, I am Master Greenhorn, I don't know so much.' Nagendra saw that nothing would be accomplished unless he could meet one of the gentlefolk. Many gentlefolk lived in the village. Nagendranath went to the house of an important man. The master of that house was Ramakrishna Ray, the village physician. Seeing that a Babu had arrived, Ramakrishna Ray courteously settled Nagendra in an armchair. Nagendra asked for news of the brahmachari. Ramakrishna

Ray said, 'The brahmachari Brahmin is not here.' Nagendra was very disappointed. He asked, 'Where has he gone?'

Ramakrishna answered, 'I cannot say. We do not know where he has gone. He does not stay in any particular place; he moves around continually from place to place.'

Nagendra asked, 'Does anyone know when he will return?'

Ramakrishna said, 'I have some important business with him myself, too. So I have asked for word of him. But no one can say when he will return.'

Nagendra was very disappointed. Again he asked, 'How long ago did he leave here?'

Ramakrishna said, 'He came here in the month of Shravan. He left in the month of Bhadra.'

Nagendra said, 'Well, can someone show me where in this village is the house of Haramani Vaishnavi?'

Ramakrishna replied, 'Haramani's house was right beside the road. But that house is no more. It has been destroyed by fire.'

Nagendra pressed his brow. In a feeble voice he asked, 'Where is Haramani?'

Ramakrishna said, 'That, also, no one can say. She fled away somewhere on the night fire broke out in her house. Some say that she herself set fire to her own house and fled.'

Nagendra said, brokenly, 'Was there a woman who went to live in her house?'

Ramakrishna said, 'No, only from the month of Shravan there had been a strange woman in her house, who had arrived suffering from an illness. The brahmachari brought her from somewhere and left her there. I heard that her name was Suryamukhi. She was suffering from tuberculosis—it was I who treated her. I had nearly cured her—when—'

Nagendra, breathing hard, asked, 'When what—?'

Ramakrishna said, 'When that woman was burned to death in the fire at Hara Vaishnavi's house!'

Nagendra fell from his chair. He suffered a severe blow to the head.

From that blow, he lost consciousness. The physician tended to him.

Who desires to live? This world is full of pain. There is a poison tree in everyone's courtyard. Who desires to love?

38
Eventually, Everything Was Lost

AFTER SO LONG, EVERYTHING WAS LOST. WHEN, IN THE EVENING, NAGENDRA Datta climbed into the palanquin to leave Madhupur, he was saying this to himself, 'After so long, I have lost everything.'

What was lost? Happiness? That had been lost the day Suryamukhi left home. Then what was lost now? Hope. While people have hope, nothing is lost; once hope is lost, everything is lost!

Now Nagendra had lost everything. Because of this, he went back to Govindapur. He did not go to live in the house at Govindapur; he went to take leave once and for all of his responsibilities as a householder. This was a complicated task. He had to arrange for the distribution of property and possessions. The landholding, the household and all the other immovable possessions he had acquired he would make over by deed of gift to his nephew, Satishchandra—that had to be done in writing at a lawyer's office. He would give all his moveable possessions to Kamalamani—he had to arrange for them all to be sent to her house in Kolkata! He would keep only a few bonds—he would support himself by means of these for the few years he remained alive. He would send Kundanandini to Kamalamani. He had to explain all the accounts of his property and possessions to Shrishchandra. And he would lie down and weep, once, on the bed on which Suryamukhi used to lie. He would take Suryamukhi's ornaments with him. He would not give these to Kamalamani—he would keep them. Wherever he went he would take them with him. Then, when the time came, he would die looking at them. Once he had done all these necessary things, Nagendra would leave his ancestral home once and for all and take up his wanderings again. And he would pass his days, as many of them as he had to live, hiding himself somewhere in some corner of the world.

With these thoughts, Nagendra travelled on in the palanquin. The doors of the palanquin were open, the night was filled with the moonlight of the month of Kartik; there were stars in the sky; the telegraph wires beside the main road sounded in the wind. In Nagendra's eyes that night, not a single star seemed beautiful. The earth was very cruel. Why did the beauty which in his happy days pleased the mind show itself now? Those moon beams reflected in the long grass used to refresh the heart; why was that grass still so bright? The sky was still as blue, the clouds as white, the stars as bright, the wind as playful, the animals roamed in the same way, people were as engaged in frolic and fun; the earth was as ceaselessly active; the current of the world as irresistible. Why did not the earth open and swallow Nagendra and his palanquin together?

Nagendra, thinking, realized that everything was his own fault. He had reached thirty-three years of age. In that span he had lost everything. Yet, nothing of that which God had given to him had been lost. All those things which make people happy had been given to him by God in a measure which is given to few. Riches, possessions, prosperity, respect—he had received all these in uncommon measure from his birth. Without intelligence, all these do not produce happiness—God had not been miserly in that respect either. His father and mother had not neglected his education—who was as well-educated as he? Beauty, strength, health, love: nature had given him those, too, without stint; even that rarer treasure—that single, priceless possession in this world—an endlessly loving and faithful wife—this too had been his happy fate. Who else on earth had so many of the sources of happiness? And now, who on earth was so unhappy? Now, if by giving everything he had—wealth, possessions, respect, beauty, youth, learning and intelligence—he could change places with one of the bearers of his own palanquin, he would consider this to be divine happiness. A bearer? He thought, 'Is there any murderer in the government's jails who is not happier than I? Not more innocent than I? He has killed some stranger, I have slain Suryamukhi! If I had controlled my mind, why would Suryamukhi have gone away to be burned to death in a hut? I am Suryamukhi's killer—who of those who kill father, mother, or son, is a greater sinner than I? Was Suryamukhi only my—wife? Suryamukhi was my—everything. In union, a wife; in fellow-feeling, a brother; in caring, a sister; in hospitality, a kinswoman; in affection, a mother; in devotion, a daughter; in enjoyment, a friend; in advice, a teacher; in attendance, a servant. My Suryamukhi—who was like her? My companion in the world; the Lakshmi of my home; the religion in my heart; the necklace around my neck! The pupil of my eye, the blood in my heart; the soul of my body; the all of my life! The joy of pleasure; my peace in suffering, the intelligence of my mind, the inspiration of my work! Is there another such in the world? The light of my sight; the music of my ears; the breath of my faith; the world of my touching. My present happiness, my past memory, my future hope; my virtue in the world to come! I am a swine—how would I recognize a pearl?'

Suddenly it occurred to him that he was riding at ease in a palanquin, whereas Suryamukhi had fallen ill walking the roads. So Nagendra got off the palanquin and went on foot. The bearers brought the empty palanquin along behind him. He left the palanquin at the market they reached in the morning, and dismissed the bearers. He would go the rest of the way on foot.

Then he thought, 'I will offer penance in this life for slaying Suryamukhi. What penance? I will renounce all the pleasures which Suryamukhi was deprived of when she left home. I will have no more to do with wealth, possessions, servants, friends and relations. All the troubles which Suryamukhi suffered after she left home, I will suffer. When I set out from Govindapur, from that day on I will go on foot; I will eat bad food, I will sleep under trees or in huts. What other penance? Whenever I see a helpless woman, I will give my life to help her. I will use the money I keep to live on for bare subsistence, and spend the rest to help destitute women. I will write into the deed of gift that half of the money I am giving to Satish must be spent, as long as I live, to help destitute women in the world. Penance! There is penance for sin. There is no penance for misery. Only death is the penance for misery. In death, misery dies. Why do I not do that penance?' Then Nagendranath covered his eyes with his hands, called on the name of God, and longed for death.

39

All Was Lost, But Not Suffering

IT WAS ONE PRAHAR INTO THE NIGHT, AND SHRISHCHANDRA WAS SITTING alone in his reception room when Nagendra arrived there and threw down the carpet bag he had been carrying in his hand.

Shrishchandra, seeing his stricken, dirty face, was afraid; he did not know what to ask. Shrishchandra knew that Nagendra had received the brahmachari's letter at Kashi, and that, having received it, he had set out for Madhupur. Now, seeing that Nagendra was saying nothing of his own accord, Shrishchandra went and sat by Nagendra, and, taking his hand, said, 'Dear Nagendra, seeing you silent makes me anxious. Did you not go to Madhupur?'

Nagendra only said, 'I did.'

Afraid, Shrishchandra asked, 'Did you not see the brahmachari?'

Nagendra said, 'No.'

Shrishchandra said, 'Did you get news of Suryamukhi? Where is she?'

Nagendra pointed upwards and said, 'In heaven.'

Shrishchandra was silent. Nagendra bowed his head and was silent too. After a moment, he lifted his head and said, 'You do not believe in heaven—I do.'

Shrishchandra knew that previously Nagendra did not believe in heaven; he understood that now, he did. He understood that this heaven was the creation of love and hope. The words 'Suryamukhi is nowhere' could not be borne—there was much more happiness in the thought that Suryamukhi was in heaven.

The two of them sat in silence. Shrishchandra knew that this was not the time for words of consolation. Talk of others, now, would feel like poison. Converse with others was poison. Understanding this, Shrishchandra got up to see to the preparation of a bed and so on for Nagendra. He did not dare ask about food; he thought he would give that responsibility to Kamala.

Kamala heard that Suryamukhi was no more. Thereupon, she accepted no responsibility of the hostess at all. Leaving Satish alone, she was seen no more that night.

Seeing Kamalamani lying on the floor, with dishevelled hair, weeping, a maidservant brought Satishchandra, left him there, and withdrew. Satishchandra, seeing his mother all dusty and weeping silently, first sat quietly beside her. Then he put a small finger, sweeter than a flower, on her chin and tried to raise her head to look at her face. Kamalamani lifted her head but did not speak. Then Satish, wanting his mother to be happy, kissed her. Kamalamani caressed Satish's limbs with her hands, but did not kiss him, or speak. Then Satish lay on his mother's lap, put his arms around her neck, and wept. Who, other than God, could enter the child's heart and discern the reason for his weeping?

Shrishchandra, relying perforce on his own judgement, brought a little food himself and placed it before Nagendra. Nagendra said, 'There's no need for food—but sit down. I have much to say to you—that is why I came here.'

Then Nagendra told Shrishchandra all that he had heard from Ramakrishna Ray. After that, he told him all that he planned to do.

Shrishchandra said, 'It is very surprising that you did not meet the brahmachari on the way. For he set out yesterday from Kolkata for Madhupur in search of you.'

Nagendra exclaimed, 'Is that so! How did you find the brahmachari?'

Shrishchandra said, 'He is a very great man. When he received no answer to his letter, he himself went to Govindapur in search of you. He did not find you at Govindapur either, but he heard that his letter had been sent on to Kashi. You would receive it there. Therefore, without fuss, and without saying anything to anyone, the excellent man set out. From there he returned again to Govindapur in search of you. He received no news of you there—he heard that he would get news of you from me. He came to me. He arrived the day before yesterday, and I showed him your letter. Then, yesterday, he left in the hope of meeting you at Madhupur. You should have met him last night at Raniganj.'

Nagendra said, 'I was not at Raniganj yesterday. Did he say anything to you about Suryamukhi?'

Shrishchandra said, 'I will tell you all that tomorrow.'

Nagendra said, 'You think that it will increase my distress to hear it. My distress cannot be further increased. Tell me.'

Shrishchandra told Nagendra what he had heard from the brahmachari of how he had come across Suryamukhi on the road, of her illness and the treatment she had received, and how she had almost recovered. He left out much—he did not say how much Suryamukhi had suffered.

When he had heard all this, Nagendra went outside. Shrishchandra got up to go with him, but Nagendra angrily forbade this. For two prahars, Nagendra wandered on the roads like a madman. He wanted to lose himself in the flow of people. But the flow of people had by then abated—who could lose themselves in it? He returned to Shrishchandra's house. Shrishchandra again sat by him. Nagendra said, 'There is more. The brahmachari must certainly have heard from her where she went, and what she did. Did he tell you?'

Shrishchandra said, 'What is the use of all this now? Be calm now, and rest.'

Nagendra frowned and said in a loud voice, 'Tell me.' Looking at Nagendra's face, Shrishchandra saw that he was like a madman; his face was as dark as a lightning-filled cloud. Afraid, Shrishchandra said, 'I will tell you.' Nagendra looked pleased. Shrishchandra said, briefly, 'Suryamukhi went by land, slowly, from Govindapur, first on foot, in this direction.'

Nagendra asked, 'How far did she go each day?'

Shrishchandra said, 'A mile or two.'

Nagendra said, 'She did not take even a paisa with her—how did she live?'

Shrishchandra said, 'Some days she fasted—some days she begged—you are mad!'

With these words, Shrishchandra rebuked Nagendra. For he could see that Nagendra was choking himself with his own hands. He said, 'Will you find Suryamukhi by dying?' Saying this, he took Nagendra's hands and held them in his own. Nagendra said, 'Tell me.'

Shrishchandra said, 'Unless you listen calmly, I will tell you nothing more.'

But Shrishchandra's words no longer reached Nagendra's ears. His consciousness had faded. With eyes closed, Nagendra was contemplating the form of Suryamukhi, ascended into heaven. He saw that she was seated on a jewelled throne; from all around, cool, fragrant breezes stirred her hair; on all sides, birds made of flowers were flying and singing to the sound of the veena. He saw that hundreds of red lotuses bloomed beneath her feet; a hundred moons burned in the moonlight of her lion-throne; hundreds of stars burned on all sides. He saw that he himself had fallen into a place of darkness; there was pain in his limbs; demons were beating him with canes; Suryamukhi was stopping them with a gesture.

With great care, Shrishchandra brought Nagendra back to consciousness. Regaining consciousness, Nagendra called in a loud voice, 'Suryamukhi! Dearer than life! Where are you!' Shrishchandra was astounded and frightened at this outcry. Gradually, Nagendra came back to himself, and said, 'Tell me.'

Shrishchandra, afraid, said, 'What else shall I tell you?'

Nagendra insisted, 'Tell me, or I will die this instant.'

Shrishchandra, frightened, began to speak again: 'Suryamukhi did not suffer thus for long. A wealthy Brahmin was travelling with his family to Kashi. He was going as far as Kolkata by boat, and one day, when Suryamukhi was lying under a tree by the river, the Brahmin family came ashore there to cook. The mistress talked with Suryamukhi. Seeing Suryamukhi's condition, and pleased with her character, the Brahmin woman took her with her on the boat. Suryamukhi had told her that she too was going to Kashi.'

Nagendra said, 'What was the Brahmin's name? Where was his home?'

'I don't know,' Shrishchandra said.

Making up his mind about something, Nagendra asked, 'And then?'

Shrishchandra said, 'Suryamukhi went with the Brahmin as one of his family as far as Barhi. To Kolkata by boat, from Kolkata to Raniganj by rail, from Raniganj by bullock-train; thus far, she didn't need to walk.'

Nagendra said, 'Did the Brahmin then say farewell to her?'

Shrishchandra said, 'No; Suryamukhi herself said farewell. She was no longer going to Kashi. How long could she go without seeing you? Intending to see you, she set out from Barhi on foot.'

As he spoke, tears came to Shrishchandra's eyes. He looked at Nagendra's face. Seeing Shrishchandra's tears, Nagendra dissolved into tears himself. He clung to Shrishchandra's neck, and, laying his head on his shoulder, wept. Until his arrival at Shrishchandra's house, Nagendra had not wept—his grief was beyond tears. Now his pent-up grief streamed out. With his face on Shrishchandra's shoulder, Nagendra wept for a long time like a child. By this, his suffering was greatly alleviated. Grief without tears is a messenger of death.

Once Nagendra had become a little calmer, Shrishchandra said, 'There is no point now in going over everything that happened.'

Nagendra said, 'What more is there to tell? I can imagine what else happened. She went from Barhi to Madhupur on foot. Suryamukhi fell ill from the effort of walking, from hunger, from sun and rain, from lack of shelter and from her mental suffering, and was facing death.'

Shrishchandra was silent. Then he said, 'Brother, why should we needlessly go over these things any more? You are not at all to blame. You did nothing without her consent or against her word. It is not sensible to repent for that which was not your fault.'

Nagendra did not accept that. He knew that all the fault was his alone: why had he not uprooted the seed of the poison tree from his heart?

40
The Fruit of Hira's Poison Tree

HIRA HAD SOLD A GREAT JEWEL FOR A FARTHING. VIRTUE IS MAINTAINED BY constant effort, but is destroyed in one day's carelessness. So it had been with Hira. The gain for which Hira sold this great jewel was a useless farthing. For Devendra's love was like the water of a flood; as fleeting as it was muddy. In three days, the water of the flood retreated, leaving Hira stuck in the mud. As certain individuals, miserly yet greedy for fame, who have for so long guarded the wealth they have amassed, at the risk of their lives, spend it all for a day's happiness on the occasion of a son's wedding or some other such festival, so Hira, having spoiled her long and carefully preserved virtue for one day's happiness, found herself standing, like a miser who has given up all his money, on the path of eternal regret.

At first, Hira—abandoned by Devendra like an unripe, barely-tasted mango thrown away by a playful boy—felt great pain in her heart. But she was not only abandoned—the way she had been abandoned and mortified by Devendra was even more deeply unendurable for a woman.

When, on the last day of their meeting, Hira fell at Devendra's feet and said, 'Do not abandon your slave,' Devendra told her, 'It was only in the desire for Kundanandini that I have honoured you so much—if you can arrange a meeting with Kunda for me, then I will talk to you—otherwise this is the end. I have requited you for your pride. Now put this disgrace in your offering tray and take it home on your head.'

Rage darkened Hira's sight. When her head cleared, she stood before Devendra with frowning brows and reddened eyes, and rebuked him volubly—as only sharp-tongued, sinful women can. This put Devendra out of patience. He kicked Hira and drove her away from the flower-garden. Hira was sinful—Devendra was sinful and a brute. This is what the vows of eternal love of the two of them had ripened into.

Hira, spurned, did not go home. A Chandal physician used to practise in Govindapur. He only treated Chandals and other such low-caste people. He knew nothing about treatment or medicines—he put an end to people's lives with the help of poisonous pills. Hira knew that he kept a collection of quick-acting poisons: plant poisons, mineral poisons, snake poisons and others. That very night, Hira went to his house, called him, and said in a whisper, 'Every day a jackal comes and eats from my pot. Unless that jackal dies, I can't go on. I thought that I would mix poison with the rice—then when it came to eat from the pot, it would eat the poison and die. You have many poisons; can you sell me a poison that will act quickly?'

The Chandal did not believe the story of the jackal. He said, 'I have what you want, but I cannot sell it to you. If they find out I have sold poison, the police will seize me.'

Hira said, 'Don't worry. No one will know that you have sold it to me—I swear it by my god and by the Ganga. Give me enough poison to kill two jackals and I will pay you fifty rupees.'

The Chandal was certain that she was going to kill someone. But he could not resist the temptation of earning fifty rupees. He agreed to sell the poison. Hira fetched the money from her house and gave it to him. The Chandal wrapped some strong poison, fatal for humans, in a paper and gave it to Hira. Hira said as she left, 'Take care you don't tell anyone about this—if you do, it will be worse for both of us.'

The Chandal said, 'Mother! I do not even know you.' Then Hira, relieved of fear, went home.

When she reached home she wept for a long time with the packet of poison in her hand. Then she wiped her eyes and thought, 'For what crime should I take poison and die? Why should I die without killing him who killed me? I will not take this poison. I will give it to him who has put me in this condition; or else I will give it to his lady-love, Kundanandini. I will kill one of them, and then I will die when I must.'

41

Hira's Grandmother

Hira's granny's old.
There's cow-dung in her basket.
She walks bent over.
She cracks pebbles in her teeth.
She eats thirty jackfruits.

HIRA'S GRANDMOTHER WAS GOING ALONG, BENT OVER, USING A STICK, AND a flock of boys were dancing behind her, clapping their hands in rhythm and reciting this strange little poem.

It is doubtful whether there was any particular condemnation in this poem or not—but Hira's grandmother became very angry. She ordered the boys to go to the house of Yama—and prescribed very unjust food and so on for their forefathers. This used to happen nearly every day.

When she reached Nagendra's gates, Hira's grandmother was delivered from the hands of the boys. When they saw the glossy black beards of the gatekeepers, they broke off the battle and fled. As they fled, one boy said:

Ramacharan the gatekeeper
Sleeps in the evening
If a thief comes, where will he run?

Another said:

Ram is a poor rustic
He goes around with a stick on his shoulder
If he sees a thief he runs off to the pond's bank.

Another said:

Lalachand Singh
Dances around skipping,
No dal or bread, but, at work, horses' eggs.[15]

The boys, called by the gatekeepers various words not found in the dictionary, ran away.

Tapping with her stick, Hira's grandmother made her way to the doctor's office in Nagendra's house. Seeing the doctor, the old woman said, 'Oh, sir—where is the doctor?' The doctor said, 'I am the doctor.' The old woman said, 'Sir, I can't see well any more—I'm one or two score and three-quarters old—what can I say of my sorrows—I had a son, and gave him to Death—now I have a granddaughter, and she, too, has—' and she began to wail and weep noisily.

The doctor asked, 'What has happened to you?'

Without answering this, the old woman started to tell her life's story, and when, after much weeping, she had finished, the doctor had to ask again, 'What do you want now? What has happened to you?'

Then the old woman started the strange story of her own life all over again, but abandoned it as the doctor grew angry, and started to recount instead the life-stories of Hira and Hira's mother, and Hira's father, and Hira's husband. The doctor had great difficulty in understanding the gist of these—for they were mixed with a great deal about herself and a bit of weeping.

The gist was this, that the old woman wanted some medicine for Hira. Her illness was that she was behaving oddly. While Hira was in the womb, her mother had become insane. Become insane, and after suffering from her mental illness, had eventually died from it. From her childhood, Hira had been very intelligent—there had never been any sign of her mother's disease to be seen in her, but now the old woman had some doubts. Hira now sometimes laughed when she was alone—wept alone, or sometimes danced through the doors of the house. Sometimes she cried out. Sometimes she fainted. The old woman wanted medicine for this from the doctor.

The doctor considered and said, 'Your granddaughter has hysteria.'

The old woman asked, 'Oh, sir! Is there no medicine for wish-juice?'[16]

The doctor said, 'Certainly there is medicine for it. Keep her warm, and take this castor-oil and give it to her every morning. Later, I will give you some other medicine.' This was as far as the doctor's medical knowledge went.

The old woman went away, tapping with her stick, the phial of castor-oil in her hand. On the way, she met one of her neighbours. This woman asked, 'Well, then, Hira's grandmother, what is that in your hand?'

Hira's grandmother said, 'Hira has got wish-juice, so I went to the doctor, and he gave me some Krishna-juice. Is it true that Krishna-juice is good for wish-juice?'

The neighbour thought for a long time and said, 'That could be so. Krishna is everyone's wish. His treatment could be good for wish-juice. Well, Hira's grandmother, where did your granddaughter get so much juice from?' Hira's grandmother said, after much thought, 'It's because of her age.'

The neighbour said, 'Give her the urine of a new-born calf to drink. I've heard that that will help to digest lots of juice.'

When the old woman reached home, she remembered that the doctor had talked of warmth. The old woman brought a pan of coals and put it in front of Hira. Hira said, 'Help! Why the fire?'

The old woman said, 'The doctor told me to keep you warm.'

42
Dark House—Dark Life

IN GOVINDAPUR, THE DATTA'S GREAT ESTABLISHMENT, THE SIX-PART HOUSE—without Nagendra and Suryamukhi all was dark. The clerks sat in the office building, and in the inner building there was only Kundanandini, living with the kinswomen who were always to be provided for. But in the moon's absence, is the sky's darkness lessened by the moon-god's wife? There were spider webs in the corners—heaps of dust in the rooms, pigeons' nests on the cornices, sparrows in the rafters. In the gardens there were piles of dead leaves, and algae in the lake. There were jackals in the courtyards, wilderness in the flower-gardens, and rats in the storerooms. Things were draped with covers. On many, fungus had taken hold. Much had been gnawed away by rats. Muskrats, scorpions, bats and flittermice wandered about day and night in the darkness. Cats had eaten most of Suryamukhi's tame birds. Their remains were lying here and there. The geese had been killed by jackals. The peacocks had become wild. The bones of the cows stood out—they no longer gave milk. Nagendra's dogs had no spirit—they did not play or bark but remained tied up. One had died—one had gone mad, one had run away. The horses were suffering from various illnesses—or were beyond illness. In the stables, straw, dried leaves, grass, dust and pigeon feathers were everywhere. The horses sometimes got grass and grain, and sometimes not. The grooms hardly showed their faces in the stables; they stayed in their married quarters. In places, the parapets of the buildings were broken; in places, the stucco had fallen off; in places, window panes, Venetian blinds and railings were broken. There was rainwater on the matting, marks on the paint on the walls, weevils' nests on the bookcases, the straw of sparrows' nests on the chandeliers' shades. There was no Lakshmi in the house. Without Lakshmi, even Vishnu's abode is wretched.

As a single rose or lily-of-the-valley sometimes flowers in a garden without a gardener, which has become overgrown with grass, Kundanandini lived alone within this household. Kunda ate what everyone else ate. If someone spoke to her as to the mistress of the house, Kunda would think, 'They are mocking me.' If the steward sent to ask about something, Kunda's breast would thud with fear. In fact, Kunda was very afraid of the steward. There was a reason for this, too. Nagendra did not write to Kunda; therefore, Kunda used to ask for the letters Nagendra wrote to the steward, and read them. Having read them, she did not return them—reading them had become akin to reading the scriptures for her. She was always afraid lest the steward should ask for them. Because of this fear, Kunda's face paled at the very sound of the steward's name. The steward had learned of this from Hira. He did not ask for the letters. He used to keep copies of the letters himself before he gave them to Kunda to read.

Suryamukhi had indeed suffered—was Kunda not suffering? Suryamukhi had loved her husband—did Kunda not love him? Within that little heart was immeasurable love! Because she did not have the power to express it, it was constantly belabouring that heart of Kunda's, like a confined wind. Before the marriage, Kunda had loved Nagendra since childhood—she had told no one, no one had known. She had not intended to win Nagendra—neither had she hoped to do so: she had borne her own despair by herself. The moon in the sky had been put into her hand. After that—where was the moon now? For what fault had Nagendra spurned her? Day and night Kunda thought of this, and day and night she wept. Well, then, let it be that Nagendra did not love her. He might come to love her; Kunda's fortune could be thus—why did Kunda not get to see him even once? Only that? He thought that it was Kunda who was the cause of all this trouble; everyone thought that it was Kunda who was the cause of the damage. Kunda thought, 'For what fault am I the cause of all the damage?'

In an evil hour, Nagendra had married Kunda. As they who sit under the upas tree die, so those who were touched by the shadow of this marriage were ruined.

Again, Kunda thought, 'Suryamukhi's situation is because of me. Suryamukhi saved me—she loved me like a sister—I made her a beggar on the roads; is there anyone else as luckless as I am? Why did I not die? Why do I not die now?' Again she thought, 'I will not die now. Let her come back—let me see her once more—will she not come back again?' Kunda had not heard the news of Suryamukhi's death. So she said to herself, 'Why should I die now, for nothing? If Suryamukhi returns, then I will die. I will not be a thorn on the path of her happiness any more.'

43
Return

THE THINGS TO BE DONE IN KOLKATA HAD BEEN DONE. THE DEED OF GIFT had been drawn up. In it were special provisions for rewarding the brahmachari and the unknown Brahmin. It was to be lodged at the Haripur registry, so Nagendra returned with the deed of gift to Govindapur. Shrishchandra had made great efforts to prevent him from arranging the deed of gift and so on, and from travelling on foot and other such actions; but these efforts had been fruitless. Perforce, he followed him, by river. Kamalamani could not do without her counsellor, so she too, without being asked, went on board Shrishchandra's boat, taking Satish with her.

Kamalamani had been to Govindapur earlier, and at the sight of her it seemed to Kundanandini that there was again one star in the sky. Since Suryamukhi had left home, Kamalamani had been very angry with Kundanandini; she had refused to see her. But this time, when she arrived and saw Kundanandini's pale figure, Kamalamani's anger evaporated—she was saddened. She tried to cheer Kundanandini up, and when she told her that Nagendra was coming, she saw a smile on Kunda's face. Following that, she had to give her the news of Suryamukhi's death. At this, Kunda wept. Hearing this, many of the fair readers of this book will laugh to themselves, and say, 'The cat weeps at the fish's death.' But Kunda was very stupid. It did not occur to her dull mind that the death of a co-wife was to be greeted with laughter. The foolish girl wept a little for her co-wife. And you, lady! You who say, laughing, 'The cat weeps at the fish's death'—if you weep a little when your co-wife dies, I shall be very pleased with you.

Kamalamani calmed Kunda. Kamalamani herself had become calm. At first, Kamala had wept and wept—then she had thought, 'What will I achieve by weeping? If I weep, Shrishchandra becomes unhappy—if I weep, Satish weeps—weeping will not bring Suryamukhi back; so why do I make them weep? I will never forget Suryamukhi; but if I laugh Satish will laugh, so why should I not laugh?' Thinking thus, Kamalamani left off weeping, and became her former self.

Kamalamani said to Shrishchandra, 'The Lakshmi of this abode of Vishnu has left it. So if my brother goes there, will he sleep on a banyan leaf?'

Shrishchandra said, 'Come, let us all put it in order.'

So Shrishchandra set masons, labourers, cleaners and gardeners to work wherever there was need. Meanwhile, under Kamalamani's stern eye, there was great consternation amongst the muskrats, bats and flittermice in the buildings; the pigeons flew cooing from this crevice to that; the sparrows were anxious to escape—where the windows were closed they were circling around trying to open a way through by pecking at the glass; the maidservants, with brooms in hand, were hastening to conquer everything and everyone. Soon the house was again smiling with pleasure.

Finally, Nagendra arrived. It was evening by then. As a river flows very swiftly in its first spate, but when the flood is at its height the deep water assumes a peaceful aspect, so the full flow of Nagendra's grief had now developed an appearance of deep peace. Nothing of his sorrow had diminished, but his restlessness had abated. He spoke calmly with the people of the house and inquired after everyone. He spoke of Suryamukhi with no one—but, seeing his calmness, everyone was saddened by his grief. The older servants, going to offer their respects, wept spontaneously. Nagendra wounded only one heart. He did not visit the ever-sorrowing Kundanandini.

44

By the Dim Lamp

BY NAGENDRA'S ORDERS, THE SERVANTS HAD PREPARED HIS BED IN Suryamukhi's bedroom. When she heard of this, Kamalamani shook her head.

At night, when all the inmates of the house were asleep, Nagendra went to Suryamukhi's bedroom. He did not sleep—he wept. Suryamukhi's bedroom was very spacious and pleasing; it was the temple of Nagendra's overflowing happiness, so he had furnished it with care. The room was spacious and high; the floor was laid with black and white marble. On the walls, blue, yellow and red creepers, fruits, flowers and so on were painted; perched on them were different kinds of small birds, eating the fruit. On one side was a costly bed, made, with artistry, of wood inlaid with ivory; on the other side were several kinds of seats covered with many-coloured cloth, and other furnishings including a large mirror. Several paintings hung on the walls. These paintings were not European. Suryamukhi and Nagendra had together chosen the subjects of the paintings, and had them painted by a Bengali painter. The Bengali painter was the student of an English painter; he drew well. Nagendra had had them framed in expensive frames and hung in the bedroom. One painting was taken from the *Kumarasambhava*. Shiva sat meditating on a dais on the top of a mountain. At the entrance to a bower was Nandi, with a golden ferrule in his left hand—with a finger to his mouth he was forbidding sound in the forest. The forest was still—the bees hid in the leaves—the deer were sleeping. Into this scene had come Madan, to break Shiva's meditation. With him came the dawn of spring. Parvati, adorned with spring flowers, had come forward to make obeisance to Shiva. She was depicted stooping before Shiva, one knee on the ground, the other on the point of touching it, head and shoulders bent. One or two red flowers were falling from the ringlets over her ears, dislodged by the bending of her head; her dress had fallen a little from her breast, and from a distance Madan, hidden in the spring-blossomed forest, one knee on the ground, was fixing a flower-arrow to his elegant, full-drawn, flowery bow. In another painting, Rama was bringing Sita back from Lanka; the two of them sat in a bejewelled chariot, travelling through the sky. Rama had one hand on Sita's shoulder, and with the other was pointing out the beauties of the earth below. On all sides of the flying chariot, multicoloured clouds—blue, ruddy and white—were moving, tossed up in thick waves. Below, other waves were breaking in the wide, blue sea—the waves were sparkling like diamonds in the rays of the sun. On one side was 'Lanka, adorned with many buildings'—the gold-ornamented tops of its palaces were sparkling in the sun's rays. On the other side, was the darkly beautiful 'azure with tamal and tal forests' seashore. In-between, in the sky, lines of swans were flying. In another painting, Arjuna was carrying off Subhadra in his chariot. The chariot was travelling through the sky among the clouds; behind it, countless Yadavi soldiers were running: in the distance could be seen their banners and the clouds of dust they raised. Subhadra herself, as charioteer, was driving the chariot. The horses had turned their heads towards each other, and were pounding the clouds with their stride; Subhadra, delighted with her skill as a charioteer, had turned her head and was looking sidelong at Arjuna; she was biting her lower lip with her jasmine-white teeth in suppressed laughter; in the wind of the chariot's speed, her tresses were flying—one or two locks of hair, damp with perspiration, lay in ringlets on her forehead. In another painting, Ratnabali, dressed as Sagarika, under a tamal tree in the clear sky, was preparing to hang herself. A creeper full of bright flowers was trailing from the branches of the tamal tree; Ratnabali was with one hand draping the end of the creeper round her throat, and with the other hand wiping tears from her eyes; the flowers of the creeper beautifully adorned her tresses. In another painting, Shakuntala was taking an imaginary sharp blade of kusha grass from her foot in order to look at Dushyanta—Priyamvada was laughing without malice—Shakuntala, from anger and shame, did not lift her head—she could not look in Dushyanta's direction—neither could she go away. In another painting, the mighty prince Abhimanyu, like a young lion, dressed for battle, was taking leave of Uttara to go to war—Uttara would not let him go and was standing at the door herself, keeping it closed. Abhimanyu, seeing her fear, was laughing, and playfully showing her how he would break the lines of battle, drawing on the ground with the point of his sword. Uttara was seeing nothing of this. She was weeping, with both hands over her eyes. In another painting, Satyabhama's weighing-vow was depicted. There was a wide courtyard of stone; on one side, the king's city was shining with the golden tops of the beautiful buildings. In the middle of the courtyard, a great silver weighing machine had been set up. Filling one side of it sat Krishna, Lord of Dwarka, adorned with many ornaments, in his mature aspect, like a cloud burning with lightning. That side of the scales was touching the ground; on the other side were piled heaps of gold and jewels, but the first side was not rising at all. Beside the scales was Satyabhama; Satyabhama was mature, beautiful, with upright figure, with a ripe grace, enhanced with much tending, with eyes like lotus petals; but seeing the position of the scales her face had become pale. She was taking the ornaments from her limbs and throwing them into the scales; with her champak-white fingers she was taking the jewels hanging from her ears; from shame, drops of perspiration were on her brow, tears of misery had come to her eyes, her nostrils were flaring with anger, she was biting her lower lip: in such a state the painter had drawn her. Behind, like a golden image, Rukmini was watching. Her face, too, was sad. She, too, had taken the ornaments from her limbs and was giving them to Satyabhama. But her eyes were on Krishna; she was glancing sidelong towards her husband and smiling just a little with the corners of her lips, yet Krishna saw clearly the joy of the co-wife in that smile. Krishna's face was grave and still, as if he knew nothing; but he too was looking sidelong towards Rukmini, and there was in that sidelong look, too, a little smile. In the middle was the sage Narada, in white clothes, beautiful as the evening star; he was watching everything as if delighted, and his scarf and beard were flying in the breeze. All around, the many members of the household, dressed in various clothes and ornaments, brightened the scene. Many Brahmin beggars had come. A number of the household guards were quelling the hubbub. Under this painting, Suryamukhi had written with her own hand, 'As the deed, so the result. Are gold and silver equal to a husband?'

More than two prahars of the night had elapsed when Nagendra entered the room, alone. It was indeed, a terrible night. From evening onwards, little by little, rain had started to fall, and the wind had risen. Now rain was falling repeatedly, and the wind had gained a furious force. Where doors were open in the house, they were banging with a noise like thunder. The windows were all rattling. When Nagendra entered the room, he closed the door. The sound of the gale was then reduced. Beside the bed another door was open—no wind was coming through it, and that door remained open.

Having entered the bedroom, Nagendra sighed deeply and sat down on a sofa. No one knew for how long Nagendra wept, sitting there. How many words of happiness had he spoken, sitting with Suryamukhi, how many times, face to face on that sofa.

Again and again, Nagendra kissed that inanimate sofa. Lifting his head again, he looked towards Suryamukhi's beloved paintings. A bright lamp was burning in the room—in its restless rays, all the painted figures seemed alive. Nagendra saw Suryamukhi in every painting. He remembered that one day Suryamukhi, looking at Uma's adornment of flowers, had felt the desire to wear flowers herself. Nagendra had gathered and brought flowers from the garden himself, and with his own hands had decked Suryamukhi with blossoms. How happy Suryamukhi had been at that—is any woman decked with jewels as happy as she was? Another day, looking at Subhadra's charioteering, Suryamukhi wanted to drive Nagendra's carriage. Nagendra, loving his wife, at once had two little Burmese horses harnessed to a small carriage and brought into the garden of the inner courtyard for Suryamukhi to drive. The two of them got into the carriage. Suryamukhi took the reins. The horses started to move of their own accord. Suryamukhi, like Subhadra, turned her face towards Nagendra, and bit her lower lip in suppressed laughter. Seeing the main gateway close by, the horses took this opportunity to go right out into the open road with the carriage. Then Suryamukhi, distressed by the fear of public disgrace, drew her veil. Seeing her unhappy state, Nagendra took the reins in his own hands and brought the carriage back to the inner courtyard. And when they both got off, how much they laughed. Going to her bedroom, Suryamukhi shook her fist at Subhadra's image and said, 'You are a causer of great ruin and a source of much danger.' How Nagendra wept, remembering this. Unable to bear more pain, he got up and began to pace about. But in whichever direction he looked—there were signs of Suryamukhi. The creeper that the painter had drawn on the walls—Suryamukhi had drawn a creeper in a desire to imitate it. It was still there. One day, during Holi, Suryamukhi had thrown gulal at her husband—it had missed Nagendra and hit the wall. The mark of the red powder still remained. When the room had been finished, Suryamukhi had written in one place with her own hand:

In the year 1854
THIS TEMPLE
was established
for the installation of
HER DEITY
her husband
by his servant Suryamukhi

Nagendra read this. How many times Nagendra read it—his longing was not quenched by reading—again and again tears blurred his vision—wiping his eyes, he read again. He turned and saw that the lamp was on the verge of going out. Then Nagendra sighed and went to lie down on the bed. Just as he sat down on the bed, the storm blew up with suddenly increased force; from all sides came the sound of doors protesting. The lamp, empty of oil, was nearly extinguished—only a little light, like that of a fire-fly, remained.

In that light, little better than darkness, something extraordinary came within his sight. Startled by the noise of the rain and wind, he turned his eyes towards the open door beside the bed. Through that open door, in the dim light, he saw a shadow-like figure. The shadow had the form of a woman, but at what else he saw, Nagendra's flesh prickled and his limbs trembled. The woman-shaped image had Suryamukhi's figure. As Nagendra identified this as Suryamukhi's semblance, he fell from the bed to the ground and started to run towards the shadow. The shadow disappeared. At the same time, the light went out. Then Nagendra cried out and fell fainting to the ground.

45
Shadow

When Nagendra regained consciousness, the bedroom was still in deep darkness. Gradually, he came back to his senses. When he remembered his fainting, amazement gave birth to even greater amazement. He had fallen fainting to the ground; then where had the pillow under his head come from? Again a doubt shook him—was it a pillow? He touched the pillow—and found that it was not a pillow. It was somebody's lap. From its softness he realized that it was a woman's lap. Who had come and, while he was in a swoon, taken his head on her lap? Was it Kundanandini? To dispel his uncertainty, he asked, 'Who are you?' She who was cradling his head gave no answer—only several warm drops fell on Nagendra's forehead. Nagendra realized that whoever she was, she was weeping. Receiving no answer, Nagendra touched her limbs. Then suddenly Nagendra's senses became disoriented and his flesh prickled. He lay for a while inactive and inanimate. Then slowly, holding his breath, he lifted his head from the woman's lap and sat up.

The storm had now stopped. There were no more clouds in the sky—dawn was lightening the east. Outside, there was a considerable amount of light—even within the room a little light was coming through the windows.

Sitting up, Nagendra saw that the woman had risen to her feet—she was going slowly towards the door. Nagendra realized that this was not Kundanandini. It was not yet light enough to recognize anyone. But shape and posture were to some extent perceivable. Nagendra looked hard for a moment at the shape and posture. Then, he fell at the feet of that standing woman. 'Whether you are goddess or human, I fall at your feet: speak to me just once. Otherwise I shall die.'

What the woman said, Nagendra was not destined to understand. But as the sound of her words reached his ears he swiftly got up to his feet. Then he went forward to embrace the woman. But then both his mind and body were overwhelmed with faintness—like a creeper falling from a tree, he fell once more at the feet of that bewitching figure. He said no more.

The woman sat down, and again took his head on her lap. When Nagendra rose out of swoon or sleep, day had dawned. There was light in the room. Outside the room, in the garden, the birds were warbling in the trees. From its path of light above, the rays of the young sun were falling into the room. Nagendra realized that his head was once again resting on someone's lap. Without looking, he said, 'Kunda, why did you come? I have been dreaming of Suryamukhi all night. In my dream I saw that I had laid my head on Suryamukhi's lap. What joy it would be if you could become Suryamukhi!' The woman said, 'If you would be so happy to see that unfortunate woman, then I have become her.'

Nagendra looked up. Astounded, he sat up. He rubbed his eyes. Again he looked. He held his head in his hands. Again he rubbed his eyes and looked. Then, bending his head once more, he said softly to himself, 'Have I gone mad—or is Suryamukhi alive? Is this my final fate? I have gone mad!' With these words, Nagendra lay on the ground, covered his eyes with his arms and wept again.

Now the woman took hold of his feet. Hiding her face at his feet, she bathed them with her tears. She said, 'Rise, rise! My life's all! Rise from the ground and sit. Now all the sorrow I have suffered is ended. Rise, rise! I did not die. I have come back to serve you.'

What misapprehension was left? Nagendra held Suryamukhi in a close embrace. And leaning his head on her breast he wept, wordlessly, ceaselessly. Then, with their heads on each other's shoulders, how much they both wept. Neither spoke—how much they wept! What joy was in their weeping!

46

What Had Happened

IN DUE COURSE, SURYAMUKHI ALLAYED NAGENDRA'S CURIOSITY. SHE SAID, 'I did not die—what the physician said about my dying—that was not true. The physician did not know. When, through his treatment, I regained strength, I became very anxious to come to Govindapur to see you. I pestered the brahmachari. Finally, he agreed to take me to Govindapur. One day, after the evening meal, I set out with him for Govindapur. When we arrived, we heard that you were not in the area. The brahmachari, introducing me as his daughter, left me at a Brahmin's house six miles away from here, and went in search of you. He went first to Kolkata and met Shrishchandra. From Shrishchandra he heard that you were going to Madhupur. Hearing this, he went back to Madhupur. In Madhupur, he learned that on the very day we had left Haramani's place, her house had burnt down. Haramani had been burnt to death in the house. In the morning, people looking at the burned body could not recognize it. They worked out that there had been two people in the house and that one had died and the other was not there. So they supposed that one had escaped and survived—and the other had burned to death. The one who had escaped was fit, the one who was ill was unable to escape. In this way they decided that Haramani had escaped and I had died. What was at first a mere inference, gradually became proclaimed as a certainty, as it was passed on. It was this that Ramakrishna Ray heard and told you. The brahmachari, learning all this, heard further that you, having gone to Madhupur and heard the news of my death, had come in this direction. Being very concerned, he returned in search of you. Yesterday afternoon he reached Pratappur; I, too, had heard that you would reach home within a day. In that expectation, I came home the day before yesterday. I have no difficulty now in walking six miles—I have learned how to walk the roads. You had not arrived, the day before yesterday, and hearing this I returned, and, after meeting the brahmachari again yesterday, I came back to Govindapur. When I arrived here, it was one prahar into the night. I saw that the back door was still open. I entered the house—no one saw me. I stayed hiding under the stairs. Then when everyone was asleep I climbed the stairs. I thought that you would certainly be sleeping in this room. I saw that this door was open. I peeped through the door—you were sitting with your head in your hands. I longed very much to fall at your feet—but I was extremely afraid as well—the wrong that I had done you—what if you did not forgive that? I was happy just seeing you. I watched you from the shelter of the door; I thought, now I will show myself. I was coming forward to show myself—but as soon as you saw me in the doorway, you fainted. Then I sat down and took your head in my lap. I had not known that this happiness was in my destiny. But, fie! You do not love me. You did not recognize me even when your hand touched my body—I would know you from the feel of the very air your body displaced.'

47
The Simple-hearted and the Snake

WHILE NAGENDRA AND SURYAMUKHI, FLOATING ON AN OCEAN OF HAPPINESS, were having this life-restoring conversation, in another part of the house a life-destroying conversation was taking place. But first, it is necessary to say something about the previous night.

When he arrived at the house, Nagendra did not speak with Kunda. In her own bedroom, Kunda wept all night with her face in her pillow. She did not weep the easy tears of girlhood—she wept wounded to the heart. If anyone has, in childhood, given themselves unreservedly to someone and, in return for the priceless heart, received only disregard, they will know how this weeping cleaves the heart.

Then Kunda lamented, 'Why have I stayed alive, longing for the sight of my husband?'

She thought, further, 'In the hope of what happiness do I stay alive?'

After a night of wakefulness and weeping, sleep came to Kunda at dawn. Overcome by sleep, she had for the second time a vivid dream.

In it, the light-filled figure that had taken her mother's shape and appeared to her in a dream as she slept her father's deathbed in her father's house, four years before—that same light-filled, calm figure appeared again above Kunda's head. But this time she was not within the flawless bright circle of the moon. She was descending, riding in a dense blue raincloud. All around her, waves of deep blue vapour full of darkness were thrown up; within that darkness, a human form was smiling slightly. Gradually it lightened. Kunda saw with fear that this smiling face was that of Hira. She saw further that her mother's compassion-filled beauty was now informed with seriousness. Her mother said, 'Kunda, you did not come with me—have you now seen sorrow?'

Kunda wept.

Then her mother spoke again, 'I told you that I would come once again; so I have come. Now if you have had your fill of earthly happiness, come with me.'

Then Kunda, weeping, said, 'Mother, take me with you. I do not want to stay here any longer.'

Hearing this, her mother was pleased, and said, 'Then come.' With these words the shining one vanished. When she awoke, Kunda remembered her dream, and prayed to the deity, 'This time may my dream bear fruit.'

In the morning Hira entered the room to serve Kunda. She saw that Kunda was weeping.

Since Kamalamani's arrival, Hira had behaved meekly to Kunda. The cause of this was the news that Nagendra was coming. As if in expiation for her ancestors' behaviour, Hira indeed spoke even more sweetly and was even more obedient to Kunda than before. Anyone else would have able to see through this trickery—but Kunda was unusually simple and easily satisfied—so she was not suspicious or displeased at Hira's new agreeableness. Hence Kunda now considered Hira to be as worthy of trust as before. She had never considered her untrustworthy apart from her rough-speaking.

Hira asked, 'Mistress, why are you weeping?'

Kunda said nothing. She looked at Hira. Hira saw that Kunda's eyes were swollen, and her pillow soaked. Hira said, 'What is this? Have you wept all night, then? Why, did the master say something?'

Kunda said, 'Nothing.'

With these words she began to weep again with increased force. Hira saw that something particular had happened. Seeing Kunda's distress, her heart was flooded with joy. Donning a sorrowful expression, she asked, 'Did the master speak to you when he came home? He spoke to the maidser vants.'

Kunda said, 'He said nothing.'

Astonished, Hira, said, 'What is this, mistress! Seeing you after so long! He said nothing at all?'

Kunda said, 'He has not seen me.'

As she said this, Kunda's weeping became unrestrainable. Hira was secretly pleased. Smiling, she said, 'Fie, mistress, what is there to weep at that? How many great sorrows fall on how many people's heads—and you are weeping because of a small delay in seeing him?'

'Great sorrows' of what sort, Kunda could not at all understand. Then Hira said, 'If you had had to bear as much as I have—then you would have committed suicide long since.'

The great, ominous word 'suicide' sounded terribly in Kundanandini's ears. She sat shuddering. In the night she had thought many times of suicide. Hearing that word on Hira's tongue seemed to underline it.

Hira said, 'Then listen while I tell you the story of my sorrows. I, too, once loved someone more than my life. He was not my husband—but what is the point of hiding from you the sin I committed—it is good to confess it clearly.'

Kunda did not hear these shameless words. The word 'suicide' was resounding in her ears. It was as if a spirit was saying in her ears, 'You can commit suicide; which is better, this suffering, or death?'

Hira said, 'He was not my husband; but I loved him more than a hundred thousand husbands. He did not love me. I knew that he did not love me. And he loved another sinner, a hundred times inferior to me.' Saying this, Hira shot one sharp, angry, sidelong look at downcast-eyed Kunda, and then said, 'Knowing this, I did not approach him; but one day we both became foolish.' Beginning thus, Hira gave Kunda a brief account of her own great suffering. She used no names; Devendra's and Kunda's names both remained unspoken. And she said nothing by which Hira's beloved, or that beloved's beloved, could be identified. Everything else she briefly disclosed. Finally, after recounting that she had been kicked, she said, 'What did I do then, do you think?'

Kunda said, 'What did you do?'

Hira, with animated face and hands, went on, 'I went straight to the Chandal physician's house. He has all the poisons which will kill a person as soon as they take them.'

Calmly, mildly, Kunda said, 'And then?'

Hira said, 'I bought the poison in order to kill myself with it, but in the end I thought, "Why should I die for someone else?" Thinking this, I put the poison in a little container and put it away in a box.'

With these words, Hira fetched the box from within her room. Hira kept the box there to hide in it gifts from the master's house, rewards, and things she had stolen.

In that box, Hira had kept the little packet of poison she had bought. Opening the box, Hira showed Kunda the little packet of poison within its small container.

Like a cat greedy for meat, Kunda looked at it. Then Hira, as if absent-mindedly forgetting to lock the box, began to console Kunda. Just then, suddenly, in that morning in Nagendra's house, there rose the auspicious sounds of the conch, and of women ululating. Astonished, Hira ran to see. Ill-fated Kundanandini took that opportunity to steal the packet of poison from its container.

48

Kunda's Prompt Action

WHEN HIRA ARRIVED AND SAW WHAT THE CAUSE OF THE CONCH-SOUND was, she could not at first understand it at all. She saw that the women of the household, and the children, all mingled together, were circling around someone in a large room, and making a great uproar. The person around whom they were clamouring—that was a woman—Hira could only see her hair. Hira saw that Kaushalya and other maidservants had oiled that hair with the finest oil, and were colouring it with hair dye. Among those who were circling her, some were laughing, some weeping, some chattering, some invoking blessings. The children were dancing, singing and clapping their hands. Circling everyone, Kamalamani was blowing the conch, and ululating, and laughing as she wept—and, sometimes, looking this way and that, giving one or two skips.

Watching this, Hira was astonished. Hira craned her neck within the circle, and peered. She was overwhelmed with astonishment at what she saw. She saw that Suryamukhi was sitting on the floor, smiling sweetly and affectionately. Kaushalya and the others were smoothing her rough hair with flower-scented oil: someone was colouring it; someone was cleansing her body with moist body-oil. Someone else was putting on her all her abandoned ornaments. Suryamukhi was speaking sweetly to everyone—but smiling an abashed, somewhat guilty, sweet smile! Tears of affection were falling down her cheeks.

Suryamukhi had died; that she had returned and was again in the house, smiling a sweet smile, Hira could not at once believe, even seeing it. In a muffled voice, Hira asked one of the women of the house, 'Who is that, then?'

The words reached Kaushalya's ears. Kaushalya said, 'Do you not recognize her? The Lakshmi of our house, and for you, Death.' For so long Kaushalya had been like a thief in fear of Hira, today she turned her eyes frankly towards her.

When she was dressed, and had finished speaking with everyone, Suryamukhi said in Kamala's ear, 'Let us come and see Kunda. She has done nothing wrong to me—nor am I angry with her. She is now my younger sister.'

Kamala and Suryamukhi went alone to greet Kunda.

They were there for a long time. At last Kamalamani, with a fear-stricken face, came out of Kunda's room. And in great anxiety she sent for Nagendra. When Nagendra came, summoned by the women, she showed him Kunda's room.

Nagendra entered it. At the door he met Suryamukhi. Suryamukhi was weeping. Nagendra asked, 'What has happened?'

Suryamukhi said, 'Disaster. I have known for a long time that there is not even one day's happiness in my destiny—otherwise why, as soon as I become happy again, would such a disaster happen?'

Afraid, Nagendra asked, 'What has happened?'

Suryamukhi, weeping again, said, 'I brought Kunda up from girlhood; now she is my little sister; I came back longing to cherish her like a sister. That longing has turned to ashes. Kunda has taken poison.'

Nagendra exclaimed, 'What?'

Suryamukhi said, 'Stay with her—I will fetch the doctor.'

With these words Suryamukhi went away. Nagendra went alone to Kundanandini.

When he went in, Nagendra saw that darkness had pervaded Kundanandini's face. Her eyes were lustreless; her body, exhausted, was failing.

49
After So Long, Speech

KUNDANANDINI WAS SITTING ON THE FLOOR, RESTING HER HEAD ON A side-post of the bed—when she saw Nagendra approaching, her eyes overflowed. When Nagendra was standing by her, Kunda fell forward like a creeper from a tree, her head at his feet. In a voice blurred with emotion, Nagendra said, 'What is this, Kunda! For what fault are you leaving me?'

Kunda would never answer her husband—now, at the time of death, she spoke to her husband in a free voice; she said, 'For what fault did you leave me?'

Then Nagendra, having no answer, sat down near Kundanandini with his head bowed. Kunda said again, 'If, when you arrived yesterday, you had once called my name like this—if you had once, yesterday, sat down near me like this—then I would not have died. I had you just for a few days—I have not yet had enough of seeing you. I would not have died.'

At these love-filled, painful words, Nagendra rested his forehead on his knees, and remained silent.

Then Kunda said again—Kunda was now very talkative; she would have no further days in which to speak with her husband—Kunda said, 'Fie! Do not remain silent like that; if I do not see your smiling face as I die—then even in my death there will be no happiness!'

Suryamukhi, too, had spoken in this way; at the time of death, all are equal.

Then Nagendra, wounded to the heart, said in a pained voice, 'Why did you do such a thing? Why did you not once call me?'

Kunda smiled a soft, sweet, heavenly smile, like lightning within a cloud lying in dissolution on the ground, and said, 'Do not think that. I only said what I did out of passion. I had already decided, before you came, that after seeing you I would die. I had decided that if my elder sister should ever return, I would leave you with her and die—but seeing you I do not want to die.'

Nagendra could make no answer. Now he was without answer before Kunda, the girl unskilled in speech.

Kunda was silent for a while. She was losing the power to speak. Death was taking possession of her.

Then Nagendra saw the fullness of love in that death-shadowed face. The smile that he saw then on that afflicted face, like dim lightning, remained engraved on his heart until the end of his days.

Kunda rested for a while longer, and then as if unsatisfied, breathing painfully, spoke again, 'My thirst for speech is not allayed—I thought of you as a god—I never had the courage to open my mouth and speak to you. My longing is not fulfilled—my body is becoming exhausted—my mouth is drying up—my tongue is stiffening—I have no more time.' With these words, Kunda relinquished the support of the bed, lay on the floor, rested her head on Nagendra's body and, closing her eyes, remained silent.

The doctor came. When he had seen and heard what he had to, he offered no medicine—seeing that there was no hope, he went away sorrowfully.

Feeling the time near, Kunda asked to see Suryamukhi and Kamalamani. When they both came, Kunda took the dust of their feet. They both wept aloud.

Then Kundanandini hid her face in her husband's feet. Seeing her silent, they both wept aloud again; but Kunda spoke no more. Gradually losing consciousness, her face still between her husband's feet, in the freshness of youth, Kundanandini relinquished life. Barely opened, the Kunda-blossom withered.

Checking her first tears, Suryamukhi looked towards her co-wife and said, 'Fortunate one! May my fate be as happy as yours. May I die thus with my head on my husband's feet.'

With these words, Suryamukhi took her weeping husband by the hand and led him away. Later, Nagendra took Kunda, who had suffered so much, to the river-bank and, after a cremation in accordance with custom, committed that incomparable heavenly image to the water.

50

Conclusion

AFTER KUNDANANDINI'S DEATH, EVERYONE STARTED TO ASK WHERE Kundanandini had obtained poison. Everyone suspected that this was Hira's doing.

Then, not having seen Hira, Nagendra sent for her. She could not be found. Since Kundanandini's death, Hira had disappeared.

From then on, no one in that region saw Hira. Hira's name was forgotten in Govindapur. Only once, a year later, she showed herself to Devendra.

Devendra's poison tree was then bearing fruit. He had fallen ill with a loathsome disease. On top of that, because of his failure to abstain from wine, the disease had become difficult to treat. Devendra was on his deathbed.

Within a year of Kundanandini's death, Devendra too was at death's door. Several days before his death, he was lying on his sickbed in the house, unable to rise—when there was a great commotion at the gate of the house. Devendra asked, 'What is it?' The servants said, 'A madwoman is asking to see you. She won't accept a refusal.' Devendra ordered, 'Let her come in.'

The madwoman entered the room. Devendra saw that she was a poverty-stricken woman. No particular indication of her madness could be seen—but it was clear that she was a very poor beggar. She was young, and there were still signs of her former beauty. But now she was in a very pitiable state. Her clothing was very dirty, torn in a hundred places, patched in a hundred places, and so meagre that it did not reach below her knees and did not cover her back and head. Her hair was rough, undressed, and grey with dust—even somewhat matted. There was a dry crust of dirt on her oil-less limbs, and mud as well.

The beggar-woman came close to Devendra and gave him a sharp look of such a kind that Devendra could see that what the servants had said was true—this was a madwoman.

The madwoman looked at him for a long time and then said, 'Do you not recognize me? I am Hira.'

Devendra saw that it was indeed Hira. Amazed, he asked, 'Who brought you to this state?'

Hira, with a look blazing with anger, biting her lip, struck Devendra with her clenched fist. Then, becoming calm, she said, 'You ask me—who brought me to this state? It was you who brought me to this state. Now you do not recognize me—but there was a time when you flattered me. Now you do not think of it, but there was a time when in this very room you sat and held this foot (as she said this, Hira placed her foot on the bed) and sang:

Allayer of love's poison, place on my head
your beautiful, lotus-like feet.'

Reminding him thus of so many things, the madwoman went on, 'Since the day you abandoned me, kicked me, and drove me away, I have become mad. I was going to poison myself—but a joyful idea came into my mind—I would not take the poison myself but would give it to you or to your Kunda. In that hope I somehow hid my disease for some days—this illness of mine sometimes surfaces, sometimes goes. When I was demented I would stay at home; when I was well, I did my work. Finally, I relieved my mind's misery by getting Kunda to take the poison; after I saw her die my illness increased. I would no longer be able to hide it—realizing that, I left the region. I no longer had food—who gives food to a madwoman? Since then I have begged—when I am well, I beg; when my illness presses on me I lie down under a tree. Now, hearing that you were near death, I came rejoicing for once to see you. I pray that your place will not be in hell too.'

With these words, the madwoman got up, laughing loudly. Devendra, afraid, moved to the other side of the bed. Then Hira danced out of the room, singing:

Allayer of love's poison, place on my head
your beautiful, lotus-like feet.

From then on, Devendra's deathbed was full of thorns. A little before his death, in the delirium of fever, Devendra said only, 'Beautiful, lotus-like feet', 'Beautiful, lotus-like feet'.

After Devendra's death, for many days the guards heard in the garden at night a woman singing—

Allayer of love's poison, place on my head
your beautiful, lotus-like feet.

I have concluded *The Poison Tree*. I hope that from it, in many households, there will come nectar.

Endnotes

1. A Babu is a respectable person. The term is usually applied to an upper-class bhadralok. It is also used for the higher classes generally—zamindars, lawyers and rich, professional people. A Babu in a village was the zamindar of the village. But the word Babu is also used for English-educated Bengalis, and in this context it can have negative connotations, referring to anglicized Bengalis who had adopted such practices as drinking alcohol. (See Chapter 10.)
2. 'Grants-in-aid' refers to the British education policy in India as enunciated by Sir Charles Wood's Education Despatch of 1854. Under this system, the British government in India encouraged private schools and colleges for English education with substantial grants. Many schools and colleges were established in the seventies of the nineteenth century under this scheme.
3. The Brahmo Samaj was a reformist Hindu sect established by Raja Rammohun Roy (c. 1772–1831) in 1828. One of their magazines, the *Tattvabodhini*, established in the forties of the nineteenth century, propagated social and religious reform in Bengal.
4. According to a traditional Bengali proverb, it is in the nature of thieves and stray animals to enter homes without permission.
5. Panchalis were moral tales from traditional Bengal. In the nineteeenth century, one of the authors and singers of panchalis was Dasharath Roy.
6. Vaishnavis often invoke the name of Radha when they meet, or enter someone's house.
7. Gopal Ure and Nidhu Babu were famous singers of popular (often considered vulgar by the bhadralok) songs in nineteenth-century Kolkata.
8. After a serious devotional song, a khemta, sensual dancing music of nineteenth-century Kolkata, would be considered most inappropriate.

9. Ishvar Chandra Vidyasagar (1820–91) was a nineteenth-century Bengali social reformer and a great Sanskrit scholar. He started a campaign for widow remarriage; he proved through his researches that although custom did not permit it, widow remarriage was allowed by the ancient Hindu shastras. In 1856, he persuaded the government to enact a law to legalize widow remarriage.
10. Bhattacharya Brahmins were mostly priests famous for their Sanskrit scholarship.
11. 'Govinda the Prince' was a drama popular in Kolkata in the early nineteenth century.
12. This is a parody of a Sanskrit hymn invoking the goddess Durga.
13. It was an old custom in rural Bengal for women to establish formal friendships by giving each other pet names. 'Ganga Water' is such a name.
14. *Vidyasundara* is part of an eighteenth-century narrative poem by Bharatchandra, often staged as a drama. It was notorious for its erotic poetry.
15. 'Horses's eggs' means nonsense, a mare's nest.
16. 'Wish-juice' is the English of 'ishti rasa', which is how Hira's grandmother hears the English word 'hysteria'; and she hears 'castor-oil' as 'kestha rasa', which means 'Krishna juice'.

Indira

1
I Am to Go to My Father-in-law's House

I WAS GOING, AT LAST, TO MY FATHER-IN-LAW'S HOUSE. I HAD TURNED nineteen, but I had not yet taken up my position as wife in that house. The reason for this was that my father was rich and my father-in-law was poor. Several days after the wedding, my father-in-law sent people to fetch me, but my father did not let me go. He said, 'Tell her father-in-law that my son-in-law must first learn how to earn some money—then he may take the bride: if he takes her now, will he be able to feed her?' Hearing this, my husband was extremely mortified—he was then twenty years of age, and he resolved that he would himself earn enough to support a family. With this in mind, he travelled to the west. There was then no railway—the way to the west was very difficult. He went on foot, without money, without any attendant, he was long on the way and finally he reached the Punjab. He who could do this could also make money. My husband started to make money—he started to send money home—but for seven or eight years he did not come home or ask for any news of me. I was overcome with anger. How much money did we need? I was very angry with my father and mother—why had they raised the disgraceful issue of earning money? Was money more important than my happiness! There was a lot of money in my father's house—I used to squander it. I used to think, 'One day I will spread out money to lie on, and see if that is happiness?' One day I said to my mother, 'Mother, I will spread out money to sleep on.' My mother said, 'Where has this lunatic come from!' My mother understood. I cannot say what tricks or strategems she employed, but a little before the history I am beginning to narrate, my husband came home. The rumour sprang up that he had returned with untold wealth from working in a commissariat (have I got that word right?).[1] My father-in-law wrote to my father, 'By your blessing, Upendra (my husband's name was Upendra—I have used his name; may older women forgive me, but the present custom permits me to refer to him as 'my Upendra') is competent to support his bride. I have sent a palanquin and bearers; please send the bride to this house. Otherwise, if you permit it, I will arrange another alliance for my son.'

My father saw that here indeed was a newly-risen important man. The interior of the palanquin was covered with brocade; on top were bits of silver; on the handles were silver sharks' heads. The servant women who had come wore silk and had necklaces of thick gold beads. Four black-bearded men from Bhojpur had come with the palanquin.

My father, Haramohan Datta, of an old aristocratic line, laughed and said, 'Mother Indira! I can no longer keep you. Go now, and I will come soon to fetch you.[2] Mind that you don't laugh at the upstart.'

I answered my father's words in my mind. I said, 'I think my spirit has become an upstart; may you understand this, and not laugh.'

My younger sister Kamini understood, I think. She said, 'Didi! When will you come back?' I pinched her cheek.

Kamini said, 'Didi, do you know anything about your father-in-law's house?'

I said, 'I do. It is in a delightful forest; there, the god of Love, with arrows of parijat flowers, makes people's lives complete. As soon as women set foot there they become heavenly nymphs, and men become sheep. There, the kokil always sings, the south wind blows in the winter, and the full moon rises in the new moon's place.'

Kamini laughed and said, 'Oh, go on with you!'

2

I Go to My Father-in-law's House

WITH THIS BLESSING FROM MY SISTER, I SET OUT FOR MY FATHER-IN-LAW'S house. My father-in-law's house was at Manoharpur. My father's house was at Maheshpur. There were twenty miles of road between the two villages; therefore, we set out after the morning meal, and I knew that it would take two or three hours after dark for us to arrive.

On that account, a few tears came to my eyes. I would not be able to see well at night what he was like. And he would not be able to see well at night what I was like. My mother had dressed my hair with great care—twenty miles of travelling would loosen my chignon, my hair would all fall out of place. I would perspire within the palanquin and become ugly. The red tint of paan on my lips would dry from thirst, tiredness would deprive my body of grace. You are laughing? I adjure you not to laugh: I was in the fulness of youth, going for the first time to my father-in-law's house.

On the road, there was a wide lake called the Black Lake. It was nearly a mile across. Its banks were as tall as hills. There was a path through them. On all sides were banyan trees. Their shade was cool, the water of the lake was like blue clouds; the sight was very appealing. Few people came there. There was only one shop on the landing. The village that was nearby was also called Black Lake.

People were afraid to come to this lake alone. For fear of brigands, people preferred to come here only in groups. So people called it 'Brigand Lake'. It was said that the shopkeeper was an ally of the brigands.

I was not afraid of all this. There were many people with me—there were sixteen bearers, four guards, and several other people.

When we reached there, it was midday. The bearers said, 'If we don't have some refreshment, we can't go on.' The guards forbade this—they said, 'This is not a good place.' The bearers answered, 'There are so many of us—why should we be afraid?' The people with me had not eaten anything all this time. Finally, they all agreed with the bearers.

The palanquin was put down on the landing, under a banyan tree. I was enraged. Here I was, obeying my father-in-law, and coming speedily, and here the bearers were, putting down the palanquin, stretching their legs, twirling their dirty napkins and taking the air! But shame! Women are very selfish! I was travelling on others' shoulders; they were bearing me on their shoulders; I was travelling in the flush of youth to see my husband—they were travelling with empty bellies, in pursuit of a handful of rice; was I angry at them for twirling their dirty napkins and taking a little air! Shame, O youth!

Thinking this over, I became aware after a while that my people had left the palanquin. Then, taking courage, I opened the door a little and looked at the lake. I saw that the bearers were all sitting in front of the shop, under a banyan tree, eating. That spot was about half an acre away from me. I saw that in front of me, like a dense cloud, the lake was spread out; on all sides, as high as a line of hills, yet with a beautiful covering of soft, deep green grass, were its banks. On the stretch of earth between the banks and the water were rows of tall banyan trees; many young heifers were grazing on the banks; water-birds were disporting themselves on the water; the gentle waves from a gentle wind were breaking like crystal; sometimes the water-moss and the leaves and flowers of the water-plants swayed with the knock of the small waves. I could see that the guards had descended to the water and were bathing—white strings of pearls were scattered over the water from the beating of their limbs.

I looked at the sky—what beautiful blueness! How beautiful was the diversity of forms that the layers of white clouds made against each other—how graceful against the sky were the small, soaring birds, like a collection of dark dots scattered amongst the blueness! It came into my mind to wonder, was there not some knowledge whereby a human being could become a bird? If I could have become a bird, I would instantly have flown up to reach the ever-desired place!

Again I looked towards the lake—and now I became a little nervous. I saw that alongwith the bearers, all the other people accompnaying me had gone down to bathe as well. The two women with me—one from my father-in-law's house, one from my father's—were both in the water. A little fear came into my mind: no one was near me, the place was evil; this was not good. What was I to do; I was a girl from a respectable family: I could not put out my head to call someone.

At this point, I thought I heard a sound from the other side of the palanquin. It was as if something heavy had fallen from a branch of the banyan tree above. I opened the door panel on that side a little and looked. I saw that it was a black, monstrously-shaped man! In fear I closed the door; but then I realized that it would be better to leave the door open—but before I could open the door again, another man jumped down from the tree. As I watched, another, and another! In this way, four men almost simultaneously jumped down from the tree and lifted the palanquin to their shoulders. Then they ran off with it, panting.

I could see my guards running from the water, raising an outcry.

Then I realized that I had fallen into the hands of brigands. Then what was the use of modesty? I opened the doors of the palanquin. I wondered whether I could escape by jumping, but I saw that all the people with me were running after the palanquin, making a great uproar. That raised my hopes. But these hopes were quickly dashed. A great number of brigands jumped down from the nearby trees and showed themselves. I have said that there were rows of banyan trees beside the water. The brigands were taking the palanquin through those trees. Men leaped down from all those trees. Some had bamboo clubs in their hands, some had branches of trees.

Seeing so many men, the people with me fell back. Then, bereft of hope, I determined to jump. But the palanquin was being carried along at such a speed that leaping from it was likely to give a severe jolt. Moreover, a brigand, showing me a club, told me, 'If you jump I'll break your head.' Therefore, I desisted.

I saw that one of the guards, in the lead, had reached and seized the palanquin; then one of the brigands struck him off with a club. He fell unconscious to the ground. I did not see him get up again. Perhaps he never did get up again.

Seeing this, the remaining guards gave up. Those carrying me took me away without hindrance. They carried me thus until dusk, and then finally put the palanquin down. I saw that the place where they had put it down was dense forest—and dark. The brigands lit a torch. Then they said to me, 'Give us everything you've got, or we'll kill you.' I gave them my ornaments and other things—and I took off the ornaments on my limbs and gave them away too. I only left the bangles on my arm—but they snatched those from me as well. They gave me a torn, dirty piece of cloth; putting that on, I removed my costly garments and handed these over. Having taken everything I had, the brigands broke up the palanquin and took off the silver. Finally, they lit a fire and burnt the broken-up palanquin, and hid all signs of brigandry.

Then they too went away, and seeing that they were leaving me in that deep forest, in the dark night, to the mercy of the wild animals, I started to weep. I said, 'I fall at your feet, take me with you.' I had become desirous of even the brigands' company.

An old brigand said, in a sympathetic manner, 'Child, how can we take such a beautiful girl with us? It would instantly proclaim us as brigands—people would instantly seize us.'

A young brigand said, 'Never mind if I go to jail for taking her, I can't let her go.' I cannot write what else he said—and now I cannot even bring it to mind. The old brigand was the leader of that group. He shook his club at the young one and said, 'I will leave you here with this club in your broken head. Are we capable of such sin?' Then they went away.

3
The Pleasure of Travelling to My Father-in-law's House

HAS SUCH A THING EVER HAPPENED? HAS ANYONE EVER SUFFERED SUCH danger, such misery? There I had been, going to see my husband for the first time—wearing jewelled ornaments on every limb, hair bound up with so much longing, pure lips reddened with paan prepared with longing, virginal body made delightful with fragrances, nineteen years old, going to see my husband for the first time, thinking as I went of what I would say as I offered this priceless jewel at his feet; and suddenly into this, what a thunderbolt! They snatched all my ornaments away—so be it; made me wear a torn, dirty, ill-smelling cloth—so be it; left me to the mercy of tigers and bears—so be it; I was dying of hunger and thirst—let it be so—I no longer wanted life: if life left me now, that would be good; but if life did not leave me, if I lived, then where would I go? And I had not seen him—I supposed that I would not see my father and mother again, either! I could not weep enough.

So I decided not to weep. My tears did not cease in the least, but I was making an effort—when, from some distance, came a loud roar. I thought, a tiger. A little joy came to my mind. If a tiger ate me, all suffering would come to an end. It would break my bones and drink up my blood; I thought that I would endure this; it was only physical pain. To be able to die was the greatest happiness. So I stopped weeping, became a little cheerful, and remained still, waiting for the tiger. Every time the leaves rustled, I thought, that's the sorrow-destroying, spirit-soothing tiger coming. But much of the night passed and still the tiger did not come. I was crestfallen. Then it occurred to me that where there were jungle thickets, there could be snakes. In the hope of setting my foot on a snake's neck, I went into the thickets and wandered around in them for some time. Alas! Seeing a person, they all fled—within the forest I heard many rustling, hissing and tapping sounds, but my feet did not fall on any snake; many thorns pierced my feet, many nettles stung them; but woe! snakes did not like them! Crestfallen, I turned back again; I had grown weary from hunger and thirst—I could no longer wander around. Seeing a clear spot, I sat down. Suddenly, a bear appeared in front of me—I thought I would die at the hands of a bear. I called out to the bear and prepared to die. But alas! The bear ignored me. She went and climbed up a tree. From the tree, after a while, came the buzzing sounds of a thousand bees. I realized that there was a beehive in that tree and the bear knew this; she had renounced me in her desire to steal honey.

At the end of the night a little sleep came—as I sat leaning against a tree, I fell asleep.

4

Now Where Do I Go?

WHEN I WOKE UP, THE CROW AND THE KOKIL WERE CALLING—RAYS OF sunlight were coming through the bamboo leaves and dressing the earth with jewels and pearls. In the light I saw first that there was nothing on my arms; the brigands, snatching all the ornaments from my arms, had dressed me as a widow. There was a bit of iron on my left arm—but nothing on my right. Weeping, I tore off a bit of creeper and bound it round my arm.[3]

Then, looking around in all directions, I saw that near to where I was sitting, many of the trees' branches had been cut; some trees had been cut down completely, with only the roots remaining. I thought, woodcutters must come here. Then there must be a path to a village. Seeing the light of day, I once again felt the desire to live—hope dawned again—I was no more than nineteen! Looking around, I found the very faint line of a path. I followed it. As I went, the line of the path became distinct. I began to hope I would reach a village.

Then another difficulty occurred to me—I could not go into a village. The torn, worn-out bit of cloth which the brigands had given me and forced me to wear covered me only from my waist to my knees—my breast was uncovered. How could I show myself, brazen-faced, amongst people? I could not go—I would have to die where I was. This is what I decided.

But seeing the earth glowing in the sun's rays, the flowers swaying on the creepers, I felt my desire to live strengthen again. Then I tore some leaves from the trees, threaded them together on strips of bark and tied them round my waist and neck. Modesty of a sort: but I looked like a madwoman. Then I went along the path. After a while, I heard the mooing of cows. I realized that the village was near.

But I could go no further. I had never been accustomed to walking. On top of that was my wakeful night, with its unbearable mental and physical suffering, and hunger and thirst. I lay down exhausted under a tree beside the path. I had no sooner lain down than sleep overcame me.

As I slept, I dreamed that I had gone to my father-in-law's house up above the clouds, in the place of the gods. It seemed that the god of Love himself was my husband, and his consort was my co-wife—I was quarrelling with him over a parijat flower. At this point, someone's touch woke me up. I saw that a young man, who looked to be of some low caste, such as a coolie or labourer, was pulling at my arm. By good fortune, a piece of wood had fallen nearby. I picked it up, swung it round, and hit the sinner on the head. I do not know where I got the strength; the man clapped his hands to his head and ran away breathlessly.

I did not throw away the piece of wood; I went ahead, leaning against it. After walking a long way, I met an old woman. She was driving a cow along.

I asked her, where was Maheshpur? Or, where was Manoharpur? The old woman said, 'Mother, who are you? Is such a beautiful girl wandering alone on path and landing? Oh, my life, what a beautiful body! Come to my house.'[4] I went to her house. Seeing that I was suffering from hunger, she milked the cow and gave me some milk to drink. She knew Maheshpur.

I told her, 'I will see that you get some money if you take me there.' To that she said, 'How can I go and leave my house and family?' Then I set out on the path she showed me. I walked until evening—I became extremely tired. I asked someone on the road, 'How far is Maheshpur from here?' He looked at me stupefied. After much thought he said, 'Where have you come from?' I told him the name of the village where the old woman had shown me the path. At that, the traveller said, 'You have mistaken the way; you have been going in the wrong direction all the time. Maheshpur is a day's walk from here.'

My head spun. I asked him, 'Where are you going?' He said, 'I am going to the village of Gouri, which is close by.' Having no choice, I followed him.

When we came into the village, he asked me, 'Whose house are you going to?'

I said, 'I do not know anyone here. I will lie down under a tree.'

The traveller said, 'What is your caste?'

I said, 'I am a Kayastha.'

He said, 'I am a Brahmin. Come with me. Your garment is dirty and worn out indeed, but you are the daughter of an important house. Such beauty is not found in low-class houses.'

Ashy beauty! Hearing this 'beauty, beauty', I became vexed, but this Brahmin was old; I went with him.

For the next two days, I rested in the Brahmin's house. This kindly old Brahmin was a priest. Seeing the condition of my clothes, he was astonished and asked, 'Mother, why are your clothes in such a state? Did someone take away your clothes?' I said, 'Yes, sir.' He obtained many clothes from the people whose priest he was—he gave me two saris with narrow red borders. There were conch shell bracelets in his house, too; I took these, also, and wore them.[5]

I did all this with great difficulty. My body was exhausted. The Brahmin's wife gave me some rice—I ate. She gave me a mat; I spread it out and lay down. But even with so much trouble taken, I did not sleep. I could only think of how I was ruined for life—that it would be better if I was dead. I could not sleep.

At dawn I slept a little. Again, I dreamed. I saw in front of me the dark-filled form of Death, smiling and showing his great rows of teeth. I slept no more. When I got up the next morning, I found that my body hurt. My feet were swollen, and I did not have the strength to sit up.

For as long as I needed to recover physically, I stayed perforce in the Brahmin's house. The Brahmin and his wife took great care of me. But I saw no way of returning to Maheshpur. Some of the women did not know the way; or would not agree to go. Many of the men offered—but I was afraid to go with them alone. The Brahmin too, forbade it. He said, 'They are not of good character: do not go with them. It is not clear what their intentions are. I cannot let a child of gentlefolk, as beautiful as you, go with them anywhere.' So I desisted.

One day, I heard that a gentleman by the name of Krishnadas Basu was going with his family to Calcutta. When I heard this, I thought that here was a good opportunity. It was true that both my father's house and my father-in-law's house were a long way from Calcutta, but my father's brother lived there, for his business. I thought that if I went to Calcutta I could certainly find my uncle. He could certainly arrange for me to go back to my father's place. Or if not, he could send word to my father.

I told this to the Brahmin. The Brahmin said, 'You have judged well. Krishnadas Babu is one of my people. I will tell him to take you with him. He is old, and he is a very good man.'

The Brahmin took me to Krishnadas Babu. The Brahmin said, 'This is a daughter of gentlefolk, who has fallen into danger, lost her way, and come to these parts. If you take her with you to Calcutta, this helpless one will be able to return to her father's house.' Krishnadas Babu agreed. I went into his inner chambers. On the following day, with the women of his family—even though I was not well received by his family—I set out for Calcutta. On the first day, after walking for nine or ten miles, we reached the bank of the Ganga. The next day we boarded a boat.

5
'We Will Make Our Anklets Sound as We Go'

I HAD NEVER SEEN THE GANGA. NOW, SEEING THE GANGA, MY SPIRIT WAS filled with joy. For the moment, all my sorrows were forgotten. The peaceful heart of the Ganga! On it were small waves: the sunlight sparkled on them. As far as the eye could see, the water ran, gleaming; on the banks, like arbours, were endless lines of well laid out trees; on the water were so many boats of so many kinds; there were the sounds of oars on the water, the sounds of the oarsmen and the boatmen, noise and bustle on the water, noise and bustle on the landings on the banks; so many kinds of people were bathing in so many ways. Again, in places there were endless stretches of sandy beach, like white clouds: on these, so many kinds of birds were making so much noise. The Ganga was truly full of virtue. For some days I watched her with insatiate eyes.

The day before we reached Calcutta, there was high tide a little before evening. The boat had stopped. It had been moored near the stone-built landing of an upper-class village. I saw so many beautiful things; I saw the fishermen with nets, like spiders, in dinghies, catching fish. I saw pandits, sitting on the terraces beside the landing's steps, discussing the shastras. So many beautiful women, with ornaments in their hair, came to fetch water. Some threw water, some filled pitchers, some emptied them out again, filled them again, laughed and told stories, again threw out the water, again filled their pitchers. As I watched, an old song of mine came to mind,

I take the pitcher on one hip. I fill it with water,
Within the water is the dark prince!
Making waves with the pitcher, I no longer see anyone,
Krishna is hidden again in the water.[6]

That day I saw two little girls there whom I will never forget. They were seven and eight years old. They were pleasant to look at, though not really beautiful. But they were well-dressed. There were earrings in their ears, and an ornament each on their arms and neck. Their hair was adorned with flowrs. Each wore a shiuli-flower-dyed orange sari with a black border. There were sets of four anklets on their legs. Each had a little pitcher on her hip. When it was time to come down to the landing's terrace, they came down singing a song of the high-tide's water. I remember the song: I thought it was very sweet, so I have written it here. One of them sang one verse, the other sang the next. I learned that their names were Amala and Nirmala. They sang:

Amala:
In the fields of rice waves have risen
the water has reached the bamboo grove
Come, my friend, let us fetch water,
let us go and fetch water.

Nirmala:
Spreading over the landing, surrounding the trees
masses of flowers have opened.
Come, my friend, let us fetch water,
let us go and fetch water.

Amala:
In pleasant clothes smiling sidelong,
we will laugh gently.
Carrying our pitchers, we will with pride
make our anklets sound as we go.
Come, my friend, let us fetch water,
let us go and fetch water.

Nirmala:
With ornaments on our bodies, lac-dye on our feet

and saris with embroidered borders,
With gentle movement we will in rhythm
make our anklets sound as we go.
Come, my friend, let us fetch water,
Let us go and fetch water.

Amala:
All the boys leave their games
and come back in groups.
The old women, the grim old women,
will carry so much water,
We will smile sidelong, in our pleasant clothes
and make our anklets sound as we go,
We will make our anklets sound as we go,
Friend, make our anklets sound as we go.

Both:
Come my friend, let us fetch water,
let us go and fetch water.

This life is somewhat soothed when it is steeped in the essence of girlhood. I was listening intently to this song when I saw that Basu Babu's wife was asking me, 'Why are you listening again with gaping mouth to that trashy song?' I said, 'What is the harm in it?'

Basu Babu's wife said, 'These girls are shameless, aren't they? A song about making anklets sound!'

I said, 'It is true that these words would not sound well in the mouths of sixteen-year-old girls, but they sound well in the mouths of seven-year-olds. Cuffs and slaps from the hands of stout young men are not good, it is true, but cuffs and slaps from the hands of a three-year-old boy are very sweet.'

Basu Babu's wife said nothing more, but sat there morosely. I started to think. I thought, 'Why is there this difference? Why does the same thing appear in two different lights? Why is the gift to the poor which is accounted as virtue, considered to be flattery if it is given to the great man? Why does truth, the primary virtue, become according to circumstances the sin of self-praise or of slander of others? Why is forgiveness, which is a prime virtue, a great sin if it is directed towards a criminal? People do indeed call someone who leaves a woman in the forest a great sinner, but Ramachandra left Sita in the forest. Why does no one call him a great sinner?'

I decided that all this happens because of differences in circumstances. This idea stayed in my mind. After this, I would remember it before I spoke, ever, of shameless deeds. So I have written down this song here.

When I saw Calcutta from a distance as the boat approached it, I was amazed and frightened. Building after building, mansion on top of mansion, mansion behind mansion, and behind them, mansions, a sea of buildings—endless, countless, limitless. At the sight of the forest of ships' masts, my faculties were thrown into confusion. Seeing the countless, endless lines of boats, I thought, 'How can men have built so many boats?'[7] As we came closer, I saw that carriages and palanquins were moving like lines of ants along the main roads on the banks—there are no words for the number of people who were on foot. Then I thought, 'How can I search out my uncle from within this? How can I search out one particular grain of sand from among the piles of sand on the river's beaches?'

6
Subo

KRISHNADAS BABU HAD COME TO CALCUTTA TO WORSHIP AT KALIGHAT. HE lived in Bhowanipore. He asked me, 'Where is your uncle's house? In Calcutta or in Bhowanipore?'

I did not know.

He asked me, 'In what part of Calcutta does he live?'

I knew nothing of this—I had thought that Calcutta was simply a small village, as Maheshpur was. People would direct you if you merely asked for a gentleman by name. Now I saw that Calcutta was like a sea of endless buildings. I saw no way of searching for my uncle. Krishnadas Babu searched extensively on my behalf but what could a search for a man from an ordinary village achieve?

Krishnadas Babu planned to go to Kashi after Kali Puja. He offered his worship, and was preparing to go to Kashi with his family. I wept. His wife said, 'Listen to me. Take up service now in someone's house. It is said that Subo is coming today; I will tell her to employ you as a servant.'

Hearing this, I threw myself to the ground and wept aloud—'Am I finally fated to become a servant!' I bit my lips till they bled. Krishnadas Babu was, no doubt, compassionate, but he said, 'What can I do?' This was true: what could he do? It was my fate!

I went away to a room and fell in a corner and wept. A little before evening, Krishnadas Babu's wife called me. I came out and went to her. She said, 'This is Subo. If you are willing, tell her that you will work as a maid in her house.'

If I did not become a maid I would starve to death. I had realized that; but now I did not think of it—now I took one look at Subo. When I had heard the name 'Subo' I had thought it was a question of some 'Sahib Subo'[8]—I was a country girl then. I saw that this was not so: it was a woman—and a sight to see. I had not seen such a good thing for a long time. She would have been of my own age. Nor was she any fairer in complexion than I. Her dress and ornaments were not so much, she wore some earrings, bangles, a necklace, and a black-bordered sari. That in itself was a sight to see. And I had never seen such a face. It was as if a lotus had blossomed—and all around it, curling hair like the raised heads of snakes surrounded the lotus. Huge great eyes—sometimes steady, sometimes laughing. Her two lips were turned up like the petals of a delicately coloured reddish flower, her face was small, just like an opened flower. What her general form was like I could not grasp. As the slender branches of a mango tree play in the wind, so all her limbs played—as waves play in the river, so was there play in her body—I could not perceive anything, it was as if something spread over her face bewitched me. The reader will not need to be reminded that I was not a man, but a woman—I myself had some pride of beauty. Subo had a three-year-old boy: he too was just such a half-opened flower. Getting up, falling, sitting, playing, swinging, dancing, laughing, prattling, hitting, he was cajoling everyone.

I had been looking at Subo and her son unthinkingly; and Krishnadas Babu's wife became irritated and said, 'Answer the question, then—what do you think?'

I asked, 'Who is she?'

The mistress said, reprovingly, 'What can be said to that? She is Subo, who else?'

Then Subo laughed a little and said, 'Oh, Aunt, surely something can be said? She is a stranger; she does not know me.' Saying this, Subo looked towards my face and said, 'My name is Subhashini—she is my aunt; they have called me Subo since I was a child.'

After that, the mistress took the thread of the conversation into her own hands. She said, 'She is married to the son of Ramram Datta of Calcutta. They are important people. She has lived in her father-in-law's house since she was a child—I never get to see her. Hearing that we had come to Kalighat, she came to let me see her for once. They are important people. Can you work in the house of important people, then?'

I was the daughter of Haramohan Datta, I had wanted to sleep on a pile of money—could I work in the house of important people, then? Tears came to my eyes and a smile to my lips, at the same time.

No one else saw this—but Subhashini did. She said to the mistress, 'Let me speak with her a little in private. If she agrees, then we will take her with us.' With these words, Subhashini took my hand and drew me into a room. No one was there. Only the little boy came running after his mother. A plain cot was there. Subhashini sat down on it—drawing me by the hand, she made me sit, too. She said, 'I have told you my name without being asked. What is your name, sister?'

'Sister!' I thought that if I could at all do the work of a maidservant, I could do it for her, and answered, 'I have two names—one is generally used, one not. I have told them the one not generally used, so I will tell you that one, for now. My name is Kumudini.'

The little boy said, 'Kunutini.'

Subhashini said, 'Without hearing your other name now, is your caste really Kayastha?'

I laughed and said, 'We are Kayasthas.'

Subhashini said, 'I will not ask you now whose daughter you are, whose wife, or where your home is. Now, listen to what I say. You are the daughter of an important man, I can see that—there are still the marks of ornaments on your arms and neck. I will not tell you to do the work of a maidservant—you know something of cooking, don't you?'

I smiled. 'I do. I was particularly renowned for my cooking, in my father's house.'

Subhashini said, 'In our house, we are all cooks.' (The little boy said, innocently, 'Muvver and I cook.') 'But following the custom of Calcutta, we have employed a cook. That woman is about to visit her home.' (The little boy said, 'Bisit hobe.') 'Now I will tell Mother that I will keep you in her place. You do not have to cook like a cook. We will all cook, and you will cook for one or two days a week. Don't you think that's best?'

The little boy said, 'Guest! She guest?'

His mother said, 'You are a pest!'

The little boy said, 'I Babu. Favver is pest.'

'Don't talk like that, child!' Having said this to the child, Subhashini looked towards me, laughing, and said, 'He talks all the time.' I said, 'I agree to work even as a maidservant for you.'

'Why do you speak so formally to me, sister? If you must speak like that, speak like that to Mother. There is a little difficulty with Mother. She is a bit peevish—she will have to be managed. You will be able to do that—I know people. Do you agree?'

I said, 'If I don't agree, what will I do? I have no other recourse.' Tears again came to my eyes.

She said, 'Why have you no recourse? Wait here, sister, I have forgotten the main thing. I will come back.'

Subhashini darted away to her aunt. She said, 'Well, now, who is she to you?'

I could hear this much. I could not hear what her aunt said. Probably she told the little she knew. It is unnecessary to say that she knew nothing; only as much as she had heard from the priest. This time the little boy had not gone with his mother—he was playing with my hands. I talked to him. Subhashini returned.

The little boy said, 'Muvver, see pretty hands.'

Subhashini laughed and said, 'I have seen them long since!' To me, she said, 'Come, the carriage is ready. If you don't come, I'll take you! But remember what I said—Mother will have to be managed.'

Subhashini drew me with her into the carriage. I was wearing one of the red-bordered saris the priest had given me—the other was drying on the line—there was no time to take it with me. In its place I took Subhashini's son on my lap and kissed him as we went along.

7
A Bottle of Ink

'MOTHER' WAS SUBHASHINI'S MOTHER-IN-LAW. SHE HAD TO BE MANAGED—so as soon as we arrived I paid my respects to her and took the dust of her feet; and then, in one glance, I saw what kind of a person she was. She was on the roof, in the darkness, lying on a mat with her head on a bolster, with a maid massaging her feet. It seemed to me that she was like a tall ink bottle, filled to the brim with ink, which had tilted and fallen on the bolster. Her grey hair was like the bottle's beautiful tin lid.[9] The darkness increased.

Seeing me, the mistress asked her daughter-in-law, 'Who is this?'

Her daughter-in-law said, 'You were looking for a cook, so I have brought her for you.'

The mistress said, 'Where did you find her?'

Subhashini said, 'My aunt brought her.'

The mistress said, 'Brahmin or Kayastha?'

Subhashini said, 'Kayastha.'

The mistress said, 'Ah! Your aunt is unlucky! What can I do with a Kayastha girl? If we have to feed a Brahmin one day, what will we do?'

Subhashini said, 'We don't have to feed Brahmins every day—never mind about those few days—and then, if we get a Brahmin girl we will have to keep her—Brahmin girls are very fastidious—if we go into their kitchen they throw away all the utensils—and come again to give offerings of food! Why—are we of low caste?'

Silently, I praised Subhashini—I saw that she knew how to bring the tall bottle of ink into the palm of her hand. The mistress said, 'That is true, indeed—such self-conceit on the part of unimportant people is not to be borne. Let us keep the Kayastha girl for a few days, and see. What wage does she want?'

Subhashini said, 'She hasn't said anything about that to me.'

The mistress said, 'Ah me, you girl of this degenerate age! You bring me a person to keep, and have said nothing about her wages?'

The mistress asked me, 'What will you accept?'

I said, 'Since I have come to take refuge with you, I will accept what you give.'

The mistress said, 'We would have to pay more for a Brahmin girl, it is true, but you are a Kayastha girl—I will give you three rupees a month, and your food and clothing.'

It was enough that I should have found a refuge—so I agreed. It is unnecessary to say that my spirit wept at hearing that I was to accept monthly wages. I said, 'I accept.'

I thought that the fuss was now finished—but this was not so. There was a lot of ink in the tall bottle. She said, 'How old are you, then? It is too dark to see how old you are—but your voice sounds like that of a child.'

I said, 'I am between nineteen and twenty.'

The mistress said, 'Then, child, go and look for work somewhere else. I do not keep young people.'

Subhashini said, innocently, 'Why, Mother, cannot young people work?'

The mistress said, 'Stupid girl, daughter of a madwoman! Are young people any good?'

Subhashini said, 'What is this, Mother! Are all young people in the country bad?'

Now I could not restrain myself. Weeping, I got up and went away. The bottle of ink asked her son's wife, 'The wench has gone away, has she?'

Subhashini said, 'It seems so.'

The mistress said, 'Let her go, then.'

Subhashini said, 'But should she go from our house without eating? I will give her something to eat before sending her away.'[10]

With these words, Subhashini got up and came after me. She seized me and took me to her own bedroom. I said, 'Why do you still hold me back? Neither hunger nor desire for life will permit me to listen to such words.'

Subhashini said, 'It's not a matter of staying. But for my sake, stay tonight.'

Where could I go? So I wiped my eyes and agreed to stay for that night. After speaking of this and that, Subhashini asked, 'If you don't stay here, where will you go?'

I said, 'To the Ganga.'[11]

Now Subhashini, too, wiped her eyes a little. She said, 'You mustn't go to the Ganga; wait a little and see what I can do. Don't make a fuss—listen to me.'

With these words, Subhashini sent for a maid called Haramani. Haramani was Subhashini's special maid. Haramani came. She was sturdy, of a shining dark complexion, more than forty years old; her face could not contain her laughter, all of her laughed. She was inclined to be restless.

Subhashini said, 'Send for him to come.'

Haramani said, 'Will he come now, at this unlikely time? How will I send for him?'

Subhashini frowned and said, 'However you can—go and call him.'

Haramani went away, laughing. I asked Subhashini, 'Call whom? Your husband?'

Subhashini said, 'Would I call the neighbourhood grocer here tonight?'

I said, 'I asked because I wanted to know whether I should go away.'

Subhashini said, 'No. Stay here.'

Subhashini's husband came. He was a very handsome man. As soon as he arrived, he said, 'Why am I here?' Then he saw me and said, 'Who is this?'

Subhashini said, 'I called you because of her. Our cook is going home, so I have brought her from my aunt's place to keep her here. But Mother doesn't want to keep her.'

Her husband said, 'Why doesn't she want to?'

Subhashini said, 'Because she's young.'

Subhashini's husband smiled a little. He said, 'So what must I do?'

Subhashini said, 'You must keep her.'

Her husband asked, 'Why?'

Subhashini went closer to him and said in a low voice so that I should not hear, 'Because it's my command.'

But I did hear. Her husband, speaking in the same way, said, 'Yes, mistress.'

Subhashini said, 'When can you do it?'

Her husband said, 'At mealtime.'

When he had gone, I said, 'He may arrange for me to be kept, but how can I bear such harsh words?'

Subhashini said, 'We'll consider that later. The Ganga is not going to dry up in one day.'

At nine o'clock in the evening, Subhashini's husband (his name was Raman Babu) came for his meal. He sat down near his mother. Subhashini drew me with her and said, 'Come and watch what happens.'

From concealment we watched; various dishes were presented, but Raman Babu, having tasted a little, left everything else. He ate nothing. His mother asked, 'You are eating nothing, son!'

Her son said, 'Not even ghosts and ghouls could eat this food. If I go on eating this Brahmin cook's food, I will die from loss of appetite. I think that from tomorrow I will go and eat at my aunt's house.'

Then the mistress shrank. She said, 'Don't do that, darling! I will get another cook.'

The Babu washed his hands, and got up and went away. Seeing all this, Subhashini said, 'For our sakes, sister, he has eaten nothing. That won't do—we must fix that.'

While I, embarrassed, was wondering what to say, Haramani came and said to Subhashini, 'Your mother-in-law wants you.' Saying this, she looked towards me and laughed a little, without cause. I understood that laughing was a habit with her. Subhashini went to her mother-in-law, and I listened from concealment.

Subhashini's mother-in-law said, 'Has that Kayastha wench gone away?'

Subhashini said, 'No; she still hasn't eaten, so I haven't sent her away.'

The mistress said, 'How well does she cook?'

Subhashini said, 'I don't know.'

The mistress said, 'Don't let her go away yet. Tomorrow we will try one or two of her dishes.'

Subhashini said, 'Then we will keep her.'

With these words, Subhashini came to me and asked, 'Sister, you do know how to cook, then?'

I said, 'I do.'

Subhashini asked, 'But can you cook well?'

I said, 'You will be able to tell that tomorrow.'

Subhashini said, 'If you are out of practice, tell me, and I will sit with you and teach you.'

I laughed. I said, 'We'll consider that later.'

8
The Pandavas' Queen[12]

THE NEXT DAY, I COOKED. SUBHASHINI CAME TO HELP; AT THAT POINT I chose to fry some chillies—she got up, coughing, and went away, saying, 'Oh help!'

When I had finished, the children ate first. Subhashini's son did not eat much, but Subhashini had a five-year-old daughter. Subhashini asked her, 'How is the cooking, Hema?'

She said, 'Good! Good, oh, good!' The little girl loved to recite poetry, and she said again, 'Good, oh, good,

Good cooking, bound hair,
garland of bakul flowers.
Red sari, pot in hand
the cowherd's daughter cooks.
At this point, the flute sounds,
under the kadamba tree.
Making the boys weep, abandoning her cooking,
the cook comes to the water.'[13]

Her mother reprimanded her, 'Stop that poetry.' The little girl feel silent.

After that, Raman Babu sat down to eat. We watched from concealment. We saw that he took helpings of everything and ate them all. The mistress's face could not contain her smiles. Raman Babu asked, 'Who did the cooking today, Mother?'

The mistress said, 'A new person has come.'

Raman Babu said, 'She cooks well.' With these words he washed his hands, got up and went away.

After that, the master sat down to eat. I could not go there—following the mistress's orders, the old Brahmin cook took the master his rice. Then

I thought I knew the mistress's area of concern, and why she would not keep a young woman. I vowed that as long as I was there, I would not intrude in that direction.

Later, I heard people talk of the master's character. Everyone knew that he was very much a gentleman—and the master of his senses. But the bottle of ink was filled to the brim with ink.

When the Brahmin cook returned, I asked her, 'What did the master say when he tasted the cooking?'

The Brahmin cook went red with anger; she shouted, 'Oh, now, you cooked well, you cooked well. We, too, know how to cook; but once we're old, what are we worth! Now youth and beauty are needed to cook.'

I understood that the master had spoken well of the cooking. But I felt like making a little fun of the Brahmin cook. I said, 'Of course youth and beauty are needed, sister Brahmin! At the sight of an old woman, who feels like eating?'

In a very harsh voice, showing her teeth, the Brahmin cook said, 'Do you think your youth and beauty will last? That your face won't decay?'

With these words, her anger at its height, the lady cook struck a pot with her hand so that it fell and broke. I said, 'See there, sister! Without youth and beauty, pots break in the hand.'[14]

Then the Brahmin cook, in a murderous state, took up the tongs and came charging to hit me. Because of her age, she was a little hard of hearing, and probably had not heard all I said. She made some very ugly retorts. My anger rose, too. I said, 'Sister, stop. The tongs had better stay in your hand.'

At this point, Subhashini came into the room. In her anger, the Brahmin cook did not see her. Chasing me again, she said, 'Pig! Say what you want! The tongs won't stay in my hand—will you put them at my feet? I am mad!'

Then Subhashini frowned and said to her, 'Who are you to call a person I have brought, a pig? Go away from my house.'

Then the cook hurriedly threw down the tongs and said, weeping, 'Oh, Mother, what words are those! When did I say "pig"? I have never uttered such a word. You astonish me, Mother!'

At these words, Subhashini started to giggle. Then the Brahmin cook stopped screaming and started to weep—she said, 'If I have said "pig", then I am ruined—'

(I said, 'God forbid! May Goddess Shashti protect you!')[15]

'I might as well die—'

(I said, 'What is this, sister; so soon! Fie, sister! Stay a couple of days yet.')

'There won't even be a place for me in the nether world—'

This time I said, 'Do not say that, sister! What is hell, if they don't eat your cooking there?'

The old woman, weeping, went to Subhashini and complained, 'She says what she wants to me, and will you say nothing? I am going to the mistress.'

Subhashini said, 'Well, in that case I will have to tell her that you called this person a pig.'

Then the old woman protested vociferously: 'When did I say "pig"—When did I say "pig"!!—When did I say "pig"!!!'

Then we started to console the old woman. First, I said, 'Yes, young mistress—when did you hear her say "pig"? When did she say this? I did not hear it.'

Then the old woman said, 'You hear that, young mistress! Could such a word come out of my mouth!'

Subhashini said, 'That must be so—I must have heard someone outside abusing someone else. Is the Brahmin cook such a person! Did you taste her cooking yesterday? No one else in Calcutta can cook like that.'

The Brahmin cook looked at me and said, 'Do you hear that?'

I said, 'Everyone says that. I have never tasted such cooking.'

The old woman laughed heartily and said, 'Of course you say that, Mother! Since you are daughters of good people, you know cooking. Aha! Can I rebuke such girls—girls of such a great house. Don't think that, sister; I will teach you how to cook and serve, before I go.'

So a compromise was reached with the old woman. For many days I had done nothing but weep. Now, after such a long time, I had laughed.

That laughter and fun was as sweet to me as riches to the poor. That is why I have written out the old woman's words in such detail. I will not forget that laughter in this lifetime. I will never again receive such happiness from laughing.

After that, the mistress sat down to her food. While she sat, I served her dishes with care. The woman consumed a lot. Finally, she said, 'This cooking is good! Where did you learn to cook?'

I said, 'In my father's house.'

The mistress said, 'Where is your father's house, then?'

I said something untrue. The mistress said, 'This is like the cooking from an important man's house. Was your father an important man?'

I said, 'He was.'

The mistress said, 'So why have you come here to cook?'

I said, 'I have fallen on hard times.'

The mistress said, 'Then stay with me, and you will be all right. You are the daughter of an important man, you will live like that in my house.'

Then she sent for Subhashini and said to her, 'Bouma, see that no one speaks rude words to her—and don't you do so, either; treat her as someone like yourself.'

Subhashini's little boy was there. He said, 'I will speak food words.'

I said, 'What will you say!'

He said, 'Food, pan, pot—and what else, muvver?'

Subhashini said, 'And your mother-in-law.'

The little boy said, 'Where is muvver-in-law?'

Subhashini's daughter pointed to me and said, 'She is your mother-in-law.'

Then the little boy said, 'Kunutini muvver-in-law! Kunutini muvver-in-law!'

Subhashini was looking for a way of establishing a relationship with me. Hearing her son and daughter saying this, she said to me, 'Then from now on you are my son's mother-in-law.'

After that, Subhashini sat down to eat. I sat near her, too, to serve her. As she ate, she asked, 'How many weddings have you had?'

I understood her words. I said, 'Why, does the cooking seem to you like that of Draupadi?'

Subhashini said, 'Oh, yes! The Pandavas' queen was a "first class chef". Do you now understand my mother-in-law, then?'

I said, 'Not very well. Everyone makes a distinction between the daughter of a poor man and the daughter of an important man.'

Subhashini started laughing. She said, 'Oh, go on with you! Do you think that? Do you think she treated you well because you are the daughter of an important man?'

I said, 'Then what?'

Subhashini said, 'Her son ate to capacity, that is why she is treating you so well. Now, if you use a bit of skill, you can double your wages.'

I said, 'I do not want wages. If my not taking them would cause trouble, then I will accept wages. I will entrust them to you, and you can give them to the poor. It is enough for me that I have found a refuge.'

9

A Grey-Haired Person's Happiness and Sorrow

I HAD A REFUGE. AND I HAD ANOTHER PRICELESS JEWEL—A COMPANION who wished me well. I saw that Subhashini genuinely loved me—she treated me like a sister. Her skilful management ensured that the servants, too, were not disrespectful to me. Meanwhile, I also found some happiness in cooking and serving. The old Brahmin cook—she was called Sona's mother[16]—did not go home. She thought that if she went, she would not have the job any more; I would become permanent. Thinking this, she did not, on various pretexts, visit her home. On Subhashini's recommendation, we both stayed. She explained to her mother-in-law that Kumudini was the daughter of gentlefolk, and could not do all the cooking alone—and

Sona's mother was an old woman: where would she go? Her mother-in-law said, 'Can we keep both of them? Who will supply so much money?'

Her daughter-in-law said, 'If we are to keep only one of them, it must be Sona's mother. Kumu cannot do it all.'

The mistress said, 'No, no. My son cannot eat Sona's mother's cooking. Then let them both stay.'

Subhashini had employed all these strategies in order to save me trouble. The mistress was a puppet in her hands; for she was Raman's wife—who would ignore Raman's wife's words? Again, Subhashini's nature was as beautiful as her intellect was keen. Having such a friend, I found some happiness in those days of sorrow.

I cooked fish and meat, or a couple of special dishes. And the remaining part of the day, I spent with Subhashini: I talked to her children, or even played a few tricks on the mistress myself. But from this last, a great disturbance arose. The mistress believed that she was young, only by mischance a few of her hairs had gone grey, and if she pulled these out, she could again be young. Hence, when she could get the person and the opportunity, she would sit and have her grey hairs pulled out. One day, she seized me for this forced labour. I was speedily, with swift hands, clearing the month of Bhadra's grassy fields.[17] Seeing this from a distance, Subhashini beckoned to me. I left the mistress and went running to her daughter-in-law. Subhashini said, 'What deed is this! Why are you reducing my mother-in-law's head to hairlessness?'

I said, 'It is better to finish that sin in one day.'

Subhashini said, 'Then what money will you have? Where will you go?'

I said, 'My hands do not stop.'

Subhashini said, 'Oh, help! Pull out one or two, and then come away!'

I said, 'Your mother-in-law won't let me go.'

Subhashini said, 'Oh, then tell her that you can't see any more grey hairs—and come away.'

I laughed, and said, 'How can such banditry be done in daylight? What will people say? It's like the banditry I suffered at the Black Lake.'

Subhashini asked, 'What banditry at the Black Lake?'

I used to become a little forgetful in talking to Subhashini—suddenly, unguardedly, the reference to Black Lake had come from my lips. I repressed it. I said, 'I will tell you that story another day.'

Subhashini said, 'Why don't you try saying what I said, just once? At my request?'

Laughing, I went back to the mistress and sat down again to pull out grey hairs. Having pulled out several, I said, 'I can't see any more grey hairs. There are only one or two left; I will pull them out tomorrow.'

The woman laughed heartily. She said, 'And the girls say all of them are grey.'

From that day, I was treated even more cordially. But I determined to arrange things so that I did not have to sit day after day pulling out grey hairs. I had received some pay; I took one rupee from it and put it in Haramani's hand. I said to her, 'Get someone to buy a phial of hair dye and bring it to me.' Haramani convulsed with laughter. When she stopped laughing, she said, 'What will you do with the hair dye, then? Whose hair will you put it on?'

I said, 'The Brahmin cook's.'

Now Haramani sat plump down, laughing. At this point, the Brahmin cook arrived. Then Haramani stuffed the end of her sari into her mouth to stop her laughter. Being quite unable to stop, she fled. The Brahmin cook said, 'Why is she laughing so much?'

I said, 'As far as I can see, she hasn't anything else to do. I said just now, why not put hair dye on the Brahmin cook's hair? That's why she was laughing.'

The Brahmin cook said, 'Then why so much laughter? What would be the harm in it? The children provoke me by calling me Grass-seed head, Grass-seed head! I would escape that trouble!'

Subhashini's daughter, Hema, spontaneously started,

'The old woman goes, a grass-seed head,
bell-flowers in her hair,
Stick in hand, rope round neck,
in her ears a pair of rings.

Hema's brother said, 'Dings!' Then, lest 'dings' fall on anyone, Subhashini took him away.

I understood that the Brahmin cook wanted the hair dye very much. I said, 'Very well, I will give you some hair dye.'

The Brahmin cook said, 'Very well, give it to me. May you live, may you have gold ornaments. May you learn a lot about cooking.'

Haramani might laugh, but she was competent. She speedily brought me a phial of the best hair dye. I took it in my hand and went to pull out the mistress's grey hairs. The mistress asked, 'What is that in your hand?'

I said, 'An essence. If you spread it on your hair, all the grey ones come out, and all the dark ones stay.'

The mistress said, 'Really! I have never heard of such a marvellous essence. Good, spread it on and let me see. Mind that you do not use hair dye.'

I carefully spread the hair dye on her hair. When I had finished, I said, 'There are no grey hairs left,' and went away. When the set time had elapsed, all her hair turned black. By misfortune, Haramani saw this as she was sweeping the room. She let fall the broom, stuffed the end of her sari in her mouth and went laughing to the outer building. When there was a disturbance of 'Where's the maid? Where's the maid?' she went back to the inner chambers, and, stuffing her sari in her mouth, went up to the roof. Sona's mother was drying her hair there; she asked, 'What has happened?' Haramani could only indicate her head with her hand. Unable to understand anything from this, Sona's mother went down and saw that the hair on the mistress's head was all black—and she started to wail aloud. She said, 'Oh, Mother! What is this that has happened, then! All the hair on your head has gone black, then! Oh, Mother, someone must have given you some potion!'

At this point, Subhashini came and seized me—laughing, she said, 'Wicked girl, did you do that, did you put hair dye on Mother's hair?'

I said, 'Yes.'

Subhashini said, 'Plague take you! Look what you've done!'

I said, 'Don't worry.'

At this point, the mistress herself summoned me. She said, 'Well, then, Kumo! Did you put hair dye on my head?'

I saw that the mistress had a very pleased expression on her face. I said, 'Who told you such a thing, Mother!'

The mistress said, 'Sona's mother told me.'

I said, 'What of Sona's mother? That was not hair dye, Mother, it was a potion of mine.'

The mistress said, 'It is a good potion, child. Bring a mirror and let me see.'

I brought a mirror and gave it to her. When she had looked in it, the mistress said, 'Oh God! All my hair has gone black! You ill-fated wench, now people will say you have used hair dye on me!'

The mistress's face was all smiles. That evening, she praised my cooking, and increased my wages. Moreover, she said, 'Child! You go around with only glass bangles on your arms, which is distressing to see.' With these words, she presented me with a pair of gold bangles of her own, which she had long since given up wearing. I was ashamed to take them—I could not restrain my tears. So I did not have the chance to say, 'I will not take them.'

When she had the chance, the old Brahmin cook took hold of me. She said, 'Sister, is there any of that potion left?'

I said, 'Which potion? The one I gave to the Brahmin woman to subdue her husband?'

The Brahmin cook said, 'Certainly not! That is a childish thought. Have I any such thing?'

I said, 'No? Is that so? Not even one?'

The Brahmin cook said, 'I suppose you have five of them?'

I said, 'If not, how could I cook as I do? Unless one is Draupadi, good cooking is lost! Get five of them, and people will fall in love with your cooking.'

The Brahmin cook sighed deeply. She said, 'There isn't even one available—let alone five! Muslims are allowed to, but for the daughters of Hindus it is a sin. And what good would it be if there were? With this grass-seed hair! That is why I was asking if there was any more of that potion which makes hair black?'

I said, 'Is that what you mean! Certainly there is!'

Then I gave the phial of hair dye to the Brahmin cook, and went away. In the night, after the meal, at bedtime, in the dark, the Brahmin cook spread it on her hair; some went on her hair, some did not, some went on her face and eyes. When she appeared in the morning, her hair looked like the fur of a tortoiseshell cat: some white, some red, some black; and her face looked somewhat like a monkey's and somewhat like a cat's. As soon as they saw her, the people of the house laughed aloud. That laughter did not stop. Whenever someone looked at the cook they laughed. Haramani, out of breath from laughing, threw herself at Subhashini's feet, and said, gasping, 'Mistress, let me go, I can't stay in such a house of laughter—some day I'll choke to death.'

Subhashini's daughter, too, vexed the old woman; she said, 'Old Aunt—who made you up?

Death said, Golden moon,
come into my house.
So she decorated the cremation ground
with vermilion and cow-dung.'

One day, a cat had eaten a fish from the pot, and had got soot on her face. Subhashini's son had seen this. When he saw the old woman, he said, 'Muvver! Ole Aunt has eaten ve pot.'

But, following my instructions, no one let on to the Brahmin cook. Unperturbed, she showed that splendid mixture of monkey and cat to everyone. Seeing them laugh, she asked everyone, 'Why do you laugh, then?'

At my instruction, everyone said, 'Didn't you hear what that boy said? He said, "Ole Aunt has eaten ve pot." Everyone is talking about who went to your kitchen to eat from the pot last night; and saying, would Sona's mother do such a thing at her age?'

Then the old woman started a string of abuses—'Shameless ones! Cursed ones! Unfortunate ones!' with these and many other such incantations she invited Yama many times to come and take them and their husbands and children—but the King of Death showed no eagerness in the matter for the time being. The Brahmin cook's countenance remained as it was. In that same condition, she went to serve Raman Babu's meal. Seeing her, Raman Babu, suppressing his laughter, choked on his food, and ate no more. I heard that when she went to serve Ramram Datta his meal, the master chased her away.

Finally, Subhashini had pity on her, and said to the old woman, 'There is a big looking-glass in my room—go and look in it.'

The old woman went and looked at herself. Then she started to weep loudly and abuse me. I tried to explain that I had told her to spread the stuff on her hair, not on her face. The old woman did not understand. She invited Yama again and again to eat my head. Hearing this, Subhashini's daughter recited this verse—

She whom Death calls
is the most beautiful.
Let ashes fall on her face.
Old woman, why won't you die.

Finally, that three-year-old son-in-law of mine got a piece of firewood and put it on the old woman's back. He said, 'My muvver-in-law!' Then the old woman fell down and started weeping loudly. The more she wept, the more my son-in-law danced round her, clapping his hands and saying, 'My muvver-in-law, my muvver-in-law!' I went and took him on my lap and kissed him, and then he stopped.

10
The Lamp of Hope

THAT SAME DAY, IN THE AFTERNOON, SUBHASHINI TOOK ME BY THE HAND, drew me to a secluded place, and made me sit down. She said, 'My son's mother-in-law! You said you would tell me the story of the banditry at the Black Lake—you still haven't done so. Tell me now—I want to hear it.'

I thought for a long time. At last I said, 'It is the story of my misfortune. I have said that my father is an important man. Your father-in-law is also an important man—but there is no comparison. My father is still alive—he still has his immeasurable wealth; there are still elephants in his elephant stalls. That I am earning my living by cooking is because of the banditry at the Black Lake.'

After these words, we were both silent. Then Subhashini said, 'If it distresses you to talk of it, then don't: when I asked for the story, I didn't know.'

I said, 'I will tell you everything. You care for me so much, and have done so much for me, that there is no distress in telling you.'

I did not tell her my father's name, nor the name of the village where my father's house was. I did not tell her the names of my husband or father-in-law. I did not tell her the name of the village where my father-in-law's house was. I told her everything else, up to the time of my meeting Subhashini. As she listened, Subhashini wept. It is unnecessary to say that I, too, wept from time to time as I told my story.

So much for that day. The next day, Subhashini again took me to a secluded place. She said, 'You must tell me your father's name.'

I told her.

'You must also tell me the name of the village where his house is.'

I told her that, too.

Subhashini said, 'Tell me the name of the post office.'

I said, 'The post office! The name of the post office is "post office".'

Subhashini said, 'Oh, wicked one! The name of the village where the post office is.'

I said, 'That I don't know. I only know "post office".'

Subhashini said, 'Tell me, is the post office in the same village where your home is, or in another village?'

I said, 'I don't know.'

Subhashini was depressed. She said nothing more. The following day, again in private, she said, 'You are the daughter of an important man. For how long will you earn your living by cooking? If you go away I will weep a lot—but I am not such a sinner as to ruin your happiness for the sake of my own. So we advise you—'

I interrupted her to ask, 'Who are "we"?'

Subhashini said, 'I and R. Babu.'

'R. Babu' was Raman Babu. Subhashini used to refer to him thus in our conversation. She went on, 'Our advice is that we should write a letter to your father saying that you are here; that is why I was asking you yesterday about the post office.'

I said, 'So you have told him everything?'

Subhashini said, 'Yes—was that wrong?'

I said, 'Not wrong at all. And then?'

Subhashini said, 'We concluded that there must now be a post office at Maheshpur, and sent the letter there.'

I said, 'The letter is already written?'

Subhashini said, 'Yes.'

I was beside myself with joy. I calculated how many days it would be before an answer came to the letter. But no answer came. I was ill-fated—there was no post office at Maheshpur. At that time, every village did not have a post office of its own. There were post offices in certain villages—I was the pampered child of the king—I did not know of such things. Without the address of a post office, Raman Babu's letter was opened at the main post office in Calcutta, and returned to him.

I started to weep again. But R. Babu was persistent. Subhashini came and said to me, 'Now you must tell me the name of your husband.'

I had learned to write. I wrote down my husband's name. Then she asked, 'And your father-in-law's name?'

I wrote that down too.

'The name of the village?'

I told her that, as well.

'The name of the post office?'

I said, 'Do I know that?'

I heard that Raman Babu sent a letter there, also. But no answer came. I became very depressed. But then something occurred to me; overwhelmed by hope, I had not forbidden the letter-writing. Now I thought, 'I have been abducted by bandits: what caste do I have?[18] Surely my husband and father-in-law will reject me because of this. That being so, it was not a good idea to write those letters.' When Subhashini heard this, she was silent.

Then I understood that I had no further hope. I went and lay down.

11
A Stolen Glance

ONE DAY, WHEN I GOT UP IN THE MORNING, I SAW THAT SOME EVENT WAS being prepared for. Raman Babu was a lawyer. He had one very important client. For a couple of days we had been hearing that he had come to Calcutta. Raman Babu and his father were continually going to and from his house. The reason for his father's going was that he had some connections with him involving business. Now I heard that he had been invited for the midday meal. So special preparations for cooking were going on.

I liked to cook—so most of the responsibility for cooking fell on me. I cooked with care. The meal was being served in the inner chambers. Ramram Babu, Raman Babu and the guest sat down to eat. Serving was the old woman's responsibility—I never served people from outside the house.

The old woman was serving—I was in the kitchen—when a disturbance broke out. Raman Babu was scolding the old woman severely. At that point, one of the kitchen servants came and said, 'They are deliberately embarrassing her.'

I asked, 'What has happened?'

The servant said, 'The old woman was putting dal in Brother-Babu's plate (she was an old servant, she called him Brother-Babu)—and he put out his hand, saying, "No, no!"—and all the dal fell on his hand.'

Meanwhile, I could hear Raman Babu scolding the Brahmin cook: 'If you don't know how to serve why do you come? Can't you give that duty to someone else?'

Ramram Babu said, 'It is not your work! Go and send Kumo.'

The mistress was not there: who could forbid it? Meanwhile, there was the command of the master himself—how could I disregard it? I knew that if I went, the mistress would be very angry. I explained to the old woman several times—I said, 'Put things down carefully'—but from fear she would not agree to go out again. Therefore, I washed my hands, wiped my face, cleaned myself, arranged my clothing properly, veiled my face a bit, and went to serve the food. Who foresees that such things will happen? I know that I am very intelligent—I did not know that Subhashini could sell me in one market and buy me in another.

I was veiled, but a woman's nature is not covered up by a veil. From within the veil I took one look at the guest.

I saw that he was about thirty years old; he was fair-complexioned and very well-built; one could see that he would be very attractive to women. As if startled by a flash of lightning, I became somewhat preoccupied. I stood staring there for a while holding the dish of meat, and as I looked at him from within my veil, he raised his head—he could see that I was looking towards him through my veil. I did not intend to give him any kind of a significant look. So much sin was not in my heart. Yet I suppose that the snake, too, may not intend to raise its hood; when an occasion arrives for the hood to be risen, it raises itself of its own accord. The snake, too, may not have a sinful heart. I suppose that something of the sort happened. I suppose he would have seen a significant look. Men say that, like a lamp in the darkness, the sidelong look of a woman from within a veil shows more clearly. Probably he, too, would have seen it like that. He smiled gently, just a little, and bent his head. Only I saw that smile. I put all the meat on his plate and came away.

I was a little ashamed, a little unhappy. Although I was married, I was living as a widow. I had seen my husband only once, at the time of our marriage—so youth's desires were all unsatisfied. Thinking how the waves rose at the casting of the net into such deep waters, I became gloomy. In my mind, I cursed myself a thousand times, in my mind I suffered.

When I returned to the kitchen it came to me that I had seen him before somewhere. To confirm my suspicion, I went to see him again, from concealment. I looked at him carefully. I said to myself, 'I know him.'

At this point, Ramram Babu called to me to bring more food. I had cooked many preparations of meat—I took them out. I saw that the guest remembered my sidelong look. He said to Ramram Babu, 'Ramram Babu, please tell your cook that the cooking has been very skilfully done.'

Ramram Babu understood nothing of the underlying situation, and said, 'Yes, she cooks well.'

I said in my mind, 'I will cook your head.'

The guest said, 'But it is very surprising that in your house a couple of the dishes have been cooked in the fashion of my region.'

I said to myself, 'I know him.' Indeed, I had cooked a couple of dishes according to the custom of our own region.

Ramram Babu said, 'That could be; she is not from this region.'

The guest took this opportunity, and, looking towards me, asked, 'Where are you from, then?'

My first problem was whether to speak or not. I decided to speak.

My second problem was whether to tell the truth or not. I decided not to. He who has made women's hearts fond of artfulness and inclined to take roundabout paths knows why I decided thus. I thought that it was necessary to keep the truth in my hand, and to see now what came of saying something else. With this in mind, I answered, 'I come from Black Lake.'

He was startled. After a while he asked, in a gentle voice, 'Which Black Lake, the bandit's Black Lake?'

I said, 'Yes.'

He said nothing more.

I took a plate of meat in my hand and stood there. I forgot that it was improper of me to stay standing there. I quite forgot that I had cursed myself a thousand times. I saw that the guest was no longer eating well. Seeing this, Ramram Datta said, 'Upendra Babu, please eat.' That was all I needed to hear. Upendra Babu! I had known before hearing the name that he was my husband.

I went back to the kitchen, dropped the plate, and sat down, rejoicing for once, after such a long time. Ramram Datta said, 'What fell?' I had thrown down the plate of meat.

12

Haramani's Laughter Is Checked

FROM NOW ON IN THIS CHRONICLE, IT WILL BE NECESSARY TO MENTION MY husband's name hundreds of times. Now, I need half-a-dozen women to sit together as a committee and advise me on how to refer to him. Shall I pain the ears by saying 'husband', 'husband', hundreds of times? Or, following the example of the play 'Jamai Barik',[19] shall I start to call my husband 'Upendra'? Or shall I scatter such expressions as 'Master of my life', 'Beloved of my life', 'Lord of my life', 'Ruler of my life' and 'Dearer than my life' all around? There is not a word in this afflicted country's language by which to call him who is dearer to us than anyone else to address, whom we wish to call at every moment. A friend of mine (imitating the servants) used to call her husband 'Babu'—but just 'Babu' did not sound very sweet—finally, in her mental distress, she started to call her husband 'Baburam'. I have chosen to do the same.

After I had thrown down the plate of meat, I said to myself, 'If Providence has returned what was lost—it must not be thrown away. Let me not spoil everything with maidenly modesty.'

With this in mind, I stood in a place where someone going from the dining room to the drawing room, who looked around as he went, could see me. I said to myself, 'If he doesn't look around as he goes, then I have learned nothing of men's characters in my twenty years.' I speak plainly: you must forgive me—I stood there with very little cloth over my head. I am ashamed, now, to write this, but consider what my need was then.

Raman Babu came first; he looked all around as if he was investigating who was there. After him came Ramram Datta—he did not look around at all. After him came my husband—his eyes looked all around as if searching for someone. His eyes fell on me. I could tell that it was I for whom his eyes were searching. As soon as he looked towards me, I chose—what shall I say, I am ashamed to say it—as the snake's hood expands of itself, so with our sidelong looks. Why should I not cast a little more poison at him whom I knew to be my own husband? Perhaps 'the master of my life' went out injured.

Then I decided to seek Haramani's help. As soon as I sent for her in private she came, laughing. Laughing loudly, she said, 'Did you see the Brahmin cook's humiliation when she was serving?' Without waiting for an answer, she let out another cascade of laughter.

I said, 'I know, but I didn't send for you for that. Do me one good turn, only one. Bring me word quickly when that guest is going to leave.'

Haramani stopped laughing altogether. So much laughter, covered as a fire is blanketed by the darkness of smoke. Haramani said, 'Fie! Mistress! I did not know you had this disease.'

I laughed. I said, 'People's days are not all the same. Put aside your preaching—tell me whether you will do this for me or not.'

Haramani said, 'I will play no part in such a thing.'

I had not come empty-handed to Haramani. There was the money of my wages; I put five rupees of it into her hand. I said, 'Eat my head, but you must do this for me.'

Haramani was about to throw the money down, but instead she put it on a basket of earth which stood nearby for swabbing down the stove. She said, very seriously, with no more laughter—'I was going to throw your money down, but the noise might have given rise to some scandal, so I have put it down gently here—you gather it up. And don't say such things anymore.'

I fell to weeping. Haramani was reliable, everyone else was unreliable; whom else could I call on? She did not understand the real meaning of my weeping. Yet she had pity on me. She said, 'Why do you weep? Do you know the man?'

At first I thought I would tell Haramani everything. Then I thought, 'She will not believe it, she will create some trouble.' After some thought, I decided that I could do nothing without Subhashini. She was my intelligence, she was my rescuer—I would go to her, tell her everything, and ask her advice. I said to Haramani, 'I know him, indeed—I know him very well; you would not believe it all if I told you, so I am not telling you everything. There is nothing wrong in it.'

When I had said, 'nothing wrong',, I considered a little. There was nothing wrong from my point of view, but from Haramani's point of view? There was indeed something wrong.

So why involve her in something wrong? Then I remembered, 'We make our anklets sound as we go.' I persuaded my mind with a sophistry. Those in an unfavourable position resort to sophistry for deliverance. I said to Haramani again, 'There is nothing wrong in it.'

Haramani asked, 'Must you see him?'

'Yes.'

'When?'

'In the night, when everyone is asleep.'

'Alone?'

'Alone.'

'No one could do it,' Haramani said.

'And if the young mistress commands you?' I asked.

'Have you gone mad? She is the well-born wife of a well-born family—Sati and Lakshmi! Would she put her hand to such a thing!'

'Will you do it if she doesn't forbid it?'

'I will. Can I refuse her command?'

'If she doesn't forbid you?'

'I will go, but I will not take your money. Take your money back.'

I said, 'Very well; I will call you later.'

Then I wiped away my tears and went in search of Subhashini. I found her in a secluded place. When she saw me, Subhashini's beautiful face blossomed with gladness, like a lotus in the morning, like a gardenia in the evening—her whole being bloomed with joy like an open shephalika flower, like river currents at moonrise. Laughing, Subhashini brought her face close to my ear and asked, 'How did you recognize him, then?'

I was struck with amazement. I said, 'What is this? How did you know?' Subhashini rolled her eyes and pursed her lips and said, 'Aha! Did you think that your golden moon had let itself be seized of its own accord? It is because we know how to spread a net in the sky that we caught and brought your moon from the sky!'

I said, 'Who is "we"? You and R. Babu?'

Subhashini said, 'Who else would it be? You remember that you gave us the names of your husband, your father-in-law and their village? When he heard them, R. Babu recognized them. Your U. Babu was one of his important clients—on that pretext, he wrote to your U. Babu to come to Calcutta. Then he invited him here.'

'And then he spread out his hand to receive some dal from the old woman?'

'Yes, we plotted that, too.'

'Have you told him anything about me?'

'Oh, destruction! Could we do that? You were abducted by bandits, and after that who knows the details of where you went? If he had news of you, would he accept you into his house? He would say that you were manipulating him. R.Babu says that now you can do something.'

I said, 'I will try my best once and for all—and if I don't succeed I will drown myself. But if he doesn't see me, what can I do?'

Subhashini said, 'When will you meet him, and where?'

I said, 'If you have done so much, then give me a little help in this matter, too. I can't meet him by going to his house—who would take me, or let me see him? I must meet him here.'

'When?'

'At night, when everyone is asleep.'

'In a love-tryst?'

'What other way is there? Is there anything wrong in it—he is my husband.'

'No, there's nothing wrong in it. But in that case, he must be detained for the night. His house is nearby; how can this be managed? I'll see what R. Babu advises.'

Subhashini sent for Raman Babu. She came and told me of their conversation. She said, 'What R. Babu can do is this: he will not yet look at the client's papers—he will set them aside on some pretext. He will fix a time later in the evening to look at them. When your husband arrives, he will look at the papers. This will take some time. When it gets late, he will ask for some food. But after that, what does your learning suggest? How can we ask him to stay the night?'

I said, 'You do not have to make that request. I will do it myself. I have done what will make him heed such a request. I have thrown him a couple of glances and he has returned them. He is not a good man! I will write a brief note. Who is there to take it to him?'

'Send it by some servant?'

'Even if I never get a husband in this life, I can't speak of this to any man.'

'No, indeed. Which maidservant, then?'

'Which maidservant is reliable? If she creates a disturbance, I will lose everything.'

Subhashini said, 'Haramani is reliable.'

I said, 'I spoke to Haramani. Because she is reliable, she is unwilling. But if she gets a sign from you, she will go. But how can I ask you to give her such a sign? If I die, at least I'll die alone.'

Again tears came to my afflicted eyes.

Subhashini said, 'What did Haramani say concerning me?'

I said, 'If you don't forbid it, she would feel able to go.'

Subhashini thought for a long time. She said, 'Tell her to come to me for that word, after dusk.'

13
I Am Given an Examination

AFTER DARK, MY HUSBAND CAME, BRINGING HIS PAPERS TO RAMAN BABU. When I heard this, I pleaded with Haramani once again. Haramani said, 'If the young mistress doesn't forbid it, I will do it. But I must know that there is nothing wrong in it.' I said, 'Do what you must—I am in great distress.'

At this indication, Haramani laughed a little and ran off to Subhashini. I waited for them. I saw her come running back, panting, tousled, holding her hair and clothes together, and letting loose a fountain of laughter. I asked her, 'What, then, why do you laugh?'

Haramani said, 'Sister, is a person to be sent to such a place? My life is lost!'

I said, 'Why, then?'

Haramani said, 'I know there is no broom in the young mistress's room; when it's needed, we take a broom with us and sweep the room. Today, I see that someone has left a broom just near the young mistress's hand. When I went and said, "Shall I go?" the young mistress took the broom and came chasing to hit me. Fortunately, I know how to run away, so I ran away and escaped. Otherwise wouldn't I have been beaten to death? But I think one blow fell on my back—have a look and see if there is a mark or not?'

Laughing, Haramani showed me her back. She was fibbing—there was no mark. Then she said, 'Now, tell me what must be done—and I will do it.'

'Because of the broom?'

'The broom hit—it didn't forbid. I said that if I wasn't forbidden, I would do it.'

'Isn't a broom a forbidding?'

'Ha! Look, sweet sister, when the young mistress lifted the broom, I saw a little smile at the corners of her mouth. So tell me what is to be done.'

Then I wrote on a scrap of paper.

'I have given my heart and soul to you. Will you accept them? If you will, then sleep in this house tonight. Let your door remain unlocked. The cook.'

When I had written this letter, I wanted, for shame, to sink into the pond's water, or to hide in the darkness. What could I do? Providence had sent me good fortune! I suppose that no such misery has ever fallen to the lot of a well-born woman.

Folding up the piece of paper, I gave it to Haramani. I said, 'Wait a little.' I said to Subhashini, 'Send for your husband. Say something to make him excuse himself.'

Subhashini did so. When Raman Babu came, I said to Haramani, 'Go now.' Haramani went, and soon came back with the piece of paper. In one corner of it was written, 'Very well.' Then I said to Haramani, 'Since you have done so much, you must do a little more. At midnight you must come and show me his bedroom.'

Haramani said, 'Very well; and there's nothing wrong in it?'

I said, 'Nothing at all. He was my husband in another life.'

Haramani said, 'Another life, or in this life: I can't quite work it out.'

I laughed and said, 'Silence.'

Haramani laughed, and said, 'If he is of this life, then I will take a present of five hundred rupees; otherwise, my broom-wounds won't get better.'

Then I went to Subhashini and told her all this. Subhashini went and said to her mother-in-law, 'Kumudini is not well today; she will not be able to cook. Let Sona's mother cook.'

Sona's mother went to cook—Subhashini took me into her room and shut the door. I asked her, 'What is this, why the prison?' Subhashini said, 'I am going to dress you.'

Then she wiped my face clean. She put fragrant oil on my hair and carefully bound it into a chignon; she said, 'This chignon is worth a thousand rupees: when the time comes, send me this thousand rupees.' Then she took one of her own fresh, beautiful saris and put it on me perforce. She tugged with such force that, in fear of being left naked, I was obliged to wear it. Then she brought out her own ornaments to put on me. I said, 'I will not wear any of these.'

There was considerable dispute over this—then, seeing that I could by no means accept, she said, 'I have another set: wear them.'

With these words, Subhashini took mallika flower buds from a jardinière and made me bangles of them, anklets and bracelets, and a double garland for my neck. Then she brought out a pair of new gold earrings and said, 'I got R. Babu to buy these with my own money—to give to you. Whenever and wherever you may be, think of me when you wear them. I do not know, sister, if I will see you again after this—may God arrange it—so I will give you these earrings to wear now. Do not say anything more of it.'

As she spoke, Subhashini wept. Tears came to my eyes, too, and I could say no more. Subhashini put the earrings on me.

When I was fully dressed, a maid brought Subhashini's son. I took the little boy on my lap and told him stories. After a few stories, he fell asleep. Then a sad thought rose in my mind; nor, in the midst of this happiness, could I refrain from telling it to Subhashini. I said, 'I have been overjoyed, but I blame him, a little, in my mind. I recognized that he was my husband; that is why I do not think that what I am doing is wrong. But there is no possibility that he can have recognized me. I saw him when he was of age. That is why I suspected the truth at once. He saw me only as an eleven-year-old girl. I have seen no sign of him recognizing me. So I blame him a lot in my mind that, knowing me to be another's wife, he was eager for my love. But he is my husband, I am his wife—because it is improper for me to think badly of him, I will not consider this any more. I have decided that if I ever have the chance, I will make him renounce that practice.'

Subhashini listened to my words, and said, 'You are worse than any monkey in the trees; it is as if he has no wife.'

I said, 'Have I a husband or not?'

Subhashini said, 'Oh, destruction! Men are not the same as women! I don't see you earning money working in a commissariat?'

I said, 'Let them produce a human being by carrying a child in their belly and giving birth, and I will go and work in a commissariat. Each does as they can. Is it so difficult for men to control their senses?'

Subhashini said, 'Very well, first get your house and then set fire to it. Leave all that. Will I examine you on how you will bewitch your husband's heart? You have no other recourse than that.'

After some thought I said, 'I have never studied this matter.'

'Then learn from me. You know that I am an expert in this shastra?'

'I can see that.'

'Then learn. Imagine you are a man. Watch how I bewitch your heart.'

With these words, the shameless woman, veiling her face a little, brought me some scented paan, prepared with her own hands, and gave it to me. She kept this paan for Raman Babu alone, and gave it to no one else. She did not even take it herself. Raman Babu's hookah was there, its bowl in place; only ashes in it: Subhashini held it before me, pretending to let me puff. Then she took in her hand a palm-stalk ornamented with flowers and began to fan me. The bracelets and bangles on her arm jingled sweetly.

I said, 'Sister! This is just serving—have I kept him here today just to show him how much I know about serving?'

Subhashini said, 'Are we not servants, then?'

I said, 'When his love awakens, that is the time for serving. Then I will fan him, massage his feet, prepare his paan and offer it to him, and offer him tobacco. Now is not the time for all that.'

Then Subhashini, laughing, came and sat close to me. She took my hand between hers and started to speak sweet words to me. At first, laughing and chewing paan, her earrings swinging, she spoke according to the pretence she had set up. But as she spoke, that mood was forgotten. She started to speak as a woman friend. She spoke of my going away. A teardrop sparkled in her eye. Then, to cheer her, I said, 'What you have taught me are indeed the weapons of women, but will they prevail now with U. Babu?'

Then Subhashini laughed and said, 'Then learn my divine weapon.'

With these words, the woman circled my throat with her hands, raised my face and kissed me on the mouth. One teardrop fell on my cheek.

With a gulp I suppressed my tears and said, 'Oh, sister, you are teaching me to offer a reward without a commitment.'

Subhashini said, 'But you will not have the skill. Demonstrate and let me see what you know. Imagine I am U. Babu'—saying this she disposed herself splendidly on the sofa; she could not help laughing, and stuffed the end of her sari in her mouth. When her laughter had stopped, she gave me one stern look—and then immediately fell back laughing again. When that laughter had ceased she said, 'Demonstrate!' Then I made Subhashini acquainted a little with that skill of which the reader will later have some acquaintance. Subhashini pushed me off the sofa—she said, 'Away with you, sinful one! You are a regular cobra!'

'Why, sister?'

'Can a man endure that laughing glance? He would be slain.'

'Then I pass the examination?'

'A high pass—the one hundred and sixty-nine men of the commissariat, too, have never seen such a laughing glance. If the fellow's head spins, give him some almond oil.'

'Very well. I can tell by the sounds that the Babus have finished their meal. It's past time for Raman Babu to come: I will take my leave now. Of what you have taught me, one thing was particularly sweet—that kiss on the mouth. Come and teach me again.'

Then Subhashini clasped my neck, and I clasped hers. In a close embrace we kissed each other, and clasped each other round the neck; we both wept for a long time. Is there any other such love? Does anyone else know how to love like Subhashini? I may die, but I shall not forget Subhashini.

14
My Vow to Cast Off This Life

AFTER CAUTIONING HARAMANI, I WENT TO MY OWN BEDROOM. THE BABUS had finished their meal. At this point, there was a great commotion. Someone called for a fan, someone called for water, someone called for medicine, someone called for a doctor: that kind of confusion. Haramani arrived, laughing. I asked, 'What is all the commotion about?'

Haramani said, 'The guest had a fainting fit.'

'And then?' I asked.

'Now he has recovered.'

'And?'

'Now he is very exhausted—he couldn't go home. At this very moment he is lying in the room next to the big reception room.'

I understood that this was a ruse. I said, 'When all the lights have been extinguished, and everyone is in bed, come back.'

Haramani said, 'But I'm sick.'

I said, 'Sick, your head! And the heads of five hundred ladies, if I have the chance!'

Laughing, Haramani went away. Later, when all the lights had been extinguished and everyone was in bed, Haramani came and took me with her and showed me the room. I entered the room. I saw that he was lying there alone. There was no sign of exhaustion; there were two big lamps burning in the room: he was lighting up everything with his own beauty. I, too, was pierced as if by an arrow. My body was flooded with bliss.

This was my first conversation with my husband since I had grown up. How can I say what happiness it was? I am very talkative—but when I first tried to speak to him, no words at all came out. My throat closed up. All my limbs trembled. My heart started to pound. My mouth dried up. Because no words would come, I fell to weeping.

He did not understand those tears. He said, 'Why do you weep? I did not send for you—you came of your own accord—so why the weeping?'

My heart was deeply wounded by this severe speech. That he thought me a loose woman—at that my tears flowed faster. I thought to myself, 'Now I will make myself known—I cannot bear this pain any more'; but then it occurred to me, that if he said to himself, 'She comes from Black Lake; she must have heard the story of my wife's abduction and now, in the desire for riches, is passing herself off as my wife'—how would I convince him? Therefore, I did not make myself known. I sighed deeply, wiped my eyes, and started to converse with him. After a while, he said, 'I was astonished to hear that you came from Black Lake. I never even dreamed that such a beautiful woman could be born at Black Lake.'

I saw that he was looking at me with great amazement. I made up an answer to his words and said, 'I may or may not be beautiful. In our region, it is your wife's beauty that is celebrated.' Turning the conversation to his wife by this stratagem, I asked, 'Has there been any trace of her?'

He said, 'No. How long have you been away from the region?'

I said, 'I left the region after all that business. Then perhaps you have married again?'

He said, 'No.'

I saw no chance of his answering on important matters. I had come voluntarily, as one seeking a love-tryst—there was no chance of his treating me with respect, either. He was looking at me in amazement. He said, just once, 'I have never seen a person with so much beauty.'

I had been very glad to hear that I did not have a co-wife. I said, 'Since you are important people, you should be prudent in this matter. Otherwise, if, later, you should find your wife, the two co-wives will come to blows.'

He laughed gently and said, 'There is no fear of that. Even if I found that wife, it is not likely that I would accept her. She would have to be considered as having lost caste.'

I was thunderstruck. So much hope and expectations was spoilt. Then, even if he came to know who I was, and recognized me to be his own wife, he would not accept me. This rebirth of mine as a woman was in vain.

I took courage, and asked, 'If you saw her now, what would you do?'

He said, with a cheerful face, 'I would cast her off.'

What heartlessness! I was stunned. The world spun before my eyes.

That night, sitting on my husband's bed, looking at his flawless, enchanting form, I vowed, 'He will accept me as his wife, or else I will cast off this life.'

15
A Loose Woman

THEN THOSE THOUGHTS LEFT ME. I HAD KNOWN BEFORE THIS THAT HE WAS enchanted by me. I thought to myself, if it is no sin for a rhinoceros to use its horn, if it is no sin for an elephant to use its tusks, a tiger its claws, a buffalo its horns, then it would be no sin for me either. I would use all the weapons God had given me, for the good of the two of us. If there was ever a time to go 'making our anklets sound', it was now. I went away from him and sat down at a distance. I started to talk cheerfully to him. He came close to me, and I said to him, 'Do not come close to me; I see you are under a misapprehension.' (I smiled as I said this, and as I spoke I unloosed my hair [if I do not speak truly, who will understand this story?] and sat binding it up again.) 'You are under a misapprehension. I am not a loose woman. I came only to hear from you some news of the region. I have no immoral intentions at all.'

Perhaps he did not believe this. He advanced, and sat down. Then I said, smiling, 'You did not listen to me, so I will go; our meeting is at an end,' and with these words, looking at him as the situation required, I got up, swaying a little like a spring creeper in the evening breeze, and, as if carelessly, letting my sleek, curling, scented tresses touch his cheek.

Seeing that I really had got up, he was mortified, and came and took my arm. His hand fell on the bracelets of mallika buds. Keeping hold of my arm, he gazed at it as if astonished. I said, 'What are you looking at?' He said, 'What is this flower? This flower is not fitting. The person is more beautiful than the flower. This is the first time I have seen a person more beautiful than the mallika flower.' Angrily, I tore my arm away, but I smiled and said, 'You are not a good person. Do not touch me. Do not think me immoral.'

With these words, I moved towards the door. My husband—as yet, to think that word brought sorrow—he joined his hands together and called, 'Heed my words, do not go. I have become maddened by your beauty. I have never seen such beauty. Let me see it a little longer. I will never see such beauty again.' I came back again—but I did not sit down—I said, 'Dearer than life! I am nothing; understand that my mental anguish is because I am leaving a jewel like you. But what can I do? Virtue is our only great wealth—I will not give up virtue for one day's happiness. I came to you thoughtlessly, without realizing. I wrote to you thoughtlessly, without realizing. But I will not go to my downfall. The way to safety is still open. It is my good fortune that I have remembered this now. I am going.'

He said, 'You know your virtue. I have fallen into such a state that I no longer know virtue or sin. I swear to you that you will be the mistress of my heart for ever. Do not think that this is only for one day.'

I smiled, and said, 'I have no faith in men's oaths. Can so much have happened in a moment's meeting?' With these words, I moved away again—I reached the door. Then, unable to contain himself any longer, he held my face in his two hands and blocked my way. He said, 'I have never seen anyone like you.' He let out a heart-piercing great sigh. Seeing his state, I, too, became sorrowful. I said, 'Then let us go to your house—if you stay here, you must give me up.'

He immediately agreed. His house was in Simla, very close by. His carriage was waiting, and the gatekeepers were asleep. We silently opened the gate and got into the carriage. When we reached his house, I saw that it was of two buildings. I entered one room first. As soon as I entered, I bolted the door. My husband lay down outside.

From outside, he spoke in supplication. I said, laughing, 'I have now become your servant. But I want to see whether the force of your love will last until morning or not. If I still see such love tomorrow, then I will talk with you again. This is all for now.'

I did not open the door; perforce, he went elsewhere to rest. Tell me: if you sat a terribly thirsty, sick person down on the bank of a resevoir of cool water in the unbearable heat of the month of Jyaishtha, and bound their mouth so that they could not drink—would their love of water increase, or not?

Well after daylight, I opened the door and saw that my husband was standing by the door. I took his hand in my own, and said, 'Lord of my life, send me back to Ramram Datta's house; or else do not talk with me for eight days. These eight days are your testing.' He consented to the eight days' test.

16
Having Committed Murder, I Am Hanged

FOR EIGHT DAYS, I INFLAMED MY HUSBAND WITH ALL THE MEANS WHICH Providence has given women to inflame men with. I am a woman—how can I divulge these things? If I had not known how to ignite flames, he would not have been so enkindled during the past nights. But by what means I ignited those flames, by what means I fanned them, by what means I inflamed my husband's heart, I cannot, for modesty, say anything about these. If any of my women readers have taken a vow to destroy a man, and have succeeded, they will understand. If any of my male readers have ever fallen into the hands of such a destroyer of men, then they will understand. It can be said that it is women who are earth's thorns. More harm on earth is caused by us than by men. It is fortunate that not all women have this man-destroying knowledge, or else the earth would by now be unpopulated.

For those eight days I stayed constantly with my husband; I spoke caressingly to him; I said not a single unpleasant thing. Smiles, glances, gestures—these are ordinary women's weapons. On the first day, I spoke caressingly; on the second day, I showed signs of affection; on the third day, I started to act as his housewife; I started to do that by which his meals, his sleeping, his bathing would be orderly, and in every respect good; cooked with my own hands, and prepared everything, down to the toothpicks. If I saw him a little unwell, I would stay awake all night to serve him.

Now, with joined hands, I humbly beg you not to think that all this was pretence. There was enough pride in Indira's heart to prevent her from doing all this only from a desire for security, or a desire to be the mistress of her husband's wealth. I could not have manifested a pretended love in the desire to get my husband—or, indeed, even to become the consort of Indra. I could use smiles and glances in order to enchant my husband, but I could not simulate love in order to enchant him. God did not make Indira of such clay. The unfortunate ones who cannot understand this—the heroines who will say to me, 'You may set traps of smiles and glances, you may let loose your hair and bind it up again, with a trick of words you may let your curling locks touch the unfortunate fellow's cheek and make him shiver—and you may even massage his feet or prepare his hookah!'—the unfortunate ones who will say such things to me: let those miserable things not read this chronicle of my life.

Still, there will be a handful of you women (I am not thinking of men readers—how would they understand about these weapons?) to whom I can explain the truth. He was my husband: to serve my Lord was my joy, so it was no pretence; I did it with my whole heart. I thought to myself, 'If he does not accept me, then at least for these few days let me fill my soul with, and taste, that which for me is the world's best happiness—which will not happen ever again, cannot happen ever again.' So, filling my soul, I served my Lord. The measure of my happiness in this, some of you will understand and some will not.

I will take pity on my men readers and explain only the principles of smiles and glances. It is not possible to instil the theory of devotion to one's husband into a mind whose limits are reached merely in sitting for college examinations, which sees the winning of ten rupees in a court of law as evidence of world-conquering genius; and whose absence is respectfully received in a court of justice. Will those who say, 'Let widows marry; do not let women marry until they are grown up; let women, like men, become learned in the various shastras,' understand the principles of devotion to one's husband? Yet the reason I have said that I will, having mercy, explain the principles of smiles and glances is that these are very simple. As a mahout controls his elephant with an ankush, a coachman controls his horses with a whip, a cowherd controls his cows with a rod, and the Englishman controls a party of Babus with his reddened eyes, so we can control you with smiles and glances. Our devotion to our husbands is our virtue: that we are reviled for our smiles and glances is your sin.

You will say, 'These are very arrogant words.' That is so—we, too, are earthenware pitchers, a blow with a flower can crack us. I was receiving the fruit of this pride in my own hands. The god who has no limbs, but a bow and arrow—no parents,[20] but a wife—an arrow of flowers, yet with that even mountains are split; that deity is the diminisher of women's pride. Setting the traps of my own smiles and glances to catch another, I caught the other and was caught myself, also. Setting a fire, I burned another, and burned myself, as well. On the day of Holi, going to redden another in the play with red powder, I became flushed with love myself. I went to commit murder, and was hanged. I have said that his form was enchanting—I learned again that he whose beauty this was, was my treasure—

I am beloved in his love
I am beautiful in his beauty.[21]

Then, there was the scattering of this fire. I knew how to smile; were there no answers to these smiles? I knew how to glance; were there no counter-glances? My lips, longing from a distance for a kiss, were swollen, petals of a flower-bud opening; did his soft lips, like a blossoming red flower, not know how to turn in my direction, with petals also thus opening?

If I had seen in his smiles, his glances, his longing for kisses, only signs of sensual longing, I would have been the victor. That was not so. In these smiles, those glances, that trembling of his lips, was only tenderness—boundless love. So it was I who lost. Losing, I acknowledged that this was earth's full measure of happiness. It serves that deity right, who brought physicality into this, that his own body was burned to ashes.[22]

The time of testing was accomplished, but I had become so tamed by his love that I had decided in my own mind that when the period of the test was over, I would not leave even if he beat me and drove me away. So even if, when he learned who I was, he did not accept me as his wife, if I could stay with him even as his mistress, I would do that; if I could have my husband, I would not fear public disgrace. But in the fear that even that was not in my fate, I used, when I had the chance, to sit down and weep.

But I understood this also, that my husband's wings were clipped. He no longer had the power to fly. Into the fire of his passion much sacrificial ghee had fallen. Now, doing nothing else, he only gazed at my face. I would do the housework—he would go around with me, like a little boy. I could see the unruly force of his thoughts at every step, yet at just a sign from me he was still. Sometimes he would touch my feet and weep, and say, 'I will honour your word for these eight days—do not leave me.' So I saw that if I left him, he would be in a very bad state.

The test failed. When the eight days had elapsed, we were each, without speaking, under the control of the other. He knew me as a loose woman. I endured that, too. But I understood that whatever I was, I had put chains on the elephant's legs.

17
After the Hanging, the Lawsuit's Investigation

WE SPENT MANY DAYS IN CALCUTTA IN HAPPINESS AND HARMONY. THEN ONE day, I saw my husband looking very miserable, holding a letter in his hand. I asked, 'Why are you so sad?'

He said, 'A letter has come from home. I must go.'

I said spontaneously, 'But what about me!' I had been standing—I sat down abruptly. I dissolved into tears.

Affectionately, he took my hand, drew me up, kissed me and wiped away my tears. He said, 'I, too, was thinking of that. I cannot go and leave you behind.'

I said, 'How would you introduce me there? How and where would you keep me?'

He said, 'That is what I am considering. The town is not such that I could keep you in another place, and no one would know much about it. Under my parents' eyes, where could I keep you?'

I asked, 'Can you not go?'

He said, 'I cannot.'

I said, 'When would you return? If you will return soon, then never mind about me, leave me and go.'

He said, 'There is no hope that I should return soon. We rarely come to Calcutta.'

I said, 'You go—I will not be a trouble to you. (I said this weeping profusely.) That which is in my fate must happen.'

He said, 'But if I do not see you I shall go mad.'

I said, 'Look, I am not your married wife (my husband shivered a little)—I have no rights over you. Send me away now—'

He would not let me say more. He said, 'There is no point in talking about it any more now. Now let me think. I will tell you my decision tomorrow.'

In the afternoon, he wrote to Raman Babu to come. He wrote, 'There is a private matter. Unless you come it cannot be told.'

Raman Babu came. I listened from the shelter of the door to hear what was said. My husband said, 'That cook of yours—the young one—what is her name?'

Raman Babu said, 'Kumudini.'

Upendra asked, 'Where is she from?'

Raman Babu said, 'I cannot tell you at present.'

'Has she a husband or is she a widow?'

'She has a husband.'

'Who knows her husband?'

'I do.'

'Who is he?'

'I am not at liberty to say, at present.'

'Why, is there some mystery about it?'

'There is,' Raman Babu said.

Upendra asked, 'Where did you get her?'

'My wife got her from her aunt.'

'Let that go—those are all trivial things. What is her character like?'

'Blameless. She used to tease our old cook a lot. Apart from that, she has not a single fault.'

'I am asking about her character faults as a woman.'

'No more excellent a character could be found.'

'Why can you not say where she is from?'

'I am not at liberty to say.'

'Where is her husband's house?'

'The same answer.'

'Is her husband alive?'

'He is.'

'Do you know him?'

'I do.'

'Where is this man now?'

'In this house of yours.'

My husband was astounded. Astonished, he asked, 'How did you know?'

Raman Babu said, 'I am not at liberty to say. Has your cross-examination ended?'

Upendra said, 'It has. But you have not asked why I asked you all these questions.'

Raman Babu said, 'I did not ask, for two reasons. One is this, that if I asked you would not answer. True or not?'

'True. What is the second reason?'

'That I know why you are asking.'

'You know that, too? Tell me and let me see.'

'I will not say.'

'Very well; can what I intend come to pass or not?'

'It can very well come to pass. Ask Kumudini.'

'Another thing. Can you write all that you know of Kumudini on a piece of paper and sign it?'

'I can—on one condition. I will write it, seal it in a packet and leave it with Kumudini. You will not be able to read it now. When you go home, you will read it. Do you agree?'

My husband thought for a long time and said, 'I agree. Will it further my intentions?'

'It will.'

After speaking of various other things, Raman Babu got up and left. Upendra Babu came to me.

I asked, 'What was all that for?'

He said, 'Did you hear everything?'

'Yes, I did. I was thinking that I had killed you and been hanged. Why the investigation after the hanging?'

He said, 'According to today's laws, that can happen.'

18
Plans for a Great Deception

THAT DAY, DAY AND NIGHT, MY HUSBAND WAS PREOCCUPIED IN THOUGHT. He did not say much to me—only, if he saw me he would keep looking at my face. I had more things to think of than he did; but at the sight of him thinking, a great pain arose within my soul. I suppressed my own pain and tried to cheer him up. I made flower-garlands and nosegays and so on of various forms and presented them to him, I prepared various kinds of paan, and made various kinds of good things to eat; I was weeping myself, but I put forward entertaining stories of different savours. My husband was a man who liked possessions—above all, he loved to manage property; with this in mind, I introduced the topic of managing property: I was Haramohan Datta's daughter; I knew about the management of estates. Nothing availed. Tear upon tear fell from my eyes.

The next day, in the morning, after bathing and eating, he made me sit by him, and said, 'I am sure that you will answer truthfully whatever I ask you?'

Then I remembered the cross-examination of Raman Datta. I said, 'What I say will be true. But I cannot answer everything.'

He asked, 'I have heard that your husband is alive. Will you divulge his name and address?'

I said, 'Not now. Some time must pass first.'

'Will you say where he is now?'

'Here in Calcutta.'

He said, somewhat startled, 'You are in Calcutta, your husband is in Calcutta, so why do you not live with him?'

'He does not know me.'

Notice, reader, that everything I was saying was true. My husband was astonished to hear this answer, and said, 'Husband and wife do not know each other? This is a very surprising thing!'

I said, 'Does everyone? Do you?'

Somewhat abashed, he said, 'That is because of misfortune.'

I said, 'Misfortune is everywhere.'

He said, 'Let that go: is there any likelihood of his claiming any rights over you in the future?'

'That is in my hands. If I make myself known to him, who knows what would happen.'

'Then let me tell you everything; I have learned that you are very intelligent. I will listen to what you advise.'

'Tell me.'

'I must go home.'

'I understand that.'

'Once I go home, I shall not be able to return soon.'

'I know that, too.'

'I cannot go and leave you behind. I should die.'

My heart rose into my throat, but I said, with a burst of laughter, 'Ah me! If rice is scattered, will there be any lack of crows?'

'Crows are no substitute for the kokil. I will take you with me.'

'Where will you keep me? Under what guise?'

'I will prepare a great deception. I thought about it yesterday. I have not spoken of it to you.'

I said, 'You will say, "This is Indira—I found her at Ramram Datta's house."'

'Oh, ruination! Who are you?'

My husband, stock-still, lifted his eyes and gazed at my face. I asked, 'Why, what has happened?'

He said, 'How did you know the name Indira? And how did you know my secret intention? Are you human, or some enchantress?'

I said, 'I will tell you later. Now I will return your cross-examination: answer in the same way.'

He said fearfully, 'Speak.'

'You told me once that even if you found your wife, you would not accept her because she had been abducted by bandits, and you would lose caste. Why are you not afraid of that if you take me home with you as Indira?'

He said, 'Not afraid of that? I am very afraid of that. But that will not endanger my life: now my life is in danger. Is caste more important than life? And it is not such a terribly acute danger, either. The bandits at Black Lake who were responsible were caught. They confessed. They said in their confession that they had only taken Indira's ornaments and other valuables, and had abandoned her. Only no one knows where she is now and what has happened; if she is found, it is easy to prepare and tell a blameless story. I hope that what Raman Babu writes will support this. If something is questioned, suspicion can be allayed by having some ceremony in the village. We have money—everyone can be controlled by money.'

'If that objection is met, then is there any other?'

'Suspicion about you. You are a counterfeit Indira—what if you are found out?'

'In your house, no one knows either me or the real Indira; for you all saw her only once, when she was a child; so why would I be found out?'

'By what you say, a strange person disguising herself as a known person can easily be found out through what she says.'

'Why don't you teach me everything?'

'That is what I have been thinking. But I cannot teach you everything. Remember that if something which I have forgotten to teach you comes up, then you will be found out. Remember that if the real Indira ever arrives, and judgement is made between the two of you, if there are questions about the past, you will be found out.'

I laughed a little. In such a situation, laughter is spontaneous. But it was not the time to make my true self known. I smiled, and said, 'No one can outwit me. You were asking me just now whether I was a human being or an enchantress. I am not human (hearing this, he shivered); I will tell you later what I am. I will tell you only this, now: no one can outwit me.'

My husband was astounded. He was an intelligent, active man. If not, he would not have been able to make so much money in so short a time. Outwardly, he was a little dry—with a wooden manner, if the reader will understand that—but inside he was very sweet, very soft, very tender; but he did not have the 'higher education' of Raman Babu or of today's young men. He believed strongly in the gods. He had travelled in various regions and heard stories of ghosts, witches, enchantresses and so on. He believed a little in all these. Moreover, he remembered now how he had become enchanted by me; he remembered what he had called my unusual intelligence; he remembered what I could not tell him. So he believed me a little when I said, 'I am not human'. For a little while, he was astounded and afraid. But after that, pushing away that vestige of belief with the force of his own intelligence, he said, 'Very well, will you tell me what I ask and let me see how much of an enchantress you are?'

'Ask.'

'You know that my wife's name is Indira. What is her father's name?'

'Haramohan Datta.'

'Where is his house?'

'In Maheshpur.'

'Who are you!'

'I told you that I would tell you that later. I am not human.'

'You said that your father's house was at Black Lake. A person from Black Lake could know all this. Now, tell me—what direction does the gate of the outer building of Haramohan's house face?'

'To the south. There is a lion on each side of a big portico.'

'How many sons has he?'

'One.'

'What is his name?'

'Basantakumar.'

'How many sisters has he?'

'At the time of your wedding, there were two.'

'Their names?'

'Indira and Kamini.'

'Is there any lake near his house?'

'There is. It is called Goddess Lake. Many lotuses bloom in it.'

He said, 'Yes, I have seen it. Were you once at Maheshpur? What is strange about that? That is how you know so much. Let me see what else you can tell me. At Indira's wedding, where did the giving of the bride to the bridegroom take place?'

'In the north-west corner of the puja hall.'

'During the women's rites, someone pulled my ear very hard. I remember her name. Let me hear you say her name.'

'Bindu—she had big eyes, and red lips. She was wearing a huge, old-fashioned nose-ring.'

'Correct. You must have been present at the wedding. You are a kinswoman of theirs, then?'

'Ask me a couple of things which neither kinswoman, maidservant nor cook would know.'

'On what date was Indira's wedding?'

'On the 27th day of the month of Baishakh, on the thirteenth day of the bright lunar fortnight.'

He was silent, in thought. Then he said, 'Reassure me, that I may ask two more questions?'

'I reassure you. Speak.'

'When everyone had left the bridal chamber, I said something to Indira alone, and she answered. What were these words, can you tell me?'

There was a little delay before I spoke. The reason for this was that I was restraining the tears which were coming to my eyes. He said, 'This time you have been outwitted! I live again—you are not an enchantress.'

Forcing back my tears, I said, 'You asked Indira, "Tell me then what relationship is there now between you and me?" Indira said, "From now on you are my god and I am your servant." That was one question, then. What is the other?'

He said, 'I am afraid to ask another question. I think I have lost my wits. Yet tell me. On the day of the flower-bed ceremony,[23] Indira, in fun, rebuked me, and I punished her, too. Can you tell me what these words were?'

'You held Indira's hand with one hand, and with the other on her shoulder you asked, "Indira, tell me, who am I to you?" To that Indira answered, "I have heard that you are my sister-in-law's bridegroom." As punishment, you lightly boxed her cheek, and seeing her a little abashed, you kissed her on the mouth.'

As I spoke, my body was flushed with a strange joy—that had been my first kiss. After that, there was the nectar of Subhashini's. Between them there had been a great drought. My heart had dried and cracked.

As I was thinking of this, I saw that my husband had slowly laid his head down on the pillow and closed his eyes. I said, 'Will you ask me something else?'

He said, 'No. Either you are Indira yourself, or else some enchantress.'

19
Demi-Goddess

I SAW THAT NOW I COULD EASILY REVEAL MY IDENTITY. MY IDENTITY HAD been uttered by my husband's own mouth. But I decided not to make myself known while any doubt at all remained. So I said, 'Now I will tell you who I am. I come from Kamrup.[24] I live by the great temple of Mahamaya. People call us Mahamaya's witch-attendants, but we are not witches. We are demi-goddesses. I offended Mahamaya, and for that was put under a curse and took this human form. The occupation of cook, and the position of a loose woman were also in Mahamaya's curse. So all this happened according to my fate. Now the time has come for me to be free of the curse. The goddess has said that if I please her by singing hymns in her praise, then I need only see her in her Mahabhairavi manifestation to obtain my freedom.'

He said, 'Where is that?'

I said, 'The temple of Mahabhairavi is in Maheshpur, to the north of your father-in-law's house. It is their place of worship: there is a road to and from it from the house, through the postern gate. Come, let us go to Maheshpur.'

He said, thoughtfully, 'You may indeed be my Indira. If Kumudini is Indira, what happiness! If that should be so, who on this earth would be as happy as I?'

I said, 'Whoever I am, if I go to Maheshpur, everything will be resolved.'

He said, 'Then go; let us set out from here tomorrow. Beyond Black Lake, I will send you on to Maheshpur, and go home myself, for the time being. After one or two days there, I will go to Maheshpur. I beg you, with joined hands, whether you are Indira, or Kumudini or a demi-goddess, do not leave me.'

I said, 'No. When I am free of the curse, I may, by the mercy of the goddess, have you again. You are dearer than my life to me.'

'That is not the speech of a witch.' With these words, he went to the outer building. Someone had arrived there. It was none other than Raman Babu. Coming with my husband into the inner chambers, Raman Babu gave me a small, sealed packet. He gave me the same instructions concerning it as he had given my husband. Finally, he said, 'What shall I say to Subhashini?'

I said, 'Tell her that tomorrow I am going to Maheshpur. When I go there, I will be freed from the curse.'

My husband said, 'Do you know all about that, then?'

Clever Raman Babu said, 'I do not know everything, but my wife Subhashini does.'

Going out, my husband asked Raman Babu, 'Do you believe in witches, Mahamaya's attendants, demi-goddesses and so on?'

Raman Babu knew something of the secret; he said, 'I do. Subhashini says that Kumudini is a demi-goddess under a spell.'

My husband said, 'Please ask your wife particularly whether Kumudini is Indira.'

Raman Babu stayed no longer. He went away laughing.

20

Disappearance of the Demi-Goddess

IN DUE COURSE, AFTER THIS CONVERSATION, WE BOTH SET OUT FROM Calcutta. After he had taken me past that lake of ill-fortune called Black Lake, my husband set off towards his own home.

The attendants took me on to Maheshpur. I told the bearers and guards to stay outside the village, and entered the village on foot. When I saw my father's house before me, I sat down in a secluded place and wept for a long time. Then I entered the house. I saw my father in front of me, and touched his feet. When he saw who I was he was overcome with joy. There is not enough space to speak about all that here.

I said nothing of where I had been for so long, or how I had come. When my father and mother questioned me, I said, 'I will tell you later.'

Later I told them the essentials of my story, but I did not tell them everything. I explained that I was finally with my husband, and that I had come with him. And that he, too, would arrive in one or two days. To Kamini I told every detail. Kamini was two years younger than I. She loved pranks very much. She said, 'Sister! Since the son of the Mitras is so very soft-hearted, why don't we play a prank on him?' I said, 'I, too, would like to do that.' Then both of us discussed and laid out plans. We instructed everybody carefully. We even instructed our parents a little. Kamini explained to them that I had not yet been publicly accepted. That was to happen here. We would organize that. But when their son-in-law arrived, they were not to tell him that I had come.

The next day, the son-in-law arrived. My father and mother received him very cordially. He did not hear on anyone's lips the news that I had arrived. Kamini asked him many questions; he answered mechanically. Standing in concealment, I heard and saw everything. Finally, he asked Kamini, 'Where is your sister?'

Kamini let out a great sigh, and said, 'Do I know where? After the disaster that happened at Black Lake, we have not been able to get any further news.'

His face fell. He could say nothing more. He must have thought, 'I have lost Kumudini', for he dissolved into tears.

Checking his tears, he asked, 'Has a woman called Kumudini arrived here?'

Kamini said, 'Whether she was Kumudini or not I can't say, but a woman did arrive in a palanquin the day before yesterday. She went straight on to the temple of the Great Goddess and touched the goddess's feet. Immediately an amazing thing happened. Suddenly it was dark with clouds and a shower rain came up. The woman took a trident in her hand and went burning up away into the sky.'

The Lord of my life stopped eating. He washed his hands, clasped them to his head and sat there for a long time; after a long time he said, 'Can I see the place where Kumudini disappeared?'

Kamini said, 'Why not? It's dark now—let us take a light.'

With these words, Kamini signed to me—'You go first. I will bring Upendra Babu after you, with a light.' I went ahead to the temple and sat on the veranda.

Thither came Kamini, holding a light (I have said that there was a path from the postern gate) bringing my husband to me. He fell at my feet. He called, 'Kumudini, Kumudini! If you have come—do not leave me again!'

After he had said these words again several times, Kamini said, angrily, 'Come, sister! Come away! This fellow knows Kumudini, he does not know you.'

Eagerly he asked, 'Sister! Who is your sister?'

Kamini said furiously, 'My sister is Indira! Have you never heard the name?'

With these words, the mischievous girl put out the light, seized my hand and pulled me away. We ran very fast. Recovering his senses somewhat, my husband ran after us. But it was dark—the path was unknown to him; he stumbled slightly over the threshold. We were close by: we seized him, one on each side, and lifted him up. Kamini said, in a whisper, 'We are demi-goddesses—we are accompanying you to protect you.'

With these words, pulling him along, we arrived at my bedroom. A light was burning there. Seeing us, he said, 'What is this? You are Kamini, and you are Kumudini!' Kamini, even more angrily, said, 'Ah, miserable one! Have you earned a living with these wits? Do you wield a spade? This is not Kumudini—this is Indira—Indira—Indira! Your wife! Can you not recognize your wife?'

Then my husband, silly with joy, went to take me on his lap and took Kamini on his lap instead. She gave him a cuff on his cheek and went away laughing.

I cannot describe the joy of that day. There was great festivity in the house. That evening there were about a hundred battles of words between Kamini and Upendra Babu. Every time it was my husband who lost.

21
How It Was Then

NOW MY HUSBAND HEARD FROM ME EVERYTHING THAT HAD BEEN MY FATE after the banditry at Black Lake. He heard, too, about the plot Raman Babu and Subhashini had contrived in order to bring him to Calcutta. He was even a little angry about this. He said, 'Was it necessary to pull me to and fro so much?' I explained the necessity to him. He was satisfied. But Kamini was not satisfied. Kamini said, 'I blame my sister a little that you were not ground like oilseeds. And then, didn't you make that childish assertion that you would not accept her! See here, fellow, when you men can not live without our lac-dyed lotus feet, why do you boast so much?'

Upendra Babu this time ventured an answer. He said, 'I could not know you then! What chance was there of recognizing you?'

Kamini said, 'Providence has not written in your fate whom you will recognize. Haven't you heard the play? It says,

The white cow said, Dark One, who recognizes you!
I recognize only the fresh grass on the Yamuna's banks.
I seek your footprints, I hear your flute.
The auspicious marks on your feet are there,
but does a cow know them?'[25]

I could no longer restrain my laughter. Upendra Babu, abashed, said to Kamini, 'Go, sister, don't pester me! You have recited from the play; now take this paan as a reward and go away.'

Kamini said, 'Oh, sister! I can see that this son of the Mitras does have a little sense after all.'

I said, 'What sense do you see?'

Kamini said, 'He has kept the container of paan and given me just one: is this not sense? Now you do something; make him put his hand to your feet occasionally—then his hand will be generous.'

'Can I make him put his hand to my feet? He is my god of a husband.'

'When did he become your god? If a husband is a god, then for all this time with you he has been a demi-god.'

'He became my god when his demi-goddess disappeared.'

'Aha! It is just as well, Master Mitra, that you could catch the demi-goddess. For if you were caught for your knowledge and work you would be in great trouble.'[26]

I said, 'Kamini, you exaggerate! Are you implying he is a low-caste thief?'

Kamini said, 'Is the fault mine? When Master Mitra worked for the commissariat he was committing theft. And as for low caste—when he was supplying provisions to the army, he was acting as a low-caste man, too.'[27]

Upendra Babu said, 'Let her speak—she is only a child. It is said that: 'Tis sweet to hear a child a-babbling.'

Kamini said, 'Of course. When you were a-taming your demi-goddess, your wits were a-begging. I will return—Mother is a-calling me.'

Indeed, our mother was calling.

When Kamini returned from our mother, she said, 'Do you know why she was a-calling? You will be a-staying another two days—if you are not a-staying, we will be a-keeping you by force.'

We looked at each other.

Kamini said, 'Why are you a-looking at each other?'

Upendra Babu said, 'We are a-thinking.'

Kamini said, 'Leave a-thinking till you are home. These two days are for a-eating, a-giving, a-laughing, a-pleasing, a-playing, a-dusting, a-leaning, a-swinging, a-dancing, a-singing—'[28]

Upendra Babu said, 'Kamini, will you dance?'

Kamini said, 'Go away with you, why me? I have kept what chains I have bought—you dance.'

Upendra Babu said, 'You have made me dance ever since I arrived—how much more will you make me dance—now you dance a little!'

'If I do, will you stay?'

'I will.'

Not in the hope of seeing Kamini dance, but at the request of my parents, Upendra Babu agreed to stay for another day. That day, too, was very joyful. The women of the neighbourhood came in groups, and, after dusk, surrounded my husband. The women gathered in a room in a corner of the great house.

I did not count how many women came. So many shapely eyes with bee-black pupils, in rows, playing like saphari fish in a clear lake; so many forelocks coiled like hooded snakes, twining and expanding and swaying like forest creepers in the rainy season, as if black she-snakes, terrified at Krishna's subdual of the serpent Kaliya were twisting and turning in the waters of the Yamuna—so many ears, ear-hoops, studs, earrings, ear-drops played in so many cloud-like piles of hair, like lightning within clouds—so many kinds of wave-like lips moving, as so many rows of pearl-like teeth between reddened lips, chewed so many packets of scented paan—the love god, caught in the snares of so many hoop-nose-rings freed himself by responding with his arrows: with the flinging up and down of so many ornament-adorned plump arms, that room acquired an unearthly, restless beauty, like a garden full of wind-stirred flowering creepers, resounding with jingles and tinkles like the humming of bees; so much sparkle in necklets, beauty in necklaces, necklaces outshining the moon; the sparkle of anklets as feet moved! So many Benarasi, Baluchari, Mirjapuri, Dhakai, Shantipuri, Simla, Pharasdanga saris[29]—different kinds of silks—full of colour, striped, fluttering, floating, chequered—with those, some had veils, some were obliquely veiled, some half-veiled—some had only their chignons covered—and some not even that.

The Lord of my life had brought home money by conquering many platoons of white men—he had deprived many colonels and generals of their wits and brought home a share of the profits—but seeing this platoon of beauties he was terrified. In the place of the cannons' fire, that of the great cannons of the eyes; instead of the black-toothed coiling clouds of smoke, these black-toothed coiling clouds of lovely hair; instead of the clash of bayonets, this tinkling of ornaments; instead of the music of the war drums, the jingling of anklets on lac-dyed feet! The man who had seen Chilianwala—he was bereft of hope. Seeing me beside the door, he signed to me to save him on this great battlefield—but I, like the Sikh army-leader, betrayed him—I did not help him in this battle.[30]

In truth, I knew that much shameless behaviour took place in all these gatherings. So Kamini and I did not attend—we remained outside. We occasionally peeped in from the doorway. If you say, why are you engaged in describing something at which shameless behaviour took place, my answer to that is that I am a Hindu woman, and all these are shameless in my view. But the prevailing view today is that of the English, and if judged from the English viewpoint, there was nothing shameless at all in this behaviour.

I have said that Kamini and I peeped in. We saw that Yamuna, a lady of the neighbourhood, was sitting in splendour, presiding over the assembly. She was more than forty-five years old; her complexion was softly dark; her eyes were small, but a little heavy-lidded; her lips were thick, but full of colour. Her clothes and ornaments were ostentatious—there was a display of red lac-dye on her feet, red on the black, like hibiscus on the Yamuna itself—on her head, a display of hair reinforced with a hair-piece. Seeing the uncommon width and circumference of her body, my husband ridiculed her by calling her 'nadirupa mahishi'.[31] Mathurans call the Yamuna river Krishna's 'Queen in the form of a river' and it was from taking note of this that my husband made his joke. Now, our Yamuna had never been to Mathura, and did not know of this, and did not know of this meaning of the word mahishi. The only meaning she knew for the word mahishi was 'female buffalo', and hearing her body compared to that of this beast she was beside herself in anger. In retaliation, she referred to me insinuatingly, before my husband, as 'cow'; at this point I put my head round the door and asked, 'Sister Yamuna! What are you talking about?'

Yamuna said, 'A cow, sister.'

I asked, 'Why a cow?'

Kamini said from beside me, 'Sister Yamuna's voice has become dry from calling. Give her something to drink.'

The presider over the assembly was diminished by laughter's wounds; angry with Kamini, she said, 'Insignificant girl, why is your stick in everyone's pot, Kamini?'

Kamini said, 'Well, no one else can cook your cow-fodder.'[32]

With these words, Kamini fled, and so did I. When we came back again and peeped in, we saw that grandmother Piyari, of the neighbourhood, a Vaidya by caste—sixty-five years old, and a widow for twenty-five of them—had come dressed up like Radha; with cymbals, and ornaments on every limb. When she noticed my husband, she wandered around that forest of kamini flowers saying, 'Where is Krishna? Where is Krishna?'

Kamini said, 'What are you looking for, Grandmother?'

She said, 'I am looking for Krishna.'

Kamini said, 'Go to the cowherds' house—this is a Kayastha house.'

The elderly jokester said, 'It is in a Kayastha's house that my Krishna is to be found.'

Kamini said, 'Oh, Grandmother, are you available to all castes, then?'

Now, there had once been some talk about Piyari being connected with the oilmen's caste. At these words, she flared up angrily and started to shout taunts and abuses at Kamini. In order to stop her I pointed out Yamuna and said, 'Why are you angry? Your Krishna has jumped into that Yamuna. Come, let us stand by the verge and weep.'

Yamuna was as knowledgeable about the meaning of the word 'verge' as she was about the meaning of the word for 'queen, she-buffalo'. She thought that I was referring to someone called Verge and casting aspersions on her stainless chastity (stainless by reason of her figure). She said angrily, 'Who is this Verge then?'

As a result, I, too, felt the urge to make a little joke. I said, 'He on whose body Yamuna dashes billows day and night, he is called Verge in Brindavan.'[33]

There was more destructive dashing of billows—Yamuna understood nothing of this and said angrily, 'I do not know your Billows, I do not know your Verges and I do not know your Brindavan. I suppose you learnt all these funny names from the bandits.'

There was a girl called Rangamayi in the gathering, of my own age. She said, 'Why are you so angry, Sister Yamuna! The sand-banks on the sides of the river are called verges. Are there sand-banks on each side of you?'

Yamuna's sister-in-law, Chanchala, was sitting behind in a veil; from within that veil she said in a soft, sweet voice, 'If there were sand-banks, I would survive. I would be able to see some light. Now, only the dark water of the dark river murmurs.'

Kamini said, 'Why are you dropping our Sister Yamuna on the sand-banks like this!'

Chanchala said, 'Perish the thought! Goddess! Why would we drop the lady in the middle of a sand-bank? We will clasp her brother's feet and tell him to put her on a cremation ground in the fields.'

Rangamayi said, 'What is the difference between the two?'

Chanchala said, 'On the cremation ground she would benefit the jackals and dogs—on the sand-banks cows and buffalo graze—what use would she be to them?' As she said the word 'buffalo' she lifted her veil a little and cast a smiling, sidelong look towards her sister-in-law.

Yamuna said, 'No, I don't want to hear that word another hundred times. Let those who like buffaloes say "buffalo, buffalo, buffalo" a hundred times.'

Piyari had not been listening much—she asked, 'What is this talk of buffaloes?'

Kamini said, 'We were talking of countries in which the oilmen use buffaloes to turn the grinding block.'

With these words, Kamini fled. It was not a good thing to keep bringing up the subject of oilmen—but it was impossible to see Kamini as bad. Piyari became dark with anger, said nothing more, and went to sit near Upendra Babu. Then I called Kamini and said, 'Kamini! Come and see! Now Piyari has found Krishna.'

Kamini said, from a distance, 'It is about time.'

Then we heard a clamour. I heard my husband's voice—he was reprimanding someone in Hindi. I went to see. I saw that a bearded Moghul had entered the room; U. Babu was scolding him and ordering him to go away; the Moghul was not going. Then Kamini called from the door, 'Master Mitra! Is there no strength in your body?'

Master Mitra said, 'Of course there is.'

Kamini said, 'Then push the Moghul fellow away by the neck.'

At these words, the Moghul fled away breathlessly. As he fled, I caught hold of his beard—a false beard came away. The Moghul said, 'Oh help! How can you set up house with a fool like this?' With these words he fled. I threw the beard to Yamuna, as a gift. Upendra Babu asked, 'What's the matter?'

Kamini said, 'The matter? Put on a beard, go on four legs and start grazing in the pasture.'

Upendra Babu said, 'Why, was the Moghul a fake?'

Kamini said, 'Who could say such a thing! Could Anangamohini be a false Moghul! He was a genuine import from Delhi!'

There was a burst of laughter. I was approaching, a little subdued, when Brajasundari, a woman of the neighbourhood, in a worn-out sari, with a little boy on her hip, started to weep words of sorrow to Upendra

Babu. 'I am very poor; I get nothing to eat; I cannot raise my son.' Upendra Babu gave her something. We were one on each side of the door. As she was passing through the door, Kamini said to her, 'Sister beggar! Don't you know that if you get something by begging from an important man you must give a bribe to the doorkeepers?'

Brajasundari said, 'Who are the doorkeepers?'

'The two of us.'

'How much do you want?'

'What did you get?'

'Ten rupees.'

'Then give us eight rupees plus eight rupees, that is, sixteen rupees before you go.'

'Not a bad profit!'

Kamini said, 'Why should you worry about profit and loss when you are begging at an important man's house? In season and out of season something has to be given out from the house.'

Brajasundari was the wife of an important man. She quickly brought out sixteen rupees and gave them to us. We gave these sixteen rupees to Yamuna saying, 'Get some sandesh to eat, with this money.'

My husband said, 'What is going on?'

Meanwhile, Brajasundari sent away the child and came back wearing a Benarasi sari. Another amusing thing happened.

Upendra Babu said, 'Is this a play?'

Yamuna said, 'What else is it? Don't you see that some are acting the story of Krishna's subduing of Kaliya, some the story of the restoration of Radha's good name, some the story of Brindavan's sorrow at Krishna's departure for Mathura—and some have only the play of escaping from the plays.'

Upendra Babu said, 'Whose is the play of escaping from the plays?'

Yamuna said, 'Why, Kamini's! Hers is only the play of escaping from the plays.'

Kamini ignited everyone with words; she pleased everyone by distributing paan, flowers, and perfume. Then everyone joined together, seized her and said, 'Are you wandering around escaping, then?'

Kamini said, 'If I don't flee, won't I have you to be afraid of?'

Master Mitra said, 'Kamini! Sister, isn't there an agreement between us?'

'What agreement, Master Mitra?'

'That you would dance.'

'Well, I have danced.'

'When did you dance?'

'At noon.'

'Where did you dance, then?'

'In my room, with the doors closed.'

'Who saw you?'

'Nobody.'

'That was not the agreement.'

Kamini said, 'Nothing was said about my dancing in front of you, wearing dancing-girls' trousers. I agreed to dance, and I have danced. I have kept my word. If you did not get to see me, that is just your destiny. Now what will become of the chains I have bought and kept by me?'

Kamini might have evaded the danger of dancing, but my husband was caught in the matter of singing. The order came from the gathering that he should sing. He had learned the style of singing of the west. He sang a song in the Sanadi raga. That assemblage of heavenly nymphs smiled to hear it. They put in the order, 'Badan Adhikari or Dashu Ray.'[34] Upendra Babu was unskilled in these. So the heavenly nymphs were unsatisfied.

In this way, two prahars of the night passed. I could have omitted this chapter. Yet I believe that this part of life of the women of this country has now disappeared. It is good that it should be so: for with it, indecency, shamelessness and sometimes corruption had intertwined. But I wrote this chapter in the wish to present a picture of something that has gone. Yet I do not know: these bad customs may still exist in some places. If that is so, then it is necessary to open the eyes and ears of those who do not forbid their urban womenfolk to go to see their sons-in-law. So I have shown them how to catch fish without touching the water.

22
Conclusion

THE FOLLOWING DAY, I WENT WITH MY HUSBAND, RIDING IN A PALANQUIN, to my father-in-law's house. That I was going with my husband was a joy, it is true; but when I was going there earlier, that was yet another kind of happiness. I went then in the hope of what I had never had; now I was going with what I had received tied up in the end of my sari. One is the poetry of the poet; the other is the riches of the rich. Are the riches of the rich equal to the poetry of the poet? Those who have become important by earning riches, and have lost poetry, even they do not say this. They say that it is while the flower is on the tree that it is beautiful; if it is plucked it is no longer so beautiful. Is there as much happiness in the fulfilment of a dream as in the dream itself? As the sky is not really blue, but only looks blue, so it is with riches. There is no happiness in riches; we only think that there is. It is poetry which is happiness. For poetry is hope; riches are only possessions. And even that is not in everyone's fate. Many rich people are nothing but watchmen of a treasure-store. One of my kinsmen calls them 'treasury guards'.

Yet I went with happiness to my father-in-law's house. This time, we arrived without hindrance. My husband gave his parents a detailed account of everything. Raman Babu's packet was opened. Everything I had said agreed with it. My father and mother-in-law were satisfied. Everything was made known to the people of the community, also; nothing was omitted.

I wrote a letter to Subhashini, telling her about everything that had happened. My heart constantly wept for Subhashini. At my request, my husband sent five hundred rupees to Raman Babu for Haramani. I very quickly received an answer from Subhashini. Her letter was full of joy. R. Babu had written the letter for Subhashini. But it was clear from the expression that the words were Subhashini's own. She sent news of everyone. I will quote an excerpt or two from her letter. She wrote:

'At first, Haramani wouldn't take any money at all. She said, "I would become greedy. It seems that this was a good deed to do, but this kind of deed is wrong. What if, through greed, I consented to wrongdoing?" I explained to the poor woman: "Would you have done this without the taste of my broom? Would you have a taste of my broom on every occasion? Would I give you only a taste of the broom on the occasion of a bad deed? Would you not also get a couple of rebukes? You did a good thing, so take the reward." After a lot of such instructions and explanations, she took the money. Now she is making a list of various kinds of penances to do. For as long as there was no news of you, she laughed no more; but now everyone in the house is afflicted by the blaze of her laughter.'

Subhashini wrote the news of the Brahmin cook thus: 'After you and your husband went away secretly, the old woman bragged a lot, saying, "I always knew that she was not a good person. Her ways and manners were not good. How many times did I tell you not to keep such a bad person. But who listens to the words of the poor? Everyone just talked of Kumudini, Kumudini in an infatuated way." And so on and so on. Then, when she heard that you had not gone off with just anyone, but had gone with your own husband, that you were the daughter of an important man, and the bride of another—then she said, "I have said again and again that she was the daughter of a good house; are such a nature and character found in common houses? She was as virtuous as she was beautiful—like Lakshmi! May she be well, mistress! May she be well! And see here, mistress! Tell her to send me something."'

Concerning the mistress of the house, Subhashini wrote, 'When she heard all this news of you, she expressed joy, but she rebuked me and R. Babu a little. She said, "Why did you not tell me in the beginning that she was the daughter of such a great house? I would have taken great care of her." And she reviled your husband a little, saying, "She may have been his family, but it was not well done of him to take such a good cook away from me."'

The news of the master, Ramram Datta, was in Subhashini's own scrawling handwriting. With difficulty, I read that the master had rebuked the mistress with simulated anger, saying, 'You have sent away the beautiful cook on a deceitful pretext.' The mistress said, 'I have done well; what would you do with a beautiful woman?' The master said, 'How can I say that? I can no longer meditate on your dark form night and day.' At that, the mistress went to lie down, and did not get up again that day. She did not understand at all that the master was only teasing her.

Needless to say, I sent something for the Brahmin cook, and for the other servants.

After that I saw Subhashini only once more. At her particular request, my husband took me to her at the time of her daughter's wedding. I gave Subhashini's daughter ornaments and put them on her; I gave suitable gifts to the mistress; I gave appropriate gifts and greetings to others. But I saw that the mistress was displeased with me and my husband. She told me many times that her son was not eating well. I did cook something for Raman Babu. But I did not go again. Not for fear of having to cook; for fear of upsetting the mistress.

The mistress and Ramram Datta long ago ascended to heaven. But I have not gone again. I have not forgotten Subhashini. I shall not forget her in this life. I have not met anyone else like Subhashini in this world.

Endnotes

1. In the nineteenth century, many Indian contractors amassed fortunes as suppliers of food to the army. Indira is shown here as a traditional woman who is not sure of her grasp of the English word 'commissariat'.
2. In traditional Bengal, daughters were married off young and custom demanded that they spend some time in their parental homes, away from the husband's family, during the first years of marriage. It was a parental duty to visit the 'in-laws' regularly to bring back the daughter. Here Indira's father promises to do this.
3. A married woman should never go out with bare arms, as it is a sign of widowhood, hence Indira makes a bracelet with creepers from the jungle.
4. It is customary to address a strange lady as 'mother'.
5. The Brahmin arranged for clothes and bracelets suitable for a married woman. Red is the colour of weddings, and conch shell bracelets are worn by the poor in place of gold bracelets which are symbols of the married status.
6. This is an allusion to the Puranas and the mythology of Krishna who used to play erotic games with milkmaids on the banks of the Yamuna. The 'dark prince' is Krishna.
7. The number of boats in Calcutta now is not one-hundredth of that of previous times (Bankimchandra's own footnote).
8. 'Sahib Subo' in Bengali refers to Europeans or high caste anglicized Indians.
9. Capsule (Bankimchandra's own footnote, in English).
10. No householder should let a guest or visitor leave the house without partaking of some food, or else, it is believed, it will bring misfortune to the household.

11. Going 'to the Ganga' implied jumping into the famous holy river to commit suicide.
12. 'The Pandavas' queen' refers to Draupadi, the heroine of the epic, the *Mahabharata*, who according to Indian tradition was an excellent cook.
13. The allusion is to the mythology of Krishna and his cowherd girls. Sometimes he would play the flute under a kadamba tree near the river Yamuna.
14. It is considered a bad omen to break a pot in the kitchen.
15. Goddess Shashti is the goddess of children. Childless women have no status in society and are considered to have earned Shashti's displeasure.
16. It is usual to refer to an elderly domestic female servant as her son's or daughter's mother. Sona is the child of the old Brahmin cook, hence the cook is called 'Sona's mother'.
17. This is how a witch is described in Bengali folklore.
18. Abducted women would lose their caste status and not be accepted back into society because they are suspected of having been violated or at least forced to share food with the wrong caste.
19. This refers to the Bengal dramatist Dinabandhu Mitra's (1830–73) satire 'Jamai Barik' (1872). In this play, roles are reversed for humour, and the wife calls her husband by his first name.
20. Self-created (Bankimchandra's own footnote).
21. From a medieval Bengali poem.
22. This refers to Kamadeva, the god of Love (the Hindu Eros). According to Hindu tradition, he lost his body but could still carry his bow and arrow of flowers.
23. The flower-bed ceremony takes place on the nuptial night when the marital bed is decorated with flowers.
24. In Kamrup, Assam, there is an old temple of the goddess Kamaksha or Mahamaya. According to Bengali folklore, the goddess has many demi-goddesses in the temple who live there as her companions. They often use their supernatural powers to turn men pilgrims into sheep

and keep them for fun.

25. Here Kamini is calling her brother-in-law a 'white cow' who failed to recognize the god Krishna, since he failed to recognize his wife.
26. This chapter is difficult to translate and this paragraph is particularly difficult. Here Bankimchandra is using Bengali puns. Vidhyadhari, the word for 'demi-goddess', literally means 'knowledge-holder', a combination of vidya, 'knowledge' and dhari, 'holder', from a verb meaning to catch or hold. Bankimchandra is alluding to a Bengali proverb, Churi vidya bara vidya, yadi na parey dhara (knowledge of thieving is great knowledge as long as one is not caught). Kamini is teasing Upendra who could not keep hold of his demi-goddess, or 'knowledge-holder' (vidyadhari), but is lucky he did not get caught (dhara) for his knowledge of thieving (churi vidya).
27. It was generally believed in India that army contractors amassed fortunes by dishonest means and that all kinds of provisions were supplied which customary law did not allow high-caste Hindus to handle.
28. This conversation uses 'dog-Sanskrit' for humour.
29. These are names of various regions famous for designs of expensive saris.
30. This refers to the Second Sikh War; in the battle of Chilianwala, the British army suffered a terrible loss in December 1848. In January 1849, the British conquered the Sikh kingdom of the Punjab when a Sikh general helped the British.
31. Mahishi is a word for 'queen' as well as for 'female buffalo'. The Yamuna is referred to as 'queen in the form of a river' (nadirupa mahishi).
32. This is a pun. Gai means 'cow' and also 'sing'.
33. The pun here is with the word pulin ('verge') which is often used as a proper name.
34. Badan Adhikari and Dashu Roy were two well-known Bengali singers of popular and 'naughty' Bengali songs in the nineteenth century.

Krishnakanta's Will

Part 1

1

THERE WAS A RICH ZAMINDAR FAMILY IN HARIDRAGRAM. THE HEAD OF THE family was Krishnakanta Roy. He was a very rich man; the annual income from his estate was nearly two lakhs of rupees. The estate was acquired jointly by him and his brother Ramkanta. The two brothers earned money together, and were deeply attached to one another; it never occurred to one that the other might deceive him. They lived in a joint family and the estate was bought in the name of the eldest, Krishnakanta.

In due course, a son was born to Ramkanta; he was named Govindalal. After the birth of his son, Ramkanta felt that proper legal documents should be drawn up regarding the estate acquired by him and his brother together. He was sure that Krishnakanta would not deceive Govindalal or do him any harm. He was, however, not so sure about his nephews; they might adopt a different course after their father's death. But Ramkanta could not broach the subject of legal documents easily and put it off every day. Then, once, while visiting one of their estates on business, he suddenly died.

If Krishnakanta wished, he could have deceived his nephew and appropriated the whole property. There would have been no difficulty in doing so. But he had no such evil intention. He brought up Govindalal as his own son, with his own children and he resolved to leave his nephew, by will, half the share of the property that rightly belonged to Ramkanta Roy.

Krishnakanta Roy had two sons and a daughter. The elder son was called Haralal, the younger son Vinodlal and the daughter Sailavati.

According to Krishnakanta's will, after his death, Govindalal would get eight annas of the property, Haralal and Vinodlal three annas each, and the wife and Sailavati one anna each.

Haralal was a rude, uncontrollable man, disobedient to his father and foul-mouthed. A will in a Bengali community rarely stays secret. So Haralal got to know the contents of the will. His eyes red-rimmed in anger, he abused his father, 'What is this? Govindalal gets half the property and I only get three annas?'

Krishnakanta said, 'This is right. I have given Govindalal the half of the property that belonged to his father.'

Haralal said, 'What is this about his father's share? Why should he get a share of our paternal property? And we will look after our mother and sister. Why should they get one share each? You should write down in your will that they are entitled to maintenance only.'

Somewhat angered, Krishnakanta said, 'Son, the property is mine and I shall dispose of it as I like.'

'You have lost your senses. I won't let you dispose of the property as you like.'

Krishnakanta retorted, his eyes also red with anger, 'Haralal, if you were a boy I'd call for the schoolmaster and have you caned.'

To which Haralal retorted, 'As a boy I singed my schoolmaster's moustache, and now I shall burn your will.'

Krishnakanta did not utter another word. But he tore up the will and had another drawn up. According to this new will Govindalal received eight annas, Vinodlal five annas and his wife, Sailavati and Haralal, one anna each.

In anger, Haralal left home and went to Calcutta, whence he wrote a letter to his father, which could be summed up like this: 'The pandits of Calcutta say that widow remarriage is permitted according to our shastras. I have decided to marry a widow. If, however, you change your will and leave me eight annas and register the will, I shall change my mind. Else I shall marry a widow without delay.'

Haralal hoped that his father would be alarmed and change the will in his favour. But his hopes were soon dashed when a reply came from his father: 'I have now disowned you as my son—you can marry anyone you like and I shall dispose of my property as I like. If you marry a widow I shall certainly change my will but the change will not be to your advantage.'

Soon after this, Haralal sent word that he had married a widow. Krishnakanta Roy tore up his will again and decided to make a new will.

Brahmananda Ghosh was a meek and good-natured man who lived in the neighbourhood. He used to call Krishnakanta 'big uncle' and was favoured and supported by the zamindar.

He had a good hand and all Krishnakanta Roy's legal documents came from his pen. Krishnakanta sent for him, 'Come after lunch, you have to write a new will.' Vinodlal, who was present there at the time, asked, 'Why do you want to change the will again?' Krishnakanta said, 'This time your elder brother will get nothing in his share.'

Vinodlal said, 'That is not right. Maybe he is guilty. But he has a son, and the little boy is innocent. What about him?'

'I shall give him one pie.'

'One pie is not enough.'

Krishnakanta said, 'The income from my estate is two lakhs of rupees. One pie of that is three thousand rupees. A householder can live comfortably on this. Anyway, I shall give no more.'

Vinodlal argued for a long time, but the old man did not change his mind.

2

BRAHMANANDA, AFTER HIS DAILY BATH AND LUNCH, WAS ABOUT TO TAKE HIS siesta, when he was surprised to see Haralal Roy, who came in and sat at the head of the bed.

Brahma said, 'Hello! Is it you, "big" babu? When did you get home?'

Haralal said, 'I haven't been home yet.'

'So you came straight here! When did you arrive from Calcutta?'

'Two days ago. I was in hiding. I understand a new will is to be made!'

'So I hear.'

'This time nothing in my share.'

'The master said so in anger, but he will change his mind.'

'I understand that it will be written this afternoon, and you are going to write it.'

'What am I to do? I cannot say "no" to the master's command.'

'Well! It is not your fault. Now, do you wish to earn something?'

'What! Slaps and blows? Go ahead and hit me.'

'No! One thousand rupees.'

'How? By marrying a widow?'

'Yes!'

'Oh! I am too old for such a thing.'

'Then do something else and start now. Let me give this to you as an advance.'

So saying, Haralal placed a five hundred rupee note in Brahmananda's hand. Brahmananda looked at it carefully, turning it over and over, and said, 'What shall I do with this?'

'Keep it as a saving and give ten rupees to Mati, the milkwoman.'

Brahmananda said, 'I have no business with the milkwoman or anyone else! But what do you want me to do?'

'Mend two pens so that they write exactly like each other.'

Brahma said, 'All right, friend, whatever you say.'

Saying this, the son of the Ghosh family (Brahmananda) mended two pens and trying them, he saw that they wrote exactly alike.

Then Haralal said, 'Put one pen in your box. When you go to write the will, use this one; with the second pen we shall write something here. Have you got good ink?'

Brahmananda took out his inkpot and showed it to Haralal, who said, 'Good! Take this ink with you when you go to write this will.'

'Is there no pen or ink in your father's house that I must carry all these with me?'

Haralal said, 'Don't worry. I have a plan. Otherwise why would I give you so much money!'

'I thought as much; you have got it all planned.'

'Someone may wonder why you have brought your own pen and inkpot today. To convince them you must curse the ink and pen from the steward's office.'

'I can curse the steward, not just his pen and ink.'

'That won't be necessary. Now let us get down to the real job.'

Then Haralal gave Brahmananda two sheets of 'general letter'. Brahmananda said, 'Why, this is government paper.'

Haralal said, 'No. This is not government paper. This is the paper used in attorney's offices. The master uses such paper for his wills. That's why I got it. Now you write what I tell you, using this pen and ink.'

Brahmananda wrote the will as Haralal dictated it. The substance of the will was thus: Krishnakanta Roy decided that after his death, Vinodlal should receive three annas of his estate and one pie each for Govindalal, Krishnakanta's wife, Sailavati the daughter and Haralal's son; the remaining twelve annas would go to Haralal, the eldest son.

When he finished writing, Brahmananda said, 'The will is written. But who signs it?'

'I do,' said Haralal, and he signed Krishnakanta's name and names of four witnesses.

'This is forgery,' cried Brahmananda.

'No, this is the genuine will. The will that you will write this afternoon is the forgery.'

'How?'

'When you go to write the will, take this will, hidden in your coat pocket. While there, write a will as my father dictates, but using this ink and this pen. The paper, pen, ink and writer of the two wills will look alike. After my father's will has been read out and signed, you take it back to sign it yourself. Turn your back to the others when you are signing it and take the opportunity to exchange the wills. And give the master my will and bring his will back to me.'

After some thought Brahmananda said, 'Whatever one may think, there is no doubt that this is a clever plan.'

Haralal said, 'Then what is in your mind?'

'I am tempted to do it but I am afraid. Take back your money. I won't be involved in a forgery.'

'Then return my money,' said Haralal and put out his hand. Brahmananda returned the note. Haralal got up and was about to leave, when Brahmananda said, 'What! Going already, my friend?'

'No, I am not,' said Haralal.

'You gave me an advance of five hundred rupees. What more will you give?'

'Another five hundred after you bring me the other will.'

'That is a lot of money. It is difficult to resist temptation.'

'Then you agree?'

'What else can I do? But how do I change the wills? They will certainly catch me out.'

'Why should they? Here, I will change them before your own eyes. Catch me out if you can.'

Haralal was not an educated man. He had no particular skill, but he was a clever trickster. He put the will in his pocket, took out another sheet of paper and proceeded to write on it. How, in the meantime, the paper went from his hand into his pocket, and the will from his pocket into his hands, Brahmananda did not see. He praised Haralal's skills.

'I shall teach you,' Haralal said, and he showed Brahmananda how the trick was done. Brahmananda mastered the trick after some practice. Then Haralal took his leave.

'I shall go now, but I shall be back with more money in the evening.'

Soon after Haralal's departure, Brahmananda was seized with fear. He realized that he had agreed to commit a serious crime, which was punishable by law. Who knows, he might have to spend the rest of his life in prison. What if he were caught while changing the wills? Why should he do it? But a thousand rupees was within his grasp; he could not let that go while he lived.

Alas! The anguish that the prospect of a ritual feast has brought to many a poor Brahmin! He may be suffering from infectious fever and an enlarged spleen which fills his stomach when an invitation to a ritual feast arrives. His eyes feast on many delicacies such as luchi, sandesh, mihidana and sitabhog, served beautifully on brass dishes or plantain leaves. What should a poor Brahmin do? Should he eat them or leave the feast? I can swear that the holy Brahmin will not be able to solve this knotty problem even if he ponders over it for a thousand years. Unwillingly, he must put the food in his mouth.

This is exactly what happened to Brahmananda. He knew that the money offered by Haralal could land him in prison, but his greed was as great as his fear of the consequences. Like the poor Brahmin, he could not make a rational decision, his heart was set on the money.

3

AFTER WRITING THE WILL, BRAHMANANDA RETURNED HOME IN THE EVENING and found Haralal waiting for him.

'What happened?' Haralal asked.

Brahmananda was fond of poetry. Forcing a smile he recited,

I stretched my hands to catch the moon,
But the thorns of babla scratched my fingers.

'So, you could not do it?'

Brahma said, 'My friend, I was nervous.'

'You could not do it!'

'No, I could not. Here—take your counterfeit will and your money.' And he took out Haralal's will and his note for five hundred rupees and returned them to him.

Haralal's eyes turned red and his lips trembled with anger. 'Fool! Incompetent fool! You could not do what an ordinary woman could do. I am going. But be careful, do not utter a word about it to anyone, else your life is in danger.'

'Do not worry; I shall keep quiet about it.'

Haralal went to the kitchen. Since Haralal was almost a son of the family, he had access to all parts of the house. He found Rohini, Brahmananda's niece, cooking there.

Now, this Rohini has a special role to play, and I must, therefore, say something about her appearance and her character—although these days there is not much demand for descriptions of beauty and it is risky under recent laws to describe anyone's character but one's own. But I have to say this: that Rohini was then in the full bloom of youth, and overflowing with beauty like the harvest moon in autumn. She had become a widow in her early youth, but had acquired some improper habits for a widow: she wore a black-bordered dhoti, bangles on her wrists and took up chewing betel leaves. On the other hand, she excelled in cooking—she was like Draupadi: all Bengali vegetarian dishes, jhol, ambal, charchari, ghanta, dalna, etc. received a special flavour in her hands. She had no rival in needlework, in decorating with rice paste and in flower decoration. She was the only one who was in demand in the neighbourhood for dressing women's hair and arraying brides.

Rohini, the raving beauty, was stirring dal in the pot with a wooden spoon—and now and then darting bitter-sweet glances at a cat which sat at some distance, its pads on the floor. Rohini was trying to find out whether animals were thrilled by provocative flashes from the corners of a woman's eyes. But the cat, taking these glances as an invitation to eat the fried fish, was advancing slowly.

Just then, Haralal entered the kitchen, with his shoes squeaking. The cat, frightened, bolted, abandoning its hunt for fried fish. Rohini got up, put back the stirrer, washed her hands and pulled the end of her dhoti over her head in modesty. Rubbing her fingernails, she asked, 'When did you get in, Big Uncle?'

'Yesterday. I want to have a word with you.'

Rohini shivered in expectation. 'Will you have a meal here? Shall I put some fine rice on the fire?'

'Put it on if you like. But that is not what I wanted to talk about. Do you remember what happened to you one day some time ago?'

Rohini stood silently looking at the ground. Haralal continued, 'Remember that day when you were coming back from bathing in the holy Ganga and got separated from your fellow pilgrims?'

Rohini, holding the fingers of her left hand with her right hand and looking down, said, 'I remember.'

'Remember! You lost your way and found yourself in a field and a group of ruffians followed you?'

'Yes, I remember.'

'Who rescued you then?'

'You. You were going somewhere on horseback . . .'

'I was visiting my sister-in-law.'

'You rescued me and sent me home in a palanquin. How can I forget that? I can never repay that debt.'

Haralal said, 'You can repay it today. You can put me in your debt for the rest of my life.'

'Tell me how. I shall give my life to help you.'

'Whether you help me or not, do not mention to anyone what I tell you now.'

'Never, not as long as I live.'

'Swear to it.'

Rohini swore. Then Haralal told her about the will and the counterfeit will and said, 'You have to steal the genuine will and replace it with the counterfeit will. You move freely in my father's house and you are intelligent, you can do it easily. Will you do it for me?'

Rohini shuddered. 'Steal? I couldn't do it even if I were cut into pieces.'

'Women are really such worthless creatures! Mere masses of words. Is this why you said that you would not be able to repay me in this life?'

'Ask me anything else, I will do it; if you want my life, I will die for you.

But I cannot betray my benefactors.'

Having failed to persuade Rohini in any other way, Haralal offered Rohini a thousand rupee note. 'Take this as an advance. You must do it.'

Rohini refused. 'I do not care for money. I wouldn't do it even if you offered me all your father's estate. I would do it if it were possible, just for your asking.'

Haralal sighed deeply and said, 'I thought you were my friend and well-wisher. But I am nothing to you. If my wife were alive today I wouldn't come to you. She would have done it for me.'

Now Rohini laughed a little.

'Why are you laughing?' Haralal asked.

'Hearing you speak of your wife reminded me of your proposed widow marriage. Do you still intend to marry a widow?'

'I do, but where can I find a widow to my liking?'

'Well, widow or married woman—I mean widow or unmarried woman, it would be good to see you settled as a family man again. We, your friends and relatives, would be delighted.'

'You see, Rohini, widow remarriage is allowed by our sacred books.'

Rohini said, 'So they say now.'

'You can also marry again, and why shouldn't you?' Rohini pulled her dhoti over her head and turned around. Haralal continued, 'You only call me uncle because we are your neighbours; there is no blood relationship, nothing to prevent us from getting married.'

Now Rohini covered her head fully, sat down by the oven and started stirring the dal. Haralal, disappointed, turned to go. When he reached the door, Rohini called, 'You may leave the paper, I will see what I can do.'

Haralal took the counterfeit will and the note and left them near Rohini.

'Not the note; only the will,' said Rohini.

Haralal left the will, took back the note and left.

4

THAT DAY, AT ABOUT EIGHT O'CLOCK IN THE EVENING, KRISHNAKANTA ROY was in his bedroom, sitting up in bed resting his back on a pillow. He was smoking and dozing under the influence of that medicine, the best of intoxicants—opium. In that state of stupor, he imagined that his will had suddenly become a deed of sale, and Haralal had bought up his entire estate for three rupees, thirteen annas and one pie. Someone said that this was not a deed or gift, but a bond. Instantly he registered that this bond was executed by Vishnu, son of Brahma, when he borrowed a box of opium. In fact, Vishnu gave Mahadeva the mortgage on the universe, which Mahadeva forgot to foreclose, being under the influence of hemp.[1]

At that moment, Rohini came slowly into the room, and said, 'Are you asleep, Grandfather?'

Still dozing, Krishnakanta said, 'Is it you, Nandi? Ask your master to foreclose now before it is too late.'

Rohini understood that Krishnakanta was under the influence of opium, and said, 'Who is Nandi, Grandfather?'

Without raising his head, Krishnakanta said, 'You are right; in Brindavan he ate up the milkman's butter and till today has not paid a penny for it.'

Rohini burst out laughing, which startled Krishnakanta. He raised his head and looked at her. 'Who is that—Aswini, Bharani, Krittika, Rohini . . .?'

Rohini continued the listing, '. . . Mrigasira, Adra, Punabsu, Pusya.'

'. . . Aslesa, Magha, Purvaphalguni.'[2]

Rohini then said, 'Grandfather, have I come to learn astrology from you?'

Krishnakanta said, 'True, that cannot be; then what do you want? Some opium?'

'How can I want something that you cannot part with for your life? My uncle sent me.'

'Then it must be for some opium.'

'No, no, Grandfather, it is not for opium. Uncle said that the will that was written today was not signed by you.'

'How can that be? I remember well that I signed it.'

Rohini said, 'But Uncle said that as far as he could remember, you did not sign it. In any case, why remain in doubt? Why not bring out the will and see for yourself?'

'Ah, well, hold the lamp then.'

While Rohini held the lamp, Krishnakanta got out of bed and took a key from under his pillow. With it he opened a small box and took out another unusual-looking key. With this key, he opened a drawer in the chest. After some searching he brought out the will. Then he got his glasses out of their case and tried to put them on his nose, but was some time doing it for he was still under the influence of opium. When the glasses were fixed at last, Krishnakanta looked at the will and said with a laugh, 'Rohini, you think I am old and senile, but look, here's my signature.'

Rohini said, 'Dear, dear, you aren't old. But you insist on calling me your granddaughter. Well, I had better go and tell Uncle.'

Rohini left Krishnakanta's bedroom.

Late that night, Krishnakanta was asleep; suddenly he woke up, he saw that the lamp in his room, which was always kept lighted the whole night, had been put out. At the same time, a sound came to his ears, as if someone had turned a key. It seemed that a person was moving about in the room. The person then came to the head of his bed and put a hand under the pillow. Krishnakanta was heavily under the influence of opium, neither quite asleep nor awake, incapable of perceiving anything clearly. He could not be sure that there was no light in the room—even when he was awake he could not open his eyes. When he finally opened them he saw that the room was indeed dark. But under the influence of opium, he imagined that he was in prison. He had been sent there for submitting a forged document in a lawsuit against one Hari Ghosh. He heard a faint sound as of a key turning—was it the key turning in the prison door? Startled, Krishnakanta searched for the pipe of the hookah in vain. He called out for his servant, 'Hari!'

Krishnakanta did not sleep in the inner building, nor in the outer building, but in a room situated between the two. A servant called Hari guarded him. Krishnakanta called him again, but not receiving an answer he began to doze again. Meanwhile, the genuine will had been removed and the counterfeit put in its place.

5

NEXT MORNING, ROHINI WAS BACK IN THE KITCHEN COOKING WHEN Haralal peeped in again. Luckily Brahmananda was out, otherwise he might have wondered.

Rohini did not look up as Haralal approached. 'Your pot won't crack if you look up,' he said. Rohini looked up and smiled. 'Have you done it?' asked Haralal.

Rohini got up and fetched the stolen will and gave it to him. Haralal read it and realized that this was the genuine will. Then, beaming with joy, he said, 'How did you get it?'

Then Rohini began telling a tale which bore no semblance to what had really happened. As she was telling the story, she took the will from Haralal to show how it had dropped on an inkstand. When she finished telling her story, Rohini suddenly left the room with the will. When she returned, Haralal noticed that the will was not with her.

He asked, 'Where have you left the will?'

Rohini said, 'I have put it in a safe place.'

'What for? I must go now.'

'Must you? What's the hurry?'

Haralal said, 'I can't stop.'

'Then go!'

'What about the will?'

'It should stay with me.'

'How's that? You won't give it to me?'

Rohini said, 'It's the same whether you keep it or I do.'

Then Haralal asked, 'If you won't give it to me, why did you steal it?'

Rohini said, 'I stole it for you and I shall keep it for you. When you marry a widow I will give the will to your wife. You can then tear it up.'

Haralal understood. 'It cannot be, Rohini. Whatever money you want I will give you.'

'Even a lakh of rupees won't do. You must give me what you said you would.'

'That cannot be. I forged and stole for myself; for whose gain did you steal?'

Rohini went pale and looked down.

Haralal continued, 'Whatever else I am, I am Krishnakanta Roy's son, I will never marry a thief.'

Rohini suddenly stood up, threw back her dhoti from over her head, and looked at Haralal full in the face. 'I am a thief? And you are a saint! Who told me to steal? Who tempted me? Who deceived a simple woman? You are a son of Krishnakanta Roy, but you cheated me. You said things which the vilest of men would not say, you are a cheat and a liar. And you say that I am not worthy of you! There are no such wretched women as will have a scoundrel like you. If you were a woman I would give you the broom. Since you are a man, leave now, before I tell you what I really think of you.'

Haralal realized that he had got what he deserved. He left with what was still left of his honour, and with a sly smile on his lips. Rohini, too, realized that Haralal had got what he deserved—but so had she—they both had. She tightened her braid, which had come loose in her anger; she sat down to cook. But tears filled her eyes.

6

YOU ARE KOKIL, THE BIRD OF SPRING. SING TO YOUR HEART'S CONTENT, I have no objection. But I have a particular request to make—please choose a good time for your songs. It is no good singing all day without some consideration for your listeners. As I sat down to write the story of Krishnakanta's will, having found pen and ink after a long search, you sang out from the sky—Kuhoo! Kuhoo! Kuhoo! I admit that you have a good voice, but that does not give you the right to call out to people while they are busy at work. For me, whose hair is grey and pen active, your singing matters little. But sometimes when you sit on the broken wall of an office and sing 'Kuhoo! Kuhoo!', just when the young clerk is racking his brains over his accounts—the result is that he fails to balance his book. And when a beautiful woman, saddened by her lover's absence, sits down to a meal after a day's work with a pot of kheer in her hand and you call out 'Kuhoo! Kuhoo!', she forgets to eat her kheer or eats it with salt.

However that might be, there certainly was enchantment in the kokil's voice when it called from the bakul tree as Rohini made her way to fetch water with a pitcher on her hip . . . but first let me tell you about Rohini fetching water.

Well, it was like this. Brahmananda Ghosh was poor and could not afford to keep a maidservant. Whether that was an advantage or disadvantage, I cannot say. But a house which has no maidservant has no deceit, no falsehoods, no quarrels and no dirt; the goddess called maidservant is the creator of these four evils. The house with many maidservants is a field on which epic battles, like the one in Kurukshetra or the one in Lanka where Ravana was killed, are fought daily. Some maidservants strut alone, broom in hand, like Bhima with his club, while others are like King Duryodhan, Bhima's rival, admonishing his generals, like Bhishma, Drona or Karna. Yet others are like Kumbhakarna, they sleep for six months and eat everything in sight when they wake up. Some are like Sugreeva, stretching their necks, planning to kill Kumbhakarna.[3] Brahmananda, however, was free from these afflictions. But it meant that all domestic chores, including fetching water and washing dishes, had to be done by Rohini. She used to fetch water in the afternoon when she had finished her other domestic chores. The following day, after the events which I have already described, Rohini, with a pitcher on her hip, was going to fetch water at the usual hour. She always went to Varuni, a large tank with clear and sweet water. Other girls of the village went in a group. They were light-hearted girls, full of light-hearted laughter, with light pitchers to bring water. Rohini went alone, her pitcher was heavy, her manner somewhat solemn. Maybe this was so because she was a widow. Although, to look at her you would not think so: her lips were tinged red with betel leaves, she wore bracelets on her wrists, her very attractive plait lay on her neck like a black snake. She carried a brass pitcher on her hip; it swayed gently and rhythmically like a swan swaying on soft ripples. Her feet fell softly on the ground like blossoms falling from trees; she moved like a ship in full sail. So, lighting up the path to the tank, beautiful Rohini was walking along to fetch water, when from the bough of a bakul tree, the kokil sang: 'Kuhoo! Kuhoo!'

Rohini looked around. I can swear if that little bird had seen Rohini's uplifted restless glance, it would have been immediately struck by her look as by an arrow, and since birds are small creatures, the kokil would have plumped down, head over heels, feet drawn in. But the bird's fate decreed otherwise, it was not linked with the eternal chain of cause and effect. The bird had earned no merit from previous births to deserve such an ending. So the foolish kokil sang again: 'Kuhoo! Kuhoo!'

'Go away, Blackface!' Rohini exclaimed, and went on her way. But she could not forget the kokil. It's our firm belief that the bird had called at an inauspicious moment. It should not have called when a poor, young widow was going alone to fetch water. The song of the kokil brings to mind some queer thoughts—something has been lost, the loss has made one's life a waste—the lost object can never be found. There is something or somebody missing, something has not happened and will remain unrealized. We then feel that we have lost a jewel and must cry—that our life has been in vain, our cup of happiness has never been full, we have tasted nothing of this endless, beautiful world.

Again the bird sang 'Kuhoo! Kuhoo!' Rohini looked up and saw the clear, blue, endless sky, silent yet attuned to that kokil's song. She saw the new mango blossoms, pale-gold, cool-scented, among layers of green leaves, buzzing with honeybees and bumblebees. They too seemed attuned to the 'Kuhoo' sound of the kokil. On the other side of the tank was Govindalal's flower-garden, where myriads of flowers bloomed in cluster on cluster, row upon row, on every branch and every leaf; white, red, yellow, blue, large and small. Some had honey bees on them, others bumblebees, their buzzing too was attuned to the kokil's song. The breeze was bringing the strong scent of the blossoms across the tank, which too was attuned to the call of the bird. There, in the shade of a flowery grove, stood Govindalal himself; his thick, black hair fell in curls over his shoulders, golden brown as the champak flower, and a flowering creeper swayed over his tall figure, more beautiful than a tall flowering tree. This too seemed in keeping with the mood of the kokil's song. The kokil sang out again, this time from an ashoka tree.

Just then Rohini was descending the steps of the tank. She reached the end of the steps, floated her pitcher, then sat down and began to cry. I cannot say why Rohini started crying. How can I say what a woman thinks? I suspect the wicked kokil made Rohini cry.

7

I AM FACING A LOT OF TROUBLE WITH THE VARUNI TANK; I FIND IT HARD TO describe. The tank was very large; it resembled a blue mirror framed by a border of grass. Beyond this frame was the frame formed by the garden on all four of its sides; trees and walls appeared endless there. This was an impressive frame, enamelled with flowers of many colours—red, black, green, rose, white and saffron, and studded with many fruits, as with gems. Here and there, the white pleasure houses glittered like diamonds in the rays of the setting sun. The sky above was framed by the garden; it too was a blue mirror. The sky, the grass frame, the garden, the flowers, fruits, trees and houses were all reflected in the blue water. Now and then the kokil called. All this I can describe, but I cannot describe the connection between Rohini's mind and that sky, that tank and the kokil's voice. That is why I said I am facing a lot of trouble with the Varuni tank.

Like me, Govindalal was also in trouble. Govindalal, standing behind the flowery creeper, saw Rohini weeping on the steps of the tank. He concluded that Rohini must have had a row with some girl from the neighbourhood. We should not pay too much attention to Govindalal Babu's conclusion. Rohini continued to cry.

I cannot say what was in Rohini's mind, but it must have been something like this:

'For what fault was I destined to become a widow while still a child? Have I committed more sins than others that I should be deprived of all worldly pleasures? What is my fault that although I am young and beautiful, I am condemned to live the rest of my life like a dried-up piece of wood? People who have all the happiness that life can give—take Govindalal's wife for instance—what virtues do they have that I have not? What spiritual merits have they acquired that they should have so much happiness while I have none? I do not really grudge them their happiness, but why are all paths closed to me? What shall I do with my unhappy life?'

Well, I told you, Rohini was not a nice person. See how jealous she could be over small matters. She had many faults: do you feel like crying at the sight of her tears? No, you do not. Maybe it is better to cry at the sight of her tears than to judge her; gods do not withhold rain from thorny fields.

Say a kind word for Rohini. She is still there on the steps of the tank, weeping, with her head in her hands, while the empty pitcher on the water dances in the breeze.

At last the sun went down; and slowly a dark shadow fell over the blue water. As darkness fell, birds flew back to their nests and the cattle turned homewards. The moon rose, shedding a soft light on the darkness. Rohini was still crying, her pitcher still floating on the water. As Govindalal started for home, he saw Rohini still sitting there on the steps, alone and weeping.

He reflected, this woman may be good or bad, but she is a humble creature of God; I too, am a humble creature of God, hence she is my sister. If I can relieve her sadness, why should I not do it?

Govindalal descended the steps, and quietly stood beside her like a statue in the champak moonlight. Rohini was startled. He said, 'Rohini, why have you been crying?' Rohini stood up but remained silent. Govindalal continued, 'Won't you tell me what's troubling you? I may be able to help.'

Rohini could speak like a shrew to Haralal, but now, standing beside Govindalal, she could not utter a word. She stood like a sculpted figure, enhancing the beauty of the steps. In the clear water of the tank, Govindalal saw the reflection of that figure, the full moon and the gold-flowering trees. Everything is beautiful, only cruelty is ugly. Creation is kind, only human beings are unkind. Govindalal read clearly the book of nature. He spoke again, 'If you are in any trouble, let me know soon. If you cannot speak to me directly, then let me know through one of the ladies of our house.'

Then Rohini spoke, 'Some day I will tell you. Not today. Some day you must hear what I have to say.'

Govindalal nodded and went home. Rohini stepped into the water and filled her pitcher. I know that empty vessels, whether earthen or human, make a lot of noise in protest if one tries to fill them. When the pitcher was filled, Rohini came out of the pond, neatly covered herself with her wet dhoti and slowly walked home. A dialogue then took place between the pitcher, the water in the pitcher and Rohini's bracelets. And Rohini's mind joined in.

Rohini thought, 'Stealing the will.'

The water said, 'Chalat.'

Rohini felt, 'It wasn't right.'

The bracelet spoke, 'Thin-thina, no indeed it wasn't.'

Rohini wondered, 'What should I do now?'

The pitcher said, 'Thanak-dhanakdhan, use me with a cord. Tie a rope around yourself and me.'

8

THAT EVENING, ROHINI FINISHED HER COOKING EARLY, FED BRAHMANANDA; then without eating anything, she went into her bedroom and closed the door; she went to bed, not to sleep, but to think.

Reader, leave the opinions of your philosophers and scientists for a moment and listen to a few plain words of mine. A goddess named Sumati (good counsel) and an ogress named Kumati (bad counsel) dwell in human hearts, and they are always at war. As two tigresses fight for the carcass of a cow or two she-jackals for a human corpse, so do these two fight for living human beings.

Sumati asked, 'Is it right to ruin such a nice man?'

Kumati said, 'I did not give the will to Haralal. So how have I ruined Govindalal?'

'Return Krishnakanta's will to Krishnakanta.'

'Ha! What shall I tell Krishnakanta when he asks me where I got this will and how the counterfeit came to be in his drawer? What shall I say, then? What a strange thing to suggest! You want me and my uncle to go to prison?'

'Then tell Govindalal everything, throw yourself at his mercy. He is a kind man, he will surely protect you.'

Kumati said, 'That is right. But Govindalal will have to tell Krishnakanta about it, otherwise the wills cannot be exchanged. If Krishnakanta calls the police, then how can Govindalal protect you? But I have another plan. Say nothing till Krishnakanta's death, then give Govindalal the genuine will and throw yourself at his mercy.'

Sumati argued, 'It will be useless then. The will that will be found in Krishnakanta's drawer will be accepted as genuine. And Govindalal will be accused of forgery if he produces the other will.'

'Keep quiet, then—what is done is done.'

So Sumati kept quiet. She was defeated. The two made peace and united. They started something else. They conjured up the god-like champak image of Govindalal, as he stood in the moonlight by the tankside. Rohini gazed at it with her mind's eye for a long while until tears flowed from her eyes. She did not sleep that night.

9

FROM THAT DAY, ROHINI WENT DAILY TO THE VARUNI TANK TO FETCH WATER. Every day the kokil called, every day she saw Govindalal, every day Sumati (good counsel) and Kumati (bad counsel) made war and peace—war between Sumati and Kumati is acceptable to mankind. Peace between the two, however, is dangerous. Then Sumati takes the form of Kumati and Kumati works like Sumati. Then we cannot distinguish between the two and people follow Kumati mistaking her for Sumati.

The image of Govindalal was imprinted in deep colours in Rohini's heart. Whether it was the work of Sumati or Kumati, I cannot say. The picture of Govindalal was bright on a dark canvas; day by day the canvas grew darker while the picture got brighter. Then the world in Rohini's eyes—no, we should not repeat the old story. Rohini suddenly and secretly fell in love with Govindalal.

I cannot understand, nor can I explain why after such a long time this calamity befell her. Rohini had known Govindalal since they were children, but she had never been attracted towards him. I do not know why she should suddenly fall in love with him now. I am only narrating what happened. The call of that wicked kokil; that time when Rohini wept by the tank; the time and the place; Govindalal's unexpected kindness; and, above all, Rohini's harmful action against innocent Govindalal. The conjunction of all these factors over a short time gave Govindalal a big place in her heart. I do not know what will come of it; I only narrate incidents as they occur.

Rohini was very intelligent—she knew that the matter was one of life and death for her. If Govindalal had the slightest inkling of her feelings for him, he would never again tread on her shadow—he would perhaps even send her away from the village. Rohini realized that she must not breathe a word about it to anyone. So, with great effort, she kept it hidden in her heart. But she was consumed inwardly with this fiery passion. Life became too painful for her—she prayed for death day and night.

Who can keep count of the people who wish to die? I believe that there are many happy and unhappy people who wish heartily to die. In this world there is no pure happiness, it is full of pain; no happiness is complete. So many who are happy still wish for death. The unhappy wish for death for they are unable to carry the painful burden of unhappiness.

Those who seek death rarely find their wish fulfilled. Death comes not to those like Rohini but to those who are happy, beautiful, young, hopeful, and look upon this earth as the heavenly garden. On the other hand, humankind is too weak to bring about its own death. One can end this perishable life with the prick of a needle or half a drop of poison and merge this restless bubble with the sea of time. There are some who can do it, but Rohini was not one of them.

Yet Rohini had made up her mind on one point—the forged will must not be passed. There was one easy way out of this. Rohini, or someone, could tell Krishnakanta that his will had been stolen; one need not tell him the identity of the thief. Once his suspicion was aroused, Krishnakanta would open his drawers and find the forged will there. He would certainly have another will drawn up and Govindalal's estate would be saved. No one would be any the wiser about the identity of the thief. But there was a danger in this plan. As soon as he read the will, Krishnakanta would recognize that it was written by Brahmananda. So no one must know that the counterfeit will lay in Krishnakanta's chest of drawers. Hence, Rohini could not undo the wrong she had done to Govindalal when she was tempted by Haralal. She had to protect her uncle, although she now wanted to help Govindalal. In the end, she decided to steal the counterfeit and substitute it with the genuine will, in the same way that she had stolen the genuine will.

So, one night, summoning up all her courage, with the will in her hand, Rohini went alone to Krishnakanta's house. As she found the back door closed, she entered through the front gate. She confronted the gatekeepers, sitting on their charpoys, eyes half closed, humming Pilu in most unmusical voices. They stopped her, 'Who are you?' 'Sakhi,' Rohini replied. Sakhi was one of the maids of the family, so the gatekeepers let her pass. She knew her way around the house well, and she reached Krishnakanta's bedroom without trouble. This room was never locked, since the house was well protected. Rohini listened carefully; Krishnakanta was snoring loudly. When she was sure, the will-thief entered the room slowly and quietly. She blew out the lamp as soon as she entered the room. Then, as on the previous occasion, she took the key and, feeling her way in the darkness, opened the drawer.

Rohini was very careful, the movement of her hand very gentle, yet the key in turning made a click which woke Krishnakanta. He was not sure about the nature of the noise; he did not respond but listened intently. As the snoring stopped, Rohini realized that Krishnakanta was awake. She stood still, making no noise. Krishnakanta called out, 'Who's there?' No one answered.

Rohini, meanwhile, was beginning to feel feeble, worried, unbalanced and perhaps a little frightened. Her breathing was faintly audible and reached Krishnakanta's ear. He called out for Hari several times.

Rohini, if she had wanted to, could have run away. But that would have left unrepaired the damage she had done to Govindalal. She thought, 'I had the courage to do the wicked deed that night, why should I not have the courage to do a good deed tonight?' She decided to stay.

Krishnakanta's repeated calls brought no answer from Hari who had gone elsewhere seeking pleasure, promising to return soon. Then the master took out a matchbox from under his pillow and struck a light. In the light he saw a woman standing near the drawers. Krishnakanta lit the lamp and asked, 'Who are you?'

Rohini came closer to him and said, 'I am Rohini.' Surprised, Krishnakanta said, 'What are you doing here at this hour of the night in the dark?'

'I was stealing,' Rohini replied.

'Stop joking, and tell me why I find you like this. I cannot believe that you are a thief, but it looks as though you came to steal.'

Rohini said, 'Then let me complete the work that I came to do. I shall do it in front of your eyes. Afterwards you can treat me as you think fit. I am caught now, I cannot escape, nor will I try to escape.'

Saying this, Rohini returned to the chest of drawers. She opened the drawers, took out the forged document and replaced it with the genuine will. Then she tore up the counterfeit will.

'Hey, hey! What are you tearing, let me see,' Krishnakanta shouted, while Rohini burnt the fragments of the forged document in the flame of the lamp.

'What did you burn?' Krishnakanta asked, his eyes blazing with anger.

'A counterfeit will.'

Krishnakanta shuddered, 'Will! Will! Where's my will?!'

Rohini said, 'Your will is in the drawer. Why don't you see for yourself?' Krishnakanta was astonished at her coolness and confidence. He wondered if some goddess had not come to play tricks on him. He opened the drawer, and finding the will, took it out. Once he found his reading glasses, he read it and was sure it was the genuine will. Surprised, he asked again, 'What did you burn?'

Rohini replied, 'A forged will.'

'A forged will? Who made it? Where did you find it?'

Rohini said, 'I cannot say who made it, but I found it in the drawer.'

'But how did you know that there was a counterfeit will in the drawer?'

Rohini said, 'That I cannot say.'

Krishnakanta thought for a while and then said, 'Do you think that I could manage such a large estate for so long if I could not see through the little cunning of a woman like you? This counterfeit was made by Haralal. You took money from him and came here to exchange the documents. Then when you were caught you tore up the counterfeit. Am I right?'

'No, that is not true.'

'Then what is the truth?'

Rohini said, 'I shall not say anything more. I came here as a thief. Deal with me as you think fit.'

Krishnakanta said, 'There is no doubt that you came here with evil intentions, otherwise why should you enter the house like a thief? I shall make arrangements for the punishment that you deserve. I shall not call the police. Tomorrow I'll have you turned out of the village, with your head shaved and whey poured over it. Until then you will be locked up.'

That night Rohini remained locked up.

10

THE NEXT MORNING, GOVINDALAL STOOD BY THE OPEN WINDOW OF HIS bedroom. It was not quite light yet; the kokil had not given its first call from the kamini shrub in the courtyard. The koel, however, had already started singing. As the cool breeze of dawn rose, Govindalal opened the window to enjoy the fragrance of mallika, gandharaj and kutaja flowers it brought with it. A slender girl came up and stood beside him.

'Why are you here?' asked Govindalal. 'Why are you here?' the girl replied. It is unnecessary to point out that the girl was Govindalal's wife.

Govinda said, 'I am here to take the air; you can't bear that, can you?'

The girl said, 'Why should I? You are always taking things. You are not satisfied with taking things from home that you must take things from the hills and fields.'

'What have I taken from home?'

'Why, you have taken my scolding just now.'

'You know, Bhomra, Bengali men can take a lot of scolding. If they could not, then the whole race would have died of indigestion. Bengalis can digest a scolding easily. So shake your nose-ring and scold me again.'

We do not know for certain whether Govindalal's wife's name, as given by her parents, was Krishnamohini or Anangamanjari or something like that. The real name was obsolete from disuse. Her pet name was Bhramar or Bhomra; the name was suitable for the Bhramar (bumblebee) is black.

Bhramar objected to her husband's suggestion that she shake her nose-ring. As a sign of protest, she took it off and hung it on a hook and then tweaked Govindalal's nose. Then she looked at him with a gentle smile as if she had done something really wonderful. Govindalal too looked at her with admiring eyes. Just then the first rays of the sun appeared in the eastern sky and their tender shafts fell on the earth. As Bhramar was facing east, the sunlight fell on her face. The dawn light, falling on that bright, clear, soft, dark-toned, beautiful face, shone on the dancing, playful eyes and glowed on the smooth cheek. Her smile, her look, the morning sun, the morning breeze and his love—all blended together.

Then there arose a commotion from the maidservant's quarter. As they were awake now, they started sweeping floors, sprinkling water, scouring pots and pans, and attending to other domestic chores. Together they made a great noise—sap-sap, chap-chap, jhan-jhan, khan-khan. Suddenly it all stopped, and instead there arose voices, mimicking, mocking and laughing, 'Oh God!', 'What's new!', 'What a calamity', 'How impudent', 'What audacity'. Bhramar came out of her room to see what had happened.

The maidservant community did not pay much attention to Bhramar. There were many reasons for this. To start with, she was too young and not the mistress of the household since her mother-in-law and sister-in-law were still there. Moreover, Bhramar was generally inclined more to laugh than to rule. The clamour increased as she approached.

The first maid she encountered asked, 'Have you heard, young mistress?'

The second maid said, 'No one has ever heard such an awful thing.'

The third maid said, 'What audacity! I will go and take the broom to that woman.'

The fourth maid commented, 'Only broom! If you just say the word, I will go and cut her nose off!'

The fifth maid said, 'You can never tell what is inside anyone.'

Bhramar laughed and said, 'First tell me what has happened. Then you can all go and do as you please.' The clamour began all over again.

The first maid said, 'Haven't you heard? The whole neighbourhood is in turmoil over this!'

'A hyena in a tiger's den,' commented the second maid.

The third maid said, 'I can beat the venom out of her with a broom.'

'A dwarf reaching for the moon,' said the fourth maid.

The fifth maid said, 'It is not difficult to detect a wet cat—a rope round her neck.'

Bhramar said, 'A rope round your necks.'

Then the maids cried with one voice, 'Why do you blame us? What have we done? Yes, we know, whenever somebody does something wrong somewhere, we are blamed. We are poor women, we have to work hard so that we can eat.' When this speech was over, some covered their eyes and began to cry. One of them wailed for her dead son. Bhramar was moved but could not stop laughing: 'I said that you deserve a rope round your necks because you haven't told me what it's all about. What has happened?'

Then again voices rang out from all quarters. With great difficulty, Bhramar gathered from the endless talk the essential information that a theft had taken place in the bedroom of the zamindar. Some said it was not a theft but a robbery, another called it a burglary, while someone else said that four or five thieves had come and taken away government paper worth a lakh of rupees.

Bhramar asked, 'What happened then? Who is this wretched woman whose nose you wanted to cut off?'

The first maid said, 'Mistress Rohini's, who else's?'

The second maid said, 'That shameless woman is the cause of all this trouble.'

The third maid added, 'They say it is she who brought the gang of robbers.'

The fourth maid commented, 'She will now pay for her misdeed.'

The fifth maid said, 'Now she will rot in prison.'

'How do you know that Rohini came to steal?' asked Bhramar.

'Why, she was caught and is locked up in the cutcherry jail.'

Bhramar went back to Govindalal and reported the story. He shook his head thoughtfully.

'Why do you shake your head?' asked Bhramar.

Govindalal said, 'I do not believe that Rohini came to steal. Do you?'

'You tell me why you don't.'

'I shall tell you some other time, but you tell me first.'

Bhramar said, 'No, you tell me first.'

Govindalal laughed and said, 'You tell me first.'

Bhramar asked, 'Why should I?'

Govinda said, 'I'd love to hear it.'

'You want the truth?'

'Yes.'

Bhramar tried but could not say it and then shyly bowed her head. Govindalal understood, he understood it from the beginning, that is why he was pressing so hard for an answer. Bhramar believed in Rohini's innocence as much as she believed in her own existence, but for that there was no reason except that Govindalal said Rohini was innocent. Govindalal's belief was Bhramar's belief. He understood that for he knew her. That is why Govindalal loved this dark girl so much.

Govindalal said, teasing, 'Shall I tell you why you are on Rohini's side?'

Bhramar said, 'Yes, tell me.'

Govinda said, 'Because she calls your complexion "bright brown", not "black".'

'Go away,' Bhramar said with a frown.

'I am going,' replied Govindalal and was about to leave when she pulled his garment and asked, 'Where are you going?'

Govinda said, 'Tell me where I am going.'

'Shall I tell you now?' asked Bhramar.

'Yes, tell me.'

'To save Rohini,' said Bhramar.

'That's right,' said Govindalal and kissed Bhramar. A compassionate heart understood another compassionate heart. That is why he kissed her.

•

11

GOVINDALAL WENT STRAIGHT TO THE CUTCHERRY WHICH WAS LOCATED IN the anterior portion of the house. Krishnakanta was already there. He was sitting on a high seat arranged like a throne, smoking ambergris-scented tobacco from a hubble-bubble with a golden tube; he was enjoying the pleasures of heaven on earth. To one side of him were bundles of records, ledgers, account books, receipts, rent rolls, registers of land transactions, assessments and cash books, and on the other stood his stewards, agents, overseers, clerks, cashiers, surveyors, footmen and tenants. And in front of him stood Rohini, her face downcast and veiled.

Govindalal was Krishnakanta's favourite. On entering the cutcherry, he asked, 'What has happened, Big Uncle?' As she heard his voice, Rohini opened her veil a little and gave him a look. Govindalal wondered what that look meant. It was a sad and imploring look. But what did she want? It must be her appeal to save her from this trouble. Then he remembered their conversation on the steps of the tank. He had told her she could speak to him if she was ever in trouble. Now she was in trouble. That's what she told him by that look. He thought, 'I wish you well, for there is no one who can help you here. But it won't be easy, for the man who is holding you is a strong-minded person.' As he was pondering about the 'look', Govindalal paid no attention to what Krishnakanta was saying, so he repeated his question, 'What has happened, Big Uncle?' The master had already told him what had happened the night before, but as his nephew repeated his question he said to himself, 'This young man has lost his head at the sight of this pretty face.' He, however, told the whole story again and added, 'It is that rascal Haralal's doing. I think that this wretched woman took a bribe from him to replace the genuine will with a forged one. Once she was caught she tore up the forged will in fear.'

Govinda asked, 'What does Rohini say?'

Krishnakanta said, 'What can she say? She says that that was not how it happened.'

Govindalal turned to her, 'If it was not so, then how was it, Rohini?'

Rohini, without lifting her head, answered in a choked voice, 'I am in your hands, do what you like. I shall not tell you any more.'

Krishnakanta said, 'See! The wickedness!'

Govindalal said to himself, 'Not everyone is wicked in this world. There may be something other than wickedness in her.' He asked his uncle, 'What orders have you given? Are you going to send her to the police?'

Krishnakanta said, 'What have I to do with the police? I am the police, magistrate and judge in this estate. Will it help my manliness if I were to send this unimportant woman to prison?'

'Then what will you do?' asked Govindalal.

'I will have her winnowed out of the village, having had her head shaved and whey poured over it. She will never be able to return to my estate.'

Govindalal turned to Rohini and said, 'What have you got to say?'

Rohini said, 'It would do me no harm.'

Govindalal was astonished. After a little thought he said to his uncle, 'I have a request to make.'

'What is it?'

'Please free her for a little while. I stand surety and shall bring her back by ten o'clock.'

Krishnakanta said to himself, 'Just as I thought: my nephew is interested in this woman.' Then he said to Govindalal, 'Where will you take her and why should I let her go?'

Govindalal said, 'It is our duty to find out the truth. She will not talk in front of all these people. I shall take her to the women's quarter and question her in private.'

Krishnakanta said to himself, 'To hell with his questioning. The boys of today are shameless. But wait, you rascal, I will go one better.' He said to Govindalal, 'Very well', and then he ordered one of his footmen, 'Take this woman, send her with a maidservant to Bhramar's quarter and make sure that she does not escape.' The footman took Rohini away. Govindalal too left. Krishnakanta invoked Goddess Durga, 'What's come over the younger generation!'

12

GOVINDALAL ENTERED THE INNER BUILDING AND SAW BHRAMAR SITTING with Rohini in silence. She wanted to comfort Rohini but was afraid of making her cry. So Bhramar sat there in silence. She was relieved to see Govindalal; moving quickly towards him, she gestured to him. As he came near, Bhramar asked him in a low voice, 'What is Rohini doing here?' Govindalal replied, 'I want to ask her some questions in private. Afterwards, let fate decide her future.'

'What do you want to ask her?'

'What's on her mind. If you are afraid to leave me alone with her then you may listen from behind the door.'

At this, Bhramar hung her head in embarrassment. She went straight to the kitchen, pulled the hair of the cook and said, 'Cook, tell me a fairy tale.'

In their room, Govindalal asked Rohini, 'Will you tell me everything?'

Her heart was bursting to tell him everything but she was the daughter of an Aryan, the race who would mount funeral pyres alive. 'You have heard what the master said,' Rohini replied.

Govindalal said, 'The master said you came to put in a forged will and steal the genuine one. Is that right?'

Rohini said, 'No, that is not right.'

'Then how was it?'

'What good will it do if I tell you?'

'It may be for your own good.'

'You may not believe me.'

'If it is believable, why should I not believe it?'

'It is not believable.'

'I know what I should believe and should not believe. How would you know what I might consider believable? There are times when I believe in unbelievable things.'

Rohini thought, 'Why else have I courted death for you? But I will put you to a test before I die.' Then she said to him, 'That is because you are very kind. But what's the use of my telling you this sad story?'

Govinda said, 'I may be able to help you.'

'How will you do that?' asked Rohini.

Govinda thought, 'I have not met anyone as difficult as this one. But I must be patient, for she is in real trouble.' He said to her, 'I shall request the master and he might let you go.'

Rohini asked, 'If you do not make that report, what will he do with me?'

Govinda said, 'You have heard that already.'

Rohini answered, 'He would have my head shaved and whey poured on it and then throw me out of the village. I see neither good nor bad in that. After this disgrace I do not wish to live here. If I am not thrown out I shall leave the village of my own will. How can I show my face here? Pouring whey on one's head is not a severe punishment, it would wash off. As for my hair'—Rohini cast a glance at her dark, rippling hair—'as for my hair, fetch me a pair of scissors and I will cut it off to make plaits for your wife.'

Govindalal was distressed. With a deep sigh he said, 'I understand, Rohini. The disgrace is your real punishment. If you can't be saved from it, you don't care what's done to you.'

Now she cried; in her heart Rohini thanked him a thousand times. 'Since you understand, tell me how you can save me from this disgrace.'

Govindalal thought for a moment and said, 'I cannot say. But if I knew what really happened, then I could say something.'

Rohini said, 'Tell me what you want to know.'

'What was it you burnt?'

'The forged will.'

'Where did you find it?'

'In the drawer in the master's room.'

'How did the forged will get there?'

'I put it there. The night of the day when the will was written. I stole the genuine will and replaced it with a forged one.'

'Why? Why did you do that?'

'Haralal requested me to do so.'

'Then why did you come back last night?'

'To replace the forged will with the genuine one.'

'Why? What was in the forged will?'

'Haralal would get twelve annas and only a pie for you.'

'Why did you come to replace the will? I did not ask you to.'

Rohini started to cry again. With some effort she regained control. 'No, you did not request me to do so. But you gave me something which I never had in this life and I shall never get again in this life.'

'What was that, Rohini?'

'You remember—on the bank of Varuni tank.'

'What?'

'What was it? I shall not be able to tell you in this life. Please say no more about it. There is no treatment for this disease. I shall never be free of it. If I could come by a poison I would take it, though not in your house. The only way you can help me is to let me go and have a good cry. Then if I am still alive, send me out of the village with my head shaven and whey poured over it.'

Govindalal understood. He saw her heart as clearly as if it were an image in a mirror. He realized that the spell that had charmed Bhramar had also charmed this snake. He was not pleased but neither was he angry, his loving heart surged with compassion. 'Maybe death is the best solution for your problem. But one must not take one's life. We have all come to this world to do our work. Why should you take your life without completing your work?' He hesitated.

'Please go on,' Rohini insisted.

Govindalal said, 'You must leave the village.'

Rohini asked, 'Why?'

'You said yourself that you wanted to go.'

'That was because of my disgrace. Why do *you* want me to go?'

'We must not meet again.'

Rohini saw that he understood. She was embarrassed but very happy. She forgot her pain, she wanted to live again, and not go away. Human beings are very dependent. 'I am willing to go at once,' she said, 'but where shall I go?'

Govindalal said, 'Calcutta. I will give you a letter of introduction to a friend of mine. He will buy you a house. You do not have to spend any money.'

'What will happen to my uncle?' asked Rohini.

'He will go with you, otherwise I would not have suggested this to you,' said Govindalal.

'But what will he do there?'

'My friend will find him a position.'

Then Rohini said, 'Why should my uncle agree to go?'

Govindalal asked, 'Can you persuade him about this?'

'I suppose I can. But who will persuade your uncle? Why should he let me go?'

Govindalal said, 'I shall request him.'

'That will mean disgrace upon disgrace. Your disgrace will add to my disgrace.'

'That is true. I shall ask Bhramar to talk to the master. Now go, and find Bhramar, send her to me and stay in the house so that I can send for you.'

Rohini, with a tearful glance at Govindalal, went out to look for Bhramar. Thus in disgrace and in shame Rohini first spoke of her love.

13

BHRAMAR WOULD NOT AGREE TO SPEAK TO HER UNCLE-IN-LAW ON ROHINI'S behalf; she was too shy.

So Govindalal was compelled to go himself. Krishnakanta was half reclining on his bed, with the pipe of his hubble-bubble in one hand; he was already asleep, having had his midday meal. He snored, and as he did so his nose played a trill with melody and gradual modulation like many classical tunes. On the other hand, his mind, thanks to opium, was riding the mythical horse which travels through wonderful places in the three worlds. It seemed that the old man was also under the spell of that moon-like face of Rohini. Does not the moon rise everywhere? Otherwise why should Krishnakanta linger on the shoulders of Sachi, Indra's wife? Krishnakanta dreamt that Rohini, who had suddenly turned into Sachi, had gone to steal Shiva's bull from his cowshed. Nandi, with trident in hand, had gone to feed the bull. Having found Sachi/Rohini there, he seized her by her curly hair that reached down to her ankles. The peacock of Karttikeya, son of Shiva, came to eat up the curls, mistaking them for snakes. Karttikeya, outraged by this, went to complain to Shiva, calling him, 'Big Uncle'.

Krishnakanta could not understand why his son, Karttikeya, should call him 'Big Uncle'. But the son did it again. Krishnakanta, annoyed, raised his hand to pull his ears. The pipe of the hubble-bubble fell from his hand on to the betel box with a clang, the betel box fell with a louder clang—jhan-jhan-jhanat on the spittoon, and the three rolled on the floor. The commotion disturbed the old man; he opened his eyes and saw that Karttikeya was indeed standing before him.

It was Govindalal, looking as handsome as the temple image of Karttikeya, saying, 'Big Uncle.' Krishnakanta sat up in a flurry and asked, 'What is it, my son?' The old man was very fond of his nephew.

Govindalal, somewhat embarrassed, said, 'Please go back to sleep, I have not come about anything very important.' He then stood the spittoon upright, put the betel box in its proper place and the tube of the hubble-bubble in the old man's hand. Krishnakanta was a tough old man, not easily taken in. 'The rascal has come again to plead for that pretty face,' he said to himself and then to Govindalal, 'I have had enough sleep, I shall not sleep more.'

Govindalal was confused. In the morning, he had had no hesitation in speaking about Rohini; now he found it hard to broach the subject. Perhaps it was because of his conversation with Rohini about what had happened by the Varuni tank.

The old man enjoyed the game. Since Govindalal could not say what he had come to say, Krishnakanta talked about the estate, family problems, court cases and did not mention Rohini once. His nephew could not bring himself to talk about her. Krishnakanta laughed in his sleeve; he was a wicked old man. In desperation, Govindalal decided to leave—then the old man called him back, 'That wretched woman for whom you stood surety, has she confessed anything?' Govindalal briefly stated Rohini's story. He, however, said nothing about the conversation he had had by the tank. Krishnakanta asked, 'What do you wish to do with her?' At this Govindalal embarrassedly said, 'Whatever you wish, we also wish.' Laughing to himself, but with no outward sign of laughter, the old man said, 'I do not believe her story. I say that she should be turned out of the village, with head shaved and whey poured over it. What do you say?' Govindalal was silent. Then the wicked old man added, 'But if you think her innocent, then let her go.'

Govindalal heaved a sigh of relief and escaped from the old man.

14

WITH GOVINDALAL'S PERMISSION, ROHINI WENT HOME TO MAKE arrangements to leave the village with her uncle. She said nothing to her uncle, went into her room and sat down on the floor to weep.

'I cannot leave Haridragram, I shall die if I do not see him. If I go to Calcutta I shall not see Govindalal again. I will not go. This village is my heaven and Govindalal's temple. This is my cremation ground. I shall be cremated here. There is no one more unfortunate than the one who cannot be cremated in his own cremation ground. If I do not leave Haridragram, what can they do to me? Krishnakanta Roy might throw me out of his estate, with my head shaved and whey poured over it. But I will come back. Govindalal might get angry with me. At least I will be able to see him. They cannot gorge my eyes out. I will not go—will not go to Calcutta—I will go nowhere. I would rather die than leave this village.'

Having resolved not to leave the village, Rohini got up, opened the door and went, like a moth to the flame, to see Govindalal again. As she went, she prayed, 'Oh Lord of the world, protector of the poor, sole refuge of the unhappy. I am very unhappy. I am in great trouble—protect me—stamp out this fire of passion in me. Do not burn me any more. The sight of the person I am going to see gives me eternal happiness and unbearable pain. I am a widow. I am about to lose my virtue, my happiness and even my life. I shall have nothing left that I want to keep—Oh Lord! Oh God! Oh Durga! Oh Kali! Oh Jagannath! Advise me, comfort my heart. I cannot bear this pain any longer.'

But that bursting, stricken heart, overflowing with endless love, was not appeased. Now she thought of taking poison; next she thought of throwing herself at Govindalal's feet and opening her heart to him; then she thought of drowning in the Varuni. Sometimes she tl ought of throwing virtue to the wind and eloping with Govindalal.

Rohini appeared before Govindalal, still weeping.

Govindalal said, 'Well, have you arranged to leave for Calcutta?'

Rohini said, 'No.'

'How can that be? A little while ago you agreed to leave.'

'I cannot go.'

'I do not know what to say. I have no right to force you to go, but it would be better for you to leave.'

'Why better?'

Govindalal hung his head. Who was he to speak openly on such a matter?

Rohini returned home, secretly wiping her tears. Govindalal was deeply troubled and was thinking about the matter. Just then, Bhramar came dancing in and asked, 'What are you thinking about?'

Govindalal said, 'You tell me.'

'My black beauty.'

'Ha!'

Then Bhramar said angrily, 'What! You are not thinking of me. Have you any other thought but me?'

'Of course I have. You think you are omnipresent! I was thinking of someone else.'

Bhramar put her arms round Govindalal's neck and kissed him. Melting with love, she said in a half audible, gentle, smiling voice, 'Tell me who this someone else is.'

'What's the use of telling you?'

'Please tell me.'

'You will be angry.'

'Perhaps I will be angry, but I still want to know.'

'Go and ask about dinner.'

'I shall see to it soon, but tell me first.'

'You are a thorn in my flesh! I was thinking of Rohini.'

'Why were you thinking of her?'

'I do not know.'

'Yes, you do know, tell me.'

'Should not one person think of another?'

'No! You think of somebody if you love the person. You think of me and I think of you.'

'Then I love Rohini.'

'Liar! You love me. You should love no one else. Please tell me why you were thinking of her.'

'Should a widow eat fish?'

'No.'

'A widow should not eat fish, then why does Tarini's mother eat fish?'

'She is wicked, she does what she should not do.'

Govindalal said, 'I am also wicked. I am doing what I should not do. I love Rohini.'

Bhramar suddenly pinched his cheek, lightly, and said angrily, 'I am Bhramar, your wife, you dare lie to me?'

Govindalal accepted defeat. He put one hand on her shoulder, held her sweet lotus-like face in the other, and said in a soft, grave and troubled voice, 'Yes, it's a lie. I do not love Rohini, but she loves me.'

Bhramar freed herself from him and said with great anger, 'The wretch, the black-faced monkey, may she die, die, die!'

Govindalal laughed, 'Why abuse her so? She hasn't yet taken from you your priceless jewel.'

Bhramar said, somewhat embarrassed, 'No, I do not mean that, she cannot take you away from me. But that wretched woman should not pronounce her love to you so openly.'

Govindalal said, 'You are right. She should not have said it to me. I have been thinking about that. I suggested that she should leave for Calcutta and offered her financial help.'

Bhramar asked, 'What then?'

'She did not agree.'

'Well, can I give her some advice?'

'You can, but I must hear it.'

'Wait and see.'

Then Bhramar called Khiri, her maidservant. Khiri, alias Kshirodamani alias Kshiradhitanaya, appeared; she was short and stout, wore anklets on her feet and a chain round her waist, and she had a face full of smiles. Bhramar said, 'Khiri, can you go at once to that wretched Rohini?'

Khiri said, 'Certainly I can, what should I tell her?'

Bhramar said, 'Tell her to go and kill herself.'

'Only that? I am off then.' Khiri set off, jingling her anklets. 'Come back and tell me what she says,' Bhramar added. 'Very well,' Khiri said and went. She came back in a short time and said, 'I told her.'

'What did she say?' asked Bhramar.

'She said you must tell her how she should kill herself.'

Bhramar replied, 'Then go again and tell her to drown herself in the Varuni tank in the evening with a pitcher tied to her neck. Do you understand?'

'Very well,' said Khiri and went again.

When she came back Bhramar asked, 'Did you tell her about the tank?'

'Yes I did,' Khiri said.

'What was her answer?' Bhramar wanted to know.

'Very well,' Khiri said.

Govindalal said, 'Shame on you, Bhramar.'

'Do not worry, she will not die; the woman is in love with you, she won't kill herself.'

15

HAVING COMPLETED HIS DAILY CHORES, GOVINDALAL WENT, AS WAS USUAL, to stroll in the flower-garden by the Varuni tank. He took great pleasure in this. He would linger under every tree. But we shall not speak of that now. By the tank, in the centre of the garden there was a platform made of stone. In the middle of it stood a marble statue of a woman, half draped, with downcast eyes, pouring water on her feet from a jug. On the pedestal surrounding the statue, there stood many brightly coloured small pots with geranium, verbena, euphorbia, chrysanthemum and rose. Around the base there were rows of sweet-scented kamini, juthika, mallika, gandhraj and other native flowers perfuming the air. Beyond that were rows of shrubs, native and foreign, with leaves of many colours—blue, yellow, red and white—which delighted the eye. Govindalal loved to sit here. Some moonlit nights he would bring Bhramar here for a stroll in the garden. Bhramar used to mock the half-draped statue, saying, 'Shameless woman.' Sometimes she would cover it up with the hem of her sari or with some rich garment brought from home. Sometimes she would pull at the jug in its hand.

This evening as Govindalal sat there he watched the beauty of the mirror-like water of Varuni. As he was watching the tank, Govindalal saw Rohini with a pitcher on her hip descending the broad stone steps of the tank. It is possible to live without many things, but not without water. So even on such an unhappy day, Rohini had come to fetch water. Govindalal thought it improper to stay in sight in case Rohini wanted to have a bath—he moved away.

After wandering for a while in other parts of the garden, Govindalal decided that Rohini must have left by now. He came back and sat at the feet of the marble beauty, taking in Varuni's pleasant view. There was no one there, no Rohini, no man or woman. The place was empty, but a pitcher was floating in the water.

Whose pitcher was that? He became suspicious. The thought flashed across his mind that someone might have drowned. Rohini was there a little while ago. Then he suddenly remembered what had transpired in the morning. Bhramar had sent word to Rohini that the latter should drown herself in the Varuni tank in the evening with a pitcher round her neck, and Rohini had said 'Yes'. Govindalal immediately went to the steps of the tank. As he descended to the last step, he examined the tank closely. The water was as clear as glass. One could clearly see the bottom. There he saw Rohini, lying under the water like a golden image set in crystal, her body lighting up the bed of dark water.

16

GOVINDALAL AT ONCE DIVED INTO THE WATER AND BROUGHT ROHINI UP and laid her on the steps. He was not sure that she was still alive; she was unconscious, she had stopped breathing. Govindalal called a gardener. With his aid, he took Rohini into his garden house for first aid. Thus, whether dead or alive, Rohini entered Govindalal's garden house for the first time. No woman other than Bhramar had ever entered this house until now.

He put Rohini's drenched champak flower-like body on a couch. It looked still brighter in the lamplight. Her long, dark, curly hair was now straight since it was wet; water dripped from it like rain. Her eyes were closed and the eyebrows were now a deeper black, being wet. Her calm broad forehead suggested no shame or fear but some unexpressed feeling. Her cheeks were still bright; the lips still sweet and their redness shamed the red of the bandhuli flower. Govindalal wept, 'Alas! alas! Why did God send you with so much beauty? Why did He not make you happy if He made you so beautiful? Why are you leaving us this way?' His heart broke for he knew that he was responsible for her suicide.

If Rohini was still alive she must be saved. Govindalal knew how to save a drowning person. It was relatively easy to get the water out of her system. He made her throw up the water she had swallowed by putting her now in a standing, now in a sitting position and by turning her about from side to side. However, she did not resume her breathing. That was a difficult task.

Govindalal knew what was to be done—her lungs had to be dilated by slowly raising her arms and having air blown into them through her mouth. Her arms were then to be lowered so that the lungs, contracting, would expel the air that was blown into them. This process of artificial respiration had to be continued until natural respiration was restored. Someone had to raise Rohini's hands while someone else would blow into her mouth. Who would blow into those plum-like red lips which were still full of nectar, a pitcher full of intoxicating sensual desires, like poison. Who should do this dangerous deed, touch those sweet, red lips with his lips?

All other servants had left the garden except the gardener. Govindalal asked him to blow into Rohini's mouth while he raised her arms. The gardener refused and said in his native Oriya, 'No, my master. I cannot do that.'

He would rather kiss the holy stone than blow into those lips. The gardener began to sweat, then he said definitely, 'Not those lips.'

I think that the gardener was right. To see Rohini again after she had been restored to life, to see her going home, her pitcher on her hip, with her red lips, would have made it impossible for him to carry on at his job. It would have made him throw his tools in the Varuni tank and run for his native town, maybe drown himself in the Subarnarekha on the way.[4] I do not know if the gardener thought of all this, but he definitely refused to blow into Rohini's mouth.

Since there was no other way out, Govindalal decided to blow into Rohini's mouth and the gardener agreed to raise and lower her arms. Then Govindalal put his soft, red, cherry-like lips on her soft, red, cherry-like lips and blew into her mouth. At that very moment, Bhramar, trying to hit a cat with a stick, hit herself on the forehead instead.

The operation of moving Rohini's arms up and down and blowing into her mouth continued for two or three hours, at the end of which she breathed and came back to life.

17

AS ROHINI STARTED BREATHING, GOVINDALAL GAVE HER A STIMULANT TO restore her strength. Her strength slowly returned and she opened her eyes. She saw the beautiful room cooled by the breeze coming in through the window. On one side was a lamp in a crystal container, shedding a soft light, and on the other was Govindalal, the lamp of her life. She was restored to life by Govindalal's medicine, which he gave her to drink, and by his words, which she drank through her ears. Her consciousness had returned after her breathing had been restored, and then she had opened her eyes; her memory revived next, and finally her speech: 'I was dead; who brought me back to life?'

Govindalal said, 'That is not important. All that matters now is that you are saved.'

Rohini asked, 'Why did you save me? Am I your enemy? You won't even let me die.'

'Why do you wish to die?'

'Have I no right to kill myself?'

'No one has the right to sin—suicide is a sin.'

'I don't know anything about merit and sin. Nobody taught me. In fact, I do not believe this. I have committed no sin but I have suffered so much. I cannot possibly suffer more if I commit a sin. I will kill myself. You saved me this time because you saw me. Next time I shall take care not to be seen by you.'

Govindalal was distressed, 'Why do you want to die?'

'It is better to die in one go than to die slowly every day, every hour and every moment.'

'What's hurting you so much?'

'My heart is burning with desire, there is cool water in front of me. I cannot touch it, not in this life. I cannot even hope to touch it.'

'Enough of this kind of talk; come, let me take you home.'

'No, I shall go alone.'

Govindalal respected her decision and said no more. Rohini went alone.

Then, in that deserted room, Govindalal suddenly threw himself on the floor and started to cry. He hid his face on the floor, and with tears streaming from his eyes he called out, 'Oh Lord, save me from this danger. I shall not be able to save myself unless you give me strength. I shall die, Bhramar too will die. Abide in my heart—with you I can conquer my weakness.'

18

WHEN GOVINDALAL RETURNED HOME, BHRAMAR ASKED, 'WHY WERE YOU in the garden for so long tonight?'

Govindalal said, 'Why do you ask? Have I never been late before?'

'You have, but from the look on your face and the tone of your voice, I feel that something has happened tonight.'

'What has happened?'

'How can I say what is wrong if you do not tell me? I was not there.'

'Why can't you tell from the look on my face?'

Bhramar said, 'Stop joking. I can tell from your face that something is wrong. Please tell me. I am very worried.'

As she spoke, tears fell from her eyes. Govindalal caressed Bhramar, wiped her tears and then said, 'I shall tell you some other day, but not today.'

Bhramar persisted, 'Why not today?'

Govinda said, 'You are young and it is not a matter for a young girl like you to hear.'

'Shall I be told tomorrow?'

'No, I shall not tell you tomorrow, but in two years' time. Please do not ask me more now.'

Bhramar sighed. 'Ah well, then let it be after two years. I wanted very much to know, but how can I know if you don't tell me? I feel so sad.'

A deep sorrow darkened Bhramar's mind. As the sudden appearance of a cloud blots out the bright blue and beautiful spring sky, so this sadness blotted out Bhramar's cheerfulness. Tears came rolling down from her eyes. She thought that she was crying for nothing, she was wicked and her husband would be angry. So, still crying, she went out, found a corner and sat down with her feet outstretched to read Annadamangal. I cannot say if she enjoyed it but the black cloud did not lift from her heart.

19

GOVINDALAL DECIDED TO TALK TO HIS UNCLE ABOUT THEIR FINANCIAL AFFAIRS. He started asking about various estates. Krishnakanta was pleased that Govindalal was showing an interest in the family's property. 'It would be good if you boys take an interest in the business of running our estates. I may not live long and if you were to learn the management of our property, it would be good for the future. I am too old to travel to inspect all our estates and there are disturbances in some of them.'

Govindalal said, 'If you were to send me there, I would be happy to go. In fact, it is my wish to visit all our estates.' Krishnakanta was very pleased. 'I am very happy to hear this. At the moment there is some trouble in Bandarkhali; the steward says that the tenants are on a rent-strike. The tenants say that they have been paying the rents regularly but the steward does not give them proper receipts. If you wish to go there, I can make the necessary arrangements.'

Govindalal agreed. This was really the reason why he went to see

Krishnakanta. He was in the prime of his youth, with excitable desires like the waves of a turbulent sea and he had a strong passion for beauty. Bhramar could not satisfy this passion. Rohini's beauty was like the first cloud in the blue summer sky. Govindalal beheld her beauty as the chatak bird beholds a raincloud. His heart danced at the sight of Rohini like a peacock dances at the sight of the first rain. When he became aware of his own feelings, he swore to himself that he would rather die than be unfaithful to Bhramar. He resolved to forget Rohini and put his mind to work. He was sure that once he had gone away he would forget her. That's why he started talking about the estates, and when Bandarkhali was mentioned, he was eager to go.

When Bhramar heard that her husband would be leaving to visit a country estate, she insisted that she too should go with him. She pressed hard. She cried and went to her mother-in-law for support. The old lady would not let her go. So Govindalal kissed Bhramar, and with the boat ready and surrounded by servants, he set out on his ten-day journey to Bandarkhali.

Bhramar lay down on the floor and cried. Then she got up, took her copy of Annadamangal and tore it up. She opened the bird's cage and let the bird fly out, drowned her dolls and cut all the flowers in the flowerpots. She lost her appetite, flung her food at the cook, pulled down the maidservants' braids, and quarrelled with her sister-in-law. Having done such naughty things, Bhramar lay down in bed, pulled the sheet over her head and began to cry. Meanwhile, propelled by a favourable wind, Govindalal's boat went its way over the waves of the river.

20

AFTER GOVINDALAL LEFT, NOTHING SATISFIED BHRAMAR. SHE TOOK DOWN her bed because it was too soft, and the fan above it because the air was fiery hot. She forbade her servants to bring flowers to her for there were insects in them. She stopped playing cards; she told her friends that her mother-in-law did not approve of such games; she gave away her needles, cotton, wool and patterns to the girls in the village on the grounds that they made her eyes ache. If someone asked about the unwashed clothes that she had taken to wearing, she blamed the washerman; yet her wardrobe was full of clean clothes. She would hardly touch her hair with a comb, it looked more like a field of thatching grass ruffled by the wind; if anyone drew her attention to it she would laugh and bundle it up. She was difficult at mealtimes; she would say, 'I cannot eat, I have a fever.' Her mother-in-law got a doctor, who prescribed some pills and potions for Bhramar. She got Khiri to see to it that Bhramar took these medicines regularly. Bhramar received the pills and potions and then threw them out of the window.

Before long, these excesses became unbearable for Khiri. 'Whom do you pine for, my young daughter-in-law mistress?' she asked. 'Does he, for whom you are crying yourself to death, think of you for a moment? While you are crying he is probably meditating on mistress Rohini's beauty, with a hubble-bubble in his hands.'

Bhramar was very free with her hands—she slapped Khiri's face with a strong hand. Then she said, weeping, 'How dare you speak to me like that? Get out of my sight.'

Khiri said, 'Can you stop people talking by slapping me? We do not say anything, for you would get angry. But we must tell you, and you must know. Call Panchi, the low-caste woman, and ask her whether she did not see Rohini coming out of the second young master's [Govindalal's] garden house late at night.'

Khiri was unlucky to have spoken this way to Bhramar in the morning. Bhramar stood up and showered slaps and blows on Khiri, knocked her down, pulled her hair and at last burst into tears.

Khiri was used to Bhramar's occasional slaps but today the young mistress had gone too far, so she got angry and said, 'What's the use of beating us? If we say anything it is for your own good, for we cannot bear to hear people gossiping about you. If you don't believe me, then send for Panchi and ask her yourself.'

Crying in anger and sorrow, Bhramar said, 'You go and ask a low-caste woman about my husband. How dare you talk to me like that? I will tell my mother-in-law and have you thrown out of the house with a broom. Now get out of my sight.'

Then Kshiroda alias Khiri the maid left, boiling with anger at the unnecessary beatings she had received.

Bhramar, looking up with folded hands and tears in her eyes, called out to Govindalal, 'O preceptor, teacher, you are conversant with righteousness and are my sole truth. Is this what you concealed from me the other day?' Deep in her heart, in that secret place which no eye could penetrate and where there was no self-deception, Bhramar found no distrust of her husband. Only once did the thought come to her mind, 'If he is unfaithful to me—but then I shall not suffer much. If I die, the suffering will also end.' To a Hindu woman, death appears very easy.

21

KHIRI THOUGHT THAT THIS WAS INDEED THE KALI AGE—WHY ELSE WOULD a slip of a girl like Bhramar disbelieve her? Kshiroda in her simple heart bore no real grudge or malice against her mistress; in fact, she wished her well. But she found it intolerable that Bhramar should not believe her story. She oiled her smooth body, put a coloured towel on her shoulder and with a pitcher on her hip, she went to bathe in Varuni.

On her way she first met Haramani Thakurani, a cook in the zamindar's household, who was coming back from Varuni. As soon as she saw her, Khiri started speaking loudly to herself, 'It is said that the person for whom you steal calls you a thief. I cannot work in a rich man's house any more; you never know what mood they are in.'

Haramani, sensing a quarrel, shifted the wet garment she had washed during her bath from her right hand to her left and asked, 'What is it, Khiri? What's up?'

Khiri proceeded to unburden her heart, 'The shameless hussies of the neighbourhood would visit our master's garden house, but we servants must not tell our mistress.'

Hara asked, 'What is this? Who is this hussy?'

'Who but that wretched Rohini?'

'Oh Lord! How long has she been carrying on? And with whom?'

Khiri whispered Govindalal's name, then they exchanged sly glances and smiles and went their different ways. A little way down the path, Khiri met Ram's mother, stopped her with a smile and told her about Rohini's misdeeds. The two exchanged meaningful looks and smiles, then they went their ways.

And so Kshiroda unburdened herself to Haramani, Ram's mother, Shyam's mother, Hari, Tari, Pari and everyone else she met. At the end of it she felt better and with a happy heart she went to bathe in the crystal waters of Varuni. In their turn, Haramani, Ram's mother, Shyam's mother, Hari, Tari and Pari told everyone they met that Rohini had been in Govindalal's garden house. Zero added to one made ten, zero added to ten made a hundred and zero added to a hundred made a thousand. The sun, whose rays were not too warm when Khiri first spoke of Rohini to Bhramar, had not set yet when it was proclaimed in every house that Rohini was favoured by Govindalal. The tale of Rohini's visit to Govindalal's garden led to the tale of the unbounded passion that had grown between them and this in its turn led to the tale of the countless pieces of jewellery he had given her. To this, many other details were added, but I, as a humble truth-telling male writer, shall not presume to elaborate on these to you ladies, highly skilled in the art of talking and spreading scandal.

By and by the news reached Bhramar. First Vinodini came and said, 'Is this true?' with a pale face and a heart about to break. Bhramar asked, 'Is what true?' Vinodini contracted her eyebrows like Cupid's flowery bow and flashed a bolt of lightning from the corner of her eye, put her boy on her lap and said, 'I am talking about the Rohini affair.'

Bhramar could not reply. She drew the child towards her and with a girlish trick made him cry. Vinodini left giving the boy her breast.

Suradhani came next. 'Didn't I tell you to put a spell on your husband? After all, you are not of fair complexion, you cannot win a man's heart just with words, you need beauty and other qualities. God knows, Rohini is very clever.'

'What do you mean, Rohini is clever?'

Suradhani hit her brow with her hand, 'Hard luck! Everyone knows except you that your husband has given Rohini seven thousand rupees worth of jewellery.'

Bhramar was angry. In her mind she sent Suradhani to the land of Yama. Wringing the neck of one of her dolls, she said, 'I know that. I saw his account book. We are down by fourteen thousand rupees worth of jewellery.'

After Vinodini and Suradhani, a host of Bhramar's other women relatives and friends came in singly, in twos and threes, to tell this poor and distressed girl that her husband was in love with Rohini. Young, middle-aged and old, they all said, 'It is not at all surprising. Could there be a woman who would not fall in love with such a handsome man? Is it any wonder that he fell for such a beautiful woman as Rohini?' In love or hatred, in jest or anger, in joy or sorrow, with laughter or tears, they all said, 'Bhramar, you are ruined.'

Bhramar had been the happiest girl in the village and other women were jealous of her happiness. Why should a dark-complexioned, plain-looking girl be so rich? Why should she have a husband with whom no scandal was attached and who was worthy of a goddess? Why should a simple aparajita flower be valued like a lotus and smell like jasmine? The women of the village could only bear so much. So they came in flocks and herds with their children or their sisters, with their hair done up or while in the act of doing it up or with their hair loose. They all came to tell Bhramar that her happiness was at an end. No one felt for her, no one considered that Bhramar was an innocent girl, unhappy due to the absence of her husband.

Bhramar could not take this torture any more. She closed her doors, and threw herself on the floor. As she rolled on the floor, she cried for her husband, 'You, who are dearer than life, you alone can remove my doubt. You are my doubt but you are also my faith. Whom should I ask now? I don't believe what they are saying, but they are all saying it, and why should they do so if it weren't true? Who will allay my fears? You are not here, why don't I die as my suspicion is not removed? How can I live with this doubt? Why don't I die? When you come back, Lord of my life, don't reproach your Bhomra for having died without letting you know.'

22

NOW ROHINI ALSO SUFFERED FROM THE SAME GOSSIP AS DID BHRAMAR—all the tales from the village reached her ears. She heard the scandal that Govindalal was her slave and had given her seven thousand rupees worth of jewellery. Rohini did not know how this gossip had started; she made no inquiries about the source of this scandal. She jumped to the conclusion that Bhramar must have started the rumour, for she was the one who was most interested in Govindalal. It was unbearable for Rohini to be involved in such a scandal so soon after being taken for a thief. She decided to leave the village but resolved to get even with Bhramar before she left.

We have already seen that for Rohini nothing was impossible. She borrowed a Benarasi sari and a set of gilt jewellery from a neighbour. In the evening, she wrapped the sari and the jewellery in a parcel and went to the women's quarter of the zamindar's house. Bhramar was lying on the floor, now weeping, now wiping her eyes and gazing at the ceiling thoughtfully, when Rohini entered her room and sat beside her with her parcel. Bhramar was astonished to see Rohini; she felt that her whole body burned as if it were poisoned. 'You came here the other night to steal from the master's room. Have you entered my room tonight for the same purpose?'

'I have come to ruin you,' Rohini said to herself, and then said aloud to Bhramar, 'There is no need for me to steal now. I have no need of money—by your husband's favour, I have enough to live on. But of course people exaggerate.'

'Get out of here,' Bhramar cried. Rohini paid no attention to Bhramar's protest and went on, 'People exaggerate, they say that I have got seven thousand rupees worth of jewellery. In fact, it is only worth three thousand rupees and I have received this sari. I have come to show them to you. Why do people say that it is worth seven thousand rupees?'

Then she opened her parcel and displayed the contents. With a kick, Bhramar sent the pieces of jewellery flying.

'You must not put your foot on gold,' Rohini said as she retrieved the pieces quietly; she then packed up her parcel and left the room.

We greatly regret that Bhramar, who gave Khiri many blows, did not give Rohini even one. I have no doubt that my lady readers would have hit her had they been present at the scene. We admit that one should not strike a lady, but it does not mean that one should not strike a female fiend or a demon. I can, however, tell you why Bhramar did not strike Rohini. She struck Khiri for she loved her maidservant. But Bhramar did not love Rohini, that is why she did not strike her. When two children fight, a mother strikes her own child, not the other.

23

BEFORE THE NIGHT WAS OVER, BHRAMAR SAT DOWN TO WRITE A LETTER TO her husband. Govindalal had taught her how to read and write but she had never mastered the skill. She was more interested in her flowers, dolls, birds and husband than her studies or housework. When she had to write a letter, she would scrap many sheets of paper because of the blots and crosses she made, and in the end she would put it off for another day. Normally it would take her two or three days to finish a letter, but it was different tonight. She did not care at all about her handwriting or spelling. She wrote down whatever came from her pen. Her 'm's looked like 's's, 'dh's like 'ph's and often there were no joint letters. But she did not care, although there were some corrections, for instance 'Bhomra' became 'Bhramar', 'dasyo' became 'dasya' and so on. A more refined and corrected version would have read like this:

> You did not tell me why you stayed so long in the garden the other night. You said you would tell me after two years, but through bad luck I have heard it sooner. Not only did I hear it, I have also seen it. Rohini herself has shown me the sari and jewellery you gave her. You probably think that my devotion is unshakeable and my faith in you is unbounded. I too used to think so. But I now know that it is not so. I was devoted to you so long as you were worthy of my devotion. I had faith in you so long as you deserved it. Now I have neither devotion nor faith in you. I shall not be happy to see you. Please let me know before you come home so that I can go away to my father's house. Nothing can stop me here.

The letter reached Govindalal in due course. He was thunderstruck when he read its contents. Only from the handwriting and the spelling was he sure that Bhramar had written the letter. Even so he had doubts; he could scarcely believe that Bhramar was capable of writing such a letter.

There were other letters in the same post; but Govindalal remained motionless for a long time. Then he started reading the other letters. Amongst them was one from Brahmananda. Poetry-loving Brahmananda wrote, 'My friend, a battle between kings is the death of the ulu grass! Your wife may play tricks on you, why can't she leave us poor people alone? She has spread the rumour that you have given Rohini some seven thousand rupees worth of jewellery and has circulated many other ugly tales. I am too ashamed to write about them. I write to you so that you can put matters right. Otherwise I shall have to leave the village.'

Govindalal was astonished again. 'Bhramar has spread such rumours?' He could not comprehend it at all, and decided to go home. He ordered his boat to be made ready. 'I cannot stand the climate here. I shall go home tomorrow.'

Next day, he climbed into the boat and set out for home in a state of dejection.

24

DO NOT LET THE PERSON YOU LOVE OUT OF YOUR SIGHT. KEEP SHORT THE cord that ties your love if you wish to keep your bond strong. Never let your lover go out of your sight, because of the tragedy that separation breeds. You will shed bitter tears at the time of parting, and will feel that you will not be able to live without your sweetheart; but when you meet again after some years you will merely say, 'Are you well?' Maybe the separation will have gone so deep that you will say nothing at all, and in pride and anger will not even see each other again. Even if things do not go so far, they will never be the same after the separation as they were before. What goes never comes back; what breaks can never be whole again; rivers that flow away from each other do not mingle their waters again.

Bhramar was wrong to let Govindalal go away. Had they been together no misunderstanding would have arisen, and the truth would have come out in their heated verbal exchanges. Bhramar would not have been so wrong and so angry and this tragedy could have been averted.

After Govindalal set out for home, his steward sent word of the fact to Krishnakanta. The postal service moved faster than the boat; the steward's letter reached the zamindar four or five days before Govindalal's proposed date of arrival. As soon as she heard that her husband was returning, Bhramar sat down to write another letter, this time to her mother. Having smudged and wasted many sheets of paper, she managed to complete her letter in about four hours. It said, 'I am very ill. If I could come home I would get better. Don't delay else my illness will get worse and incurable. Send for me tomorrow if you can and don't tell anyone here about my illness.' She managed to get the letter off secretly through Khiri.

Anyone other than Bhramar's mother would have seen through Bhramar's deception and would not have been so worried about Bhramar's health. But the mother was very distressed by the news of her daughter's illness. She called Bhramar's mother-in-law many names and her husband a few, and shed many tears. The following day she sent a man and a maidservant with a palanquin and bearers to bring her daughter home. Bhramar's father sent a letter to Krishnakanta, in which he carefully avoided saying anything about Bhramar's illness. Instead he wrote, 'Bhramar's mother is ill and she wishes to see her daughter.' He instructed the servants to that effect.

Krishnakanta found himself in a dilemma. It would be wrong to let Bhramar go as his nephew was coming; on the other hand, it would be wrong not to let her go as her mother was ill. After some consideration, he let her go on the understanding that she would be back after four days.

Govindalal arrived on the fourth day. He heard that a palanquin was to be sent to fetch Bhramar. He understood why she had gone and he was very angry with her. 'Such mistrust! She left without questioning me, without letting me explain! I shall never see her face again. There is life without Bhramar.'

Govindalal asked his mother not to send for Bhramar; he gave no reason for it. Getting the impression that the nephew would like her to stay on, Krishnakanta made no further arrangements to bring her back.

25

THUS A FEW DAYS PASSED; NO ONE SENT FOR BHRAMAR, NOR DID SHE come. Govindalal felt that Bhramar must be punished, for she was so defiant and unjust. But tears came to his eyes at the sight of their empty room, and at the thought of her lack of faith in him and the misunderstanding that had arisen between them. But as he wiped his tears, he became angry and tried to suppress all thoughts of her. How difficult it is to forget! Happiness goes, its memory stays, a sore heals but its mark stays, and a man goes but his name is left behind.

At last, the stupid Govindalal thought that the best way to forget Bhramar was to fill his mind with thoughts of Rohini. Until now, the thought of Rohini's beauty had never left him, and however hard he tried to forget her, she was there in his heart. In old stories, we read of evil spirits who go in and out of houses day and night while exorcists try to expel them. In the same way, the fiend Rohini used to go in and out of Govindalal's heart and he used to try to exorcize her. In his heart there was no real Rohini, only her shadow, the same way as one only finds the reflection of the sun and the moon in a pool of water, not the real sun and moon.

Govindalal thought that since he must now forget Bhramar he should think of Rohini, otherwise there would be no end to his unhappiness. There are some quacks who often use strong poison to cure common ailments. Govindalal too proceeded to use strong poison for his small ills and thus courted disaster.

At first Rohini was a memory, then she became a sadness and finally a desire. Govindalal was regretting this desire while sitting in the pavilion of the Varuni tank. It was the rainy season, the sky was overcast, the rain was incessant—now soft, now hard. It was nearly dusk, the encroaching darkness of the evening and the darkness of the clouds obscured the view of Varuni. Govindalal dimly perceived the figure of a woman descending the steps and was reminded of Rohini doing the same. The rain had made the steps very slippery. Fearing that the woman might slip and fall into the water, Govindalal called out, 'Hey you, do not go down the slippery steps, it is dangerous.'

I cannot say whether the woman understood him clearly in the loud patter of rain. She put her pitcher down, climbed the steps, entered the flower-garden and stood before Govindalal. It was Rohini.

Govindalal asked, 'How did you get here, all wet?'

Rohini said, 'Did you call me?'

'No, I was just warning you about the slippery steps. But why are you getting wet standing outside?'

Gaining courage, Rohini entered the pavilion. 'What will people say if they see us now?' Govindalal asked.

'They are already saying things. I wanted to talk to you about it one day.'

'I have to ask you about that too. Who spread the rumour? Why do you blame Bhramar?'

'I shall tell you everything. But should I do that now standing here?'

'No, come with me,' said Govindalal and took Rohini into his garden house. I have no desire to repeat what was said there. I will only go so far as to say that that night when she went home, Rohini knew that Govindalal was enchanted with her beauty.

26

ENCHANTED WITH BEAUTY? WHO IS NOT ENCHANTED WITH THE BEAUTY OF something or someone? I am enchanted by the beauty of this blue and green speckled butterfly. You are enchanted by the beauty of a flowering kamini bough. There is no harm in that, since beauty is meant to enchant.

These were the first thoughts in Govindalal's mind. When a virtuous man puts his foot on the first step to vice, this is how he thinks. But as it is with gravitation in the outer world, so it is with vice in the inner world; the fall accelerates with every step down. Govindalal's fall was very rapid, because his heart had been long parched with the thirst for beauty. We can only shed tears for him, we cannot describe his fall.

Before long, Krishnakanta heard people coupling Govindalal and Rohini's names. He was distressed that his nephew's character was stained. He wanted to reproach him for it, but of late he had been ill and could not move out of his bedroom. Govindalal visited him every day, but Krishnakanta was always surrounded by his attendants and others, hence he could not speak to his nephew alone. As his illness grew worse, Krishnakanta suddenly realized that Chitragupta was about to settle his accounts with him, that his river of life was about to merge with the sea of eternity.[5] He could not put it off any longer. He decided to speak to Govindalal. One evening, Govindalal came home late at night from his garden and went to visit his uncle. Krishnakanta asked his attendants to leave the room and when Govindalal, somewhat embarrassed, asked how he was, the old man said in a feeble voice, 'Not very well. Why are you so late tonight?'

Without answering, Govindalal took his uncle's wrist in his hands and felt his pulse. He turned pale as he did so. Krishnakanta's life stream was flowing much too slowly. 'I shall be back soon,' Govindalal said and went immediately to the doctor's house. He told the surprised doctor, 'Come immediately with some medicine, my big uncle's condition is very serious.' The doctor hurriedly collected some pills and the two went running to Krishnakanta's bedroom.

Krishnakanta was a little frightened, and as the doctor felt his pulse he asked, 'Is there any danger?' The doctor replied, 'When is the human body free from danger?' Krishnakanta understood. 'How long have I got?' he asked. 'I shall be able to tell you after I give you the medicine,' the doctor said. He prepared the medicine in a small mortar and gave it to Krishnakanta. The old man took the mortar and after touching it to his head, he threw its contents into his spittoon.

The doctor was distressed. The zamindar reassured him. 'Don't be distressed, medicine cannot prolong my life now. I would much rather recite God's name. Go on, recite God's name, I want to hear it.'

No one except Krishnakanta recited God's name—they were all astonished, frightened and stunned. The old man alone was fearless. 'The key to my drawer is at my head, take it out,' he instructed his helpers.

Govindalal took the key from under the pillow.

'Open the drawer and take out my will,' said Krishnakanta.

Govindalal got the will out, then the old zamindar ordered, 'Send for my estate officers, clerk and about ten bhadralok from the village.'

Almost immediately, the room was filled with Krishnakanta's officers and village gentlemen. He asked one of the clerks to read out his will. When this was done, he said, 'This will is to be destroyed. Write a new will.'

'What shall I write?' the clerk asked.

'Everything as it is except—'

'Except what?'

'Strike out Govindalal's name, put Bhramar's name instead and add that Govindalal will receive half the share after Bhramar's death.'

No one uttered a word. The clerk looked at Govindalal who gestured to him to write.

The clerk wrote out the new will. When it was done, Krishnakanta signed it. The witnesses signed it and Govindalal also signed it without being asked to do so.

In the will, a half share was left to Bhramar and not a farthing to Govindalal.

That night, reciting God's name under the sacred tulsi plant, Krishnakanta passed away.

27

KRISHNAKANTA'S DEATH WAS MUCH LAMENTED BY THE PEOPLE IN THE PART of the country where he had lived. Some compared the event to the fall of Indra, some to the death of a dikpal, some to the crumbling of a mountain peak. Krishnakanta was a wealthy man, but he was also an honest and generous man. He gave generously to the poor, Brahmins and pandits. So he was mourned by many.

However, it was Bhramar who mourned him the most. Her mother-in-law sent for her the next day and she arrived in tears.

We cannot say for certain whether Govindalal and Bhramar would have had a quarrel over Rohini at their first meeting, but it was buried for the moment under their sorrow for Krishnakanta. They met when Bhramar was still crying for her uncle-in-law. The sight of him made her cry even more. Govindalal too wept.

Thus, the possibility of a big row was averted by the general confusion stemming from Krishnakanta's death. They both understood that this was not the time for their row. Since the first meeting passed off smoothly, they decided they should let the funeral rites and the mourning period pass unimpaired. With this in mind, Govindalal chose a suitable moment to speak to his wife, 'Bhramar, I have something to discuss with you, although it will break my heart to do so. I am now weighed down by grief; this grief is heavier than that I felt at the loss of my father. I shall tell you all about it when the funeral rites are over and I suggest that we avoid the topic till then.'

Bhramar said, restraining her tears and remembering the deities, Kali, Durga, Shiva and Hari, 'I too have something to tell you; ask me about it when you have some free time.'

Nothing further was said. Days passed as they used to; and it seemed nothing had changed. The servants, the mistress, relatives and neighbours, no one realized that there was a cloud in the sky, an insect had entered the flower, a woodworm had lodged itself inside the beautiful love-image. Govindalal and Bhramar would now smile at each other as before, but it no longer came spontaneously to their lips when their eyes met. It was no longer half-laugh and half-love as it had been; nor did the smile speak of happiness and an intense desire for more happiness. The look in their eyes had changed. She no longer saw the beauty in his eyes, the beauty which was like a boundless and fathomless sea that she could never swim across. No more did he see in her eyes the goodness that had made him oblivious of the world. Gone too were the loving words, ever new, ever pleasing, ever colourful; words that they used to address each other with—new pet names like 'Bhomra', 'Bhom' and 'Bhum' or 'darling' or 'hey' or words with which he used to tease her like 'darkie' and 'dark gold'. They would no longer call each other for nothing, as they did before; or have those arguments which led nowhere. Their mode of speech too had changed—words that used to flow abundantly had to be searched for now. Gone too was the language of constant communication which was partly words, partly looks and partly kisses; the language that did not need to be more articulate to be understood. Formerly, when they were together, if someone called, Govindalal would not go easily, Bhramar would not go at all. But now one or the other would get up to go under the pretence that it was very hot or someone was calling. The full moon was hidden by a cloud, the autumnal moon was eclipsed. Someone had cut the strings of the tender musical instrument.

Those bright hearts, which were bright like the midday sun, were now filled with darkness. To light up the darkness, Govindalal thought of Rohini, and Bhramar of Yama, the God of Death. Home for the homeless, help for the helpless, love for the loveless—death comforts the heart, ends sorrow, relieves distress. It is solace for the poor, hope for the hopeless—Yama, the God of Death. Bhramar prayed that He take her.

28

THE FUNERAL RITES OF KRISHNAKANTA ROY WERE PERFORMED WITH GREAT pomp. Even his enemies said that it was grand, but had only cost between five to ten thousand rupees. His friends, on the other hand, put the expenses upto one lakh and his heirs mentioned privately that they were about fifty thousand. We have seen the accounts; the total expense was thirty-two thousand three hundred fifty-six rupees and twelve and a half annas.

Be that as it may, the commotion lasted for quite a few days. Haralal, being the eldest son, came to perform the rituals. For days, nothing could be heard in the village except the buzzing of flies, the clatter of pots and pans, the clamour of beggars and the disputes of logicians. There were loads of sweetmeats, hordes of beggars, crowds of Brahmins with tikis and namavalis, and no end of relatives, relatives of relatives and their relatives. The boys threw around sitabhogs and mihidanas as if they were playing ball. The women, knowing that coconut oil was dear, put ghee, already used for frying luchis, on their hair. The opium dens were closed as the addicts went to the feast. The liquor stores were closed as the customers went to receive customary gifts at the funeral feast, disguising themselves as Brahmins. The price of rice went up; there was a shortage of flour; there was also a shortage of ground rice as the grocers tried to pass it off as flour. The patients could not get castor oil as the grocers used it for adulterating ghee which was consumed in large quantities. The milkmen had no whey, having already sold it as curd for the feast; they said that their whey had turned into curd by the blessings of the Brahmins who had it at the feast.

When at last the din of the funeral ceremonies was over, a meeting was called for the reading of Krishnakanta's will. Haralal realized that the will bore many signatures and could not possibly be contested. He went back where he had come from.

When the reading of the will was over, Govindalal came to Bhramar and asked, 'Have you heard about the will?'

'What about it?' asked Bhramar.

'A half share to you.'

'To me or to you?'

'Now there is a difference. The property is not mine but yours.'

'In that case, it is still yours.'

'No, I shall not accept your property.'

Bhramar felt like crying, but her pride restrained her from doing so. 'What will you do, then?'

'I shall find a way of earning a livelihood,' said Govinda.

'What way?'

'I shall travel from place to place seeking work.'

'The half share is your father's. Your big uncle had no authority to will it. My father explained this to me when he was here during the funeral ceremonies. The half share is yours, not mine.'

Govindalal said, 'My big uncle was no fool. He knew what he was doing. The property is yours, not mine; he left it to you.'

Bhramar said, 'If you are in doubt I shall make it over to you.'

'I shall not accept your charity.'

'What's the harm in that? Am I not your slave?'

'That sort of talk does not become you now.'

'What have I done? I don't care for anyone in the world but you. I was married when I was eight and now I am seventeen. In these years I have cared only for you; I am dependant on you, I am your toy. What have I done to offend you?'

Govinda said, 'Just try to remember.'

'I went away when you were coming. I admit to my fault and I ask a thousand pardons for it. It was my love for you that made me angry.'

Govindalal did not speak. At his feet lay his seventeen-year-old wife, distressed, hair dishevelled, enchanted by his beauty and now weeping uncontrollably. Govindalal remained silent. He thought, 'She is dark, Rohini is so beautiful; Bhramar has virtue, Rohini beauty. So far I have served virtue, now I shall enjoy beauty and I shall spend as I choose this worthless, hopeless, motiveless life. After that I shall end this earthen pot-like life, a life without purpose!'

Bhramar was still crying, clasping his feet, 'Forgive me, I am only a girl.'

Her cry was heard by God, that omniscient dispenser of joys and sorrows and the friend of the distressed; but not by Govindalal.

Receiving no reply, Bhramar said, 'What do you say?'

Govindalal said, 'I forsake you.'

Bhramar released his feet and got up to go outside. But she stumbled on the threshold and fell down unconscious.

29

'WHAT HAVE I DONE TO MAKE YOU ABANDON ME?'

Bhramar could not bring herself to ask this question of Govindalal. But she kept asking herself, 'What was my fault?' The question was in her thoughts every moment since that last encounter.

Govindalal too asked himself what her fault was. In a way, he was convinced that she had committed a grave offence, but he did not know what it was. When he thought about it, he blamed Bhramar for her lack of trust in him, for writing a harsh letter to him, for not verifying the truth about the 'gossip between him and Rohini'. 'I loved her so much, but she did not trust me, that is her real fault.' We have already spoken of Kumati (bad counsel) and Sumati (good counsel). Now we shall relate a conversation they had while seated beside each other in Govindalal's heart.

Kumati argued, 'Bhramar's first offence is her lack of trust.'

Sumati said, 'Why should she not distrust a person who deserves it? You are enjoying Rohini's company now. How can you blame Bhramar for suspecting you of doing so?'

'I may be unfaithful now, but I was innocent when she distrusted me.'

'You have committed an offence. What does it matter at what time you become unfaithful—now or two days ago? Why blame her for suspecting you, who is capable of such an offence?'

'I am guilty now because Bhramar thought that I was guilty. If you call an honest man a thief, he becomes a thief.'

'So you blame Bhramar for calling you a thief when it is you who are the thief.'

'I cannot argue with you. But can you not see how she insulted me? When she heard that I was coming back from the country estate, she left for her father's house.'

'She did the right thing, for she firmly believed that you were attracted to another woman. Is there a woman who would not be angry if her husband started an affair with another?'

'She was wrong to believe it and that's her offence.'

'Have you asked her about it?'

'No.'

'You are angry but you never questioned her about it? Bhramar is only a girl. She was angry with you without questioning you. But that is not the real cause of your anger. Shall I tell you what it is?'

'Yes, tell me.'

'The real cause is Rohini. You've set your heart on Rohini, so the dark Bhramar no longer pleases you.'

'How is it then that Bhramar pleased me for so long?'

'Because you did not have Rohini for so long. Everything can happen in time. There is sunshine today but that does not mean there won't be floods tomorrow. Not only that, there is something more.'

'What else?'

'Krishnakanta's will; the old man knew that if he left the property to Bhramar it would go to you. He also knew that Bhramar would transfer the property in your name within a month. But because you had strayed into an evil path of late, he wanted to reform you. That's why he tied up your property in this manner, so that you would be close to Bhramar. You do not understand this and you are angry with Bhramar.'

'That's true. Do I have to live on a monthly allowance from my wife?'

'It is your property. Get Bhramar to transfer it in your name.'

'Do you want me to live on my wife's charity?'

'Oh Lord! What a lion of a man you are! Then take Bhramar to court and claim your own paternal property.'

'You want me to start a legal battle with my own wife?'

'Then what will you do? Go to the dogs?'

'That's what I am after.'

'Will Rohini go with you?'

Then Kumati and Sumati started fighting, pulling each other's hair and exchanging blows.

30

IT IS MY BELIEF THAT IF GOVINDALAL'S MOTHER HAD BEEN AN INTELLIGENT mistress of the household then the black cloud would have blown away and the crisis could have been averted. She knew that a disagreement had arisen between her son and his wife—women always know such things—and she could have sorted things out, by good counsel, affectionate words and other womanly devices. But Govindalal's mother was not a clever mistress. Moreover, she had a grudge against her daughter-in-law. She did not love Bhramar, hence she was not one of her well-wishers. She could not bear to think that her daughter-in-law should inherit the property when her son was still alive. She failed to understand the motives behind Krishnakanta's actions. The old man wanted to teach Govindalal a lesson and bring him back from his evil ways and he assumed that the young ones would always live together. She should have realized that Krishnakanta acted somewhat unwisely during the last moments of his life when he changed the will. She only dwelt on the injustice that she felt had been done; she was now entitled to a bare subsistence and was one of the many dependants in her daughter-in-law's household. So she resolved to leave the family. Ever since the death of her husband, this self-centred widow had wanted to go and live in Kashi. It was because of her love for Govindalal that she could not leave the family. Now her desire had intensified.

She told Govindalal, 'The master of the household has now gone to heaven. My time is approaching. Do a son's duty. Send me to Kashi.'

Govindalal instantly agreed. 'I shall take you to Kashi myself.'

Unfortunately, at that time Bhramar was away at her father's house. Hence, arrangements for a visit to Kashi were made without her knowledge. Govindalal had some private property in jewellery, gold and other valuable possessions. He secretly sold them all, and in this way he collected about a lakh of rupees. He thought that he should be able to live on it in the future.

Then, having decided upon a date for their departure, he sent for Bhramar. When she heard that her mother-in-law was leaving for Kashi, Bhramar hurried back home. She threw herself at her mother-in-law's feet and tearfully entreated her to stay. 'Mother, I am only a young girl, do not leave me. I know nothing of running a household—a household is like a sea, do not leave me drifting alone in it.' The mother-in-law replied, 'Your elder sister-in-law is going to stay. She will look after you and you too have become a mistress now.' Bhramar understood nothing.

She saw danger ahead. Her mother-in-law was leaving her; there was the possibility that her husband, accompanying her, would not return. Clasping Govindalal's feet, Bhramar asked, 'When will you come back?'

Govindalal said, 'I can't say. I have not much desire to come back.'

Bhramar let go of his feet and got up. 'What do I fear,' she said to herself, 'I can take poison.'

Then, at last, the chosen auspicious day for the journey arrived. A short distance had to be travelled by palanquin before taking the train to Kashi. Everything was ready—the bearers carried heavy chests, trunks, boxes, bags and bundles. The servants who were to accompany them were neatly dressed in clean, freshly washed clothes, their hair neatly done, and they stood about chewing betel leaves outside the main door. The boys and girls of the neighbourhood came to see what was happening. The gatekeepers buttoned up their chintz coats and, lathis in hand, started altercations with the bearers. Govindalal's mother did her pranams to the family deity, said goodbye to all the inmates of the house and got into the palanquin with tears in her eyes. Everybody wept. She left first; Govindalal was to follow on horseback.

Meanwhile, Govindalal bid farewell to all the other women members of the family and then went to his bedroom. There he found Bhramar weeping. Seeing her so distressed, he could not say what he had come to say. Instead he said, 'I am taking Mother to Kashi.'

Wiping her tears she said, 'Mother will stay there, but will you return?' As she spoke, she stopped crying. Govindalal was amazed at the gravity and steadiness of her voice and the steely determination on her lips. He could not reply. As he was silent, Bhramar continued, 'It is you who taught me that truth is the sole dharma and the sole happiness. Do tell me the truth, do not deceive me, I am a young girl dependant on you.'

Govindalal spoke at last, 'Then hear the truth; I have no wish to come back.'

Bhramar said, 'Won't you tell me why you do not want to come back?'

'If I stay, I live as your dependant.'

'What harm can come of that? I follow your commands.'

'Bhramar, who obeyed my commands, would have watched by the

window for my homecoming instead of going away to her father's.'

To that Bhramar said, 'How often have I begged to be forgiven for that offence? Can't you forgive me?'

Govindalal said, 'There will be hundreds of such offences in the future. You are now the owner of the property.'

'No, that is not so. See what I have done with the help of my father during my last visit to his house.'

She showed him a paper. 'Read it,' she said.

Govindalal read it; it was a deed of gift on duly stamped paper and registered. Bhramar had made over her whole property to her husband. After reading it he said, 'You have done what you thought right. But what is the basis of our relationship? It's that I should give you ornaments and you should wear them. It is not that you should give me property and I should enjoy it.' He tore the valuable deed of gift to pieces.

'My father said that it is useless to tear that up, for there is a copy of the deed in the government office,' said Bhramar.

'Then let it stay there. I am leaving.'

'When will you return?'

'Never.'

'Why? I am your wife, your pupil, your dependant, and I am your slave who begs a word of you. Why won't you come back?'

Govindalal said, 'Because I don't wish to.'

'Have you no sense of duty? Have you no dharma?'

'Maybe I do not.'

Bhramar restrained her tears with much effort. With folded hands and in a firm voice she said, 'Then go. If you do not wish to come back, then don't come back. If you want to leave me for no fault of mine, then leave me. But remember that the gods above us are watching, remember that one day you will weep for me. One day you will search for a genuine, beautiful love. By the gods I declare that if I have been a faithful wife, if I have been devoted to you with my body and soul and if there are gods above, then we shall meet again. I shall live with that hope. Now go, and say if you wish that you won't come back. But I tell you that you will come back, and call me and weep for me one day. The gods are false, dharma is false and I am unchaste if this does not happen. Go now. I am not unhappy for I know you are mine, not Rohini's.'

After that speech, Bhramar touched her husband's feet with reverence and left the room. She walked into another room and closed the door.

31

BEFORE THE BEGINNING OF THIS STORY, BHRAMAR HAD HAD A SON WHO HAD died within a few days after delivery. Now, behind the closed doors, she threw herself on the floor, and rolling in the dust and choking with sobs, she began to lament for her dead son: 'My butter doll, my beggar's gold, where are you now? If you were here, he could not have deserted me. He has ceased to love me but he could not have stopped loving you. I am ugly, but who could have called you ugly? Who could be more beautiful than you? Show yourself: in this time of trouble, appear once at least. After death can you appear no more?'

She put her hands together, looked up and called out to her gods in an indistinct voice, 'Tell me what wrong I have done that I should suffer so much. I am only seventeen. I have lost my son and my husband has deserted me. I have cared for nothing in this world except my husband's love. Why should I be deprived of it when I am still so young?'

She concluded that the gods were cruel. What can men do when the gods are cruel? They can only cry. So she cried and cried for a long time.

Meanwhile, Govindalal, having said farewell to Bhramar, walked slowly to the outer building. To tell you the truth, Govindalal too was weeping. He remembered that he had been so happy with Bhramar. That simple, sincere, childlike but invaluable love, how it had inspired her every word and flowed incessantly like a stream. He knew that he could never get back what he was now giving up. But he also thought that what he had done could not be undone. He thought it would be difficult to go back now, so he decided to continue on the course he had taken.

All would have been well if he had gone back, pushed Bhramar's door open and said that he would return. He wanted to do so but shame stood in his way and his sense of guilt deprived him of courage. He thought there was no hurry—he could return whenever he wished. So he abandoned the idea, came outside, mounted the saddled horse and gave it the whip. As he rode out, his thoughts turned to Rohini's beauty.

Part 2

1

GOVINDALAL SENT NEWS THAT HE, HIS MOTHER AND THE PARTY HAD SAFELY reached Kashi and that they were all well. All correspondence was between him and the estate office. There was no letter for Bhramar, and she was so hurt that she did not write either.

At last the steward was told that Govindalal had left Kashi and was coming home. Bhramar knew that Govindalal had said that only to deceive his mother, for he was really going elsewhere. She did not think he would come home.

Now she secretly started making inquiries about Rohini. There was nothing unusual about Rohini's life. She still performed her daily chores—cooking, bathing, washing, fetching water and so on. Then one day Bhramar heard that Rohini was ill and confined to her room where she lay all wrapped up. It was so bad that Brahmananda had to cook and look after himself. Then came the news that Rohini was somewhat better but not fully cured. Her condition of colic pain needed specialized treatment. Rohini was going to go to the famous temple at Tarakeswar and had taken a vow so that she could get the god's blessing for a divine cure. Finally, the report reached Bhramar that Rohini had left for Tarakeswar; she had gone alone for there was no one to accompany her.

Meanwhile, there was no news of Govindalal; nearly six months passed and still no news. There was no end to Bhramar's tears, no end to her worries—where was he, how was he? Even the barest news would have enabled her to live. Why was it withheld from her?

At last she got Sailavati to write to her mother-in-law. After all, she was his mother. She must have some news of her son. Her mother-in-law wrote back that she had indeed heard from Govindalal, who was now in Delhi, having visited Allahabad, Mathura, Jaipur and other places. He was not staying in one place for long and would be leaving Delhi soon.

Rohini too did not return. 'God knows where she has gone,' Bhramar thought. 'I am a sinful creature and will not utter a word about my suspicions.' She was unable to bear the situation any longer. With tears in her eyes, she went to her father's house in a palanquin. But it was more difficult to get news of her husband there and so she returned to Haridragram. She asked Sailavati to write again. Her mother-in-law replied that Govindalal no longer wrote to her and she did not know where he was. Thus passed the first year. At the end of that year, Bhramar was lying ill, in bed. The aparajita flower had begun to wither.

2

BHRAMAR'S FATHER CAME TO SEE HER WHEN HE HEARD THAT HIS DAUGHTER was very ill and bedridden. We have so far not given an account of Bhramar's father. We shall do so now. Madhavinath Sarkar, Bhramar's father, was forty-one and very handsome. There was considerable difference of opinion about his character; many praised him very highly while others thought him to be a wicked man. But all agreed that he was a very clever man and all feared him, even those who praised him.

When he saw her, Madhavinath could not stop weeping. He found that his beautiful, dark girl, who had shapely limbs, was now pale and thin; the bones on her neck protruded and her lotus eyes had sunk in their sockets. Bhramar too shed many tears. After they had both recovered, Bhramar spoke, 'Father, my days are numbered. Help me prepare for some religious rites. I am young but I am dying. I don't have much time left to perform these rituals. I have so much money. I want to spend it on religious duties. You must organize them for me. Who else can help me?'

Madhavinath could not answer; the pain of seeing his daughter so unhappy was unbearable. He left her room. He sat down in the outer building and cried for a long time. Then the pain in his heart turned into burning anger. 'Is there no one in this world who can punish the man who has tormented my daughter?' he wondered. Then with red-rimmed eyes he vowed determinedly, 'I shall destroy the person who has destroyed my daughter.'

After a while, having regained his composure, he went to his daughter. 'I was thinking of what you said about religious rites. Such rituals will involve much fasting. You cannot fast now, in your present condition, but only when you are a little better.'

'Shall I ever be better?'

'Of course you will. You are not seriously ill. You are not getting proper medical treatment here and that is your problem. You have no father-in-law, no mother-in-law and no one else to help you. I want you to come home with me and you will be treated there. I'll stay here a couple of days and then take you to Rajgram.'

Rajgram was Bhramar's paternal home.

Madhavinath left his daughter and went to the estate office. He asked the steward, 'Do you get letters from the young master?'

'No,' said the steward.

'Where is he now?' Madhavinath asked.

'None of us can tell you that, he does not send us any news.'

'Who can give me some news?'

'If we knew that we would have made inquiries ourselves. We sent a man to Kashi to ask the old mistress about her son. Even she does not know his whereabouts. The young master is living somewhere secretively,' answered the steward.

3

MADHAVINATH RESOLVED TO AVENGE THE WRONG DONE TO HIS DAUGHTER. He knew that Govindalal and Rohini were at the root of all this mischief. He vowed to find those two sinners, otherwise the wicked would go unpunished and Bhramar would perhaps die.

They had completely hidden themselves, cutting off every thread and effacing every footprint. Madhavinath said to himself that he would find them if he had any pride in his manhood. With this firm resolve, he set out alone from the Roy house.

There was a post office in the village. With a cane in his hand and a betel leaf in his mouth, Madhavinath went inside the office, looking meek and innocent.

This office was managed by a deputy postmaster whose salary was fifteen rupees per month. It was dark inside the thatched post office. On a broken mango-wood table, lay some gum in an earthen saucer, a pair of scales, a seal and some other articles.

In this atmosphere, the postmaster—or the post-babu as he was often called—solemnly ruled over the postman, who received a salary of seven rupees per month. For the postman, the difference between him and the postmaster was no more than the difference between seven annas and fifteen annas. For the postmaster, however, the difference was similar to that between heaven and earth. He considered himself Lord of his subordinate in life and death. To prove it, he constantly scolded the postman, who gave back at least half of what he received.

The postmaster was weighing a letter and scolding the postman when Madhavinath's calm and smiling face appeared before him. So the postmaster stopped shouting and gaped at the visitor instead. He recognized the visitor as a gentleman, and vaguely thought that civility demanded that he greet the visitor, but he did not know how to offer his greetings.

Madhavinath saw that he stood before a monkey. 'Are you a Brahmin?' he asked the postmaster.

'Yes, and you?'

Suppressing a smile, Madhavinath bent his head and touched his forehead with folded hands, 'My morning's respects to you.'

'Please sit down.'

This created a problem for Madhavinath. Where was he to sit? The only seat available was an ancient three-legged chair, which was already occupied by the postmaster. Then the postman, who was called Haridas Bairagi, removed a heap of torn books from a wooden stool and offered it to Madhavinath. 'Hallo, how are you? Haven't I seen you somewhere?' the visitor asked Haridas, fixing him with his eyes.

'Yes, sir, I deliver the letters.'

'Ah! That's how I know you. Do you think that you could prepare a hookah for me?'

In fact, Haridas had never met Madhavinath. They lived in different villages. But the poor postman thought that this strange gentleman would give him a baksheesh if he did him a favour. So he ran out to prepare a hookah for the visitor. Madhavinath did not smoke—he asked for the hookah to get rid of the postman.

After Haridas had left the room, Madhavinath said to the postmaster, 'I have come here to ask you some questions.'

The postmaster could not help smiling to himself. He was from Bikrampur, a town in East Bengal; however crude he was in matters of civility, the postmaster was a shrewd man when it came to serving his own interests. He guessed Madhavinath's purpose. 'What do you want to know?' he asked.

'Do you know Brahmananda Ghosh?'

'Maybe I do.'

Madhavinath realized that the postmaster was about to show his true colours. 'Do any letters come to your office addressed to Brahmananda Ghosh?'

'Don't you know Brahmananda Ghosh?'

'Never mind whether I do or don't. I came to ask you.'

The postmaster remembered his high office and replied in a solemn and somewhat angry voice, 'We are forbidden to give out such information.' He started to weigh his letters.

Madhavinath smiled to himself and said, 'My dear man, I knew you would say that, so I have come prepared. I will give you something before I go. Now answer me truthfully.'

The postmaster, beaming with expectation, said, 'What do you want to know?'

'Do you get letters addressed to Brahmananda?'

'We do.'

'How often?'

'I have not yet been paid for what I have said. Produce the money, then ask another question.'

Madhavinath planned to leave some money for the postmaster, but the latter's attitude annoyed him. 'My dear man, it seems that you are a stranger here; do you know who I am?' he asked.

'No, I don't. But it does not matter who you are, we do not give out official information to anybody and everybody. Anyway, who are you?'

'My name is Madhavinath Sarkar and I am from Rajgram. Do you know how many armed men I employ?'

The postmaster was now frightened; he had heard of Madhavinath and his power; he could not speak.

So Madhavinath continued, 'Mind you answer me truthfully, whatever I ask. I won't give you a pie if you try to deceive me. If you refuse to speak, or tell a lie, I'll burn down your house and after robbing your post office I'll produce evidence in court to prove that you had it done by your own agents. Now will you speak?'

The postmaster was trembling with fear.

'Please do not be angry, sir. I did not know who you were. I thought that I was speaking to a common man, that's why I spoke like that. As your honour is here in person, I'll tell you whatever you ask.'

'How often do letters come for Brahmananda?'

'About once a month. I am not sure.'

'Are they registered letters?'

'Yes.'

'In what office are they registered?'

'I do not remember.'

'Surely you keep receipts of all your registered mail.'

The postmaster, after searching for sometime, found a receipt and read it out, 'Prasadpur.'

'In what district is Prasadpur? Check your list.'

The postmaster, still trembling, looked at his list and said, 'Jessore.'

'Check if there are other letters for Brahmananda from some other places. Examine all the receipts.'

The postmaster found that all the letters lately received had come from Prasadpur.

Madhavinath put a ten-rupee note in the postmaster's trembling hand and left. Haridas had not yet turned up with his hookah. Madhavinath left a rupee for him with the postmaster who, it is needless to say, kept it for himself.

4

MADHAVINATH WENT BACK SMILING. HE HAD KNOWN ABOUT THE CLANDESTINE affair between Govindalal and Rohini. He was certain that those two were living secretively together somewhere. He also knew about Brahmananda; he had no relatives except Rohini. So when Madhavinath learnt from the post office that registered letters were sent to Brahmananda every month, he concluded that either Rohini or Govindalal was sending her uncle a monthly allowance. Letters came from Prasadpur, so they must be living somewhere near there, or in that town itself. But he wanted to be doubly sure. So when he reached the Roy household, he sent a messenger to the police station with a letter to the sub-inspector, asking him to send a constable. Madhavinath sent word he might be able to help the police about some stolen goods.

The sub-inspector knew Madhavinath well, and was afraid of him. He immediately dispatched a constable named Nidra Singh.

Madhavinath gave Nidra Singh two rupees and said, 'Look, my dear man, don't try your Hindi with me, but do as I tell you. Go and hide under that tree, but make sure that you can be seen from here.' Nidra Singh did as he was told.[6] Then Madhavinath sent for Brahmananda, who came and sat next to him.

There was no one else there. After exchanging greetings, Madhavinath said, 'My daughter's in-laws considered you one of their near relatives. They are all dead now and my son-in-law is away. So I thought that it was my duty to help you when you are in danger.'

Brahmananda went pale. 'Danger! What danger?'

Madhavinath replied in a grave voice, 'You are indeed in danger.'

'What danger, sir?'

'You are in grave danger for the police have learned that you are in possession of a stolen note.'

Brahmananda was thunderstruck. 'Stolen note! In my possession, how?'

'You may not know that the note was stolen. Someone else might have given you the note.'

Brahmananda said, 'How can that be, who would give me a note?'

Lowering his voice, Madhavinath said, 'We know all about it. The police too know about it. In fact, it is the police who told me about it. The stolen note comes from Prasadpur. Look, there is the policeman who has come to get you. I paid him something to hold back for a while.' Then he pointed to the policeman under the tree. He stood with a baton in hand, his bearded face lowered like a dark cloud; he looked formidable to Brahmananda. He burst into tears. Trembling all over, he clasped Madhavinath's feet and cried, 'Save me.'

'Don't be frightened. Just tell me the number of the latest note you received from Prasadpur. The police have given me the number of the stolen goods. If your note does not bear that number then you have nothing to fear. Even if it does, we can always change the number. Please go and fetch the latest letter and the latest note from Prasadpur and let me check the number.'

But how could Brahmananda go? He was afraid of the policeman under the tree.

'Have no fear. I shall send someone with you.' Then Madhavinath ordered one of the gatekeepers to accompany the frightened man. Brahmananda came back with the note and the letter. The letter gave Madhavinath the information he wanted. Returning the letter and the note he said, 'The note received does not bear the number of the stolen one. You're quite safe and you can go home. I'll send the constable away.'

Brahmananda breathed again and went back home as fast as he could.

Madhavinath took Bhramar home and arranged for proper medical treatment for his daughter. After that he left for Calcutta. Bhramar raised objections but Madhavinath went, promising to return soon.

In Calcutta, Madhavinath had a friend called Nisakar Das, who was about ten years younger than him. Nisakar had inherited some property and had a private income. He did not have to work for a living, so he spent his time with music and travel. Madhavinath went to see him. After they had talked about various matters, Madhavinath asked, 'Would you like to accompany me on a journey to Jessore?'

'Why there?'

'I want to buy an indigo factory.'

'Let's go, then.'

Then, after completing the necessary preparations—which took them a day or two—the two friends set off for Jessore, en route to Prasadpur.

5

SEE HOW GENTLY THE LEAN RIVER CHITRA FLOWS. ON THE BANKS ARE MANY trees—aswatha, kadamba, mango, date and others. You can hear the birds, like the kokil, papiha and koel singing from these trees. There is no village nearby, and the small market of Prasadpur is about two miles away. Finding this a secluded spot, well suited for committing sinful acts with impunity, a European indigo planter had built a factory here many years ago. Now the planter and his wealth had long gone and all his underlings had met the doom they deserved. A Bengali had recently bought this secluded house. He had furnished it beautifully with flowers, statues, seats, mirrors and pictures. As we enter the large room on the first floor, we notice the pictures. Some are beautiful, while others are so offensive as to be indescribable. We see a bearded Muslim music teacher, sitting on a soft cushion, tuning a tambura, while a young woman, sitting next to him, is playing a tabla, her golden bracelets tinkling with the movement of her hand. We see the reflections of these two in two large mirrors standing close to them. Through the open doorway we see a young man in the next room, reading a novel and occasionally looking at the young woman to see how she is getting on with her lesson. After much plucking and tightening of the strings, the music teacher has decided that the tambura is in tune with the tabla. Then he begins to sing. His snow-white teeth gleam out of the darkness of his beard and moustache, and his face breaks into many contortions as he bellows like a bull. Then the young woman, taking her cue from the grimaces of her teacher, begins to sing in her own soft voice. Then their two voices, one light, the other heavy, unite like gold and silver threads, creating some peculiar music.

Here we would have liked to let the curtain fall, for we do not wish to show anything that is unseemly and impure. We must tell you what is absolutely necessary. But there was beauty here. The call of the kokils and the humming of bumblebees from the ashoka, kutaja and kurbak groves; the geese babbling on the river; the scent of juthi, jati, mallika, madhumalati and other flowers; the sunlight coming into the house through the blue panes; the flowers in silver and crystal vases; the various colourful objects in the house; and the pure sound that poured forth from the music teacher. I have a special reason for mentioning all this, for all this beauty was connected with the young man who was looking with so much interest at the wandering eyes of the young woman. It was her beauty that made them so beautiful to his eyes.

The young man was Govindalal and the young woman was Rohini. Govindalal had bought the house and the two of them were living here.

Suddenly, Rohini's tabla played out of tune, a string snapped off the music teacher's tambura and he stopped singing. The novel fell from Govindalal's hands. An unknown young man appeared at the doorstep of this pleasure-house. We know him. He was Nisakar Das.

6

ROHINI LIVED ON THE UPPER FLOOR OF THIS TWO-STOREYED HOUSE IN semi-seclusion—half pardanasin. The ground floor was occupied by the servants. In this secluded spot, scarcely anyone came to visit Govindalal, so there was no outer building for visitors. If, once in a while, a tradesman or someone else came to see Govindalal, word was sent to him upstairs and he came down and received his visitor in a room which had been set apart for the purpose on the ground floor.

Nisakar shouted, 'Is someone at home?' as he reached the door.

Govindalal had two servants called Sona and Rupo. The two came to the door as they heard someone calling, and were surprised to see Nisakar, whom they at once took to be a highly respectable gentleman. Nisakar had taken particular care to put on very fine clothes. Never before had such a person crossed the threshold of this house; so the servants stared at each other in astonishment. Sona asked, 'Who are you looking for?'

'You, inform your master that a gentleman wishes to see him.'

'What name shall I give?'

'No need for that, just say a gentleman wishes to see him.'

The servants knew that Govindalal did not receive visitors—that was not his nature. So they were unwilling to announce Nisakar. Sona was hesitant. Rupo said, 'You have come in vain—the master does not see anybody.'

'Then you stay here, I'll go up unannounced.'

The servants were now in trouble. 'No, sir, please don't. We will lose our jobs.'

Then Nisakar produced a rupee. 'Whoever announces me will get this rupee.' While Sona pondered, Rupo pounced like a kite, took the rupee from Nisakar's hand and went up to tell the master.

There was a beautiful garden surrounding the house. Nisakar tipped Sona a rupee and said, 'I shall be in the garden. Call me when the master sends for me.'

Govindalal was busy and Rupo had no opportunity of telling him about the visitor. Meanwhile Nisakar, as he was walking in the garden, looked up and saw a very beautiful woman watching him from the window.

Rohini saw Nisakar and thought, 'Who is he? It is clear from his appearance that he does not belong to this area. It is also clear from his clothes that he is very rich. He is handsome too—more so than Govindalal? No, that's not true. Govindalal is of fair complexion but this man has a beautiful face and eyes, yes, those eyes—oh! what a beautiful pair of eyes. Where does he come from? He cannot be from Haridragram. I know everyone there. Can't I speak to him for a while? There is no harm in that. I shall never be unfaithful to Govindalal.'

These were the thoughts racing through Rohini's mind when Nisakar looked up and their eyes met. I do not know if their eyes spoke to one another, nor would I care to say if I knew. But I have heard that eyes do speak.

Now Rupo had an opportunity to tell Govindalal that a gentleman was waiting to see him. Govindalal said, 'Where does he come from?'

Rupo said, 'I do not know.'

'Why did you not ask him before you came to tell me?'

Rupo saw that he was about to prove himself a fool, but he had sufficient presence of mind to say, 'I did ask, but the gentleman said he would only tell you.'

'Then go and tell him that I cannot see him.'

Meanwhile, Nisakar had begun to suspect that Govindalal had declined to see him for the servants did not come for him. 'But why should I be civil to an evil-doer? Why shouldn't I go up without being asked?' he thought and without waiting for the servants' return, he re-entered the house. He saw no one downstairs, so without hesitation he went upstairs and appeared in the room where Govindalal, Rohini and Danesh Khan, the music teacher, were sitting. Rupo pointed out Nisakar to Govindalal. 'That's the gentleman who wanted to see you.'

Govindalal was very annoyed, but seeing that the visitor was a gentleman, he asked him who he was.

Nisakar gave his name as Rashbehari Dey and said that he was from Baranagar. Then he planted himself on a seat, knowing that the master of the house would not offer him one.

'Whom do you want to see?'

'You.'

'If you had waited a little, instead of forcing yourself into my room, you would have heard from the servants that I have no time to see anyone.'

'But I see you have plenty of time. I wouldn't have come to see you if I were a man who is put off so easily. Since I am here, you can't get rid of me until you have heard my business.'

Govindalal said, 'I do not wish to hear it. But if you can get it over in a couple of words, you may as well do so before you go.'

Nisakar said, 'It will only take me a couple of words. Your wife Bhramar wishes to lease out her property.'

The music teacher, Danesh Khan, was putting a new string to his tambura. While he continued with the task, he held up a finger of the other hand, and said, 'That's word number one.'

Nisakar continued, 'I wish to take it.'

Lifting another finger, Danesh Khan said, 'Word number two.'

'For that purpose I went to your house at Haridragram.'

Danesh Khan said, 'You have had two words. That makes three.'

Nisakar asked, 'Are you counting pigs, maestro?'

With anger in his eyes, Danesh Khan asked Govindalal to send the ill-bred visitor away. But Govindalal was deep in thought and did not speak.

Nisakar continued, 'Your wife has agreed to give me the lease but we need your consent. She neither knows your address nor wishes to write to you, so the task of consulting you fell on me. After much search I have found you and I am here to seek your consent.'

Govindalal did not answer. His mind was elsewhere. He had heard Bhramar's name after a long time, after nearly two years—his own Bhramar.

Nisakar understood that something was going on in Govindalal's mind so he continued, 'If you agree, just give me a line to say so and I'll go.'

Govindalal said nothing. Nisakar understood, and he repeated everything all over again. This time, Govindalal, having controlled his feelings, listened carefully. Reader, know that Nisakar had made up what he said; Govindalal, however, was not aware of this. In a more mellow tone he said, 'You do not need my permission. The property belongs to my wife, it is not mine; you should know that. She can lease it out to whomsoever she likes. I cannot permit it, nor can I forbid it. Perhaps now you will excuse me.'

Nisakar had no choice but to go. After he had gone, Govindalal asked Danesh Khan to sing something. The master had just finished tuning his tambura. He asked his patron, 'What shall I sing?'

'Whatever you like,' Govindalal said as he started drumming the tabla. He had learnt to play the tabla many years ago, but he had now become an expert. Today, however, he could not keep time with the maestro. There was no accompanist with his song and tambura. Danesh Khan was annoyed. He put down his tambura and stopped singing; he excused himself, saying that he was tired. Then Govindalal tried to play the sitar, but could not remember the melody. He left the sitar and started reading his novel. But he was not able to concentrate on what he was reading; he put that down too. He went into the bedroom and he did not see Rohini there. He told Sona, who was at hand, that he was going to have a nap and must not be disturbed.

Having said this, Govindalal entered the bedroom and closed the door. The evening was nearly done. He did not sleep. Sitting on the bed, he covered his face with his hands and wept. We do not know why he cried, whether it was for Bhramar or for himself. Perhaps it was for both.

We do not see that there was anything else for him to do but cry. After what he had done, how could he go back to Bhramar or show his face in his village? Now there were thorns on his path to Haridragram. There was nothing for him to do but cry.

7

WHEN NISAKAR CAME AND SAT IN THE LARGE HALL, ROHINI WENT TO ANOTHER room. She was out of sight but not out of hearing, and in fact she listened to everything that was said in the hall, very attentively. She even moved the door curtain a little so that she could see Nisakar. He was well aware that a pair of wide and beautiful eyes were watching him from the other side of the curtains.

She heard that Nisakar had been to Haridragram. Rupo was also there and had heard the conversation between his master and the visitor. As soon as Nisakar left, Rohini beckoned Rupo and whispered in his ears, 'Can you do something for me? The master must not know and you will get five rupees baksheesh.'

Rupo thought it was his lucky day. He was earning a lot of money. Poor people like him needed all the extra money they can get, so he said, 'I'll do whatever you ask.'

'Follow that gentleman downstairs. He is from my native village. I never get any news from there. I am worried about my people, I need to ask him about them. The master sent him away angrily. Go down and ask him to stay, but take care that neither the master nor anybody else knows anything about it. I shall go to see him as soon as I can without being noticed. If he hesitates, persuade him to stay.'

Sensing baksheesh, Rupo ran off to carry out Rohini's order.

With what objective Nisakar had come to deceive Govindalal I cannot say, but his conduct as he came downstairs would have aroused grave suspicions in any intelligent person. He had started examining the wood and the bolts and hinges of the front door. And then Rupo came down and asked, 'Do you wish to smoke, sir?'

'The master did not offer me this, should I accept it from his servant?'

'Perhaps not, but I need to speak to you in private. If you would not mind coming with me . . .'

Rupo took Nisakar to his room. Nisakar had no objection. Having offered him a seat, Rupo gave him Rohini's message. Nisakar thought that the moon was within his reach. A very easy way of accomplishing his task appeared before him. 'My dear man,' he said to Rupo, 'your master has thrown me out. How can I stay on in this house?'

'The master will not know anything about it. He never comes down to this room.'

'Maybe he does not, but when the mistress comes down to see me, he may wonder about that and follow her downstairs. Just imagine what will happen to me if he finds her with me.'

Rupo kept silent. So Nisakar continued, 'In this secluded place, he could lock me up, murder me and bury my body in the garden. I could not even call for help. You yourself might give me a blow or two. No, I can't stay here. Go and tell your mistress why I can't. Tell her also that I have an important message for her from her uncle. I could not give it to her because the master threw me out.'

Rupo saw the five rupees receding from his grasp. 'If you can't stay here,' he said, 'what about waiting for her somewhere outside?'

'I was thinking of that. As I came I noticed a landing ghat on the river bank under two bakul trees not far from this house. Do you know it?'

'I do.'

'I'll go and wait there; it is dark, nobody can see me there now. If your mistress can come, I'll give her all the news from her village. If there is any trouble, then I can run away from there. I do not particularly fancy being locked up and being beaten like a dog.'

Rupo went up and told Rohini what Nisakar had said.

Now, I cannot say what went on in Rohini's mind. A human being does not even know his own thoughts, so how would I know Rohini's? I cannot say that she was so fond of her uncle that she would throw discretion to the winds to get news of him, and I suspect she had quite different reasons for wanting to meet Nisakar. The two had exchanged glances and divined each other's thoughts. She had noticed that he was handsome, had a beautiful pair of eyes and was a prince among men for his manliness. She had resolved not to be unfaithful to Govindalal—but this was quite different from being unfaithful.

This wicked woman might have thought, 'If a hunter sees a deer off its guard, doesn't he shoot an arrow at it? If a woman sees a vulnerable man, doesn't she wish to make a conquest? A tiger does not eat all the cows it kills. Women conquer men solely for pride and the pleasure of conquest. Many people catch fish and shoot birds solely for love of sport. One hunts for sport, not food, and that's why hunting is such fun. Since this large-eyed deer has strayed into my woods, why should I let it go without piercing it with an arrow?' I am not sure that Rohini's thoughts were exactly these, but she agreed to see Nisakar at the ghat by the river bank of Chitra.

Rupo reported this back to Nisakar, who stood up in delight when he heard it.

8

AFTER RUPO HAD GONE, NISAKAR CALLED SONA. HE ASKED HIM, 'HOW LONG have you been working here?'

Sona replied, 'Ever since the master came here.'

'Not very long, then. What does he pay?'

'Three rupees per month, plus food, shelter and clothes.'

'How do you manage with such a low wage, since you are such a good head-servant?'

Sona, melted by such kind words, said, 'What can I do? Who will give me a higher wage in this place?'

Nisakar said, 'You need not worry about a good job. If you were to come to my part of the country, you'd be snapped up and easily earn five, seven or even ten rupees per month.'

'If you would be so kind as to take me with you.'

'How can I take you? How can you leave your master?'

'The master is all right, but the mistress is awful.'

'I have first-hand proof of that. Are you sure that you want to come with me?'

'Of course I am sure,' said Sona.

'Then do your master a favour before you leave. Can you do this?'

'If it is something good, of course I can.'

'It is good for your master but very bad for your mistress.'

'In that case tell me at once. I am very eager to do it.'

'Your mistress sent word that she would meet me secretly at the ghat on the banks of the Chitra. Do you understand that? I have agreed to keep the appointment with the purpose of opening your master's eyes. And I want you to inform him on the quiet.'

'I will do it at once. I will do anything to get rid of that wicked woman.'

'No, not yet, wait till I have gone to the ghat. Keep your eyes open; when you see the mistress setting off for the ghat, then go and inform your master. Then come and join me.'

'As you wish,' Sona said, and touched Nisakar's feet. Then Nisakar walked slowly and with a stately gait to the ghat, from where one could enjoy the beauty of Chitra, and sat down on the steps.

Chitra was flowing silently under the stars. Jackals, dogs and other animals were howling all around. Somewhere in the distance, a fisherman on a boat was loudly singing a song in praise of the goddess Kali. There was no other sound in that isolated place. As he listened to the song and gazed at the bright light that came from a window of a room on the first floor of Govindalal's house, Nisakar thought: 'I am a cruel man. How cruel of me to lay such schemes for ruining a woman! Or is it really cruel, is it not my duty to punish the wicked? I promised my friend I would do this to save his daughter's life, and so I must carry out my promise, but I am not happy about it. Rohini is wicked and it is my duty to punish wickedness and check its course. Then why am I so unhappy and worried? Can it be because I haven't been fair? Yes, it is the unfair means which I have adopted that are raising these doubts. Moreover, who am I to punish wickedness and reward virtue? He who punishes wickedness and rewards virtue will also judge Rohini. I cannot tell, but maybe He has appointed me to carry out His plans.'

Since you, Krishna, are always in my heart,
I only do what you tell me to do.

Nisakar spent the first quarter of the night with such reflections. Then he saw Rohini approaching the ghat with silent steps. She came and stood beside him. To be doubly assured he asked, 'Who is it?'

To be doubly sure, Rohini also said, 'Who is it?'

'I am Rashbehari.'

'I am Rohini.'

'Why are you so late?'

'I had to watch my steps in case someone saw me. I am sorry you have been put to so much trouble.'

'No trouble at all. I thought you'd forgotten.'

'I wouldn't be in this sorry plight if I were one of those who can forget. I came to this place because I could not forget someone. And now I am here because I could not forget you.'

Even before she could finish speaking, someone came from behind and caught her by the throat. Startled, she asked, 'Who is that?' A solemn voice replied, 'Your death.' Rohini recognized Govindalal's voice. Almost blind with fear of imminent danger, she said, her voice trembling, 'Let go, let go, I had no evil intention in coming here. Ask this gentleman if you do not believe me.'

She pointed to the spot where Nisakar had been sitting. No one was there now. Nisakar had vanished the moment he saw Govindalal. Rohini said in astonishment, 'Why, there is no one there.'

Govindalal said, 'There is no one here; come with me.'

Rohini slowly and sadly returned home with Govindalal.

9

WHEN THEY REACHED THE HOUSE, GOVINDALAL FORBADE THE SERVANTS TO come upstairs. The maestro had already gone back to his lodgings.

Govindalal took Rohini to their bedroom and closed the door. She stood before him, trembling like a reed in a stream.

'Rohini,' he said in a low voice.

'Yes?'

'I want to have a few words with you.'

'What about?'

'What are you to me?'

'Nothing. I am your servant so long as you let me serve you, otherwise I am nothing.'

'You are not my servant. I was yours. My princely fortune, my princely estate, my unstained character—I sacrificed everything for you. Who are you, Rohini, that I left everything for you and now live in exile? Who are you, Rohini, that I deserted Bhramar, incomparable Bhramar, who was my happiness and nectar in sorrow, for you? Why?' Unable to control his anger and sorrow, Govindalal kicked her. Rohini sat down and wept without a word. He did not see her tears.

'Rohini, stand up.'

She stood up.

'One day you tried to kill yourself. Have you still the courage to die?'

Rohini, at that moment, wanted to die. She said in a feeble voice, 'Why shouldn't I wish to die now, my fate is sealed.'

'Then wait here, don't move.'

Rohini stood there while Govindalal got hold of a pistol case and took out a pistol. It was loaded, as it always was. He held it in front of her and said, 'Well, have you the courage to die?'

Rohini was thinking. She could not remember the day she had gone to drown herself in the Varuni, easily and calmly. She was then very unhappy, so she had had the courage. Now she thought, 'Why should I die? If he wants to leave me, let him do so. I shall never forget him, but that's no reason to die. If I live, I shall at least have the pleasure of thinking of him; I will be poor, but I shall have the pleasure of thinking of him and the happy days that I spent in Prasadpur. That is some kind of happiness and some kind of hope. Why should I die?'

Rohini said, 'I don't want to die. Don't kill me. If you don't want me, let me go, please.'

Govindalal raised the pistol, aimed it at her forehead, and said, 'I will let you go.'

'Don't kill me,' Rohini cried out. 'I am young, I have just tasted happiness. I'll never come near you, never cross your path again; I'll leave you at once. Do not kill me.'

The click of the pistol was heard, then a bang, and all was dark. The lifeless body of Rohini felt on the floor. Govindalal threw down the gun and ran out of the house.

The servants, hearing the gunshot, rushed upstairs. They saw her body on the floor. It was like a lotus ravaged by the fingernails of a boy. Govindalal was nowhere to be seen.

10

Second Year

THAT NIGHT, THE VILLAGE WATCHMAN REPORTED AT THE POLICE STATION that a murder had been committed in the indigo planter's house in

Prasadpur. Fortunately for Govindalal, the police station was twelve miles away and so the police inspector could not get to the scene of the crime to begin investigations till nine o'clock the next morning. He made an on-the-spot investigation, examined the body and then sent in a report. He put the body, duly sheeted and tied, in a bullock cart, and sent it, in charge of the watchman, to the morgue. He then took his bath and his midday meal and at his leisure began searching for the murderer. But where was the murderer? Govindalal did not re-enter the house after he had killed Rohini. Who could say how far he had gone in the night that had passed? He had not been seen by anyone, anywhere. In Prasadpur, no one knew Govindalal's true identity. He was known there as Chunilal Datta. Not even his own servants knew where he had come from. The inspector spent a few days interrogating a few people. But nobody could help him. In the end, he sent in a report that the culprit had absconded.

Then a very able detective inspector called Fichel Khan was sent in from Jessore. There is no need to describe in detail Fichel Khan's methods of investigation. But after thoroughly searching the house, he found a number of letters and that helped him identify the culprit and his native village. Needless to say, Fichel Khan went to Haridragram in disguise; but Govindalal was not there. The detective inspector returned without success.

After leaving Rohini to her fate on that cruel deadly night, Nisakar returned to their lodgings in Prasadpur Bazaar, where Madhavinath was waiting for him. Madhavinath had not gone himself as Govindalal would have recognized him. Nisakar told him what had happened. Madhavinath said, 'You should not have done that. He might kill her.' The two friends stayed on secretly in Prasadpur, awaiting further news. Next morning, they heard that Chunilal Datta had indeed murdered his wife and absconded. This greatly alarmed and distressed them. They were worried about Govindalal. But they heard that the inspector had failed to discover Govindalal's whereabouts. Somewhat relieved, but still unhappy, they returned to their respective homes.

11

Third Year

BHRAMAR DID NOT DIE. I DO NOT KNOW WHY. ONE OF THE SADDEST ASPECTS of this world is that no one dies at the right time, that everyone dies at the wrong time—either too early or too late. That may have been the reason why Bhramar did not die. However that may be, Bhramar had recovered from her serious illness and was not living at her father's house any more.

Madhavinath brought news of Govindalal. He told his wife, who secretly communicated the news to their elder daughter, Yamini. Yamini told Bhramar about it privately.

Yamini said to Bhramar, 'He can now come and live in Haridragram. He should be out of danger here.'

'Why would he be in no danger here?'

'He lived in Prasadpur under an assumed name, no one knew him as Govindalal Babu of Haridragram.'

Bhramar said, 'Have you not heard? The police came to the village looking for him; so they must know.'

'Suppose they do know. He will have money when he takes possession of his property, and Father says that the police are open to bribery.'

Bhramar burst out in tears, and said, 'Who will give him this advice? We need to find him. Father traced him once; he could do it again, couldn't he?'

'How can Father find him, when the police, who are so good at tracing people, have failed? But I think that Govindalal Babu will return to his native village of his own accord. He hasn't done so already because people will find out that he was living in Prasadpur. He will come now.'

'I have no such hope.'

'But he will come.'

Bhramar said, 'If it is safe for him to come, I pray with all my heart that he comes back. But if it is safer for him not to come, I pray with all my heart that he may never again set foot in Haridragram. May God direct him to whichever is the safer course.'

Yamini said, 'Sister, it is my view that you should go and live in Haridragram. Who knows, one of these days he might turn up there. He is in need of money. Suppose he does not trust the employees of the estate and so does not show himself to them? Won't he go away if he does not see you there?'

'I am so ill, my life so uncertain, who will look after me there?'

Yamini said, 'If you so wish, then one of us will come with you. In any case, you should be on the spot.'

Bhramar thought over Yamini's suggestion, then agreed. 'Yes, I will go to Haridragram. Tell Mother to make the arrangements to send me there tomorrow. There is no need for any of you to come now, but you must come if I am in trouble.'

'What trouble, sister?'

Bhramar replied, weeping, 'If he comes back.'

Yamini said, 'How can that be a problem? What greater joy can you have than to recover your lost treasure?'

'Joy! I have no joy any more, sister.'

Bhramar said no more. Yamini understood nothing of her feelings, nothing of her heart's sorrow. Bhramar had a premonition of what would happen in the future, but Yamini could not see that. Yamini did not understand that Bhramar could not forget that Govindalal was a murderer.

12

Fifth Year

BHRAMAR WENT TO LIVE IN HER FATHER-IN-LAW'S HOUSE. THERE SHE LIVED in daily expectation of her husband's return. Days and months passed—he did not return, nor was there any news of him. Thus the third year passed and so also the fourth. Meanwhile, Bhramar's cough and asthma got worse and she began to waste away rapidly. Yama, the god of Death, was approaching so swiftly that she feared she would never see her husband again.

In the fifth year, there was a great commotion in the village, as news of Govindalal's arrest reached there. He had been living in Brindavan, disguised as a mendicant, but the police had apprehended him and brought him to Jessore for trial.

The news reached Bhramar as a rumour. It originated in a letter which Govindalal had written to the chief steward, in which he had said, 'I am about to be taken to prison. If it be thought to spend some of the income from my paternal property on my defence, then it should be done now. I know I do not deserve this and I do not wish to live. But I beg to be saved from the gallows. Tell the people in the house that you heard the news—do not let it be known that I wrote to you.' The chief steward did as he was told, sent the news to Bhramar as a rumour, and said nothing about the letter.

Bhramar immediately sent for her father, who lost no time in coming. Bhramar gave him fifty thousand rupees in notes and said with tears in her eyes, 'Father, do what can be done to save him, otherwise I shall kill myself.' Madhavinath too was crying and said, 'My child, don't be anxious. I'll go to Jessore this very day. Don't worry. There's no proof that Govindalal committed the murder. I promise you that I'll bring back my son-in-law and forty-eight thousand of your money.'

At Jessore, Madhavinath discovered that the evidence against Govindalal was very strong. Inspector Fichel Khan had investigated the case and sent the witnesses. He found no trace of Rupo, Sona and others, who knew the facts of the case. Sona was with Nisakar; Rupo had left the area and nobody knew where he had gone. Since the evidence was very weak, Fichel Khan had manufactured evidence with bribes. He sent up three witnesses who had deposed before the magistrate that they had gone to the house to hear Danesh Khan sing and had with their own eyes seen Govindalal, alias Chunilal, shoot Rohini. The magistrate was an Englishman, highly esteemed by the government as a good administrator. He committed Govindalal for trial at the sessions on the basis of the evidence produced by Fichel Khan's witnesses.

Govindalal was rotting in prison when Madhavinath reached Jessore. He was saddened to know the unhappy state of affairs. He got hold of the names and addresses of the witnesses and visited them at their homes. He told them, 'My friends, what you said before the magistrate is over and done with. Now you must say something very different before the judge. You must say that you know nothing of the case. Here are five hundred rupees in cash. There will be another five hundred after the defendant is released.'

'We will be punished for perjury,' the witnesses said.

'Have no fear,' Madhavinath assured them. 'I shall bribe witnesses to give evidence that Fichel Khan beat you up and forced you to give false evidence before the magistrate.'

The witnesses had never seen a thousand rupees all at once. They readily agreed.

The day of the trial arrived. The defendant stood in the dock. After the first witness took the oath, he was asked by the government prosecutor. 'Do you know Govindalal, alias Chunilal?'

The witness said, 'No, I do not think so.'

'Have you ever met him?'

'No.'

'Do you know Rohini?'

'Which Rohini?'

'The one who lived in Prasadpur.'

'I have never been to Prasadpur. I have never heard of the place.'

'How did Rohini die?'

'I heard that she committed suicide.'

'Do you know anything of the murder?'

'Nothing at all.'

The prosecutor then read out the deposition that the witness had made before the magistrate. 'How now? Did you not say all that before the magistrate?'

'Yes, I did.'

'Why did you if you did not know anything about the murder?'

'Because Fichel Khan beat me, he left no bone unbroken in my body.'

Then the witness shed a few tears. A few days ago, in a dispute over a plot of land, he had received a few blows from his brother, the marks of which were still visible on his body. Without blushing, he showed them to the judge as evidence of Fichel Khan's beatings.

Much embarrassed, the crown prosecutor called the second witness. He too had a similar story to tell. He had made some sores on his back with the juice of leadwort—anything can be done for a thousand rupees. He showed his sores to the judge as evidence of Fichel Khan's beatings.

The third witness followed the path trodden by the other two. The judge discharged the defendant for lack of evidence and was highly displeased with Fichel Khan. He directed the magistrate to hold an inquiry into the conduct of the detective inspector.

Govindalal was surprised to find the witnesses so much in his favour, but he understood it all when he saw Madhavinath in the crowd. After being acquitted, Govindalal had to go back to prison to await the order for his release. As he was being taken back, Madhavinath came up to him, and whispered the address of his lodgings and asked him to meet him there after Govindalal was released.

But Govindalal did not go to his father-in-law's lodgings after he was released. He disappeared, and nobody knew where he had gone. Madhavinath searched for him in vain. Thus, he was obliged to go back to Haridragram alone.

13

Sixth Year

MADHAVINATH CAME BACK TO BHRAMAR AND TOLD HER ABOUT GOVINDALAL'S release and disappearance. After he had gone, Bhramar cried—I know not why.

Meanwhile, Govindalal went straight to Prasadpur, where he found his house deserted and stripped. He was told that some of his possessions were stolen while others had been sold as unclaimed property. Only the house was still standing—even the doors and door-frames had been lifted. He stayed at the bazaar a few days and sold the house, or rather whatever was left of it, for a trifle. Then he went to Calcutta. In Calcutta, he lived very modestly and secretly, unknown to even his friends.

But the little money he had brought from Prasadpur did not last long; after the end of a year, he realized he had no money. So he thought of writing to Bhramar—Bhramar, with whom he had not been in touch for nearly six years.

He sat down with pen, paper and ink. But to tell the truth, he started crying before he could put his pen to paper. As he wept, a thought occurred to him. Bhramar might not be alive. To whom should he write then? Later he said to himself, 'I may as well write. At the worst, my letter will come back to me. I shall know, if it comes back, that Bhramar is no more.'

He spent a long time wondering what to write; then he thought, 'I could not hurt her more by writing than I have done by deserting her.' So he decided to put down anything that came to his mind. He wrote:

> Bhramar, this wicked man is writing to you after six years. You can read the letter or you can tear it up unread. I expect you know all that has happened to me. If I say that I brought it on myself, you may think that I am trying to please you, for I am about to beg something of you. I have nothing to live on. I have kept myself alive by begging.

> It was possible to live by begging in places of pilgrimage. Here I get nothing and am facing starvation. I had only one refuge, my mother in Kashi. But I expect you know that she is dead and I have nowhere to go now, nothing to live on. So I thought of showing this guilty face in Haridragram, else I must die of hunger. One who deserted you, took another woman and killed her—how can I feel shame? How can a starving man feel shame? I can show you my face, but you, who are owner of a property and a house and I have wronged you—can you give me refuge? Won't you help one whom hunger has brought to your door?

After much hesitation, Govindalal posted the letter, which reached Bhramar in due time.

Bhramar recognized his handwriting. She trembled as she opened the letter. She entered her bedroom and closed the door. Then she read the letter over and over again as tears streamed down her face. That day she did not open her bedroom doors. When she was called to come for a meal, she replied she had a fever and did not feel like eating. As she often had fever, they all believed her.

Next day, Bhramar got up from bed. She had not slept a wink. She really did have a fever. But she was calm and had a clear head. She had already decided what to write in reply. She did not have to think again. She had even decided how to write it.

She did not write 'your servant', as was customary in addressing one's superiors. But since a husband is to be revered in all circumstances, she used the form, 'After a thousand salutations I beg to state'. Then she wrote:

> I have received your letter. The property is yours. Although it was left to me, I gave it to you. You may remember the deed of gift which you tore up before you left here. The copy of this deed is in the registry office, so the gift was valid. So you can easily come back to Haridragram and enjoy your property. The house is yours. In these last five years I have saved some money. That too is yours. Of that

money, I beg a small portion of eight thousand rupees. I shall use three thousand rupees to build a house by the banks of the river Ganga and the rest to live on. I shall make all arrangements for your return and then I shall go to my father's house. I shall stay there until my own house is built. It is not likely that we shall meet again in this life. I am content with that, and I am sure that you too are content with it. I await your second letter.

In due course, Govindalal got Bhramar's letter. 'What a terrible letter,' he thought. 'There is no tenderness, no mention of six years of separation. I mentioned that in my letter. Is it the same Bhramar?'

Govindalal replied, 'I shall not go to Haridragram. Send me a monthly allowance so that I can live here.'

Bhramar wrote back, 'I shall send you five hundred rupees monthly. I could send more but I fear it would be squandered. I think that it would be better if you were to come here and enjoy the income of your property. You must not leave your native village for me. My days are coming to an end.'

Govindalal stayed on in Calcutta. Both felt it was the best thing to do.

14

Seventh Year

BHRAMAR'S DAYS REALLY WERE COMING TO AN END. HER TERRIBLE ILLNESS could no longer be kept in check with medicines, as it had been for so long. She was wasting away. In the month of Aghrayan, she took to her bed and never again left it. Madhavinath himself came to stay with her and organize medical treatment, all in vain. Yamini too came to nurse her sister at the last stage of her life.

Bhramar did not respond to treatment. Thus passed the month of Poush. In Magh, Bhramar gave up taking medicines; 'I won't take medicines any more,' she told Yamini. 'Next month is Phalgun.[7] I wish to die on the full-moon night. See to it, sister, that a full-moon night does not escape me. And if I survive the full-moon night, ensure my death by giving me a secret pinch. I must die that night. Please do not forget that, sister.'

Yamini wept, but Bhramar refused medicines. Her illness got worse but she was calm. She had not laughed or made jokes for the last six years, but now she was full of laughter and fun, like a lamp flaring up before it finally goes out.

During the last few days, Bhramar seemed calm, contented and cheerful. At last the terrible day arrived. From Yamini's tears, from the agitated look of the other people in the house, from the pain in her own body, Bhramar knew her time had come. She called her sister. 'Sister, this is my last day.' Yamini wept and did not reply. Bhramar continued, 'I have some requests to make and you must grant them today. My first request is that you must not cry today. You can cry when I am dead. I can't come back to stop you. But today I want to say a few words to you, when I am still capable of saying them, before I die. My second request is that you alone stay with me now. I shall see everyone in time, but I wish to be alone with you now. Make sure that nobody comes here. This is my last chance to speak to you alone.'

How much longer could Yamini keep back her tears?

Gradually the day ended and it was night. 'Is it a moonlit night?' Bhramar asked.

Yamini opened a window and said, 'There is a beautiful moonlight outside.'

Bhramar said, 'Then open all the windows. Let me die looking at the moonlight. Are there any flowers below that window over there?'

This was the window at which Bhramar and Govindalal used to stand in the morning and talk. For seven years, Bhramar had not gone near it nor opened the window. After some effort, Yamini opened the window. 'There is no flower-garden here,' she said, 'only weeds and dead plants, no flowers or green leaves.'

'There was a flower-garden there seven years ago,' Bhramar replied. 'It has died for lack of care. I have not looked after it for seven years.'

After a long silence, Bhramar spoke again. 'Get me some flowers from wherever you can. Can't you see, this is my bridal night. I need a flowery bed.'[8]

At Yamini's orders, servants brought heaps of flowers into the bedroom.

'Scatter them on my bed. This is my "flowery-bed" night.'

Yamini scattered the flowers on her bed. Bhramar's eyes were streaming with tears. 'Why do you cry, sister?' Yamini asked.

'I have a great sorrow. The day he left for Kashi, I implored the gods with folded hands and tears in my eyes that they must grant me one more meeting with him. I proudly said that if I were a chaste woman we should meet again. But we have not met. Today, on the day of my death, if only I could see him once, I could forget my seven years' sorrow.'

'Do you wish to see him?'

'What do you mean?' Bhramar said, astounded.

'Govindalal,' Yamini said calmly. 'He's here. Father sent him news of your illness. He arrived here today—he has come to see you. I was afraid to tell you in your present condition. He too has not the courage to come in.'

Bhramar cried out, 'Let me see him once, once more in this life, once again before I die. Let me see him.'

Yamini left and after a while, Govindalal came in quietly. He was entering their bedroom after seven years. Both wept and were unable to speak.

Bhramar gestured to her husband to sit on the bed. He sat down, weeping all the while. She asked him to come closer. As he came closer, she stretched her hands to touch his toes. 'Forgive all my faults and bless me that I may be happy in another life,' she said.

Govindalal could not speak, but he took her hand in his and held it there for a long time. Bhramar silently passed away.

15

BHRAMAR WAS CREMATED ACCORDING TO THE CUSTOMARY RITES. Govindalal came back from the cremation ground but did not speak to anyone.

The night passed and the sun rose on the morning after Bhramar died, as it always does. The leaves of the trees glistened in the shade, the dark water of the tank threw up little ripples which glittered in the sun, and the dark clouds in the sky turned white. Nature followed its routine as if Bhramar had not died. Govindalal walked out of the house.

He had loved two women, Bhramar and Rohini, both of whom were now dead. He was attracted to Rohini's beauty. He could not control his unsatisfied desire for beauty. That is why he had forsaken Bhramar and had taken up with Rohini. As soon as he started life with Rohini, he realized that Rohini was not Bhramar; he recognized the difference between love and passion, between happiness and enjoyment, between nectar and poison. He had to drink Rohini's love, which was poison, but like Nilakantha of Indian mythology, though Govindalal took the poison, he could neither swallow it nor could he spit it out—the poison stayed in his throat. But then the nectar of Bhramar's love stayed in his heart day and night. When he was in Prasadpur, engrossed in music with Rohini, Bhramar was in his heart. Even while Rohini was near, Bhramar was in his heart. Bhramar was unobtainable but Rohini could not be abandoned; even then Bhramar was within while Rohini was without. This is the reason why Rohini had to die so soon. I hope the readers have understood that, else this story has been written in vain.

If only Govindalal, having made proper arrangements for Rohini, had gone to Bhramar and sought forgiveness; if only he had said to her, 'Forgive me, give me a place in your heart. I don't deserve to be forgiven but you are full of goodness, you can forgive me', Bhramar would have forgiven him, for women are forgiving, kind and affectionate; women are God's highest creation, His own shadow, while men are God's common work.

Women are lights and men their shadows. Can Light forsake her Shadow?

Govindalal could not do that; partly because of pride, which man is so full of, partly because of the shame which is the evil-doer's punishment, and partly because of fear which prevents the sinner from facing the virtuous. So it was that Govindalal could not come before Bhramar, he could not face her. After he murdered Rohini, he abandoned all ideas of seeing her. How could darkness come before light?

Even then Govindalal was consumed every day, every moment, by an unquenchable desire to see her. Had he not possessed and lost a treasure, the like of which no one before had ever possessed and lost? Both he and Bhramar had suffered, but she had been happy in comparison with him; his suffering was beyond human endurance. Death had come to her help, but not to his.

The earth was smiling in the sunlight when Govindalal walked out into the garden. He was thinking of how he had killed Rohini with his own hands and how he had indirectly killed Bhramar.

We do not know what sort of a night he had spent but it was probably a terrible night. As he opened the door, he saw Madhavinath. The father-in-law looked at Govindalal's face. It seemed to bear the shadow of a disease beyond human remedy. Madhavinath walked away. He had resolved not to speak to his son-in-law again in this life.

As he came out of the house, Govindalal went into the garden below Bhramar's bedroom. Yamini was right in saying that it was no longer a flower-garden but a jungle of grass and weeds. A few hardy and half-dying plants were still standing, but they bore no flowers. He walked there a long while, until it was late morning and the sun very hot. Feeling tired, Govindalal left the garden.

He walked to the Varuni pond, speaking and looking at no one. It was already half past ten in the morning. The deep, dark Varuni was glittering in the strong sunlight. Many men and women were bathing, children were swimming, raising crystal sprays as they did so. Govindalal did not like the crowd. He left for the spot where his beautiful flower-garden used to be. He saw that the cast iron railing was broken, the iron gate was no more and it had been replaced by a bamboo hedge. Bhramar had carefully preserved all his property except this garden. When Yamini asked her about it, she said, 'Sister, I am going to the land of Yama, so let my earthly paradise go to ruin. I have no one to whom I can leave it.'

Govindalal found no gate and no railings in the garden. There were no flowering shrubs now, only coarse ulu grass and weeds. The creeper-covered pavilion had fallen down. The stone statues were all broken. Some of the statues, or what was left of them, were standing, while others lay on the ground overrun by creepers. The roof of his pleasure garden was broken, the Venetian blinds and sashes were also broken or taken away, the marble floor removed. Here no flowers bloomed, no trees bore fruit and maybe the good wind blew in this garden no more.

Govindalal sat down at the foot of a broken statue. The strong sun burnt down on his head at midday, but he felt nothing. He felt as if he would die. Since the night he had been thinking of nothing but Bhramar and Rohini, and had seen their forms alternating with one another before his eyes. The world now seemed filled with those two figures, every tree took the form of Bhramar, and Rohini sat in its shadow; Bhramar appeared before him one moment, only to disappear the next, and Rohini did the same. He heard their voices in every sound; when bathers in Varuni spoke to one another, he heard Bhramar or Rohini or both of them speaking; the rustle of dry leaves sounded like Bhramar coming, the buzz of insects like Rohini running away. The swaying of boughs sounded like Bhramar sighing, the call of the koel sounded like Rohini singing. The world was full of Bhramar and Rohini.

Twelve noon; half past one: Govindalal was still there, at the foot of that broken statue, in that world filled with Bhramar and Rohini. Much later, Govindalal, who had not bathed nor had his midday meal, was still there; in that world filled with Rohini and Bhramar, in that pit of fire. The day came to an end but he did not get up. He was not aware where he was. The people in the house, not having seen him all day, thought he had gone back to Calcutta. So they did not search for him. As evening fell, the garden turned dark, stars appeared in the sky, and the world became silent.

Govindalal was still there.

Suddenly, in that dark, silent, isolated spot, Govindalal became delirious and heard Rohini say aloud, 'Here.'

He could not remember that Rohini was dead and asked, 'Here, what?'

Rohini's voice said, 'At this time.'

Mechanically he said, 'Here, at this time, what, Rohini?'

The delirious Govindalal heard Rohini say, 'Here, at this time, in that water, I drowned myself.'

Hearing these words, the fiction of his own mind, Govindalal asked, 'Shall I drown myself?'

Again he heard an answer invented by his deranged mind. 'Yes, come, Bhramar sends word from heaven that her virtue has power to redeem us. Atone, die.'

He closed his eyes and fell down, exhausted and trembling, unconscious, on the stone steps.

In that state of unconsciousness, he saw Rohini suddenly disappear into the darkness. Illuminating the horizon by degrees, the radiant figure of Bhramar appeared before him. She said, 'Why should you die? Do not die because you have lost me. There is One who is dearer than I, live and find Him.'

That night Govindalal lay there unconscious. He was found by his people and taken home. Even Madhavinath felt sorry for him, so bad was his condition. They put him under medical care and he recovered in two or three months. Everyone expected him to live at home, but he did not. One night, without telling anyone, he went away and no one heard from him any more.

When seven years had passed, they presumed that he was dead and funeral rites were performed.

EPILOGUE

GOVINDALAL'S COUSIN SISTER'S SON,[9] SACHIKANTA, WHEN HE CAME OF AGE, inherited his uncle's property. Every day, Sachikanta would take a walk around the garden which was once Govindalal's. Now it was a thick jungle of weeds. He had heard the sad story of Govindalal in every detail. As he recalled the story on his daily walks, he decided to restore the garden. He put up another beautiful railing and built a splendid flight of black marble steps going down to the Varuni; he built up a well-laid garden again, but he was careful not to have shrubs that bore coloured flowers. Among the indigenous plants, he chose bakul and kamini and among the foreign plants he had cypress and willows. In place of the pleasure house, he erected a temple, and placed in it, instead of a deity, an expensive golden statue of Bhramar. The base of the statue bore the following inscription: 'To her who will equal Bhramar/In joy and in sorrow/In merit and demerit/I shall give the golden statue.'

Twelve years after Bhramar's death, a mendicant appeared at the door of the temple. Sachikanta was there. The mendicant said, 'I wish to see what is inside this temple.'

Sachikanta opened the door and showed the visitor the statue. The stranger said to the young man, 'This Bhramar was mine; I am Govindalal Roy.'

Sachikanta was astounded. He could not speak for a while. When he recovered, he touched Govindalal's feet and invited him to come to the house. Govindalal declined his invitation. 'I have come here to give you my blessings. Today is the last day of my twelve years' life in obscurity.[10] I shall go away, now that I have blessed you.'

'But you must stay and enjoy your own property.'

'I have found a treasure which is greater than all properties and estates, one that even Kuber, the god of Wealth, could never possess, and it is sweeter and more holy than Bhramar. I have found peace. I have no need of property. Let it remain yours.'

Sachikanta inquired humbly: 'Have you found peace in asceticism?'

Govindalal answered, 'No, never. I only put on this garment because it is suited to a life of obscurity. Only by offering one's mind at the feet of God can one find peace. He alone is now my property, my Bhramar and more than Bhramar.'

With these words, Govindalal left and was never seen in Haridragram again.

Endnotes

1. Brahma, Vishnu and Mahadeva (Shiva) are the 'Holy Trinity' of Hindu mythology. They are the manifestations of the three aspects of God—the Creator, the Protector and the Destroyer, respectively. In mythology, however, they were related; Brahma and Vishnu were married to Shiva's daughters. Nandi was the famous mythological bull who carried Shiva through the universe. In this humorous piece, he is Shiva's companion.
2. These are the names of various stars in Sanskrit, and are important for Indian astronomy and astrology.
3. The author is referring humorously to various characters and events in the two great epics of India, the *Mahabharata* and the *Ramayana*. Sugreeva was the king of the monkeys who helped Rama conquer Lanka and kill Ravana. His name means 'good neck', hence the pun.
4. The gardener came from Orissa, a neighbouring state south-west of Bengal. He would have to cross the river Subarnarekha to reach his home town, Cuttack.
5. In Hindu mythology, Chitragupta is the accountant of the god Yama (Death) and keeps a book for all the creatures of the universe. The account is settled after death and decisions about heaven, hell and rebirth are made according to this book.
6. In nineteenth-century Bengal, most police constables came from Bihar and other Hindi-speaking provinces of British India.
7. Eighth, ninth, tenth and eleventh months of the Bengali calendar, covering the period from mid-November to mid-March.
8. In traditional Bengal, on the nuptial night, the bride and bridegroom slept on a bed decorated with flowers, so the wedding night was usually called 'flowery-bed night'.
9. In Bengali society, cousins are referred to as sisters and brothers. Since Govindalal had no children, his property passed to his nephew,

Sachikanta, who was the son of Govindalal's female cousin, Sailavati, Krishnakanta Roy's daughter.

10. For atonement of serious sins, Hindu tradition often demanded twelve years in obscurity and exile. The epics provide many examples of this. Govindalal lived as a mendicant for twelve years for the sins he had committed.

Rajani

PART I

1

YOUR PLEASURE AND PAIN CAN NEVER BE THE SAME AS MINE. YOU AND I ARE not alike. You can never take pleasure in my joys and you would never understand my sorrows. For example, I would be thrilled with the perfume of a tiny flower; but the beauty of a full moon, spread out before my eyes in all its glory, would be lost on me—would you even pay any heed to my tale? I am blind by birth.

How would you know? You have the gift of sight while my life is dark. Unfortunately, I don't even perceive it as darkness. To my sightless eyes, the dark is light. I have no knowledge of your kind of light.

Does that mean I have no pleasures? Not true. Sorrows and joys between you and me—perhaps come in equal measure. The sight of beauty pleases you and the sound of sounds gives me pleasure. The stems of these tiny flowers are so slim and even slimmer is the sharp point of the needle I hold. I pierce these tiny flowers with that needle and weave a garland—that's all I have done ever since my childhood—but no one ever wears my garlands, for they say, 'These are threaded by a blind person.'

Threading garlands is my occupation. My father has a flower-garden at the extreme end of Ballygunge. It is the sole source of his income. From the onset of spring until the time when flowers bloom, he plucks flowers and brings them to me and I thread them into garlands. My father then walks the streets of the city selling them. My mother keeps busy with all the household chores. But in their spare time both my parents lend me a hand in doing my work.

The feel of flowers is very pleasing; it must be a greater pleasure to wear them. They certainly smell delightful. But threading garlands isn't enough to live on. The tree of hunger has no blossoms. Hence, we are quite poor. We live in a plain, earthen hut in Mirzapur. It is in a corner of this house that I sit with piles of flowers spread out before me, and weave garlands out of them. Once my father leaves the house, I sing: *On this, my favourite morning, there isn't a bloom to be found.*

Oh dear Lord, I still haven't told you if I am a man or a woman. But—if you haven't been able to guess that yet, it's better left unsaid. I shall not tell you now.

Whichever one I am, marriage is a vain fantasy for a blind person. I have not got married yet because I am sightless. Any sensible person with a head on their shoulders can decide for themselves if that is fortunate or unfortunate. Many a renowned beauty, when they heard of my obligatory chastity, have said, 'Oh, I wish I were blind too.'

I had overcome my regrets about never being able to experience marriage. But I had given myself to a husband of my choice nonetheless. One day I was hearing descriptions of Calcutta from my father. I heard that the Monument was a huge and weighty sight. Taller than ever, unmoved, immovable, invincible—a Lord in his own rights. In my heart of hearts, I wedded the Monument. Who was greater than my husband? I was Lady Monument.

But it was not just this once that I found for myself a husband. When I married the Monument, I was fifteen years old. At the age of seventeen, I am ashamed to say, as a still-married woman—another marriage came to pass. Very close to our house lived a gentleman called Kalicharan Basu. He owned a toy shop in China Bazaar. We were of the same caste and hence there was some familiarity between our families. He had a four-year-old son called Bamacharan. This child often came to our house. One day a groom and his band passed by our house, like a slow-moving typhoon. Bamacharan asked, 'Who's that?'

I said, 'That's a groom.'

Bamacharan wailed, 'I want to be a groom.'

Trying to stop his tears and failing miserably, I said as a last resort to pacify him, 'Don't cry, you can be my groom.' I handed him a sweet and asked, 'Will you be my groom, then?'

The child stopped wailing when he got the sweet and said, 'Yes.'

After some time, when the sweet was eaten, he asked, 'Well, what exactly does a groom do?' Perhaps he believed with all his heart that a groom merely ate sweets. If that were the case, he was ready to start on the next one. Gauging his thoughts I said, 'A groom gathers up the flowers for me.' Bamacharan was quick to understand the duties of a husband and he began to gather up the flowers and hand them to me. Ever since that day I call him my groom and he gathers and hands the flowers to me.

These are my two marriages. Now my question is to the misses and the ladies of this day and age: am I a chaste woman or not?

2

DELIVERING FLOWERS TO THE BIG HOUSE WAS A TROUBLESOME CHORE. IN the olden days, Malini Aunty used to supply flowers to the palace but then she died. Vidyasundar got the nectar and Hira the flower woman got the blows; all because she supplied flowers to the palace. Sundar got the kingdom of his dreams, but Malini's, the vanquished, never came back to life.

Father hollered 'Beli flowers' and sold them among the music-loving connoisseurs. Mother used to supply flowers daily to a few non-connoisseur households. Of them, Ramsaday Mitra's house was the most important. Ramsaday Mitra had four and a half horses (four good steeds and a pony for the grandchildren) and one and a half wives. One acting lady of the manor and the other ailing and old. Her name was Bhuvaneshwari, but the wheezing of her croaky voice only brought to mind the name Rammoni.

The whole and acting lady of the manor was called Labangalata. That's what everyone called her, but her father had named her Lalitlabangalata and Ramsaday Babu lovingly said, 'Lalitlabangalata [the pretty creeper vine], darling of the gentle summer breeze.' Ramsaday Babu was elderly, nearly sixty-three years old. Lalitlabangalata was young, about nineteen years old and she was his second wife—she was the apple of his eye, the jewel in his crown, the feather in his cap, the complete mistress of his heart. She was Ramsaday's vault-key, his bedcover, the lime paste on his betel leaf, and the water in his glass. She was the quinine to his fever, the ipica to his cough, the flannel to his arthritis and the soup for his convalescence.

I am blind; so I've never seen Lalitlabangalata. But I've heard that she is beautiful.

But forget beauty, I have heard of her talents. In truth, she is very talented. She's flawless in household chores, generous to a fault, simple at heart, but—endowed with a venomous tongue. Amidst the abundant gifts that Labangalata had, one was that she truly loved her husband who was old enough to be her grandfather—loved him perhaps more than a young wife would love her young husband. Since she loved him so, she tried to dress him up as a young man—oh, how can I describe those larks? She dyed his grey hair black every day with her own hands. If ever Ramsaday, out of sheer modesty, donned a plain white dhoti, she would take it off with her own hands and replace it with dhotis that had thick and decorous borders and donate the plain dhoti immediately to the nearest poor widow. At his age, Ramsaday ran a mile at the sight of a bottle of attar—but Labangalata would douse him in it as he was sleeping. Often she would steal his glasses, take out the bit of gold in it and donate it to someone who had a daughter of marriageable age. If he ever snored as he slept, she took out her heavy anklets, wore them on her feet and jangled around all over the room until he woke up.

Labangalata used to buy flowers from us. She took flowers worth four annas and paid us two rupees for it. The reason: I was blind. When she held the garland she always cursed and said, 'Why have you given me such worthless flowers?' But when she paid for it, she would always hand some notes with the coins. If I ever went back to return the extra money, she would shoo me off saying, 'That's not my money.' And if I went back a second time, she'd curse me till I left. Any mention of her generosity would always entail a venomous attack. If truth be known, but for Ramsaday Babu's household, we would not have had enough to live on. But since one shouldn't milk the milch cow too hard, mother never took too much from the lady. We were happy if we could make ends meet. Sometimes, Labanga bought piles of flowers from us and decked Ramsaday Babu with them, saying, 'That's my Cupid.' Ramsaday Babu said, 'That's your Hanuman.' Such was the harmony of minds between two people of different generations. They could read each other as clearly as a mirror. Such was the way of their love—

Ramsaday: Lalitalabangalata, darling of the—

Labanga: Yes, my grandfather, your maid is at your service.

Ramsaday: If I were to die?

Labanga: I'd take your wealth and run.

To herself she'd say, 'I'd rather die than go on living.' And Ramsaday knew that very well.

Labanga used to pay me so generously. So then, why was it a bother going to the Big House to give flowers? Hear me out.

One day, Mother had fever. Father, like other male outsiders, was not allowed into the inner chambers. So who else could go and give the flowers to Labangalata but me? I took the flowers for her and set off. Blind I may be, but I knew every corner of the roads of Calcutta. I could go anywhere with my cane in hand and never had I come in front of a motor car or tram. Sometimes though, I have stumbled onto another pedestrian; the reason for that is that some people go mum when they see a young blind girl. Instead they jostle you and then shout, 'What's the matter—can't you see? Are you blind or what?' I'd murmur to myself, 'It works both ways, doesn't it?'

I took the flowers to Labanga. She saw me and said, 'Well, well, blind child, why have you come here again with your ugly flowers?' The words 'blind child' used to set me on fire. I was thinking up a suitable and nasty enough reply when suddenly I heard some footsteps. Someone came in. The one who came in, said, 'Who is this, Chhoto-ma?'

Chhoto-ma! So then it was one of Ramsaday's sons. But which one? I had heard his elder son's voice one day—it wasn't as sweet as this, neither did it fill the heart with such joy. I guessed that this was the young master.

Chhoto-ma answered, in honeyed tones this time, 'She is the blind flower girl.'

'Flower girl! I thought she was a lady.'

Labanga said, 'Why, my dear, can't a flower girl be a lady as well?'

The young master was embarrassed. He said, 'Why not? She does appear to be of genteel birth. So what made her blind?'

Labanga said, 'She was born that way.'

The young master said, 'Let me see?'

I had heard that he was very proud of his education. Like many other fields in which he had acquired his skill, he had devoted himself to the science of medicine with equal dedication, without any thoughts of gain to himself. People even said that Sachindra Babu (the young master) was studying medicine only to be able to treat the poor and needy free of cost. 'Let me see,' he said to me. 'Could you please stand up?'

I stood up in a huddle.

He said, 'Look at me.'

How could I!

'Turn towards me.'

With my sightless eyes I shot an arrow in the dark, aiming at the sound. It didn't satisfy him. He held my chin and turned me to face him.

I wish I could do something very bad to the field of medicine! That touch alone was my death.

It was gentler than flowers; I smelled the perfumes of all flowers merged into one in that one touch alone. I felt there were flowers all around me, on my head, at my feet, all over my body and deep in my heart. Oh dear, dear me! Which of the many gods had created this flower-like touch? I have already told you that you wouldn't understand the joys and sorrows of the blind. Oh my, my—it was as soft as butter, ever-young, perfumed and like a musical note, that touch. How can a person, who isn't blind, ever understand a touch being like a musical note? Let my joys and sorrows stay buried in my heart. What would you—the proud owner of large, expressive eyes—know of the veena notes that tinkled in my ears every time I thought of that touch?

The young master said, 'No, this blindness is beyond cure.'

Yes, that was keeping me awake at nights all right!

Labanga said, 'So what if it is incurable—is it impossible for a blind girl to get married even if enough money is spent?'

The young master said, 'Why, isn't she married?'

Labanga said, 'No. Will money solve the problem?'

He asked her, 'Would you like to spend money for her marriage?'

Labanga was angry now, 'I have never seen such a boy! Do I have that kind of money to spare? All I want to know is if it's possible. I'm a mere woman and there's so much that I don't know. Can it happen?'

The young master knew his Chhoto-ma all too well. He laughed, 'Mother, you keep your money. I'll fix a groom for her.'

I began to curse the living daylights out of Labanga in silence as I fled from the room.

Now you know why I said carrying flowers to the Big House was a troublesome chore.

Oh earth, who nurtures us all, what do you look like? What do the varied creations, animate and inanimate, and the immense and abundant strengths that you hold, look like? All things that are perceived as beautiful—how do they look? How do the creatures with varied qualities, that roam your fields, appear to the eye? Tell me, Mother, how does the male species, dwelling in your heart, look? Among them, O Mother, show me the one whose touch feels so sweet? Show me, Mother, how it feels to see. What is sight? How is sight? What pleasure does it bring? Just for an instant, can I not 'see' this pleasurable touch? Show me, Mother! Let my corporeal eyes stay closed. Grant me eyes within my heart so that I may conceal myself within myself and just this once, fill my eyes with a sight of him so that I forever remain grateful to be born a woman. Everyone can see—why can't I? I believe even insects and worms can see—so why can't I? Just plain seeing—no harm to anyone, no grief caused to anyone, no sins committed, they all take sight for granted—what is my sin that I shall never be able to see?

No! No! Fate grudges me. I probed my heart—sound, touch and smell were all I came up with.

My heart is rent with a shattering cry, 'Show me, someone, please show me the beauty.' But no one understood! No one paid heed to the blind one's sorrow.

3

SINCE THAT DAY, I WENT NEARLY EVERY DAY TO RAMSADAY MITRA'S HOUSE to sell flowers. But I do not know why. Why this urge in one who had no eyes? I would never see, and could only anticipate a few words from him. Why would Sachindra Babu come and speak to me? He lived in the main house and I went to the inner chambers. If he was married, he may have come that way sometimes. But a year or so before, his wife had passed away and he had not married again. So that hope too—of his coming to the inner chambers—was gone. Seldom, if ever, some business brought him to his mother's. What were the chances even then that he'd happen to come by exactly when I took the flowers into the house? Hence, my anticipation of a few words too was in vain. Yet, the blind one took the flowers there every day. With what vain hopes, I do not know. As I came back disappointed, every day, I asked myself why I went there. Every day, I vowed never to go back. And each day that vow put me to shame. Daily I went back, as if someone was dragging me there by the hair. Again the same disappointment, and the vow, and then breaking it—thus passed my days.

I would often ask myself why I went back there—I'd heard that women fell in love with a man for his good looks. I am blind and that doesn't hold true for me. So why did I go? To hear him speak? Has anyone ever heard that a woman had lost her heart to someone by just hearing his voice? Is that what had become of me? Was it even possible? If that were true, why didn't I visit musicians? Was Sachindra's voice sweeter than the sitar, violin, sarangi and esraj? That would be a lie.

So then, was it the touch? Was his touch softer than the piles of flowers that surround me day and night, that I hold in my heart and press to my heart? That's not true. So, what was it? Who could tell this blind girl what it really was?

You do not know it yourself—so what can you tell me? You have sight and all you see is beauty. I know that beauty is a mere illusion of the beholder—the same as sound. Beauty is not in the person, but in the eyes of the beholder—otherwise, why do people perceive it in different degrees in different people? Why don't we all fall in love with the same person? Similarly, the effect of a sound too is in your mind. Beauty is a mere gratification of the eyes and sound for the ears and touch for the skin. If I was to remain ignorant of the pleasures of beauty, why wouldn't sound and touch provide me with the same pleasure instead?

When a fallow land gets her first drops of rain, she blossoms. Parched wood blazes into life at the first touch of a spark. When an idle female heart comes into contact with a handsome male, by sight, or touch or smell, love becomes a foregone conclusion. Flowers bloom in the dark of night as well, the moon roams the sky even if clouds shield it from view, the koel sings in the woods even if there is no one about, the pearl still grows in the womb of the ocean where no one man would ever go, and love blossoms in the heart of the blind girl too; why shouldn't my heart respond, just because my eyes are sightless? Certainly it should, but merely to torture me. Poetry for the mute, love of music for the deaf, are merely instruments of their own torture; their own song is denied to them. Love, within my heart, was something like that. I have never set eyes on my own form, let alone that of my beloved. Beauty, form! How do I look? On the face of this earth, how does the tiny speck called Rajani appear to the eye? Has anyone ever wanted to take a second look at me? Is there any such, lowly, tiny form that has ever found me beautiful? A woman without her eyes has no beauty to speak of—I am sightless—but then, why does the sculptor sculpt the female form and give her vacant eyes? Am I then as rock-hewn as that? Why then did God grant me this heart full of sorrows and joy and the desire for love? If I received the misery of stone, why didn't I get its bliss as well? Fate can be so cruel and unfair! Even the worst of criminals gets to see and I was refused that right even before I was born—for what sins, I wonder. This world is devoid of gods, justice, trophies and penalties for virtue and sin—I wish I were dead.

I have lived for many years and will probably live for many more years; every year has many days, every day has many minutes and every minute has many seconds. Of them, not even for a single second, for an instant, could I not have the gift of sight? If only I could, I'd have taken a look at this world full of sound and touch, seen what I looked like, what Sachindra looked like.

4

I TOOK FLOWERS THERE EVERY DAY; AND MOST OF THE TIME I DIDN'T GET TO hear the voice of the young master. But some days, on rare occasions, I did. That joy which I experienced when I heard him defies description. I felt the same as the rain-laden clouds that thundered, growled and finally gave way to a downpour. I wanted to thunder and rumble as ecstatically as that. Every day I wanted to go and give a select bunch of flowers to him. But I could never do it. For one, I was shy, and then, even if I did, I felt he'd like to pay for them—how would I stop him? Dismal and desolate I'd come back home and try to make his form with my flowers—I do not know what shape it took, I've never seen.

Meanwhile, all my visits had borne an incredible fruit of which I knew nothing. I came to know of it first from my parents' conversation. One evening I had dozed off as I was weaving garlands. Voices woke me up—I heard my mother and father speaking. Perhaps the lamp had gone out and they didn't seem to realize that I was awake. When I heard my name being spoken, I lay still. Mother was saying, 'So it is fixed?'

Father replied, 'Of course. There's no going back when a big man like him has given his word. The only flaw my daughter has is that she is blind; otherwise such a bride would be a godsend to anyone.'

Mother asked, 'Why would someone else do so much for us?'

Father replied, 'You do not realize that they are not so starved for money like us. To them a few thousand rupees is nothing. Since the day that Ramsaday Babu's wife broached the topic of marriage for the first time, Rajani began to visit her every day. She had asked her son, 'Would money be of any use to get a blind girl married?' At this perhaps our daughter's hopes rose that this lady would be generous enough to fund a wedding for her. From that day on, Rajani has been going to her every day. At this Labanga understood that the girl was very keen on marriage—and why not, she is old enough. So, the young master has paid some money to Haranath Basu to agree to a match between his son Gopal and Rajani. Gopal is also agreeable.

Haranath Basu was Ramsaday Babu's manager. I knew a little bit about Gopal. He was thirty years old, married but childless. In the sense of companionship, he had a wife, but I suppose he was agreeable to taking another one, albeit blind, for the sake of a child. Moreover, Labanga had promised him money. From my parents' conversation, I gathered that my marriage was fixed with Gopal—the lure of money had even got him to accept a twenty-year-old blind girl. The money would buy him status. My parents seemed to be relieved that in this life at least their blind daughter had found her salvation. In fact, they sounded delighted. I felt my world was caving in.

The next day I decided never to go to Labanga again. In my heart I called her all manner of names. I wanted to die with shame. I was so angry that I wanted to hit Labanga. I was so upset I wanted to cry. What had I ever done to Labanga that she was so inclined to harm me? If her status as a rich woman entitled her to harm others and take pleasure in it, couldn't she find anyone else to inflict her tortures upon? Did it have to be this blind, hapless girl? Then I decided to go there just one more time and curse her to my heart's content—after that I'd never go that way again. I'd never sell her flowers, never take money from her—if mother sold her flowers and brought back money, I'd refuse to eat off it, even if it killed me. I thought I'd tell her that wealth doesn't give you the right to torment others; I'd say, I may be blind, but don't you have a heart? What pleasure do you gain from hurting someone who has no joy in life? The more I thought of the things I'd say, the more tears welled up in my eyes. I was afraid I'd forget everything when it was time to talk to her.

At the usual time, I went to Ramsaday Babu's house again. I had thought I wouldn't take flowers, but I felt shy to go there empty-handed. As before, I took some flowers. But today I didn't tell Mother I was going.

I gave the flowers and sat down beside Labanga, ready to curse her. How would I bring up the subject? Oh dear Lord, how would I begin? Where did it all begin? The fire was raging all around me, but where did I have to pour the first bucket of water? I could say nothing; I couldn't even broach the topic. Tears came to my eyes.

Fortunately, Labanga herself brought it up, 'Hey you, blind girl, you're going to be married.'

I flared up and said, 'Nonsense.'

Labanga said, 'Why? The young master will supervise it himself, why won't it happen?'

I flared up some more and said, 'What have I ever done to you?'

Labanga was angry too, 'My oh my, so you don't want to get married, do you?'

I shook my head, 'No.'

Labanga was angrier, 'You good-for-nothing, why won't you get married?'

I said, 'My wish.'

Perhaps Labanga felt I wasn't chaste, or why else would I refuse to get married? She blazed in anger and said, 'For shame, get out this instant or I'll throw you out myself!'

I got up. My two sightless eyes were brimming with tears that I hid from Labanga. I turned to go. On my way out I hesitated for a while on the stairs as I realized I hadn't spoken a word of what was on my mind. At this moment, I heard footsteps. A blind person's hearing acquires extraordinary prowess. I realized immediately whose footfall I was hearing. I sat down on the steps. The young master came up to me and halted. Perhaps he could see the tears in my eyes. He asked, 'Is that you, Rajani?'

I forgot everything! The anger, the insults, the misery, everything. The only words ringing in my ears were, 'Is that you, Rajani?' I didn't answer; I wanted him to ask a few more times, so that my ears could feast on his voice.

He asked, 'Rajani, why are you weeping?'

My heart began to overflow with joy and the tears welled up even more in my eyes. I didn't speak—let him ask more questions. I felt I was so lucky to be just blind and not deaf.

He asked again, 'Why are you crying, has someone said something?'

Then I answered. If I were to have the pleasure of a conversation with him in this lifetime, why should I let the chance go? I said, 'Chhoto-ma has scolded me.'

He laughed, 'Don't take her words to heart, she has a vile tongue, but she's good at heart. Come along with me—she'll speak to you nicely this very instant.'

Why wouldn't I go along with him? When he called out for me, all my anger vanished. I got up to go with him. He went on ahead and I followed right behind. But he said, 'You cannot see—how will you take the stairs? If you cannot, then take my hand and let me help you.'

I trembled; my entire body felt exhilarated. *He* would hold my hand! Let him. Tongues would wag. Let them. At least I'd be grateful for this birth as a woman. I am capable of roaming the lanes of the city without any aid, but I didn't tell him that or stop him. The young master—how shall I say it, I am lost for words—took my hand in his.

It was as if a freshly bloomed lotus had looped its stems around my wrist, as if someone had woven a garland of roses and wound it around my hand! I remember nothing else. Perhaps at that instant I had wanted to die; perhaps had melted at that moment; perhaps I had wished that Sachindra and I would become two flowers, and hang from the same bough of some tree in the woods. I do not remember what else I felt. When he let go of my hand at the head of the stairs I heaved a sigh—all of this world came back to me and at the same time the thought came, 'What did you just do, O Lord of my heart? Unthinkingly, what have you just done? You have taken my hand. Now whether you accept me or not, you are my husband and I am your wife. In this lifetime at least this blind flower girl will not have another as her husband.'

Was it at that moment that the evil eye fell on me? Perhaps.

5

THE YOUNG MASTER WENT UP TO CHHOTO-MA AND ASKED, 'WHAT HAVE YOU said to Rajani? She is weeping.' Chhoto-ma was discomfited to see my tears; she spoke to me kindly and made me sit by her side. She could not reveal all to her stepson, who was older than her in age. When he saw that his Chhoto-ma's anger had subsided, he went on his way to his own mother. I too came back home.

Meanwhile, arrangements were under way for my marriage to Gopal Babu. The date was fixed. What was I to do? I stopped weaving garlands. My every thought was centred upon a way to stop this wedding. But Mother was happy, Father excited, Labangalata concerned and the young master was the matchmaker—this one fact pained me the most, that *he* was the matchmaker. Me, a solitary, blind girl—how could I fight all this? No salvation came to mind. I left my flowers untended and my parents thought it was because I was so lost in the thoughts of marriage.

But the Lord brought me an aid. I had mentioned earlier that Gopal Basu was married. His wife's name was Champa—her father had named her Champaklata. She was the only one who was not happy about this marriage. Champa was a determined lady; she left no stone unturned in seeing to it that her husband didn't bring home a second wife.

Champa had a brother named Hiralal, he was a year and a half younger than Champa. Hiralal liked his alcohol and in no small amount. I had heard that he was also addicted to drugs. His father had not educated him; he could barely sign his own name. Yet Ramsaday Babu got him a clerkship somewhere. But his drinking habits cost him that job. He talked Haranath Basu into setting him up in a shop. But far from making profits, the debts mounted up and the shop wound up. Thereafter, in some village, Hiralal became a teacher at a salary of twelve rupees. But he ran away from there because alcohol was not available there. Then he brought out a newspaper. For some time it made good profits, the cash registers kept ringing—but the police began to interfere on charges of obscenity. Frightened, Hiralal closed down the paper and went underground. He surfaced after some days and began to hover around the young master. But when he realized Sachindra was not into alcohol, Hiralal slipped away on his own. All else having failed, he began to write plays. Not a single one sold. But since the publisher didn't ask for his money back, his skin was saved this time around. At this point, seeing no other salvation in this world, Hiralal caught hold of his Champa-didi and discussed his position with her.

Champa employed Hiralal to get her work done. He heard her out and finally asked, 'Is it true about the money? Whoever marries the blind girl gets the money?'

Champa reassured him on that count. Hiralal needed money urgently. He arrived at my doorstep as soon as he could. My father was at home, and I was in the next room. When I heard an unfamiliar male voice speaking to my father, I pricked up my ears and began to listen. What a hoarse, ugly voice Hiralal had!

He said, 'Why do you want to give your daughter to a married man?'

Father was sad as he said, 'What can I do, that's the only way to get her married; it didn't happen all this while.'

Pretending ignorance, Hiralal asked, 'Why, what's the problem in your daughter's marriage?'

Father laughed, 'I am poor; we live off these flowers. Who will marry my daughter? Add to that the fact that she is blind and quite old too.'

Hiralal said, 'But, grooms are available in plenty. If you ask me, I'd be willing to marry her. Nowadays everyone wants grown up girls. When I was the editor of the *Stushchubhishchashat* magazine, I wrote so many articles propagating the marriage of girls after they mature—it made people sit up. Child marriage! Shameful. Girls are meant to marry after maturity. Come on, let me set an example to the people of this country—I shall marry this girl.'

At that point we had been unaware of Hiralal's character; that realization came later. My father hesitated. He probably nursed the regret that such an erudite groom may slip away from him. Finally he said, 'Now the word has been given—it cannot be broken. Especially when the main hand behind this marriage is that of Sachindra Babu. They are arranging this wedding; their wish is my command. They are the ones who have brought forth this match.'

Hiralal tried again, 'How would you know what goes on in their minds? It's very difficult to fathom the heart of the rich man—don't put all your faith in them.'

Then Hiralal whispered something to Father at which Father said, 'What! No, no, my daughter is sightless!'

Thereafter, Hiralal looked around the room gloomily and said, 'Don't you have any alcohol in your house?'

Father was surprised and said, 'Alcohol? Why would I keep it?'

When he realized there wasn't any, Hiralal pretended to be very wise and said, 'I just wanted to warn you; now you are going to strike up relations with high society, see that those things are not there.'

My father didn't like these words. He was silent. Having failed to set an example in either marriage or drink, Hiralal went away unhappily.

6

THE DAY OF THE WEDDING WAS DRAWING CLOSE—IN FACT, I WAS TO GET married just a day later. No way out! No help at hand! The crushing waves rushed forth from all sides—drowning was inevitable.

I gave up on shame and fell flat at my mother's feet. I wept as I said with folded hands, 'Don't get me married—let me stay unmarried!'

Mother was astounded. 'Why?' she asked.

Why? I had no answer to that. I could just plead with folded hands and go on weeping. Mother was annoyed—she flared up and cursed me. Finally she told Father. He too cursed me and came to slap me. I had to keep quiet.

No way out! No hope for salvation! I was drowning!

That evening I was alone at home; Father had gone to collect some funds for the wedding and Mother was shopping for essentials. At such times I usually bolted the door or Bamacharan came to give me company. Today it was the latter. Suddenly, someone pushed open the door and stepped into the house. The footsteps were unfamiliar. I asked, 'Who is that?'

'Your death,' came the reply.

The words were livid, but the voice belonged to a woman. I was not afraid. I laughed and said, 'Does my death truly exist? Where were you all these days then?'

The woman's anger did not abate, 'I'll tell you in a minute! Dying to get married, eh! Rascal, good-for-nothing!' A string of curses poured forth from her mouth. At the end of it all, the soft-spoken lady said, 'Let me warn you, blind girl, if you do get married to my husband, then the day you come into the house will be the day I shall poison you.'

I realized this was Champa. I requested her to have a seat and said, 'Listen to me, I need to talk to you.' When she found such eager welcome in answer to her vicious curses, Champa cooled down a bit and deigned to sit.

I said, 'Listen, I want this marriage as little as you do. I am ready to do anything to stop this wedding. Could you give me an idea?'

Champa was surprised, 'Why don't you tell your parents?'

I said, 'I have, a thousand times—all in vain.'

Champa then asked, 'Why don't you go to the Big House and plead with them?'

'Same results,' I responded.

Champa gave it some thought and said, 'Then, there is one thing you could do.'

'What is that?' I asked eagerly.

'You could hide for a few days,' suggested Champa.

'But where would I hide? I have nowhere to go.'

Champa thought some more and said, 'You could go to my parents' home.'

I thought, not a bad idea. There didn't seem to be any other way out. I said, 'I am blind. Who will guide me there and why would they let me stay there?'

Champa had truly come as my nemesis to drag me into hell. She said, 'Don't you worry about that; I'll take care of all that. I shall send someone with you and I shall tell him what to say. Will you go?'

Like a straw to the drowning man, this appeared to me as the best way out. I accepted immediately.

Rising up to leave, Champa said, 'Then be prepared; when everyone sleeps at night I shall knock on the door. Come out with me.'

I agreed.

At two o'clock at night, I heard a knock on the door. I was awake. I picked up a change of clothes, opened the door and walked out. I saw Champa waiting outside. I went away with her. I didn't think twice, never gave a thought to the wrong I was doing. I did feel sad for my parents, but at the time I believed I'd be away for a few days only. Once the talk of marriage subsided, I'd come back.

When I arrived at Champa's house—my soon-to-have-been marital home—she gave me an escort and sent me packing right away. She hurried because she was afraid her husband would wake up. I had strong objections to the escort she gave me—but she was in such a hurry that my protests were swept away. Can you guess who she sent with me? Hiralal.

At the time I still didn't know anything of Hiralal's sterling reputation. That wasn't the cause of my objections. He was a young man and I was a young woman—how could I go with him, unchaperoned? That was my objection. But at the time who paid any heed to what I said? I was blind, the road was unfamiliar and I had stepped out at night—hence the normal signals by sound that I mark along a new road had been absent; so I could not go back home without help, and even there all that awaited me was that sinful marriage. Consequently, I had to go with Hiralal. I felt, 'Even if there's no one to come to a blind girl's aid, there's a God above. He would never torture the wounded like Labangalata does. He is kind and strong, He'll surely have mercy on me—if not, what use is mercy?'

At the time I didn't know that the Heavenly Will worked differently from the laws of this world; what we call mercy is not the same before His omniscience, and what is torture to us is not the same before the all-knowing God. I also did not know that the karmic wheel of this world was devoid of mercy and pity; that wheel turned on its familiar path in a set pattern. Whoever or whatever came in its hurtling path—be they blind, lame or wounded—would be ground to a pulp. Just because I was blind and helpless, why would the karmic wheel move from its path?

I set off on the road with Hiralal. I followed his footsteps. Somewhere, a clock struck one. No one was about, not a sound. A few vehicles were heard, a few drunkards in the grip of alcohol, singing a few lines here and there. Suddenly I asked Hiralal, 'Hiralal Babu, how strong are you?'

He was a little surprised, 'Why?'

I said, 'I'm asking.'

He replied, 'Well, not very little.'

'What's the staff in your hand made of?'

Hiralal replied, 'Palm wood.'

'Can you break it?' I asked him.

'Not a chance,' said Hiralal.

'Just hand it to me once.'

Hiralal handed me the staff. I broke it into two. He was probably astounded to see my strength. I handed him one half and kept the other half to myself. He must have also been annoyed to see that I'd broken his staff. I said, 'Now I can relax—don't be upset. You've seen my strength, you've seen this half of the staff in my hand—even if you so desire, you wouldn't dare do me any harm.'

Hiralal was silent.

7

HIRALAL AND I BOARDED THE BOAT AT THE JAGANNATH GHAT. IT WAS NIGHT and the southern breeze puffed up the sails. Hiralal told me that their home was in Hooghly; I'd forgotten to ask that earlier.

As the boat moved over the waters, Hiralal said, 'So now that your marriage to Gopal is off, why don't you marry me?' I said, 'No.' Hiralal began to argue. His intent was to prove to me that he was the best possible groom on this earth, and also that I was the worst possible bride. I acceded to both, but still I maintained, 'I shall not marry you.'

At this, Hiralal got really angry. 'Who wants to marry a blind girl, anyway?' he asked of the world and fell silent. Thus the hours crawled away.

Suddenly, towards very early morning, Hiralal ordered the boatmen to draw up to the bank. They followed his orders. I could hear the boat pull up to the bank. 'Get down,' Hiralal told me, 'We have reached.' He took my hand and helped me ashore. I stood on the bank. Then I heard sounds of Hiralal getting back to the boat. He said to the boatmen, 'Go on, set sail again.'

I said in alarm, 'What's this—why are you setting sail after dropping me off?'

Hiralal said, 'Find your own way now.' The boatmen began to row; I heard the oars splashing through the water. I pleaded pitifully, 'Please, I beg of you, I am blind—if you must leave me behind, at least take me to someone's home. I have never come here before, how will I find the way?'

'Will you marry me, then?' he asked.

I wanted to weep. I did cry for some time; but I was also really angry—I said to Hiralal, 'Go away; it would be wrong to be indebted to you. When the night ends, I shall meet hundreds of men kinder than you. They'd surely have pity on a blind girl.'

'That's if you meet them,' he retorted. 'This is an island, there's water all around. Will you marry me?'

I could make out that Hiralal's boat had already gone some distance. Hearing was my livelihood, my ears did the work of my eyes. When someone spoke, I could gauge from how far or from which direction the voice came. I made a guess regarding the distance of Hiralal's boat, got into the water and began to run, meaning to catch the boat. I was neck-deep in water, but didn't get a hold on the boat; it was further away. If I tried to catch it, I'd drown.

The palm wood staff was still in my hand. Once again I estimated from how far and from which direction he'd spoken. I stepped back and waded up to waist-high water once again, gauged the distance and hurled the staff with all my might.

Hiralal screamed as he fell down on the boat's deck. 'Murder, murder,' the boatmen shouted and picked up anchor. In reality that rascal wasn't dead; I heard his sweet voice in a minute as the boat rowed away and he cursed me at the top of his voice. With the foulest and most hideous language, he polluted the Ganga as he sailed on her. I also heard his voice—loud and clear across the water—threatening to start up his newspaper again and to write articles defaming me.

8

THERE I WAS, A BLIND YOUNG GIRL STANDING ALONE ON THAT ISLAND THAT night, hearing the waters of the Ganga lapping at her feet.

Alas, the life of man! It is so futile—why does he come, stay or go? Why such a grief-stricken life? The thought of it is so pointless. One day Sachindra Babu had been explaining to his mother that everything follows a law. This life of a person—was it a corollary of this law? The laws that made flowers bloom, clouds glide, the moon rise, water-bubbles float, laugh and vanish, that made the dust particles flutter, the grass burn, the leaves fall, did the same laws govern, complete and conclude a human life? Was it the same law that made the crocodile crouch in the water for its prey, that made all other insects on this island hunt their quarry, and was it the same law that was making me willing to give up my soul for Sachindra? Shame on giving up my soul! Shame on romance! Shame on this life! Why don't I give it up on the banks of this river?

My life was bleak, but not because all joy was missing from it; the rose plant will yield rose blossoms and nothing else. A life of misery will be sorrowful and that doesn't qualify it as bleak. But I call it bleak because my misery seems to be an end in itself, and there doesn't appear to be anything beyond it. I have the sole benefit of the misery of my soul; no one else knows of it, comprehends it; I cannot express it because I do not possess the skill to do so. There is no audience and so no one witnesses it or understands it. From one rose plant several rose plants may rise; but how many other people would share in your grief? How many such others have been born who can plumb the depths of the misery of another? Who on the face of this earth will understand the grief of a blind flower girl? Who can follow the waves of sorrow and joy that rise every moment in every word, every sound and every letter that this insignificant heart utters? Sorrows and *joys*? Yes, there are those too. When, at the onset of spring, along with the piles of flowers the bees buzzed into our home, who could even guess just how the sound thrilled my heart? No one knew how it delighted me when the sounds of music from the musicians' home floated on the gentle breeze into my ears. One cannot comprehend the joy that rushed through me when Bamacharan spoke his first words, when he said 'totter' for water and 'Jonji' for Rajani. Hence, who could fathom my misery? Who would know the grief of not being able to see; that may even be comprehensible, but would he understand my sorrow at never being able to express my grief? Would he know how sad it is that sorrow has no language in this world? You do not appreciate plain people saying big words—how can I express deep sorrow in plain words? Such is my grief that even if my heart bursts away, I myself cannot gather all of my sorrow into it at one time.

In the human language there are no such words, in the human psyche there are no such thoughts. I suffer my agony, but I can scarcely fathom it. What is my angst? I do not know, but my heart is rent asunder by it. You may often notice that your body grows thinner, you lose your strength, but you cannot perceive the cause; similarly, sometimes it happens that grief is tearing away at your heart, threatening to rip away your soul and send it heavenward, but you do not understand what you are sad about. If you cannot fathom it yourself, how can anyone else? This is no simple grief. No wonder I say this life is bleak!

If this life is so miserable, why am I so keen on holding on to it? Why don't I just give it up? Here I stand in the heart of a flowing Ganga—two steps further and death could be mine. Why don't I take those steps? What's the use of this life? Let me end it!

Why was I born? Why am I blind? If I had to be born, why couldn't I be a match for Sachindra? And since I am not his equal, why did I have to fall in love with him? If I had to fall in love with him, why couldn't I stay near him? Why did I have to bear him in my heart and leave home? Helpless and sightless, why did I have to come to these banks to die? Why did I have to float like the proverbial straw against the currents of this life, along uncharted waves? There are many sad people in this world, but why am I the saddest? Who plays this game—the gods? What do they gain from such pain given to man? Why would one create only to torture? Why would I worship such cruelty personified as gods? Why should I worship heartlessness? Such terrible grief in man can never be God's gift—if it were, then they are worse than demons. Is it then the fruit of my own labour? What sins have caused me this blindness at birth?

I began to take a few steps forward—death, be mine! The waves of the river crashed around my ears—perhaps death would elude me—I love sweet sounds. No, I shall die! The chin went under, the lips went under, just a little bit more. The nose went under, my eyes went under, I went under!

I went under, but I didn't die. But I do not wish to carry on with this tale of suffering. Let someone else speak.

I began to float away on those early morning currents of the river. Gradually, my breathing slowed and the senses dulled.

Part II

Amarnath

1

IT IS ABSOLUTELY NECESSARY FOR ME TO TRANSCRIBE THE TRIVIAL TALE OF my futile life. I wish to paint a picture on the screen of this world, of the exact point where the boat of my life crashed on the banks of life. Sailors of today may perhaps take heed and learn from it.

My home—or ancestral dwelling—is in Shantipur. At present, I have no fixed address. I am born into a high caste but in my ancestral family there was once a great scandal. My paternal uncle's wife had run away from home. My father was wealthy enough for me to live off it without earning anything on my own. People considered him to be well-off. He had spent a lot of money on my education. I too had acquired some knowledge, but let that subject be for now. As the king has his crown, I had my learning.

When I reached the marriageable age, many matches were brought for me. But none met my father's approval. He wanted the bride to be breathtakingly beautiful, her father to be immensely rich and for all caste restrictions to stay in place. But no such match came forth. In reality, once they heard about our family scandal, no well-settled family wished to marry off their daughter to me. Thus, as he was still searching for the right match for me, my father passed away.

Eventually, after my father was no more, one of his cousins—my aunt—brought forth a match. On the other side of the Ganga there was a village called Kalikapur. In this narration, another village called Bhawaninagar will be mentioned. Kalikapur was close to Bhawaninagar. My aunt's marital home was in Kalikapur and she had fixed a match for me with a girl of this village. Her name was Labanga.

I had met Labanga quite often even before this alliance was fixed. I used to visit my aunt quite often and on some occasions I'd seen Labanga in my aunt's house, as well as in her own home. At times I'd even tutored Labanga from the first book of letters: A for apple, B for ball. From the time that her match was brought for me, she stopped appearing before me. But from that very moment, I too became increasingly eager to catch sight of her. At that time, Labanga was past the age for marriage—she was a bud ready to blossom. Her eyes darted restlessly, yet timidly, her laughter was soft and shy, her quick footsteps had slowed down. I felt I had never seen such beauty before—it was a rare beauty, even for a young damsel. In effect, the beauty of childhood-past but youth-unattained, and that of a child before he learns to speak is unparalleled, even by that of youth in full bloom. In the youthful damsel, the choice of clothing, the display of smiles and peeks, the sway of braids, the swing of the arm, the slant of the neck and the whorls of her words, all adds up to a veritable showcase. And the eye with which we take in that beauty too is jaundiced. The true beauty is that in the perception of which, the senses and their related emotions are not in use.

At this point, rumours of our family scandal fell on the ears of the girl's father. The match was broken. My heart had just about installed Labangalata on its pedestal when Ramsaday Mitra from Bhawaninagar came and uprooted her from it. Labangalata was soon wedded to him. I was despondent.

A few years after this, an incident took place that I can barely describe. I do not know if I can ever describe it. Since then I left my home and began to roam from place to place without a fixed address to my name.

No fixed address, but I could have had one any time I wished. If I so desired, I could have married many more times than even a high-caste Brahmin. I had everything—wealth, status, youth, erudition, strength. By a stroke of bad luck, on a single day's misapprehension I let go of everything, the comfort of home, my life as fragrant as a garden, and took to roaming through the land like the bat driven by a fierce wind. If I'd wanted to, I could have started a beautiful life in a pretty home in my motherland, raised the flag of joy against the winds at play and shot arrows of laughter at the monster called grief. But—

Now I do wonder sometimes, why didn't I? The meting out of sorrows and joy may be in others' hands, but this heart is mine. Just because the boat went under, why did I have to follow suit? I could have easily stayed afloat. Besides, what is sorrow? It is a state of mind, which is in one's own hands. Were my sorrows and joys really in the hands of others, or in my own? Others were the doers in the external world, in my own mind I was the sole achiever. Why couldn't I be happy with my own kingdom? The material world was real, and wasn't the inner world equally real? Can't a person live with his mind alone? How many elements does your external world have that my inner self doesn't have? Could you even hope to show me in your outer world some of the things that my soul has? The flower that blooms on this soil, the breeze that blows in this firmament, the moon that rises in this sky, the ocean that dances its own merry dance in this dark, scarcely has a match in your outer world.

Why then, that night did that sleeping beauty's—oh, for heaven's sake. In one silent night this unbounded earth shrunk to the size of a dried pea in my eyes—I could barely find a place to hide. I took to roaming the lands.

2

GRADUALLY THE COOL FINGERS OF TIME PLACED ITS BALM ON MY SORE SPOT.

In Kashi, I met a genteel and very old man called Govindakanta Dutta. He had been staying there for many years.

One day, the subject of police torture came up in our conversation. Many people who were seated with us mentioned several stories related to that topic. Some were true; some must have been fabricated by the narrators. Govindakanta Babu narrated a story that went roughly thus:

'In our village there was a poor Kayastha called Harekrishna Das. He had only one offspring, a daughter. His wife was no more and he himself was ill. Hence, he had entrusted his daughter's upbringing to a near relative. His daughter owned some gold ornaments which he hadn't handed over to his relative. But when death was close, he called me, handed me the ornaments and said, "Please give these to my daughter when she comes of age. If I give it to her now, Rajchandra will sequester it." I accepted the ornaments. Later, when Harekrishna died, the parody of an inspector arrived on the scene with his joker-assistants and declared that the body was an unclaimed one. He began to confiscate Harekrishna's bowls and glasses, clothes and all material possessions as they were supposedly "not spoken for". Some people pointed out that he had a daughter in Calcutta. The inspector shut them up saying, "If she is the successor, let her present herself in court." At that point, a few of my enemies saw their chance and let it slip that Govinda Dutta held some of Harekrishna's ornaments in his keeping. I was summoned. I stood before His Highness the police inspector, palms joined in supplication. Some curses were hurled at me. It looked like I would be sent away into prison. What could I say? When blows were aimed at me, I poured out all the ornaments as well as a fifty-rupee note at the feet of the inspector and only then was I released.

'Needless to say, the inspector took the ornaments home for his own daughter to wear. To his superior he reported that Harekrishna Das owned nothing beyond a cup and a plate and that he had died leaving behind no successors.'

I had heard of Harekrishna Das. I asked Govinda Babu, 'Does this Harekrishna Das have a brother called Manohar Das?'

Govindakanta Babu said, 'Yes, how did you know?'

I didn't say much more, but merely asked, 'What is the name of this relative of Harekrishna to whom he entrusted his daughter?'

'Rajchandra Das,' replied Govindakanta.

'Where does he live?'

'In Calcutta. But I have forgotten the exact address.'

I asked, 'Would you know his daughter's name?'

Govinda Babu said, 'Harekrishna had named his daughter Rajani.'

Fairly soon after this incident, I left Kashi forever.

3

I NEED TO FIRST UNDERSTAND WHAT IT IS THAT I AM SEARCHING FOR. MY heart is despondent, this world is dark and full of despair. If I were to die today, I would not see tomorrow. If I cannot even relieve my misery, what use is my manhood? But before the disease can be cured, it has to be diagnosed. Before I aimed at ending my misery, I needed to know what was causing it.

What is sorrow? A lack. All sorrow rises from a feeling of want. Disease is grievous because of the lack of good health. Lack is not necessarily agony, and that I know. The lack of a disease would not be so sorrowful. Only certain kinds of lack brought grief in its wake.

What did I lack? What did I want? What does a man want? Wealth? I had enough of that. Fame? There is no one in the world who doesn't have that. The practised conman is notorious for his shrewdness. I have even heard of the fame of a butcher—he never cheated anyone in matters of meat; he had never handed anyone dog-meat as mutton. Everyone had fame. And then again, no one had it in full measure. Bacon was famous for corruption; Socrates' notoriety earned him a death sentence. Yudhishthira was a liar in the manner he chose to kill Drona, Arjuna was defeated at the hands of Bavruvahana. It is well known that Kaiser was also called the queen of Bethunia. Voltaire had called Shakespeare a clown. I do not crave fame.

Fame rests on the tongue of common men. But they are no one to judge anybody because common men are thick-skinned and stupid. What would I gain from being famous among the thick-skinned and stupid? No, I do not crave fame.

Respect? Who is there in this world whose respect would bring me joy? The few that are there, do respect me. From anyone else, it's nothing but an insult. Respect in the royal court is a mere symbol of your subjugation and I defy it. I do not crave esteem. I only desire it from my near and dear ones.

Good looks? How much? A little. One should not throw up at the sight of my face. So far no one has. My looks are good enough for me.

Health? As of now it is abundant.

Strength? What shall I do with it? It is necessary to beat up people. I do not wish to beat up anyone.

Intelligence? On this earth, no one has ever acknowledged a lack in that area, and neither do I. Everyone thinks he is extremely bright and so do I.

Erudition? I do accept I do not have enough. But no one has ever been unhappy for the lack of it and neither am I.

Spirituality? They say a lack of it affects one's afterlife, not the present one. In the nature of man I perceive the greater grief coming from a lack of irreligion than from the reverse. I know it's an illusion. Yet, I do not crave spirituality. That is not the reason for my melancholia.

Romance? Love? Adulation? I happen to know that its absence brings joy—to love is to suffer. Witness Labangalata.

So then, what was I sad about? What did I lack? What did I covet, that I could attain and thus lessen my misery? What was the object of my desire?

I know—it is the lack of an object of desire that is causing me such pain. I have realized that everything is futile and hence my grief is all that is genuine.

4

COULD I FIND NOTHING TO DESIRE? IN THIS ETERNAL WORLD, FULL OF abundant wealth, could I find nothing to covet? Who did I think I was? Tindle, Huxley, Durbin and Lyall sat on the same seat all their lives and analysed a tiny droplet of moisture, a minute speck of dust or the nameless wildflower and failed to describe them accurately—and here I was, with nothing to covet! What sort of a man was I?

Look here, nobody has been able to count to a man just how many people there are on this earth. Millions and millions, I am sure. Each of these millions is the holder of numerous virtues. Everyone is a holder of devotion, love, kindness, spirituality, etc.; everyone is admirable and worthy of emulation. Did I not aspire to or crave for any one? Who on earth was I?

I did have an object of desire—I still have it. But it is impossible to achieve. And for that reason alone I had cast it from my heart long, long ago. I do not wish to rekindle it. Wasn't there anything else I craved?

For a few years now I had been asking myself this question repeatedly, without receiving any answer. When I asked the few friends that I have, they said, 'If you have nothing to do for yourself, do something for others; try to help others as much as possible.'

That is an old adage. What would actually help others? Ram's mother's son has fever, check his pulse and give him some quinine. Ragho, the halfwit, has nothing to wear—buy him a blanket. Sasta's mother is a widow—give her a pension. Sunder the barber's son could not study further—arrange for his school fees to be paid. Was this called helping others?

I accept, this *is* helping others. But how much time does this take? How much time can be spent doing this? How much effort does it take and how much does this effort excite the brain? This is not to say that I do these things to the extent to which it is possible for me to do. But the little I do, leaves me feeling that this wouldn't fulfil my emptiness. I look for a chore worthy of me, something that'll hold my interest.

There is another kind of social service that is in fashion these days. In a nutshell it can be summed up as 'yabbering and dabbling'. Societies, clubs, associations, meetings, speeches, resolutions, pleas, petitions, empathy—these are not for me. Once I had seen a friend reading one such petition for a big meeting and asked him what he was reading. He had replied, 'Nothing much, just the blind beggar going a-begging.' That's all it is to my limited knowledge and perception.

This disease has one other aberration. Get the widow remarried, stop the high-caste Brahmin from being polygamous, prevent child marriages, do away with the caste system, the women who at present are tied to a pole like cows should all be let loose and left to graze on their own. I do not own any cattle and I have no interest in other people's cowsheds. I am not for abolishing the caste system, I am not yet that well educated. I am still unwilling to eat from the same plate as my sweeper, or to marry his daughter and the curses that I can willingly tolerate from the learned pandit, I am unwilling to take from my sweeper. Hence, my caste should stay untouched. Let the widows remarry, let children stay unmarried, let the high-caste Brahmin suffer the agonies of monogamy—I have no objection to that; but I fail to understand what would be gained from espousing these causes.

Consequently, in contemporary Bengali society I have no work to do. Here, I am nobody, I am nowhere. I am me, and that is all. That is the cause of my pain. I have no other grief—I am not counting Labangalata's handwriting.

5

WHEN MY STATE OF MIND WAS THUS, I HEARD RAJANI'S NAME ON THE LIPS OF Govindakanta Dutta in Kashi. I felt the Lord had at last assigned me a vital task. In this world I seemed to find a responsibility. It was possible to try and be of use to Rajani to the best of my ability. I have no other work—why didn't I take this up? Wasn't this a task worthy of me?

At this point, it is important to detail some part of Sachindra's lineage. Sachindranath's father's name is Ramsaday Mitra, his grandfather was Banchharam Mitra and his great-grandfather was Kevalram Mitra. Their ancestral home was not in Calcutta; his father was, in fact, the first to live in Calcutta. Their ancestral home was in the village of Bhawaninagar. Sachindra's great-grandfather was a deprived and destitute man. But his grandfather Banchharam Mitra used his wit and amassed the fortune which was passed down to them for their enjoyment.

Banchharam had a dear friend called Manohar Das. It was with the latter's assistance that Banchharam had amassed his fortune. Though Manohar had devoted his life to acquiring wealth for Banchharam, he himself never aspired to any of it. Banchharam was eternally grateful to him for these virtues. He loved Manohar like his own sibling. And Manohar too accorded him the respect due to an elder brother. Sachindra's father Ramsaday Mitra and grandfather did not get along very well—perhaps the fault lay with both men.

Once it thus happened that Ramsaday came to loggerheads with Manohar. The latter complained to Banchharam that Ramsaday had insulted him beyond belief for some reason. After this declaration, Manohar resigned from his duties and moved away from Bhawaninagar with his family forever. Banchharam pleaded with Manohar, but the latter remained unmoved. He did not even tell anyone where he went off to.

Banchharam loved Manohar as much if not more than Ramsaday. Hence, he was extremely annoyed with Ramsaday. Banchharam cursed him no end and Ramsaday responded in kind.

The upshot of this squabble between father and son was that Banchharam disinherited Ramsaday. The son too left his father's home and vowed never to show his face there again. In anger, Banchharam made a will stating that his son, Ramsaday, would inherit nothing whatsoever from him. After the demise of Banchharam Mitra, Manohar Das and, in his absence, his successors would inherit all; thereafter Ramsaday's children and successors too would come in line, but not Ramsaday himself.

Ramsaday left his father's home and came to Calcutta with his first wife. She had some inheritance of her own. Supported by this and with the aid of a foreigner who was a businessman, he set himself up in business. The goddess of wealth smiled on him and he didn't have a day's worry over the running of his home.

If he did have to suffer, perhaps Banchharam would have been appeased. But when he heard of his son's good fortune, the little bit of love left in the old man deserted him at once. The son was also a proud man and he had decided not to go back until his father called him—so he never asked after his father's health. Banchharam felt that his son was doing this out of disrespect and indifference and so he didn't send for him either.

Hence, none of the parties abandoned their stance and the will remained unchanged. At such a point in time, Banchharam passed away.

Ramsaday was devastated. He wept for days together, regretting the fact that he hadn't made up with his father and come to see him sooner. He did not go back to Bhawaninagar. Instead, he performed his father's last rites in Calcutta, because by that time the house in Bhawaninagar, legally, belonged to Manohar Das.

Meanwhile, no one knew the whereabouts of Manohar Das. Later it came to light that even while Banchharam had been alive, no one had found out where Manohar Das was. The day he had left Bhawaninagar had been the last anyone had seen of him. Banchharam had hunted high and low for him. Finally, he added an addendum to the will by which he appointed a relative called Bishnuram Sirkar, who lived in Calcutta, as the executor of the will. It stated that Bishnuram would try his best to locate Manohar Das and thereafter hand over the property to its rightful owner.

Bishnuram Babu was a wise, unbiased and capable man. He began to search for Manohar Das as soon as Banchharam passed away. After spending much money and effort he discovered what Banchharam had not been able to find out. The fact of the matter was thus: after leaving Bhawaninagar, Manohar had lived in Dacca for some time. But he had some trouble earning a living there and so he set off for Calcutta with his entire family by boat. On the way the boat capsized and all of them met their end. There were no other living successors as far as one could tell.

Bishnuram Babu gathered hard evidence of all these facts and presented them to Ramsaday Mitra. Thereafter, Banchharam's immovable property was divided equally between Sachindra and his elder brother. Bishnuram Babu duly handed over the rights to them.

But at present, if this Rajani was alive, then the wealth that Ramsaday Mitra's sons were currently enjoying actually belonged to her. Perhaps she was destitute and needy. Let me try and find out. I have nothing else on my hands right now.

6

AFTER LEAVING KASHI AND ON REACHING BENGAL, I WENT TO VISIT A RELATIVE in a village. At dawn I went for a stroll. I came upon a very appealing, cloistered forest. The birds were chirping in harmony, there were tall trees all around, thick foliage, green and gentle; the leaves on the trees were thickly packed together, greenery was abundant everywhere—a bud here, a bloom there, a raw fruit here and a ripe one there. Suddenly, I heard a scream in the woods. I rushed towards the direction of the cry and found a grotesque looking man trying to attack a young girl.

One look and I could tell that the man was from a low caste, perhaps an untouchable; but he was built like a rock.

Slowly I crept up behind him. I snatched away the hatchet that was tied to his waist and hurled it into the distance. The rascal let the girl go and turned to face me, cursing volubly. His eyes gave me a fright. I realized that any delay could cost me a lot. I went for his throat. He unfettered himself and grabbed me. I tried to return the favour, but he was stronger. I wasn't afraid or agitated. As soon as I could, I said to the young girl, 'Run away while I see to this scoundrel.'

She said, 'Where will I run—I am blind and I do not know the way here.'

Blind! My strength doubled—I was looking for a blind girl called Rajani.

I realized that although he couldn't beat me up, my opponent was dragging me away. I understood his game, he was trying to pull me towards the area where I had thrown his hatchet. I tore myself from his clutches, ran and grabbed the hatchet first. He broke a branch of a tree, spun it around and hit me on the arm. The hatchet dropped from my hands. He picked it up and hit me in a couple of places with it and then made his escape.

I was badly injured. In great pain, I walked back towards my relative's home. The blind girl began to follow the sound of my footsteps and came with me. After some distance I could walk no further. People on the streets saw my condition and helped me back home.

I stayed there for some time. The blind girl too stayed put, because she had nowhere else to go and because she couldn't leave me in the state that I was in. After many days and much nursing, I finally recuperated. I had my suspicions ever since the girl had told me that she was blind. At the earliest moment that I could open my mouth, she came and sat by my bed. I asked her, 'What's your name?'

'Rajani.'

I asked, 'Are you the daughter of Rajchandra Das?'

Rajani was startled, 'Do you know my father?'

I did not give her a clear answer.

After I had made a complete recovery, I took Rajani to Calcutta.

7

WHILE I WAS TAKING RAJANI BACK TO CALCUTTA, I ALSO TOOK WITH ME AN old domestic called Tinkari from my relative's house as a chaperone. This step was more for Rajani's benefit. At the time of our departure, I asked her, 'Rajani, your home is in Calcutta; so how did you come here?'

Rajani said, 'Do I have to answer all the questions?'

I said, 'If you do not wish to, you needn't answer.'

In reality, the intelligence, wisdom and innocence of this blind girl really appealed to me. I did not wish to cause her any discomfort. Rajani said, 'Since you give your permission, I'd like to keep a few things in the dark. We have a neighbour called Gopal Babu. His wife is Champa. I am acquainted with her. Her father's home is in Hooghly. She asked me if I'd go to her father's house. I agreed. One day, she brought me to Gopal Babu's house, but while sending me to her father's home, she didn't come along with me. She sent her brother Hiralal with me. Hiralal set off for Hooghly with me on a boat.'

At this point, I realized Rajani was hiding facts about Hiralal. I asked her, 'And did you go with Hiralal?'

'I didn't want to, but I had no choice,' replied Rajani. 'I cannot tell you why that was so. On the way, Hiralal began to torment me. When he realized he couldn't overpower me, he dropped me off on the banks of the river and left with the boat.'

Rajani fell silent. I took Hiralal to be the heartless monster that he was and began to wonder what he looked like. Then Rajani continued, 'After he left, I wanted to drown in the Ganga and stepped into the water.'

I said, 'Why? Did you love Hiralal so much?'

She frowned darkly and said, 'Not one bit. There's no one in the world that I hate more.'

'Then why did you wish to drown?'

'I cannot tell you what ails me.'

'All right, carry on.'

'I tried to drown, but I floated. A stage-boat was passing by; the passengers in the boat saw me floating and hauled me up on the boat. The village where I met you was where one passenger got off. Before getting off he asked me, "Where are you going?" I said I'd go wherever I was taken. He asked me again, "Where is your home?" I said, "Calcutta." He said, "I will go to Calcutta tomorrow. You come with me today; you may stay in my house today and tomorrow I'll take you with me." I got up to go with him, feeling very relieved. The rest you know.'

I said, 'The man I rescued you from—was that him?'

'The same.'

I brought Rajani to Calcutta and found the address given by her and met Rajchandra Das. I took Rajani there.

Rajchandra was very happy to get his daughter back. His wife wept copiously in joy. They heard Rajani's story from me in detail and expressed their gratitude to me.

Later, I took Rajchandra aside and asked him, 'Do you know why your daughter left her home?'

Rajchandra said, 'No. I ponder over it at all times, but I can never really decide why.'

I said, 'Do you know what caused Rajani to want to drown herself?'

Rajchandra was surprised, 'I do not know what great anguish she could have. It is true that she is blind and that pains her, but why would she wish to drown herself after so many years? But then, she is a grown girl and still unmarried. But that can't be the reason. I was trying to get her married to a good match. She ran away the night before her wedding.'

I found a new link and asked, 'She ran away from home?'

'Yes.'

'Without telling you?'

'Not a soul knew,' said Rajchandra.

'Who were you marrying her to?'

Rajchandra said, 'Gopal Babu.'

'Which Gopal Babu?' I asked. 'Champa's husband?'

'You seem to know everything—yes, the same.'

I glimpsed a ray of light. So then Champa, for fear of competition, had betrayed Rajani and sent her off to Hooghly with her brother. Perhaps she had even inspired Hiralal to attempt to destroy Rajani.

I concealed my thoughts from Rajchandra and said, 'I do know everything. I shall also tell you much more that I know. Don't hide anything from me.'

'What would you like to know?' asked Rajchandra.

'Rajani is not your daughter,' I said quietly.

Rajchandra was surprised. He said, 'What? Whose daughter is she, then?'

'Harekrishna Das's.'

Rajchandra was silent for some time. Finally he said, 'I do not know who you are. But I beg of you, please don't let Rajani come to know this.'

I said, 'Perhaps not now, but I will have to tell her later. First, answer me honestly—when Harekrishna died, did Rajani have any ornaments that belonged to her?'

Rajchandra was now a little fearful. He said, 'I know nothing of her ornaments—no, there weren't any.'

But I persisted in my quest. 'After Harekrishna died, did you ever go to his home in search of his inheritance?'

'Yes, I did,' said Rajchandra. 'But I was told that the police had confiscated all his belongings.'

'What did you do, then?'

'What could I do? I am very scared of the police. At the time of Rajani's stolen-bangles case itself I had suffered a lot. When I heard about the police confiscating the remaining gold after Harekrishna's death, I held my peace.'

'Rajani's stolen-bangle case—what's that?' I asked, startled at the new revelation.

Rajchandra elaborated, 'At the time of Rajani's annaprasan, her bangles were stolen. The thief was caught. The case came up in Bardhaman. I had to go from Calcutta to Bardhaman as a witness. It was a terrible time.'

I kept quiet. I could see my plan clearly.

Part III

Sachindra

1

THIS TASK HAS FALLEN TO ME—THIS PART OF RAJANI'S LIFE-STORY MUST BE written by me. I shall do so.

I had made all arrangements for Rajani's marriage. But on the morning of the wedding I heard that Rajani had run away and she was nowhere to be found. I searched for her, but all in vain. Some said she was not chaste; I did not believe them. I had seen her many times. I could swear that she was innocent. But it was possible that while being unmarried, she had lost her heart to someone and fearing a wrong match, she had run away from home. But there were two questions that raised their heads. One was: how would a blind girl trust anyone enough to leave her home? Two: is it possible for a blind girl to fall in love? Impossible, I felt. Please don't laugh at me, there are many a fool just like me. We may have read a book or two or three and we feel we have in our grip the deepest of deep knowledge of this world—that, whatever doesn't come within the sphere of our beliefs cannot possibly be true. We refuse to accept God because such metaphysics goes beyond our tiny frame of thoughts. How would I then comprehend the romantic inclinations of a blind girl?

As I continued my search for her, it came to light that on the same night that Rajani had disappeared, Hiralal too had vanished. Everyone said she had eloped with Hiralal. Consequently, I came to the conclusion that Hiralal had betrayed Rajani into eloping with him. Rajani is exceedingly beautiful. Albeit blind, there isn't a man around who wouldn't be taken up by her beauty. Hiralal must have fallen for her looks and cheated her into running away. It is obviously very easy to deceive the blind.

A few days later Hiralal turned up. I asked him, 'Do you have any news of Rajani?'

'No,' he said.

What could I do? Complaints and entreaties were useless. I asked my elder brother for advise; he said, 'Beat up the rascal.' But how would that help? I began to advertise in the newspapers and announced a reward for anyone bringing news of Rajani. But it yielded no results.

2

RAJANI WAS BORN BLIND. BUT HER EYES GAVE THE LIE TO THAT FACT. VISIBLY, there was nothing wrong with her. Her eyes were blue, almond-shaped with irises as dark as the bee. Very pretty eyes—but lifeless. She was blind through the fault of optic nerves. The passivity of the nerves had rendered mute the image-signals from her retina to her brain. Rajani was undoubtedly beautiful. Her complexion was fair as the golden hued, brand new banana leaf, her form as complete as the river after the rains, her visage solemn, her pace, her movements, all gentle, calm and due to her blindness, always hesitant; her smile was wan. Sometimes, the sight of those sightless eyes lodged in this matured, beautiful form brought to mind the stone statue of a woman sculpted with great care by a skilful sculptor.

The moment I set my eyes on Rajani I had felt that though attractive, her beauty wasn't addictive. Rajani was eye-catching, but her beauty would never drive someone mad. She lacked a sparkle in her eyes. People would praise her beauty, perhaps wouldn't even forget it in a hurry. That still, sombre form did have a fascinating quality. But that fascination was different—not sensual in any way. Rajani's beauty had nothing to do with Cupid's arrows. Or did it?

Whatever be it—I did often wonder what would happen to Rajani. She was born to a low-caste family. But she didn't appear to have a single lowly thought in her head. She could only be married to someone of her class. But even that had not happened till date. The poor man's wife was meant to work in the house. If her blindness came in the way of housework, which poor man would want to marry her? But if it weren't for an indigent man, who would marry this girl who worked for a living? To cap it all, she was blind too. Even with such a husband, Rajani's life too would be a living hell. Just like a tender blossom blooming amidst the thorny bushes, Rajani was born into this flower-seller's home. She would die her death amidst the thorns. Why then was I so eager to get her married to Gopal? I am not sure. But Chhoto-ma was very insistent; it was her perseverance that had urged me to arrange this match.

Besides, how shall I say this—if I couldn't marry someone myself, I at least wanted to get her married.

At this, many a beauty may smile sweetly and say, 'Do you have any secret longings to marry Rajani yourself?' No, that I don't. She may be beautiful, but she is also blind. Rajani is the daughter of a flower-seller and she is illiterate. I cannot marry Rajani and neither do I wish to. I am not averse to marriage—but I haven't yet found the girl of my dreams. The woman I shall marry must be as attractive as Rajani and also the proud owner of lightning glances; by birth she should be of royal or very prestigious stock; in erudition, she should be Goddess Saraswati doing her penance on earth; her chastity should be as legendary as Savitri's; in grace, she should be the equal of Lakshmi; her culinary skills should match those of Draupadi's; her hospitality should be as cordial as Satyabhama's and in housework she would have to be as skilled as Gada's mother! When I wanted my betel leaf, she'd take the clove out of it, when I wanted to smoke the hookah, she'd warn me if there was no tobacco in it, when I ate my fish, she'd pick out the bones for me and when I had my bath she'd check if I had dried myself properly. She'd keep a lookout so that I didn't stir my inkpot with a spoon while drinking tea, or dip my pen into the teacup. She'd rebuke me gently so that I didn't leave my wallet in the spittoon and spit in the drawer instead. If I wrote a letter to my friend and addressed it to myself, she'd correct me as she would if I handed over notes instead of coins and while joking, if I named my pious neighbour instead of my in-law she would point it out immediately. She would always be on her toes so that I didn't drink castor oil instead of the tonic, or called out the name of a colleague's wife instead of the maid's. If I find such a girl, I'd marry her like a shot. Why are you all giggling and winking at one another? If there is among you, a girl who is the holder of all these virtues, please let me know—I shall send for the priest.

3

EVENTUALLY, RAJCHANDRA DAS INFORMED US THAT RAJANI HAD BEEN FOUND. But his behaviour with us thereafter was very strange indeed. He didn't tell us a word of where and how Rajani was found. We asked him repeatedly, but he refused to divulge any information. We asked after the reason for her leaving home, and he was silent on that too. His wife was the same. Chhoto-ma usually entered into people's minds like a needle. But she, too, could get nothing out of Rajani's mother. Rajani herself had stopped visiting our house. As to the reason for her behaviour, we were in the dark. Gradually, Rajchandra and his wife too stopped coming to our house. Chhoto-ma was a little upset at their withdrawal from our lives and she sent people to their house. They came back to say that they had all moved from their home, without leaving a forwarding address.

A month later, a gentleman came to see me. He introduced himself saying, 'I am not from Calcutta. My name is Amarnath Ghosh and I live in Shantipur.'

I soon got talking with him but I could not suddenly ask him why he had come. He too did not volunteer the information. Hence, we began to discuss social and political subjects. From his talk and manner, I came to the opinion that he was quite sensible in his thoughts, well rounded in his knowledge and far-sighted in his vision. When there was a lull in the conversation, he began to turn the pages of the Shakespeare volume on my desk.

In the meantime, I began to study Amarnath. He was handsome, fair, a little short, neither fat nor thin, with large eyes and thin hair that lay in well-arranged waves; his clothes and habit were not overly ostentatious, but neat and clean. His manner of speech was very pleasant and his voice was very sweet. I also realized this was a very shrewd man.

Once he finished turning the pages of Shakespeare's work, he began to discuss the illustrations in the book instead of stating his business. He argued that whatever has been expressed by words and action, can never be truly replicated in imagery. Illustrations would never give the whole sense and hence they were quite incomplete. He pointed to Desdemona's picture and said, 'In this drawing you can see patience, sweetness and humility. But where is that courage, that pride in her chastity?' He pointed to Juliet and said, 'This may be the drawing of a youthful girl, but do you see here in this picture that playful impatience of Juliet that characterizes her youth?'

Thus he continued to speak; from Shakespeare's heroines we moved on to Shakuntala, Sita, Kadambari, Basavadatta, Rukmini and Satyabhama. Amarnath analysed each of these characters in turn. From ancient literature, we wandered into the arena of ancient history and thereof came some penetrating analysis of Tacitus, Plutarch, Thucydides, etc. From his discussion of Comte, we came to his critics Mill and Huxley; from Huxley to Owen and Darwin and from Darwin to Buchnaire, Schopenhauer, etc., they all came to be discussed. Amarnath's amazing erudition fell upon my ears like music, and wonderstruck, I forgot to ask him the real question—the purpose of his visit.

When it was late in the day, Amarnath said, 'I shall not keep you any longer. I am yet to state the purpose of my visit. Rajchandra Das, the man who sold flowers in your house, has a daughter.'

I said, 'Probably he does.'

Amarnath smiled a little and said, 'Not probably, he does. I have decided to marry her.'

I was surprised. Amarnath spoke on, 'I had gone to Rajchandra to place this proposal before him. I have done that. At this moment, I have something to discuss with you as well. This topic should perhaps be broached to your father, because he is the master. But what I have to say may be a cause of your ire. You are the most composed and judicious of the lot and so I am telling you all.'

'What is it, sir?' I asked.

Amarnath said, 'Rajani owns some property.'

'Really? But isn't she Rajchandra's daughter?'

'She is his adopted daughter,' replied Amarnath.

'But then, whose daughter is she?' I asked. 'And how did she come upon the property? Why didn't we hear of it before?'

'The inheritance that you are enjoying happens to be Rajani's. She is the daughter of Manohar Das's brother.'

For an instant I was shocked. Then I realized I had walked into the trap of a conman, a cheat. I laughed out loud and said, 'You, sir, appear to have nothing to do. I, on the other hand, am a busy man. At this moment, I do not have the time to play games with you. Please go home.'

Amarnath said, 'In that case you will hear it all from the lawyers.'

4

MEANWHILE, BISHNURAM WHO WAS THE EXECUTOR OF MANOHAR DAS'S WILL sent word to us that Manohar Das's successor had appeared and that we would have to give up the inheritance. So then, it seemed as if Amarnath was not a cheat after all.

At first, Bishnuram Babu did not state who the successor was. But I remembered Amarnath's words. Perhaps Rajani was the one. I went to Bishnuram Babu to ascertain whether he had any proof that the person who claimed to be the successor was in fact the genuine inheritor. I said, 'Sir, you had said earlier that Manohar Das had drowned in the river with his entire family and you have proof of that. So where is the successor coming from now?'

Bishnuram Babu said, 'Perhaps you know, he had a brother called Harekrishna Das?'

'Yes, I know that, but he too is dead, isn't he?' I asked.

'Certainly, but after Manohar's death. Therefore, he died after he became a successor to the property.'

'That's fine, but Harekrishna also wasn't survived by anyone, was he?'

Bishnuram said, 'That's what I thought at first and I let the property go to you. But now I have come to know that he had a daughter.'

'Why then was there no mention of this daughter in all these days?'

'Harekrishna's wife died before him. Unable to raise his infant daughter, Harekrishna gave her away to his wife's sister, who raised the child as her own and calls her as such. After Harekrishna's death, his body was declared to be unclaimed and his belongings obtained by the magistrate and so I assumed he was survived by no one. But as of now, a neighbour of Harekrishna has presented himself to me and made me aware that he had a daughter. I have conducted the necessary investigations and come to the conclusion that what he said is indeed true.'

'Any shrewd and clever man can catch hold of any girl and present her as Harekrishna Das's daughter. Is there any proof that she is indeed the one?' I said, still unconvinced of the matter.

'Yes, there is,' said Bishnuram.

He handed me a piece of paper and said, 'Each and every verification attained in the course of these investigations has been noted on this paper.' I took the paper and began to read it. I came to know from it that Harekrishna Das's wife's sister was married to Rajchandra Das and Rajani was Harekrishna's daughter.

The proof before my eyes was indeed conclusive. For so many years we had been enjoying the wealth that belonged to the blind Rajani, all the while pitying her and looking down upon her.

Bishnuram handed me a true copy of a testimony and said, 'Now take a look and tell me whose testimony is this?'

I read it. It was a testimony by Harekrishna Das given before the magistrate, a testimony concerning a case of some stolen bangles. In the testimony, Harekrishna's name and address was also mentioned. It was the same as that of Manohar Das's father. Bishnuram asked me, 'Do you not agree that this is a testimony given by Manohar Das's brother Harekrishna Das?'

I said, 'Yes, I do.'

Bishnuram said, 'If you have any doubts, they'll be dispelled in an instant. Continue to read.'

I read on. It said, 'I have a six-month-old daughter. A week ago, I celebrated her annaprasan, and on the same evening her gold bangles were stolen.'

At this point, Bishnuram said, 'Just check how long ago this testimony was made.'

I glanced at the date—it was nineteen years ago.

Bishnuram said, 'In that case how old would that girl be now?'

'Nineteen years and a few months—almost twenty,' I replied.

'How old is Rajani?' asked Bishnuram.

'Almost twenty.'

'Go on reading. A little later, Harekrishna mentions his daughter's name.'

I read on. At one point, after getting back the stolen bangles, Harekrishna clarified, 'These belong to my daughter Rajani indeed.'

There wasn't much room for doubt. Still, I read on. The defendant's lawyer was asking Harekrishna, 'You are a poor man—how did you give your daughter gold bangles?'

Harekrishna replied, 'I may be poor, but my brother Manohar Das earns ten rupees a month and he has gifted these bangles to my daughter.'

So now all doubts were dispelled about the relationship between Manohar and Harekrishna Das.

The lawyer had further asked, 'Has your brother ever given you or any member of your family any jewellery before?'

The answer was 'no'.

The lawyer continued to question Harekrishna, 'Does he contribute to the household expenses?'

'No,' answered Harekrishna.

'So, why is he giving gold ornaments to your daughter for her annaprasan?'

Harekrishna said, 'My daughter is congenitally blind. My wife always weeps for that reason. My brother and his wife took pity on us, and wishing to alleviate our sorrow somewhat, they gifted these ornaments to my daughter.'

Blind at birth! Then there was no doubt at all that this was the same Rajani.

I handed back the testimony with an air of dejection and said, 'I have no more doubts.'

Bishnuram said, 'I do not ask you to be content with such little proof. Take a look at the copy of another testimony.'

The second testimony was also regarding the case of the stolen bangles. Here the speaker was Rajchandra Das. He was the only living relative of Harekrishna Das and hence he was present at the annaprasan. In his testimony, he declared himself to be a relative of Harekrishna and detailed everything as a witness to the theft.

Bishnuram now told me, 'The present Rajchandra is the same as this one. If you are in doubt we can send for him and ask him.'

'No need,' I said.

Bishnuram showed me a few more documents, the details of which would bore most of my readers. It is suffice to say that I was left in no doubt that this Rajani Das was the daughter of Harekrishna Das. I also realized that with ageing parents, I would now be hard put to earn a living!

I said to Bishnuram, 'Contesting this would be pointless. The inheritance belongs to Rajani and we shall give it back to her. But my elder brother has an equal share in all that I own. I need to consult with him first.'

I dropped in at the courts and took a look at the original testimonies. Nowadays they tear up the old documents, but earlier they used to preserve them. I discovered that there was no difference between the original and their copies.

We gave up our inheritance to Rajani.

5

WE GAVE IT UP TO RAJANI, BUT NOBODY CAME UP TO CLAIM IT.

Rajchandra Das came to meet us one day. He said that he had purchased a house in Shimla and he was now living there with his wife and Rajani. I asked him where he got the money to buy a house from. He said that Amarnath had given it as a loan, to be recovered later from the inheritance. I asked him the reason for which they had not claimed the property. He replied, 'All those things are known to Amarnath Babu.' Was Amarnath Babu now married to Rajani? Rajchandra said, 'No.' As our conversation meandered along I asked, 'Rajchandra, why were you not to be seen for some time?'

He said, 'I was lying low for some time.'

'What have you stolen and from whom, that you needed to lie low?'

'Why would I steal?' asked Rajchandra, 'But Amarnath Babu had said that since the property was being fought over at this point, I should lie low. After all, we all have our pride and considerations.'

'Meaning, in case we requested you to let some of it go—well, Amarnath Babu is indeed a wise man. So, why have you surfaced now?'

Rajchandra said, 'Your father has sent for me.'

'My father? How did he know where to find you?' I asked in surprise.

'Oh, he searched and searched.'

'Why was all this searching needed? Is it because he wants you to share the inheritance?'

Rajchandra said, 'No, no, oh no, why should that be the case? It is about something else. Now that Rajani has some assets to her name, we are getting offers from everywhere. I have come to seek your advice on where to get her married.'

'Why, the wedding was fixed with Amarnath Babu, wasn't it? He went to such lengths to rescue Rajani's inheritance, who else is more deserving of her hand?' I said.

Rajchandra said, 'What if there's a better groom?'

'Where would you find a better choice than Amarnath?'

'Perhaps, someone like you—if I get you as a possible match?'

I was taken aback. I said, 'I wouldn't be a better choice than Amarnath. But, let the clichés be—have you come here to suggest an alliance between Rajani and me?'

Rajchandra was a little embarrassed, 'Yes, that's right. Your father has sent for me to discuss this very matter.'

I felt as if I was being hurled from the sky as I realized Father had been impelled to make this match because the sight of the demon called poverty, awaiting around the corner, had scared him badly. If I married Rajani, the inheritance would stay within the family. By selling me to the blind flower girl, my father would reacquire the inheritance that had slipped out of his reach. I felt mortally offended.

I said to Rajchandra, 'You go on home now; I shall speak to Father about this.'

Seeing my agitated state, Rajchandra went to Father. I do not know what transpired between them. After sending him on his way, Father called me. He begged and pleaded with me—I must marry Rajani. Or else, we would all die of hunger—what would we eat? But his sorrow and piteous state did not melt my heart. I was only angered all the more and I walked away.

From my father's hands, I fell into Mother's. I could show my temper to my father, but not to my mother. Her tears drove me to misery. I ran away from her too. But my vow was firm—how could I now marry the same Rajani who I had arranged for Gopal to marry, that too, just because she had come into some money?

In my time of need I remembered Chhoto-ma, and sought refuge with her. She was the brightest in the house and I went to her with some hope.

'Chhoto-ma, do I have to marry Rajani? What is my crime?'

She was silent.

'Are you of the same opinion, then?'

'My child, Rajani is of good Kayastha stock, isn't she?' asked Chhoto-ma, the implication of her question being quite clear.

'So what?' I asked stubbornly.

'I know she is virtuous.'

'I have no doubts about that,' I said.

'Rajani is also very beautiful.'

'Lotus-eyes!' I muttered, more to myself.

Chhoto-ma pounced on what I let slip. 'My child, if you really want lotus-eyes, what's to stop you from marrying again?'

'What is this, Mother! Would you have me marry Rajani for her money, take her inheritance from her and then push her away to bring in someone else?' I asked.

'But why would you push her away? Is your mother pushed away?' she countered.

I could not bring myself to answer this question in Chhoto-ma's presence. She was my father's second wife and I could not discuss the pitfalls of polygamy in front of her. I avoided the question and said, 'I cannot go through this marriage—please save me! You can do everything.'

'It is not that I do not understand. I know all about it. But if you do not marry her, we will all die of hunger. I can take any hardship, but I cannot watch you all going hungry. May you live a hundred years, but you have to agree to this match,' she said with an air of finality.

'Is money so important?' I asked, not willing to give in.

'Perhaps not to you and me, but certainly to them who mean everything to us; and consequently also to us. Look here, for you the three of us can give up our lives. And for our sake, could you not marry a blind girl?'

And with that I lost the debate with Chhoto-ma. This only made me angrier. I knew in my heart of hearts that it was wrong to marry Rajani for the sake of money. So I declared proudly, 'Whatever you all say, I shall never go through with this marriage.'

Chhoto-ma wasn't one to accept defeat, 'Whatever you claim, if I am born to a Kayastha household, I shall see to it that this marriage happens.'

I laughed, 'Then you must be low born because this you will not succeed in.'

She said, 'No, my child, I am definitely high born.'

Chhoto-ma was very smart; by calling me her child she turned the table on me.

6

A SANYASI USED TO COME AND STAY IN OUR HOME EVERY NOW AND THEN. Some called him a hermit, some a saint. He wore saffron robes and had rudraksh-beads around his throat, his hair was unkempt but not matted, and on his forehead was a tiny dot of red sandal-paste. He was not very keen on getting rough and muddied—within the hermit clan he seemed a bit fashion-conscious. His sandals were made of sandalwood and ivory. Whatever he may be, he was called the sanyasi by the children and that's what I shall call him too.

Father had once brought him from somewhere. I guessed Father believed the saint to possess some tantric powers and have knowledge of ancient medications—these powers were to be of some use as my stepmother was childless.

My father's largesse had led to the sanyasi occupying a roomy quarter upstairs. This was a source of irritation for me. Moreover, at dusk, the sanyasi would look to the setting sun and chant the stotras in Sarang ragini. I could barely tolerate the hypocrite. I went to him one day with every intention of exposing him for what he was. I said, 'Revered sanyasi, what nonsense were you muttering on the terrace?'

The sanyasi was from northern India. But the language in which he spoke to us was nine-tenths Sanskrit and the rest a mixture of Hindi and Bengali. He replied, 'Why, don't you know what I mutter?'

I asked, 'Ved-mantras?'

'Could be,' he said vaguely.

'What's the use of chanting them?' I asked.

'Nothing,' he replied.

The answers won him the first round—I had not expected this. I asked him, 'Why then do you utter them?'

'Is it painful to your ears?'

I admitted, 'Not really, especially from your mellow voice. But if it yields no results, why would you do it?'

'If it doesn't harm anybody, what is wrong with doing it?'

I had come to make a statement, but I realized that I was pushed back a little. So I had to go on the attack. I said, 'No harm indeed, but no one does anything needlessly; if the Ved-mantras are pointless, why do you chant them?'

He said, 'You are a learned man. Tell me, why does the koel sing upon the branches?'

I was in a fix. There were two answers: one, 'Therein lies the koel's pleasure,' and two, 'In order to mate with the female koel.' Which one should I say? I chose the first, 'It pleases the koel to sing.'

'It pleases me to sing,' he said simply.

'But why Ved-mantras when there are more challenging forms of music, like tappa, thumri, etc. available?'

'Which words bring the greater joy—the description of prostitutes and their nature or that of gods and their deeds?' he asked casually.

Beaten, I chose the second answer and said, 'The koel sings to impress his mate. There's a tangible pleasure in the act,which brings joy to the living being. The pleasure of the voice is related to that tangible pleasure. Who are you trying to impress?'

The hermit laughed, 'My own heart. The heart is not a lover or benefactor of the soul. I sing to hold sway over my mind.'

I argued, 'You philosophers consider the heart and the soul to be separate entities. But I cannot agree with it. It is the heart and its work that I witness—wishes, proclivities, sorrows and pleasure are all in my heart. Why then should I take the soul to be larger or transcending the bounds of this heart? I shall accept whatever I can see or feel.'

'Then you may as well say that the heart and the body are one,' said the sanyasi. 'Why should I take them to be different? All the work that you see—is all done by the body, where is the heart?'

'Thinking, inclination and sensory acts are all born out of the heart,' I replied.

'How can you tell those are not done by the body?'

'True enough. The heart can be a function of the brain,' I conceded.

'Good, good, come a bit further, then,' he said. 'Why don't you say that the body is also a mere extension of the five elements? I have heard that many young people like you are believers of multiple elements; fair enough, why don't you take the body to be an extension of these various elements? The very fact that you are talking to me now can be taken as some of these elements speaking to me instead of Sachindra alone. Why imagine there to be a body or a heart? Outside the elements, I do not accept the existence of a Sachindra.'

Totally defeated, I folded my hands respectfully and left the sanyasi alone. But since then I grew a little more tolerant of him. Often I went and sat with him and discussed philosophy. I noticed that he indulged in many kinds of charades. He gave away medicines, he did some palmistry and sometimes he even conducted a prayer by the sacred fire; he read the moving iron rods, caught thieves by prediction and had so many other pretences. One day I could take it no longer and said, 'You are a greatly learned man. Why do you perform these charades?'

'Which charades?' he asked.

'All this—the rods, palmistry, etc.'

'Some of these are a bit vague, but nevertheless a duty,' he admitted.

'When you know it is ambiguous, why do you cheat people?'

'Why do you dissect corpses?' he countered.

'To learn.'

'Even after your learning is done, why do you do it?' he persisted.

'For investigation.'

'That is precisely why we do it too. I have heard many Western scientists claim that the structure of a man's skull can say a lot about his character. If the skull can reveal so much, why can't the lines on one's palm? I accept that till date no one has been able to predict the future very accurately from the lines on a palm alone. But that could be because we are yet to discover the precise code for this science and gradually perhaps, with repeated performances, the code will probably be perfected? That's why I look at the palm whenever one is offered to me.'

'What about the iron rods? I asked.

'You pass messages all over the world through iron rods, and we move them to tell us something! You all have one problem, you believe that whatever the English know is true and whatever they don't know is untrue, that it is beyond human information and it is impossible. That is not true. Knowledge is infinite. Some I know, some you know and some others know, but no one can claim that they know everything and nobody else knows more. Some knowledge the English have, some our ancestors had. What the English know, the saints of yore did not and what the saints knew the English still don't know. Those ancient arts and skills are now extinct. Some of us know one or two that we keep hidden—we do not reveal it or teach it to anyone.'

I laughed. The sanyasi said, 'You do not believe me—would you like some proof?'

I said, 'That may help.'

'I'll show you later,' he said. 'Right now I have an important matter to discuss with you. Since I have come close to you, your father has asked me to motivate you to get married.'

I laughed and said, 'There's no motivation needed, I am ready for marriage. But—'

'But what?' asked the sanyasi.

'Where's the girl? There is a blind girl, but I won't marry her.'

'Is there no bride worthy of you in all of Bengal?'

'There must be thousands. But how shall I choose? How would I know, which one of these hundreds and thousands of girls, would love me all her life?'

'I do know one arcane art,' he divulged. 'If there is someone on this earth who loves you to death, you can see her in your dreams. But as to someone who doesn't love you right now, but will do so in future, I am powerless to reveal that.'

I scoffed at him. 'This is not a great skill. Most naturally, everyone always knows who loves them.'

'Really? The hidden love is the most common of all. Do you know who loves you?'

'I do not know of anyone special besides my family.'

'You wanted some proof of my skills—why don't you try this today?'

'Why not?' I agreed with some interest.

'Call me when you are about to sleep.'

My bedroom was in the outer sections of the house. I called for the sanyasi before my bedtime. He came in and asked me to lie down. Then he said, 'As long as I am here, do not open your eyes. After I leave, if you are still awake, you may look.'

So I closed my eyes. I do not know what tricks he played, but I was fast asleep before he left the room.

The hermit had said that I would dream of the one person who love me to death. I did dream of her. The Ganga was flowing rapidly and at one end of her banks, half immersed in water—who was that? *Rajani*.

The next morning the sanyasi asked me, 'Who did you dream of ?'

'The blind flower girl,' I answered.

'Blind?'

'From birth,' I clarified.

'Strange! But whatever it is, she is the one who loves you the most in this world.'

I was silent.

Part IV

Everyone

1
Labangalata

WHAT A FIX! HERE I AM TRYING MY BEST, BEGGING AND PLEADING WITH THE sage, to get him to make Sachindra fall in love with Rajani. He has great powers; with the Mother's blessings, he can do whatever he sets his mind to. The fact that my husband, at his age of sixty plus, is still so in awe of me is perhaps more to the hermit's credit than to mine. I leave no stone unturned in serving my husband and the sage takes the same care to keep up the sacrificial fires and the mantras. Whatever he has tried to do for anyone, has always happened. He turned the blacksmith woman's bronze basket into a gold one. There is nothing that is beyond him. I have no doubt that with his efforts, Sachindra would fall in love with Rajani and wish to marry her. But still there was a hitch and that concerned Amarnath. Now I have come to know that Rajani's marriage is fixed with Amarnath.

Rajani's uncle and aunt, Rajchandra and his wife, were initially on our side. That is because my husband had promised them the matchmaker's fees if the marriage materialized. That was a mere euphimism, hinting at a large sum of money. But it was all in vain. For, Amarnath wouldn't let go. He was determined to marry Rajani.

Just great! Who was Amarnath? The decision rested after all, on the bride's guardians—Rajchandra and his wife. If they were on our side, what did Amarnath's persistence matter? He may have retrieved the inheritance for them, but for that he could be paid a generous sum of money and sent on his way. How dared he get in the way of the girl whom I had decided to bring home as a bride for my son? This was too much! At one point of time

I had taught Amarnath a lesson—perhaps it was now time for more. I vowed to myself that if I was born to a Kayastha, I would succeed in snatching Rajani away from Amarnath and marrying her to my son.

I knew all about Amarnath. He was very cunning. A war with him meant extreme caution on all sides. I took every precaution and set to work.

First I sent for Rajchandra's wife, the gardener's wife (that's what we still called her, more when we were angry than when we were not). She came and asked, 'What is it?'

I said, 'I believe you are getting your daughter married to Amar Babu?'

'That's how it seems now,' she replied.

'But why? What did we all decide?' I demanded of her.

'What can I do, ma'am; I am just a woman, what do I know?'

The woman's thickheadedness made me so angry. I said, 'What is this, gardener's wife? If we women don't know about it, who does—the men? What do they know of relationships and marriages? They are only good for earning the money and bringing it home. What do they know of the real action?'

The dull-witted woman must have found my words offensive; she smiled a little. I said, 'What does your husband say—does he want Amarnath as the groom?'

She said, 'No, he doesn't. But Amarnath Babu has retrieved Rajani's inheritance. It is only fair to abide by his wishes.'

I had to try another line of attack. 'Then you go and tell Amarnath Babu that Rajani has not yet got hold of her inheritance. It belongs to us and we shall not leave it. If you can, you fight us in court and take it!'

'You could have said this earlier. By now the court order would have come.'

'A court case is not a simple matter; it costs money. How much has Rajchandra Das earned from selling flowers?' I asked, determined to win the argument.

The gardener's wife began to rumble in fury. To tell you the truth, I wasn't a bit angry. She controlled her temper somewhat and said, 'If Amar

Babu becomes my son-in-law, he will get the entire inheritance; he will then have the power to finance a court case.'

She was about to get up and leave. I pulled her sari and held her back. She sat back again. I said, 'What do you stand to gain if Amar Babu fights the case and takes the money?'

'My daughter will be happy.'

'And will she be unhappy if she marries my son?' I retorted.

'No, not at all. But wherever she is, my daughter should be happy.'

'And you? Don't you want to be happy?'

'My daughter's happiness is all I want,' she stated.

'And the matchmaker's fees?'

The gardener's wife gave a sly smile. She said, 'Shall I tell the truth, milady? My daughter doesn't want to marry here.'

'What! What does she say?'

'Whenever the subject of this household comes up, she says why bother with a blind girl's marriage?'

This was news to me. 'And whenever Amarnath is mentioned?'

'Then she says, in his hands rests my life. I have to do his bidding.'

'Well, what does it matter what the bride says? It is the parents' opinion that counts.'

'Rajani is not a little girl and neither is she born to me. Besides, the inheritance is hers. If she sends us packing, what can we do? On the contrary, these days we are doing her bidding mostly,' she argued.

I gave it some thought and asked, 'Does Rajani meet Amarnath often?'

She said, 'No. He doesn't see her.'

'May I meet with Rajani once?' I requested of her.

'That is what I want too,' she said. 'If you could coax and convince her it would help—she really holds you in high esteem.'

'Well, I could try. But how can I see her? Could you send her over here tomorrow?'

'Why not, she has almost grown up in this house. But when a girl's match is being talked of, it doesn't look good for her to come to the same house at any odd hour of the day before the wedding.'

Oh damn! More work for me! With no other option left to me, I said, 'Fine, if Rajani cannot come, could I come to your house once?'

In disbelief she cried, 'Oh my Lord, can we really have the good fortune of your hand knocking on our humble door?'

'If the marriage happens, many other hands will come a-knocking. Why don't you extend the invitation to me today?'

Rajani's mother seemed to find my eagerness to visit them a bit far-fetched, for she asked dubiously, 'But will the master agree to sending you to our home?'

'What does he have to do with it? The woman's word is always the man's word, too.'

The gardener's wife invited me with folded hands and went away laughing.

2
Amarnath

PERHAPS MANY OF YOU ARE SURPRISED TO HEAR THAT IN SPITE OF ALL MY efforts to retrieve Rajani's inheritance, and in spite of the Mitras letting go of it without a struggle, it had not yet been claimed. I too was in the same boat. The property was not mine and I was not the one to claim it. It belonged to Rajani and if she did not claim it, no one could say anything. But she seemed totally averse to claiming it for herself. She kept postponing it by a day here, a day there and many other excuses. Far from claiming it, I was now trying to fathom why a poor woman would have so little interest in riches. Rajchandra and his wife too had entreated Rajani to this end, but she seemed most reluctant to claim what was rightfully hers. What was the sense in this? Why then had I laboured so hard?

I went to see her, with the intention of thrashing things through to an end. Ever since the topic of my marriage to her had been broached, I had avoided going to see her, because these days she was very shy in my presence. But today it was imperative that I talked to her, so I went to meet her. The doors of that house were always open to me. I went looking for Rajani, but didn't find her in her room. I was on my way back when I saw Rajani coming upstairs with another woman in tow. I could recognize the other woman instantly—I hadn't seen her for some years, but I knew immediately, that indolent walk belonged to none other than Labangalata.

Rajani had dressed in rags on purpose I think and she wasn't talking properly to Labanga, perhaps out of embarrassment. But Labanga was laughing and bubbling with delight; her face bore no trace of ire or irritation.

I hadn't heard this laughter for many years. It was the same as ever—like the tiny waves on a full-moon ocean, like the sway of a spring creeper in blossom, dripping with exhilaration.

I stood in stunned surprise, with a wildly beating heart, analysing the mental faculties of this unconventional woman. Labangalata was so hard to understand. She had fallen from immense riches to instant penury—yet the same delighted smile; she was stepping into Rajani's house, conversing with that same woman who had brought about this state in her own life and yet—the delighted smile. I stood right before her, and yet—the delighted smile! But I knew for a fact that Labanga had not forgotten a single thing.

I stepped into the next room. Labanga followed suit. Without a stroke of hesitation, like a commanding queen, she said, 'Rajani, go away for some time, I need to speak to your groom. Don't worry, he may be handsome, but my old husband still beats him hollow.' Rajani looked embarrassed as she strolled away unmindfully.

Labangalata crinkled her brows, donned the same sweet smile and took up position in front of me like the queen of all she surveyed. Except for that one instance long ago, no one had ever seen Amarnath bemused, lost for words. But now, once again, I forgot myself. Then too it was Lalitlabangalata, now too, it was Lalitlabangalata.

Labanga smiled and said, 'Why are you staring at my face? To gauge whether I have come to seize your acquired wealth? I could do that if I so desired.'

I said, 'You can do many things, but not that. If you could, you wouldn't have given away your wealth to Rajani and then cooked for your husband's first wife every day with your own hands.'

Labanga laughed aloud in glee, 'Do you think that will pinch me? It is truly bothersome to have to cook for my husband's other wife; but if I call the guards and hand you over to them now, I could once again employ five cooks.'

I said, 'The property belongs to Rajani. What's the use of getting rid of me? The owner of the inheritance will continue to enjoy it.'

Labanga said cunningly, 'You have never really understood women. If they love someone, they'd give away their last cent to protect him.'

'Meaning in order to save me, she'd bribe you with the property?'

'Exactly,' replied Labanga.

'So all these days you haven't claimed that bribe because we weren't married? And the moment we are, you'll come and stake your claim?' I asked incredulously.

'How would a lowly vermin such as you ever know how we work? Thieves like you wouldn't know that it's a sin to keep what belongs to another. Even if I could, why would I keep Rajani's inheritance?'

I said, 'If you were not like this, why would I have had such a bad idea at the time? If you have forgiven me so much, then I have one more request. If you haven't confided what you know to anyone else, then don't say it to Rajani either.'

The haughty Labanga's brows danced—what a graceful movement it was! She said, 'Am I a cheat! Have I come here to cheat the woman who is to become your wife?'

She laughed. I have never been able to make sense of her laughter. She was really quite angry. But her laughter washed her anger away. It was like the shadow of a cloud drifting away from the water's surface and the laughter glinting on it like the unadorned full moon. I have never been able to fathom Labangalata.

She smiled, 'Then let me go to Rajani.'

'Go.'

Lalitlabangalata sashayed away like a graceful creeper, true to her name. A little later she sent for me. I went and found Labangalata standing and Rajani weeping at her feet. Labanga said to me, 'Listen to what your future wife has to say—I refuse to hear such things unless you too hear them.'

Astounded, I said, 'What?'

Labangalata said to Rajani, 'Go on, say it; your husband is here—'

Rajani's eyes were swimming with tears as she touched Labanga's feet and pleaded, 'I have just one request. All that I have acquired through the efforts of this gentleman here, I'd like to hand over to you with proper legal documents. Will you please do me the favour of accepting it?'

Delight coursed through my entire being. I felt all my efforts, all the sacrifices I made on Rajani's behalf were truly successful. I knew at the very outset, and now it was even more obvious, that amongst women on this earth the blind Rajani was a priceless gem. Even Labangalata's scorching lustre was put to shame. I had, in the meantime, drowned myself in the sightless eyes of this woman—today I became her slave for free. I would illuminate my dark abode with this dazzling jewel and live my life in great joy. Would the gods allow me that fate?

3
Labangalata

I HAD ENVISAGED AMARNATH HEARING RAJANI'S WORDS AND WITHERING like a banana leaf held over the fire. But no, that didn't happen. His face, instead of wilting, actually grew more cheerful. Stunned and astonished, whatever be it, was only my expression.

At first I took it for a joke. But Rajani's insistence, tears and firmness finally convinced me that she was sincere. I said, 'Rajani, you are indeed unique, there's no one like you. But I cannot take your donation.'

Rajani said, 'If you refuse, I shall give it away to charity.'

'What about Amarnath Babu?' I asked.

'Perhaps you do not know him very well. Even if I were to give it to him, he will not take it.'

'What do you say, Amarnath Babu?' I asked, hoping that he would refuse to marry Rajani in the event of the property slipping out of his reach.

'I am not a part of this conversation, what can I say?' he asked me in return.

I was in a fix. Rajani's eagerness to give away the inheritance was indeed surprising. But it was even more shocking that Amarnath, who had gone to such lengths to retrieve this property, for the lure of which he was even prepared to marry Rajani, was actually quite happy to see it whisked away and given to someone else. What was the matter here?

I asked Amarnath to leave so that I could have a heart to heart talk with Rajani. He left instantly. Then I asked Rajani, 'Do you really want to give away the wealth?'

'Absolutely. I can swear by the sacred waters of the Ganga.'

'I can take your charity if you take some of mine.'

'I have taken enough,' she said.

'You have to take some more.'

'You may give me a sari as a token,' said Rajani with some reluctance.

'Not that. You have to take whatever I give you.'

'And what is that?'

Here was my chance. 'I have a son called Sachindra. I shall give him away to you. You must take him as your husband. If you accept him, I shall accept your wealth.'

Rajani had been standing, but she sat down slowly and closed her sightless eyes. Then she began to weep silent tears, unending—they streamed down without a pause. I was in a real quandary. Rajani was silent, and weeping. I asked, 'Why do you weep thus?'

Rajani spoke through her tears, 'That day, beside the Ganga, I had tried to drown myself. I did succeed, but people dragged me out. It was all for Sachindra. If you said to me, you are blind, I shall grant you sight, I'd have refused it and asked for Sachindra instead. I know nothing beyond him on this earth—my life is at his feet like the flowers at the feet of the idol of God. If I get a place at his feet, my life would be complete. Will you listen to this blind girl's tale of misery?'

I was moved by her grief and said, 'I will.'

Then Rajani unburdened her heart even as she wept; she told me all. Sachindra's voice, Sachindra's touch, the blind girl's desire, her escape, the drowning, her rescue—everything. Finally she said, 'Ma'am, you are blessed with sight. Is it possible for those with eyes to adore so passionately?'

To myself I murmured, 'Ye blind one—what do you know of love's hunger? You are a hundred times happier than Labangalata!' But overtly I said, 'No, Rajani, my husband is an old man and I do not know these things. So it is decided that you will marry Sachindra?'

She replied, 'No.'

I was astounded. 'What? Then what were you saying all this while, why did you weep so hard?'

'I wept because fate has denied me these pleasures.'

'But why? I shall give you away.'

But Rajani didn't find it as simple as that. 'You will fail. Amarnath has done everything for me. What he has done to retrieve my inheritance is something no one would ever do for a stranger. Even if I discount that, he has saved my life at his own risk.'

Rajani then narrated that incident to me and said, 'I shall abide by whatever he says since I am thus indebted to him. Since he has had a wish to place me at his feet, I shall serve him and no one else.'

Oh dear Lord, why did I get the hermit to cast his spell on my poor child! Even without a wedding, the property could have been recovered. Rajani was willing to hand it back anyway. But shame! How could I take Rajani's cast-offs? I'd rather beg for a living! I have declared that if I didn't make this marriage happen I am not a Kayastha woman! I shall see to it that my word is kept. I said to Rajani, 'In that case I refuse to take your charity. You may give it away wherever you wish.' I rose to leave.

Rajani said, 'Please sit down. I shall make my request once more through Amarnath Babu—let me get him.'

I too wanted one more meeting with Amarnath. So I sat down. Rajani fetched him.

Once he came in, I said to Rajani, 'If Amarnath Babu really wants to make his case, will he be able to speak freely in your presence? Why do you want to listen to your own praise?'

Rajani went away.

4

Labangalata

I ASKED AMARNATH, 'DO YOU WISH TO MARRY RAJANI?'

'Yes—it's decided,' he said.

'Is it now? Even though she is handing back her property to me?'

'I shall marry Rajani, not her inheritance,' he stated.

'But you *had* wanted to marry Rajani for her wealth, isn't it?' I asked, not to be outdone.

'Women have such vulgar minds!'

'Since when have you hated us so much?'

'Not hatred—or I wouldn't be all set to marry,' he said.

'But why have you hand-picked a blind girl? That's why I brought up the topic of inheritance,' I explained.

'Why have you hand-picked the geriatric?'

'It is not good manners to call someone's husband geriatric in her presence. Why are you picking on me? Aren't you afraid of the vile tongue of the foul-mouthed woman?'

(I did so want an argument.)

Amarnath said, 'Of course I fear it, and I haven't said anything offensive. I love Rajani just as you love Mitra Babu.'

'Is it her playful eyes?'

'It's the lack of artifice in them. You too would have been more beautiful if you were blind.'

'I shall surely put that question to my husband, not to you. Lately I too have begun to love Rajani the way you love her.'

'Do you also wish to marry her?' he asked with veiled sarcasm.

'Almost. Not personally, but I'd like to see her marry well. I shall not let her get married to you,' I asserted.

'I am a good match. Rajani is unlikely to find a better one.'

'You are a bad match. I shall find her a good one.'

'Why am I a bad match?' he asked, genuinely puzzled.

'Why don't you take off your shirt and show me your back?'

Amarnath's face crumpled as he spoke wretchedly, 'Shame, Labanga!'

I too was upset, but I didn't let his misery get to me. I said, 'Shall I tell you a story?'

He thought I was changing the subject so he agreed. 'Fine,' he said.

I began to speak, 'When I was in the bloom of youth, people found me a striking—'

Amarnath interrupted me, 'If that's fiction, what's a fact?'

'Just hear me out,' I said. 'My beauty ensnared a thief in its grip. He stole his way into the room in my father's home, where my maid and I slept.'

At this point, he broke out in a sweat and said, 'Please forgive me.'

I continued, 'The thief broke into my room. The lamp was burning and I recognized him. Scared, I woke the maid. She did not know the thief. So, I spoke to him politely and made him take a seat.'

Amarnath said, 'Forgive me, but I know all this.'

'Still, I need to refresh your memory,' I objected. 'A little later, as per my signal, the maid left the room quietly and called the watchman. They stood at the mouth of the thief's escape route. At the right moment, I too made an excuse and left by the only door to the room, locking it from without. Did I do it right?'

'Why are you repeating all this to me?'

'Can you guess how the thief finally left the room? I called everyone in the area. The stronger men seized him. The thief covered his face in shame. I took pity on him and let that pass. But I took a heated iron rod and with my own hands I branded his back with the word *thief*. Amar Babu, do you ever take off your shirt even in the worst of summer days?'

'No,' Amarnath said in misery and defeat.

'Labangalata's handwriting is hard to erase. I had every intention of narrating this story to Rajani today. But I shall desist. You are not worthy of Rajani. Do not try to marry her. If you do not cease your efforts, I shall be forced to reveal all,' I told Amarnath.

He heard me and sat in silence for some time. Finally he spoke dejectedly, 'You may do as you wish. Whatever you do I shall confess everything to Rajani today. After knowing all my flaws and virtues, she may accept or reject me—it is her choice. I shall not dupe her.'

I must say I lost this round. In my heart, I gave a million thanks to Amarnath and went back home, feeling a mixture of sorrow and joy.

5
Sachindra

SOME DAYS AFTER THE LOSS OF OUR WEALTH, I FELL ILL. I DO NOT KNOW IF it was a result of some anxiety about the sudden change of state from riches to poverty. But I can describe the symptoms to you.

When the blatant heat of the sun had mellowed in the late afternoon, I sat on the terrace reading. I had been reading all day, trying to make some sense of the most complex mysteries of our existence, but I had failed miserably. Nothing seemed to make sense, but the yearning remained. The more I read, the more I wanted to read. Eventually I grew tired. I held the book in my hands, closed my eyes and began to ruminate. I was a little drowsy. It wasn't as pleasant or gratifying as a real sleep. The book slipped from my tired hands. My eyes were open and all things visible, but if you asked me what I saw, I would not be able to tell you. Suddenly, in front of my eyes there was the restless, swirling waters of a river at dawn. It felt as if the first rays of the sun were just brightening the eastern sky. And on the banks of that Ganga stood Rajani! She was walking into the river! Slow, slow, ever so slow! Blind and yet frowning brows, disabled and yet composed, as serene and unruffled as that flowing river at dawn, yet as tumultuous and strong within as the same river. Slow, slow, ever so slow—there, she walked into the water! She was so beautiful! Like the fading fragrance of the flower dropping from the bough, like the last note of a concluding melody, Rajani was stepping into the water ever so slowly! Slow, Rajani, go slow! Let my eyes have their fill of you. Once I had not known your worth and I hadn't spared you a glance. Now, let me look to my heart's content.

I fainted. I do not remember anything after that. There is no point in repeating what I was told later. But when I regained consciousness, it was late in the night and there were many people beside me. But I did not see any of them. All I saw was that gently rumbling Ganga and that softly treading Rajani, slowly stepping into the waves. I closed my eyes—it was still the same sight. I opened my eyes again and it was still the same sight. I looked to the distant horizon, and it was again Rajani, slowly wading into the water. I looked upwards and it was that same river flowing in the heavens and Rajani treading the clouds to step into the water. I tried to think of other things, but it was all the same. I gave up. The doctors began to treat me.

My treatment continued for many days, but the visage of Rajani never left my vision for even a second. I do not know for which disease the doctors were treating me. The face that never left my eyes and her name was something I did not tell anyone.

6
Sachindra

HEY THERE, RAJANI, SLOW, GO SLOW! STEP INTO THE TEMPLE OF MY HEART ever so gently. Why do you hurry thus? You are blind, you do not know the way! This abode is constricted and dark, bleak and gloomy—forever in darkness. Please enter it like the burning wick of the lamp and illuminate it. Burn yourself away like the wick, but please light my heart.

Hey there, Rajani, slow, go slow! Light this abode, but why do you make me burn? Whoever knew that cool marble could also be set on fire? I had taken you to be carved from stone, and hard-hearted; who knew that stone could also blaze? And again, whoever knew that stone, when it caused friction to iron, could very well ignite? The more I see of your beauty, fair as marble, cool as marble and sculpted from marble, the more I wish to gaze at it. Although I look at it every second of the day, every single day, I feel as if I've hardly seen you. The craving remains just as strong.

When I was unwell, I barely spoke to anyone. If anyone came to converse to me, I didn't welcome it. I never brought Rajani's name to my lips, but I cannot say what I spoke in my delirium. It was a common enough state with me.

I hardly ever left the bed. As I lay there, the sights that defy description flashed before my eyes. Sometimes I saw the battlefield where Greeks were being slain and blood was flowing like a river. Sometimes I saw a diamond tree in distant lands where row upon row of diamonds were in bloom. Once I saw that Saturn with its eight moons had landed with a thud upon Jupiter with its four moons and also saw all the planets in the galaxy shattering into a million pieces, thus blazing into a brilliant conflagration and hurtling about all over the galaxy. Yet another time, I saw that this earth was peopled with radiant, magnificent, divine beings who moved about the skies every now and then, dazzling me with their pleasant fragrance. But whatever I saw, in the centre of it all remained that image of Rajani, like a marble statue. Alas Rajani! Such fire trapped in stone!

Slow, Rajani, slow—ever so slowly open those sightless eyes of yours. Look, look at me and let me look at you! There, I can see your eyelids fluttering open and slowly, ever so slowly I can see your lotus eyes. Who on this earth doesn't have eyes—even dogs, cows, lambs and the lowest of the low have eyes—but you don't? No, you don't—then, I don't either. I do not want my eyes.

7
Labangalata

I KNEW FOR SURE SACHINDRA WOULD GET HIMSELF INTO TROUBLE. IT WASN'T right to do so much thinking at such an early age. Didi (his mother) never looks at him twice, and what's the use of my saying something, for no one pays attention to the stepmother's words. Such boys are very difficult to handle. Now the burden is mine. The doctors have failed to bring about a cure and they do not even know what the disease is. The disease, I am sure, is in his mind—what would they learn from his hands, eyes and tongue? If, like me, they ever lay in wait and watched the boy up to his tricks, they may perhaps have had an inkling of what was wrong with him.

What were the words? 'Slow, Rajani, go slow!' The boy muttered them whenever he was alone. Was this the effect of the hermit's medication? Why, for the love of God, did I think of doing this? Will it help if I made Rajani sit at his bedside for some time? But, I had gone to Rajani's house and yet she never visited me even once since then. If I sent for her, would she stay away? I decided to risk it and so sent a messenger to her home, saying I needed her urgently and could she please come once?

I decided to mention Rajani to Sachindra first so that it would be apparent if there was any connection between his illness and the girl. Hence, I went and sat near him. After talking of this and that I spoke of Rajani but Sachindra merely gazed at me mournfully without a word passing through his lips. He grew restless, he reached for something, broke something else and thus he went on. Finally, I began to criticize Rajani, calling her a mercenary. There was no one else in the room. The poor child looked up like a startled swan and glanced at my face. I continued, saying that Rajani and her family were ungrateful to us. Sachindra appeared to be displeased by such sentiments but he did not express anything in words.

I was certain now that this was the hermit's doing. At present, he was travelling, but he was expected back shortly. I began to await his return. But the doubt niggled in my mind whether he'd be able to do anything. I was a foolish, short-sighted woman who had brought this trouble on her own head due to her yearning for wealth. At the time I was sure that Rajani would be my daughter-in-law. Who knew then that even a blind flower girl would be so hard to get? How was I to know that the hermit's medication would go wrong thus? I had not known just how tiny the woman's brain was; I stood corrected. Why didn't I die before I had such a foolish idea? Now I did wish I could die, but I couldn't as long as I didn't see that Sachindra was on the road to recovery.

A few days later, the hermit reappeared seemingly out of nowhere. He said he had heard about Sachindra's illness and had come to see him. He did not reveal from where he had got the news.

He first acquainted himself with all the details of Sachindra's illness. Then he sat near Sachindra and began to talk of many things. Finally, I sent for the hermit in order to take his blessing. After doing that, I asked after his health and then said, 'You are omniscient, oh sage; there is nothing beyond your ken. I am sure you know what ails Sachindra?'

He replied, 'It is a very difficult malady indeed.'

I said, 'Why then does Sachindra always mention Rajani?'

He said, 'You are a child, you wouldn't understand—' (Dear Lord, me a child! I am Sachi's mother!) 'One of the symptoms of this disease is that every desire, every unconscious thought comes to the forefront of the brain and grows stronger by the day. Once when Sachindra wanted to test my divine powers, I had performed a ritual whereby he would dream of the one person who loved him the most. Sachindra dreamt of Rajani. It is an innate law of nature that we tend to start loving someone if we come to know of their love for us. Therefore, that night, the seeds of passion for Rajani were sowed secretly in Sachindra's subconscious. But Rajani being blind and born to a low caste, his fondness remained concealed even to himself. Even if he perceived some signs of his own fondness for her, he refused to acknowledge it. Gradually, the spectre of penury loomed large on the horizon of this family. That upset Sachindra the most. In order to forget his woes, he turned to his books. He began to study in real earnest. A profusion of this reading made his heart grow restless. That, in turn, caused this mental collapse. With the aid of this breakdown, his hidden desire for Rajani made itself felt in his conscious mind. Now Sachindra lacked the mental strength to fight this growing love and to banish it from his heart. Especially since, as I mentioned earlier, the desires that come forth during this illness tend to take a strong hold upon the mind. Then it takes the form of a delirium and that's what has happened to Sachindra.'

I was beside myself with worry as I asked, 'Is there a cure for this illness?'

The hermit said, 'I know nothing of medical science and I do not know if it has the means to effect a cure. But I have never heard of doctors being able to cure this kind of a disease.'

I said, 'Many doctors have been consulted, but no cure has been found.'

'In my experience, even our native form of medicine will prove to be quite ineffective for this.'

'So then, is there no way out?' I asked in despair.

'If you so desire, I can prescribe a cure,' he said.

'What could be better than that? You are everything to us—please give us the cure for this malady.'

'You are the mistress of this house. I can work the cure only if you give permission. Sachindra is also in your sway. He will take my medication on your orders alone. But medication alone will not help. For a mental illness we need a psychological solution—we need Rajani.'

'She will come—I have sent for her.'

'But, it is debatable whether her presence would prove to be a blessing or a bane,' he cautioned me. 'It is possible that the arrival of Rajani, when he is in this state, would only serve to entrench his feelings for her more strongly in his heart. If his marriage to Rajani is unlikely, then perhaps it is better for her to stay away.'

'There is no time now to debate on the good or evil of Rajani's presence—there she comes now.'

At that moment Rajani arrived, accompanied by a maid. On hearing of Sachindra's illness, Amarnath himself had arrived with Rajani. He stayed back in the outer chambers and sent Rajani indoors with the maid.

Part V

Amarnath

1

I DON'T KNOW WHAT SPELLS THIS BLIND FLOWER GIRL CAN CAST. WITH HER sightless eyes, she had enslaved a hermit like me. I had thought I could never love anyone after Labangalata. But pride comes before a fall. Others may have failed, but I fell in love with this blind flower girl quite easily.

I had thought this life would be like a new-moon night—that it would pass in darkness. But suddenly the moon rose in my sky. I had thought I'd have to swim my way across the ocean of life, but suddenly a golden bridge appeared before me. I had thought this desert of a life would stay barren forever, but Rajani suddenly created an oasis in its midst. My joy knew no bounds. It was like that of a man who had lived in a dark cave all his life and suddenly came upon this sunlit, verdant earth full of people. In loving Rajani, my pleasure was the same as his who, blind from birth, has suddenly been granted sight.

But I cannot say where this enchantment will lead. I am a thief! On my back was branded the word *thief* in fiery letters. The day Rajani's fingers traverses those letters and she'll ask me what they say, what will I say to her? Will I be able to say they mean nothing? She was blind, she'd never know. But how could I deceive the one person with whom I was planning to regain my paradise on earth? Perhaps some men can. When I could, I had attempted far more daring deeds, and suffered for them. Why again? I had said to Labangalata that I'd confess to Rajani, but I hadn't been able to do it yet. Now I will!

The day that Rajani came back after seeing Sachindra, I went to her in the afternoon intending to confess to her. I found her sitting alone and weeping. Without saying a word to her, I asked her aunt why she was crying. Her aunt said she didn't know, and that Rajani had been weeping ever since she came back from the Mitra residence. I had not visited Sachindra personally because he was cross with me, and I feared my presence could aggravate his illness. So I did not know what took place there. I asked Rajani why she was crying. She wiped her eyes and kept quiet.

I was disconsolate. I said, 'Rajani, whatever your sorrow is, if I come to know of it I shall do my best to eliminate the cause. Won't you tell me the reason why you are crying?'

She began to weep again. Then she checked herself with great effort and said, 'You are so generous to me, but I am not worthy of it.'

'Why do you say that, Rajani? I know for a fact that it is I who isn't worthy of you and that's what I have come to tell you,' I said.

'I am a serf at your feet—why do you say such things to me?' she pleaded.

I began to open my heart out to her. 'Listen to me, Rajani—it is my heart's desire that I shall marry you and spend the rest of my life in happiness. If my hopes are dashed, I may even die. But I have come to tell you of the obstacles in the way of my dreams. Speak only after you hear me and not before that. In the first flush of youth, once upon a time, I had been dazzled by beauty—senselessly, I had committed a crime and I bear the marks of that deed upon my body to this day. That's what I have come to tell you.'

Then I narrated the whole sorry tale slowly, aided by patience and nothing else. I could do it only because she was blind. If our eyes had met, I would have failed.

Rajani remained silent. I said, 'Rajani, I was swayed by corporeal beauty and in the first flush of youth, just once, I committed this crime. Never ever have I done anything wrong again. I have paid for that one instance every day of my life. Will you accept me?'

Rajani was weeping as she said, 'Even if you have been looting, killing or pillaging all your life, you would still be a god to me. If you make room for me at your feet I am ever willing to serve you. But I am not worthy of you. You are yet to hear that tale.'

'What is it, Rajani?' I asked in anxious anticipation.

'This sinful heart of mine belongs to another,' she said quietly.

I got a jolt of shock, 'What!'

Rajani went on, 'I am a woman—what more can I say to you? But Labangalata knows everything. If you ask her, you will know everything. Please tell her that I have asked her to tell you all.'

I went to the Mitra mansion immediately. I shall not waste time on trivial matters by describing how I came upon Labangalata. I found her lying on the floor and weeping for Sachindra. The moment she saw me, she grabbed my feet and wept even louder saying, 'Forgive me, Amarnath! Forgive me. Fate is punishing me for torturing you once. Sachindra, a son dearer to me than one from my own womb would be, is about to lose his life through my fault. I shall take poison and die—I'll do it right now, in front of you!'

My heart shattered. Labanga was weeping, Rajani was weeping! They were women, used to shedding tears. My tears were checked but Rajani's words had raised a storm of tears in my bosom. Labanga wept, Rajani wept, I wept—and Sachindra was sick—who said life was good? It was depressing at best.

I put away my woes and asked after Labanga's woes first. She then began to weep as she described Sachindra's illness. Labanga described everything, starting with testing the hermit's powers to the meeting with Rajani at his bedside.

Then I asked her about Rajani's tale. I said, 'Rajani has asked you to tell me everything, so please tell me.'

Labanga then narrated all that she had come to know from Rajani.

Rajani belonged to Sachindra, Sachindra belonged to Rajani; what was I doing there?

Now I hid my face in my shirt and sobbed as I walked back home.

2

I HAD TO WIND UP SHOP FROM THIS MARKETPLACE CALLED LIFE. FATE HAD not decreed joy for me—how could I rob another of his joy? I decided to return Sachindra's Rajani to him and to get away from this life. I would quit the marketplace, I would punish this heart and I would submit myself at the feet of Him who is beyond all pain and pleasure.

Lord, I have hunted for you high and low, where are You? You are not present in philosophy or science. You are not there in the knowledge of the erudite or in the contemplation of the saint. You are beyond proof and hence there is no proof of You. This blossoming heart is the sole proof that You exist—please ride on it. Let me cast away the blind flower girl from it and replace her with Your image.

You do not exist? Doesn't matter—I shall make everything in Your name.

The infinite universe, pervaded completely by You, I bow before it—and so saying I shall cast away this sullied body of mine. Will You not take back that which is Your bequest? You must, or who else can restore the purity to this burden of sins?

Lord, I have but one request to You! Who has sullied this body—You or I? I am dishonest and foolish—is it my fault or Yours? Who has furbished this shop of mine—You or I? I shall return to You that which you have set up—I shall no longer ply this trade.

Joy! I have looked for you everywhere, you have eluded me. If there is no joy, what use is hope? What is the use of setting up a kitchen in a land devoid of fire?

I vowed to give up everything.

*

The following day I visited Sachindra. I found him to be comparatively calmer, looking a little more cheerful. I conversed with him for some time.

But I realized that he was still plagued by some ire towards me.

The next day I went to see him again. I began to visit him every day. Sachindra's paleness and malaise did not go away but he began to appear more composed. The delirium vanished and gradually he began to recover.

I had never heard him mention Rajani. But I realized that he had started on the road to recovery on the same day that Rajani had visited him.

One day, when the room was empty of other people, I brought up Rajani's name gingerly, without preamble. I talked of her blindness and its sorrow, her deprivation of the pleasure of visual beauty, of the sight of her loved ones. Sachindra turned his face away; his eyes were full of tears.

Fondness for sure!

Then I said, 'You are a well-wisher of Rajani and I have come to seek your advice on a matter regarding her. Rajani is already tormented by fate; moreover she has received some grief at my hands, too.'

Sachindra turned towards me and glared at me angrily.

I said, 'If you would care to listen to the tale patiently, I would like to narrate it to you.'

'Please,' he said.

'I am quite greedy and selfish,' I confessed. 'I was impressed by her nature and wished to marry her. She was bound to me by strong ties of gratitude and hence she had accepted.'

'Sir, why are you telling me all this?'

'I have come to realize that the hermit that I am, I roam all over the country and how would the blind Rajani go along with me? Now I wish some other gentleman would marry her. I would like to see her marry well. I am telling you all this in case you have someone in mind.'

Sachindra spoke a trifle hurriedly, 'There's no dearth of grooms for Rajani.'

I understood who he had in mind.

3

THE NEXT DAY I REAPPEARED AT THE MITRA HOUSE. I TOLD LABANGALATA that I was leaving Calcutta with no chance of returning soon. She had once been my student and I wanted to bless her before I left.

Labangalata met me. I asked her, 'Have you heard what I said to Sachindra yesterday?'

'I heard,' she said. 'You are beyond compare. Please forgive me; I wasn't aware of your virtues.'

I was silent. In that pause she asked, 'Why did you request a meeting with me? I heard you are leaving Calcutta?'

'Yes,' I said.

'Why?' she asked.

'Why not? There is nobody to stop me.'

'If I were to stop you?'

'What am I to you that you'd do such a thing?' I asked her.

'What are you to me? That I do not know. In this world you are nothing to me, but if there is another life—' She left the sentence hanging.

I waited for some time and then asked, 'If there is another life, then what?'

Labangalata said, 'I am a woman—easily swayed. Why do you want to test my strength? All I can say is I shall always wish you well.'

I was a little upset, 'I do believe that. But I have never really understood one thing; if you truly are my well-wisher, why did you mark me so hideously? This doesn't go away—it can never be erased.'

Labanga was embarrassed. She thought for some time. She said, 'You had done something wrong. In my childish way so did I. Each crime should be left in fate's hands for the proper judgement, who am I to judge? Now I have my regrets. But let us not talk of that. Will you forgive me my crime?'

I hastened to reassure her, 'That was done long ago, even before you asked. And what is there to forgive—you gave an apt punishment; you were not at fault. I shall never come back and I shall never see you again. But if ever in future you come to hear that Amarnath is not a bad man, will you feel just the tiniest bit of affection for me?'

'That would mean my fall from grace,' she pointed out.

'No, I do not aspire to those affections anymore. But in this heart of yours, like an ocean in magnitude, don't you have any place for me?'

'No. For the one who once craved my affection outside the bounds of matrimony, I have no place in my heart, even if it was one of the gods himself. In this life I shall never feel even the tiniest bit of affection for you, not even what one feels for a caged, pet bird.'

'This life' once again. Anyway, I cannot say that I understood her words. And but she certainly did not understand mine. Yet, I noticed she had tears in her eyes.

I said, 'Let me finish saying what I came to say. I have some land and assets. They are of no use to me. I wish to donate them before I go.'

'To whom?'

'To the man who will marry Rajani.'

'All your material wealth?' she asked, quite overwhelmed by my offer.

'Yes. You will keep the documents of that gift in great secret. Do not reveal their existence until the day Rajani is married. After the wedding, hand over the papers to Rajani's husband.'

With these words, I dropped the papers near her and walked away without waiting for her response. I had everything arranged. I did not go back home. I proceeded to the station and boarded a steam engine and set off for Kashmir.

The business was sold!

4

ABOUT TWO YEARS AFTER THIS INCIDENT, IN THE COURSE OF MY TRAVELS, I decided to visit Bhawaninagar. I heard that someone from the Mitra family was living there. Out of curiosity, I went there to have a look. At the entrance of the once-disputed estate I met Sachindra.

He recognized me and after embracing and welcoming me, he took my hand and seated me. We conversed at length. From him I came to know that he had indeed married Rajani. But he feared that people in Calcutta would look down upon her as an erstwhile flower girl. So they had moved to this house. His father and brother still lived in Calcutta.

Sachindra pleaded with me to take back my own property. But needless to say, I paid no heed to it. Finally, he requested me to meet Rajani. I too wanted that. Sachindra led me indoors.

Rajani appeared, bowed down and touched my feet respectfully. I noticed that she did not fumble around in the natural way of the blind as she bent to touch my feet. She went straight to the right spot. I was a little surprised.

She stood up after saluting me. But her head was bowed. My surprise increased. The blind felt no shyness to meet the eye. The awkwardness of eye contact was absent in their case and hence they never hesitated to meet the eye. I asked something, and in response Rajani looked up once and glanced down again. I saw—for sure—those eyes had life!

So then, was the congenitally blind Rajani now gifted with sight? I was about to ask Sachindra when he asked Rajani to give me a seat. She began to lay out a mat on the floor, but at that spot there was a drop of water. She kept the mat aside and wiped the water first with her sari and then laid out the mat on that spot. I had noticed for a fact that she had stopped short of laying the mat without even touching the drop of water. Hence, she could not have guessed by touch that there was water there. Obviously she had seen it.

I couldn't keep my emotion in check; I asked, 'Rajani, are you able to see now?'

Rajani bowed her head, smiled slightly and said, 'Yes.'

I looked at Sachindra in amazement. He said, 'Surprising, but there is nothing that is impossible with divine grace. In India, there are some incredible cures available to the ancient art of medicine that will never be known to the Western world, however hard they labour. Why just medicine, it goes for every branch of learning. But these secrets are now extinct; some parts of it can still be found, guarded zealously by a few hermits and sages. One such hermit is an occasional visitor in our house and he is fond of me. When he heard that I was going to marry Rajani, he said, "How will the auspicious first sight of bride and groom take place—the girl is blind!" I said in jest, "Why don't you cure her blindness, then?" He said, "I will—in a month's time." He treated her eyes and within a month he granted her sight.'

I was truly astounded and said, 'I would not have believed this if I had not seen it. This would be unheard of in European medical science.'

We were talking thus when a one-year-old child came into the room, stumbling and fumbling, crawling and walking. He came and fell at Rajani's feet, tugged at her sari and pulled himself up, and hiding his face between her knees, he gurgled cheerfully. Then he stared at me for some time, waved me away and said, 'Do [Go].'

'Who is this?' I asked.

Sachindra said, 'Our son.'

I asked, 'What have you named him?'

'Amarprasad,' he replied.

I did not stay there any longer.